This book is dedicated to my wife, Rosemary

John Gordon Davis

John Gordon Davis was born in Zimbabwe and brought up in South Africa. He did his schooling in the Transkei, and was a student at Rhodes University in the Eastern Cape, where he took a degree in Political Science, before moving on to the University of South Africa, Pretoria, where he qualified as a lawyer. He spent his university vacations as a deckhand with the British and Dutch merchant navies. He worked as a lawyer in Rhodesia and later in Hong Kong. The international success of his first novel, *Hold My Hand I'm Dying,* allowed him to take up writing full time. His twelve novels include *Cape of Storms, Leviathan, Years of the Hungry Tiger, Typhoon, The Land God Made in Anger* and *Talk to Me Tenderly, Tell Me Lies.* He and his Australian wife Rosemary divide their lives between their farm in southern Spain and Africa.

Roots of Outrage

'John Gordon Davis has hit the jackpot again. Highly recommended . . . this epic volume cries out to be filmed.'
Natal Mercury

'Captures perfectly the emotions, hopes and fears of a very explosive yet exciting time. It is a story so well told you can smell and feel Africa on every page.'
African Panorama

'A sweeping history, politically questioning and charged with passion.'
The Star

'Great holiday reading. This is a huge saga of history, politics, romance and adventure set against the turbulent background of South Africa.'
Eastern Province Herald

'*North and South* and *Gone With the Wind* wrapped into one. A great read.'
Sunday Tribune

ACKNOWLEDGMENTS

This is a novel, not a history, but I am indebted to many learned authors – too numerous to list – whose works I researched for historical background. Numerous friends – they know who they are – from all shades of the political spectrum also gave me much help. In addition, I am particularly indebted to the people listed below, who advised me on aspects of the story. Any factual errors, however, are my own responsibility, and interpretations of events articulated by my characters are not necessarily the views of my advisors.

Chris Munnion, formerly the Africa correspondent for the *Daily Telegraph* for over twenty years, for much advice on past and current affairs, and for checking my typescript; Professor Christopher Hummel, of Rhodes University, for historical guidance; similarly Professor Simon Bekker of the University of Natal and Professor Janis Grobelaar of the University of South Africa; Jacques Pauw and Max du Preez, formerly of Vrye Weekblad, for much background advice; Dirk Coetzee, formerly of the South African police; political analysts Dr Wim Booyse and Jan Taljaard; Brian Currin, of Lawyers for Human Rights, for describing his organisation's work; Barney Cohen of Drum, for describing his magazine's background; the editors of the South African Institute of Race Relations, for their excellent annual surveys of political events; the Human Rights Commission and the Community Agency for Social Enquiry, for their literature; veteran journalists Patrick Lawrence of the *Star*, Gavin Evans of *Weekly Mail & Guardian*, Marichen Waldner of *Rapport*, for their wisdom; Eugene Terreblanche of the Afrikaner Weerstandsbeweging (AWB), Robert van Tonder of the Boerestaat Party, Koos van der Merwe, former Member of Parliament, for explaining their respective different movements and views; numerous officials of the African National Congress, South African Communist Party, the Congress of South African Trade Unions, Inkatha Freedom Party, National Party, Democratic Party, Conservative Party, and the Freedom Front Party, for providing me with their literature and much other information; Anna Boshoff and officials of the Afrikaner Volkswag, for explaining their policy, and for making me welcome in Oranje; the library staff of the *Star*, the *Natal Witness*, Rhodes University and the Africana Library of the Johannesburg City Council, for allowing me to use their research facilities; Buck Buchanan, Cyril Wilkinson, Dr Donald Clark, Michael Shafto, Roger Webber, Dr Michael Hurry, Jeff Rann, the David Hilton-Barber family and the Bill Jackson family, for much encouragement and for opening many doors.

But my greatest indebtedness is to my wife, Rosemary – for everything.

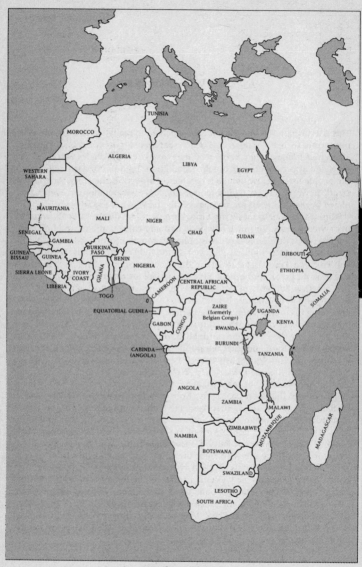

Modern Africa

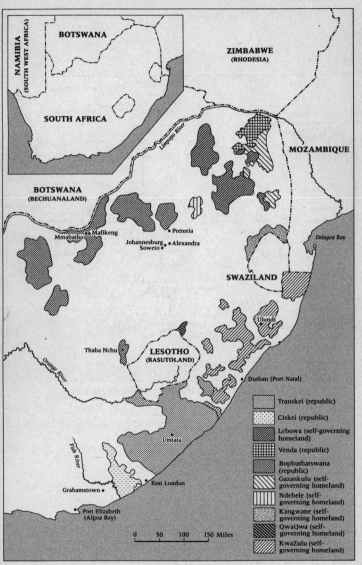

The African 'Homelands' of South Africa

Transkei (republic)

Ciskei (republic)

Lebowa (self-governing homeland)

Venda (republic)

Bophuthatswana (republic)

Gazankulu (self-governing homeland)

Ndebele (self-governing homeland)

Kangwane (self-governing homeland)

QwaQwa (self-governing homeland)

KwaZulu (self-governing homeland)

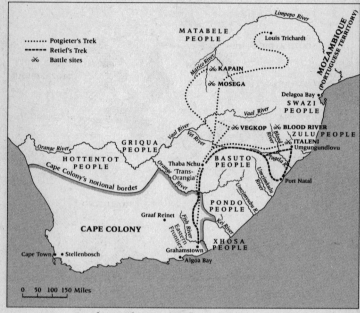

········· Potgieter's Trek
– – – – – Retief's Trek
⚔ Battle sites

MATABELE PEOPLE

Limpopo River

Louis Trichardt

Marico River

⚔ KAPAIN

⚔ MOSEGA

MOZAMBIQUE (PORTUGUESE TERRITORY)

Delagoa Bay

SWAZI PEOPLE

Vaal River

GRIQUA PEOPLE

Vaal River

Vet River

⚔ **VEGKOP**

⚔ **BLOOD RIVER**

ZULU PEOPLE

⚔ **ITALENI**

Blood River

Umgungundlovu

Orange River

HOTTENTOT PEOPLE

Cape Colony's notional border

Orange River

Thaba Nchu

'Trans-Orangia'

BASUTO PEOPLE

Tugela R.

Umzimkulu River

Port Natal

PONDO PEOPLE

Umzimvubu R.

Graaf Reinet

Fish River

Kei River

CAPE COLONY

Eastern Frontier

XHOSA PEOPLE

Cape Town ● Stellenbosch

Grahamstown

● Algoa Bay

0   50 100 150 Miles

Southern Africa at the Time of the Great Trek

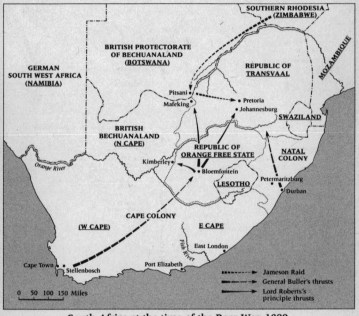

South Africa at the time of the Boer War, 1899
(Modern names of provinces/countries are underlined)

The story of South Africa is real.
The characters, with obvious exceptions, are fictitious.

PROLOGUE

The gallows stood ready, silhouetted. These hard, rolling hills of the eastern frontier of the Cape Colony were soaked in the blood of the Kaffir Wars, and today more blood was to be spilt at the execution of the five ringleader Boers of the Slagter's Nek rebellion – at the very place where they had taken the oath to drive the British into the sea.

The hangman, who had journeyed up from the coast, had brought only enough rope to hang one man at a time, so the magistrate had acquired more, but unbeknownst to everybody it was rotten. Now five nooses dangled, and gathered around were the relatives of the condemned, the other rebels who had been sentenced to imprisonment and the Dutch farmers from miles around who had been ordered to attend to witness how seriously the British took rebellion. And now, from the direction of the military post, came the beat of drums, and the wagon bearing the condemned.

The drummers slow-marched. Slowly they advanced up the rise to the gallows. The condemned men climbed down off the wagon and mounted the scaffold. One after the other, the hangman tied their ankles, slipped the nooses over their necks. When all was ready, the Reverend Harold led the assembly in prayer. The magistrate ordered the drums to roll: softly, then louder and louder. The plank was kicked away, the men plunged into their death-fall, there came the dreadful wrench on their necks, and four of the ropes snapped.

The condemned men lay writhing in the dust, choking, as pandemonium broke out all around them: the shrieks of joy that the hand of God had intervened, people rushing to the struggling men, wrenching loose the nooses, the priest in the midst of them gabbling his prayers. Then the magistrate bellowed above the uproar: *'Bring more ropes!'*

The uproar redoubled, the priest in the forefront – *'God Himself has intervened!'* The magistrate had to shout at the top of his voice that it was not within his power to grant pardons.

By the time the horseman came galloping back with more ropes order had been restored. The condemned were clustered under the gallows in the arms of their wives and friends, surrounded by a ring of soldiers. While the hangman rigged new nooses the priest led the emotional people in prayer again. Then the condemned men sought permission to sing a hymn. This was granted, and the tearful cadence rose up. Then one of the condemned asked permission to say a few last words, and in a shaking voice he urged his brethren to heed his unhappy fate. They mounted the scaffold again. The magistrate ordered another roll of drums. The platform was kicked away.

This time the ropes held: the men hung, their eyes bulging and their tongues sticking out, excrement dripping down their kicking legs, and a howl of anguish went up from the people.

King Henry the Navigator called it the Cape of Good Hope, for he was sure it was the sea-route to China, but despite its mercantile importance this southern tip of Africa lay unoccupied until, in 1652, the Dutch East India Company established a small revictualling station for its ships there, called Cape Town. The Company had no intention of colonising the interior, but within a hundred and fifty years Dutch farmers had, in defiance of Company edicts, wandered six hundred miles along the rugged coastal hinterland with their cattle, building mud and thatch homesteads, then wandering on after a while. They were called *Trekboers*, and a new language evolved, a bastard Dutch called Afrikaans.

Theirs was a good life, called the *Lekker Lewe*, of limitless land, adequate slave labour and security, for they met no Caffres – as black men were then called – the hinterland being empty but for small bands of nomadic Bushmen who were soon driven out. But finally they came to the big river called the Fish, and beyond were many warlike Caffres, the Xhosa, and they were also cattle men.

The Company forbade the Trekboers to cross the Fish River, to have any contact with the Xhosa. But there was always cattle thievery, followed by raids to recover the cattle (and probably a few more besides), and by the time the British occupied the Cape in 1806 to protect her Far Eastern trade against Napoleon there had already been three bloody, full-scale 'Kaffir' Wars.

The British were mighty unwelcome amongst the rough and ready Boers. And with the Redcoats the Age of Enlightenment arrived at the wild and woolly colony, in the form of the London Missionary Society and British justice. The missionaries blamed the frontiersmen for the Kaffir Wars, and the British magistrates busied themselves with cases of mistreatment of slaves and servants, which was deeply resented. A handful of Boers plotted a rebellion after one of their number was shot dead resisting arrest, and their leader stole across the Fish River to make a treasonous pact with the dreaded Xhosa: Join forces with me, together we'll drive the British into the sea and then divide the land between us. The wily Xhosa chief declined. The rebellion was quickly put down by the redcoats, but the British took treason seriously and their ringleaders were sentenced to death. Their ghastly public execution at Slagter's Nek followed.

It is bitterly remembered to this day. And history was to repeat itself.

At about the same time, far away on the lush coast of south-east Africa, there arose a warrior king called Shaka, who welded together the nation of the Zulus, the 'People of Heaven'. The Zulus made war on neighbouring tribes, who fled and made war on their neighbours, all killing and plundering for food. This period was called the Mfecane, which means the 'crushing'. It was a time of chaos, the veld blackened with burnings and littered with skeletons. One of Shaka's generals, Mzilikazi, rebelled and led his people up onto the highlands, making mayhem more terrible, and established a new nation called the Matabele, which means the 'destroyers'. The dislocations pressed upon the Xhosa, who had no place to go but across the Fish River into white man's land; the cross-border thieving, raids and counter-raids got worse.

The government decided to settle thousands of British immigrants on farms along the Fish, to form a buffer zone, and forts were built; but the thieving continued and in the next decade there were two more full-scale wars. The missionaries blamed the frontiersmen and raised a furore in London, so the imperial government hesitated to act decisively against the Xhosa. And then the missionaries forced the repeal of the Vagrancy Laws, so now blacks roved the frontier at will, thieving. And then the Abolition of Slavery Act was passed: all slaves throughout the British Empire would be emancipated at midnight 31st December 1834. This would wreak great hardship on the Cape's frontier. On Christmas Day 1834, six days before the slaves were to be freed, the Sixth Kaffir War broke out. It was the bloodiest of all.

As the frontiersmen celebrated Christmas, there was a massive eruption of Xhosa warriors across the Fish, burning, killing, plundering. They swarmed over thousands of square miles before they were driven back across the Fish by British troops and frontier commandos. It was the costliest war in the frontier's bloody history; eight hundred farms destroyed, hundreds of thousands of cattle stolen. It took six months to drive them further back across a distant river, for the British commander intended to create a militarised cordon sanitaire to keep the races apart. There was rejoicing on the frontier, for it looked as if a new order was being ushered in at last.

But it was not to be. The missionaries blamed the frontiersmen for the war, and so the imperial government ordered that the newly annexed buffer zone be abandoned. It seemed towering folly: the thievery and wars would continue. There was outrage on the frontier. And then the news came that the British government had reneged on its promise to compensate slave-owners fairly: the sum of three million pounds that had been allocated for the purpose was reduced to one million, and would only be given to those who journeyed to London to claim it.

The sense of outrage redoubled on the frontier, amongst Boer and Briton alike, for who would leave his farm unprotected from marauding Xhosa for a year to make an expensive journey to London?

And so the Great Trek began. And Ernest Mahoney, from New York, enters our story.

The Great Trek was not a sudden, stormy mobilization of an angry people, as romantic chroniclers like Ernest Mahoney have suggested, it was the slow culmination of bitter debate that had been going on since the terrible Slagter's Nek hangings: the thievery, the repeal of the Vagrancy Laws, the 'ungodly' attitude of the British towards master-and-servant relationships, the injustice of the missionaries, the Abolition of Slavery Act which defrauded them, the terror and devastation of Kaffir Wars, the British government's refusal to fight them decisively. The Great Trek was a gradual consensus of people who had been bitterly tried, God-fearing folk who knew little other than the Bible and the gun, who had finally had enough of their incompetent, duplicitous government. In part it was the old trek spirit of their forefathers coming back, the quest for pastures new and the *Lekker Lewe*, but more important was the resentful determination to set their world to rights. One after another the hardy Boers packed up their wagons, rounded up their herds and set off. Out of the mauve hills of the frontier they rolled northwards, up into the highveld of Trans-Orangia, to find their Promised Land.

It was in Piet Retief that the people found their Moses. It was he who published the Voortrekker Manifesto:

> . . . *We despair of saving this country from the threat posed by vagrants* . . . *nor do we see any prospect of peace for our children* . . . *Be it known that we are resolved, wherever we go, that we will uphold the just principle of*

liberty; but whilst no one shall be in a state of slavery, it is our determination to maintain such regulations as may suppress crime and preserve proper relations between master and servant . . . We shall not molest any people, nor deprive them of the smallest property; but, if attacked, we shall consider ourselves fully justified in defending our persons and effects to the utmost . . .

It was a profession of faith, an enunciation of constitutional principles for a democratic Boer republic. Much of the turbulent story of South Africa is a betrayal of that manifesto.

Enter Ernest Mahoney of New York, sent thither by the Harker-Mahoney Shipping Company to investigate trading opportunities in this opening-up of the African hinterland. A hundred and twenty years later, when Ernest's great grandson, Luke Mahoney, read his forebear's journals of that epic time, he could visualise the meeting of shareholders in New York, the rotund old chairman, Ernest's grandfather, saying:

'The Mahoneys were amongst the first to transplant the principles of our magnificent American Revolution across the oceans . . . Amongst the first to seize the unspoilt virtue of our frontier heritage and reject the wiliness of the Old World, "its useless memories and vain feuds", amongst the first to shun the tawdry lures of Europe and export our American Enlightenment by the adventurous prows of the Harker-Mahoney clippers to replace wars and so-called diplomatic treaties with the benign embrace of commerce . . . the first to join with those Massachusetts poets in their cry:

> *Preserve your principles, their force unfold*
> *Let nations prove them and let kings behold.*
> *EQUALITY, your first firm-ground stand;*
> *Then FREE ELECTIONS; then your FEDERAL BAND.*

'We were amongst the first to see that political happiness would eventuate throughout the world from the simple principle of free oceans, free trade, and the free dissemination of American inventiveness by Yankee vessels, and that, in return, the world would unfold its treasures . . . The Mahoneys were amongst the first to turn America's eyes to the Pacific, and to Africa, to probe dark regions of alien religions which would, through our worthy commerce, fall to the influence of our Enlightenment . . . And we all know what the result is: Harker-Mahoney has, without firing a

*shot except in self-defence, an empire upon which the sun never sets . . .
And now there is a new frontier for Harker-Mahoney to add to their
empire, brethren shareholders! It is the hinterland of southern Africa!*

*'"The hinterland"? you ask. We have traded profitably with the
Cape of Good Hope for years, but how do we penetrate the hinterland?
Ah . . . It is being penetrated for us by the Dutch Boers, just as our west
is being opened up by our pioneer wagons! Whole new lands that will
one day stretch to the Nile, vast new untapped markets for our goods,
vast new resources, lands bigger than the whole of China . . . '*

And so now here is nervous Ernest Mahoney, twenty-two years old,
lanky, wan – a graduate of a Presbyterian seminary but feeling unable
to take holy orders because of lusts of the flesh – disembarking with a
big bagful of silver dollars, buying two horses, hiring a Dutch guide
(paying twice what he should and thinking it cheap), setting off timidly
into the wilderness to spread the American Enlightenment through
worthy commerce. Ernest riding up into the highveld, overtaking Boer
wagon trains, eventually coming upon the high mountain called Thaba
Nchu, the foregathering place. The hundreds of wagons outspanned,
the thousands of Boers waiting for their leader, Hendrik Potgieter, who
had trekked on to the north to explore, for Piet Retief to come up from
the south. There is Ernest fearfully riding on north with his guide to
look for Hendrik Potgieter's wagon train, following his tracks; the veld
is littered with evidence of the Mfecane, whitened skeletons, burnt
huts. Ernest eventually finds Potgieter and his people feverishly preparing for an imminent attack by Mzilikazi, lashing their wagons into a
circle, stuffing thorn branches into the gaps. And so Ernest, four weeks
in Africa, never having fired a shot in anger, who just wants to get the
hell out of this land, finds himself plunged into one of South Africa's
most famous battles. And he meets Sarie Smit, the feisty Boer girl
assigned to him as a loader because she speaks English.

The Battle of Vegkop. The veld black as ink with five thousand of
Mzilikazi's warriors loping across the veld chanting *Zhee Zhee*, encircling
the wagons, sharpening their assegais, humming, humming for hours
until Potgieter tied a red rag to a stockwhip and waved it above the
wagons as a challenge. Then their terrifying battle charge, thousands of
glistening warriors hurling themselves at the laager, stabbing, slashing,
hurling, the wagons shaking under their tumult midst the cacophony
of the trekkers' muzzle-loaders, the smoke and stink of gunpowder.
And there is Ernest, sick-in-his-guts terrified, blasting straight into the
savage faces through the thorn branches, thrusting the spent gun at
Sarie and grabbing the reloaded one she thrust back – *bang – grab – bang*

8

– *grab* – *bang* – There is sweaty Sarie Smit and her mother pouring the powder down the hot muzzles, ramming in the lead with a wad of cotton on top, thrusting the gun in Ernest's trembling, outstretched hand – *bang grab bang* . . . For hours the cacophonous battle rages, and the bloody black bodies are piled high around the laager before Mzilikazi's warriors withdraw, round up all the voortrekkers' thousands of cattle and drive them off northwards. Potgieter sends horsemen galloping back to Thaba Nchu to call for oxen, and Ernest volunteers to ride with them. It is regarded as a courageous offer, for more Matabele impis may be waiting, but Ernest just wants to get the hell out of there. And when, eight days later, he arrived at Thaba Nchu, he would have kept going, heading south to the faraway sea to take the first ship back to America, except that no way was he going to ride alone through this fearsome country.

Piet Retief had arrived at Thaba Nchu, where he had been elected Governor of the 'United Laagers', and he sent oxen up to Vegkop to haul Potgieter's wagons back. But the United Laagers were disunited at the outset, a characteristic of the Boers throughout their history. Retief wanted to establish the republic in the east, with a land grant from the Zulu king, while Potgieter wanted to recover his cattle stolen by Mzilikazi, drive him from the land and establish the republic in the north. So there is vengeful Potgieter setting out northwards to deal with Mzilikazi, there is Piet Retief setting out eastwards to the land of the fearsome Zulus. And with Retief's wagons rolls that of Sarie Smit's family. And Ernest rides with them. And his fate is sealed.

'*I at last know the meaning of love,*' Ernest breathlessly confides to his journal. There is Ernest having the first real live sexual affair of his life, waiting excitedly each night outside the glow of the laagers' campfires for Sarie to come creeping out. There is Ernest earnestly proposing marriage in the moonlight (after praying to the Lord for guidance), '*begging her to return with me to the comfort and security of America once my duties are completed – but alas, she insists her loyalties are to her volk . . .*' There is Ernest travelling on his delicious illicit honeymoon across the highveld until Retief's convoy of wagons stands on the lip of the towering Drakensberg, looking down on vast, misty, mauve Zululand far below. Ernest looks down at the daunting descent, at the long shadows cast by the mountain, and he is filled with foreboding: '*Woe unto the land whose borders lie in shadow*' he records.

Ernest's sense of duty to Harker-Mahoney compelled him to ride down with Retief's advance party to parley with King Dingaan for a grant of land. The foreboding stayed with him as they picked their way down into rolling, wooded Zulu country. After many days they arrived at Dingaan's royal kraal of Mgundgundlovu, 'the place of the Elephant'.

'A mighty circular village,' Ernest records, *'fenced with high poles, in side of which are many concentric rows of beehive-shaped huts all dominated by the Great Place, the huge hut of the king, surrounded by those of his many wives . . . Beyond is the Hill of Executions where vultures circle, feeding on the bodies of people slaughtered daily. I am filled with trepidation as we wait outside for the king to receive us . . . '*

Ernest's fear was well founded: King Dingaan was afraid of these Amaboela, these white men who rode swift 'hornless cattle' and used strange weapons with devastating effect; men who – his spies told him – had recently routed Mzilikazi, and who now wanted to settle on his borders. When Dingaan finally received these people midst great pomp and praise-singing he spent three days impressing them with his might, by military displays and frightening dancing by his magnificent regiments, the earth shaking under the synchronised stamping of their feet, their battle cries rising up to the skies. But finally he announced he would consider the request for a land grant favourably if Retief recovered cattle that had been stolen by a distant tribe.

Retief and his men were in high spirits as they set out to fulfil the bargain, but Ernest was a very worried young man: he was fearful of the Zulus, *'deeply suspicious at how simply a grant of land the size of England was arranged. The whole thing reeks of blood . . . '* When Retief set off he sent two horsemen back to the Drakensberg with the tidings and Ernest seized the opportunity to ride with them, to persuade Sarie to leave this frightening land and go back to America with him.

The voortrekkers' joy was unbounded when the horsemen toiled up the last crest of the Drakensberg with the news, but the most joyful was Sarie Smit, who had big news for Ernest: 'I am pregnant . . . '

Love-sick Ernest was overjoyed. But Sarie refused to go with him to America: her place was with her volk. And so, because his heart and honour ruled his head, Ernest Mahoney went back down the Drakensberg Mountains. And the roots of the Mahoney clan in Africa were set down.

Retief recaptured the stolen cattle and returned to Dingaan's royal kraal to claim his grant of land. Dingaan made his mark on the deed Retief proffered, then leapt up and shouted: *'Kill the wizards!'* Warriors fell on Retief and his men from all sides, dragged them up to the Hill of

Executions and clubbed them to death. Then, plumes dancing, assegais flashing, the impis set out across the land to slay the voortrekkers encamped at the foot of the Drakensberg. Hundreds were slain in the terrible massacre that followed, hundreds of wagons burned, twenty-five thousand head of cattle driven off. Ernest and Sarie survived because they were encamped miles from the main killing grounds but the whole of her family was butchered. The surviving voortrekkers were in a dreadful plight as they awaited the next onslaught and desperately hoped for reinforcements to arrive from the highveld. *'Is there a curse on this land that lies in shadows?'* Ernest chronicled.

At last, the prestigious Boer Andries Pretorius descended the Drakensberg and rallied the beleaguered trekkers. He mounted a commando of five hundred men and set off to do battle with Dingaan. En route a Holy Covenant was taken that if God gave them victory they would forever hold the anniversary of the battle-day hallowed, that they would build a church in thanksgiving and forever live according to His laws.

Pretorius chose his battleground on the banks of the Blood River, where two sides of his laager were protected by the confluences. In the ensuing battle five hundred Boers defeated twelve thousand magnificent Zulu warriors, killing three thousand of them as they hurled themselves against the laager. Not one Boer life was lost. And thus was the conviction born amongst these simple, God-fearing folk that God had entered into a covenant with them, as He had with Moses and his Israelites, and that henceforth everything they did would be with His blessing. Thus was a theocracy born. It was to survive a hundred and fifty years.

Ernest took part in the Battle of Blood River. That night he wrote in his chronicle:

> . . . *while I am as thankful to the Lord as any, it can only be said that it was not a battle in the normal sense, but a mass execution of a magnificent army heroically taking on superior weapons. No army of white men, I believe, would have been so valiant, so disciplined, as these Zulus today . . . The Boers are convinced that the Lord has accepted their Covenant. But as a trained theologian, albeit a poor example, I am by no means sure: it was surely the musket that won the day – as it is winning in America against the Indians, for why should the Lord make a bargain with one tribe at such tremendous and heartless expense of another? And while I admire these Boers, and applaud their piety, it worries me that they are fond of referring to Genesis where it says that God made the sons of Ham black, to be hewers of wood and drawers of water* . . .

11

And so the Boers set up their republic of New Holland, electing their volksraad, building their church. Ernest married his beloved Sarie ('*Such happiness as I have never imagined possible . . .*' his chronicle records). They built a hut as storage for Harker-Mahoney and began to trade in ivory and hides with what few vessels braved the sandbars. Sarie was pregnant again when the British came sailing up the coast to put an end to this impertinent new republic.

The Boers are outraged. They left their farms in the Cape Colony and trekked into the savage unknown because of Britain's unjust maladministration, they braved the dreaded Mzilikazi, overcame the steep Drakensberg Mountains, suffered the bloody treachery of Dingaan, braved his fearsome Zulus at Blood River, and now that they have at last got their republican freedom along come the lordly British to take it all away. Personally, I understand the British view-point: the Boers are Her Majesty's subjects who have established an illegal regime and, I hear, have seized Zulu children to work as 'apprentices' in a thinly disguised form of slavery . . . But my Sarie does not understand: she rode over to the beach as the British disembarked and, astride her horse, pointed at her swollen belly and informed the commanding officer and his admiring men that her forthcoming son was not only an American citizen but a Boer to boot and that they would have to trample over her dead body, and numerous of their own, if they imagined that the young Queen Victoria was going to deprive her unborn child of its republican birthright. 'I would rather walk barefoot over the Drakensberg again than submit to British rule!' cried she . . .

The Boers furiously laid siege to them at the lagoon, but reinforcements arrived overland and the Boers were defeated. And Sarie Mahoney kept her pledge.

So the Boers abandoned their new homesteads, trekked back over the Drakensberg and established their republics on the highveld, the Orange Free State, and the Transvaal Republic. The British government was unwilling to spend money on military campaigns and administration so, after a few skirmishes and considerable bluster, it formally recognised the legal independence of these two republics, in 1852 and 1854.

And so the Great Trek was over, twelve years after it began. The Boers at last had their republican freedom, without the accursed British laying down the law, without missionaries meddling and blaming them for the savagery of Africa, without vagrants roaming unpunished. There was no more egalitarian nonsense: a black man knew his place again. It was the *Lekker Lewe* once more, limitless land again, proper labour again, and security at last. Mzilikazi had fled across the Limpopo, and the distant Zulus were the British government's problem now, like the infernal Xhosa.

And a problem they were: in the following decades the British had to fight three more Kaffir Wars and re-annex the land across the Fish right up to the border of the new colony of Natal. And the British had plenty of trouble with the Zulus too. Dingaan's grandson, Cetshwayo, began to weld his people back together, and there was cattle-thieving, and warlike noises again. Then, on the eastern frontier, came the Great Cattle Killing, and there was chaos.

It was a desperate act by the Xhosa to rid themselves of the British: it was national self-immolation. A Xhosa girl had a vision that if the Xhosa nation slaughtered all their cattle and destroyed all their crops, all would return a hundred-fold on 18th February 1857, all the ancestors would return from the dead, soldiers from Russia would arrive, and together they would drive the British into the sea. So the destruction began. The grazing lands became littered with rotting carcasses, the clouds of smoke barrelled upwards. The colonial government sent officials across the Fish to dissuade the Xhosa, but there was only black euphoria that paradise was at hand. On 17th February the last beasts were slain, the last maize burned, and the people waited for the glorious morrow.

The great day dawned silently, for there was no lowing of cattle or bleating of goats to be heard. The people searched the horizon for the hordes of ancestors driving great herds of cattle. As the sun approached its zenith excitement was intense, but the sun began to descend and no hordes appeared, no Russian ships were sighted. Then sunset came, and panic swept the land, weeping and wailing. The promised day was gone, the country was devastated, and tomorrow the starvation would begin.

The months that followed were horrific. Out there beyond the Fish the stench of decomposing flesh fouled the air, blackened maize fields turned to dust; eighty thousand Xhosa died of starvation, their unburied corpses rotting amongst the carcasses of their animals. And across the river staggered the wretched starving people, begging the colonists for food. Harker-Mahoney had opened a branch on the eastern frontier; the manager wrote to Ernest in the Transvaal:

> *. . . once fed, they plead to stay but we have to deny them, and they stagger on towards the Cape. I have heard reports of cannibalism, and starving children abandoned by their parents. My neighbour, McPherson, has found a Xhosa baby left by his mother in a fork of a tree . . .*

What could he do with a starving abandoned baby but take it in? He named the boy Felix. Several years later, visiting American preachers converted Mr McPherson and his family to Mormonism, so they decided to emigrate to America, where the religion had taken strong root. So Felix became the first Xhosa to emigrate to America. Many years later his great granddaughter was to return to South Africa to set it to rights.

But the crisis of the Great Cattle Killing had little impact on the Boer republics in the north – that was Britain's problem now.

It was a rough-and-ready but pleasant life up there; the republics were bankrupt and inefficient, but it was the *Lekker Lewe* again. Farming was the only real economy. In the pleasant village of Pretoria, the capital of the Transvaal republic, Ernest had established a trading depot for Harker-Mahoney, exporting cattle, hides and ivory, and importing American products. Life in southern Africa muddled along in comparative peace after Britain gave up on the bankrupt Boer republics. And then diamonds were discovered, and then gold. Fortune hunters from around the world descended, and the Boer War came about.

Gold – that was the reason the mighty British Empire waged war on the tiny Transvaal Republic. The whole balance of power in the region had changed, Britain was in danger of losing her paramountcy in southern Africa to these undeserving Boers, and Britain needed gold to maintain her position as the leading banker in an industrially expanding world. Further, she intended to extend her colonial power from Cape Town to Cairo, and this tinpot Boer republic stood in her way. The only solution was to make it part of the empire. First Britain tried economic strangulation, encirclement to cut the Boers off from the sea so that they would be forced to rejoin the Cape Colony. When that failed Britain promoted a rebellion by the foreigners on the gold reefs, demanding the vote. When that was crushed Britain mobilised her imperial army on the excuse that British subjects were being treated 'like helots'.

It was a vicious, scorched-earth war the British waged: Boer farms

14

were put to the torch, their crops and homesteads sent up in smoke, their livestock shot or driven off, their women and children herded off to concentration camps where twenty-eight thousand of them died of malnutrition and disease. For three years the war raged, 1899 to 1902. Only devastating attrition drove the Boers to discuss peace. The British offered the Boers financial aid and self-government in a few years in a union with the Cape and Natal colonies; but the most significant concession concerned the status of black people: the question of whether blacks would be given the vote in the new South Africa would be decided only *after* self-government had been granted.

The bitter-enders wanted to fight on: not to do so meant that almost a century of suffering had been in vain – Slagter's Nek, the Kaffir Wars, the Great Trek, the battles of Vegkop, Blood River, this terrible war, their whole hard-won independence . . . But the British pressure was now overwhelming, the countryside was exsanguinated, their very livelihoods destroyed, their women and children dying. Was it not better to lose the war but win the peace? They would get their self-government, albeit in a union with Cape and Natal colonies – and the dreaded question of the voting rights of natives would be decided by *them*, not by the British. And would not the Boers come to dominate the union government – would they not then have beaten the British at their own bloody game?

The debate was angry, but finally the bitter-enders threw in their hand so as not to split the volk further. And the commandos rode back to what was left of their farms, to try to rebuild their devastated lives.

Ernest and Sarie Mahoney died before the Boer War, but their son William, and his son Hector, both fought on the side of the British.

'What was it all for . . . ?' William Mahoney demanded in his journal shortly before his death. *'The British thought it was going to be a "tea-time" war – instead it taught them "an imperial lesson", in the words of Rudyard Kipling.'*

Writers from around the world were there: not only Rudyard Kipling, the immortal poet of Empire, but also Winston Churchill, Conan Doyle, Edgar Wallace, Banjo Patterson, who became Australia's poet laureate, and John Buchan. The American and European press fiercely condemned the British as monsters who laid waste, starved women and children; the Boers they described as heroes. The greatest were General de Wet, General Smuts, General de la Rey, General Louis Botha, all of them fighting courageous running battles.

It was the longest, costliest, bloodiest, most humiliating war she fought in almost a hundred years. Over 450,000 British troops took almost three years to defeat a mere 87,000 combatant Boers who were reduced finally to a few thousand commandos. 22,000 British soldiers lost their lives, over 400,000 horses were killed, 15,000 innocent natives, over 27,000 Boer women and children died in the concentration camps. And most survivors were left destitute. The hideous scars will last a very long time: a nation of embittered paupers has been created.

And after the British soldiers sailed home, Sir Alfred Milner, supreme ruler of all the South African colonies, determined to crush the Boer spirit, culture and language, to turn the two old republics into real British colonies. He Anglicised the civil service and decreed that all education be in English. Boer children who used their mother tongue had to wear the label around their necks: '*I am a Donkey: I spoke Dutch today.*'

. . . and the Boer bitterness grew: not only had he been conquered for his gold, not only had he been brutally vandalised, not only had he lost loved ones in the dreadful concentration camps, but now his very culture was being humiliated. He now belonged to a volk of poor-whites: impoverished by the British scorched-earth policy, many were driven to the towns. There, poorly educated, unable to speak the language of his oppressor, regarded as a country bumpkin, he had to sell his labour in competition with the ubiquitous black man. And so, to his old fear of the black man as a warrior, as the Black Peril, was now added the fear of being swamped by him economically.

But Britain's greatest injustice was to the black people. In order to woo the Boers into surrender, the peace treaty had agreed that the thorny question of the black man's vote would be shelved until *after* responsible government – knowing that there was no likelihood of the Boers granting the franchise to the 'kaffirs'. And, predictably, they did not. In short, the British purchased peace at the expense of the black man, and opened the door to legalised racial prejudice.

I have no doubt that this dereliction of British duty will plague South Africa for years to come . . . I hear that the natives are deeply hurt that they have been treated so badly. An organization has been formed, called the 'African National Congress', to work for their political rights and a fairer distribution of land . . .

And so the Boers lost the war but won the peace. When the first elections were held and the new Union of South Africa came into being in 1910, the Boer War hero, General Louis Botha, was the first prime minister, and he was a segregationist. His successor was General Jan Smuts, also a Boer War hero, also a segregationist, but Britain was rewarded for her duplicity by having a South African government who believed its best interests lay in being a member of the Empire. But vast numbers of Afrikaners believed they were being sacrificed in favour of English-speakers, and the Black Peril remained. The National Party was formed to pursue Afrikaner interests vigorously. Then along came World War I, and rebellion.

William Mahoney's grandson George did not join Harker-Mahoney – he had the gift of the gab rather than the commercial instinct, and he became a lawyer and, in due course, a member of parliament. He kept up the tradition of the family journals, even when he was fighting in World War I. His journal continues:

> *Many Afrikaners hated to fight on the side of the hated British against the Germans who had been their allies in the Boer War a scant twelve years ago. A group of army generals tried to mount a coup d'état to recover the independence of their old republics. The battles were fast and furious, Afrikaner fighting Afrikaner. They lasted three months before General Smuts crushed the rebellion. And the scars of the Boer War were split wide open.*

In 1918 a secret society called the Broederbond was formed to promote the domination by Afrikaners in all walks of life. When World War II came, and South Africa again went into battle on the side of the hated British against the Germans, Afrikaner nationalists who called themselves the Ossewa Brandwag hatched a plot with Hitler to assassinate General Smuts, mount a coup d'état and harness South Africa's goldfields to the Third Reich. The plot was foiled but many Afrikaners had to be interned in concentration camps, including three future prime ministers.

And then the war ended in 1945, and the same old troubles resumed that had plagued the land since the Kaffir Wars and the Great Trek: the 'native problem', the 'Black Peril'. The poor-white Afrikaner was still struggling, the English-speakers still dominated the land economically. And then came the fateful elections in 1948 . . .

General Smuts, the hero of the Boer War, was an old man, worn out by fifty years of bloody fighting for and against his Afrikaner volk. And although he was a segregationist, he was a paternalistic one who believed the problem had to be solved 'by future generations.' His weary policies were no emotional match for the strident National Party whose policy was immutable segregation as ordained in the Bible, and as envisioned in the Covenant taken by their forefathers at the Battle of Blood River: the immutable segregation of blacks from whites, territorially and politically. It was a strong, self-righteous policy of 'South Africa for the White Man' – which meant, more specifically, 'South Africa for the Afrikaner'.

It was called Apartheid

PART I

And so *Apartheid* entered political science, and the dictionary. It means 'apartness', and it is pronounced 'apart-hate'. Although it was not the intention to generate hate, that is what happened, and numerous attempts to change the name – to 'Separate Development', 'Plural Democracy', 'Self Determination' – failed to eradicate the original connotation. Nor did the claims by the political architects that it was designed with the laudable motive that one race should not interfere with another's cultural and political needs hold water.

As George Mahoney thundered in parliament: 'The roots of this mad science, Mr Speaker, lie not in pious guff the Prime Minister gives us about apartheid being God's will and a "mighty act of creation"; the roots of apartheid lie in racial prejudice and in the trekboers' insatiable quest for the *Lekker Lewe* – the Good Life of *Land*, *Labour* and *Security* . . . '

Exclamations of *Onsin* (nonsense) rang out from the government benches, cheers from the opposition benches. Sitting in the stranger's gallery of the august oak-panelled chamber, young Luke Mahoney looked down on his father with pride. George Mahoney was a stocky, handsome, square-faced man with bristling moustache and eyebrows.

'The *Lekker Lewe*, Mr Speaker!' he continued. 'That's why the voortrekkers trekked away from the *insecurity* of the Kaffir Wars in 1836, trekked away from the British administration's new regulations about master and servant. And the establishment of the Boer republics achieved this *Lekker Lewe*, Mr Speaker, until the Boer War – '

Cries of *Onsin*, and groans.

'But then came Union, Mr Speaker, and the Boers were on top again and they immediately resumed their pursuit of the Good Life: the *land* they now had – indeed the *whole* of South Africa! The *security* they now had, so it only remained to secure the *labour* – cheap labour for the farmers, for the industrialists, for those mines! And it is this unsavoury matter of cheap *labour* that has motivated the government ever since. The motive of filthy *lucre*, not high-falutin' notions of God's will – '

'*Skande!*'

'Oh yes, Mr Speaker, it *is* scandalous! Let's first look at the Group Areas Act. This wicked legislation divides South Africa up into white zones and black zones – giving eighty-seven per cent of the land to the whites, and thirteen to the blacks! Can this be God's will – that a mere four million whites, twenty per cent of the total population, receive eighty-seven per cent of God's land? No, it is cynically, *scandalously* unjust! Now, from *that* unjust, sick starting point let's review the rest of this rotten apartheid structure.

'This Group Areas Act has resulted, predictably, in massive over-crowding of black land. This has resulted in blacks drifting onto white farms as squatters, where they are often tolerated in exchange for seasonal labour. But this uncontrolled squatting is anathema to this orderly minded government, so last year it passed the Prevention of Illegal Squatting Act! And this, too, it claimed as God's will. In terms of this act, "surplus" blacks – surplus to the farmers' labour require-ments, that is – are forcibly removed back to their black zones. But who are these *"surplus"* people? Are they the healthy young men and women who can turn in a good day's work for the white farmer? No, they are the *dependants* – the old, the infirm and the children – who are deported. And what is the result? The creation of squalid villages of old people and children who *cannot* work, cannot contribute to the overall economy, who are therefore helpless. This is a sick economic base, Mr Speaker, doomed to the creation of poverty and despair. And it is on this *sick* economic base that this government is bent on effecting the biggest social engineering exercise devised by man – and the result is absolutely predictable: *failure*, Mr Speaker – this policy is doomed!' George's face was getting flushed. His finger shot up. 'It will result in degradation of the earth upon which these impoverished, overcrowded people try to scratch their living. And it will lead to *hate* – this govern-ment is creating hate against itself while trying to dress itself up in the shining raiments of God's will. And,' he shook his glowering face, 'mark my words, this hate will one day rise up against this government and strike it down.'

Groans from the government benches. As the Speaker restored order, George Mahoney continued relentlessly: 'And the same failure, and disaster, will arise from apartheid laws applicable in the towns, Mr Speaker! The philosophy in this unchristian country has always been that the towns are the white man's creation and that the blacks have no right to be there, except in so far as they serve the interests of the white man! And so we have the Native Urban Areas Act, which removes blacks from the towns into "locations" outside town. But there is insuf-ficient housing in these locations, Mr Speaker, so shanties develop –

and it is this government's *policy* to keep housing in short supply, *deliberately*, in order to create a feeling of impermanence. And so people are dumped on the bare veld with only communal water points and told to build their own houses. What cynical callousness! What materials are these poor people supposed to use? There are none! So they have to build out of cardboard and sacks and flattened tin! And the result is *slums*, shanty-towns. And slums are not only unhealthy, they breed crime and discontent!'

He frowned around the chamber in wonder. 'Is *this* the way a sensible, Christian government treats its citizens, Mr Speaker? Is it *sensible* for a government to treat its subjects like *scum*! Is that likely to breed peace? Prosperity? A contented, cooperative people? Or is it likely to breed *hate* for those who forced this misery and poverty upon the people!' He glowered, then his finger shot up again and he cried: 'This government, Mr Speaker, is *brainlessly* creating an immense social crisis for itself and using the will of God to justify it!'

Groans from the government benches. George Mahoney shook his head angrily, then continued witheringly: 'And another disastrous result of this inhumane policy, Mr Speaker, is the hostel system which requires blacks who have lived in the location for less than ten years to live as bachelors in squalid hostels without their wives and families, who must remain back in the homeland. Deprived of their family bonds, these overcrowded hostel-dwellers have become a social problem – men without their women, Mr Speaker, become restless, discontented, form gangs, prowl. Fight. Rape. Steal. These squalid hostels are *hotbeds* of trouble and crime! And because of the tribal nature of the African, these hostels become divided into Xhosa hostels and Zulu hostels, which leads to inter-tribal fighting. And these hostels become hotbeds of political discontent. It is *crazy* politics for any government to deliberately turn the labour force into political malcontents, ripe for rebellion! Not only is it cruel, it is insane!' He raised a finger and cried: '*This government is self-destructing!*'

Jeers and groans from the government benches. The Speaker, seated on his carved throne, nodded wearily at George Mahoney.

'And hand-in-hand with this crazy policy is the government's inhuman policy of pass laws, to control the flow of labour for their precious *Lekker Lewe*. What other country in the world says that its citizens may not go out to look for work unless they have permission from an official? But that is the cruel lot of the poor black South African citizen – before he can look for work he must get a permit, a pass, which he probably cannot read. And these passes are only valid for fourteen days – if he has not found work in fourteen days the poor man must go back to his homeland empty handed. And if he does not go he is thrown in jail! *Jail?!* For the offence of looking for work in his own country to feed himself and his family! What staggering cruelty, to deny a man a proper chance of earning a livelihood. And then say it's God's will.' He shook his head. 'It's a massive waste of the taxpayers' money, because the police, who should be catching crooks, spend vast amounts of time and energy catching unfortunate peasants who haven't got a valid pass! And the courts, which should be dispensing justice, are clogged up with these pass offenders! And the jails are overflowing!' He stabbed the air with his finger. 'It's *madness*, Mr Speaker. And the further result of this monumental stupidity is *massive* black resentment. Even if the pass laws were *humanely* enforced they would lead to massive resentment, but as they are enforced by our totally Afrikaans police force – the entrance qualifications for which are low in order to provide employment for poor whites – '

Angry cries from the government benches.

George Mahoney shouted: ' – enforced by our Afrikaner police force, the pass laws have become instruments of racial *persecution*, bringing justice into disrepute, turning millions of innocent black men who only want a job into potential subversives! Mr Speaker, these black people will one day rise up against this stupid, cruel injustice and bring this government to its knees!'

Cries of *Never! Nonsense!* The Speaker sighed and nodded. George Mahoney shook his head disparagingly, then continued: 'And what does the unfortunate black man encounter when he's got his precious pass? *Job reservation!* Apartheid in employment to protect the white worker from black competition – particularly the poor unskilled Afrikaner! *Job* reservation – no, Sambo, you can't be a bricklayer because that job is reserved as *white* man's work! No, Sambo, you can't do an apprenticeship to become a mechanic, or a plumber, or an electrician, because that job is reserved for white men. No, Sambo, you can only dig ditches or be a garden boy or work on the mines because we want to enjoy our *Lekker Lewe* at your expense!'

A government backbencher shouted: 'What work did the black man have before the white man came – he was only a cattle-herder and his wives hoed the fields – '

'The Honourable Member,' George Mahoney cried, 'is quite right for once. But the white man came some centuries ago, and in those days the white man was also only a cattle-herder, Mr Speaker. But then civilization changed the economy, although the Honourable Member hasn't noticed as he is still only a cattle-herder at heart. But we white men have resisted this change by imposing job reservation, and though the Honourable Member can't grasp the folly of it, being a cattle-man, it will result in an unhealthy economy and eventual rebellion which will, sure as God made little green apples, destroy not only the honourable member but the *Lekker Lewe* he so recklessly, mindlessly, *brain*lessly cherishes!'

George Mahoney smiled sadly at the boos and derisive laughter, spread his hands and appealed theatrically to the heavens for help. Up in the stranger's gallery, young Luke Mahoney was grinning with pride. His father continued: 'Alas, Mr Speaker, half of the government benches are occupied by brainless, blind, silly asses!'

Midst outcries the Speaker thundered: 'The Honourable Member for Transkei will withdraw that remark!'

George Mahoney held up his palms. 'Mr Speaker is quite right, of course. And I do withdraw it: *Half* of the government benches are *not* brainless, blind, silly asses!'

Anger and laughter. Mr Speaker banged his gavel. George Mahoney went on happily: 'And now look at this wondrous God's will in the field of education in this wondrous Malice in Blunderland of ours.' He frowned. 'If this government knew anything about economics it would realize that a well-educated populace is the *essential* requisite of a nation's prosperity nowadays. Repeat *nowadays*, Mr Speaker – not the age of the oxwagon, the *voorlaaier* and the Great Trek in which the government is still living. I'm speaking of the *real* world, the world of telephone, radio, the atom bomb and, would you believe, this new thing called television – which the government does not allow us to have lest it corrupt our tiny minds. The new world of the Cold War, in which communist Russia is *exploiting* the anger of the underdog and promoting world revolution! That is the dangerous world we live in and this *real, dangerous* world is best met by a prosperous people. Which means a labour force which is properly educated, fairly treated, and fairly paid!' He frowned around the government benches in wonder. 'But what does this government do? *Does* it educate its populace properly?' He held up a finger. 'Ah yes – it educates its *white* populace very well! But what does it give to its black populace? Only such education necessary to equip them for their role as "hewers of wood and drawers of water"!'

'Quite right too,' shouted a member of the government benches.

George Mahoney punched his finger at the floor and cried: 'This government intends to keep the blacks as perpetual serfs, to serve the *Lekker Lewe*! To supply labour for menial tasks, as they think befits the Sons of Ham! What unchristian arrogance! And what utter folly to imagine that they, a minority of Afrikaners, can keep a majority of blacks suppressed forever, and insult their intelligence – '

25

'*What intelligence?*' a government frontbencher shouted.

'You see, Mr Speaker – that's how the Honourable Member thinks. And it will lead to this country's downfall, for not only will they create an ill-educated populace which cannot contribute properly to a modern economy, but sure as God made little green apples these black students will one day rise up in rebellion – '

'And we'll be ready for them! Who's paying for their education – the white taxpayer!'

George Mahoney's bushy eyebrows shot up. 'Ready for them? With your *kragdadigheid* – your batons and guns! Is that the way a sensible government runs its country? No, it is a *crazy* way, to have to rely on force! It is moonshine *madness* to spend the taxpayers' money in such a way that the country is angry, resentful, bitter, rebellious!'

He glowered, then went on with withering scorn: 'As it is moonshine *madness* to antagonise the populace by cruel social engineering which attempts to stop human relationships between the races! *Punishes* people who fall in love across the colour bar! The Population Registration Act classifies each one of us into card-carrying racial groupings and thereafter determines who may do what to whom for the rest of our lives! The Prohibition of Mixed Marriages Act forbids people of different races to marry – and if they were already married before that date they either have to divorce or the white spouse has to be reclassified as non-white and thereafter live in a non-white area!' He spread his hands in appeal. 'What kind of a law is it that says you *must* divorce? Is it a *Christian* law? No – it is the law of the devil! And even the children can receive different racial classifications depending on their appearance – and families have had to split up and live in different areas! I ask you, Mr Speaker – is it a Christian law that forces a family to split up?' He punched his palm. 'No, it is a *diabolical* law! And the Immorality Act punishes people of different pigmentation who have sexual intercourse! Throws them in jail! Drags them before the courts for public humiliations, brings scandal upon their families, ruins their careers! It has driven people to suicide. What kind of country makes sexual intercourse between consenting adults a crime? It is *grotesque.*'

'Immorality is against the word of God!'

'Then so is *all* sexual intercourse unless the parties are married! Okay – if *that* is the will of God, I challenge this government to make *all* sexual intercourse outside wedlock a crime! I defy them! Come on! Make a *total* laughing stock of yourselves!'

The Speaker pounded his gavel. 'I warn you, Mr Mahoney, that personal insults will not be tolerated.'

'"*Personal* insults"?' George Mahoney echoed, astonished. 'But these laws *are* personal insults, Mr Speaker, and just as insulting, just as humili-ating, just as unchristian, just as stupidly cruel, are the laws governing public places! *Petty* apartheid. The Separate Amenities Act is the most conspicuous form of insult, made in public for all the world to see! The petty apartheid, designed by petty minds and strictly enforced by petty policemen, the notices that insist on separate amenities like public lava-tories, benches, playgrounds, beaches, railway coaches, entrances to public buildings, separate libraries, cinemas, bars, hotels, eating estab-lishments, buses – even separate *elevators*, for God's sake, Mr Speaker!'

'The Honourable Member for Transkei will kindly not blaspheme!'

'If that is blasphemy, I repent. But the legislation is a tremendous blasphemy itself. How unchristian it is to say to our fellow citizens: You are not good enough to sit next to me on a train or bus or a barstool or in a restaurant or to swim in the same surf or read in the same library – '

'They have their own amenities,' a government backbencher shouted, 'separate but equal!'

'"*Equal*"?' George echoed. 'Then whites are much more equal than non-whites in this mad-hatter country of ours, Mr Speaker! Because any fool with one eye can tell you that not only are all the non-white amenities inferior to the whites', but there are much fewer of them! Yet there are many more non-whites than whites! This is *equal*? The honourable member should look up the word "equal" in the dictionary, if he has one. He could look up the word "Christian" at the same time and really have a confusing day.'

He shook his head. '*Why*, Mr Speaker, does this government insist on in*sulting* the majority of the populace in this manner? *Why* does this government in*sist* on courting hatred? On courting *rebellion*? On court-ing its own *destruction*?' He looked around, his bushy eyebrows raised. 'Is it because the government is so *stupid* that it believes that political *chaos* will ensue if a non-white sits next to me on a bus, or barstool, or enjoys the same surf, or buys his ice-cream at the same kiosk, or his postage stamp at the same post office window? Is it *credible* that this government is *so* stupid, when you bear in mind that there are certain things that even *this* government has failed to segregate – roads for example. Sidewalks. Pedestrian crossings. Traffic lights. Shop windows. *Shops* – it is still legal for a black lady to walk into Woolworths, stand beside me and buy the same socks I do – though she better not try subversive stuff like that if she buys a postage stamp, no *sir!*'

He nodded theatrically, and dropped his voice to a growl. 'Yes, of *course* it is credible, and this government probably hopes to segregate the sidewalks, roads, and Woolworths too when their Clever Chaps Department can dream up the tricky legislation.' He beamed sadly at the prime minister; then replaced his scowl and thundered: 'But that stupidity is only half of the appalling unchristian reason! The other half is even *more* awful, and it will be the downfall of this whole country. And that reason is *racial prejudice*, Mr Speaker!' He glowered around. 'Indeed racial *hatred*. Belief in racial *superiority*! It is the government's belief that they are the master race and that it is wrong for a non-white person to sit beside them in a bus, or swim in the same surf! It is a belief in *Baaskap*, in Bosshood – I am the boss, and you inferior mortals are not as human as I, not worthy to be near me except as my servant, my garden boy, my child's nursemaid, my farm labourer, the man who shovels rocks on the mines!' He jabbed his finger again. '*That* is the rotten basis of this *petty* apartheid – apart from the towering political and economic injustices of *grand* apartheid – and *that* rotten base will rot the whole country, for our racial prejudice is breeding racial hatred in return – the Afrikaner has sown the seeds of his own destruction!'

Mutters and groans from the government benches. George Mahoney cried: 'Oh yes, Mr Speaker – we've already had the massive Defiance Campaign in 1952 when hundreds of thousands embarked on Gandhian civil disobedience to throw the administration into confusion – for months we had thousands of protesters defying apartheid and curfews and pass-laws so as to invite arrest – over eight *thousand* people were convicted and thirty-two people lost their lives in confrontations with police, including six whites, including a nun, Sister Aiden – '

'And who killed her?' demanded a backbencher. 'The very same blacks she was trying to help – brutally murdered her, cut out her liver for medicine. Savagery killed her, not apartheid – '

'*That* type of savagery,' George Mahoney cried, 'is what apartheid will provoke, again and again – confrontation and mob violence!' He glared around the chamber. 'What a tragedy! And what a *waste*. Of energy and money! The vast body of law that this mad science has built has required tremendously hard work by the police, by the courts, by the legislator, who should have his well-paid mind on beneficial projects, not destructive ones. It's all a *profligate* waste of money which could be spent on black *betterment* schemes, making them better citizens – instead of making them our enemies! And not only is it a *stupid* waste, not only is it *dangerous*, it brings the whole nation into international disrepute!' He paused, glowering at the government benches, then ended: 'For these *compelling* reasons, Mr Speaker, I move a vote of no confidence in this government.'

Luke Mahoney wanted to burst into applause.

2

Out there in the tribal lands there had been troubles for years arising out of the Bantu Authorities Act, which resulted in indirect Pretoria rule through subservient chiefs; but in the black urban areas resistance to apartheid had waned after the failure of the Defiance Campaign. And so the ANC and Indian Congress issued a 'Call to a Congress of the People' to be convened on 26 June 1955, at Kliptown, near Johannesburg. Volunteers across the land canvassed opinions and collected grievances at furtive meetings, and on the appointed day three thousand delegates of all races from scores of organizations converged on the football stadium at dusty, wintry, joyless Kliptown.

Amongst them was a beautiful young Indian schoolgirl, called Patti Gandhi, who had journeyed up from the faraway Transkei by bus on her own initiative to listen to her heroes, in particular to hear a young man called Nelson Mandela who hailed from the same part of the land as she.

In the centre of the football pitch on a platform with microphones stood the convenors; about them the sea of delegates. The proposed Freedom Charter was read out, each clause followed by a rousing speech from the platform. That night Patti Gandhi read it aloud to herself, over and over, until she knew it by heart.

WE THE PEOPLE OF SOUTH AFRICA DECLARE FOR
OUR COUNTRY AND THE WORLD TO KNOW:

That South Africa belongs to all who live in it, black and white, and that no government can justly claim authority unless it is based on the will of all the people;

That our people have been robbed of their birthright to land, liberty and peace by a form of government founded on injustice and inequality and that our country will never be prosperous or free until all our people live in brotherhood . . .

That only a democratic state can secure all their birthright without distinction of colour, race, sex or belief.

And therefore we, the people of South Africa, black and white together – equals, countrymen and brothers – adopt this Freedom Charter:

THE PEOPLE SHALL GOVERN!

Every man and woman shall have the right to vote . . .

ALL NATIONAL GROUPS SHALL HAVE EQUAL RIGHTS!

. . . all apartheid laws and practices shall be set aside.

THE PEOPLE SHALL SHARE IN THE COUNTRY'S WEALTH!

. . . the mineral wealth beneath the soil, the banks and monopoly industry shall be transferred to the ownership of the people.

All other industry and trade shall be controlled . . .

THE LAND SHALL BE SHARED AMONG THOSE WHO WORK IT!

. . . and all the land re-divided . . . to banish famine and land-hunger . . .

All shall have the right to occupy land wherever they choose . . .

ALL SHALL BE EQUAL BEFORE THE LAW . . .

No one shall be imprisoned, deported or restricted without a fair trial . . .

ALL SHALL ENJOY EQUAL HUMAN RIGHTS!

. . . all shall be free to travel from countryside to town . . . and from South Africa abroad; pass laws, permits and all other laws . . . shall be abolished.

THERE SHALL BE WORK AND SECURITY!
THE DOORS OF LEARNING . . . SHALL BE OPENED!
THERE SHALL BE HOUSES, SECURITY AND COMFORT!
THERE SHALL BE PEACE AND FRIENDSHIP . . .

Let all who love their people and their country now say, as we say here:

THOSE FREEDOMS WE WILL FIGHT FOR, SIDE BY SIDE,
THROUGHOUT OUR LIVES, UNTIL WE HAVE WON OUR LIBERTY!

The Freedom Charter was adopted by popular acclaim, though a group called the *Africanists* rejected it because of its multi-racialism: they wanted Africa for the Africans, and they broke away from the ANC to form the Pan Africanist Congress. The next day the people reconvened. That day the South African police struck, with a crack of thunder.

Suddenly the stadium was surrounded, and into the mass went the police. They photographed every individual, and they seized thousands of documents, looking for evidence of treason. Hundreds were arrested. Thus began the infamous Treason Trial.

It was held in the cavernous Johannesburg Drill Hall, remodelled to provide a massive dock to hold 156 accused, sitting in tiers. One of them was the young Xhosa lawyer called Nelson Mandela. The trial was to last for five years, the longest trial in history.

In those days the wind of change was starting to blow in Africa. In Kenya the Mau Mau rebellion was raging; in Ghana the Great Redeemer, Kwame Nkrumah, was demanding independence from Britain, proclaiming himself leader of the Pan African movement; in Nigeria and Tanganyika independence was being loudly demanded; in the Federation of Rhodesia and Nyasaland a policy of 'Partnership' was being attempted but black politicians were demanding immediate majority rule. The Cold War was raging and Russia was providing arms and training, inspiration and indoctrination to the black nationalists. The Western colonial powers, exsanguinated by two world wars, alarmed by the Cold War, had lost their will to govern, appeasement was becoming the order of the day, and the white settlers were afraid, and angry. But in South Africa the government said it had the answer to this *Swart Gevaar*, this Black Peril: they were building a model state which would keep the races apart, each to develop in its own way, enforced by *kragdadigheid*, strength-to-do, and South Africa would be the bastion against communism.

In those days the Mahoneys lived in a big old Victorian house near the centre of Umtata, capital of the Transkei. The garden occupied half a suburban block and Mrs Mahoney hired black convicts, called Tame Bandits, from the prison to keep it neat. George Mahoney had his law office in Main Street, which was wide enough to turn a wagon drawn by sixteen oxen, and there were hitching posts for horses. There were always many Xhosa in their red blankets in Main Street, smoking their long pipes, looking in the Victorian shop windows. The big old Victorian courthouse was set in large lawns, where crowds of Xhosa would sit, waiting for court to begin. On the benches outside George Mahoney's office there were always dozens of Xhosa, waiting to consult the white lawyer who always won cases.

'But there's no money in being a small-town attorney, son,' George told Luke. 'None of my clients has much money. You're going to be an *advocate*, son, in the big city, get amongst the big stuff.'

'But he doesn't want to be a lawyer,' Mrs Mahoney said, 'he's talking about being a journalist.'

'That's this week. Next week it'll be law again. I tell you, this son of ours is going to be a bloody good lawyer.'

'But I don't think it's right for a boy of fourteen to be spending his afternoons and holidays in a stuffy law office.'

'If I was a farmer my boy of fourteen would be ploughing the land. If I was a shopkeeper he would be helping behind the counter. There is no finer training for a law student than to sit in my office and watch how it's done. Life in the raw! Crime, divorce, debt-collecting, he'll have seen it all by the time he leaves school. The boy's a natural.'

'Well, I'm sorry but I really don't think it's right to spend so much time in court, hearing all those sordid details – '

'The world is sordid and the best place to learn about it is the court-room – the forum of human drama, learning to sift the wheat from the chaff, strong points from weak points – '

Beyond the courthouse was the Bhungha, an imposing white build-ing which used to be the Native Representative Council until apartheid put an end to that; and opposite was the school for whites. Umtata had a population of only three thousand whites, but the school taught almost one thousand because most of the pupils were the children of the traders who lived way out in the rolling hills that stretched from the Kei River in the west to the Umzimvubu in the east, from the Indian Ocean in the south to the Drakensberg in the north, a territory almost the size of Scotland, of which George Mahoney was the parlia-mentary representative. On the other side of town, down near the winding Umtata River with its weeping willows, was the poorer part of town, where most of the Afrikaners lived, mostly artisans and railway workers, with chickens and maybe a cow in the backyard. Beyond them, on the very edge of town, lived the Coloureds, the half-castes, and this is also where Patti Gandhi lived.

Legally speaking, the Gandhi family should not have lived in a Coloured area, but in an Asian area, but as there were no other Indians in town the mentors of the Group Areas Act had not yet got around to zoning a separate residential area for them. Mr Gandhi was not allowed to trade in Main Street, which was a white area, but his store two streets back, where he had his small clothing factory, was also tolerated. It was in a grey area which the scientists in Pretoria would have to clean up one day, but until then the police did not know what to do with them.

For the same reason Patti Gandhi's attendance at the white convent, St Mary's College, had to be tolerated although she wasn't even a Christian: the Coloured school was quite inadequate, and of course the government high school, which Luke Mahoney attended, was out of the question. It was George Mahoney who persuaded the police commandant to turn a blind eye, 'until such time as this bloody government builds an Asian school just for her!'

'She should be sent to school in Natal, where all the Indians are,' Colonel Visser said uncomfortably.

'For God's sake, Colonel, you can't tear a family apart! The girl's in her formative years, the Gandhis are a very law-abiding family and it's a great expense to send your child away to school!'

'Old Gandhi's got more money than you and me put together, sir, and I don't know how law-abiding he is – look at that swank house he's built illegally in the Coloured area.'

'The man's got to live somewhere and as the government hasn't yet told him where that is, he's perfectly entitled to build a decent house on the land he's owned for decades. And *that*, you can take it from me,' he said with more conviction than was warranted, 'is the law.' He appealed: 'If the servants of God are prepared to help her, so should you.'

'Okay,' the colonel sighed, 'I saw nothing. But – ' he held up a warning finger – 'no sport, hey. No swimming, no hockey, no socializing, none of that nonsense. And *one* complaint and she's on the bus to Natal.'

'On my head be it!' George Mahoney beamed. 'She'll cause no trouble. She's exceptionally intelligent . . .'

And she was exceptionally good-looking. As a little girl she was angelic, as a nymph of twelve she was beautiful, as a fifteen-year-old she was gorgeous. She was tall and smooth of movement, with long black shiny hair that reached to her waist, long golden legs under her demure gym-skirt, a face to make one stare, big almond eyes and a smile, when she gave it, to melt the heart. And she caused plenty of trouble in the loins of the boys of Umtata High School. But they seldom saw her: her father drove her to and from school so she would be seen as little as possible in her convent uniform lest a complaint be raised. If the boys wanted to see her they had to go to the Gandhi Store, where she worked after school: but how many excuses could a lad find for buying in a 'kaffir store'? She often worked in her father's garment factory, but what excuse could a schoolboy find for visiting that? And when she was seen that beautiful smile was seldom given: she was an aloof, haughty girl.

'She hasn't got much to smile about, has she?' Luke's sister Jill said. 'No friends.'

'Aren't your friends at the convent nice to her?' Mrs Mahoney asked.

'I mean after school.'

'Well, she should be grateful she's getting a decent education – and these people prefer their own company anyway.'

'But there *are* no other Indians for her to be friends with. Can I invite her home one day to have a swim?'

Ooh, yes please, Luke prayed. *Patti Gandhi in a swimsuit . . .*

'Definitely *not*. I'm not having Indians in our pool!'

Only one Indian . . . Mahoney prayed.

'Mother, she's perfectly clean, you know!' Jill cried.

'The subject,' Mrs Mahoney said, 'is closed.'

'Well,' Jill sulked, 'can I at least invite her to my birthday party?'

Mrs Mahoney sighed. 'No darling – she'll be like a fish out of water. Who'll dance with her?'

Me – me – me . . . Mahoney prayed.

'I'm all for giving the girl a good education, but socializing with her is something entirely different. And what *good* will it do her? She can't keep the friendships up afterwards – it's even *unkind* to her . . .'

Jill turned in appeal to her father: '*Daddy*?'

George Mahoney sighed. 'I think your mother's right, my dear – if for different reasons. I promised Colonel Visser there'd be no socializing. I've got no objection to the girl coming to your party – and, by the way it's not illegal – not yet – but that *is* socializing, and it'll get back to your friends' parents, and somebody may kick up a fuss, and it'll get to the police and, well, I'll have broken the bargain, won't I, and Patti Gandhi could well be told to leave the convent. It could cause trouble, without her being in any way to blame . . .'

But Patti Gandhi was to blame for the trouble. It happened in Luke's second-last year at high school. That was the year the government translocated the people of Sophiatown, the black spot in white residential Johannesburg, to Soweto, the sprawling black township on the out-skirts of the golden city. The year of the heartbreak of Sophiatown, the destruction of a whole teeming city within a city, a whole way of life, to replace it with a white middle-class suburb to be called *Triomf*, meaning Triumph. For months the government had been warning the people of Sophiatown that the day was approaching when vehicles would come to move them; it was the day the lorries and bulldozers arrived that Patti Gandhi, fifteen years old, walked into the public library in Umtata, took a book off the shelf and sat down to read.

'Excuse me,' the librarian, nice Mrs van Jaarsveld, whispered, 'but this library is for whites only.'

Ten minutes later Mrs van Jaarsveld felt obliged to fulfil her threat to call the police. An hour later Patti Gandhi was released by a fed-up Colonel Visser into the custody of her father with a stern warning not to try any funny business like that again. By nightfall it was the talk of the town.

'Oh, *hell*!' George Mahoney groaned.

The next day was Saturday, when the boarders at the girls' hostel and the boys' hostel were allowed into town. The big topic of conversation was what that Indian girl, Patti Gandhi, had done. At mid-morning she walked into the Rex Café, where the boarders were all tucking into their ice-creams and milk-shakes and, midst the ensuing sudden silence, sat down at an empty table, held out her money and asked the Coloured waitress for a Coca-Cola. The waitress called the owner. The owner called the police. 'What,' the Afrikaner constable demanded, 'are you doing here, hey?'

'I am endeavouring,' Patti Gandhi said, 'to quench my thirst.'

'Well, jus' you ender- whatchacallit along with me, hey . . .'

This time Colonel Visser was really angry. 'Is this how you treat my kindness?' He telephoned her father to come. 'This is her last warning! Next time it's straight into Juvenile Court! I hope you give her a bladdy good hiding, hey!'

'I will, sir, thank you, sir,' Mr Gandhi said.

He did not give her the hiding 'which you deserve' – 'Don't you realize we have no rights to even *be* here under the Group Areas Act?'

'That's exactly what I realize. And nor do the people of Sophiatown have any rights!'

'*Sophiatown!*' the old man shouted. 'I'm sick of hearing about Sophiatown! Just thank your lucky stars you're not in Sophiatown but in Umtata where people are kind to us!'

'*Kind?*' She rolled her flashing eyes. 'God help us when they get unkind!'

'Here we can *survive*, because of nice people like Mr Mahoney and Colonel Visser whose hand you bite – '

'"*Bite!*" Reading a book is a *bite*? Asking for a Coca-Cola!' She bared her teeth. 'Just wait till I *do* bite . . .'

'Don't you threaten me!' Mr Gandhi wanted to slap her face but checked himself. 'Don't you threaten our existence! We've survived and that is an achievement! Your grandfather came here as a coolie to cut cane for a rupee a day, and now look at us! Look at this house! Look at our factories!'

'And look at my great-uncle! He ended up liberating India from the British!'

'And I suppose you want to liberate South Africa with your library books and Coca-Colas!'

'Yes!' Patti hollered. 'Yes, yes, yes!'

Quivering with rage, her father sent her to bed for the rest of the day. But as soon as he had gone back to the factory she climbed out of the window, and cycled to her father's store. She unlocked the back door and went to the hardware counter. With bolt-cutters she sliced off two metres of chain. She selected two stout padlocks and a pair of pliers. Then she rode across town to the municipal swimming pool.

Saturday was a big day at the municipal pool. In the afternoons most of the girls from the high school and convent came to meet their boyfriends. The fenced lawns around the pool were choked with young bodies when Patti Gandhi arrived. She parked her bicycle with the others, then set off to approach the area from the back.

She crept up the storm-water culvert that led up the side of the big fence, then into the shrubbery beyond. She crept up to the hedge that lined the mesh-wire fence. With the pliers she cut a hole.

Nobody noticed Patti Gandhi wriggling through, nobody noticed her until she strolled across the lawn, her lovely young body golden, her breasts bulging and her hips slowly swinging, her soft thighs stroking each other, her long black hair down to her waist, her seldom-seen smile all over her beautiful face: then every head was turning. Patti Gandhi sauntered across the lawn, carrying a little hold-all, her towel trailing languidly, making for the high-diving board. She climbed up it, two hundred pairs of astonished eyes upon her. She had reached the top and sauntered out to the end of the board when the pool manager, Frikkie van Schalkwyk, came bustling out of his office.

'Hey!' he shouted furiously. 'Hey! Get out of here, man!'

Patti gave him a wave and her magnificent smile, dropped her hands to her knees, stuck out her beautiful backside at him and shook it. And a gasp went up from the white boys and girls, then laughter, then scattered clapping that gathered momentum. Patti Gandhi stood on the tip of the diving board, grinning and waving and blowing kisses, and Frikkie van Schalkwyk, of the Umtata Municipality Recreation Department, gave a roar of outrage and charged.

Frikkie ran up the steps onto the lawns, puffed around the top end of the pool, leaping over the gleeful white bodies, heading for the high-dive on the other side. He scrambled furiously up it, huffing his municipal outrage, and as he reached the top Patti blew him a splendid kiss, and she dived.

Patti Gandhi dived in a beautiful beaming swallow, just as Frikkie burst onto the board to roars of derision. She disappeared under the water in a streaming of long black hair. Frikkie blundered to the end, furiously shouting at the water, torn between diving in after her and retracing his outraged steps to confront her on the other side with the long arm of the law. Patti broke surface in the centre of the big pool, tossed back her long hair like a whiplash and beamed up at Frikkie: *'Come in! The water's lovely!'*

And Frikkie hurled himself in after her. He landed in a mighty belly-flop to roars of delight and *'Go, Frikkie, Go!'* and *'Faster, Frikkie, Faster!'* from the gleeful teenagers. Frikkie van Schalkwyk thrashed with all his might across the pool to apprehend the delinquent Patti Gandhi, and Patti Gandhi laughed and reached the ladder on the other side just as Frikkie was reaching the middle.

She scrambled lightly up it, her golden body glinting, and she skipped joyfully to the head of the pool to draw Frikkie that way and cried: *'This way, Frikkie –'*

Frikkie changed direction and thrashed towards her, and Patti skipped back the other way and shouted: *'Over here, now, Frikkie, over here –'*

But Frikkie van Schalkwyk, custodian of the Municipality of Umtata Bye-Laws (Recreational Facilities) (Swimming Pool) as amended, was no fool, hey. Not for him to thrash this way and that to the tune of a cheeky bladdy Coolie, hey: he heaved himself up the ladder in a furious gush, and stomped off to summon the police, to laughter and cries of 'Spoil-sport.' Patti Gandhi sauntered back to the high diving-board, grinning, and began to climb again.

Luke Mahoney was near the foot of the ladder. He watched Patti climb, looking up at her legs, and the beauty of what he saw, her lovely rounded bottom, her golden thighs, the sheer female magnificence of her, was to stay with him for the rest of his life.

Patti reached the top, unzipped her little hold-all, and pulled out the chain. She wrapped it once around her waist, and padlocked it into position. She wrapped the other end around the ladder, and padlocked that. She picked up both sets of keys and slipped them into the panties of her bikini. Then she lay down decorously to sunbathe while she waited for the police.

'Where're the keys?' the sergeant demanded.

'Up my pussy,' Patti smiled.

It took an hour to get Patti Gandhi down because the police had to retreat to find bolt-cutters. She was sorely tempted to push the policeman off the high-dive into the water, uniform and all, but she resisted it: *No violence*, great-uncle Mahatma Gandhi had said, *Passive resistance only* . . . But passive resistance meant she had to be carried down the ladder over the shoulder of the sergeant (who enjoyed clutching her lovely thigh), had to be carried bodily out of the swimming pool grounds.

She made a very dramatic spectacle, her beautiful buttocks up in the air, her long black hair hanging down the policeman's rear, sweeping the ground, being carried away by the long arm of the law to face justice. There was no more laughter: a silence that was almost awe had descended on two hundred white teenagers, almost shame. Patti Gandhi had made her point. Her great-uncle would have been proud of her.

Luke Mahoney pulled on his clothes, jumped on his bicycle and rode flat out up the hill to the golf club to find his father, his face suffused with anger, his heart bursting with guilt, and pity. 'I'll finish my game,' George said, on the tenth green, 'it won't do her any harm to spend a few hours in the cells before I get her out. It may save her from many, many more in the future. That girl is headed for big trouble . . . '

'*She's in very big trouble now!*' Colonel Visser said furiously. 'Christ, man, Mr Mahoney, I've turned a blind eye to the convent, and I've given her two chances in two days! *Christ*, girl, what have you got – a death wish?!'

'On the contrary, sir,' Patti said quietly, 'I have a life wish.'

'A *life* wish . . . ' Colonel Visser groaned. 'Christ, young lady, I've tried to *give* you a decent life, and to do that I risked *my* life – *my* career. *Got*, man, if my superiors in Pretoria knew that *I* knew about that convent business, I would face disciplinary proceedings, hey!' He held a finger out at her nose. 'I risked my career for you, because your father here has never given us any trouble! But *you*! You're a disgrace to your family and your *race*! . . . '

'Oh my goodness gracious me, sir,' Mr Gandhi said, 'I apologise for my daughter, sir . . . '

'Apologise to the magistrate on Monday!' Colonel Visser shouted at Patti, 'apologise for all the trouble you've put us to! And the trouble you've caused Mr Mahoney! Apologise for the shame you've caused your father, who's never put a foot wrong in his life here!' He wagged a finger: 'Take my advice and throw yourself on the mercy of the court, young lady, and *apologize*. And maybe that will save you from reform school!'

Patti looked at the good colonel with big beautiful almond eyes: '*Reform* school?'

'Yes! Because you're a born troublemaker if ever I saw one – '

'Trouble?' Patti said with big eyes. '*I'm* causing trouble?'

'Yes! Breaking the law deliberately! Christ, man, can't you see what *trouble*, what . . . *chaos* people like you could cause in this town – in this *country*! Christ, man, we live surrounded by millions of kaffirs! Can you imagine the *trouble* if millions of kaffirs came into this town and tried to swim in our swimming pool! Or went to the library and demanded books?! Or went to the Rex Café, hey, man?! *Got*, man, there would be *chaos*, hey! And that's why these laws are *necessary!* Yes, necessary! There must be *order*, hey! And *you*, young lady – ' he jabbed his finger at her – 'are trying to destroy this order with your bladdy silly nonsense!'

He turned to George Mahoney: 'No, sir, I can't withdraw the charges this time! Okay, I'll give her bail, but it's Juvenile Court on Monday! And then she's on that bus to Natal to the other Indians if she wants any further education, hey! No more convent, thank you very much! Not only does she bite the hand that helps her, she commits malicious damage to property, cutting a hole in the Municipality's fence!'

Patti leapt to her feet. '"Malicious Damage to Property"?' she cried. She pointed north furiously: 'At this moment, as we speak, the bulldozers of the South African government are smashing down the whole of *Sophiatown!*'

3

Sophiatown. A teeming black city within the golden city of Johannesburg, a sprawling mass of run-down houses and shacks, grubby shops and fly-blown markets, bleak churches and mosques, bazaars and shebeens and brothels and sweatshops and junkyards and outdoor lavatories, a slum city of rutted lanes that turned to mud in the rains and swirling dust in the hot dry winds of the highveld winter, a sprawling slum of blacks and Coloureds and Indians and Chinese and poor-whites, mangy dogs and scrawny chickens, riddled with gangs of tearaways and petty criminals, a city of thieving and robbery and knifing and murder and fighting and trickery and protection rackets and disposal of stolen property, drug-dealing and the illegal brewing of the fire-water called *skokiaan*: Sophiatown was an eyesore, insanitary, an offence to the exquisite sensibilities of the new social science called Apartheid.

'But only because it's in the wrong place in terms of this dreadful Group Areas Act!' George Mahoney thundered in parliament. 'If

Sophiatown were safely out of sight beyond the mine-dumps it would not matter a jot to this government that it is an insanitary place, Sophiatown could then rot in Hell for all this government cares!'

'Is the Honourable Member for Transkei aware that Sophiatown is also a den of iniquity where so-called liberal young whites, such as university students, think it's funny to go dancing to black music, dancing *amongst* blacks, dancing *with* blacks even, and drinking illegally in their shebeens, and smoking dagga and even contravening the Immorality Act with black prostitutes, hey!'

'Good gracious me!' George Mahoney cried. 'What *will* these students think of next!'

Yes, Sophiatown was also fun. A fun place to go slumming, if you had the nerve. To risk your skin and risk the cops. A place of jazz bands, zoot suits, rock and roll, gambling dens, American cars, snazzy girls and with-it wide-boys, beauty competitions and prize-fighting, Miss Sophiatown and Mr Wonderful, striptease, six-guns and flick-knives and Hollywood heroes, Porgy and Bess, James Cagney and Louis Armstrong, Harry Belafonte and Humphrey Bogart, hard drinking and dangerous living. Chicago, Africa-style. Live hard, die young and leave a good-looking corpse: that was the hip attitude and tempo that was captured in *Drum*, the glossy magazine written and published in Johannesburg that had made Sophiatown glamorously infamous.

'Does the Honourable Member for Transkei – wherever that is – honestly think that it is *proper*, that it is *right*, that it is *Christian*, that white people go and degrade themselves in a place like that? What I cannot understand is the Honourable Member's objection to implementing God's will by the orderly eradication of sin, and social upliftment! And they had plenty of warning!'

'"*Social upliftment*"?!' George Mahoney roared. 'How about social *impoverishment*?! How about social *destitution!* How about . . . government *profiteering! Yes, profiteering,* Mr Speaker! Despicable, money-grubbing, corrupt, mendacious profiteering by this government at the expense of the poor for the benefit of the rich! Why do I make this serious allegation? *Because* this government has compulsorily bought up Sophiatown, plot by plot, at its present slum value, and then, having evicted the poor unfortunate black owner who did *not* want to sell, it has sent in its big yellow bulldozers to raze his hovel to the ground. Then, waving the magic wand of the Group Areas Act, it has declared the area a white suburb, put in tarred roads, sewers and electricity, and sold the self-same plots for a *fortune*. For ten-fold! For twenty-fold! 'He glowered around, then appealed: 'Is this not *despicable*? What kind of government is it who takes advantage of its poorest citizens by first *legislating* that they must sell cheap, and then *legislating* that the new owner, this government, will sell *expensive*!' He spread his hands to the heavens and cried: 'Good God, Mr Speaker, I tell you that this government is the government of *Ali Baba!'*

Uproar. Outrage. Honourable Members wanting to leap over their benches and get their hands on the Honourable Member for Transkei.

Social upliftment? A whole society, a whole way of life, a whole livelihood was broken up and the pieces dumped out there in the bare veld beyond the horizon where it wouldn't be seen. The convoys of government lorries arriving in Sophiatown, the hordes of policemen, the civil servants with their clipboards, the loudspeakers blaring instructions, the bulldozers rumbling, waiting. The army on standby. The poor people filing down the lanes to their designated vehicles, carrying their pitiful possessions, loading them on, climbing up; the waving goodbye, the weeping, the stoicism. *'Hurry up, please, hurry along there, please!'* Those who refused to cooperate were carried. *'Come along, please, no nonsense now!'* The convoys rumbling out, the bull-dozers rumbling in, the crunch of walls coming down, the dust rising up. The long convoys with their police escorts wound through Johannesburg, piled high with people and their belongings, out towards the sprawling black city of Soweto – bureau-speak for South Western Townships – past the vast rows of identical little joyless cottages, the spread-eagled squatter shacks, and on into the veld beyond. And awaiting them were row upon row of numbered wooden pegs in the ground, and government officials with their lists, allocating the little plots. The goods and chattels were dumped on the bare ground, and the vehicles turned back to Sophiatown for the next load of human despair.

'Social upliftment?' George Mahoney roared. 'How about social *cruelty*?! Dumped in the bare veld, their goods and chattels exposed to the elements! And for this piece of dirt these poor people must now start paying *rent*! Dumped without a brick or a plank to start building even a shack! Dumped without toilets, with only one communal water-tap every so many hundred yards! Dumped without light, without fuel, miles from their employment, miles from shops, miles from the bus or train station. Dumped *heartlessly, callously* – and the Honourable Member has the towering *brutality* to call it social *upliftment!'*

He clutched his head: 'Mr Speaker, the destruction of Sophiatown is not social upliftment, it is a stinking, reeking *indictment* of this govern-ment! And it shows this government is not only cynical and cruel, it is *brainless* . . . !'

Uproar.

'It is *stupid*, Mr Speaker, to generate hatred amongst the people – especially as they are the majority! And it is *stupid* to bulldoze down one slum only to create another in the bare veld! But Sophiatown is only *half* the awful story – only a *fraction* of it! The rest of the story is even more tragic. Because the horror-show of Sophiatown is only the *beginning* of this government's crazy plans of Grand Apartheid! As we speak the mad scientists in Pretoria are poring over maps and plotting more diabolical translocations of blackspots, more bulldozer jobs, more convoys, marking out more chunks of bare veld beyond the horizon upon which to dump its black population, to make more despair, more slums, more vice, more degradation, more bitterness, more hatred, more trouble for the white man in the future. Sophiatown is only the beginning! For as long as this government is in power we are going to see the heartbreak of Sophiatown repeated, from the northern Transvaal down to the Cape, from the Indian Ocean to the Atlantic we are going to see the heartlessness of Sophiatown repeated, whilst this government relentlessly, suicidally, systematically turns the vast majority of its citizens into its enemies, guaranteeing that they will one day rise up and destroy the white man who thrust such injustice upon them!' He stabbed at the heavens. 'This government is busily, stupidly, blindly, self-destructing!'

Boos and laughter from the government benches.

'Self-destruction by the government, Mr Speaker,' George Mahoney shouted, 'would be fine with me! The sooner the better! But the tragedy of it is that in so doing they will destroy the whole country too . . .'

4

Beyond the poor-white houses of Umtata, beyond the Coloureds' area, where the grand house of Mr Gandhi stood out like a sore thumb, was the black Anglican Mission school, St John's College, or St John's Porridge as it was called, for African porridge is made of 'kaffir corn', which is brown. By law the two schools were forbidden to have anything to do with each other; but twice a year they did play a cricket match, illegally, for that had been a tradition pre-dating apartheid.

The St John's Porridge team was not much good, except for one boy called Justin Nkomo. He had no style whatsoever, but what he could do was *hit* a ball. Any ball: fast, slow, off-spin, leg-spin, googlies, full tosses. Justin stood there in his tattered khaki shorts, holding his bat like a club, as the best high-school bowlers came thundering up to the wicket, and Justin swiped and the ball went sailing up into the wide blue yonder. He always hit the ball in the meat of the bat; he never edged it or blocked it – he *smote* it. The only way to get him out was to catch him on the boundary. St John's Porridge put Justin Nkomo in as opening bat, and he stayed there while the rest of his team were dismissed. *'Get Nkomo!'* was the message the high school team received from their cricket coach. 'He's *your* kitchen boy, Mahoney, can't you sabotage him somehow?'

It was in Luke's final year at school, the year after Patti Gandhi disappeared in the bus bound for Natal, the year Luke became head prefect and was nominated for a Rhodes Scholarship, that Justin Nkomo became the Mahoney's kitchen boy, in the sense that he exchanged a few hours' household work every night for free board and lodging in the servants' quarters. It was a fashionable act of charity to thus sponsor a St John's College boy, but it was of questionable legality because under apartheid only bona fide full-time servants were allowed to reside on white property. Colonel Visser turned another blind eye, however, 'as long as there're no complaints, hey.'

Mrs Mahoney said to her son: 'But, please, no cricket with this boy behind the garage wall; he's here to work and study and I won't have any familiarity.'

But there was cricket behind the garage wall and that was definitely illegal: bona fide kitchen boys don't play cricket. Luke and Hendrik Visser, the police commandant's son, and David Downes, the district surgeon's son, had rigged some nets behind the garage and, when his mother wasn't home, Luke would call Justin out of the kitchen to bat. They would hurl ball after ball down, but they could never knock those stumps over. Once David brought a real American baseball-bat along, to see what Justin would do with it, and he did the same. They tried to teach him a bit of style, to make him hold his bat straight, step forward to long balls, back for short balls, and though he tried, to be polite, within a minute he was back to his slugging style. They asked him how he did it and he replied it was 'just easy'.

The other thing Justin Nkomo found easy was studying. His English was stilted when he first came to work for the Mahoneys – 'Please scrutinise my endeavours, Nkosaan' – but he soon became idiomatic. In the evenings, after he'd helped the cook, he was allowed to study at the kitchen table, for there was no electric light in the servants' quarters, and he sometimes sent a message to Luke via the houseboy to come to the kitchen to help him. Luke found it easy to help him because, although they were both in their matriculation year, Justin's curriculum was inferior. 'Nkosi, what did Shakespeare mean when Macduff tells Macbeth that he "was from his mother's womb untimely ripp'd"?'

Luke said, 'Well, you remember that the three witches have told Macbeth that no man of woman born can kill him? Well, Macbeth and Macduff are now fighting, and Macbeth is confident that Macduff cannot kill him, because of the witches' prophecy, right?'

'Correct.'

'But now Macduff announces that he was not born of a woman in the normal way – so he *can* kill Macbeth. Because he was born by a Caesarean operation.'

The next night Justin said: 'Our English teacher says you're right.' He added: 'Shaka once had a hundred pregnant women slit open so he could examine the foetuses.'

'Shaka did?' Shaka, the Zulu warrior-king of the century, was one of Luke's military heroes and he was interested in any new information about him. 'Why?'

'Because he was a stupid butcher.'

'He was also a military genius.'

'Then why didn't he get guns? There were traders in those days who would have sold him guns. All Zulus are stupid.'

'But the Xhosa didn't get guns either, and they had more opportunity to get them than the Zulus – they fought *nine* Kaffir Wars against the white man.'

'And you still didn't beat us, Nkosi – we committed suicide in the Great Cattle Killing. But only four hundred Boers beat the Zulus at the Battle of Blood River.'

'And why did the Xhosa commit national suicide – wasn't that stupid?'

Justin Nkomo looked at the young master. 'No, Nkosaan, because the girl prophet told them it was the right thing to do.'

'But it was nonsense.'

'Yes, because she was a false prophet.'

'So if she *hadn't* been a *false* prophet all the dead warriors of nine wars *would* have risen from the grave and the white man's bullets *would* have turned to water?'

'Yes,' Justin Nkomo said.

'And the Russians would have come?'

'Yes.' He added, 'And one day the Russians will come. Like they have come to help the Mau Mau in Kenya.'

Mahoney was taken aback by this. He had heard such wisdom from his father, but coming from the kitchen-boy it was bad news. 'Who says?'

'My history teacher. Haven't you heard of communism? The South

African Communist Party? And the ANC, the African National Congress?'

'Of course. But what do you know about them?' They were talking a mixture of English and Xhosa now.

'Communism,' Justin said, 'is good. Soon the whole world will be communist. Soon there will be a revolution all over the world. Like is happening now in Kenya with the Mau Mau, where your aunt comes from.'

'Your history teacher says this?'

'Yes. And then we will all be rich like you. Everybody equal.'

'How am I rich?'

'You have a bicycle,' Justin Nkomo said.

'And when we have communism will they give you a bicycle?'

'Yes.'

'Everybody?'

'Yes.'

'And cattle?'

'Yes.'

'And who will own the land?'

'The people. Land is not *owned*, Nkosaan. Land is like the sun. And water. It belongs to the people. Only capitalism says land can belong to rich people who buy it.'

It was the tradition of the Mahoney household that dinner was devoted to intellectual discussions. Any subject was entertained provided it was supported by intelligent argument. If not, it was thrown out ('Like in the courtroom.'). That night Luke mentioned this conversation at dinner. Aunt Sheila McAdam from Kenya was staying, making her annual visit to South Africa.

His mother said: 'Typical. Nice boy, goes to a mission school, but believes in witchcraft. And gets his head stuffed full of communist nonsense.'

'Unfortunately it's not nonsense,' George Mahoney said. 'Apartheid will drive the blacks into the arms of the communists.'

'Like's happened in Kenya,' Jill pronounced gravely.

'Not quite – ' Luke began.

'No, we've got no apartheid in Kenya,' Aunt Sheila said. 'The Mau Mau rebellion was *fostered* by Russia, through Jomo Kenyatta who was befriended by the communists when he was in England.'

'But the whites stole the blacks' land?' Jill persisted.

'No, the Kenyan government *bought* the land from the Kikuyu, including land which the Kikuyu had never even occupied and to which they had no right. The Kikuyu were left with plenty of land, in guaranteed reserves. The land issue was an excuse dreamed up by Russia and Jomo Kenyatta to make the Kikuyu rebel and start taking those frightful oaths to kill the white settlers, so that the communists can take over – and then spread revolution down the whole of Africa, so Russia can take over.'

'What was so frightful about the oaths?' Jill demanded. 'Drinking blood and all that?'

'And the rest,' Aunt Sheila said. She was a weathered, robust English matron, married to Uncle Fred, who managed the East African end of Harker-Mahoney.

'Please,' Mrs Mahoney said, 'not during meals.' She was the opposite of Aunt Sheila: an English rose.

'Cutting up people and eating them?' Jill said hopefully.

'*Please*,' Mrs Mahoney said.

'Why did they make the oaths horrid?' Jill demanded.

George Mahoney said to his daughter: 'I've got a book you can read, Jill, called *Something of Value* by Robert Ruark . . . '

'You know how superstitious the blacks are,' Aunt Sheila said. 'They utterly believe. The missionaries come and convert them to Christianity, teach 'em readin', 'ritin' and 'rithmetic, put 'em in pants and – bingo – they imagine they've done the trick of turning the black man into a civilized man.' She shook her head. 'No such thing. He *may* – re*luct*antly – come to accept the white man's God – usually because of an uneasy feeling that the white man's magic is pretty strong medicine – but he still also believes in Ngai, his own god, who lives up there on Mount Kenya, and in his ancestors who walk along behind him giving him a hard time, and in all the evil spirits, *and* in all the spells and curses a witch or wizard can place on him.' She spread her hands. 'Of course you *do* encounter some *real* Christian converts who have staunchly refused to take the oaths and suffered terribly for it – had their wives and children butchered in front of their eyes, and so on. But for most of them the whole raft of superstitions are still as real to them as the trees and the rocks and Mount Kenya.'

'But what's the oath?' Jill demanded.

George Mahoney looked at his wife. 'She's old enough to learn about the darker side of the Africa she lives in.'

'Well,' Sheila said. She got onto her hobby horse. 'Well, it's that superstitiousness that the Mau Mau oath plays on. The oaths were dreamed up by Jomo Kenyatta and his Russian friends – our future president. Anyway, the Mau Mau oath has its strength in the fact that it *desecrates* all the Kikuyu believes in, all his taboos. It's as if you, a

Christian, broke all your principles and taboos by taking an oath to the Forces of Darkness. So the person who takes the oath becomes an *outcast* from his people, which means that the only brotherhood he belongs to which can protect him is the Mau Mau – the Devil. And they believe that the oath will kill him – and his family – if he breaks it, or disobeys orders. And of course the Mau Mau *will* kill him. So, we are fighting completely degenerate, *desperate* blood-soaked savages.'

George said: 'And the Mau Mau work on a secret-cell system, don't they?'

'Yes. Devised by the Russians. The oath-administrators initiate the members of a cell – for example, the labour force on a particular shamba. He charges ninety shillings per person – and if they refuse to take the oath they're hideously killed, as an example to the rest. The administrator keeps thirty shillings, and the rest goes to Mau Mau funds. The oath administrator gets rich and has every incentive to keep initiating people, so it's spread across the colony until now over a million Kikuyu have taken the oath. They started with initiating a few bandits in the forests, then it spread to the shambas, the farms, and then into the towns. Now it's spreading into Tanganyika. The Russians' plan is that it will spread right the way down through South Africa to Cape Town, right across the continent.'

'Do they make human sacrifices when they do the oath?' Jill demanded.

'*Please* . . . ' Mrs Mahoney said.

'Much worse than that,' Aunt Sheila murmured.

Much worse than that, Luke knew: he had read the book. The purpose was to shock, to horrify, to degrade, to defy all taboos. So the oath had to be disgusting. Each oath administrator was instructed to dream up more horrifying oaths with which to terrify the people, to pass on his new ideas to the other administrators. Human sacrifice was always one ingredient. And animal sacrifice. Blood and body-parts mixed in the ground into a kind of soup. Brains of the persons sacrificed mixed in. Woman's menstrual blood. Urine. Semen. Human shit. Maggots. Putrefied human flesh exhumed from graves. Pus from running sores. Eyeballs gouged out, intestines cut open. Drinking the vile brew while you repeat the oath. Public intercourse with sheep and adolescent girls. And all the time the dancing and the drums and the bloodcurdling mumbo-jumbo, all at dead of night in the spooky forest, all the oath-takers in a trance. All with the purpose of irrevocably committing the oath-taker to killing Europeans, burning their crops, killing their cattle, stealing their firearms, killing to order even if the victim is your own father or brother – and always to mutilate, cut off the heads, extract the eyeballs and drink the liquid. 'If I am ordered to bring my brother's head and I disobey, this oath will kill me. If I am ordered to bring the finger or ear of my mother and I disobey, this oath will kill me. If I am ordered to bring the head, hair or fingernail of a European and I disobey, this oath will kill me. If I rise against the Mau Mau, this oath will kill me. If I betray the whereabouts of arms or ammunition or the hiding place of my brothers, this oath will kill me. When the reed-buck horn is blown, if I leave the European farm before killing the owner, may this oath kill me. If I worship any leader but Jomo Kenyatta, may this oath kill me . . . '

The Mau Mau had completely shattered the average African's spiritual equilibrium, absolute sin had created a new barbarism, a fanatic who massacred whole villages, decapitating and mutilating, cutting babies in half in front of their mothers, hanging people, slitting pregnant women open, hacking heads off with pangas, cutting the ears off people so they can be easily identified later. And now cannibalism had been introduced. The victim's head chopped open, the brains dried in the sun, the heart cut out and dried, steaks cut for food when the Mau Mau gang was on the move. In each gang there was an executioner who acted as butcher. The *Batuni* Oath, by breaking every tribal taboo, ostracised the oath-taker from all hope, in this world and the next. The result was a terrorist organization composed not of humans fighting for a cause, but of primitive beasts.

'Your cook-boy tried to kill you, didn't he, Aunt Sheila?' Jill said proudly.

'No, darling.' Aunt Sheila smiled. 'It was my *house*boy. Old Moses, my cook, he's loyal, and he's a devout Christian. Not that that's any guarantee these days,' she added. 'The Mau Mau *modus operandi* is to kill Moses's family if he refuses to kill me. So, I'm well armed at all times. If this was Kenya, we'd all be sitting with our pistols on the table. And your servants would be locked in the stockade at this hour.'

'So you have to serve your own dinner?' Jill demanded, perturbed.

'No, Moses and the new houseboy sleep in the kitchen, but the rest are locked in the stockade, which has a high fence around it, and a deep wide trench with sharpened bamboo stakes. We muster them at six o'clock, roll call, then shepherd them in.'

'Don't they mind?' Jill demanded.

'*No*. The stockade is to protect them from the Mau Mau. They have their huts and families inside. And their own armed guards. And of course our homestead is also surrounded by a security fence now. With two high towers where our Masai guards sit all night with searchlights and machine guns. With rope ladders, so the Masai can pull it up after them. The searchlights can reach the labour stockade *and* the new cattle pens where we have to lock up our animals at night now, or the Mau Mau cut the udders off, and hamstring them, slash their hind legs. Terrible.'

'Oh!' Jill was wide-eyed.

Mrs Mahoney said: 'Your Masai are reliable?'

'Oh yes, they're the traditional enemies of the Kikuyu, they hate the Mau Mau. In one operation, the police and army sent the Masai into the forest to ambush a huge band of Mau Mau they were flushing out. The Masai attacked in full regalia and killed them all, the army just watched. The Masai went home very happy – because, of course, the government had put a stop to tribal warfare long ago.'

'Divide and rule,' George Mahoney murmured. 'Works every time in Africa.'

'Tell us about when you were attacked, Aunt Sheila.' Jill pleaded.

Mrs Mahoney raised her eyebrows, but George said, 'She's old enough.'

'Well,' Sheila said, 'it was before we'd put up the security fence and the watchtowers. Fred and I were having dinner. The houseboy – our last houseboy – brings in the soup. Fred tells him to taste it, in case it's poisoned. The houseboy starts trembling and tries to run to the kitchen. Same moment the door to the kitchen opens and in burst three Mau Mau with pangas. The dogs fly at them and Fred opens up with his pistol and kills the first two dead, but the third comes at me with his panga. I shoot him in the chest but he keeps coming and one of the dogs gets him in the . . . er, groin. Fred shoots him dead, then charges to the kitchen and there's the cookboy with his skull split open, and there's the houseboy standing with a panga and he swipes at Fred's collarbone. I burst into the kitchen and shoot the houseboy in the heart. Lucky shot.' She closed her eyes and sighed. 'Oh, what a mess. Blood and brains and bodies everywhere . . . '

'*Please* . . . ' Mrs Mahoney said. 'That's enough.'

'What happened to Uncle Fred?' Jill was wide-eyed.

'Well, I loaded him into the Land-Rover and rushed him to hospital in Nyeri. He was okay. Tough old bugger, Fred. But when he came out a few days later, with his arm stuck out in plaster like a Heil Hitler salute, the swines struck again. We were still erecting our security fence and watchtowers – our labour had just knocked off for the night. Fred and I were sitting having our well-earned sundowners. Suddenly – *bang bang bang* – windows smashing, and the bastards are attacking with firearms this time, from all sides. And Fred and I dive for cover and grab the rifles and start blasting out the windows, bullets flying everywhere, and there's poor old Fred firing with one arm, the other stuck out, and these two great brutes come charging through the front door and luckily I mowed them down with the new Sten gun the police had given me.'

'Wow!' Jill whispered.

'Anyway,' Sheila ended, 'after that we finished the fence and watchtowers quick-smart. And bought new dogs. The Mau Mau mutilated all our other dogs. Stuck them on spikes. Alive. Now we've got four new ones – Dobermans. Trained. Accept food from nobody but me. Only let out at night. And,' she added, 'now we've got the Masai guards. We're pretty safe. But the swines still come down out of the forests to maim our cattle.'

'And how's Fred now?' Mr Mahoney said.

Sheila smiled wearily. She took a sip of wine and her glass trembled. 'Tough as nails, my Fred. I haven't seen him for three weeks. He's up in Aberdere Forests – in freezing mist, ten thousand feet above sea level. On patrol, looking for Mau Mau hideouts. Comes back after weeks, wild and woolly and reeking and exhausted, gets roaring drunk, then off he goes to join another patrol.'

Jill demanded: 'What does he do when he finds Mau Mau hideouts in the forest?'

Sheila looked at George Mahoney. He said: 'This is her Africa.'

Sheila sighed. 'To cut a long story short, they spend days, *weeks*, tracking down their hideouts. Then they ambush. And kill them.'

'How? Machine guns and hand grenades and all that?'

'Yes.' Sheila turned to George. 'And? Do you think the same could happen in South Africa?'

'Guaranteed,' George sighed. 'This government will drive the blacks to bloody revolution. And be ruthless in trying to stamp it out. So it's going to be a much worse bloodbath than Kenya. But that'll be some time coming, the government has got an iron grip at the moment.' He added: 'The tragedy is that the bloody excesses of the Mau Mau create the impression that the South African government is right. The man on the street looks at Kenya and says, hell, the blacks are savages, so the South Africans are right.'

Sheila said: 'And who'll start it? This African National Congress? What do you make of them?'

George nodded pensively. 'I like them,' he said. 'They've been around a long time, since 1912 you know, ever since the British gave them a raw deal at the end of the Boer War. They're reasonable people. Indeed, they even supported the Smuts and Hertzog governments for a while, because they thought the Natives Land Act may give them a fair deal. Then they seemed to give up. Then apartheid seemed to revitalise them. Now they've issued their Freedom Charter, but they're non-violent. For the moment – this government will probably drive them to violence soon. But right now they're the very opposite of the Mau Mau. The people to worry about are the PAC, the Pan-Africanist Congress, under Robert Sobukwe, who split away from the ANC over the multi-racialism of the Freedom Charter – they're the people who want "Africa for the Africans". The only problem with the ANC is they're clearly socialists. The "commanding heights of industry" must be nationalised, they say. That would be disastrous. And that, unfortunately, is the influence of the communists in their ranks. The South African Communist Party has been banned since 1950 and gone underground, and it's no secret *their* policy is to ride to power on the back of the ANC. And their orders come direct from Moscow. So the ANC is in danger of becoming a communist organization unless their leadership is careful.'

'And, how good is that leadership?'

'Pretty good,' George nodded. 'I like this guy Nelson Mandela – he's head of the ANC Youth League, a potentially powerful branch of the movement. He's very intelligent, and he's a lawyer. My firm has had some dealings with his firm in Johannesburg. Sensible chap, he's a Xhosa, comes from this neck of the woods – ' he waved a finger over his shoulder – 'I believe he's of "royal blood" in that he's heir to the chieftancy of the clan. And he's recently married a very nice lass from these parts who's a fully qualified social worker. The leadership impresses me as reasonable, totally unlike the sort of people you're dealing with in the Mau Mau.' He added: 'Nelson Mandela's law partner is the acting president of the ANC, a chap called Oliver Tambo, also a Xhosa. Or a Pondo, they're the sort of poor country cousins of the Xhosa – '

Mrs Mahoney said to Sheila, 'The Pondos are the ones who wear the blue blankets, whereas the Xhosa wear the red blankets – '

'Except, of course,' George Mahoney smiled, 'neither Mandela nor Tambo wear blankets now, they wear pin-striped suits!'

Everybody laughed; then Mrs Mahoney said to Sheila: 'And is the Mau Mau crisis affecting Harker-Mahoney?'

Sheila sighed. 'Terrible labour shortage. The Kikuyu who haven't taken the oath have fled back to the reserves in terror. HM Shipping is still going strong. And most of the stores, because Kenya is swarming with the British Army and Air Force now, fighting the Mau Mau. But our coffee plantations are virtually at a standstill. No labour.'

'And how's business in West Africa?' George said.

'Well, I'm not au fait with HM's offices in Ghana and Nigeria. But

Fred says things are looking shaky there too, with independence.' She rolled her eyes. 'Kwame Nkrumah, the Great Redeemer.'

'*Why*?' Mrs Mahoney groaned. '*Why* is the British government hell-bent on giving these people independence, willy-nilly?'

Sheila said: 'The Tories have lost their nerve . . . the government's full of pinkoes.'

'They must *know* they're not ready to govern themselves yet.'

'I wonder if they *do* know,' Sheila said. 'They meet a few smart ones, like Jomo Kenyatta and Kwame Nkrumah, and think the whole of Africa is composed of charming black Englishmen. They don't realize that the rest have only recently dropped out of the trees. Independence will be the biggest failure since the Groundnut Scheme.'

Luke glanced at his father and the old man gave him a conspiratorial wink. 'What's the Groundnut Scheme?' Jill demanded.

Sheila began to speak but George Mahoney said, 'Luke, explain to your sister.'

'Well,' Luke said, 'after the war there was a food shortage. So the British government started a massive project planting peanuts, because they're very nourishing, and it was called the Groundnut Scheme. They sent out all the seeds and fertilizer and tractors and stuff and hired thousands of blacks. But they made a terrible botch of it because nobody knew about peanuts, and in places they even ploughed cement into the soil instead of fertilizer because they couldn't read. But the biggest problem was that they couldn't persuade the blacks to stay on the job because they didn't understand what money was. They didn't understand that their wages could buy things, because there were no shops out there in the bush. So the whole scheme collapsed. Cost millions of pounds.'

Jill said, 'Is that why that book about the Mau Mau is called *Something of Value*? Things in the shops?'

George Mahoney smiled. 'Luke? You've read the book.'

Luke said: 'What the book says is that if you take away a man's tribal customs, *his* values, you must expect trouble unless you give him something of value in return. *Your* values. But if he cannot accept your values, because he is uneducated, then he is lost. Neither one thing nor the other. And that causes trouble. And that is what is happening in Africa.' He looked at his father for confirmation.

'Right,' George said to his daughter. 'The white man came along and said to the blacks: "You must not worship your gods, you must worship my God." Then, "Now that you worship my God you cannot have more than one wife." And, "Now that you worship my God you must stop selling your daughters into marriage." And, "Now that you worship my

God you must stop fighting, you must turn the other cheek, you must stop carrying your spears and shields, even though these are symbols of your manhood." And, "Now that you worship my God you must be *industrious*, you must stop making your wives do all the work, and you must stop drinking so much beer, and of course you must stop following your traditional laws and obey the white man's laws, and if you do not we will put you in jail." Et cetera. And, after a while – decades in the case of Kenya, a hundred and fifty years in the case of South Africa – the black man eventually says: "Very well, now that I have given up my values I want all the advantages attached to your values – I want a good job and lots of money." And the white man says, "I'm afraid you're uneducated so the only job you can get is as a labourer, working for me." And so this uprooted man has received nothing of value. His politicians say: "Then we want the *power* that is attached to your values, *we* want to be the government." But the white man says, "Sorry, you'll ruin the country." So the black politician says: "We must rise up and drive the white man into the sea and *then* we'll get something of value, because we'll all be rich with a white man's house and a car and a bicycle and a radio."'

'"And the nice Russians,"' Aunt Sheila said, '"will help us get rid of the white man." And the simple black man believes it all.'

Jill sighed, wagging her golden pigtails. 'So if we *can't* give him something of value it's better to leave him in his tribe.'

George smiled. 'That's the African dilemma, isn't it, my darling? But we *didn't* leave him alone – we're *here*, and we can't undo that fact. The question is what do we do *from* here, to give him something of value?'

'Not apartheid,' Luke said.

'So you want to give them all the vote?' Aunt Sheila asked.

'*No*,' Luke said. 'Because they're still too uneducated. But we should give the civilized ones the vote. "Equal rights for all civilized men", like in Rhodesia. *Gradualism*, that's the answer.'

'And what constitutes "civilized"?' his mother asked.

'Education,' Luke said. 'Maybe, second year of high school. Or a certain amount of money in the bank. If a man's smart enough to make money, he's smart enough to vote. That's what they've done in Rhodesia.'

'And Rhodesia will have plenty of trouble too,' Sheila promised.

'But meanwhile,' Mrs Mahoney asked, 'what about all the ones who haven't got education or money but who're demanding the vote and a white man's job, house, car and bicycle? They won't be satisfied with your gradualism, Luke, they'll want the vote *now*. If you give the vote to some, they'll *all* want it.'

'Well,' Luke said, 'we'll just have to be strict. Strict but fair. But to be fair we must abolish apartheid.'

George Mahoney nodded judicially. Jill said: 'I agree. Apartheid,' she pronounced, quoting her father, 'stinks.'

Mrs Mahoney said: 'Choose a more ladylike word, Jill. Why do you say that? Isn't separateness the natural order of things, dear? We *are* separate, separated by civilization. The government is only legalizing the status quo.'

'It's doing a hell of a lot more than that!' George said. 'It's setting the status quo in stone, to hold them separate and down there for ever. It's damned *unnatural* to try to keep people apart – and it's asking for trouble. Let people find their own level.'

'Well, I think it's perfectly natural for a civilized people to want their standards protected by the law. And thereby *prevent* trouble.' She turned to Sheila. 'George and I don't see eye to eye on this little detail. Not that I'm a National Party lady, mark you – I'd vote for the United Party, if I dared, but George is an Independent and he'd divorce me – I'm never *quite* convinced those ballots are secret!' She grinned at her husband. 'I'd never vote for those horrid Afrikaners – I exaggerate of course – some of them are very nice – but I must say, darling, our Minister of Bantu Affairs, Hendrik Verwoerd, strikes me as a sincere man who believes he's doing his best for the blacks in the long run.'

'Hendrik Verwoerd,' George Mahoney sighed, 'is not a malicious man. And he's probably sincere when he talks about apartheid as "a mighty act of creation" and "the will of God" – he believes he's got the blueprint for successful co-existence between the races. And he *has* appointed the Tomlinson Commission to look into the viability of the black homelands becoming independent – '

'Independent?' Sheila asked, surprised.

'Yes,' Mrs Mahoney said. 'Apartheid is *evolving*, my dear, to a higher moral plane – '

'*Yes*,' George said wearily to Sheila, 'apartheid *is* evolving under Verwoerd, he *does* now talk in Parliament about giving the black homelands their independence, about dividing South Africa up into a number of black independent states and one white state, which will all live together side by side in a "constellation of southern African states", bound loosely together in a kind of common market – Verwoerd doubtless does believe his own rhetoric when he says the blacks will be eternally grateful to us. It's a pretty vision but it won't work, because the homelands are barely capable of supporting the blacks now, in thirty years' time they'll be hopelessly inadequate, because the black population will have *trebled*. How're all those people going to earn a living? They're cattle-men, not factory workers – '

Mrs Mahoney interrupted mildly: 'But he says industrialists will be encouraged with tax incentives to open up factories on the homelands' borders to provide employment – '

'Which is *bull*shit,' George Mahoney said. (Jill snickered into her hands.) 'I'm sorry, my dear, but it *is* nonsense. Because, sure, some industrialists will take advantage and open factories on the borders, but not nearly enough. The Tomlinson Commission – ' he jabbed his finger – 'showed that the homelands could only support fifty-one per cent of the black populace as farmers. What happens to the other forty-nine per cent? Find jobs in the new factories? It'll never happen. It's a Utopian dream of Verwoerd's.' He turned to his wife. 'And the hard fact remains that the black homelands are only *thirteen* per cent of South Africa's surface.' He shook his head at Sheila. 'Oh, there's nothing wrong in giving these so-called black homelands self-government – provided, as Luke says – ' he touched his son's head – 'it's supervised and done gradually, because the poor old black man has no experience of democracy – but the towering *sin* of Dr Verwoerd's new-look apartheid is that it says to the poor black man: Thou *shalt* live and vote in thy inadequate homeland. Thou *shalt* only come out of it to work in if I need you and give you a Pass. Thou *shalt* live in impermanence in locations and squatter shacks. Thou *shalt* not have thy women and children living with you. Thou *shalt* have no political or social rights in my nice white South Africa where thou workest. Thou *shalt* return to your black homeland when I've had enough of your cheap labour. Thou shalt, thou *shalt*, thou SHALT . . . '

George glared around the table, then said wearily to his wife: 'Oh, Verwoerd's vision is a fine one, on paper. But the arithmetic proves it's a recipe for black pain, and poverty, and conflict. Rebellion.' He sighed. 'I tell him at every opportunity in Parliament.'

Mrs Mahoney shifted and said: 'Darling, I'm all for the underdog. But I don't consider that saying a black can't be my next-door neighbour and keep his cattle in his backyard is exactly making him an underdog – he's got his own territory, his own customs, and I have mine. I respect him but I do not want him as my neighbour.'

Luke said: 'Mother, you've got five of them as neighbours already, in your backyard.'

'Servants are entirely different. And talking about that, I don't mind in the least you helping Justin with his homework, dear, but I won't have him starting political discussions in my kitchen about the Russians coming, please?'

Jill said: 'Well, Miss Rousseau says the Russians are already here.'

'And she's right,' George said.

'Who's Miss Rousseau?' Aunt Sheila asked.

'Our new history teacher,' Jill said, 'and she's brilliant.' She added with a giggle: 'And Luke's in love with her!'

'I am *not*!' Luke glared. 'I only said *all* the guys think . . . have got a crush on her!'

'Except you?' his father grinned.

That was another thing Luke and Justin had in common: their enthusiasm for girls. That year both of them had their first sexual experience. Justin had been through the Abakweta ceremony, living alone in a grass hut for six weeks, daubed in white clay and wearing a grass skirt and mask before emerging on the appointed day to be circumcised in cold blood with a spear: he was now a man, eligible to buy a wife when he could afford the cattle to pay *lobola*, the bridal price. Justin had lain with women. 'Is it nice?' Mahoney asked, agog. '*Ooooh*,' Justin said.

Luke had been circumcised as an infant but *his* customs forbade him to lie with a woman yet; Luke's earliest memories seemed to be of having a persistent erection he was incapable of doing anything about, and he was desperately determined to do something about it in his final year at school. *Oooh* is what Luke felt climbing the stairs behind the girls in their short gym skirts – if you contrived to be at the bottom of the stairs as they were approaching the top you could see right up to their bloomers. *Oooh* is what he felt sitting in class waiting for the girls to reveal a bit more thigh ('beef' it was called). *Oooh* is what he felt when he was allowed to grope his girlfriend of the moment but never allowed to take his cock out for a bit of reciprocity. *Ooooooh* is what he felt as Miss Rousseau unfolded the dramas of history with her creamy smiles, her breasts thrusting against her sporty blouse as she stretched to jot her 'lampposts' on the blackboard, her skirt riding a little higher up her lovely legs – for Miss Rousseau was also the girls' gym mistress and came to school in short athletic skirts.

Luke wasn't in love with Miss Rousseau as his sister teased – not yet – he was only madly in *lust* with her. All the boys were, and the girls idolised her: 'She's such fun!' *And she didn't have a boyfriend!* Oh, she had all the young men in town after her but there seemed to be none with brains enough to hold Miss Rousseau's interest. 'She says she's very hard to please,' Jill reported with the breathless smugness of one privy to royal confidences – 'and she says *we* must all be when we grow up. *None* of *these* men are capable of having an interesting *discussion*, she says, she expects a *real* man to hold *meaningful conversations*, not just play *sport*, she says. She wants her *mind* wooed, she says . . . '

Her mind wooed . . . Miss Rousseau was very sporty and played a dashing game of hockey (you could often see right up to *her* bloomers as she dashed) and she loved watching rugby. Luke wasn't really a rugger-bugger but he played so hard that year to impress Miss Rousseau that he made it to the first team. And on Fridays after school when he and Justin fetched his parents' horses for the weekend from the country stables he rode the long way round into town in order to pass the girls' hostel (that veritable cornucopia of beef, bums and tits) because Miss Rousseau sat on the verandah marking books in the afternoons – in the desperate hopes of impressing her with a meaningful conversation about horses. But no such luck; she gave him a cheery wave, that's all. He read in bed late into the night (with a hard-on) surrounded by history books, trying to dredge up obscure points to discuss with the wonderful Miss Rousseau, to have meaningful conversations about with the divine Miss Rousseau. (It wasn't easy concentrating on all that heavy-duty history with all those hard-ons.) But it didn't work. When he did manage to put one of his obscure points to her there was no discussion because Miss Rousseau knew all the answers and all he ended up saying was, 'I see, Miss Rousseau. Thank you, Miss Rousseau.' And there was no privacy for a meaningful conversation because he could only catch her in the school corridors. *And she wasn't interested in fuckin' horses*. So how the hell could a *real* man get to *discuss* anything? And then, one night, he thought of those family journals his great great grandfather Ernest had started, and all the obscure points therein.

But of course! What historian wouldn't be interested in those rare journals? Their obscure detail was a goldmine for meaningful conversations. Burning the midnight oil, he feverishly dredged up a stockpile of obscure points before he made his move to grab the divine Miss Rousseau's interest. *And it worked.*

'What an *interesting* detail, Luke – I'll have to look it up in Theal.'

'I've checked Theal, Miss Rousseau, and he doesn't say anything about it. Nor does Walker, Miss Rousseau.'

'Where did you get your hands on Theal? He's not in this town's library.'

'My father's got the whole set of Theal histories, Miss Rousseau.'

'I *see*. How lucky you are, even I don't have the whole set. But *where* exactly did you get this detail, Luke – your great grandfather's diary, you say?'

'My great *great* grandfather's *journal*s, Miss Rousseau.' (*Stop saying Miss Rousseau every sentence!*) 'He was on the Great Trek and fought at

Blood River. *His* son, *and* his grandson, fought in the Boer War, and they kept the journals going. My father kept them up, starting with World War I.' He shrugged airily. 'And, of course, I'll keep them up, Miss Rousseau.'

'*Fas*cinating . . . ' Miss Rousseau said.

He blurted: 'You can look at them any time you like, Miss Rousseau,' (*Oh you tit . . .*)

'Oh wow – will you ask your father's permission?'

It had worked! With or without his father's permission she would see them!

'Well, all right, seeing she's a teacher,' his father said, 'but don't encourage it, son, they're very personal records.'

'My father says he's delighted you're interested, Miss Rousseau,' he said the next day when he delivered the first volume.

And was Miss Rousseau interested? '*Fascinated's* the word, Luke! I sat up in bed all night!' (*Ooh, Miss Rousseau sitting up in bed – while he sat up in his bed with a hard-on dredging up more obscure detail to woo her mind with meaningful conversation –*) 'What priceless glimpses of living history you've given me!' (*He'd* given her!) 'These belong in the archives. You *must* keep them up yourself, Luke.'

'I will, when I've done something to write about, Miss Rousseau.' (*Cut out the Miss Rousseau!*)

'Start now! You've seen the introduction of apartheid, which is the culmination of the Kaffir Wars and the Great Trek and the Boer War! *Seen* it through the eyes of a very intelligent young man of the times – your youthful evaluations will make fascinating historical material one day. I can't wait to read the next volume.'

A very intelligent young man of the times! Young *man* . . . ? And *she* couldn't wait? *He* couldn't wait. He hurried home from school, on air, locked himself in his bedroom and jerked off over the heavenly Miss Rousseau. The next day he delivered the next volume, reeking of after-shave and toothpaste. 'This one's written in an old cash ledger that Ernest Mahoney's grandfather gave him for accounts, Miss Rousseau. It starts when Ernest accompanies Retief to visit Dingaan.'

'Does Sarie wait faithfully for Ernest?' Miss Rousseau demanded.

'Not only that, she . . . They have to . . . well, they get married, Miss Rousseau.'

'Oh, what *fun*,' Miss Rousseau sparkled. (*Fun?! That's pure sex talk!*) She put her heavenly hand on his arm impulsively. 'Luke, I've been thinking – these journals, I really think your family should make a copy, in case they get destroyed in a fire or something. And I would *love* a copy for myself. Now, I've got a very good typewriter. Would you ask your father if he minds if I type them up? It's quiet in the hostel while the girls are doing their prep, and in the holidays I'll have the whole place to myself.'

Luke said casually to his father, trying not to blush: 'Miss Rousseau thinks those journals are so valuable we should have them typed up in case they're ever lost, and she's offered to do so but she hasn't got a decent typewriter and that girls' hostel is so noisy, she says, and I thought maybe she could come here and use Mother's typewriter – '

'Well, that's kind of her. But I'm not sure, son – she may make a copy and I don't like the idea of that, I want to publish them one day – '

'Oh, she wouldn't make a copy, Father!'

It was his mother who swung it. 'Well, I think it's a very good idea, darling. It's an opportunity to get her evaluation of them. Tell her to come around whenever she has time, Luke. I won't disturb her.'

That afternoon Luke and Justin fetched the horses and as they casually cantered past the hostel Luke just happened to spy Miss Rousseau sitting on the verandah, marking books. He dismounted.

'Miss Rousseau, my father is very grateful for your offer to type up the journals, and of course you may make a copy for yourself, but could you possibly come to our house to do it because he doesn't want copies lying around because they're so personal?'

'But of *course*,' Miss Rousseau said earnestly.

Oh joy! 'And,' he blurted on, 'my mother suggests you come on the afternoons she plays golf so she doesn't disturb you. That's Mondays and Wednesdays, Miss Rousseau.' (The days his sister had hockey practice). 'And,' he blurted on, 'if you'd like to have a swim, bring your costume . . . '

'Well, I'll be there!'

He galloped all the way home. He'd done it! He'd contrived to get Miss Rousseau alone! He just had to lock himself in his bedroom again and get rid of his hard-on.

Oooh, the agony of waiting for Monday . . . That Saturday he played a suicidal rugby match, to roars of applause from the grandstand, where Miss Rousseau sat. 'Brilliant game, Luke.' *Brilliant . . . ?* In his sound senses he tried to hammer it into himself that nothing would happen on Monday, but with all these erections it was possible to imagine anything. The sheer eroticism of having Miss Rousseau alone in the house! Would she have a swim? Would they have tea together? *Damn right they would!* Would she sometimes ask him to help her decipher his great great grandfather's handwriting? Would she . . . walk around the garden with him? *Would she bring her swimming costume? Would it be a bikini? Please let it be a bikini . . . !*

And it surpassed his wildest dreams. Not only did they have tea together, not only did she want to see the garden, not only did she call him to decipher his great great grandfather's handwriting sometimes . . . *but she did bring her swimming costume! And it was a bikini!* Oh, the bliss of having tea with Miss Rousseau, just the two of them, like two adults – he had dredged up a stockpile of tricky historical points to talk about. Oh, the bliss of bending over the journals beside her *(the sweet scent of her)* deciphering his great grandfather's handwriting. *And Oooooh Miss Rousseau in her bikini . . .* those lovely long legs, those ooooh-so-rounded hips and oh those tits . . . But how was he going to hide this hard-on?! And after she packed up the typing at five o'clock and drove off back to the hostel in her old Chevrolet he stood in the toilet thinking, *This is where she pulled her panties down. This is where she placed her beautiful bare bum . . .* And he just wanted to smother the seat in kisses.

It surpassed his wildest dreams when, after her fourth visit, his mother announced: 'That nice Miss Rousseau telephoned today and asked if she could possibly hire one of the horses during the school holidays – she's a keen horsewoman. Of course I said she could ride them any time free, but she asked if you would go with her the first time, until she's familiar with her mount.'

Would he go with her . . . ? 'Okay, Mother.'

'Please don't use those dreadful Americanisms, son. And, she had the highest praise for you. "Quite a remarkable historian", she said. And that you'll go a long way in life.'

Quite a remarkable historian?! Well she ain't seen nothin' yet! Go a long way? He would go all the way to the ends of the earth on his hands and knees over broken glass for Miss Rousseau . . .

It seemed an eternity waiting for the mid-year school holidays. And then Miss Rousseau surpassed his wildest wild dreams again. When they dismounted at the reservoir outside town and sat down under the trees, she gave him her creamy smile and said: 'I think that you can stop calling me Miss Rousseau, Luke. Lisa will do fine when we're alone. After all, we are partners in crime.'

Lisa! When we're alone! Partners in crime?

'What crime, Miss Rousseau?'

'Lisa.'

Oh . . . 'Lisa.' It was the most wonderful name in the world.

She smiled. 'Fraud? Copyright contravention? Your father did *not* give me permission to make a copy of those journals, did he?'

Luke was mortified. Blushing. 'How do you know?'

'When I phoned your mother about riding she thanked me for the typing and apologised that your father wouldn't allow a copy to be made because he wants to publish them one day.' She smiled. 'Why did you lie to me, Luke?'

He swallowed. 'Because . . . you're a historian, and . . . and you deserve it.'

She grinned. 'Why do I deserve it, Luke?'

'Because you're – ' (he wanted to blurt '*the most beautiful*') ' – the best teacher I've ever had.'

'An apple for the teacher?'

'No, Miss Rousseau.' He wished the earth would open.

'I'm sorry,' she said. 'And Lisa, please.'

'No, not an apple for the teacher. Lisa.'

She smiled. 'The teacher? I'm only twenty-one, you know, Luke. Only four years older than you.'

'Yes, I know . . . ' Luke croaked. 'Lisa,' he added.

'And I'm not really a teacher, you know. I only got my B.A. last year, I haven't done my teaching diploma yet.' She paused. 'And d'you know what?'

'What?' he croaked. 'Lisa,' he added.

'I've decided I don't want to teach kids, Luke. Next year I'm going back to university to do my M.A. And then a doctorate. I want to teach at university level – teaching minds like yours.'

Minds like his?! Not kids . . . !

'You've no idea how bored I've been in this town, Luke.'

Goddesses get bored? 'Really?'

'Really. In fact . . . ' She paused, then grinned at him. 'Can you keep a secret, Luke?'

A secret from Miss Rousseau?!

'Promise,' he said. 'Lisa.'

'In fact – ' she smiled her mischievous creamy smile – 'the only stimulating thing that's happened to me this year has been you and those journals.' Miss Rousseau looked at him with a twinkle in her eye: 'You and your riding past the hostel every Friday. To impress me? And undressing me with your eyes in the classroom. And – ' her smile widened – 'your monstrous erections in the swimming pool.'

Luke didn't know whether he wanted to lunge at her or the earth to swallow him up. *Monstrous erections?* His heart was pounding and he was blushing furiously and he couldn't think of anything to say except: 'I'm sorry.'

She grinned widely. 'Oh don't be sorry – it's very pleasing.'

Pleasing?! That could only mean one thing! Oh God he didn't know what he dare do!

Miss Rousseau smiled. 'Are you a virgin, Luke?'

He couldn't believe this was happening. All beyond imagination. He blushed. 'Yes . . . '

She smiled. 'Well, Luke? I seem to have taught you all the *history* you need. What shall we do about what you *don't* know?'

Luke's heart was hammering, his ears were ringing, his face on fire, his stomach was faint, his legs trembled. 'I – I don't know, Miss Rousseau.'

'Lisa.' Miss Rousseau smiled. '*Well*,' she said, 'let's think . . . Now, if I were seventeen, and not your so-called teacher, what would you do now, Luke?'

Luke looked at her with utter, confused adoration. He swallowed and whispered hoarsely: 'I'd kiss you.'

'*Very* good, Luke. So, you may kiss me, you know how to do that, I'm sure.'

He stared, then he lunged at her. He seized her and plunged his gasping mouth onto hers so their teeth clashed, and she laughed in her throat and toppled over, and he scrambled frantically on top of her, and he ejaculated. In one frantic surging the world buzzed into a blurry flame that promptly crescendoed into the most marvellous feeling in the world, that exploded into a frenetic thrusting towards the source of all joy through jodhpurs and all. Luke Mahoney pounded on top of Lisa Rousseau, exploding, and she held him tight, grinning up to the sky.

When he finally went limp, gasping, on top of her, his mind in a whirl, she smiled. '*There* . . . Now we can really talk about this like adults.' She took a handful of his hair and lifted his suffused face. 'Tonight, instead of going to the cinema, or wherever, why don't you come to see me? The hostel's empty.'

5

Those school holidays were wonderful. Wonderful, marvellous, divine, delicious, heavenly, breathtaking, walking-on-air – a head-over-heels, laughing-out-loud, do-backward-somersaults love affair, a secret so delicious he wanted to bellow it to the world.

Umtata was quiet, the school silent, the sunshine golden, the birds a-twitter, the bees buzzing. And the big girl's hostel was *empty*, except for the beautiful, long-legged, big-busted, sparkly-eyed, wonderful Lisa Rousseau. Every day they went galloping over the hills to the reservoir to make love on a blanket. Twice a week she came to the house to type up the journals ('*No, Luke – your mother may come home . . .* '), every night he climbed out of his bedroom window and hurried across town to the hostel, let himself in the kitchen door and bounded up the stairs – and there was Lisa Rousseau, a grin all over her lovely face, and he seized her in his trembling arms. And, oh God, the wonderful feel of her against him, her strong-soft athletic body, her breasts crushed against his heaving schoolboy chest, her belly and loins crushed against him, his hands frantically sliding over her, feeling, feeling, *feeling* her. Then she swept her nightdress over her head, and the sight of her nakedness, each night, took his breath away. Then she tumbled onto her narrow bed, a grin of fun all over her lovely face. 'The first one's for you; the second one's for me . . . '

So it went every night, those school holidays. The first one was over in minutes, two or three minutes of frantic thrusting, then a searing explosion of cascading joy. And Lisa Rousseau lay there, legs wide, smiling, receiving this explosive accolade, then, when that bit of heavenly nonsense was over, it was her turn. Miss Lisa Rousseau toppled him onto his back, and he lay there, exhausted, happy, wildly in love, and she began her magic. She slithered down to his loins and she grinned at him up his belly, her long hair awry and her big eyes twinkling, then she slowly, so slowly, lowered her head and, *oh*, the wonderful feel of her warm wet mouth, her teeth playfully nibbling, her full lips sucking, her warm pink tongue slithering, her eyes sparkling with the sheer fun of it all, and when she had done her magic she climbed joyfully on top of him, for her turn.

At the end of the second wonderful week Luke had a brilliant idea: his father owned a fishing camp down on the Wild Coast, sixty miles away: how marvellous to have the last week of the holidays there with Lisa all to himself, out in the wide open, *sleeping* together all night long, *swimming* naked in the crashing surf, romping together in the languid lagoon, walking along the wild deserted beach together like real lovers . . . It would be just like a real honeymoon. Lisa thought it a wonderful idea provided his parents didn't know about her being there. 'And provided we have some intellectual activity – I, my friend, am going to ensure you get an A for history . . . '

Luke said to his father: 'Can I take one of the horses down to the camp? Do some fishing before I start work on my final exams?'

'Can I come too?' Jill cried.

'No girls,' Luke said firmly.

'But what about that nice Miss Rousseau?' Mrs Mahoney said. 'She'll be disappointed if you don't go riding with her.'

'Oh, she's going off somewhere for a week to meet a friend.'

'Well,' George said, 'provided you take Justin with you . . . '

Oh *shit*.

But the sheer audacity of *living* together . . . it was the romantic stuff of story books. And it was a great adventure setting out in the pre-dawn into the land of the Xhosa, something like his great great grandfather Ernest had done into the land of the Zulus. As they rode through the rolling green hills with their Xhosa kraals, through their scattered herds of cattle, Luke could almost feel the shades of his forebear riding with him – and his heart and loins were as deliciously tumultuous as Ernest's had been over his Sarie. But this adventure required him to take Justin into his confidence.

He said soberly in Xhosa: 'Justin, I must trust you with a secret. You know the white woman, Rousseau, my history teacher?'

'I know her,' Justin said.

Luke cleared his throat. 'Well, she is going to drive down to the sea tomorrow to be with us.'

'I know,' Justin said.

Luke frowned. 'How do you know?'

'I know,' Justin grinned, 'because every night you climb out of your window and run to her house. Like this . . . ' He placed his elbow in his groin and thrust his forearm up rigidly.

'So you are a spy!'

Justin smiled, 'No, I only study till late, at my window.'

'And how do you know I go to her house?'

'Because we must ride past her house every Friday. And because when she comes to your house to work your tail wags like a dog. Like this . . . ' He put his elbow in his groin again, and shook it about. He burst into laughter.

Luke grinned sheepishly. 'She is only teaching me history!'

Justin dropped his head and laughed: '*I know* . . . '

'And she is only coming to the sea to teach me more history!'

Justin threw back his head and guffawed, white teeth flashing: '*I know* . . . '

'Do you understand that?!' Luke grinned. 'And my *parents* must know *nothing* about this.'

Justin wiped his eyes. 'I understand everything . . . '

They rode on in suppressed giggles for a moment, then Justin burst into laughter again. 'But tell me, Nkosaan – is history nice?'

'*Ooooh* . . . '

It was a wonderful week. Floating in the blue lagoon with Lisa, romping in the crashing surf, walking along the deserted beaches, sleeping all night together: not once did Luke go fishing – that was

Justin's job, to keep him out of the way. Who would want to fish when he could be with the divine Lisa Rousseau? He could not get enough of her. But the divine Lisa Rousseau did also get some brain-work out of him.

'Luke, always think of history as a series of lampposts, which you can see leading up long networks of roads to the present. The greatest value of history is that our knowledge of the past, particularly past mistakes, helps us see into the future, and hopefully avoid mistakes . . . '

And she said: 'As Ernest says, the Battle of Blood River wasn't a *battle*, Luke, it was an execution – though don't say so in your exam paper. But what's the significance of that lamppost?'

Luke said: 'It's an emotional rallying point for the Afrikaner every year when they celebrate the Day of the Covenant. He is reminded every year that God was on his side, and therefore still is. And therefore apartheid is right, God's will.'

'Yes. But the real significance, the real tragedy is that a *theocracy* was born at the Battle of Blood River, Luke. "Rule of God." Through our "divinely inspired" politicians like Verwoerd. *That's* the mentality we're up against. And we won't get rid of apartheid until a new generation comes along who doesn't believe that nonsense.'

'Or until there's an uprising. A bloodbath, like Kenya.'

Lisa shook her head. 'No, that's another myth. There may be a bloodbath, but it will be black blood that's spilt, Luke. Like at the Battle of Blood River – an execution. History repeating itself. This government is surrounding us with a ring of steel – but tanks now, not wagons. An uprising will be crushed ruthlessly – it'll solve nothing.'

'But the communists? Russia's got plenty of tanks too.'

Lisa sighed. 'Communists? That's just about everybody who opposes this government, according to our Suppression of Communism Act. As for the Russians coming, that's another bit of wishful black thinking. As happened during the Great Cattle Killing. Sure, Russia's bent on world revolution, and sure she'll train saboteurs and black freedom fighters, but Russia's a hell of a long way away, it'll be many many years before her tanks get down here. No, the change in this country must come from *here* – ' she tapped her head – 'from within. From people like you and me, Luke.'

And she said: 'Okay, the Boer War. Big lamppost. What light does it shed on today?' *Oh fuck the Boer War – he wanted to get laid again*. He trailed his hand over the beautiful mound of her buttocks. 'No, Luke, I'm determined you'll get more out of me than the facts of life.'

Luke brought his mind back to the question. 'This government is still fighting the Boer War, figuratively speaking.'

'Yes. But why? The Boer War was over fifty years ago.'

'Because of their bitterness. The injustice. The scorched earth, their women and children dying in the camps. So, now that the Afrikaner is on top at last, he intends to stay there at all costs. Hence his ring of steel. His steel laager of apartheid.'

'True. But apartheid is only directed against the blacks, the *Swart Gevaar*. You've just said the Afrikaner is still fighting the *Boer* War – and blacks weren't in that war except as labourers. So, who – and what – is the Afrikaner still fighting?'

'The English-speaking South Africans?'

'*Right*. And why? Because the English still dominate this country economically – because of the Boer War. So how is the government fighting that Boer War problem?'

'By packing the civil service with Afrikaners?'

'Right. Affirmative Action, it's called. To give Afrikaners jobs and have every aspect of government dominated by loyalists. And every aspect of business. And who is the mastermind behind all that?'

'God?' Luke grinned.

She flicked his arm. 'But who *in fact?*'

'The Dutch Reformed Church?'

'But the church only dominates the government's *thinking*, its *soul*. Who is the *physical* power behind the throne of government?'

'The Broederbond,' Luke said. 'The Brotherhood.'

'*Right* . . . Lampposts, Luke. Illumination. And what do we know about the Broederbond? Very little, because it's a secret society. But what light does the Boer War shed on it? Ah, now we can start making some intelligent deductions. The Broederbond was founded after the Boer War – after Sir Alfred Milner had made his cock-up of trying to turn us into Englishmen. It was founded to fight for Afrikaner *dominance*. In all walks of life: the Dutch Reformed Church, business, parliament, the civil service, the army, police, judiciary. And it's grown into a mighty octopus that now controls the whole country – it's an Afrikaner *mafia* now, Luke. And it is really *they* who rule the country – and they will stop at nothing to stay in power. And there'll be no reform until their power is broken.'

'And how do we do that?'

'How, indeed? Only by the pen, my friend, because they've got all the swords – all the generals are Broederbonders. But what does history teach us about Power? "Power corrupts, and absolute power corrupts absolutely." Eventually they'll corrupt themselves out of power. Become decadent.' Then she rolled over onto her back and gave her creamy smile. 'And now, about that decadent suggestion of yours . . . '

It was a wonderful time. And when the holidays were over and they went back to Umtata and the kids came pouring back to town it got even better: for now their secret was multiplied, a secret to blow a thousand tiny minds, the danger a delicious spice to the delicious forbidden fruit. Luke Mahoney walked to school feeling ten feet tall, a smile in his heart about seeing her surrounded by her bevy of adoring girls, seeing the other boys lusting after her, hearing their lecherous talk, exchanging delicious grins with her, standing in assembly looking at her up there on the staff platform, eyes locked on each other's, suppressing a grin, his heart bursting with joyous pride – *his gorgeous Miss Rousseau, acting history teacher at Umtata High School, centre of the universe* . . . And when she came striding into the classroom in her gym skirt and the muted groan went up from the boys, his bursting heart turned over. And when she began to spin her wonderful tales of history, which he already knew backwards, he just wanted to leap up and applaud, and, oh God, the joy of her legs, her breasts thrusting against her white blouse as she stretched up to write on the blackboard – sometimes, just sometimes, she locked eyes with him for a moment when all heads were down making the notes, and – oh God – the delicious secret.

When the final bell rang and she set off back to the hostel – *his hostel* – he went to his father's law office with his heart singing. After dinner he went to bed, waited, listened, then pulled on his tennis shoes and breathlessly clambered out of the window and dashed across town. Then he walked past the tall hedge of the girls' hostel, heart knocking, eyes peeled, trying to look like a schoolboy going from God knows where. The towel hanging out her window, the all-clear sign . . . Then the heart-knocking business of creeping through the hole in the hedge, followed by the dash across the garden to the drainpipe. He crouched in the nasturtiums, seized the pipe and went shinning up it desperately, hand over hand, every moment expecting a girlish cry from one of the dormitory windows. Then there was the sill and he swung his leg up and Lisa grabbed his ankle, giggling. He heaved himself over, and fell into her arms. And, oh God, the forbidden fruit was all the more delicious for the outrageous danger.

And so it went. Until the night the drainpipe broke away from the wall. He was about to grab the sill when there was suddenly this creaking sound, and he was clawing at the bricks; then slowly the pipe began to fall away from the wall like a felled tree. Luke Mahoney swooped slowly down through the night, wild-eyed. *Oh Christ, how do I talk my way out of this?* As he hit the earth with a jarring jolt, his ankle buckled, he crashed onto his side, and the pipe and masonry came crashing down on top of him.

For an instant he lay there, shocked, in agony; then windows were bursting open, lights flashing on, and he scrambled up and tried to run, and he sprawled. He had sprained his ankle. He lay for another instant, clutching his foot, then he was up again and hobbling frantically. '*Hey!*' girls shouted. '*Stop! Thief!*' He hobbled flat-out, grimacing, and he sprawled again. He scrambled to his feet once more, but as he reached the gate the hostel door burst open. Girls barrelled out, clutching hockey sticks. Mahoney staggered desperately through the gate, gasping, and the girls burst out. They sprinted after him, yelling, and the first hockey stick got him. He lurched, then another stick whacked his head and he reeled; then another, then another. Under a rain of hockey sticks he crashed into the hedge, his arms curled up over his head, surrounded by gleeful, swiping girls.

'Good God!' the head girl gasped. 'Luke!'

Luke crouched in the hedge, gasping, his head splitting, looking at the menacing silhouettes of astonished, stick-toting girls. He was about to make a plea for he knew not what when a quiet voice said: 'Leave him, girls . . . ' And there was Miss Rousseau, in her dressing gown, arms folded, a sombre smile on her lovely face. 'Go back to bed, girls.'

The excited girls reluctantly turned to leave, staring back, giggling, exchanging glances. Mahoney straightened up painfully, dishevelled. He looked at Lisa.

'I'm sorry,' he whispered.

Lisa Rousseau smiled ruefully. 'We're in trouble, Luke. Tomorrow there's going to be big trouble.'

Luke closed his eyes and shook his head.

'I am,' he said. 'Not you. There's no reason for two of us to be in trouble.'

'To talk?' the headmaster repeated furiously.

'Yes, sir.'

'To *talk*?'

'Yes, sir.'

The headmaster gave a growl. 'At midnight you're shinning up the drainpipe of the girls' hostel to *talk* to the housemistress? That's what you're telling me?'

'Yes, sir.'

George Mahoney, sitting beside his son, sighed.

'To talk about what, pray?'

'About life, sir.'

'About Life? With a capital L, of course? And what *aspect* of Life were you so desperately anxious to talk about at that hour?' He waved a hand. 'The birds and the bees, perhaps?'

'No, sir. About my career, sir.'

'Your *career* . . . ' The headmaster whispered it with the contempt it deserved. He turned and paced across his study. He turned back. 'Do you know what happens to one's *career* when one is *expelled* from a school? Do you know what a *blemish* – what a *criminal* record that is you'll carry with you for life – with the capital L?!'

'Yes, sir.'

'And you are not daunted?'

'Yes, I am daunted, sir.'

Another growl. 'And what made you think Miss Rousseau would be *willing* to talk to you at midnight about your career?'

'Nothing, sir.'

'Nothing?' Steely eyes. 'She didn't . . . *invite* you perhaps?'

'No, sir, she did not.'

'You expect me to believe that? You just took it into your head to climb up her drainpipe at midnight? Without any encouragement whatsoever?'

'Correct, sir.'

The headmaster glared at him. George Mahoney had his eyes down, a grim smile twitching his face. The headmaster stabbed the air with his finger. 'I put it to you, Mahoney, that if you *didn't* have encouragement from Miss Rousseau, your behaviour was insane! *Unless* you intended to rape her! Was that your intention?'

Mahoney was shocked. 'Absolutely not, sir!'

'To try to seduce her perhaps?'

'No, sir.'

'But to "talk"? About your career? At midnight?'

'Yes, sir.'

'"Oh, good evening, Miss Rousseau – or should I say good morning? – just dropped around – or climbed around – to have a little chat about my future career as an historian. I say do you mind giving me a bit of a leg-up over this window sill – but if you prefer I'll just cling to this drainpipe for half an hour while we 'talk' . . . "'

And Luke Mahoney, seventeen years old, in the dock without a defence, had very nearly had enough, after a sleepless night. He looked his headmaster in the eye, and his voice took on a new edge: 'Yes, sir. Exactly.'

The headmaster glared. 'Do I detect a note of aggression there?'

Luke looked the man in the eye. 'No, sir. Just a note of self-defence.'

The headmaster's glare lost its steel for a moment, then his face filled with fury: 'You describe your story as a *defence?* Would your *father* – ' he flung an eloquent hand at the lawyer – 'consider that a credible *defence*?!'

Luke Mahoney did not care anymore – suddenly he had had enough of this humiliation and he did not care that he was going to be expelled: and as he was going to be expelled why the hell was he putting up with this shit?

'Very well, sir, as you evidently don't think much of that defence, how about this one: I climbed up that drainpipe at midnight because I'm madly in love with Miss Rousseau, sir. Because faint heart never won fair lady, sir. But I absolutely assure you, sir, on a stack of bibles, that Miss Rousseau knew absolutely nothing about this passion of mine, sir. And that you have obviously interpreted her resignation as evidence of complicity is quite incorrect, and if that will be a blot on *her* copybook, if that will prejudice *her* career, if you give a bad report about her to the education authorities, that will be the grossest of injustices. That would be like the injustice suffered by an honourable woman who is stigmatised by society after being raped, sir. And I promise you I will correct that by writing to the Department of Education and confessing my guilt, sir.'

There was a silence. The headmaster was staring at him. George Mahoney was looking at his son with something approaching pride. Luke Mahoney stood there grimly – and he wasn't blushing anymore. Take it or leave it, sir, was his demeanour. The headmaster recovered, and glared:

'And what did you expect Miss Rousseau to do about that, if she had given you no encouragement?'

'I had no idea, sir.'

His father sighed. The headmaster rasped softly: 'I don't believe you, Mahoney. I find it too much of a coincidence that Miss Rousseau does not intend to press charges against you – '

'Indeed, sir, I've gathered that you don't believe me.'

'Oh? And have you also gathered that I intend expelling you?'

'I have, sir.'

The headmaster glared. Then he slumped down into his chair. He sighed, then said: 'You had a good life ahead of you, Mahoney. Brains, sportsman, personality, good looks. You had an excellent chance of winning a Rhodes Scholarship. Now? Do you realize you'll have great difficulty even finding *employment* with an expulsion record?'

Mahoney said grimly: 'Yes, I realize that, sir. So can we now please get on with it?'

The headmaster was taken aback by this impertinence. 'Get on with it?'

'My medicine, sir. The six of the best you're going to give me. And let me get on the road.'

The headmaster blinked, then leaned forward. He hissed: 'You can thank your lucky stars that *before* I formally expel you I am giving you the chance of leaving this school *voluntarily*.'

Mahoney closed his eyes. And sighed in relief. 'I am very grateful, sir.'

'I hope you're still grateful after this . . . ' The headmaster picked up a cane. 'Drop your trousers.'

Mahoney undid his belt. He pulled down his trousers. He bent over. The cane whistled.

They drove home in grim silence. George parked in the garage. He switched off the engine, then slumped. He turned to his son. 'You've been punished. I'm not going to punish you further.'

'Thank you.'

The old man nodded. 'Besides, you're not a schoolboy anymore. You're a young man now, whether you and I like it or not.'

Mahoney didn't say anything. Yes, he felt like a man, though his arse felt like a schoolboy's.

'You became a man in the headmaster's study. You stood up for yourself, you protected Miss Rousseau and took your medicine.'

Mahoney didn't say anything.

'Miss Rousseau *did* know you were coming, didn't she?'

'Yes, sir,' Mahoney said grimly.

The old man sighed. He looked away. 'But you technically saved her honour. *Just*. That was right.' He added: 'Though I'd have expected nothing less of you.'

Mahoney said nothing.

'Yes, I've noticed a sudden maturity's come over you lately. Now I know why.' The old man shook his head. 'So, she did you some good, Luke. That's the way to look at it.'

Mahoney nodded grimly. 'Yes.'

'But I hope you're not going to keep in touch with her.'

'No, sir. She and I agreed that last night.'

'Good. That's wise.' The old man looked at him. 'You're not really in love with her, are you?'

Mahoney wished he could vaporise. Maybe that would also stop his arse hurting. He lied: 'No, sir. It was just very exciting.'

For the first time the old man smiled. 'I bet it was . . . And I think you can stop calling me sir. You're out in the big wide world now. You can't stay in this town. Though you might be a hero with the boys, it'll be very embarrassing.'

'Yes.'

George sighed. 'So, young man, you're going to Cape Town, to stay with your uncle. You leave by train tomorrow. And you're going to finish your matric by correspondence course. When that's over, you'll come home and we'll review your future.' He sighed again. 'But there's no chance of sending you to Oxford now, without that scholarship. Or any other university overseas. I can't afford that.'

'Of course not, Dad.'

'And that means you're going to have to take your law degree by correspondence too, through the University of London. Because there's no point in taking a South African law degree – there's no future in this country under apartheid. You must prepare yourself for somewhere where they practise English law.'

'Apartheid can't last forever, Father.'

'No, but it could easily last half your lifetime. And it's going to collapse in a bloodbath. And when that happens you'll need an English law degree, not Roman-Dutch. I want your sister to get out too.'

'I'm not sure I want to be a lawyer.'

'Nonsense. I know talent when I see it – you've got a nose for the law, like I have. And for argument. Anyway, it's an excellent degree to have, good background for other walks of life. What the hell do you think you want to do – history?'

'Yes. Or journalism.'

The old man sighed. 'History? Look, son, you're under the influence of this woman. Sure, history's fascinating but there's no money in it and anyway you're far too brainy to be a teacher. Even if you become a university professor, there's no money in it. And as for journalism, forget it, there's no money in it either. And all newspapermen drink too much. Listen, son: you'll get enough journalism if you write up those journals and get them published one day – including your own story. The modern South Africa. In fact I want you to make me a solemn promise that you'll do that. You've got the gift of the gab *and* history. Do you? Promise?'

Mahoney looked at his good father. 'Yes, sir,' he promised.

George slapped Luke's knee: 'The *Law*, son. It's a grand profession. Get to the top! Become a QC. Then a judge. Not a country attorney like me. So, do you promise me you'll do an LLB through the University of London? I'll pay the fees.'

Luke was in no position to refuse anything. 'Yes, I promise you.'

George Mahoney nodded. 'So the next question is what job are you going to do while you're doing your LLB? You can't work for me in this town, after what's happened. I think we could get you a job with HM Shipping for a few years?'

Mahoney said grimly: 'I don't want family charity.'

'Charity? I'm sure you'd do an honest day's work, even if you are bored out of your mind. I would be too. *But* – ' he pointed out a bright side – 'I'm sure they'd give you a few trips on their freighters. See something of the world? Australia. The States.'

'I'd love that, but not at the price of being a shipping clerk.' Luke turned to his father. 'No, for those three years I'll be a newspaper reporter.'

The old man looked at his son. 'And that's a slippery slope, my boy. However . . . ' He sighed and began to get out of the car. 'We'll preview the future when you come home at Christmas. And now – let's go and face your tearful mother.'

Mahoney put his hand on his father's arm – a good man whom he'd disappointed so badly. 'Dad? I've screwed up. And I don't want you to pay for my stupidity.'

The old man smiled. 'Miss Rousseau wasn't stupidity, son. She was *Life*. The stupid part was getting caught. Remember that. Of course I'm bitterly disappointed about your Rhodes Scholarship. But don't worry about my opinion of *you*, young man. You're all right. And you only did what any young man with balls would do. And one day you and I will be laughing about this.' He looked at his son, then clapped him on the shoulder. 'And now let's go and face the music . . . '

But there was no music from his mother. Only her gaunt face, her sniffs. Only once did she start to recriminate: 'And we had such hopes that you were going to be a top lawyer one day . . . ' and George Mahoney muttered: 'And who says he won't be?' Nothing else was said throughout the meal, except Please and Thank you. The clink of cutlery, the tasteless meal. Jill glanced at her big brother with big, compassionate eyes and said not a word. Justin came in to replace plates and dishes: he knew the Nkosaan was in big shit. The whole town knew Luke Mahoney was in big shit. When the dessert was over Mrs Mahoney dabbed her eyes, and departed wordlessly.

That night, when silence had descended, there was a scratch on Luke's door, and Jill came creeping in. She pulled a letter out of her dressing gown. 'Miss Rousseau made me promise to tell nobody about this.'

Luke switched on his bedside light. He opened the envelope.

Dearest Luke

It will seem that a terrible thing has happened, but one day you
will laugh about this. Despite this setback, I am confident you will
get through the examinations ahead, and the many others you will
doubtless sit, with flying colours. You should not think of contacting
me, but I'm sure I will hear about you and I will do so with pride
and great affection. You are the most promising historian, and
young man, I have met. Work hard, and you will have a wonder-
ful life.

Love
Lisa

Jill whispered: 'Does she say she loves you?'

Luke switched out the light. 'No.'

Jill didn't believe that. 'Are you going to marry her when the exams
are over?'

Luke smiled despite himself. 'No.'

'Why not? She's so wonderful. She loves you, all the girls think so.
Did you . . . you know?'

'What?'

'*You know . . .*'

Luke put his hand on his sister's. 'No,' he smiled sadly.

Jill put her hands to her face and gave a sob.

'Oh I can't bear it! My two most favourite people leaving at once,
you and Miss Rousseau!'

Luke said softly: 'You'll be leaving too, in a few years.'

She sniffed. 'Do you promise that you'll write to me . . . ?'

Later there was a tap on Luke's window. 'Nkosi?'

Luke got out of bed and went to the window.

'Come with me,' Justin whispered. He turned and crept away
through the garden.

At this hour? It could only be Lisa. He thought she had already left
town! He scrambled into shorts and climbed breathlessly out of the
window.

Justin was waiting. 'I have a witch doctor here.'

Luke's knocking heart sank. Not Lisa . . . ? And, oh, he didn't want
medicine from any witch doctor. 'But I have no money.'

'You can pay me tomorrow. He is a very good witch doctor, from my
area; he is staying in my room tonight.'

Justin led the way down through the vegetable garden towards the
servants' quarters. Outside the row of rooms a cooking fire was glow-
ing under a big black tripod pot. Round it squatted the cookboy, and

gardenboy and their wives. And dominating them all, the witch doctor.

He was an old man. Around his neck hung the accoutrements of his office: the cloak of civet skin and monkey hide, the pig's bladder, the necklace of baboon's teeth, the pendants of bones and claws and fruit-pips, the bracelets of animal hair, the leggings. He looked up at Luke, without rising, and softly clapped his hands. 'I see you.'

Luke clapped his hands. 'I see you, nganga.' He squatted down on his haunches. The servants looked on, wide eyes white in black faces. Luke wished they were not there to hear his troubles.

The witch doctor crouched, staring at the ground for a long minute, his white head down. Luke waited, and despite himself he was in the age-old grip, in the awe of the medicine-man, the priest, the medium to the supernatural. Then suddenly the witch doctor gave a shriek, and everybody jerked, he flung out his hands, and bones scattered on the ground.

They all stared at them. The witch doctor looked at the bones intently, motionlessly: then he pointed. To one, then another, then another: then he began to chant softly. He chanted over the bones for a minute; then scooped them up and threw them again. He threw them a third time. Then he rocked back on his heels, eyes closed. For a minute he was still: then he spoke softly: 'Beware the land of twenty-one . . . '

Mahoney's heart was knocking. *Beware the land* . . . A hundred and twenty-five years ago his great great grandfather had written in his journal, *Woe unto the land whose borders lie in shadow* . . . And that prophecy had turned out to be true. The murder of Piet Retief. Blaukrans, Weenen . . . It gave Luke gooseflesh. *But the land of twenty-one?*

'Beware the woman with the red forehead.'

The red forehead . . . ?

'Beware the woman who talks of pigs . . . '

Who talks of pigs?

Then the witch doctor said: 'Stay in the land of the evening sun, or you will weep in the land that lies in shadows.'

Luke had gooseflesh. *The land that lies in shadows* . . . He wanted to ask, *Where is this land?* Justin touched his knee and shook his head, *No.* Then the witch doctor opened his eyes. He got up and disappeared into the nearest room.

Justin stood up. He beckoned to Luke. They walked back through the vegetable garden towards the house. Luke said in English: 'Please ask him where the land of twenty-one is. And about the women. Come to the window and tell me.'

'He only knows what the spirits have spoken.' Justin stopped. 'Maybe one day we will see each other again, in Johannesburg. I will pray for you.'

Luke's eyes were burning. He held out his hand.

PART II

GHANA AND NIGERIA GRANTED
INDEPENDENCE

BELGIAN CONGO TO GET INDEPENDENCE

HAROLD MACMILLAN MAKES
WIND OF CHANGE SPEECH

SHARPEVILLE MASSACRE

6

In Kenya the bloody Mau Mau rebellion had finally been stamped out, and, as Lisa Rousseau would have pointed out, referring to the Boer War, history repeated itself: having finally crushed the rebellion, Britain promptly gave independence to the blacks, and Jomo Kenyatta, the pro-capitalist but Russian-helped revolutionary, became the prime minister of Kenya and immediately instituted a one-party state. Ghana had been granted its independence, and Kwame Nkrumah had thrown his opposition into jail. The British had promised Nigeria its independence and fierce tribal fighting for dominance had broken out. In the vast Congo there were also demands for independence, the Belgian government panicked and agreed to grant it soon: there was fierce tribal fighting and looting in anticipation, and the whites were fleeing back to Europe. It was a bloody time in Africa and it was set to get bloodier.

Luke Mahoney started writing up his family's journals in the Antarctic, on the whaling ships: there was nothing else to do when you came plodding off shift through the gore. He did not enjoy whaling but the pay was good, and you had nothing to spend it on down at the Ice. For four months you waded through gore, but you had enough money to last the next eight months. Most of those months Mahoney spent doing his compulsory military training. Then he returned to the whalers and plodded through more blood. And for the next three years he also plodded through blood as a crime reporter for *Drum* at the same time as he kept his promise to his father to study for a law degree through the University of London.

Drum was a glossy English-language magazine for blacks, about black issues, black society, black fashions, black music, black beauties, black sports, black news, black views, black politics, black crime, and black gore. *Drum* was a good magazine and the publisher wanted his black readership to be mindful of the blood they shed: the blood of faction fights, witchcraft murders and the blood of political rivalry. For junior reporters like Luke Mahoney it meant the stuff of police stations, courtrooms, photographs of pathologists' tables with every glistening wound for the judge to see, the probes inserted to show the depth, the bones exposed, the gaping stomach, the severed limb, the shattered skull, and the weapons that caused it, the knives, the knobkerries, the axes, spears, screwdrivers, guns, all neatly labelled. And if there was not enough of the *right* gore, Luke Mahoney went to the black townships to look for it.

Soweto was the best place for that. Soweto, the vast black township beyond the Johannesburg horizon with its desolate rows of concrete boxes in tiny dusty yards, sprawling slumlands of shacks made of flattened tin and cardboard, the sprawling compound which supplied the labour needs of the Golden City, the grim place whites never saw where their serfs lived, the city of tsotsis who robbed and killed for a living, the city of shebeens and witch doctors and warlords and tribal fighting and just plain murder. Soweto had the highest murder-rate in the world. Usually the police telephoned the crime reporters if something worthwhile had happened because, firstly, they wanted the public to know what they were up against, and, secondly, the press were regarded as left-wing, anti-government, and the police wanted to rub their noses in the barbarity of Africa.

'Thought you might like to see some of these photographs, Mahoney . . .'

The scene-of-crime photographs, the mortuary photographs. The charred body, the flesh still smoking.

'We've got the body in the morgue right now. Like to see it?'

'Who was he?'

'Who knows? His face is burnt off. Probably somebody your ANC pals didn't like. I hope you print that. And this one,' the sergeant said, flipping the photograph, 'we've got her in the morgue here, too, you *must* see her . . .'

The inside of a squatter's shack: on the floor, in a mush of blood, the torso of a naked black girl of five, her stomach slashed open and her liver hacked out, her arms hacked off, her genitals removed.

'Muti,' the sergeant said. 'He needed her liver and arms to make medicine to win the next fight.'

'Who is "he"?'

'Her father, Mr Mahoney. Her father cut her arms off while she screamed for mercy. Her mother saw everything. She's here now, you can ask her yourself.'

'But who were they fighting?'

'An ANC gang. Unfortunately, he'll hang. The evidence is strong.'

Unfortunately . . . He wrote an article that night around that word. Two interpretations were possible: 'Unfortunately for the accused he will hang', and 'It is unfortunate that we have to hang a man who fights the ANC', which is what the sergeant had in mind. Divide and rule: 'Let 'em fight each other, the more the better.' And there was a third interpretation, Mahoney wrote, with which many South Africans would secretly agree, even though they clamoured for the end of apartheid: they were afraid of *them*, the ANC, and felt secretly sorry for the primitive man who wanted muti to enable him to fight them . . . But the editor didn't publish it: 'Good stuff, Luke,' he said, 'but we can't say it.'

And then came the famous speech in South Africa by Harold Macmillan, prime minister of Great Britain, and then came the gore of Sharpeville, and then came the gore of the prime minister of South Africa.

Harold Macmillan had just been on a whistle-stop tour through his government's colonies in Africa. He had been impressed by the level of African nationalism and he wanted to tell Her Majesty's dominion of South Africa a thing or two about their folly of apartheid.

'The Wind of Change is blowing through this continent,' he told the South African parliament, ' . . . and this growth of national consciousness is a political fact. We must all accept it as a fact and our national policies must take account of it . . . ' The third world of emergent nations, he said, were trying to choose between the models of the first, free, world of the West and the second, communist, world of the East. 'Choosing by our example.' Great Britain, he said, was granting independence to its African colonies in the belief that it was the only way to establish a free world, as opposed to a communist world. 'We try to respect the rights of individuals . . . merit alone must be the criterion for man's advancement . . . We reject racial superiority, we espouse harmony, unity and the individual's rights . . . *We in Great Britain have different views to you on this* . . . ' History, he prophesied, would make apartheid a thing of the past. Isolationism, he advised them, was out of date in the modern, shrinking world. *Ask not for whom the bell tolls, it tolls for thee* . . .

'It was a brilliant, dignified speech,' George Mahoney wrote to his son, 'and you must include it verbatim in the journals, but you can imagine that it went over like a lead balloon. The applause was, at best, mutedly polite, except from me: my clapping was thunderous. I've been telling them the same thing for years, to no avail. And old Mac's speech will avail nothing either. I regret to report that old Hendrik Verwoerd made a most clever – and *persuasive*, goddamn it – impromptu reply. He made a defence of the white man's rights as a European in the minority on a black continent, and a presentation of apartheid as a policy "not at variance with the new direction in Africa but in the fullest accord with it" – because he's going to grant independence to the black homelands exactly as Britain is doing in her black colonies! But his speech left out of account the *mathematics* – the simple fact that these black homelands are incapable of being economically self-supporting, not big enough for the ever-increasing black population – they'll be simply reservoirs of labour for white South Africa. And, of course, it leaves out of account the economic injustice and indignity of the blacks in the white urban areas. You *must* put all this in the journals, Luke . . .'

Mahoney did, with relish. And then, six weeks after Harold Macmillan's speech, came a new defiance campaign, and the massacre of Sharpeville.

It is questionable how much Harold Macmillan's speech resulted in the massacre of Sharpeville, for the new defiance campaign by the ANC had been planned for months: it had been set for 31st March. But the rival PAC decided to upstage the ANC and mount their own defiance ten days earlier, to draw new supporters. The campaign was directed against the pass laws that decreed that a black man who wished to look for work in a white area had to have a pass: if he failed to find work within fourteen days, he had to return to his native area. If found without a valid pass, he was jailed. It was the law that put the lie to Prime Minister Verwoerd's dignified and clever reply to Harold Macmillan's speech: the police cells were packed each night with pass-offenders, the courts clogged, the prisons overflowing. A cruel system: cruel to make it difficult for a man to find work, cruel to punish him if he failed to find it. And so the ANC had spread the word that on the appointed day all the people must come together in their thousands and burn their passes on huge bonfires and then march en masse to their police stations and demand to be arrested. Thus would they swamp the system and make the law totally unenforceable.

Luke Mahoney was at Sharpeville that day. His editor could have sent him to dozens of other locations, but he chose Sharpeville for Luke, the only white reporter on *Drum*, because it was a 'model location' with a reputation for little violence. But Sharpeville was not quiet on March 21 1960. A noisy mob of five thousand had almost finished burning their passes when he arrived. He threaded his way through, holding up his camera and calling out: '*Mr Drum, Mr Drum!*' People were chanting and dancing as they tossed their hated passes onto the leaping flames.

Mahoney was the only white man present, but the mob was not hostile, they wanted publicity. Then the last passes burned and the mob began to surge down the road to the police station. Mahoney was swept along in the crush as the people converged on the open ground outside it. He worked his way through the mob to the very front.

The big police compound was surrounded by a high, diamond-mesh fence, topped with barbed wire. In the centre, surrounded by lawn, was the charge office, a single-storey building; behind it were garages, cells and quarters for the black constables. Beyond them the joylessness of the model location stretched on and on. And all along the stout fence surged the chanting, dancing mob, offering themselves up for arrest.

Mahoney's impression was that the mob was not hostile. *Ebullient*, he scribbled, *cocky, noisy, taunting – but not hostile in the military sense. In fact, from what I overheard, many people were expecting to hear some important announcement from the police about the suspension of the pass laws. . .*

Suddenly out of the police station the constables came running, with rifles, and they formed a line across the lawn facing the mob. The commander strode up to the fence with a loudhailer and bellowed: 'Please disperse! Go back to your houses! This gathering is illegal!'

The shouts came back: *'Yes, we are illegal!' 'We have no passes!' We must be arrested, please!'*

The rest was confused. The people at the front were being shoved from behind, and the fence was heaving, a sea of excited, laughing, shouting, singing black faces, men, women, children, young and old pressed against it, clamouring to be arrested. Again and again the station commander bellowed over his loudhailer, and the mob yelled back. Then a black sergeant ran up to the fence in panic, shouting: *'Disperse! They're going to shoot! Disperse!'* From his position at the corner of the heaving fence Mahoney formed the impression that the vast majority of the people were just enjoying themselves at the expense of the nervous policemen inside the fence, gleeful grins on black faces.

Mahoney did not hear any order to open fire, and the commander subsequently denied ever giving one. All Mahoney remembered was the line of frightened young Afrikaner policemen, rifles at the ready, the massive mob yelling at the heaving fence, the commander yelling, the black sergeant pleading: then the first shocking shot, then the ragged volley, then the pandemonium.

The pandemonium as the mob turned to flee, screaming, shoving, trampling each other underfoot, bodies crashing, and the panicked firing continued cacophonously. Shots cracked out above the screaming chaos. Men, women, children and old people were running, stumbling, lurching, tripping, sprawling, and still the shocking gunfire continued, cracking open the heavens. Mahoney stared, horrified, his face creased up, screaming: *'No! No! No! No! No!'* And still it continued, the bodies crashing and writhing; then the commander was running amongst his men, bellowing, and the gunfire spluttered out. Then wailing rose up in its place.

Luke Mahoney stared, aghast. On the ground lay sixty-nine dead, a hundred and eighty wounded. He strode furiously from his corner, his camera and notebook on high, his heart full of outrage, and he cried out to the policemen behind the fence:

'You stupid fucking bastards!'

That evening there were furious marches at Langa, near Cape Town, protesting against the Sharpeville massacre; the police baton-charged, opened fire and killed two. That night there were riots, and municipal offices were burned down. The next day the Minister of Justice suspended pass arrests, which was interpreted as a victory for the PAC, but the next week over eighteen thousand were arrested under new emergency regulations, and the next week the ANC and PAC were banned as illegal organizations. A state of emergency was declared and the Citizen Force was called out in the Cape.

It was a bloody time, and South Africa was shaken. Then, less than three weeks after Sharpeville, came the Rand Easter Show, and South Africa got more shaken.

The Rand Easter Show in Johannesburg is a big deal, a massive agricultural fair featuring pedigree livestock, gleaming machinery, the whole range of South Africa's industrial products. There are fashion shows, horse-racing, polo, show jumping; there are acres of enclosures, pavilions, marquees, stalls, bars, restaurants; there is all the colour and fun of the fair. And the women all dress to kill. Mahoney was at the show that opening Saturday, reporting for *Drum*, because as a white man he could get into all the areas. He was directly in front of the colourful raised dais when the prime minister of South Africa, Dr Hendrik Verwoerd, was shot.

Thousands of people saw it. The prime minister's motorcade arrived at noon to roars of applause. He walked down the red-carpeted avenue of people, smiling and waving, a tall, well-built, white-haired man with pale-blue eyes and a benevolent, pasty, intelligent face. Awaiting him on the platform were rows of dignitaries. The prime minister and Mrs Verwoerd mounted the dais to applause, then sat. The Mayor went to the microphone to initiate the opening ceremony and polite silence fell.

As the Mayor began, Mahoney noticed the white man approach. He was middle-aged, neat in a well-cut suit. He approached with an air of authority. Mahoney thought he was a security officer. He walked straight to the platform and mounted the steps. Several dignitaries turned but nobody looked surprised and the Mayor continued speaking. The man walked towards the prime minister, then put his hand in his pocket. He said: 'Verwoerd,' and the prime minister turned. The man pulled out a .22 calibre pistol, levelled it at the premier's surprised head, and pulled the trigger. There was a shocking bang, gasps and screams went up, the prime minister slumped, a splat of blood on his head. The man pulled the trigger again, there was another splat of blood, the prime minister collapsed, and chaos broke out. The man was overwhelmed and disarmed.

The prime minister was rushed to hospital with two bullets in his head, but he survived. The gunman's name was Pratt: he was a successful farmer. Psychiatrists judged him mentally deranged. In his statement to the police he said he shot the prime minister because he was ruining the country with apartheid.

7

Other blood that interested the editor of *Drum* was that flowing from Grand Apartheid, and forced removals.

After more than ten years of power the government had recently passed the Promotion of Bantu Self-Government Act, which sought a 'higher morality' for the policy of 'Separate Development', as apartheid was now decorously called; but it did not diminish hardship and heartbreak. Midst fanfare the prime minister had announced in Parliament that under this act the various black 'homelands' would be prepared for self-government and, eventually, total independence. This, he explained, was the logical progression of the 'benevolent science' of Separate Development and it would result in a 'constellation of southern African states', eight black and one white, independent of each other but harmoniously cooperating in matters of mutual interest. It would be a constellation so successful, the prime minister promised, that future generations of blacks would look at us with gratitude.

It sounded fine, a worthy goal, but in fact it was a cynical attempt to shovel eighty per cent of the population into the poorest corners of the land. It was a mirage because the homelands were overcrowded, and the mirage required increased forced removals of unwanted blacks from the white urban areas back to their homelands.

'Where they are to be stripped of their present South African citizenship – such as it is, second class – and have the new citizenship of their homeland thrust upon them!' Once more George Mahoney's gravelly voice rang out in Parliament. 'So they will be *foreigners* in the rest of "white" South Africa, with no right to enter and seek work unless the white South African government decides it wants their labour! And, of course, as *foreigners*, they will never *ever* expect to get the vote in "white" South Africa, even when this government collapses! *Hey presto!* With a stroke of its pen, this duplicitous government has got rid of tens of millions of its unwanted black citizens without firing a shot, while pretending to grant them independence, and thus creating pools of cheap labour!'

'They'll have the vote in their own homelands!' a government frontbencher shouted. 'What's wrong with that?! That's what Britain's doing to her colonies!'

'What's wrong with *that*,' George Mahoney cried, 'is that it's quite immoral and quite illegal! These blacks of ours are *legally* South African citizens *now* and you intend to *strip* them of that citizenship and thrust a new citizenship of a *new* country upon them! A country which I guarantee no other state in the world will recognize – a little tin-pot "country" which cannot possibly support its people! Where they will be bottled up in impoverishment!'

'They won't be impoverished! They'll have their cattle, and the Border Industries will provide employment!'

'Not impoverished?!' George Mahoney echoed incredulously. 'Eighty per cent of the population crammed onto thirteen per cent of South Africa's surface? How can they have a cattle-based economy on crowded homelands like that?! And where are these wondrous Border Industries that are going to provide employment? How many will there be? How long before these optimistic industrialists decide to take the plunge? *Years?* Meanwhile what do our poor deportees *do*?' George shook his head. 'Mr Speaker, there is nothing wrong, *per se*, in giving the blacks local self-government in their natural homelands, such as in the Transkei and in Zululand and in Bophuthatswana, giving them valuable experience in democracy. But such local self-government cannot by any stretch of the law or morality be a *substitute* for their greater South African citizenship, the right one day to vote in the land of their birth when they are ready for that responsibility!

'And there is nothing wrong, *per se*, in the notion of a "constellation of southern African states" so mistily envisaged by the Prime Minister, where half a dozen well-run, prosperous, contented black states collaborate at this tip of Africa with our big prosperous white one in some kind of commonwealth – but that will never come to pass, because those half-dozen little black states will *not* be well run, they will be misruled because this government is not bent on *tutelage*, on giving them local self-government to teach them the ropes of democracy gradually, they are bent on *hurling* total independence on them to get *rid* of them, so the government can then piously proclaim that the remainder of South Africa is white man's land. The little black states will be misruled because the natives have no *idea* of democracy yet, and they lack the education to provide a civil service! And they will not be prosperous because their territory will be over-grazed pastoral economies riddled with soil erosion because the black man counts his wealth in cattle and daughters which he sells into marriage for more cattle. And he does not have one wife, he has *several*, he does not have two children, he has a *dozen*. The Prime Minister's "constellation of southern African states" will become a shambles of little black banana republics, ripe for communist revolution! And big fat "white South Africa" will then be surrounded by *enemies*. And no other country in the *world* will recognize this so-called *constellation*, but will damn it as the political sleight-of-hand it is!'

Rumbles of agreement from the opposition benches, groans from the government benches. George Mahoney looked around, then dropped his tone to one of sweet reasonableness.

'Mr Speaker, in the name of all South Africans, present and future, I beg this government to amend this Promotion of Bantu Self-Government Act. The purpose of it should *not* be to *get rid* of our black citizens, but to *teach* them democracy by granting them some *local* self-government. I *beg* this government not to repeat the folly of the British government, of thrusting independence prematurely on unsophisticated tribesmen as it did in Ghana and Nigeria. And I *beg* this government to abandon its *hard*-hearted, heart*less* programme of forced removals, shoving unwanted black people over the newly created borders into their impoverished tinpot "states". . . '

The *Drum* editor gave Luke Mahoney the assignment of writing a series on this 'Promotion of Bantu Self-Government Farce'. Mahoney studied his father's speeches in *Hansard*, made a study of British colonial policy, and came up with a raft of suggestions on the government's responsibilities towards 'Tutelage of the African in Democracy'.

'You're turning into a good political commentator, Luke,' the editor said, 'but, Christ, we can't print stuff like this in *Drum*.'

'Why not?'

'Because you say here that blacks are not yet sophisticated enough for democracy – the government must *"teach"* them democracy *"gradually"*. Our black readers will resent that.'

'But I clearly say that I *don't* support apartheid – I only say there should be "gradualism", and equal political rights for all civilized men, as is the policy in Rhodesia.'

'That implies that most blacks aren't civilized enough for the vote.'

'They're not.'

'Be that as it may, we can't say it. But you may be able to sell it to a conservative-minded London newspaper like the *Telegraph* or *Globe*, provided you don't tell 'em you're only nineteen years old. Now I want you to write some tear-jerking pieces on forced removals.'

The government had produced a new map of the future 'constellation of southern African states'. The present Xhosa 'homelands', where Mahoney was born and brought up, would soon become the Republic of Transkei and the Republic of Ciskei, separated from each other by a white-held corridor. Together they were bigger than Scotland. The Zulu homeland was a patchwork of black areas sprinkled down the face of Natal, each black pocket surrounded by white-held land, and it would become the independent Republic of KwaZulu. The Tswana homeland was a patchwork of black pockets spread across the western Transvaal, the Orange Free State and the northern Cape, and it would become the independent Republic of Bophuthatswana. The homeland of the southern Sotho would become the tiny Republic of QwaQwa, tucked away in the Maluti mountains, and the northern Sotho would become the tiny Republic of Lebowa. The Ndebele homeland in the north-east would become the tiny Republic of Gazankulu, and the Swazi homeland would become the minute Republic of KaNgwane. Each republic would have their own black president, cabinet, a legislature elected by one-man-one-vote, their own civil service and army – all mostly paid for by the taxpayer in the remnant white Republic of South Africa. It made a crazy piebald map.

' . . . which,' Luke Mahoney wrote, 'is bound to collapse one day under the weight of eight inefficient, expensive governments.'

The rest would become the white Republic of South Africa, and blacks working there would be foreigners with work permits.

'Sounds okay, in *principle*,' Luke Mahoney wrote. 'After all, a Spaniard cannot work in England without a permit, a Frenchman cannot live in Germany without a residence visa. But the fact is that South Africa is *one* country and blacks are our citizens by international law, but they're being made foreigners in their own land, and cannot seek work in their own country without permits. And the mind-blowing injustice is that the black man cannot get a residence permit – permission to live in a *slum* – unless he has found a job with his work permit, which is only valid for two weeks. After that he is arrested, jailed, and deported back to his soon-to-be-independent "republic".'

There were two kinds of forced removals: the 'old' kind, under the Group Areas Act, abolishing blackspots in newly decreed white zones, as in the case of Sophiatown; and the 'new' kind, removing unwanted blacks, surplus to the labour requirements of the new map of the Republic of South Africa. While removals such as the one in Sophiatown were heartbreaking, removals under the Promotion of Bantu Self-Government Act were horrendous. Millions of unwanted black people were rounded up by the police sweeps, road checkpoints and door-to-door examinations of permits; millions of people – mostly the old and children – were 'repatriated' to their future republics. Luke Mahoney followed many of the removals in his *Drum* car, driving through the highveld to the dry lands of the western Transvaal to the future Republic of Bophuthatswana, driving down into the lowveld to the future republics of Lebowa and Gazankulu, driving down into the lush hills of the future putative independent state of KwaZulu, and what he saw broke his heart.

'Economic murder,' he wrote. 'At least, in the Sophiatown removal, most people still had their old jobs to go to on Monday, even if they now had to travel miles to get there. Here they have nothing. They are taken to pre-designated vacant areas and dumped. Sometimes there are rows of tin huts pre-built by the government, sometimes they have not been built yet, sometimes they are never built. There is no work, no hope. These people have no cattle, no goats, no chickens. And no young men and women to help. Vast new communities of the aged and children are being created and sternly told to get on with the business of survival. On this sick and hopeless economic base the government is building its model dream-state, its *"constellation of southern African states"*.

'All one can say is, Christ help us all . . .'

8

That year the infamous Treason Trial finally ended after five years; all the accused were acquitted, most fled abroad, but young Nelson Mandela went underground and formed Umkhonto we Sizwe, Spear of the Nation. That year the Congo received its independence from

Belgium, and the shit hit the fan. The world stared, aghast, and South Africa gained some credibility, almost some respectability: maybe apartheid wasn't such a bad idea if this is how black democracy was.

The Congo. A vast territory, twice the size of western Europe. Fourteen million blacks from two hundred warring tribes held in check for ninety years by tiny Belgium. Vast mineral and agricultural resources. A huge network of roads and navigable rivers to extract the wealth. Being in the heart of darkest Africa, it was of great strategic importance: to Russia in her quest for African influence, and consequently to the United Nations because of the grim threat of nuclear war. The successful transition of the Congo to independence was vital to the West. Independence Day was 30 June 1960. Within twenty-four hours the Congo had burst wide open.

The electioneering was loud and furious, candidates outdoing each other in promising voters they would each get a white man's salary and house, a white wife, a white man's car, that stones buried in the ground would turn to gold, that their ancestors would be resurrected. The day following independence the banks were besieged by howling mobs demanding money – 'Print money for all' was the cry. The Force Publique was furious that they still had white officers, demanded massive wage increases, and mutinied. Thousands of mutineers ransacked Léopoldville in a drunken rage. The new prime minister, Patrice Lumumba, fired all the white officers, replaced them with sergeant-majors and promoted every soldier one rank; the Force Publique became the only army in the world without any privates. The army mutiny swept across the vast Congo. And then the black police arrested all their white officers, and massive tribal warfare broke out.

Whites were slashed with pangas and riddled with bullets and burnt alive, raped and robbed and tortured. Belgium and America sent aircraft to evacuate their nationals as all over the vast land the whites abandoned their properties and fled the country in terror, crowding the airports, driving frantically for the borders into Burundi, Uganda, Rhodesia and mobbing the ferries across the Congo river into Brazzaville, gunned down, robbed, murdered as they ran.

On the seventh chaotic day after independence, Moise Tshombe, provincial premier of Katanga, raised the first sane voice when he demanded that Belgium send troops to restore order. But that very day the Congo was taking its seat at the United Nations in New York and loss of face for Africa had to be avoided. On the eighth day Moise Tshombe unilaterally requested Belgium to send troops. On the ninth day Belgium paratroopers dropped out of the sky and fierce fighting began. On the tenth day Patrice Lumumba, infuriated by this challenge to his sovereignty, asked the United States to send its army to help him. Russia loudly objected, and President Eisenhower backed down for fear of aggravating the Cold War. On the eleventh day the Congo collapsed and Moise Tshombe proclaimed the unilateral independence of his province of Katanga.

Thus the independence of the Congo began. The chaos was to last many years. The Western world looked on in horror. And when those in the corridors of international power looked at what was happening in the Congo and in the rest of the continent – in Kenya, where the Mau Mau had raged, in Ghana and Nigeria with their riots and tribal war, in Rhodesia, where their policy of equal rights for all civilized men was under attack, mission stations burnt down, dip tanks burned, cattle maimed – there were many who wondered whether the Afrikaners might not have the right idea: maybe apartheid was not such a bad thing.

Mahoney begged his editor to send him to the Congo to cover the crisis, but the idea was turned down. He took unpaid leave and went up to witness the drama, to interview the wild-eyed Belgian refugees. He filed a long article, but his editor could not publish it.

'Great stuff, Luke, but what *Drum* wants is the blood, sweat and tears of apartheid.'

The blood that his editor particularly wanted was that which flowed from the hearts broken by apartheid – from domestic tragedies arising from the Group Areas Act which forced members of the same family to split up under the Population Registration Act, from marriages and relationships broken up under the Prohibition of Mixed Marriages Act, from indignities caused by the Reservation of Separate Amenities Act – but the most dramatic blood of all was that flowing from prosecutions under the Immorality Act. That was always news: scandal and heart-break, broken lives, broken careers, and sheer shame. Most cases were prosecutions of white men screwing black prostitutes, or knocking off their housemaids when Madam wasn't looking; but sometimes there was a case where a girl was only slightly coloured, and she was in love with a white man. That was big news. And that is how Luke Mahoney met the beautiful Patti Gandhi again.

Patti Gandhi had made news several times since she had left Umtata: as the Indian schoolgirl who walked into the Durban whites-only library; the Indian girl who climbed onto a whites-only bus and manacled herself to a stanchion; the angelic Indian girl who walked into the

Dutch Reformed church and prayed until the police were called to take her away for disturbing the peace; the impertinent Indian girl who took herself to a whites-only beach and swam until the constables had to plunge in to drag her out; the girl who had become such a problem to her father that he had finally sent her to England to finish her schooling; the beautiful Indian girl who, when she returned, had the audacity to enter the Miss South Africa contest knowing she would be barred and cause a hullabaloo. And now here in the dock of the magistrates' court, Johannesburg, looking absolutely beautiful (so said *Drum*, the *Star*, the *Rand Daily Mail*, the *Sowetan* et al), was the notorious Patti Gandhi, aged nineteen, long-legged and with a bust and face to break your heart, the great-niece of Mahatma Gandhi, charged with contravening the Immorality Act in that upon or about the 20th day of May, 1961, and at or near the city of Johannesburg, she did, being an Indian as defined by the Population Registration Act, wrongfully and unlawfully have carnal knowledge of Peter Howardson, a person defined by the aforesaid Population Registration Act as White.

All the crime reporters were in court that day. Patti Gandhi was alone in the dock because her co-accused, Mr Howardson, had broken bail and fled the country. Miss Gandhi did not have an attorney to represent her. She listened to the prosecution evidence with a little smile. When the arresting police officer, Sergeant van Rensburg, finished his evidence-in-chief, she stood up to cross-examine.

'Sergeant, how long have you been on the Vice Squad?'

'Five years.'

'My word! We assume, therefore, that you are *very* experienced in vice? So will you please define for us the word "vice".'

'Objection, Your Worship,' the public prosecutor said.

'Miss Gandhi,' the magistrate said, 'we are not concerned with the witness's ability to define abstract nouns – it's not relevant whether the police call it the Vice Squad or the Virtue Squad – we are only concerned with his evidence that on the night of 20th May you contravened the Immorality Act.'

'But it concerns his attitude to his job, Your Worship,' Patti Gandhi said politely. 'If that attitude is hostile, if it is persecutory, it reflects upon his overall credibility as to what he saw. If, for example, we were in Germany now, in 1939, and Sergeant van Rensburg were a Nazi, it would reflect on the reliability of his evidence that he saw a Jew breaking the law – '

'Miss Gandhi,' the magistrate said, 'is it part of your defence that you are a white person?'

'No, Your Worship, Heaven forbid! I am an Indian person. The real

92

thing. My great grandfather came all the way from Bombay to these blighted shores as a coolie cane-cutter. My great-uncle was Mahatma Gandhi himself – that trouble-maker.'

'Then stop talking about Nazis. Confine your questions to the evidence pertaining to the Immorality Act.'

She turned to the witness. 'Sergeant, in your five years experience in vice – which means, by the way, things that are wicked, immoral, unjust, such as dealing in drugs, prostitution, illegal gambling, protection rackets and the like – have you done many prosecutions under the Immorality Act?'

'Yes, many,' the sergeant said grimly.

'Indeed, is the Immorality Act the bulk of your job?' She added kindly: '"Bulk" means the greatest part of your job.'

'Yes, Your Worship,' the sergeant said to the magistrate.

'So when you broke into my friend's apartment – ' she indicated the empty seat beside her – 'you were using your experienced eye to look for evidence of immorality?' The witness hesitated, and she snapped: 'Yes or no?'

'What's the purpose of the question, please?' the public prosecutor asked.

'The purpose is to establish whether or not the witness was *eagerly* looking for evidence of immorality,' Patti Gandhi said.

'Very well,' the magistrate said wearily.

Patti turned back to the sergeant. 'You were *looking* for evidence of *immorality*, weren't you?'

'Correct, Your Worship,' Sergeant van Rensburg said.

'And in fact you were very confident of *finding* such evidence – otherwise you would not have taken the risk of damaging my absent co-accused's door.'

The sergeant said: 'Yes, I was confident, Your Worship.'

Patti Gandhi cried: 'So confident that you were *prejudiced*!'

The sergeant said uncomfortably: 'No, I was not prejudiced.'

'*No*? You weren't *convinced* you were right? Then why did you smash a citizen's door down?'

The sergeant said gruffly: 'Yes, I was convinced.'

'Aha! You were *convinced* you'd find evidence of immorality within. And therefore, Sergeant, your expert, five-year-experienced eye was *prejudiced* by your conviction that you would find steamy evidence of immorality.'

'I was not prejudiced . . . '

Patti started to argue but the magistrate said, 'You've made your point, Miss Gandhi, now please proceed to your next question.'

Patti Gandhi said sweetly: 'So, therefore, Sergeant, it is very appropriate – very *relevant* – to ask you what your definition of immorality is. To define to us exactly what you were looking for.'

'Objection, Your Worship,' the prosecutor said. 'Argumentative.'

The magistrate sighed. 'No, Mr Prosecutor, Miss Gandhi has squeezed the question in legitimately. Her question is: *What* was the witness looking for and *what* was going on in his mind? That's relevant.'

Patti turned back to the witness. 'So, what *is* immorality?'

'Sexual intercourse.'

Patti's finger shot up. '*Ah*! So sexual intercourse is immoral!' She turned to the magistrate. 'And he was so convinced it was taking place that he smashed a door down! If that isn't a prejudiced witness, what is, Your Worship?'

The magistrate managed a smile. 'Continue, Miss Gandhi.'

Patti glared at the witness. 'And what exactly did your *prejudiced* eyes see, Sergeant? First you saw my friend in his underpants, looking frightened, agitated.'

'Correct.'

'Wouldn't you expect *anybody* to be frightened if someone breaks into his house at midnight? And then you looked into the bedroom. But you did not see me in there, did you?'

'No, you were in the bathroom.'

'Correct. You opened the bathroom door – which is down the passage – and saw me *there*. With a towel wrapped around my chest?'

'Correct.'

'Looking frightened, too, you said. Wouldn't you expect *any* woman to be frightened – *horrified* – when a strange, *nasty* man bursts in when she's naked, about to shower.'

'You weren't about to shower,' the sergeant said wearily.

'How do you know?'

The sergeant muttered: 'It's obvious.'

'Oh, *obvious*? And you say you weren't *prejudiced*? But the bathroom is an obvious place to shower? And isn't *naked* the *obvious* way to shower?'

The sergeant sighed. 'Of course, but . . . '

'Thank you. And on the bathroom floor were my clothes, you said. Isn't that the obvious place you'd expect to find them, as I was showering in somebody else's house?'

'No, you could have undressed in the bedroom, grabbed your clothes and run into the bathroom when you heard me coming.'

'I *see* . . . But did *you* see me do that?'

'No, I told you what I saw.'

'But you *presume* I did that?'

'That's for the magistrate to decide, not me,' Sergeant van Rensburg muttered.

'Thank *goodness* for that! Now, turning to the bedroom: you say the bed was unmade, as if somebody had recently slept in it? Did my absent co-accused have a servant who makes his bed?'

'I don't know.'

'So the bed could have been unmade like that for days. So why do you say it had been "recently" slept in?'

'Because,' the sergeant said triumphantly, 'the bed was *warm.*'

'Ah, yes, so you said. Warm? You used a thermometer, of course?'

'No,' the sergeant sighed, 'I felt it with my hand.'

'Oh, yes, your hand. I suppose your five years' experience in vice has made your hand a reliable thermometer?'

'The bed was *warm,* Your Worship,' the sergeant insisted.

'How warm, Sergeant?'

'It was *warm* – it was obvious people had been lying in it.'

'*Obvious*? *People*? Not just *one* person? It was obvious the temperature was caused by two or more human beings?'

The sergeant sighed. 'The point is it was *warm.* And there were two people in the apartment.'

'And two people will *always* jump into the same bed? Two people couldn't *possibly* be in the presence of one bed without feeling irresistibly compelled to *jump* into it? Is *that* your experience?'

The sergeant sighed again. 'I'm just telling the magistrate what I saw.'

'And *felt.* With your experienced hand. So tell me, what was the temperature of the bed – in Fahrenheit. Or Centigrade.'

The sergeant muttered: 'I don't know. Just warm.'

'I see. Hold your hand up in the air, please, Sergeant.'

The sergeant did so, grimly.

'What is the temperature of the air in this courtroom?'

'I don't know, Your Worship,' he sighed. 'It's normal.'

'Normal for what? For Africa in general? Johannesburg in particular, six thousand feet above sea level? What is *normal*?'

'I don't know.'

'You *don't know*! And what is the normal temperature of a bed that has just been vacated?'

'I don't know.'

In those days *Drum* had its premises in a rundown building called Samkay House, Troy Street, in downtown Johannesburg. It was a small outfit, with sales of only 80,000 copies per month, but over a million blacks read it. There was also a Rhodesia *Drum* and a Kenya *Drum* and the publisher intended to publish from Cape to Cairo in the fullness of time. *Drum* was also strong on black culture, all aspects of black urban life: Sophiatown had been the most dramatic manifestation of that urbanization, but Sophiatown had been razed to the ground and now Soweto was *Drum*'s new focus. *Drum*'s treatment was very American in style, heavy on American movies, cars, clothes, music and rising stars like Martin Luther King, Malcolm X. In those days the ANC and PAC imagined that the repressions of apartheid would make their causes bloom into open rebellion, but the government clampdown on all dissent in pursuit of its dream state was so effective that *Drum* was the only mouthpiece the blacks had, and they loved it. In short, *Drum* owed its success to apartheid.

But *Drum* was careful. The basic, day-to-day enemy was the Police Censorship Department, the Subversive Publications Act as supported by the Suppression of Communism Act, but the editor managed to steer a precarious course through this maze of legislation. Nonetheless, every *Drum* writer – and many from the other newspapers – had received an 'invitation to tea' with BOSS, the Bureau of State Security, a branch of the South African Police. It was the week after Mahoney's story of Patti Gandhi's acquittal was published that he received his invitation.

BOSS had its offices on the eleventh floor of Marshall Square Police Station, in the heart of Johannesburg. You were escorted into the building, and you rode up in a special elevator with only one button. You passed through a security gate, walked down a row of offices to the big one, and there was Colonel Krombrink, his hand extended and a smile all over his Afrikaner face.

'Mr Mahoney, thank you for coming to see us . . . '

'Us' included a young man in plain clothes at the window, smiling faintly, holding a fat file conspicuously marked *Luke Mahoney*, which he now carefully placed before Colonel Krombrink. Tea was served on a tray by a black constable, with a saucer of Marie biscuits.

After the niceties, Colonel Krombrink said: 'Mr Mahoney, every man is entitled to his opinions, hey, provided he doesn't commit subversion, but tell me, have you read the *Communist Manifesto*, and Karl Marx's *Das Kapital*?'

Mahoney had: it was in his father's library. But now *Das Kapital* was a banned book. 'No.'

'No? That's interesting, because it strikes us here in BOSS that so many of you English journalists have had a grounding in communism, hey. Particularly you people in *Drum*. Nothing wrong, I suppose, with an intellectual inquiry, hey, provided you don't *write* about it, indirectly *encourage* it. Anyway, it's nice to chat about these things, us intellectuals.' He waved his hand at his bookcase behind him. 'I've studied just about every book that's ever been written on communism, hey. It's my business. So I'm very interested to hear what you have to say, Mr Mahoney. About our Suppression of Communism Act.'

Mahoney's heart was knocking. He said: 'I don't believe in communism, Colonel Krombrink. For what my youthful opinion is worth, I think it is doomed because it must, by definition, be repressive, imposing a one-party state on the populace. And secondly, by definition, it must also suppress the most valuable resource a nation has, namely human initiative. Ambition. The work ethic. The determination to prosper.'

Colonel Krombrink smiled. 'What big words for such a young man. But, of course, you are a journalist. And your father – ' he indicated the file – 'is a Member of Parliament, an "independent". And he is always proposing his votes of no confidence in the government, hey, so I suppose he taught you a lot of big words too.' He smiled. 'Tell me, Mr Mahoney, why don't you have confidence in our government?'

Oh Jesus, he wanted to get out of here. 'Because I think apartheid is also doomed to failure. Unworkable. And unjust.'

'Ah. But you say you're not a communist? Tell me, was – or is – Lisa Rousseau a communist?'

Mahoney was taken aback. *Lisa – they knew about her?* 'Not to my knowledge.'

'Perhaps your knowledge of her was only carnal? Oh yes, she's a communist. Do you know where she is now?'

A *communist*?! 'At the University of Cape Town, doing her doctorate.'

'She's in a *house* in Cape Town, doing her doctorate. She's been banned.' Mahoney stared. Lisa *banned*? Oh God, how awful!

'It's a terrible business being a banned person, hey, Mr Mahoney. Imagine, she's not allowed to be in the presence of more than three people, she's not allowed to make any speeches, or write anything for publication, she can't play sport, she must be in her house from five in the afternoon to eight next morning. For three years. That's a hell of a way to live, hey? It would be a pity if it happened to you. But it's necessary in her case.'

Mahoney's pulse tripped at the threat. '*Why* was it necessary?'

'That's our business. But you know she's a member of the ANC. And now the ANC is a banned organization, after Sharpeville.'

'I didn't know she was a member. But being a member of the ANC doesn't make her a communist.'

'No? Have you read the so-called Freedom Charter of the ANC?'

'Of course.'

'"Of course"?' Krombrink smiled. 'Yes, journalists love to read things like the Freedom Charter, hey. Well, the so-called Freedom Charter says, amongst other things, that the land, and the mines, banks, life insurance companies, industry, big business, they all belong to the people and will be nationalised. What's that if it's not communism, hey?'

Mahoney took a deep, tense breath. Oh, he wanted this over. 'But I think somebody like Lisa Rousseau can be a member of the ANC without supporting all its economic principles.'

'You think so? Are you a secret member of the ANC, Mr Mahoney?'

'No.' Thank God he could truthfully say that. They could have no evidence to gainsay that.

'Are you an ANC sympathiser?'

Mahoney mentally closed his eyes. And, oh God, he hated himself for being frightened of the bastards. 'No' would have been untrue. So would 'Yes'. 'Partly' would open a Pandora's box. 'No.'

'Then why – ' Krombrink opened the file – 'do you write nonsense like this, hey?' He tossed onto the desk the glossy pages of Mahoney's story in *Drum* about the Sharpeville massacre.

Mahoney looked at him grimly. 'It's news.'

'News? It's your *opinion*.' Krombrink frowned at him. 'You're nineteen years old and *your* opinion is published across the land for all these stupid blacks to take as gospel. I ask you, is that reasonable? Would any other civilized country put up with that?'

It was Mahoney's instinct to retort that the Pass Laws were not reasonable, that South Africa did not have a civilized government. 'It was also my editor's opinion – he made the decision to publish. It was also the opinion of the international press.'

Krombrink sat back in his chair and tapped the printed pages. 'Mr Mahoney, you call the Pass Laws unjust. Unfair. Cruel. And you *praise* the defiance campaign, which resulted in all these people dying, hey.' He shook his head. 'Mr Mahoney, do you realize what would happen to this country if we didn't have Pass Laws? Can't you imagine the *chaos*? The millions of blacks streaming out of their homelands to look for work? Millions of blacks roaming our streets, knocking on doors – *sleeping* in the streets. Can't you imagine the shanty towns? The *squalor*, the disease, the *crime* . . . Got, man, it would be *chaotic*! It would be asking for trouble. And so unhealthy. And for every job there would be a hundred blacks queuing up, hey – is *that* fair to them? They'll be so desperate for jobs every Jew-boy will be screwing them for cheap labour, hey? And can you imagine the security problem?' He shook his head. '*Got*, man, surely you can see that the Pass Laws are absolutely necessary for good government?'

Good government? Mahoney wanted to ask whether Job Reservation was also good government, but, oh God, what Krombrink said was also true – social chaos *would* ensue if the millions of blacks descended on the cities. Before he could muster a comment Krombrink tossed another pile of print on the desktop.

'And if you're not ANC, why do you write crap like this, man?'

It was his story of Patti Gandhi's trial.

Mahoney stared at the top page: it was dominated by a photograph of Patti, looking like a million bucks, the breeze blowing her long black hair, descending the steps of the Magistrates' Court, a smile all over her beautiful face. 'What's wrong with that story, Colonel Krombrink?'

The good colonel sat forward. 'What's *wrong* with it?' He frowned in wonder. '*Got*, man, Mr Mahoney, I admit she is a good-looking girl, hey – you get some okay-looking Indian girls, I admit. Even some Coloured girls. But *Got*, man, that isn't the point, hey.' He frowned. 'The point is we must have order. And the white man in Africa represents order. It's all in the Bible, man. And therefore the white man must keep himself *pure*, hey. Can you imagine what a tragedy if the white man went kaffir, like in Brazil. Look what a mess South America is.' He frowned again. 'Mr Mahoney, does the sparrow mate with the swallow? Does a goose mate with a duck? Does a cow mate with a kudu?' He shook his head, eyes big. 'No, man – the sparrow sticks to other sparrows, the cow sticks to ordinary bulls. Why? Because it's the *natural law*, man! *God's* law!' He stared, then raised his finger. 'An' what's the only exception – the horse! The horse will mate with the donkey, hey. And what is the result?' He looked at Mahoney sadly. 'The mule. An' we all know what a stupid animal the mule is! It can't even *breed*.' He shook his head. 'The human being is as randy as hell, hey. An' what's the result? The result is *Coloureds*, Mr Mahoney – brown people who are neither one thing nor the other. Half-castes! Neither black nor white!' He narrowed his eyes. 'And *Got*, man, we know what a problem those bastards are: drunks, liars, crooks, prostitutes . . . ' He frowned at him, then jabbed a finger. '*You* know: you've been on the whaling ships with them.'

'And most of them are perfectly ordinary people.'

'"Most" of them! Ja – and the rest? *Skollies*. Hottentots. Trouble-makers! Neither one thing nor the other! Don't know where they fit in!' He shook his head, then leant forward again. 'Mr Mahoney, surely you can see that Nature did not intend *that*. Surely you can see that that is not *God's* law. God's law is pure. Sensible. Obvious.' He held up a finger. 'It's all in the Bible, Mr Mahoney. God said unto Moses when he led them out of Egypt, *"Thou shalt not let the seed of Israel mingle with the Canaanites"!*

Mahoney sighed. How do you talk to a guy like this? He heard himself say: 'And the Sons of Ham shall be hewers of wood and drawers of water?'

Colonel Krombrink looked at him.

'Man, that's what it says in the Bible, yes. But you must admit we're being bladdy fair to them, hey, because now the Promotion of Bantu Self-Government Act is going to give them independence. That's okay, they can run themselves any way they like there. But *Got*, man, Mr Mahoney,' he frowned, 'you know bladdy well that they can't run a white man's country, hey? Do you seriously think they can? You know the Transkei, you've seen how simple they are. Stick fights and witch doctors and muti-murders. An' here in Soweto – how violent they are. *Got*, man, one side is always knocking the hell out of the other. ANC versus PAC. Xhosa versus Zulu. That's a kaffir's idea of politics, hey. That's how it's always been since Shaka. Not so?'

Mahoney sighed. Oh, the age-old argument. And, yes, Krombrink had him there. He nodded.

'Not so?' Krombrink continued. 'An' even if they *weren't* like that, even if they behaved properly instead of like animals, do you imagine they've got the know-how to run a modern country? You've seen them.' Krombrink shook his head. 'No, man, it would go to hell. Not so?'

Mahoney shifted. He began: 'Of course they haven't got the ability to run the country yet – '

'Exactly. They hadn't even invented the *wheel* when the white man came – an' even the ancient Greeks had the wheel! No, South Africa would become just another kaffir country, hey. Look at Ghana. Kwame Nkrumah makes himself President-for-life and the country goes to ratshit. Do you want South Africa to go like that?'

Mahoney said grimly: 'No, but I don't want it to become a bloodbath either.'

'Of course not, and that's exactly what we will *avoid* with our policies, because the races will be kept *apart*, to develop along their own lines in their own areas an' won't interfere with each other. One day soon each race will be looking after its own affairs, an' if they want to have a bloodbath in somewhere like the Transkei, it's their problem, hey, not ours – '

'But apartheid will bring the bloodbath right here,' Mahoney said, 'to Johannesburg. Like Kenya.'

Colonel Krombrink smiled. 'Mr Mahoney, South Africa is totally different to Kenya – there were only fifty thousand whites in Kenya, there are five *million* of us here. Here we've got control, man.'

'And Russia – can you control them? Apartheid is driving the blacks into the arms of the communists.'

The colonel shook his head. 'Mr Mahoney, it is only by apartheid that we *can* control the communists. Without apartheid there will be chaos in which communists flourish. And apartheid offers the blacks an alternative to the rubbish of communism, it offers them the goal of self-government in their own territories. Russia wants to impose a one-party communist government. To achieve this, Russia *wants* chaos, it *wants* a bloodbath so it can seize power. Russia wants our gold and diamonds, Mr Mahoney – and Russia wants the Cape Sea Route. Because with the Cape she dominates all the sea traffic to the Far East, because the Suez Canal is now controlled by Egypt, and Russia can easily dominate Egypt. With the Cape route, she'll have the whole of Africa in her hand, man. An' from Africa they start on the rest of their world revolution. Do you want that?'

Mahoney sighed. 'Of course not, but the point is – '

'*That's* the only point, Mr Mahoney: apartheid or communism. *World* communism.' He frowned. 'Are you sure you're not a communist sympathizer, Mr Mahoney?'

Oh Jesus. It was intended to intimidate, and it worked. 'Quite sure.'

'Then why do you write crap like this, man?' He smacked the Patti Gandhi story. 'Trying to make a laughing stock of the Law . . . The Afrikaner is self-destructing . . . ' Before Mahoney could muster a response he continued: 'Do you know Miss Gandhi is a communist?'

Mahoney frowned. 'No. She comes from a wealthy family of Indian manufacturers.'

'Karl Marx was well off. Engels was rich. There're rich communists too. What they want is power. What Miss Gandhi wants is revolution. She's been making trouble for years and she makes headlines because she's pretty. All that crap about going into white libraries and getting on white buses and swimming on white beaches. Even into the Dutch Reformed *church*. *Got*, man, she's got no respect for other people's feelings, she only thinks of her reputation as a trouble-maker. Then she goes to this high-fallutin' school in England and they think she's some kind of hero an' her head gets more swollen.' He frowned. 'And now she breaks the Immorality Act and people like you write crap like this about her.'

'She was acquitted!' Mahoney interjected.

'But only just! The magistrate said the evidence was very suspicious – "sinister", he said – but it was just possible she hadn't had sexual intercourse and he had to give her the benefit of the doubt! We all know she committed perjury! But you make her a heroine!' He quoted: '"Beautiful . . . gorgeous . . . brilliant cross-examination . . .

101

brilliant school record . . . *courageous".'* He frowned. *'Got*, man, that brings the law of the land into disrepute. Can't you see that's irresponsible journalism?'

Mahoney badly wanted to retort about the law of the land – but, oh shit, he just wanted to get out of here. 'My editor approved it.'

Krombrink snorted. 'Your editor, hey? That English pinko. An' all those black colleagues of yours, no doubt.' He shook his head. 'Of course they would. All those drunkards at *Drum* are ANC.'

Mahoney wanted to protest their innocence, and thereby his own, but before he could think of anything, Krombrink banged the desk and said with exasperation: *'Got*, man, Mr Mahoney, what's a well-brought-up chap like you doing working for a kaffir magazine like *Drum*, hey?! A communist *rag*, man? An' you with all the advantages! Your father a lawyer an' MP. Head prefect of your school. First class pass in matric!' (Mahoney was amazed he knew all this.) 'The Mahoney family goes back to the Great Trek days.' He shook his head. *'Got*, such a proud record, an' then you come along, a Mahoney with real *brains*, an' first you get expelled for screwing the communist history mistress, you lose your Rhodes scholarship, then you go to work for a kaffir magazine and write crap like this – ' he thumped the stories – 'about Sharpeville, and Miss Patti Gandhi.' He looked at Mahoney with grim, steely eyes; then said theatrically: 'BOSS has watched your downhill slide with great alarm. And sadness, hey.'

Mahoney's heart was knocking. The statement was loaded. Krombrink looked at him witheringly, then stood up. Satisfied. He held out his hand, unsmiling. 'Thank you for dropping round. Nice to have a chat about things of national interest. Contact me anytime you feel like another one.'

Mahoney stood up. *National* interest? Oh Jesus . . . He took the hand. 'Thanks for the tea.'

As Mahoney reached the door Krombrink said: 'Oh, Mr Mahoney?' Mahoney stopped and looked back. 'As you're *not* a communist sympathiser, or ANC, any bits of information that come your way we would much appreciate to know about.' He smiled thinly. 'Do I make myself clear?'

Mahoney looked at the man. And, oh God, he hated himself for not having the courage of his convictions, for not giving the man a withering stare and turning on his heel. 'You make yourself clear.'

He turned again, and Krombrink said: 'Mr Mahoney?'

He stopped again. Krombrink smiled: 'Remember Miss Rousseau. A Banning Order is a terrible way for a young man to live, with all those pretty girls out there going to waste . . . '

9

Colonel Krombrink was dead right: all the journalists at *Drum* were pro-ANC. What else was there to be in South Africa in those days if you were black? But none of the *Drum* writers was a communist, as far as Mahoney knew. It was true that if you supported the ANC you were indirectly sympathetic to the South Africa Communist Party because the two were partners in crime now that both were banned: the ANC relied on the communist's cell structure and experience in underground survival. And Krombrink was dead wrong when he called *Drum*'s writers crap, but he was right when he called them heavy drinkers.

Mahoney could hold his booze but those *Drum* guys had livers like steelworks. Hard living was part of the job at *Drum*, part of its black mystique: 'Work hard, play hard, die young and leave a good-looking corpse.' The ambience and prose at *Drum* was styled on the tough American journalism of the fifties, the rough scribes with hats tilted, ties loose, cigarette hanging out of the corner of the mouth, a hip-flask to hand, pounding out flash, hard-hitting copy on their beat-up Remingtons before sallying out once more into the tough, danger-ous, fun world of gangsters, shebeens, cops, jazz, politics, injustice, flash cars and fast women. Most mornings Mahoney stayed at home studying for his law degree: at lunchtime he hit the streets of Johannesburg and Soweto, the courtrooms and the copshops and the mortuaries, looking for copy, chasing blood-and-guts stories. When he got to the office for the editorial meeting the boys were already getting along with the booze as they bashed out their prose; it was against the law for blacks to drink anything but kaffir beer, but Mahoney and the boss bought it for them, or they got it illegally at the Indian and Chinese fast-food joints that did a roaring trade servic-ing the black workers in downtown Johannesburg because they weren't allowed into bars and restaurants. The editorial meetings were very stimulating, a barrel of laughs, ideas flowing as fast as the wine and whisky and brandy as the boss kicked around subjects with his scribes and dished out assignments. It was at one of these meetings that he tossed a letter on the desk.

'An application for a job from a friend of yours, Luke. Justin Nkomo, says he was your garden boy. Know him?'

'Justin? Sure! Good guy. Where is he?'

'Transkei. Says he's done a teacher's diploma but wants to try his hand at journalism. Suggests he can be our education columnist. I'm embarrassed to tell him we haven't got an education desk, none of you guys are educated enough.'

'I'm educated,' Mike Moshane said. 'C-O-A-T spells JACKET. How's that?'

Mahoney said: 'He was bloody good at English. And a marvel at cricket. Best batsman I've ever seen. Hit anything.'

'*Cricket?*' the boss said.

'I swear, if he were white he'd be a Springbok cricketer. No bowler can get him out. Even if he uses a baseball bat.'

'Baseball?' The boss looked up at the ceiling for a moment. 'Now there's an angle: "Apartheid Foils Brilliant Sportsman." If he's as good as you say we could blow it up into a big story, make the government look silly. Now, how do we test him?'

Mahoney said: 'Take him to a private cricket pitch. Like Wits University, they'd turn a blind eye for a few hours. Get their best bowlers to turn out. I guarantee he'll knock 'em for six. Invite some sportswriters from the dailies to watch.'

'Then?'

'Then,' Mahoney said, 'you invite some baseball league people along. Give Justin a baseball bat, let their best pitchers have a go at him. Invite the American Chamber of Commerce, maybe. Maybe Justin'll get a scholarship to some Yank university.'

The editor nodded pensively at the ceiling. 'Now this bears thinking about. I'll invite him to drop round, tell him to write me a piece, take it from there.' Then he tossed a second letter on the desk. 'And, you've got one other friend, Luke – nice letter from Patti Gandhi thanking us for your "excellent, witty, and sympathetic story" about her trial.'

The room resounded to ribald remarks about bearing the Immorality Act in mind when he crawled on his hands and knees to thank her for her nice thank-you letter. Then Willy Thembu said: 'Why doesn't Luke do a full-length feature on her, her whole history, a sort of "Day in the Death of an Indian Beauty under Apartheid"? *Hey* – why doesn't he talk her into screwing a few top-cops, and then we blow the story?'

'Hey, how about *that* . . . '

The boss grinned. 'But we'd be sued – and Miss Gandhi would go to jail.'

'But so would the politicians and the top-cops!' Butch Molofo said happily. 'The Afrikaner establishment would have egg all over their faces! We'd make a sort of Mata Hari out of her – a love-nest spy. I bet that girl would go for it, she's a trouble-maker. And I bet she's in the *thick* of the ANC's underground – I bet she knows what this guy Nelson Mandela's up to . . . '

But the boss shook his head. 'We're trouble-*shooters*, not trouble-makers, and we don't make ourselves accomplices to crime. Anyway,

Miss Gandhi's been over-written lately.' (Mahoney was very disappointed.) 'But what we should do is start building a profile on this guy Nelson Mandela – to be ready for the day he does something dramatic. Luke – you start on that, between other stories. Start in the newspaper cuttings; look up every reference to him and his wife, Winnie. And you're a law student – maybe it's time you wrote us a nice piece on that ridiculous Treason Trial that Mandela was involved in. "What *is* treason in this land of ours?" Reminding us how the cops broke up the Congress of the people at Kliptown when the Freedom Charter was formed, arrested thousands, put a hundred and fifty-six on trial for treason, how five years later there were only thirty-one accused left because the government had withdrawn charges against the rest due to lack of any real evidence of *treason*. Explain to us what treason now means in our poor benighted country under our new *draconian* legislation. Can do?'

'Can do,' Luke said. 'I'll get my father to check me on the law.'

'Good.' The boss looked around the table. 'So what else is happening out there?'

Fred Kalanga took his feet off the desk to pour himself another shot of brandy. 'Talking about Nelson Mandela, I've heard a bit of talk in the shebeens that we're going to start seeing a few bangs from him soon. Something about the ANC changing its policy of non-violence.'

There were some cheers. The boss said: 'Doesn't surprise me – the ANC has got to resort to violence sometime soon if it's going to retain credibility with the blacks. But *Drum* doesn't publish rumours . . . '

Two weeks later Justin Nkomo came to work for *Drum*, on probation. Mahoney was delighted to see him again but he soon concluded that Justin was not going to fit in: he was too serious and bookish. Sure, he drank, but not enough. He wrote good prose, but not flip enough. He wanted to enjoy life but he was not flash enough for Soweto. Sure, he loved women but he was not hip enough. 'Our intellectual' they called him at *Drum*.

It was a month after his arrival that *Drum* staged their debut of Our Black Springbok. Justin had been sufficiently tested at nets to convince the publisher he was on to a winner of a story. Now he persuaded the Witwatersrand University first cricket team to turn out, and the first baseball team, he invited the sportswriters of the daily newspapers to come along, and several members of the British and United States consulates in the hopes that Justin might be offered a scholarship.

'I hope to God he doesn't let us down after all this.'

Mahoney was worried too – this had been his idea. *Please God . . .* he prayed as Justin walked out onto the university cricket pitch.

It was not, of course, to be a cricket match: it was an exhibition, and a wager. The publisher had offered five hundred rands to the university cricket club if Justin failed to score a century. And what an exhibition of slugging it was! The university team were astounded – and so were the sportswriters.

'They did not know what hit them,' the *Star* reported. 'There at the crease stood this gangly young black man, holding his bat like a caveman's club, smashing the university's best bowlers to all corners of the field as if swatting flies. Having reached his century in record time – thus winning the wager for his sponsor, *Drum* – the batsman, armed now with a baseball bat, repeated the same phenomenon against the best pitchers of the university's baseball club. The man is a genius with a bat: he has little style but who needs that with an eye and brawn like his? It would be foolish to tamper with such unorthodox brilliance. If there were no apartheid in this sports-mad land of ours he would, without a doubt, be a Springbok cricketer in a year or two, if not immediately. There is every chance that if he and *Drum* play their cards right, this man Justin Nkomo will be offered a sports scholarship to an overseas university. Indeed, the United States cultural attaché, watching wide-eyed, told me that he was certain that an American university would snap him up. South Africa will be the loser. What a sporting tragedy . . .'

Three months later Justin Nkomo accepted a scholarship to the University of Miami. Many years were to pass before he returned.

10

In those days Mahoney shared a big, seedy, four-bedroom apartment with three other bachelors: Shortarse Longbottom, a tall, thin, mournful young reporter on the *Star*, Hugo Wessels, known as Huge Vessel because of his capacity for beer, who was a young reporter on an Afrikaans newspaper, and Splinter Woodcock, a law student who was justifiably pleased with his genital endowments. The apartment was on the top floor of an old apartment block in Hillbrow, on the edge of downtown Johannesburg, one of the most densely populated areas of the world. By day the area teemed with blacks, employees of the shops and restaurants and cheap hotels, and servants who worked in the cheap apartments, but at night they all disappeared back to the townships beyond the horizon.

Most of the apartment blocks had servants' rooms on the very top but 'locations in the sky' were discouraged under apartheid. There were servants' rooms on Mahoney's rooftop and it was a term of the lease that they should not be occupied, but Mahoney had purloined a key and he went up there to work when the partying got too hectic downstairs. They called the apartment The Parsonage because there was a substantial turnover of young ladies at breakfast all weekend. The parties were fine with Mahoney, because he had most mornings free, but the weekend was an important time for him to study, at least during daylight, though it was great to know the party was going strong downstairs whenever he was ready to join it.

The Parsonage piss-ups began on Friday afternoons in the staff canteen of the *Star*, where the junior reporters of Johannesburg's various newspapers gathered to solve the problems of the world and flirt with the female junior reporters, including Gloria Naidoo, who wrote for the fashion page, and Wendy Chiang, who wrote for the book page, and Innocentia Molo, who wrote for the *Sowetan*. This multi-racial gathering was not illegal, but to adjourn together across the road to the Press Bar of the Elizabeth Hotel was illegal because of the Group Areas Act and the Liquor Act. Miss Chiang, Miss Naidoo and Miss Molo were not allowed to darken its white doors, so the party usually graduated back to The Parsonage. And this, strictly speaking, wasn't illegal either: people of different races were not actually forbidden to meet in private homes provided there was no question of contravention of the Immorality Act, the Prohibition of Mixed Marriages Act, the Prohibition of Political Interference Act, the Influx of Unwanted Persons Act, the Criminal Law Amendment Act, which authorized a policeman to detain you for twelve days without trial, the Suppression of Communism Act, the Seditious Publications Act . . . It wasn't actually illegal – not yet – but Sergeant van Rensburg and his squad were very optimistically suspicious about The Parsonage. Out there in Soweto there was murder going on, but there was Sergeant van Rensburg cruising Hillbrow trying to get evidence of the English press contravening the Immorality Act with Miss Chiang, Miss Naidoo and Miss Molo. As it happened, neither Shortarse, Huge, Splinter nor Mahoney were screwing Gloria – who had the reputation of preferring ladies – Wendy or Innocentia, though not for want of trying. The three women usually left The Parsonage together in Wendy's car – she did not drink – to go home over the horizon where they belonged, but they took great delight in reeling out of the building blowing kisses up to the boys in the hope that Sergeant van Rensburg was watching through his binoculars.

It was on one of these Friday piss-ups, the week after Justin Nkomo left for America, that Gloria Naidoo said to Mahoney: 'You remember Patti Gandhi?'

'How could any man forget?'

'Well she's a friend of mine, and she'd like to talk to you – she likes the sympathetic way you wrote up her trial. I'm sure you wouldn't mind her calling you? She'll use a public phone in case her line's being tapped. I gave her the number of the *Star* canteen, she'll phone here next Friday in case your number is being tapped too. Okay?'

Was it okay?

'Of *course* I remember you,' he said when she telephoned. 'And I thought *you* were very clever. You should be a lawyer.'

'Flattery will get you everywhere. So, I have a business proposition to put to you.'

Flattery would get him everywhere?

'Is this a story?'

'That's your business, isn't it? There are no other grounds upon which we *can* legally meet, are there?'

'Where do you suggest?'

'Well, there's no bar we can legally meet in. Not even a park bench, like they do in the movies. So would you come to my shop? Where my workers will ensure the bed temperature remains normal?'

Perish the thought . . . !

Gandhi Emporium was in the Indian quarter in Diagonal Street. The streets were teeming with people and traffic at five o'clock, blacks hurrying home from work to the locations. The shop was closing up as Mahoney walked in. An Indian salesgirl led him through to the workshop, where a dozen black tailors were shutting down their sewing machines. They entered the office beyond. Patti Gandhi was descending a staircase, her hand extended. She was even more beautiful than he remembered. She wore a lime-green silk dress that flared over her breasts revealing a breathtaking cleavage.

'Thank you for coming!'

As she got a beer for him from the refrigerator Mahoney said: 'You won't remember me, but we come from the same home-town, Umtata.'

'Yes, I know, though I don't believe we met. Your father was my father's lawyer.' She smiled. 'And I've checked you out.' (Checked him out?) 'By the way, we needn't worry about Sergeant van Rensburg,' she continued matter-of-factly. 'He's not gunning for me anymore: I neutralized him.'

Neutralized him? 'How?'

She sat down on the sofa opposite him with a glass of wine and crossed her legs elegantly. 'I screwed him.'

Mahoney tried not to show his amazement. Exactly as Willy Thembu had suggested in jest. His heart was knocking in hope. She smiled. 'That's off the record, for the moment. Do I shock you?'

He was blushing. 'No . . . '

'Liar,' she said, smiling.

'I mean, why shouldn't you sleep with whoever you like?'

'But I didn't *like*. I did it for two reasons. One, to get him off my back. Two, for the future. You never know in this country when it's going to be necessary to have a few cops on your side.' She raised her eyebrows. 'Not only did he contravene the Immorality Act, he's also a married man.'

Why was she telling him this? 'I see. You're right.'

'Sure I'm right. This is a wrong country. I don't care what I've got to do to get a few levers. So look at this.'

She got up and went to a wall-safe. She took out a large envelope. She pulled out a photograph. Mahoney stared at it. It showed a couple naked on a bed, having sexual intercourse. The woman was Patti Gandhi. And the man was unquestionably Sergeant van Rensburg.

'Who took this photograph?' *And why was she showing it to him?*

'Gloria Naidoo. In my apartment upstairs.' She explained, with a wisp of a smile: 'The day after I was acquitted, who should come here but Sergeant van Rensburg? Ostensibly to warn me officially that Vice Squad were watching me. Then he got fresh and said that he could put in a good word for me. I thought fast. I said I was having my period, could he come back in two days. I set it up with Gloria, she's a photographer. We bored a hole through the spare bedroom wall. When Sergeant van Rensburg came round for his illegal goodies Gloria photographed the terrible deed. But the photos didn't come out well enough because of the light – I didn't look like an Indian. So we set it up again for two days later, and that's the result. When the good sergeant came round again, I showed him that photo and told him to get off my back, or else.' She took back the photograph and slipped it into the envelope.

Why was she telling him this?

'You're wondering why I'm telling you this.' She folded her arms. 'Well, a few nights later I was raided by the Security Police. With a warrant to search for seditious material. My apartment was swarming with detectives, led by a certain Major Kotze. They ransacked the place, but found nothing – I'm not fool enough to keep seditious material at home. And I'm sure they weren't looking for those photographs because they were even looking down spines of books. And why would Sergeant van Rensburg confide in Special Branch? No, they were looking for a connection with the ANC. Anyway, I was quite calm and I answered all Major Kotze's questions very sweetly – I even offered him a drink. Which he declined at the time. But when the boys departed empty-handed, Major Kotze stayed behind to ask a few more questions and I got the distinct impression it was because I was wearing a rather revealing sari. And I thought: Hullo, maybe this trick can work twice. And sure enough, with the minimum of provocation, he made a heavy pass at me. Again saying he could put in a good word for me.' She smiled widely. 'Again I stalled him for a couple of days. Two days later Major Kotze was back again, boots and all. And so was Gloria, in the next room, with her camera.' She grinned widely. 'And the results are in this envelope.'

Mahoney had to command his hand not to reach out for those results.

Patti grinned: 'There's no reason for you to see them now – I only showed you the first one to convince you of the truth of my story. You'll see them later, if you agree to my proposition.' She smiled. 'And it's not an *illegal* proposition, Mr Mahoney. "Blackmail" would be a most inappropriate word to describe legitimate self-defence against the injustice of apartheid. Though I admit that if the entire South African police force wants to expose themselves to blackmail I'll arrange it.'

It broke his heart to think about it, a beautiful woman like this! A brutal, shocking, wildly erotic thought.

'I understand.'

She said quietly: 'No, you don't understand, Mr Mahoney. You're white. You have all the normal privileges of a civilized Western country. I do not. You may *sympathise*, but you do not really *understand* what it is to be non-white in this country.'

'Okay, you're right, Miss Gandhi.'

'Patti,' she said. 'Please.'

'Patti. And I'm Luke.'

'Wow, first-name terms already, we're getting on like a house on fire and you've only seen me in one pornographic photo.' She smiled widely. 'I'm not really domineering, you know. I'm as soft as butter when I'm treated right. All I want out of life is justice. A good society. And cops to catch *crooks*. Is that too much for a citizen to ask?'

'No.'

'Ah, but it is, in this country. In fact it's against the law.'

'That's true.'

'So what are you going to do about it, Luke? Are you going to write courageous stuff?'

He knew now he was undergoing some kind of test. 'I do my best – for a junior reporter.'

'You do very well indeed. I've read a lot of your work, including your articles about whaling.'

The quickest way to a writer's heart. 'Thank you.'

'But if whaling is so horrific – so cruel, as you so vividly described it – why did you keep on going to the Ice?'

'For the money.'

'Ah, yes, the money . . . Well, I can't promise you any money out of the proposition I've got for you, but on the other hand you could make a *killing*, if things go wrong.'

'Go wrong?'

'If the police start persecuting me again. Because in this envelope are not only the photographs but two affidavits testifying as to how they were taken. I intend to put them into a bank safety deposit box with the story of how they came about – a well-written story, for publication in the event of my being *seriously* arrested.'

'Arrested for what?'

'For a serious matter, like "furthering the illegal objectives of the ANC". I want to be able to tell the authorities that if they persist in their persecution of me *I* will be releasing a highly embarrassing story. This envelope – ' she picked it up – 'is my insurance, Luke. *Not* blackmail – because it would be to the public benefit that everybody be informed that the custodians of the law are *breaking* the law.'

God, yes, it would be a story. Though he wasn't so sure it wouldn't be blackmail – but to hell with that for now.

'You would be performing a public service, Luke. And showing up the cruelty of apartheid. And the ridiculousness of it.'

'Yes. Except I doubt it would pull down this government.'

'No, but it would rock the police. "Senior BOSS officer in Immorality Act love nest with ANC member".' She smiled. 'It would let the cat loose amongst the BOSS pigeons: how many security secrets would Major Kotze have told the ANC through me?'

Mahoney was bemused. Almost exactly what Willy Thembu had suggested. 'But do you intend to . . . see this Major Kotze again?'

'Oh, yes.'

It shocked him. A beautiful woman like this.

She said: 'This is too good an opportunity to pass up. The job must be done properly. The scandal must be about a *love* nest, not about a one-night stand. And I *might* even get some secrets.'

Jesus. BOSS secrets in a love nest? This story was getting better and better. He said: 'Are you also a member of the Communist Party?'

Patti smiled widely. 'I'm not going to make any *unwise* confessions in my story, Luke. The only crime I'm confessing to is contravening the Immorality Act with Sergeant van Rensburg and Major Kotze. Plus whoever of the BOSS hierarchy come my way. Of course, you must write that I *was* a member of the ANC before it was banned and that's how I came to be raided by Kotze – and ended up in bed with him.' She added: 'Of course, this could be an on-going story, with more BOSS victims. But you haven't agreed to write it yet. Will you, Luke?'

Would he? Any journalist would give his eyeteeth for the story! 'Oh, I'll write it.'

'You realize you may never publish it? It'll only happen on my instructions and that'll mean I'm in big trouble.'

'Yes.' He rubbed his chin. 'But you must realize that you're taking a chance on this. I might be raided by the police and if they find the story – then you will be in big trouble.'

She shook her head. 'If your house is raided they'll find nothing to do with me. Because you're not going to work on this at home. You'll do so in a nice secure place. I won't tell you where yet. And each time you finish a page, it'll disappear.'

'I see. Does your attorney know about this?'

'Not yet.' She smiled over the rim of her wine glass. Oh, she was beautiful. 'Any questions, Luke? Aren't you going to ask me why I've asked you to do this job?'

He grinned. 'I hoped it was because of my big blue eyes.'

'Oh, yes, those too.' (That made his heart turn over.) 'Because,' she said, 'you're a very good writer, Luke. I read your stories in *Drum* every month. And I *loved* your articles on whaling in the *Star*, your descriptions of the horror of the hunt – how the mother whale tried to take her harpooned calf under her fin!' Her eyes were suddenly glistening. 'It made me cry.'

He'd made her cry? And she made *him* want to cry, thinking of those fucking hairyback policemen rumbling all over her. He heard himself say: 'But there're better journalists than me, Patti.'

'If I phoned up the editor of the *Star* and told him I had a story for his ears only, would he have come along personally to see me?'

He tried to think what that august personage would do. 'No, he'd send one of his reporters.'

'Right. And I wouldn't know that reporter. And would I *like* him?' She smiled. 'But I do feel I know you, and Gloria says you're a good guy. And she says you're studying law – that shows you're serious, even if Gloria says you're wild as hell. And,' her smile widened mischievously, 'I saw the way you looked at me during the trial. You like me.'

Oh, there was sexual teasing in that. 'Yes, I do.'

She let that admission hang, her eyes bright with amusement, then said: 'And I like you. *That's* why I asked you to do my story.' She added: 'Probably as much as you like me, Luke.'

Mahoney's heart seemed to turn over. Surely this was an invitation? But he hesitated to blunder in – he wanted to make a good impression.

She went on: 'Tell me, what is it you like about me? Apart from my body.'

Her body . . . Now he was in no doubt. His heart was hammering. *But play it cool* . . . 'Your mind. And your courage.'

'But you don't know anything about my mind yet. Except that possibly I'm a hard bitch who's prepared to screw policemen.'

Her mind was the last thing on *his* mind right now – let's get back to the bit about her body. He said: 'I saw your mind in action in the trial – you were clever. And you were courageous to make a public issue over that Miss South Africa contest.'

'And how do you like my politics?'

Oh fuck politics. The conversation, moments ago so promising, was taking an unfortunate turn. 'All I know about your politics is that you're against this government – and so am I.'

'But are you really against the government, or are you a typical schizophrenic South African liberal? All talk and no action. Against apartheid, vote for the United Party, but secretly *understand* why the government's doing what it is, because in your secret racist heart you're really scared to give the blacks the vote. Because most of them are so "primitive" and your civilization will be *swamped*.'

He wished they could get off this tack. '"Schizophrenic".' He smiled. '"Secret racist heart": I must use those expressions.'

'Well,' she smiled, 'are you?'

Was he undergoing a test to see if he deserved getting laid? He was determined to pass it. 'Absolutely not.' That was only half-true but it felt like a hundred per cent.

She grinned. 'Then you're very much an exception, Luke. Even the Indians are scared of blacks. Well, not only am I anti-government, but I'm a *do-er*, not just a talker.' She lifted her wine glass to her sensual mouth, her eyes shining with amusement. 'Well? Does that worry you?'

Worry him about what? Right now there was only one thing he wanted her to be a do-er about. Right now he didn't care if she blew the South

African government to Kingdom Come as long as she didn't involve him. 'I'm a journalist, Patti, my job is to write what's happening. I'm shock-proof.' He added for good measure: 'And I'm trustworthy.'

She threw back her lovely head and laughed. It was resonant with sex. 'Oh Luke . . . I know what you're thinking. And I like you . . . '

Now you're talking, Miss Gandhi . . .

'And I like you . . . ' he said huskily.

He was about to cross the room and take her in his arms when she said: 'Know what I like about you, despite your schizophrenia? Your boyish charm . . . In fact, your body . . . '

His body? And this was definitely it! Luke Mahoney got up out of the armchair with uncool alacrity, put his glass down, and crossed the room. And Patti Gandhi put her glass down, as if to make ready for the assault. Mahoney halted in front of her, she lifted her lovely face and he crushed her smiling mouth to his, devouring her with kisses; then he tried to heave her up to her feet.

'No, Luke!' she said, grinning.

No Luke? After that come-on? He stared down at her smiling face.

'I'm sorry, Luke, I've led you on.'

Damn right she had! And he wasn't taking no for an answer. He dropped to one knee and put his arms around her and she laughed, and stood up. She smiled down at him, holding his hands, and said: 'Not tonight, Luke. It may surprise you, after all you know about me, but I'm not an easy lay. I like you, Luke, but going to bed with me is not part of our deal yet . . . '

11

Not part of the deal *yet? When, oh when would it be?* And how long was he going to have to wait to get his hands on this story? And on that gorgeous body. He'd undertaken not to telephone her in case her lines were being tapped. It was seven long days later that Gloria Naidoo brought the message.

He was taken aback at the elaborateness of the arrangements. He could understand why she couldn't risk him writing the story at home, but wasn't this taking things too far? As instructed, he left the *Drum* offices at five o'clock and walked to the public underground parking near the City Hall. On the lowest level he located a blue delivery van. He climbed in and pulled the doors closed. He was in total darkness: the van had no windows. Half a minute later he heard the driver's door open. The van drove off. It emerged into the rush-hour traffic. About thirty minutes later the vehicle turned onto a dirt track. Not long afterwards it stopped, the rear doors opened and there stood Patti.

'Hi! Sorry about the cloak-and-dagger stuff.'

He climbed out. She was more beautiful than ever and his loins stirred. 'Where are we?'

'On a farm belonging to a friend of mine, sorry I can't tell you where. Come.' She started leading the way towards a cottage.

Was this an ANC hide-out? This was stuff tailor-made for a journalist but Jesus Christ he'd better be careful! If the cops knew about this. 'Patti, is this an ANC safe house?'

'Good Lord, no. Look it's a real *farm*. Real cows, real fields.' In the distance he could make out the roof of a farmhouse through a thicket of trees, perhaps a kilometre away, beyond a fence. 'The only reason I can't tell where we are is that I've promised the owner I wouldn't tell a soul. Because it's illegal – he's white and I'm Indian.'

'I see. Where is the owner now?'

'He only comes occasionally. You won't see him, there's a separate road and entrance he uses, on the other side of the farm.'

She led him into the living room. There were two armchairs and a dining table with a typewriter on it. Two small bedrooms led off the room – he saw a double bed in one, two iron cots in the other. There was a small kitchen. In the backyard was a small swimming pool surrounded by a wooden fence 'This was the farm manager's cottage, but he lives over at the main house now because the owner rarely uses it. He won't disturb us. I use this place as a weekend retreat. Aren't I lucky?'

Wasn't *he* lucky? 'Very . . . ' And with all his heart he just wanted to take her in his arms and feel those breasts and thighs crushed against him and carry her off to that double bed.

'What can I get you to drink?' She fetched beer and a bottle of wine, kicked off her shoes, settled in an armchair and curled her lovely legs under her as only a woman can. 'Right,' she said. 'Where do we begin?'

He sat down at the table. 'At the beginning. Childhood. Family life. Schooling. Your defiance campaign. Miss South Africa. What it's like to live under apartheid. Every detail to rouse public sympathy . . . '

That first night he only took notes, looking for angles. It was going to be a long story and, by the time he had wrung every tear and jeer out of it, a good one. The beautiful, dutiful Indian girl, great-niece of one of the most important leaders of our time, Mahatma Gandhi, the man who started the disintegration of the mighty British Empire. The highly intelligent Indian girl who always came top of her class, who started learning the family trade at age seven, working on the cutting-room floor so that one day she could take over. The defiant schoolgirl who made such a nuisance of herself she had to leave town and go to live with her relatives in Natal. The girl who continued to defy apartheid, walked into the public library in Durban and sat down to read and went to jail after telling the magistrate she 'only wanted to learn, like other children, Your Worship'. The girl who, when she was released four days later, walked straight back into the public library and got arrested again. The girl who climbed into a whites-only railway coach and padlocked herself to the stanchion. The girl who walked into the Dutch Reformed church, sat in the front pew and waited, reading a prayer book, for the dominee to enter, as worshippers stormed out until the police came in: 'I only wanted to worship, Your Worship. I wasn't disturbing the peace.'

'You're a trouble-maker,' His Worship said.

'All I did was study the prayer book. I think it's the government who's making the trouble, Your Worship.'

'You're a Hindu,' His Worship said, 'you have your own temples.'

'But I'm very interested in Christianity, this being a Christian country, and this being *my* country, where I was born – and anyway we all worship the same God, don't we? There's only one God, the Christians say, and I just wanted to worship Him, I'm sure that as a Christian you understand, Your Worship.'

'And what did the magistrate do?'

'He was in a cleft stick, wasn't he? The press were there, in force. And not even this government – *yet* – has been so stupid as to forbid multi-racial worship – though don't bank on that. I was charged with disturbing the peace.' She laughed. 'Oh boy. The *peace*? By silently reading the Afrikaans prayer book, Your Worship? If the other church-goers are so *un-Christian* that they refuse to worship God in my presence and call the police to haul me out of their Christian church, *they* are disturbing the peace, surely, *God's* peace, Your Worship, making Him jolly angry, I bet. Remember how angry the Lord got about the money-changers in the temple, Your Worship, how He threw them out, and quite rightly too? But *I* was only reading the prayer book, Your Worship, I'm quite sure the Lord wouldn't have thrown me out for *that*.'

Mahoney was furiously making notes. 'Lovely stuff,' he murmured, 'And . . . ?'

'And the magistrate had to acquit me. But not without having the stupidity to warn me not to do it again and make a public nuisance of myself. *Public nuisance . . . !* Can you imagine what the press did with *that* gaffe? "Magistrate warns Indian not to bother God"! "Worshipper is a nuisance, His Worship says"!' She grinned. 'They called me the "God-Botherer" after that . . . '

And after that, many things. The beautiful Indian girl who shamelessly walked into the public whites-only toilet, put a penny in the slot before the white attendant could stop her, pulled down her knickers and had a pee while the press waited gleefully. *'Don't you dare come in here, you perverts . . . '* she shrieked at the police. And when the woman-constable finally led her away she beamed at the cameras and said: 'What's a girl to do? When you gotta go, you gotta go!'

Mahoney grinned. 'And . . . ?'

'No option of a fine, this time, with my criminal record. A straight fifteen days.'

Fifteen days. And, when she was released from prison that time, not only were the press there to meet her but her father.

'But what did your parents think of you?'

'Oh,' she said, 'you know what parents are like . . . My family was very conservative in that they'd come up the hard way, and even though they were bitter about apartheid they didn't want to rock the boat. When their darling daughter started rocking the boat they were so worried – for me. They wanted the best for me, to finish school and take over the business and get married to a nice high-caste Indian boy, and here I was, sixteen years old and seven criminal convictions behind my name. Not good. So, when the God-Botherer waltzed out of prison the last time, beaming for the pressmen's cameras, there was my father with an air ticket to England, to finish my schooling there.'

'And how did you feel?'

'At sixteen? With my eyes full of stars about thrashing the apartheid system? I'd already spent over thirty days in jail for my various offences – I was becoming an old hand at it, and I was something of a celebrity with the local press. I wanted to carry on. There were all these other apartheid laws I hadn't defied yet. I still hadn't booked a room in a white hotel. I hadn't gone to a white cinema or played tennis on a white court. I still hadn't gone into the Orange Free State where Indians are forbidden to set foot even in transit. And,' she grinned, 'I still hadn't screwed a white Afrikaner policeman.'

'Did you really intend to do that?'

'Well, I was still a virgin. But I thought it was a bloody good idea in principle – hoist the bastards on their own petard. And I had a few chances, by the way. Anyway, although my parents were generally very supportive, they'd had enough – particularly my poor mother. So, off to England I was sent to finish my education.'

Patti Gandhi, head prefect in her final year, leading light in the debating club, victrix ludorum. And, oh, she loved it in England. Not denied buses, tea rooms, cinemas, restaurants, hotels, not told to stand in another queue at the post office or bank or railway station. 'What a novelty! I was like a kid in a candy store. Just being treated like an ordinary person.' But, ah yes, an exotic one: there were advantages to being a non-white in lily-white England, standing out in a crowd: the head-turns, the wolf-whistles. 'I felt like a million bucks for a change, knowing I could date any boy who asked me, dance with anybody, hold his hand *legally* – *kiss* him goodnight! And the girls were all super to me, invited me home for weekends, and in the summer we went on coach tours of Europe and to villas by the sea – and the Europeans seemed to go out of their way to be nice to me. And the fact that I'd been to jail for defying apartheid? Oh boy, that made me a heroine in the girls' eyes.'

It made her a heroine in Mahoney's eyes too. South Africa had plenty of liberals who said apartheid was cruel, economically unfair, and so on, but who did nothing about it – all talk and no action, as Patti said: but here was a sixteen year-old Indian girl who *did*, and did her talking in court: it took a hell of a lot of courage to take on the South African system. And when she went on to university she was even more of a hero – and belle of all the balls. *God, you're beautiful*, Mahoney thought as he looked at her photograph albums of those days: Patti Gandhi being punted down the river; Patti yelling her head off at the Oxford-Cambridge boat race; Patti in a bikini on the French Riviera; Patti in ski-gear in the Austrian Alps; Patti in her graduation gown.

But when she returned to South Africa, she wasn't a heroine anymore, she was a criminal. As the sergeant from BOSS, who was waiting for her at the airport, warned her: 'Don't think you can come back here with your fancy English ideas, hey, jus' remember this is a white man's country, hey, and we'll be waiting for you *before* you make any more bleddy trouble, hey!'

'And what did you say?'

'Just smiled sweetly and said it was lovely to be home – what else can you say to an oaf like that, his English is too poor.'

'But why had you come back? You must have been able to get a good job overseas.'

'To make trouble . . . '

The first trouble she caused was her announcement that she was entering the Miss South Africa contest. 'Not because I wanted to flaunt my flesh, but just to cause a furore.' And cause a furore she did, for by law only white girls could show off their bodies for the Miss South Africa crown. Until the big night when that was decided, however, the law could not stop her hollering her intentions from the rooftops – although a certain Brigadier van Wyk of the South African police, contacted by the *Star*, warned darkly that 'if Miss Gandhi insists on making a spectacle of herself the police will not fear to act,' and a member of the public prosecutor's staff was moved to ponder aloud to the press about 'the point at which an act of *preparation*, which is not an offence, becomes an act of *consummation* in a case like this – which *is* an offence.'

The press loved it, and the cartoonists had a field day. Overnight Patti Gandhi became a household name and face, her glamour shots drooled over in every newspaper in the land – and the international press was quick to give South Africa another tongue-lashing. Day after day the press gleefully published different pictures of her, stacking her up against other contestants, doing opinion polls, inviting letters, until an honourable member of parliament, Mr Koos van der Bergh, was moved to demand of the Minister of Police why the government was not 'putting a stop to this cheeky provocation?' But Miss Gandhi had not yet broken the law, the Minister of Police explained to honourable members, she would only be guilty of a crime when she physically showed up at the City Hall for the contest – 'which would be a contravention of the Separate Amenities Act, because the City Hall is for whites only – honourable members need have no fear that Miss Gandhi will be allowed to flout the laws of the land with her ridiculous behaviour.'

'Why not use the Riotous Assemblies Act?' the *Cape Times* ridiculed, 'which would enable the police to tear-gas and baton-charge Miss Gandhi . . . ' ' . . . and water-cannon to cool down her admirers,' the *Standard* in London added gleefully, while the *Natal Mercury* considered the Terrorism Act more appropriate for such serious cases of creating an 'explosive' situation, alternately 'spreading alarm and despondency' amongst the other contestant. The *Argus* was of the opinion that a clear-cut case lay against Miss Gandhi under the Suppression of Communism Act for impudently implying she was as pretty as the next South African.

And then, predictably, came the registered letter from the organizers of the contest regretting to inform Miss Gandhi that they could not accept her entrance application because that would be contrary to the laws of South Africa; but Miss Gandhi did not receive it because she had disappeared. She did not reappear until the big night, when she arrived in a limousine at the stage door of the City Hall, to roars of applause from hundreds of fans and the flash of pressmen's cameras, 'looking like a million bucks' as the *Argus* put it; 'absolutely gorgeous' – the *Star*; 'pure long-legged, busty appeal' – the *Rand Daily Mail*; 'devastatingly beautiful' – the *Cape Times*; '*Wow wow wow*' was how *Drum* put it. She swept through them gaily, flashing brilliant smiles and blowing kisses. And the commotion when the police arrested her surpassed Patti's wildest dreams.

She had expected to be arrested the moment she set foot across the whites-only City Hall stage-door: as the *Star* put it, the stupidity of the police was 'crass and complete' because they wanted to make a 'show of their *kragdadigheid*. They wanted all the world to see they would put up with no nonsense from pretty Indian lasses who tweaked apartheid's nose; but instead they only showed it up for the cruel, tactless, boorish system it is . . . ' The South African police waited and let the glittering pageant get under way. The show had been going for some time when the doors burst open and into the pageant strode a squad of very serious members of the South African police, and up out of the audience rose a dozen plain-clothes men – 'twenty beefy South African policemen to arrest one young unarmed Indian girl' (*Time* Magazine).

The commander strode up onto the stage, took over the microphone and announced that the proceedings were in contravention of the Reservation of Separate Amenities Act because there was a non-European on the premises. Policemen were hurrying backstage. Patti Gandhi had been standing with one of the organizers in the wings, fully clothed, watching the proceedings; now, as cops swarmed towards her, she gave a girlish cry and fled, crying '*Help!*' She ducked behind the curtains and then burst onto the stage. She ran across it, dodging lunging policemen, and plunged into the opposite wing. She dodged around the curtains again then burst back again, shrieking '*Save me!*' She made sure that she was arrested centre stage. Cops grabbed her from all sides. The audience was in uproar. And as Patti was led off the stage, gleefully crying '*Please don't hurt me!*', the punch-up started.

Midst the cheers and applause from the government supporters and the boos and cat-calls of Patti's supporters, the first fist flew and within moments one corner of the hall was a mass of brawling. It took the police ten minutes to restore order. And the press loved it. As the *Star* put it: 'They don't realize it, of course, in their mindless lust for *kragdadigheid*, but the authorities played right into Miss Gandhi's hands and they could not have made greater fools of themselves, could not have exposed their beloved apartheid to greater ridicule and contempt, if they'd sent in the Keystone Cops . . . '

And now, last month, the cops had played into her hands again. Oh, it was going to be a humdinger of a story when he'd worked it through. It was nearly midnight by the time he'd finished making his notes about

Sergeant van Rensburg of the Vice Squad and Major Kotze of the Bureau of State Security – and he was finally allowed to see all the photographs. But only briefly, only long enough to be satisfied that they existed. It was with the greatest of effort that he tore his gentlemanly eyes off them and handed them back to her. 'Okay?' she said. No, it wasn't okay. Oh, the rampant sensuality of that gorgeous golden body in the act of fucking – it was enough to make your eyes water, enough to break his heart. He *ached* to feel that gorgeous body under his . . . And now it was time either to leave or make that pass, and he had drunk enough to be emboldened.

'Right,' she said as she put his notebook into the big envelope with the photographs, 'I'll look after all this until you can come back to start writing. When? This weekend?'

Oh, the whole weekend with her? 'Fine.'

'Okay, I'll send the van to the same place on Saturday morning. Well, you must be tired. Shall I call the driver?'

And it was now or never, and he stood up and took her in his arms ardently.

And, oh, the wonderful feel of her breasts and belly and loins crushed against him, the wonderful feel of her wide warm mouth, the glorious scent of her and the smoothness of her satiny skin; with all his heart and loins he had to possess her, hurl himself on top of her and splay those gorgeous thighs and *thrust* his grateful way up into the glorious depths of her; his hand went to her breast – *oh the lovely fullness of it* – and his other slid down her satiny back – then suddenly he realized she was laughing into his mouth as they banged against the wall.

She broke the kiss and giggled into his shoulder: '*Oh, Luke . . . '* Her arms hung at her sides, her eyes bright with mirth. 'You're terribly attractive, but you're so *art*less.'

Artless? *But terribly attractive! 'Me art*less?'

She burst into new giggles and walked towards the telephone. Then she turned to him and tried to put on a straight face: 'Luke, you know that there's no future in this . . . mutual attraction?' She had to work at it to suppress her grin: 'You've just seen pornographic pictures of me . . . ' Then her face failed her and she burst into giggles again. 'Oh, it's all terribly funny, but don't you realize what a . . . *tart* I feel when you make a grab at me straight after that?'

There was a silence: Patti's eyes moist, Mahoney blushing, his heart knocking with the implied promise. 'I'm sorry.'

'Please don't be *too* sorry!' And she reached for the telephone, giggling.

* * *

121

He was driven back to town in the back of the van, riding on air. 'Please don't be *too* sorry!' And, oh, the wonderful brief feel of her; it seemed he could still taste her mouth, her lipstick, smell her scent. *Oh, it felt like love.* He could not *wait* for the weekend. It *had* to happen next weekend. And he did not care if he was playing a dangerous game.

It did happen the next weekend. And when it did, it was even more wonderful, more exciting, more erotic, more exotic than he had imagined: he was trembling with desire as he took her in his arms and crushed his mouth against hers, and, oh, the wonderful feel of her again, and this time her loins were pressed against his, she was kissing him as hard as he was her, and he peeled her dress off her golden shoulders, and, oh, the bliss as he cupped her beautiful breasts. Her dress fell off her hips in a silky heap, and there she stood, naked but for her brief panties, her glorious thighs golden and perfect, and he lowered himself to one knee and kissed down her belly and thighs, and then peeled the panties off her rounded hips, and he buried his mouth into her soft sweet pubic triangle. And she sighed, then she turned out of his embrace and walked to the sofa; she sat down, then she lifted her knees and she opened her long golden legs to him.

PART III

SOUTH AFRICA BECOMES A REPUBLIC

CONGO CHAOS CONTINUES

KENYA, TANGANYIKA, UGANDA GRANTED
INDEPENDENCE

CUBAN MISSILE CRISIS

TROUBLE IN RHODESIA

ANC ANNOUNCES ARMED STRUGGLE

NELSON MANDELA ARRESTED

POLICE FIND ANC UNDERGROUND HQ

12

A lot of things happened in the two years that followed. Prime Minister Hendrik Verwoerd led South Africa into becoming a republic, severing its ties to the Queen and the Commonwealth; the Afrikaner had thrown off the British yoke at last, the Boer War had finally ended and there was an orgy of emotion. In Kenya the last of the Mau Mau had been wooed out of the forest with an amnesty and a promise by Britain of independence, which caused outrage amongst the settlers. Tanganyika was given its independence, for the British government had lost its stomach for fighting. Immediately a new Marxist government began collectivization and villagization and communization; America was alarmed, the USSR applauded and South Africa said: 'I told you so.' Uganda was granted its independence and Milton Obote, the new prime minister, sent his army, under the command of a sergeant major named Idi Amin, to blast King Freddy, the popular monarch of Buganda, out of his throne and palace. America wrung its hands, the Soviets rubbed theirs and South Africa said 'I told you so' again. In Ghana the Great Redeemer continued throwing his opposition into jail. Nigeria was granted independence and immediately there was a military coup, the first of many. In the United Nations President Khrushchev banged his shoe on the table and sent Cuba intercontinental ballistic missiles to be aimed at America. In the Rhodesian Federation the black nationalists sent their youth about burning mission schools and dip tanks, maiming cattle and throwing petrol bombs. In the Congo chaos reigned supreme, tribalism and Marxism and nihilism and cannibalism and black magic, and Moise Tshombe defended the secessionist Katanga against this chaos with white mercenaries. In South Africa, the Spear of the Nation, under Nelson Mandela, started setting off bombs. The rival PAC sponsored a terrorist organization called Poqo, which means *We go it alone*, and random murders of whites began. The government responded with a new raft of tough legislation, the press was curbed and suspects in police custody began having fatal accidents. It was a bloody, frightening time in Africa as the colonial powers withdrew with reckless haste, and to many people all over the world the South African *kragdadigheid* seemed the only way. It was the start of the really bad times.

But to Luke Mahoney they were wonderful, exciting, happy times. And when they ended in a crack of thunder, in shock, in desperation, in running for his life, it was all the more heartbreaking because they needn't have ended that way. In the years that followed he never ceased to remember the happiness of those days. And the unhappiness.

The happiness of being head over heels in love; the happiness of knowing he had one of the most beautiful women in the world to love; the excitement of knowing that tonight they were going to make glorious, riotously sensual love. And there was the excitement of danger, of delicious forbidden fruit – the sheer *fun* of getting away with it; the breathtaking joy of making love in the apartment above her emporium, with the tailors working below, the telephones ringing; the thrill of smuggling her into The Parsonage for quickies during the afternoons, the excitement of stolen secret hours, sometimes whole perfumed nights.

The stolen nights were mostly on the farm. He was allowed to know where it was now; he drove himself, but always by a different circuitous route, always watching the rear mirror. Although she had neutralized the Vice Squad, or at least Sergeant van Rensburg, it was unwise to spend the night together in her apartment above her shop, and The Parsonage was out of the question because although he trusted the boys he could not trust the girls who emerged in the mornings. The farm was the only place they could safely do it. And did they *do* it? Oh, the anticipation of waiting for the weekend, the excitement of driving out by roundabout ways, then, when he was halfway to Pretoria, doubling back by other roads to Buck's Farm. He drove up to the cottage, grinning with anticipation, and the front door burst open and out she came, looking like a million bucks, a laugh all over her lovely face. And his heart turned over each time. And, oh, the wonderful feel and scent and taste of her. And, oh, the joy of being out in the open again, for nobody to see . . .

It was lovely to be twenty years old and head over heels in forbidden love with a beautiful woman most of South Africa knew about – *but didn't know he had*. Lovely, exciting, knowing that they had the whole weekend to themselves until Monday morning, with nobody to knock on the door. Each weekend he brought his law books – he had finished her story – and in the mornings he studied but midday found them lying beside the little pool, drinking wine, cooking on the barbecue, the sun glistening on her goldenness, her long legs so gloriously female, her tiny bikini covering her mount of Venus, the wonderful olive line where her thighs touched, her rounded soft-firm hips, her glorious breasts naked, her long black hair loose, her mouth happy below her sexy sunglasses. They were lovers who had been kept apart most of the week, catching up on each other's news, what happened at the office, who said what about whom: the delightfully important business of talking about unimportant things when out there in the rest of the land awful things were happening. It was a relief 'to get away from South Africa'. And, oh, the blissful knowledge of what they were going to do after lunch: just take each other by the hand and lay themselves down upon that big double bed with a smile of anticipation, happiness all over their faces. It seemed that each time he looked at her, her perfect body, cool and warm, the droplets of the swimming pool on her, he took a happy sigh. And she was as beautiful a person as she was beautiful. And their love-making was as beautiful as she was.

Sometimes they got away from it all by getting the hell out of South Africa. Gandhi Garments had outlets in Botswana and Mozambique, all of which fell under Patti's jurisdiction. About once a month she had to visit one of them, and they made a holiday out of it. They had to go in separate cars, because a white man leaving the country in the same vehicle as an Indian woman, particularly one as well known to the authorities as Patti Gandhi, would be a prime suspect for contravention of the Immorality Act when he returned – the wires would be hot between the border and Police HQ. So they left in separate cars and met in the hotel on the other side of the border. Patti had a cousin in Botswana whom they sometimes visited, but they always stayed in hotels. And, oh, it was a lovely feeling to be free. God knows there is nothing beautiful about the towns of Botswana, flat and dry, the sun beating down hot as hell, but to them it was lovely, freedom. Freedom to be like two people in love, to lie together by the motel pool, to have dinner together by candlelight, to dance together for all the world to see. To them Botswana was beautiful. But Mozambique was truly beautiful: the Portuguese motel on the palmy beach outside Lourenço Marques, the Indian Ocean warm and clear, the fishing boats, fooling together in the warm surf, chasing, splashing, ducking each other like two kids let out of school, pulling her bikini off midst girlish squeals, the wonderful fleeting feel of her nakedness, the laughing salty kisses, lying in the sun, her long hair shiny, her golden skin glistening. Oh God, he was proud of her; he loved the way people looked at her, stole glances at her, the furtive stares when she walked into a room.

'How does it make you feel?'

'It amuses me,' she said. 'But in South Africa it makes me angry because I'm good enough to lust after but I'm not good enough to be one of them. I'm like an Amsterdam prostitute to be drooled over and left behind in the window. In fact, I'm lower than the prostitute because it's legal to fuck *her*. I'm an Untouchable.'

'Damn right, anybody touches you and I'll break their bloody necks. Apartheid's done me a *favour* . . . '

Then there were the long languorous lunches at the beachside bistros under the palms, piri-piri prawns and fresh crayfish and barbe-cued suckling pig and chicken Portuguese style. There they would talk and talk, with the sun sparkling on the sea, the vinho verde slipping down cold and crisp, getting good and replete and sensuous in delicious anticipation of what they were going to do. And waking up in the late afternoon, in the hours after love, sweaty, replete, and diving back into the sea together to start the whole lovely process again.

'Do we make love more than other lovers, d'you think?' she asked.

'Yes.'

'Why?'

'Because we want each other more than other lovers.'

She said: 'Because we're *abnormal* lovers. We're not allowed to be normal. So every time we're together it's a honeymoon.'

'If I came home to you every night it would feel the same.'

She smiled. 'Would it, darling?' She stroked his eyebrow. 'Yes, I know how it feels. However I doubt the best of lovers could keep this up. But . . . ' she sighed, 'even if we did end up moderating our carnal appetites wouldn't it be lovely to come home to each other every night?'

Oh, it was a heartbreaking thought. With all his heart he did not want the weekend to end, he did not want to drive back alone to South Africa tomorrow, he did not want to go to bed alone in The Parsonage, he did not want to wake up on Monday morning without her, he did not want to wait for next weekend on Buck's Farm.

'Yes,' he said. 'And that's how it's going to be one day.'

She snorted softly, and stroked his eyebrow. 'One day when apartheid is gone? When it's torn us to bits? When we're old?'

It made him burn to talk like this. He *hated* those Afrikaner bastards who had done this to them. He said: 'So there's only one thing to do: get out.' He looked at her. 'Get out when I've got my LLB and we'll go and live happily ever after in another land.'

She looked at him. It was the first time he had expressed his commit-ment like that. Her face softened. 'Thank you, Luke.' Her big brown eyes were moist; then she clenched her fist and clenched her teeth and heaved herself up and clasped her knees and said to the glorious sunset: 'And I mean this too: I will never, *never* leave South Africa!' She glared at the sunset. '*Fuck* them! I'll *never* let them drive me away from the land of my birth! From my parents. From my livelihood!' She shook her head angrily. 'If we stand up to these Afrikaner bastards we can pull them down!' She glared at the sunset. 'I *hate* them! And I *love* what Umkhonto we Sizwe is doing . . . !'

Umkhonto we Sizwe – MK, for short. Spear of the Nation.

That year the ANC and the Communist Party decided violence was their only policy now that they were banned, driven underground and into exile. Mau Mau violence had worked in Kenya. All over Africa the colonies were getting their independence: the ANC could be sure of support from many places in the north. It was common knowledge that Nelson Mandela was the leader of MK, but it was the South African Communist Party who hurried to Moscow to arrange weapons and training for his new army. MK's existence was unveiled on 16th December of that year, the anniversary of the Battle of Blood River when the Boers defeated Dingaan's Zulus. That day bombs exploded in Johannesburg, Port Elizabeth and Durban, at post offices, government administration offices and electrical installations, and MK's manifesto was broadcast over Radio Freedom:

'*The time comes in the life of any nation when there remain only two choices: submit or fight. That time has now come to South Africa. We shall not submit and we have no choice but to hit back by all means within our power in defence of our people, our future and our freedom . . .* '

The recruits made their way over the border to join MK, to go for training in Eastern Europe and China and elsewhere in Africa, all arranged by the South African Communist Party. That year two hundred explosions rocked the land. The journalists called Nelson Mandela The Black Pimpernel; the police called him Public Enemy Number One, a Tool of the Communists.

That year Gandhi Garments opened a factory in Swaziland, which was a British protectorate. Swaziland was ideal for those long weekends, the border only 150 miles from Johannesburg. It is high, hilly country with forests and valleys with tumbling streams. Patti usually drove up on Friday morning and completed business in one day so they would have the whole weekend free. Mahoney followed on Friday afternoon. They stayed in the Mountain Arms, in the high forests near the border. It was lovely to sit on the verandah in the evening with a bottle of wine looking down on South Africa turning mauve, the sky turning orange red and setting the western horizon on fire. It was extraordinary that up here on this side of the border they were free to watch that romantic sunset together, to be in love, to stay in this hotel – and down there the law forbade it.

'Don't think about it,' she said. 'Or it'll drive us mad.'

'I am mad. Fighting mad.'

She smiled. 'Never be fighting mad. You've got to be cold, *calculatingly* mad in this game. And you're more valuable as a wordsmith, the pen is mightier than the sword. Leave the fighting to us.'

He looked at her. 'In what game?'

'Dealing with those bastards down there.'

'What fighting? And who's "us"?'

She smiled. 'Don't worry, I'm keeping my hands clean. If the cops had anything on me they'd have gleefully nailed me long ago.'

That was the first time he really worried.

'I don't want you involved in any of this MK business, Patti.'

She put her hand on his. 'I promise you I'm far too smart to get my hands dirty or my nose bloodied.'

'For Christ's sake, what are you talking about? "Far too smart"?'

'I simply mean we should leave the fighting to MK.' She squeezed his hand brightly. 'Now can we please stop talking about bloody apartheid?'

'No, I want to know what you mean about being far too smart to get caught.'

'I didn't say that. I said too smart to get my hands dirty.'

'Patti – are you involved in these explosions?'

'Do I look like a bomb-artist?'

'Answer me, damn it!'

She looked at him. 'No.'

He glared at her. 'But you are still a member of the ANC?'

'You know the answer to that one.'

'I mean, are you a member of an ANC underground cell?'

She smiled. 'Darling, if I were I'd be the last to admit it.'

'And that's what worries the shit out of me. Answer me, Yes or no.'

She looked him in the eye. 'No, darling. There – better?'

Not much. 'And are you a member of the Communist Party?'

She smiled. 'Darling, a Communist Party member never admits it. The membership is so secret that not even other party members know who's a member apart from their immediate cell. Not even all the members of the national executive know who's who.'

'So even the ANC executive doesn't know which of its members are also members of the Communist Party.'

'I would imagine that's right.'

She would imagine . . . 'Are you or are you not?'

She smiled. 'Would it make any difference to how you feel about me?' She held up her palms. 'And please don't let's have another argument about the failure inherent in communism – about the repression of human initiative and the dictatorship of the Party.'

'But it'd make a difference to our strategy. How careful we are.'

'Can we be more careful?'

He took a breath. 'Patti, bombs are going off all over the place. The cops are scouring the land for Nelson Mandela. Roadblocks everywhere. Midnight raids. Surveillance. Tapped telephones. Intercepted mail. Informers.' He held out a finger at her. 'If you're in *any* way involved in Nelson Mandela's fucking bombs, even as just a . . . post office box for passing on messages, you'll be nailed as an accomplice. And that's the gallows in Pretoria, Patti!' He glared at her. 'Now, do you have anything to do with that?'

She looked him in the eye with fond amusement. 'No. And now can we please stop talking about it? We're away from it. We've got two whole nights and two whole days! And tomorrow we're going to our favourite place. Please let's be happy . . .'

Their favourite place was a valley two miles from the hotel where a little waterfall tumbled into a deep pool, then swirled away over rapids of smooth stones, round big grey boulders that were warm in the sun, swirling into little bays with pebbled beaches. They had the whole glorious valley to themselves. They were free, free as the air, with nobody to see them. The forest, the waterfall, the sky so blue and the sun golden warm – it was a beautiful place to be free with the most beautiful young woman in the world, swimming naked in the pool, splashing, thrashing, ducking, the wonderful sensuous feel of her cold-warm slipperiness in his arms, her breasts and her hips and her thighs satiny smooth, her long hair floating in clouds about her shoulders.

She always had to do one dive off the top of the waterfall. It was a thirty-foot drop and it gave him the willies. She stood up there, straight, lovely legs together, arms stiff at her side, her hair plastered to her head, her breasts jutting. 'Watching?'

She looked like a goddess of the forest against the sky. 'Watching.'

Up came her arms, breasts lifting, thighs tautening, up onto her toes, then a big breath and she launched herself. Through thin air she flew, her arms out in her swallow dive, hair streaming, buttocks tight, long legs together. She arced through the sunlight, glistening, then hit the water with a splash. She broke surface, puffing. 'Were my feet together?'

'Yep.'

'Were my toes pointed?'

'I was particularly proud of your toes.'

'Shall I do another one?'

'No, that was perfect, quit while you're ahead.'

Then came the important business of building a fire. She insisted on doing it herself. Why does she love the actual making of a fire? he wondered. While he sat on a warm rock drinking cold beer she went off into the forest, wearing nothing but sunglasses, collecting wood. The blackened stones of their last fire were still there: she elaborately laid her kindling, then her bigger wood, critically rearranging it, crouching around on her haunches. Mahoney watched her, wondering at her girlish pleasure. Then, the match. Great care as she applied it to her creation: it was a matter of pride that she needed only one, and used no paper. She anxiously dropped to her knees ready to blow. Then, as flame took, great satisfaction.

'*Voilà!* Only one match!'

'Next time I want you to rub two sticks together, that'll really impress the shit out of me.'

They lay in the sun on a warm smooth rock drinking crisp wine as they waited for the fire to turn to coals, the waterfall cascading, the rapids sparkling. Then they roasted the meat, succulent lamb chops and sausages, and ate with their fingers, teeth tearing, the taste of the fire and wood-smoke, the juices on their chins – it seemed like the best food they had ever eaten. Afterwards, lying back on the warm rock, happy, free, he looked at her, her eyes closed behind her sunglasses, her hair splayed out, her breasts gently rising and falling, the sun glinting on her dark pubic triangle, her thighs glistening; she was the most naked woman in the world. He leant towards her and kissed her nipple and teased it with his tongue, and she gave a little sigh. He kissed down her breasts, and down her belly, kissing her hip, her thigh, down to her knees, then slowly up her other side, and oh the bliss of her soft inner thighs, smooth and fragrant. She lay, eyes closed, a small smile on her wide mouth, her nipples hard as he lingeringly trailed his tongue all round her mount of Venus, his breathing ruffling her silky pubic hair, then she could bear the waiting no longer and she slid her legs apart. He sank his tongue into her warm secret place, and her hand reached out for him.

Later, lying side by side, replete, he said: 'Why do you love making the fire so much?'

She smiled up at the sky.

'It's freedom,' she said. 'Being close to nature. When I was a little girl I longed to go into the bush and see the animals. I longed to go camping.

But there are no places where Indians are allowed. We aren't allowed into the Kruger National Park or the other game reserves except as day-trippers. Going to the Indian beach on the Natal coast was about as close to nature as we could get. And it was always full of other Indians with their picnic baskets and portable radios – it wasn't *nature*. And you're not allowed to build fires on the beach. So the only place you can have a fire is in your backyard – and that sure isn't nature either. That was just *frustration* when I was a girl – a mockery of freedom. So now I've got the opportunity to do it, here, in *real* nature, real forest, real mountains, it's a real treat for me. I want to run and do somersaults. Skip and play the fool.' She smiled. 'So making the fire is just responding to a childhood deprivation, I guess. That's why I get a bang out of it.'

'And that crazy swallow dive is the same?'

She smiled. 'When I was a kid I saw a movie with Jean Simmons in it, where she's shipwrecked as a girl on this desert island in the South Pacific with a boy. And they grow up not knowing anything except each other – and then they fall in love, of course, and have a baby, doing it all just instinctively. And they live off the sea and wild fruit, and they are forever diving off cliffs into this turquoise sea – and they collect pearls and don't know the value of them, until one day this ship arrives and agrees to take them back to civilization, but the wicked captain finds their pearls and he makes them dive for more, and more, and more, until they're enslaved, and they rebel and run and hide and eventually the ship sails away without them. But they are happy to be free again, living with nature, just the two of them and their baby . . .' She smiled. 'I saw that movie again and again, and I cried each time. And I longed to be like Jean Simmons, so beautiful, so free, standing there on the lip of the cliff, the wind in her hair, the turquoise water below, then launching herself so gracefully, diving like a wild creature into her underwater wonderworld, amongst all the lovely fish and coral . . . Anyway, I longed to dive like that, when I was a little girl. But there were no public pools for Indians. Now, when I'm standing up there at the top of the waterfall I feel even better than Jean Simmons. Because I'm like a bird let out of a cage. I'm *free* in real nature at last, and I'm *high*, and I'm *naked*, the sun and wind on my body, and I feel *defiant* – I want to shout, so the whole of South Africa can hear: "Look at me, I'm as good-looking and smart as you are and this is what I want to say to you all: *Fuck you!*" And then I try to do a perfect swallow, to *show* 'em.' She turned her head and looked at him. 'I guess that's what it is . . .'

13

Politics. They tried not to think about politics when they were together, but you couldn't avoid politics in South Africa, because you *lived* it. The laws of the land rubbed your nose in it every day. You worried about it, read about it, argued about it, despaired over it. Mahoney wrote about it, daily Patti seethed under it; both were the victims of it, riven apart by it.

The newspapers were full of it. Every other day, it seemed, the ANC caused another explosion, and Poqo kept striking at random. Much of this bad news was half-concealed from the public by censorship laws, but everybody knew about the terrible politics of the rest of Africa: that was not censored. The terrifying triumph of the devil in Kenya, the whites selling up their lovely farms for a song, the convoys of farmers fleeing to South Africa – *'Thank God for South Africa and Hendrik Verwoerd'*. Everybody knew about the independence of Uganda, the slaughter of his tribal enemies by Milton Obote, the chaos of his socialist policies. Everybody knew of the economic chaos of Tanzania where Julius Nyerere was uprooting whole peoples with his socialist policies of 'villagization'. Everybody knew about the chaos in the Congo, the mayhem, the murder, the rape, the looting, the arson, the cannibalism. Everybody knew about that terrifying shit happening in the rest of Africa. Everybody knew that the USSR and China were behind it all, that they intended to turn Africa into a communist continent. Everybody knew that the USSR and China were behind the ANC and PAC, that the ANC was dominated by the South African Communist Party; and everybody knew that Nelson Mandela and his MK were the bastards causing these explosions.

'He's National Hero Number One,' Patti said. 'I pray for him . . . '

Nelson Mandela, the 'black pimpernel' who flitted in and out, organizing support outside the country, training, arms, money, masterminding the sabotage inside the country. Rumour had it he moved like a fish through the waters of the people, as a tribesman, a businessman, a delivery boy, a mine worker, visiting his underground cells, reconnoitring his targets, drawing up his plans, smuggling his explosives, building his bombs, getting them to his men. His face was well-known, a handsome, intelligent face, splashed across the police posters offering huge rewards for information leading to his capture; but the bombs kept exploding, damaging electric pylons, post offices, government offices, prisons, railway installations.

'Don't you think he's a hero?' Patti demanded.

Yes, Mahoney thought Mandela was heroic. But Patti believed that Mandela's bombs would eventually frighten the whites so much it would bring about the collapse of apartheid; Mahoney did not believe that. Mandela's bombs would only frighten the whites into the government's laager, like the Mau Mau atrocities did in Kenya, like the nihilism was doing in Rhodesia. No way would Nelson Mandela's bombs bring down the South African government: they would only make the laws harsher. The only thing that would bring down the government was a full-scale invasion, and the Defence Force would shoot the shit out of that too. And who was going to support such a communist invasion in the middle of the Cold War? If America was prepared to risk nuclear war against the USSR when she tried to emplace missiles in Cuba, who was prepared to support an ANC war and place the Cape sea route in the hands of the South African Communist Party and Russia? America had just fought the Korean War, it was fighting the Vietnam War: the West had already lost most of Africa to the USSR and China – no way were they going to lose South Africa and the Cape sea route by supporting Mr Mandela and his home-made bombs. Yes, Nelson Mandela and his boys in MK were brave men taking on an unjust system, but were they not also quixotic figures?

'Quixotic!' Patti cried indignantly.

'No, look: government offices and electric pylons are important targets, but he can't win like that. The Afrikaner won't be scared away by bombs – his whole culture, his whole history is one of fighting, fighting the Kaffir Wars, trekking into the unknown, then fighting the whole mighty British Empire – so he's not going to surrender because of a few bombs, that'll only make him more repressive.'

'It's a start,' Patti said. 'Somebody's got to start hitting this government. We can't just accept our fate. And it's got great propaganda value – it shows the masses that the flame of freedom is burning brightly.'

But bombs? There was something distasteful about bombs that tarnished Mandela's image. Blowing up bridges, railway and electrical installations was legitimate in an armed struggle, but the step from there to bombs in supermarkets and hotel foyers was a short one.

'Sooner or later innocent people are going to get killed, and Mandela will lose his moral high ground.'

'It is our policy that there will be no loss of human life.'

Our policy? Jesus, that worried him. 'Patti, you aren't involved in any of this, are you?'

'Of course not, I mean it's *ANC* policy, made loud and clear at the start of the armed struggle. Mandela is a very principled man.'

'Yeah, but how principled are all his boys scattered across the country? How long before one acts on his own initiative and blows up a crowded railway station? Mandela may be smart, but he can't be everywhere at once keeping his hitmen under control.'

'"Hitmen",' she said quietly, 'is hardly the right word for freedom fighters. However, yes – there is a risk that life will be taken, and I agree that's regrettable, and it's our policy to avoid it. But history is full of human life being taken in the struggle for freedom, Luke – it's sad, but sometimes it's a risk that has to be taken. Good God, how many lives are the Americans taking every day in Vietnam, as we speak? How many lives did the British take in establishing their empire? How many lives of Aborigines did the Australians take? How many Maoris were slaughtered in New Zealand? Red Indians in America? Who started the barbaric custom of scalping in America? Not the Indians, but the white settlers, to claim a *bounty* from the government for every Indian they killed. How many lives did Castro have to take in Cuba?' (Oh Jesus, it worried him that she saw nothing wrong with communism.) 'God, how many people did the South African police shoot at Sharpeville? The history of *freedom* is soaked in blood. *This country's* history is soaked in blood. So don't expect "*us*" to be too squeamish about the risk of a little more blood – regrettable though that is.'

Regrettable . . . Jesus, she frightened him when she talked like that. Out there bombs were going off and the police were scouring the land for Nelson Mandela – and where was she five nights a week when he couldn't see her? He held a finger out at her perfect nose. 'As long as you have nothing to do with that blood.'

She pretended to bite at his finger and grinned. 'It's not the blood that worries you, is it, darling – it's me? *Us.* And the police. The Immorality Act. Boy, that's typical South African liberal schizophrenia! All talk and no do. "Blood is historically inevitable, it's *academically* necessary – as long as it's not on *my* fair hands. Oh, apartheid is brutal, oh, apartheid must be toppled, and to do so there'll be blood – but I can't lift a finger in case a spot falls on me! So, alas, I can do nothing" . . . '

'I do nothing? I write my articles for *Drum*, and the *Globe*. What I want to know is what you do, Patti?'

'*Well,*' she said reasonably, 'I run Gandhi Garments. I make nice cheap dresses and pants for "kaffirs" . . . '

'And that's all?'

'That's all, darling. Please stop worrying . . . '

14

Michael Sullivan was a geography teacher, twenty-seven years old. It was a cold winter's afternoon and he wore a hat and overcoat as he hurried into Johannesburg railway station, his collar turned up. He was carrying a large, new, cheap suitcase. He made his way to the platforms. Some white people were already waiting for the 5.15 train, where the whites-only first-class coaches would pull up. Further down the platform, where the second-class coaches would stop, a good number of Coloured people were waiting. Past them, where the third-class coaches would be, many more blacks were waiting.

Michael Sullivan walked to a bench marked 'Europeans Only', where an elderly woman was sitting with her two grandchildren. They moved up to make space for him. Sullivan placed his suitcase down beside him at the end, then moved it back to make it less conspicuous. He consulted his watch, then began to read a newspaper.

It was fifteen minutes before the first rush-hour train was due. As the minutes ticked by the long platform began to fill up. The blacks and Coloureds hurried past Sullivan, and the whites began to collect in the area in front of him, waiting impatiently. Michael Sullivan looked at his newspaper sightlessly. By five o'clock there were at least two hundred people, he estimated. Over there on the big concourse people were now hurrying in all directions to different platforms. Michael Sullivan stood up. He folded his newspaper and moved away down the crowded platform, trying to look like a man wanting to stretch his legs. He wandered off through the throng, tapping his newspaper on his leg. When he reached the concourse he increased his pace.

He strode away through the crowd, side-stepping people, until he got to the big entrance, then he broke into a run. He tried to make it a jog, like a man in a bit of a hurry – he had practised this, and timed the distances involved – but panic gripped him and he sprinted, dodging people, making for the two telephone boxes across the parking area. He raced up to the nearest box; across the dial was his handwritten adhesive tape reading 'Out of Order'. He ripped it off, rammed coins into the slot and dialled 999 feverishly.

He shouted: *'There's a bomb in a suitcase about to go off in ten minutes on Johannesburg Station! Clear the area! This is a warning from the anti-apartheid forces of freedom!'*

He slammed down the telephone, and he felt the vomit rise in his guts. He clutched his chest and reeled out of the box, taking deep breaths. But once the vomit was forced back, what he felt was elation. He had done it! He had done his duty as instructed! Only he could have done it because no black man in his cell could have sat down on a Europeans-Only bench. *He had done it!* And he'd given the bastards enough time to clear the station – a lot of Johannesburg's first-class whites-only passengers would be very late getting home tonight. He lifted his head to listen for the police sirens: but instead he heard a thud. He jerked, and looked at the big station, and he saw glass flying up into the air. He stared, horrified, aghast. Then he heard the screams, and saw the pandemonium, the people reeling out.

Michael Sullivan stared in horror. Then he vomited. He retched and staggered away into rush-hour Johannesburg.

Politics. They tried not to talk about politics, but those bombs kept going off, and now lives were going up with them. Patti was shaken when they heard of the first life lost; she was absolutely shocked by the Johannesburg Station blast that killed nine people and wounded over thirty. But she vehemently denied that any of them were Mandela's bombs – they *must* have been Poqo's, or that white student group called the African Resistance Movement.

'Our policy is no loss of life . . . And anyway what alternative is there? We can't wage a guerrilla war like Castro did because we haven't got Cuba's mountains and jungles, and South Africa is buffered by the European colonies to the north – Mozambique, Rhodesia, Angola. We have no *option* except classical *urban* guerrilla warfare.'

Jesus. *Classic* urban guerrilla warfare? 'How do you know about urban guerrilla warfare?'

'I don't know anything – you're the one who's had the military training, not me. But it's common sense – guerrillas need sanctuaries when the pressure is on, like mountains and jungles. And friendly neighbouring states where they can get supplies. Well, the ANC hasn't got that.'

'South Africa has got mountains and dense bush. The mountains of Basutoland, the Drakensberg, Swaziland, all that vast bush – '

'Yes, but we're surrounded to the north by hostile territory – the Portuguese in Mozambique and Angola, the British in Rhodesia – so it's very difficult for us to get supplies through.'

'Castro,' Mahoney said, 'had no friendly neighbouring territories either. Cuba is surrounded by sea.'

'Exactly. So he could get his supplies by sea – '

'So is South Africa surrounded by sea – almost three thousand miles of coastline.'

'But South Africa's got a powerful navy – '

138

'Bullshit, we've got a very small navy. *Castro* was faced by the United States Navy. Even a United States naval base on the island, which is there to this very day.'

She cried, 'So what's your point?'

'The point, darling, is that Castro and eighty men – only *eighty* – landed off the yacht *Granma* on the coast of Cuba and ran straight into gunfire. Only *three* years later Castro marched triumphant into Havana, despite all the odds against him.'

'*So?*'

'And Mao Tse-tung didn't have any friendly territories to supply him either. On the contrary he had the whole might of America and Chiang Kai-shek dropping bombs on him – '

'*So* – what's the point?'

He only knew that he did not accept that South Africa and its borders were unsuitable terrain for guerrilla warfare. The point was that although he rejected communism he admired Castro as a soldier. He admired Mao Tse-tung as a soldier. They had tremendous odds against them but they waged courageous and *efficient* guerrilla wars. Efficient – *that* was the point. The ANC and their MK were *inefficient*. The ANC had been in existence fifty years, apartheid had been in existence for fourteen years and all the ANC had managed was bombs. They had not liberated one square foot of territory. Bombs were bad soldiering. Oh, he admired Mandela's courage, but as a soldier he was no Castro, no Mao Tse-tung. He was pissing into the wind with his bombs – it would all come back at him. Soon he would be caught and hanged and then the police would run rings around MK; the Spear of the Nation would flap around like a chicken without its head.

'The point is bombs won't get you anywhere in this hard-arsed, well-armed, heavily policed Afrikaner country. Bombs are no good unless they're part of a well-fought guerrilla war, where they're aimed at military installations and industry – otherwise they're counter-productive, especially when they start killing people. Nobody respects a bomber, they *hate* him. Unless they wage a proper guerrilla war the ANC will lose international sympathy, and that is all they've got going for them. And bombs will only make the government more repressive.'

'Could they be more repressive?'

'Sure. How about concentration camps of suspects, like the British did during the Boer War?' He snorted. 'We've only *begun* to see apartheid legislation. If they decide to get really tough that'll be bad news for you and me.'

'So we should just give up, should we?' she countered aggressively. 'Mandela and MK are wasting their time?'

'Mandela should be devoting his considerable brainpower and courage to organizing a guerrilla army, not fucking about with home-made bombs and sticking his head in a noose. It's a quixotic waste of good manpower. And suicidal. If bombs are all MK's good for, forget about them. And forget about the ANC, because what good is a liberation movement without an army? It's a paper tiger.'

Her eyes flashed. 'Bullshit! They'll do it with *urban* guerrilla warfare!'

'They'll fail. They'll shoot themselves in the foot.'

She glared at him. 'You think the ANC are useless, don't you? You don't think they can run the country – '

'I'm not saying that – '

But, ah yes, he was saying something like that. Patti wanted one-man-one-vote tomorrow, but look at the Congo – were those blacks capable of running the country? Look at Ghana, look at Uganda . . . Of course Mahoney wanted apartheid abolished tomorrow, of course he wanted a happy multi-racial South Africa. But the only way democracy would come to Africa was gradually, with political education. One-man-one-vote tomorrow would create chaos.

'But I don't believe there'll *be* chaos,' Patti said; 'I believe the experienced ANC leadership will *prevent* the type of chaos that's happening in the Congo. But if chaos is what it takes to get rid of apartheid, so be it. If we've got to blow the whole government to kingdom come to achieve a just society, so be it.'

He smiled. No use arguing with her. 'You really are a communist, aren't you? Tear down the whole structure, rebuild on the ruins?'

'I'm a socialist, darling. Not a Marxist. And so are you, in your secret racist heart.'

'Me a socialist?'

'Of a sort. I couldn't love you if you weren't *just*. You also think there's got to be a redistribution of wealth in this country. A redistribution of *land*, for a start. Housing – why should the vast majority of urban blacks live in hovels while the whites live in nice suburbs? The state must provide decent housing. The mines, and big industry – why should the blacks, who create the wealth, receive miserable wages while the fat white shareholders get the big profits? Obviously, the commanding heights of commerce must be nationalized, like the coal and steel industry in Britain.' She spread her hands. 'That hardly makes me a communist, any more than Harold Wilson . . . ' She sat up straight. 'And now can we please stop talking about bloody politics? Weekends are supposed to be for *us* . . . '

*　*　*

140

But you couldn't avoid politics in South Africa because you lived with it. And with those bombs. And with the government's new laws to deal with it all. That year the Defence Act was beefed up to give the army wider powers to suppress internal disorder, the period of military training was extended and a police reserve was created. Police powers of interrogation, control of suspects and witnesses were drastically increased: now they were empowered to detain a suspect in solitary confinement, without access to a lawyer and without a criminal charge being laid, for successive periods of twelve days. The state already had the power to ban and banish people and organizations, but now new legislation gave them the power to condemn people to house-arrest without a trial. The Prisons Act forbade the press from reporting on conditions in jails, and new legislation empowered the state to hold suspects incommunicado, which made it impossible for a prisoner to prove he had suffered third-degree treatment. Magistrates holding inquests were frequently hearing how suspects were 'having accidents', slipping on soap in the showers, falling down staircases, 'committing suicide' by throwing themselves out of high windows, hanging themselves, being 'shot in self-defence' when attacking their interrogators, 'shot escaping custody': the new laws made it impossible to refute this new tendency of suspects to injure and kill themselves. The editor of *Drum* gave Mahoney the task of reporting on all such inquests. 'Build up a case file against the bastards.'

'God,' Mahoney said to Patti, 'it's getting like Orwell's *1984*.'

'Do you still,' Patti said, 'consider that Mandela shouldn't plant bombs?'

Oh Jesus, he didn't know anymore. He would like to see the government blown to smithereens too.

'God help Mandela when his luck runs out . . .'

It was not long before Nelson Mandela's luck did run out.

He was disguised as a chauffeur, driving a shiny Jaguar through the rolling green countryside of Natal. It was a tertiary road, only used by country folk, a needle-in-a-haystack road, which made it impossible that the police were so lucky to just pick the right one. Their ambush was massive. Mandela drove straight into it: within moments his car was surrounded by firearms.

It was an agent of the American CIA, a professional going about America's covert business, who had heard on the underground grapevine of Mandela's movements, asked President John F. Kennedy for the green light, then tipped off the South African police. Within hours the whole world knew of the triumph of the forces of law and order.

As Mahoney had said, bombs lose international sympathy.

15

The Spear of the Nation was broken. The bombs spluttered out. 'Which,' as Mahoney wrote in an article for the *Globe*, who sometimes published his work, 'is not surprising in view of the massive armoury of draconian legislation the state has assembled to suppress dissent. It can lock you up, without a trial, even *before* you have dissented. But what is surprising is the case of the State versus Nelson Mandela. The police know that he was the commander of MK, directly and indirectly responsible for the recent spate of bombings, liable therefore to the death penalty: but he was only charged with incitement and leaving the country without a passport. With the laws of human rights and habeas corpus in tatters, with suspects regularly "committing suicide" by leaping from windows, it is surprising that Mandela wasn't also a victim of Newton's law of gravity; or that evidence of his bombing was not "discovered" – a fingerprint here, a bit of explosive there, an eye-witness or two – which would have ensured he succumbed to gravity on the hangman's trapdoor. But, no: three years' imprisonment is all Mandela has received – a mere slap on the wrist.

'But as the ANC evidently rule out the possibility of a Castro-style guerrilla war because the buffer states are in unfriendly colonial hands, and as their urban guerrilla war has flapped to a standstill, they are reduced to a couple of offices in the "sanctuary state" of newly independent Tanzania and London. Doubtless they'll get a trickle of refugees from South Africa who have the guts to cross hostile territory to reach them, but what are they going to do with them? Train them in Russia, then send them back as urban guerrillas? Big deal: more cannon-fodder for the draconian security legislator.

'So, what other realistic weapon do the ANC have left? The only answer is: labour. The labour that creates South Africa's wealth, the black muscle that works the mines, industry, toils on the farms. Surely, if they withhold that labour, in the form of strikes, they will not only bring the economy to a standstill, they will also destroy the basis of the *Lekker Lewe*, the Good Life upon which this unhappy land was built. Strikes will pull apartheid down – right?

'Wrong. Why? Two reasons.

'One: strikes require organization. Leaders, shop stewards, discipline, instructions, leaflets. Sorry, folks, but the aforesaid legislation, backed up by a system of well-paid informers, will stop that at first base: twelve days' detention without trial, and twelve days and twelve days for as long as it takes, plus house arrest, banning, and banishment will nip that in the bud.

'Two: the workers want their work. If you're black, you're poor. And if you're fired, there're ten guys to take your place, and they don't only come from South Africa, they hail from Mozambique, Rhodesia and Malawi. South Africa has to patrol its borders to keep illegal black immigrants out, because lousy though the wages are they're many times better than back home.

'So my educated guess is we can forget about the ANC for the time being. The Afrikaner has finally won his long battle that began with the Kaffir Wars and the Great Trek. He's got his beloved republic and *Lekker Lewe* at last: land, security, and labour, all sewn up. The ANC, blustering a thousand miles away is, in the words of Mao Tse-tung, "the mere buzzing of flies".'

'It's good writing,' Patti said grimly, '"wise beyond your years", as your editor says. But I wish to Christ you'd stop being so disparaging about the ANC.'

'I'm sorry. I've got a lot of time for the ANC, I simply mean that they're a lame duck now. Or for a long time. Until they get their act together.'

She glared. '"Lame duck"? Far from it, pal! Let me assure you that *this* duck – ' she tapped her breast – 'is not lame!'

Oh Jesus. 'What does that mean?'

She closed her eyes. '*Nothing*,' she sighed.

'Patti? Are you up to something?'

'*No* . . . I'm just devastated by Mandela's arrest, that's all. While he was around there was *hope* – something was happening. Now?' She sighed bitterly. 'I'm angry because what you say in your article is probably true . . . Freedom: that's all I want. For everybody. Freedom to live how I want, where I can afford, to love who I like.'

They were lying beside the little pool at the cottage. 'I know the feeling.'

She shook her head, her eyes closed behind her sunglasses. 'No, you only partly *understand*, darling. You only understand the injustices of being a lusty young white man having an affair with a lusty young Indian woman, the towering injustice of not being allowed to come out in the open and just enjoy the fun of being in love. But you don't fully understand that Indian lover of yours, Luke, what it's like to *be* an Indian. Or a native, or Coloured. But an Indian is something else again – an Indian is just as sophisticated as you whites, Luke.'

'I know.'

'But you don't *know* what it's really like to be as good as the next person, even smarter, as pretty as the next girl but not allowed to stand

143

next to her in a post office queue. A bank queue. Not even ride on the same bus. Let alone live in the same suburb. You don't know how *insulted* that makes you feel, you commiserate but you don't carry away with you that appalling sense of injustice.' She sighed. 'But that's not what I'm really talking about. I'm talking about you.'

'*Me?*'

She sighed up at the sky, eyes closed. Silent a long moment. 'I really love you, Luke. I've tried not to. I've tried just to keep it a fun relationship – just a sex thing, but I failed long ago. And in fact I'm very lucky. Because, as an Indian, I had no selection at all. No choice of men. Oh, there are a dozen eligible Indian men I could have, but I just don't happen to fancy any of them. Imagine that – if the law made you choose your love-life from a dozen women you didn't fancy. Imagine the feeling of bondage, if the law did that to you. But, wow, did I fancy you! And I've got you: so I'm lucky, aren't I?'

'And so am I.' He tried to jolly her out of this mood. 'If it weren't for the law you'd have won that Miss South Africa contest and be in Hollywood now.'

'Bullshit. But, yes, we're lucky. But it's also very, very sad. Because there's no future in it.'

Oh God, he did not want to talk about the future, all he cared about was here and now, the happiness of being in love.

'No future,' she repeated. She hadn't opened her eyes. 'People say apartheid can't last much longer, but how long is that? Ten years – twenty – thirty? A twinkling of an eye in the history of a country but a lifetime for you and me.' She sat up suddenly. She swept back her hair and said: 'Shall we please stop talking about it? Can we just be happy? And have fun?'

Just fun love? He didn't want that – he wanted the real thing. Oh yes it was fun, to be in love and beating the law, these deliciously exciting lover's trysts, wine in the sun, the lovely satiny feel of her nakedness as they romped in the pool, her long black hair flared out in clouds as she floated, her lovely breasts and belly and pubic mound awash, her long golden legs glinting, and bathing together as the sun went down, legs hanging over the rim of the bath, soaping each other, drinking wine, talking.

'Just fun love,' she said. 'Look at it this way: we wouldn't make love so much if we were allowed to sleep together every night. You simply couldn't keep up this spectacular weekend performance.'

'Yes I could.'

'No you couldn't. You'd get bored. Sexually bored.'

How could any man become sexually bored with this sensual beauty, those legs, that heavenly bottom, those glorious curves, that classically lovely face, those sparkling, flashing dark eyes. 'Impossible. But maybe you'd get bored with me?'

'That hard-on? Impossible. But, you see, if it were legal, I'd want to marry you. And that's the good deed apartheid's done us – if we could get married you'd get scared and run away.'

'Bullshit.'

'Oh yes. You're far too young to get married, Luke. You haven't sowed enough wild oats yet.'

'I love you,' he said. 'Fuck the wild oats.'

She smiled sadly. 'I *am* your wild oats, Luke. Your *forbidden* wild oats. I just hope your memory will be the more vivid because of that.'

Oh Jesus. 'I love you and I love you and I love you. And I'm not going to leave you.'

'And I believe you mean it. But you cannot marry me. Illegal. So? So you're safe to be in love without the responsibility that usually entails.'

'But I do want to marry you.'

'And you're lucky. Because if you weren't screwing me you'd be screwing some nice white girl who'd be wanting you to marry her. I'm saving you all that hassle. Us women are trouble, Mahoney; remember that when you leave me.'

'You're not listening. I'm not going to leave you.'

She sighed. 'Oh, yes,' she said, 'you will leave me. And if you don't, I will leave.'

'That's a terrible thing to say.'

'I'll never want to leave *you*,' she said sadly. 'I'll be leaving . . . what? Us? But there is no "us". Because there's no future in "us". "Us" means being together forever. That means a home. Home means marriage, all the things Mother Nature designed "us" for. But all that is impossible – for us. So there is no real "us", to leave. So I will leave . . . our heartbreak.' She waved a hand at the cottage walls.

He could not bear to hear this. 'We could leave this fucking country instead!'

She snorted softly. 'Oh, don't imagine I haven't thought about it often. But I don't *want* to leave Africa. And go where?'

'Australia.'

'Australia? Never heard of the White Australia Policy? They haven't got a black problem because they shot most of them. And they don't intend acquiring a new one.'

'You're not *black*, for Christ's sake!'

She smiled. 'Oh, I know I've got a good complexion. All I've got to do is read the ads for suntan lotions. Drive along the beaches I'm not allowed to lie on and see all the pretty white girls desperately trying to get themselves the tan nature gave me. But the fact of the matter is that I'm not *white*, and Australia has a White Australia Policy. And so has Canada.'

'England then.'

She waved her hand. 'But that's not the *point*. The point is I don't *want* to leave this country, Luke! It's *my* country. I just want to change the bloody place! I want to stay right here and raise hell until they change it. I *refuse* to leave.'

Oh, Jesus. 'And how're you going to raise hell?'

She sighed, then grinned and kissed his cheek. 'Just a figure of speech. Don't worry, darling, my hands are as clean as the driven snow.'

He badly wanted to believe her. 'Tell me the truth, Patti.'

'Darling?' She looked at him with big innocent eyes. 'I *also* want us to keep a low profile so that we don't have trouble. Just examine the facts. Have I made trouble since we started going together? Have I climbed on any whites-only buses? Walked into any white restaurants? Tried to cash a cheque in any whites-only queue at the bank – or buy a whites-only postage stamp? Tried to swim in a whites-only pool? Have I?'

'No,' Mahoney sighed.

'And that used to be my stock-in-trade. Now Patti Gandhi has disappeared from the magistrates' courts. Why? Because I want to be *happy* with you. I don't want to get into trouble and spoil it. So, I suppose I've become like ninety per cent of the white South Africans. Like ninety per cent of Germany under Hitler: don't make trouble with the big bad authorities.' She looked at him with big dark eyes. 'Which is pretty despicable, I suppose, but that's where yours truly is at.' Then she flashed her brilliant smile. 'And we're not allowed to talk about politics, remember? So . . . ' She heaved herself up out of the bath, gleaming, and reached for a towel. 'So, shall we just have fun while it lasts?'

'Don't *talk* like that.'

While it lasts. Oh God, those words frightened him. But somehow he did not believe them, that these glorious days could not last, somehow they would get away with it. This apartheid craziness could not go on forever. Lying alone in his bed in The Parsonage, staring at the ceiling in the darkness, he knew that these laws would not change for a long, long time and then only because of the bloodbath, and he knew she was right when she said they were doomed, living in an unreal world. But out here on Buck's Farm, drinking wine by the pool in the sun, lying together in the slippery caress of the bath, making love on the big double bed, it felt like the real world, how people were meant to feel and live, and he could not believe it was not going to last.

Unhappiness came in the second year of their relationship. In May he was going to write his law examinations: when he had that degree what the fuck was he going to do with it? What were *they* going to do?

'You'll write the local bar exam, and practise,' she said.

'I don't want to practise law.'

'Nonsense, you'll be an excellent lawyer. You can't keep on working for *Drum*. It's been a great job but it's a dead-end.'

'I could work for the *Star*. Or the *Rand Daily Mail*.'

'Luke, you're destined for greater things than newspaper work.'

'What's wrong with being a political columnist? An opinion-maker.'

'Luke,' she said. 'With your brain and gift of the gab you should be in the courtroom fighting for justice, raising hell. Helping people who're politically *persecuted*, not being an armchair political *commentator*. We need people like you.'

'Patti, law isn't a very portable qualification – it's not like medicine or dentistry, which is the same the world over – a lawyer cannot easily uproot himself and go to practise in another country. He's got to write their local bar examinations. And one day South Africa is going to blow up. I don't want to start exams all over again in Australia or Canada.'

'That's exactly the point! Yes, this country is going to blow up. But that's when you must stay and help rebuild it after the dust settles, not run away to Australia or Canada!'

He sighed. 'Patti, when the dust settles there's going to be very little law. The policeman and the judge are the cornerstones of society, and they're going to be black.'

She said quietly: 'You don't believe that us blacks are capable of running this country, do you?'

'You're not black, for Christ's sake.'

'The point is you don't believe that we in the ANC can run a decent government, do you? You think it will be corrupt, inefficient and under-qualified.'

Mahoney sighed. True. 'Not true. I just think it will take a hell of a long time to rebuild on those ruins. And during that time I will be unable to earn a reliable living as a lawyer. So if I'm going to be a lawyer I must leave South Africa, as my father said. But if I'm going to be a journalist, a political commentator, South Africa is the best place to be. Because there's more to write about here than anywhere else.'

She looked at him narrowly with those beautiful brown eyes.

'The truth of the matter is that you're a racist, darling.'

No. A realist. The truth of that matter lay in those mortuaries, in the cloven heads, the stab and hack wounds down to the bone, the severed limbs, genitals cut off for muti; the stick fights, two, three, four hundred armed a side, all breaking loose. The truth of the matter was in the chaos of the Congo, the turmoil in Uganda, the horrors of the Mau Mau, the corruption of Ghana. The truth of the matter was Luke Mahoney liked blacks and wanted to help them: he simply did not believe they were ready yet to run the country.

'No. The solution is a policy of gradualism,' he said. 'Equal rights for all civilized men. Meanwhile let the others have a degree of local self-government in their areas, so they gradually learn the responsibilities of democracy.'

'The "civilized" ones. "Them." You really don't consider them to be ordinary people, do you? They're a different *species*. God, that's typical of the white man – even the liberal white man: the blacks are *"them"* out there picking their noses, they're not like *"us"*, though of course there are a few civilized *ones* and of course we mustn't be beastly to *"them"*.'

'I didn't mean it like that.'

'But they *are* different.'

'Of course they're different, Patti. Different cultures, different institutions, different ideas on how to live and behave.'

'And therefore unfit to govern themselves and have the vote?'

'The vote, democracy, is a sophisticated Western institution. It's alien to them, not one of their institutions. If they're going to adopt it – or have it thrust upon them – they've got to learn how to use it.'

'Become "civilized"? By *your* standards.'

'By normal standards.'

'By *normal* standards you'd have to exclude a lot of the dumb whites in this country.'

'Agreed.'

'And a hell of a lot of the peasants in Europe. So are you seriously telling me that if we were Italians, having this discussion in Rome now, you'd be recommending that we disenfranchise the peasants in the hills?'

He sighed. 'No, because there are plenty of educated Italians to run the country properly. But there are not enough educated blacks to run South Africa by Western standards – and it's *Western* institutions they *want* to take over.'

'But there are enough educated blacks to run it *their* way.'

'The African way? Sure. Shaka did it single-handed.'

'Bullshit. You wouldn't disenfranchise the Italian peasants because they're *white*, but if they were black you'd only let the elite govern Italy. Or have a benevolent dictatorship, like Franco does in Spain.'

'As a matter of fact a *benevolent* dictatorship may be good for Africa. "*Nobody* has the vote for the next thirty years until we're *all* civilized sufficiently to use it properly" – maybe that's the answer. The blacks respond well under their chiefs and behave themselves. But to answer your question: no, I would not recommend disenfranchising the Italian peasants because they do not settle their political differences with an axe. They do not chop the opposition's head open to make a point.'

'And the blacks will?'

'For God's sake, Patti, they *do*.'

'So there's no hope?'

'The hope is civilization. Gradualism.'

'And what are these normal standards of civilization?'

'Various alternatives. A reasonable level of education is obviously one. Income is another alternative. Or property – a man who owns his own house is smart enough to have the vote. Age is another one: when a man reaches say, forty – '

'Forty, huh? You're twenty, you have the vote and you're judging the maturity of a man of forty. What white arrogance – '

He groaned. 'You're looking for a fight, aren't you?'

'Me? Never.'

'For Christ's sake, Patti. I love you.'

'I love you too, big boy, so what's that got to do with democracy? Except we're not *allowed* to love each other.'

He said slowly, leaning forward: 'Patti, I loathe apartheid. Apartheid must go, immediately. But surely that doesn't mean we must reduce this country to chaos. Do you honestly believe that the ANC – or the blacks – can be relied upon – *tomorrow* – to run South Africa? With its vast civil service – its health, and railways, and airports and its judiciary and police force and its navy and its agricultural departments and its mines and industries and forests and game reserves and its economy – the whole works. Do you?'

She said angrily: 'Obviously we'll have to train a new black civil service – '

'But they wouldn't – they'd fire the whites and put their pals in office. That's why we need gradualism. For God's sake, apartheid must *go*, we *agree* on that, but I'm asking you whether, *if* apartheid was overthrown tomorrow, you honestly think that the blacks could successfully take over the administration of this country?' He shook his head. 'It would be a shambles.'

'*Anything*,' she said, 'would be better than apartheid. Like anything would have been better than the Nazis in Germany. And you, sir – ' she placed her fingertip on his nose – 'are a racist in your secret heart.'

But what the fuck were they going to do about each other? About the real world.

'Nothing,' she said. 'This *is* the real world. We'll do nothing, until we're caught and sent to jail.' She added: 'Or until you leave me.'

Oh, bullshit. 'So that only leaves one alternative: leave South Africa.'

'I'm not leaving South Africa, Luke.'

He sighed angrily. 'So that only leaves jail. And when we come out, what happens? Get caught again?'

'True. So? So there's only one thing to do.'

'And that is?'

She said solemnly: 'Capitalize and get married.'

He wondered if he had heard aright.

She smiled. 'We get married in Swaziland in a blaze of publicity. You set it up through *Drum* and we'll get other newspapers involved. "Young White Lawyer Defiantly Marries Indian Wench." We drive back into South Africa to set up our happy home, we get arrested the first night and thrown in jail. Outcry. A black eye for South Africa.'

He groaned. 'Be serious, for God's sake. We go and live somewhere else. In England. In Swaziland.'

She smiled at him. Tenderly. 'Thank you, Luke. And I love you too. But darling? This is my country of birth and I'm going to stay and see it through.'

'See what through? Our jail terms? The bloodbath?'

'I'm going to see those bastards in jail. A Nuremberg trial. Crimes against humanity.'

He took both her hands. 'We can't wait for that. We have no alternative but to leave the country.'

She sighed. 'Yes we have. And that is to quit.' She looked at him. 'Split up. Before we're caught. And never see each other again.'

He stared at her. 'You don't want that, so don't say it. Ask yourself what you *do* want. And how you can achieve it.'

'I want,' she said, 'a hell of a lot more than most women. I don't just want a nice *home* and a nice husband with a nice job and nice children – I want justice for all. Freedom. *Legal* freedom – instead of legal bondage. And how do we achieve that? By getting rid of this Afrikaner government.'

'You're preaching to the converted.'

'Yes, but you're not prepared to fight for it. I am.'

Oh Jesus. He said grimly: 'You're right, I'm not prepared to fight for it – because you can't win, because *they've* got all the big battalions. All the laws. But I'm prepared to *work* for it – '

'By leaving the country?'

'By *writing* about it. Creating a fuss, raising public awareness, *international* public awareness – '

'From outside the country.'

'Jesus *Christ*, I only want to leave so that I can live with you! As we can't do that here we've got to do the best we can from outside. You can't fight if you're in jail, Patti.' He glared at her. 'Tell me how you're going to fight, Patti.'

She said grimly: 'Ask no questions and you'll get no lies.'

Oh Jesus, words like that frightened him. 'For Christ's sake! *Tell* me what you're doing! So I can evaluate it!'

'Evaluate it? And if you don't approve?' she said grimly. 'What you don't know you can't be forced to tell Colonel Krombrink next time he pulls you in.'

'For God's sake! Do you think I'd betray you?'

'I think our cops can make anybody betray anybody. Unless you throw yourself out of one of their upper windows.'

He paced across the room. 'Patti – I can't live like this, tell me what you're doing. So that maybe I can . . . help you. Pro*tect* you.'

'Help me?' She smiled fondly 'You weren't meant to be a fighter, Luke. You're a great guy, and I love you to bits, and you're an adventurer, but you're not a warrior, you're a *worrier* – that's why you're such a good writer. You're a wordsmith – that's what nature intended you to be, and that's wonderful.'

He was stung. Not a fighter? He sat down and took her hands. 'But you *are* a fighter?'

'Yep.' Then she closed her eyes. 'Darling, I'm doing nothing.'

'I don't believe you.'

She snorted softly. 'Too bad. Nor would Colonel Krombrink.'

He glared at her. Too bad, huh? He stood up angrily. 'Okay. That's it. You don't trust me. And I don't trust you not to land us in the shit. So neither of us trusts the other. And we can't live inside the country, and you refuse to leave. So you don't love me enough. So there's no future in this relationship. So? So I'm off. I'm getting out of your hair.'

She looked up at him. 'On the contrary,' she said quietly, 'I love you with all my heart.'

'But not enough to run away with me!'

'I'm not a runner. I'm a stayer.'

He glared at her. 'Goodbye, Patti. It's been great. I really mean that.'

Her eyes were moist. She said: 'Next weekend I'll be here.'

It was a long week.

'I love you,' he said.

'I love you too,' she said. 'But as you say, there's no future in it. So let's just have fun. Fun-fucking, that's all we're really good for, Mr Mahoney. So, tell me a fantasy.'

He wondered if he'd heard that right. 'A fantasy?'

She smiled in the dark. 'A sexual fantasy. Everybody has them, so tell me yours.'

He was astonished. 'You are my sexual fantasy.'

'I can't be, because you've got me. But you can have a fantasy *involving* me. Wouldn't that be fun? Exciting?'

'*Involving* you?'

She smiled. 'For example wouldn't you like to fuck two girls at the same time – me and another girl?'

It shocked him. And it was wildly erotic.

She grinned. 'Poor baby, do I shock you?'

'Why are you telling me this?'

She smiled. 'Because for all your maturity you're a well-brought-up Anglo-Saxon who believes in love and marriage and being faithful.'

'And you don't?'

'Oh I do, I'm well-brought-up too. But I'm an Indian girl in South Africa so I'm not allowed to have love and marriage with you. I'm not allowed by *law* to be *jealous* about you. So I'm making myself bullet-proof. So, tell me your fantasies.'

'I wish we could stop talking about apartheid.'

'So do I – oh don't I just. I wish apartheid wasn't there, to be talked about, but it is. So, I can't be jealous.'

'Are you unfaithful to me?' It made his heart squeeze to think about it.

She smiled. 'Ask no questions, you'll get no lies, Mahoney.'

Oh God, not that one again. 'For God's sake. Don't you care if I'm being unfaithful to you?'

'Oh yes I *care*. But there's nothing I can do about it, I can't *compete* with another woman, I can't move in with you and make myself indispensable, I can't throw a tantrum outside your door or scratch the other woman's eyes out. So although I *care* like hell, it's impractical to have sleepless nights over it. So, I'm busy making my heart unbreakable.' She was silent a moment. 'Are you? Unfaithful to me?'

'As a matter of fact,' he said grimly, 'I'm not.'

She smiled in the dark.

'I didn't think you were. You're too honest to be much good at cheating – unless you didn't care about me.' She sighed. 'And, I'm not being unfaithful to you either. Which, in the circumstances, is dumb, Mahoney – for both of us.' She sat up and swept back her long black hair. '*Dumb*! Because . . . Oh – I'm so sick of talking about it! But dumb it is! So shall we please stop? And think about something *practical*.' She added: 'Like sexual fantasies?'

'Sexual fantasies are practical?'

'More practical than *"us"*.' She snorted. 'And the other good thing about fantasies – so I've read – is that when you *fulfil* your partner's fantasy, you'll find – ' she fluttered her eyelids – 'that they're eternally *grateful* to you.'

He didn't know what to make of this. But it was wildly erotic. 'Where did you read that?'

'In some wicked magazine smuggled into this country. Or was it Freud himself? So, what's your fantasy?' She waved a hand. 'Is it leather? Is it boots? Is it plastic raincoats? Two girls? Tell me.'

'Are you trying to make me eternally grateful?'

She looked at him with big liquid eyes. 'To stop taking each other so bloody seriously!' She glared, then strode to the bathroom. She ran the tap.

Mahoney followed her. He slipped his arms around her and cupped her breasts. He whispered: 'I love you.'

She hung her head, so her long black locks swirled in the water.

'And I love you. And that's the bloody problem – I'm not *allowed* to love you.' Then she threw back her head, so her hair flew, and looked at him in the mirror. 'So the answer is to brutalize it.'

He stared at her in the mirror. '*Brut*alize it?'

'So we stop taking each other so bloody seriously! So we just treat it as *fun*. Because there's no other way to treat it!'

He didn't want to hear. 'And how're you going to brutalize it?'

She looked at him in the mirror. 'And you're going to be eternally grateful.' She closed her lovely eyes and turned and slipped her arms round his neck and held him tight. She took a deep breath. Then, as if she'd resolved to be happy, or suddenly saw the funny side of it, she giggled. 'Gloria Naidoo, that's who we'll start with. Don't all you guys drool over Gloria?'

He was astonished. 'But she's a lesbian.'

'A bi-sexual, darling. Maybe more lezzie than bi, but bi she is.'

He grappled with all this. 'And have you and Gloria . . . ?'

She leant back in his arms. 'Ever got it together? But of course, darling!' She made big beautiful eyes. 'What do you expect two good-looking Indian girls to do in sunny South Africa where all they're allowed is nice Indian boys?' Then she dropped her head and giggled. 'The look on your *face*.' Then she kissed him hard on the mouth. 'Can we please stop taking life so seriously? And I refuse to talk about it any more . . . !'

But they had to take life very seriously indeed. Because the next week the police raided Buck's farm, and all hell broke loose.

16

The editor slammed down the telephone. 'The cops have found the ANC's headquarters on a farm in Rivonia called Lilliesleaf – grab a photographer and get your ass out there!' The name Lilliesleaf didn't mean anything to Mahoney but the sketch map the editor thrust at him sure did. *Christ*, it must be right next door to Buck's Farm! It wasn't until he saw the policemen guarding the gate that he realized Lilliesleaf *was* Buck's Farm . . . *Christ* . . . His hand was shaking as he held out his press card to the policeman. *The ANC's headquarters . . . And he'd been screwing himself flat in the middle of it.*

He drove up the track towards the main house. Over there, amongst the trees, was the cottage, two police cars parked outside it. His mind was racing – *God, had he left anything there that would identify him? Was there anything of Patti's? Oh God, he had to get to a telephone and warn her.* His heart was knocking. He crested the rise, and there was the main house. It was swarming. A dozen police vehicles, policemen everywhere, police dogs. Cars from the newspapers. He got out and walked shakily over to the group of pressmen, his face ashen. 'What's the story?'

'We're going to be briefed in a moment.'

'ANC *headquarters* . . . ? Anybody arrested?'

'Lots. They've all been whisked off to town. In irons.'

The terrible question: 'Any women?'

Then Colonel Krombrink walked towards them, a malicious smile on his weathered face. 'Ah, so *Drum* has arrived an' we can begin our little tour. How are you, Mr Mahoney?'

Mahoney felt white with fear. 'Fine thanks, Colonel.'

'Did you bring a photographer? Good. We want your black readers

154

to realize the police aren't asleep, hey, man. An' we want them to realize what the penalty for treason is – death, hey, man. Will you make sure they understand that?'

'Yes.'

'Good. So first I'll read to you the official police press release, then you can take your nice photographs.' He produced some sheets of paper and began to read in his heavy South African accent:

'On the afternoon of Wednesday 23 July 1963, the South African Police, as the result of intensive undercover investigations, conducted a raid on Lilliesleaf Farm in the Rivonia area on the fringes of Johannesburg. A hundred and ten policemen were deployed. The first party of them arrived at the farmhouse inside two panel vans, one a bakery truck, the other a laundry van. The house was stormed. Inside we arrested nine leading members of the banned African National Congress gathered around a table studying a mass of documents which cursory examination proved to be plans for military-style insurrection and sabotage within South Africa. In different rooms were found two telex machines, two powerful two-way radios capable of reaching anywhere in the world, a photocopy machine, numerous cameras and film-development equipment, filing cabinets full of documents pertaining to the ANC and the Communist Party and other subversive matters, and a large quantity of arms, ammunition, land mines, grenades and explosives, all of Russian origin. The police believe that this raid has exposed the headquarters of the ANC and the Communist Party. Investigations continue and it is expected that a large number of other persons will now be traced who will be able to assist the police in their enquiries.'

He folded up the paper with a little smile. 'Any questions, gentlemen, before you are taken over the house?'

Andy Murphy of the *Star* said: 'Who is the owner of the farm?'

'The registered owner is a certain white person whose name we cannot divulge at this time, but clearly somebody sympathetic to the ANC and SACP, who bought it on their behalf.'

'What are the names of the people arrested?'

'When their identities have been definitely established, a list will be released to the press.' He looked at Mahoney. 'How about a question from *Drum*? On behalf of all those black readers.'

Mahoney's ears felt blocked. All he could think of was Patti, all he wanted to do was get the hell out of here, grab her and run like hell. His mind fumbled: 'How big . . . a breakthrough against the ANC have you made today – do you think you've smashed them?'

'Thank you for that question.' He looked at the expectant pressmen.

'Today is a *triumph* for the forces of law and order over the forces of darkness, hey! We believe we have smashed them, yes. Of course all the documents must be evaluated, but we believe we're going to finish them off and mop up the rest with the information we've got today.'

Mop up the rest . . . Oh God, he had to get to a telephone.

The tour of the house seemed to take an eternity. A nightmare. They crowded through the rambling house, the photographers' bulbs flashing, Colonel Krombrink like a showman, showing them the dining room where the men were arrested *in flagrante delicto*. They saw the office with its two-way radios, its filing cabinets, telexes, rooms with a dozen unmade beds, the kitchen with meals still in preparation, the fingerprint experts everywhere dusting for evidence, and outside on the back verandah the weapons neatly laid out in rows, the hand grenades, the landmines, the explosives, the ammunition, all neatly labelled for the public prosecutor. 'That alone will hang 'em . . .'

Oh God, how much did Patti know about this? He just wanted to get the hell out of here.

But he was the last to leave. As the pressmen hurried back to their cars, Colonel Krombrink called: 'Meneer Mahoney?'

Mahoney turned, his heart knocking. The colonel took his elbow and led him aside. He appeared to be thinking, then he said: 'Are you feeling all right, Mr Mahoney? You're very pale, hey, man.'

Mahoney's pulse tripped. 'I'm fine, thanks.'

'Very pale, man,' the good colonel said, 'like you're sick to your stomach. Or jus' seen a ghost, hey, man. Anyway . . . ' He paced beside him pensively, down the verandah. 'Mr Mahoney, you asked if we've smashed the ANC today, an' yes we have, because we've chopped the head off the snake, hey? Quote that – the head off the snake. An' now we're going to get the rest of the snake out of its hole. Easy, man. Quote that too. Okay?'

Why was the man repeating this if it wasn't a threat?

'Okay.'

They came to some wicker armchairs. The colonel waved to one and sat down. Mahoney slowly sat down on the edge.

Krombrink said: 'But, *Got*, man, it's the *eggs* that snake laid that we've also got to find, before they hatch. An' those eggs are buried, but not in the snake's hole, hey? An' sometimes they're not so easy to find, hey?'

Mahoney knew what was coming, and he felt sick. 'Yes.'

'Yes, what?'

'Yes, I can imagine . . . '

Colonel Krombrink snorted. 'Imagine? Don't you *know*?'

Mahoney felt his guts turn over. 'Know what?'

'*Got*, man, Mr Mahoney, newspapermen are supposed to use *facts*, hey? Tell the people the *facts*, not so?'

Oh God, the facts . . . 'Yes.'

'Jus' like the judge wants. *Facts*, that's what he wants to hear. An' that's what the police have to give him, not so?'

Mahoney's nerves were stretched, as the colonel intended them to be. 'Yes, that's so.'

'Yes . . . ' The colonel sat back pensively and looked at the ceiling; then, as if a sudden thought had struck him, he continued: 'But, of course, newspapermen *do* use their imagination, hey, to get a good story. And so do policemen, to outsmart criminals, get information . . . So?' He looked at Mahoney. 'So you an' I have a lot in common, really. We *both* work with facts, but we both have to use our *imagination*. An' we both got to keep our ears open to get those facts. An' another thing, hey – we both work a lot with kaffirs, don' we? You write for them, and most of my customers are kaffirs, who're trying to ruin the country.'

He knows, he knows, and he wants to use me . . .

'Not so?' the colonel said.

Mahoney nodded, sick in his guts. 'I suppose so.'

'And,' the colonel said, as another thought struck him, 'we're both involved in the law, hey? Your father's a lawyer an' you're working on a law degree, I believe?' He spread his hands reasonably. 'We both know what the law is – about accomplices, for example. About accessories before, during, or after the fact?'

Mahoney's ears were ringing. 'Sure.'

Colonel Krombrink nodded absently. Letting the silence hang. Then, as if heaving himself out of a reverie, he sat up: 'So we've got a lot in common, Mr Mahoney. So – why don't we cooperate, hey, man?'

Mahoney had known it was coming but it was like a blow to his guts. He heard himself say: 'Cooperate how?'

The colonel said earnestly: 'Of course, being an honest South African citizen, an' an educated man, an' a responsible newspaperman, you would always cooperate with the police? I mean – ' he waved a hand – 'if you knew your neighbour had murdered his wife, you'd report it to the police, wouldn't you? That's your civic duty, hey man. Isn't it?'

'Of course.'

'Yes. *Any* crime.' The colonel waved his hand. 'And so I feel confident that you'll cooperate with us now.'

Oh Jesus, Jesus . . . 'Over what?' He tried to sound puzzled.

The colonel sat back. 'Well,' he said, man to man, 'it's about those bladdy eggs that bladdy snake's laid, hey? The problem is, this snake doesn't lay its eggs in one place, hey, like a nice ordinary viper or mamba. It lays them all over the show. An' those eggs aren't all the same *colour*, hey man. No, *Got*, they're not all black, they're also white and different shades of brown, man. Which makes looking for them quite a job, hey?'

Mahoney looked at him, his heart knocking. The colonel put his fingertips together. 'Well, you work with kaffirs, Mr Mahoney, and you must hear a lot of *talk*, hey man. A lot of . . . ' he waved a hand, *'stories*. *Information*, about crime. Tip-offs. And – ' he stared with big reasonable eyes – 'I'm sure that as a responsible citizen you will pass on such information to the police. Not so?' He paused, then leant forward. 'In fact, we're *relying* on you to do that?' He smiled.

Jesus, Mahoney feared and hated the bastard. He nodded. 'Of course.'

The good colonel nodded. 'Of course. Because anybody who *didn't* do that might be described as an accomplice, hey man . . . ' He let that hang. 'But you must also hear a lot of talk about this and that, which aren't actual crimes, hey man? Rumours, even. Like who's come back to town, maybe. Who knows who.' He shrugged. 'Who thinks what.' He looked at Mahoney, then gave a wolfish smile. 'And, of course, we want you to pass on all that too.'

Colonel Krombrink's eyes had suddenly taken on a naked menace. And Mahoney wanted to shout, in anger and self-hate. Anger that this bastard was threatening him, bullying him into becoming an informer, self-hate that what he felt was *gratitude*, like he was meant to feel. Anger that he was being softened up by fear. Self-hate that he was so easily frightened – for Christ's sake, if they knew he'd been using the cottage they'd have arrested him on sight! Self-hate that he felt prepared to agree to almost anything to save his skin.

'Colonel Krombrink, you can *r*ely on me to report any crime, as any responsible journalist would do. But no journalist is allowed to disclose the source of information . . . '

The colonel slapped his knees and stood up.

'And, of course, as a journalist, you know all about the law, which enables the police to detain any person for ninety days now, until they're satisfied he's given all the information at his disposal? But, *hell*, man – ' he slapped Mahoney on the shoulder – 'forget about depressing things like that on such a successful day! Mr Mahoney?' The colonel took him warmly by the hand. 'You're busy, an' so am I. So will you now excuse me, hey?'

17

He was still shaking when they got back to town. But what else could he have said? He had stood up to the bastard as much as anybody would dare: they were trying to bully him into being an informer, but that didn't mean they had something on him – if they knew about his criminal relationship with Patti they would have nailed him long ago; if they'd known he was using the cottage his feet wouldn't have touched the ground this afternoon. But, Jesus, he was angry: at the system that gave them such power, at the laws that made him a criminal for being in love. And, by God yes, he was angry at himself for being afraid of the bastards. By God yes, he *was* afraid . . .

He stopped at the Rosebank Hotel. He hurried to the public telephone and feverishly dialled Patti's number.

'Gandhi Garments,' she said. Mahoney closed his eyes in relief: she hadn't been arrested.

'May I speak to Mr Jackson, please?'

'I'm afraid you have the wrong number.'

'I'm so sorry.' He hung up and looked at his watch. It was a long five minutes waiting for her to get to the public telephones in the Fox Street post office. He dialled the first number: engaged. He cursed and dialled the next box.

'Hullo?'

He said: 'Don't go anywhere *near* the cottage. It's been raided, I've just come from there. Got that?'

There was a stunned silence. Then: 'Yes.'

'Did you leave anything in the cottage that's identifiable?'

Short pause. 'Don't think so.'

Thank God. 'So we've got to do some fast thinking. And the only safe place to do it is Swaziland. Meet me there on Friday night. At the hotel. Okay?'

No hesitation. 'Okay. But shouldn't we make it tonight?'

'No, they're watching me, and going to Swaziland mid-week would be unusual. Just go about your normal business.'

He hurried back to the car. He drove feverishly back to the *Drum* offices. He sat down at his typewriter, put paper into the machine and threw open his notebook. He pressed his trembling fingers to his eyes.

It was six o'clock when he crossed the border into Swaziland, his heart knocking. But the beetle-browed Afrikaner constable showed no interest. And, oh, the relief of driving across into the hilly land of the

Swazis where there was no apartheid . . . And, oh God, he didn't want to live in that land back there anymore. It was dark when he wound up the dirt road to the Mountain Arms. He ordered dinner to be served in their room at eight o'clock. He got a beer and went to sit on the verandah to wait for her.

And he waited. And waited. By the time the dinner gong rang he knew she had been arrested at the border. When the dinner hour was half over he telephoned her apartment. No reply. And he could bear the suspense no longer: he got in his car to drive back towards the border in case she had broken down. And, oh, the relief when he saw headlights coming up the road and identified her car. He stopped. She pulled up alongside him. He flung open her door and clutched her tight.

They sat at the table in their room, the food untouched. Her face was gaunt.

'Well? *Did* you know?' he asked.

She took a deep, tense breath. She said to her wine glass: 'And, *are* you? Going to be an informer?'

He stared at her. '*God!* Inform on you? Would I have *told* you what Krombrink said if I intended that?'

She sipped from her glass. 'But if I was *not* involved? Would you inform on the ANC?'

He closed his eyes. 'Oh God, this is what this country does to you. Suspicions . . . '

'Exactly,' she said quietly. 'Because in South Africa you're either on one side or the other. The police ensure that: if you don't give them information you're the enemy. An accomplice. So – would you inform on the ANC?'

Mahoney took a deep breath. 'I'm a journalist, and journalists don't reveal their sources.'

'But supposing you knew that a bomb had been planted in a supermarket? Would you tell the police?'

'What the hell are you trying to do, Patti? Test me?'

'To prove something to you. Please answer the question.'

'The answer is, of *course* I would report it to the police! I don't want innocent women and children blown up.'

'And if it was a military installation? Would you report that?'

Mahoney glared at her.

'Hypothetical questions . . . The answer, in principle, is No. Because this is a police state and any smack taken at it is fair. So, what does that prove to you?'

'But supposing innocent soldiers just doing their national service get blown up too?'

He looked at her grimly. 'Let me make one thing abundantly clear, Patti. I also want to see this government thrown out, and I accept that violence is probably inevitable. But violence should be confined to soldiers fighting each other – not killing civilians in supermarkets with urban terrorism. I want nothing to do with killing people. But yes, military installations *are* legitimate targets. Now cut out this hypothetical crap and answer my question: did you know the farm was the ANC's headquarters? And did you know about the explosives and arms?'

She looked at her drink. 'No. Does that satisfy you?'

He looked at her. 'No it doesn't.' He took a breath. 'Patti, if you knew, you were playing with fire – we could both be under arrest now on charges of treason. And that's the gallows, Patti. I had a right to know about the risks we were taking.'

'And you consider I was reckless? With your life?'

'And your *own*. Which is just as important to me!'

'Reckless? Irresponsible? Because you had the "right to know"? And, if you *had* known? Would you have dropped me like a hot potato?'

'I'd have had the opportunity to find us a safer place!'

'Where, pray? Do you think I didn't rack my brains – so that you wouldn't drop me. Where could two people of different colour find a love-nest in this country – if I enter any white house I stick out like a sore thumb. If you enter any non-white house you do the same. We'd have been busted in a week!' She glared at him defensively. 'And the cottage was almost a mile from the main house – *and* there's a fence. The cottage had nothing to do with it, except the same owner. And as for your "right", you have no *right* to know what's going on in the *flat* next door, let alone the neighbours' distant farmhouse, just because you do your fucking in the neighbourhood. And as for being reckless, I was the opposite! I checked the situation out and I was convinced it was as safe as anywhere in this God-forsaken police state! God – at first even *you* didn't know where the place was!' She smouldered at him, 'You certainly had no "*need*" to know what was going on and that's the cardinal principle of – ' She stopped.

'Of what?'

She took a deep breath. 'Haven't you read any spy-thrillers? In the cloak-and-dagger business the agents are only told as much as they need to know – so if they're caught they can't spill *all* the beans.' She looked at him grimly. 'All you need to know for our relationship is that, like you, I also want to get rid of apartheid. But, no, I don't approve of blowing up people in supermarkets either. But, yes, military

161

installations and the like are legitimate targets.' She paused. 'And I have to make something very clear, Luke. If we're going to continue our relationship, all you'll ever know about me is as much as you *need* to know. And I'll answer no other questions outside of those parameters.' Her dark eyes grim. 'I love you, Luke. I didn't mean that to happen, I intended it to be just a fun thing, but then I fell in love with you. Now the only condition upon which I can continue is the *need* to know.' She took a tense breath. 'You must decide whether you can live with that.'

'*Live* with that?' He waved a hand. 'How can any man live with not knowing whether his lover's going to be arrested for treason? Whether she's going to jail or the goddamn gallows!' He frowned angrily. 'Well I do need to know, Patti. Know what I'm up against!'

'Plenty of people have lived with not knowing what risks their loved-ones are taking – in the French underground during the war. The Irish Republican Army. All the wives of men in the CIA and KGB and MI5.'

He closed his eyes in exasperation. 'Patti, you're fighting against the might of the Afrikaner government. Against BOSS. Against detention without trial. Against the Group Areas Act and the Immorality Act which makes you a subject of suspicion because of your colour – you're not like a Frenchman in World War II who had the natural camouflage of his skin. You're conspicuous, Patti! As if you're wearing the uniform of the enemy! And I'm conspicuous, the moment I step out of my area.' He glared at her. 'You have no camouflage, Patti – if they can't prove anything against you they lock you up without trial. And now your whole underground has just been busted. Realize that you're on very thin ice indeed, and underneath it is very deep shit. And you expect me not to want to *know*? I *do* need to know!'

She put her hands to her face. '*Oh*, it will never work . . .' Then she sobbed.

He began to get up. 'Patti . . . ?'

She sobbed into her hands. 'Please don't . . . ' She took a deep breath; then raised her head. The tears were running down her face. She whispered: 'Us, darling Luke – *we* can't work. I knew it all along. And I tried.' Her lip trembled; then she swept her hand through her hair resolutely. 'I really *tried*, but it all got out of control. And my heart – ' she banged her breast – 'ruled my head!'

Mahoney put out his hand.

She held up a palm. 'Please let me finish . . . It's my fault because I knew we couldn't get away with it – I *knew* sooner or later we'd be found out and go to jail. But . . . ' Two tears brimmed down her cheeks. 'But honest to God I didn't think there was any danger of you being dragged into this other business. But now, of course, you want to know what's happening, for your own sanity. But, it doesn't work like that, darling.' She shook her head. 'I can tell you nothing. Because the police will be on to you, Luke. And if you don't tell them voluntarily you'll eventually tell them *in*voluntarily. So the less you know, the better. That's the way the system works, darling. And that's why *we* can't work, Luke. Because there'll be nothing but *tension*, and an*xiety* and naked, solid *fear* . . . and *suspicions*.' She stared at him, then she dropped her face in her hands again. 'Oh God, wasn't the Immorality Act enough to live with?'

'Patti . . . ' Mahoney stretched out his hand and she got up impulsively holding her face. She walked to the window and dropped her forehead against the frame and sobbed. 'Patti . . . ' Mahoney took her in his arms. He held her tight and whispered: 'Yes, it *can* work.'

She rested her forehead against his shoulder and took a trembling breath; she whispered fiercely: 'There's only one way it could possibly work, darling Luke. And I've just proved that can't either. And there's no way I'm going to put you through it – or us.'

'*What* have you just proved?'

She turned out of his arms, her face wet. 'So the only thing to do is to quit. Now. *Tonight.*'

He stared at her, his knocking heart breaking.

'*What* is the way that won't work?'

She tried to wipe the tears off her face. She said resolutely: 'We have only two options. The obvious one is to quit, right now. Quit, and never see each other again.' Her mouth trembled.

'And the other one?'

She closed her eyes. 'That you play the bastards at their own bloody game. Become an informer. But feed them *dis*information.'

He stared at her. Outside the night insects were crick-cricking. 'False information?'

'And I'm not going to allow that. I'm not going to put you through that – or me. It would be highly dangerous – I love you too much. And it would be terribly unfair on both of us. Because . . . ' She shook her head at him. 'Because you're not the *type*, Luke.'

'Not the *type*?'

She blurted: 'To be an activist! A spy, if you like.' She looked at him tremulously. 'And that's not a criticism – very few people are. You're too straight, Luke. And I wouldn't put you through that torment even if you were willing. And so – ' she tossed back her hair – 'And so the only thing is to stop this crazy affair right now.'

Mahoney stared, his heart breaking. And there was no way he could accept that. No way could he let her walk out of his life, never see her again. And no way could they go back to the old ways either – he could not face any more of that subterfuge, he was sick of that drama, sick of South Africa and its sick laws – it was clear as day what he had to do about it. He crossed the room and took her in his arms.

'There is a way, Patti.' He wanted to laugh it. 'And that is to get married, and never go back to goddamn South Africa.' *There* – it was as simple and as complicated as that. He held her tight. 'Just get married. Tomorrow. And live happily ever after – right here in Swaziland. Or in Botswana – I can get a job anywhere, and you've got your business.'

She had gone stock still. She slowly lifted back her head. Then she closed her eyes and burst into tears. She dropped her forehead onto his shoulder and she sobbed and sobbed. '*Oh God why is life such a pig?!*' She banged her forehead against him. '*A pig – pig – pig!*'

'Patti?' He tried to lift her head and she clutched him tighter and cried: 'Of course I want to marry you! And that's why life's a *pig*! Because how the hell can we live happily ever after in a country which forbids it?!'

'But we're not going to live in South Africa – '

She banged her forehead against his shoulder and cried: 'Like hell we're not! I refuse to run away! I want to live happily ever after right there, as is my basic human *right*! I *refuse* to let those bastards terrorize me! I *refuse* to be made a refugee!' She turned abruptly out of his arms. She swept her hand through her hair and turned to face him. She said tremulously: 'And that's the whole crux of the matter, Luke. I love you but I can't marry you – because I have to stay and fight.' She looked at him, her eyes brimming. 'And so it must end, darling Luke. It is just too dangerous. We've been blown wide open – we got away with it today by the skin of our teeth.' She shook her locks at him. 'We knew it had to end someday – and that day has come. Tonight. Not tomorrow, not next week, not after waiting to see how the land lies. *Tonight*. I'm going to go and get a hotel in town. I simply could not bear to sleep in your arms knowing I was saying goodbye forever in the morning.'

He could not believe this was happening. He started towards her, to say he knew not what, and she put her hand out on his chest, her eyes bright. He whispered: 'This is your whole *life* you're dealing with! You're going back into the lions' den!'

'The struggle *is* my life, darling Luke. And the lions' den is where it's happening.'

'For God's sake, Patti, we've got the whole world to live in.'

She took a deep breath, then put her finger on his lips. 'Goodbye, darling Luke.'

She turned to her overnight bag. She picked it up. She put her hand on the doorknob and opened it. She looked back at him, her face streaked with tears. She whispered: 'It's over, darling. Believe that.'

He looked at her, his eyes full of tears.

'Do you believe that?' she whispered.

He took a deep breath, then he shook his head. 'No.'

She cried: 'Believe it, darling! Believe it! For your sake and mine!' She turned abruptly and walked through the door. She closed it behind her with a bang.

He heard her sob once. Then there was the sound of her high heels down the corridor.

He stood there. And with all his breaking heart he wanted to run after her, to seize her and make her come back. *Drag* her back. But, oh God, he did not believe this was the end. And he needed time to think, about what she had said – about a thousand things. *Think.* About what today meant. What *Krombrink* meant. What *she* had meant. He stood there, his eyes full of tears; then he turned to the double bed and sat down and held his face.

He heard her car start, and he sobbed out loud.

18

He woke up before dawn, and he thought his heart would break. He swung out of bed, slammed on the shower and stood under cold jets, trying to knock the pain out of himself. He pulled on his tracksuit and set out into the first light, to think.

He climbed along the mountain paths, then down into the valley to their waterfall. He sat on the big flat rock where they had made love so often, and it seemed he could almost hear her splashing in the water, almost see her long black hair floating and her golden body glistening, almost hear her laughter, almost feel her satiny nakedness. When he could bear it no longer he climbed up to the very top of the mountain.

Spread out below him was the vast mauveness of South Africa, so beautiful, so quiet, and so bloody cruel, so mindless. And way over there Patti Gandhi was doing something about it, doing God knows what, but putting her freedom and life on the line for what she believed in. He admired her and loved her and, oh God, he was frightened about what could happen to her, and he despised himself for not having her guts . . .

It was midday when he came down from the mountain. He knew what he had to do: there was only one way he could live with himself, and with her – and that was to play the Afrikaner bastards at their own bloody game. No way could he turn his back on her, let her walk away into the lions' den alone . . .

In the early afternoon he drove across the border back into South Africa. His heart was knocking like a criminal's. But the young policeman showed no interest in him beyond a polite *'Goeie dag'* and the routine question, *'Iets om te verklaar?'* Anything to declare? But as he walked out of the immigration post he imagined the man reaching for the telephone. Driving through the beautiful afternoon, he tried to shut his mind to his fear and just think about her. And when the bushveld began to give way to the rolling grassland of the highveld, and the industrial satellites of Johannesburg began to loom up on the skyline, it was unthinkable that he wouldn't see her again. All he cared about was *her* and, oh, he hated this land which made it illegal to live happily ever after with her. He had to get to a phone. He saw a filling station and pulled in. He rammed his coins into the callbox and dialled.

'Hullo,' she said.

He closed his eyes in relief. *She hadn't been arrested.* She was still in the land of the living. What he wanted to say was 'I love you', but he said: 'Is that Mrs Lambert?'

There was a silence. He heard her breathing. Then she said softly: 'You've got the wrong number.' She hung up.

He walked back to the car happily.

It was not until he was winding his way through downtown Johannesburg that he was sure he was being followed. He had first seen the blue Ford about fifty miles back. Three men in it. At a set of traffic lights, where he would normally turn left to the Indian quarter, he carried straight on, towards Hillbrow, and the car followed him. His knocking heart sank.

The car tailed him all the way across town. As it pulled up behind him in front of The Parsonage, he was shaking.

The men got out and came towards him. The first said, in a heavy Afrikaans accent: 'We're police. Will you come with us to the station, please.'

His heart was pounding. 'What on earth for?'

'You either come voluntarily or we arrest you.'

'On what bloody charge?!'

'The Terrorism Act.'

He stared, white with fear. 'What bullshit . . . ' he whispered.

A policeman drove his car to Marshall Square. He went with the other two. His ears felt blocked, his mind was racing. The cars parked in the yard. One man stayed behind: he went with the other two.

They entered the same back door he had used last time he was here. The same elevator, with only one button. Nobody spoke. The top floor. The long corridor, neon lights. The security gate. A row of doors. Into an office, where they took his passport, and then his fingerprints.

'Why are you taking my fingerprints?' He tried to control his shaking hands.

'Routine.'

'But I'm not a fucking criminal!'

The man said nothing. He gripped Mahoney's fingers and rolled the tips one by one onto the pad. The other detective took the form and walked out of the room. '*Kom.*'

They walked back along the corridor. Into the lair of Colonel Krombrink, who sat behind his desk.

'Good afternoon.'

At the window lolled the same detective as last time.

'Colonel, am I under arrest?'

'Not yet.'

Not yet? 'Then why am I here? And why was I fingerprinted?'

Krombrink said quietly: 'Sit down.'

Oh Jesus, he hated the bastards! And he was scared of them. 'If I'm to answer questions I'm entitled to a lawyer. In which case he will answer them for me!'

'Mr Mahoney, you know as well as I do that you can be detained for ninety days to answer questions – without access to a lawyer. What have you got to hide, that you want a lawyer?'

'Nothing!' And he hated the bastards so much it felt like the truth.

The colonel smiled. 'Nothing we don't know already? So sit down, please.'

'Oh *Jesus* . . .'

The colonel clasped his hands. 'I'm not going to beat about the bush, Mr Mahoney. You have broken the law. And broken God's law: the Immorality Act . . .'

Mahoney closed his eyes, but in relief. If that's all they had on him . . . But he had to deny it. The colonel went on: 'We know all about you and that Indian, Patti Gandhi. We can give you dates, places, times. And you've just come back from another dirty night in Swaziland. Don't waste our time denying it.'

'I *do* deny it . . .'

Krombrink shook his head in sadness. 'And you a law student.' He looked at him. 'You're going to go to jail, Mr Mahoney. And when you come out you'll never be allowed to practise law, not with a criminal record like that, man.'

The Immorality Act . . . So they weren't going to try to use him as an informer? He said: 'This is crazy.'

The colonel said: 'What we find crazy is that a man from a good family like you, with your education, should want to con*sort* with a non-European!' He looked at him with disgust; then his eyes narrowed. 'And a *communist*. A terrorist.' Mahoney felt himself go ashen. Krombrink let it hang. 'Contravening the Immorality Act is only *one* of the charges, Mr Mahoney.'

Mahoney desperately tried to think straight. 'She's not a communist! Or a terrorist! What *preposterous* charges do you think you've got against me?'

The colonel smiled. So did the detective at the window: he muttered something under his breath. The colonel said quietly: 'Preposterous? That's a big word.' He paused. 'Contravening the Suppression of Communism Act?'

'But I'm a fucking capitalist! And so is Patti Gandhi!'

The colonel smiled. 'And how about the Terrorism Act?'

Mahoney's ears were ringing. Sick in his guts, with fear, with anger. 'Neither of us is a terrorist!'

Colonel Krombrink smiled widely. '"Us"? You make it sound like you're a couple. But the Immorality Act's the least of your worries, hey? Because the Terrorism Act isn't jail. It's the gallows in Pretoria.'

Mahoney's ears were ringing, his heart pounding. 'For doing what?'

Colonel Krombrink smiled. 'The men we arrested at Lilliesleaf Farm all face the gallows.'

Mahoney felt the vomit turn in his guts. 'I'd never been to Lilliesleaf Farm before last Wednesday.'

The colonel sighed. 'Another charge: attempted extortion.' He looked at Mahoney grimly.

Mahoney stared at him, absolutely astonished. 'Ex*tortion*?'

'Blackmail?' The colonel opened a drawer. He pulled out a folder. He pulled out a photograph and flicked it across to him.

Mahoney stared. It was the photograph of Patti copulating with Sergeant van Rensburg. He could see the stacked pages of his long story. *Her secret weapon exposed* . . .

'That's a legitimate journalist's story!'

The colonel tossed across another photograph: Major Kotze with Patti. Krombrink looked at Mahoney with disgust. 'Legitimate? How can any newspaper – even *Drum* – publish pictures like that?'

'But they would publish the *story*! The pictures are just evidence to prove veracity . . . '

The colonel held his eye. 'Then why didn't you publish it?'

'Because that was Miss Gandhi's decision. It's *her* story. Told to me in confidence. She would decide whether to publish!'

'And when was *Miss* Gandhi going to publish her story?'

Mahoney closed his eyes in fury. 'I don't know.'

'You don't *know*? Agh, come, Mr Mahoney, you expect us to believe that?' He smiled. 'When she wanted – or *needed* – to *blackmail* the police, perhaps?'

Mahoney tried to sigh theatrically. 'I'm just a journalist, and I agreed to write it for her. Miss Gandhi is not a writer – it *is* an art form, you know.'

'*Oh*, I *know* . . . ' the colonel said earnestly. The detective smirked. 'And what did Miss Gandhi give you in exchange for your art form?'

The Immorality Act was the least of his worries. He was about to say 'Nothing' then brilliance struck him. 'A case of brandy.'

'*Brandy?*' The colonel leered. 'And what else?'

'Nothing.' He added shakily: 'It *is* possible to be just friends with a woman, you know. And friendship with a non-European isn't yet an offence, is it? They haven't passed the Suppression of Friendship Act yet, have they?'

The colonel smiled. 'And it was in the name of *friendship* that you've been going out of the country with her?' He reached for the file, ran his eye down it studiously. 'Swaziland, Botswana, Mozambique. I can give you dates . . . '

Outside the country? If that's all they had against him he could laugh in their faces because there was no Immorality Act outside the country! 'So what? We're friends.'

The colonel smiled. 'And what did you two *friends* talk about?'

Mahoney forced a shrug. 'Oh, you know, this and that. Art. Poetry. Literature – '

'Politics?'

He shrugged. 'Not really, politics is so . . . predictable, in this country. So black or white – if you'll pardon the pun.'

The detective who had taken the fingerprints entered. He placed a sheet of paper in front of Krombrink then withdrew. Krombrink read it expressionlessly. Then he sat back. 'I like a man who sees the funny side of trouble.' He slapped the file. 'And *where* did you write this story?'

Mahoney's pulse tripped again. 'At *Drum*.'

'At *Drum*, hey?' The colonel flicked his thumb over the pages. 'A long story. Even you can't write such a long story in one go, man.'

'Yes, all of it.'

'Over how many sessions?'

'Three or four.' He shrugged.

'And what make of typewriter have you got at *Drum*, hey?'

Oh God, typefaces. 'A Remington.'

'Yes,' the colonel nodded. 'Not an Olivetti. And this story, Mr Mahoney, was typed with an Olivetti.'

Mahoney fumbled. 'I might have used somebody else's typewriter at *Drum* – I can't remember.'

'Yes, you *did* use somebody else's, Mr Mahoney. But not at *Drum*, hey? In *fact*,' he smiled, 'you used the Olivetti we found at Lilliesleaf Farm. In the cottage.'

It was another blow in the guts. He heard his ears ring. *'That's impossible.'*

The colonel sighed. 'Experts have compared the typeface of the Olivetti with your so-called story. And they match one hundred per cent.' He raised his eyebrows pleasantly. 'And if that's not enough evidence – which it is – fingerprints were found all over the machine, hey. And those fingerprints – ' he held up the note the detective had brought in – 'match yours.'

Mahoney stared, heart pounding. Before he could say anything Colonel Krombrink continued: 'So you *were* at Lilliesleaf Farm, Mr Mahoney. Where you wrote the *whole* – ' he flicked the typescript – '*long* story, over three or four *long* visits.' The detective at the window grinned, fixing Mahoney with a cheerful glare. Colonel Krombrink went on: 'An' before you come up with some cock an' bull story, let me advise you that your fingerprints were found on many of *these*, which we seized in the cottage.' He waved his hand like a showman and the detective held up a beer bottle triumphantly.

Mahoney's mind stuttered. And all he could think was – *oh God, what about Patti's fingerprints?* He looked desperately at Colonel Krombrink.

'*Got*, man, Mr Mahoney, you're in big trouble, hey? Exactly the same as the guys we arrested red-handed at the farm, hey. *Treason . . .* ' He let that hang, then asked earnestly: 'You know the penalty for treason?'

Mahoney was ashen, dread-filled. *'You know bloody well I haven't committed treason!'*

The colonel sighed. 'What I know is that you frequented the underground headquarters of the banned ANC and Communist Party, where the most-wanted terrorists in this country were arrested in possession of thousands of documents planning armed revolution to set up a black communist government supported by Moscow – and caught with a supply of weapons and explosives, hey. And I know that you wrote this

– ' he flicked the file – '*disgusting* story for them with the intention of blackmailing the police – and you wrote it on *their* typewriter in *their* headquarters, drinking *their* beer, and that you left the story and pornographic pictures in *their* possession – we found it buried in a box. An' I know that this Gandhi woman is a member of the ANC, an' that she's your girlfriend, an' that you went on numerous trips with her to kaffir countries which are known ANC bases where these weapons and explosives come from – *a*n' you and *Miss* Gandhi had every opportunity to bring in those explosives and weapons.'

'*Bullshit! You know it is!*'

'And you're a known troublemaker, always writing – ' he waved his hand in distaste – '*crap* about apartheid.' He shook his head sadly. '*Treason*, Mr Mahoney. And that's not just the Immorality Act, hey – that's the gallows, man.'

Mahoney scrambled to his feet and smashed his hand on the desk. '*You know I had nothing to do with explosives and treason!*'

The colonel smiled. 'You'll have to convince the judge, not me, Mr Mahoney. And,' he added, 'so will *Miss* Gandhi.'

'*She had nothing to do with that farm!*' Mahoney roared.

The colonel said softly: 'Sit down, Mr Mahoney. You make the place look untidy.'

Mahoney glared, aghast, shaking. He rasped: 'I refuse to answer any more *ridiculous* questions!'

The colonel sat back. 'Ninety days, Mr Mahoney? We can detain you ninety days for questioning. An' if we're not satisfied you're telling the truth we can detain you another ninety days. An' so on, indefinitely. Now, be a sensible chap and sit down, hey.'

Mahoney stared, heart pounding. And, oh God, he was terrified. *Ninety days and ninety days and ninety days* . . . He slowly sank back into his chair.

The colonel nodded encouragingly. Then hunched forward, hands clasped. 'Mr Mahoney, where *was* Miss Gandhi when you were working on the story on Lilliesleaf Farm?'

Mahoney closed his eyes, his mind frantically racing. *They'd said nothing about her fingerprints* . . . 'I don't know. She wasn't present.'

'So you just got in your car and drove out to the farm to write the story because it was your other office, hey? That *proves* you were one of those terrorists! Good! Thank you!'

Anger rose through the fear. 'I had no idea the farm was an ANC base! And Miss Gandhi didn't even know of the farm's *existence* – she thought I was writing the story at *Drum*!'

'I see.' The colonel nodded. 'So how did you come to write it on the farm?'

Oh Jesus. 'I decided not to write it at *Drum* in case *Drum* got raided. The same applied to my apartment. Then I met a guy who rented a cottage outside town but hardly lived there. He offered it to me. I grabbed it. Writers do that, you know – we need to get away, to work.'

'Of *course*,' the colonel said, and the other detective snickered. 'Artists are *like* that. So?'

'So this guy said I could use his empty cottage whenever I liked. He took me out there. And, it was ideal.'

'How kind of him!' the colonel beamed. 'And so you rented it?'

'No. Well, I gave him a case of wine. It was just a favour.'

'I under*stand*,' the colonel nodded earnestly. 'And the Olivetti type-writer?'

'It was already there.'

'Ah . . . So it was *absolutely* ideal, hey? An' tell me – what's this kind guy's name?'

Mahoney had managed to think this far ahead. 'Mac.'

'Mac what?'

'Not sure. I just knew him as Mac, like most MacGregors or Mackintoshes. I did know, but I've forgotten.'

'So easy to forget funny names. And where is this Mac now?'

'I don't know – I heard he's left the country.'

'Oh dear! So we won't be able to meet him – an' such a nice guy too! An' what did he *do* in this country?'

'He was looking for a job. But he seemed to have quite a bit of money – always enough to stand his round.'

'An' that's where you met him, of course – in a bar?'

'Yes. In the Elizabeth Hotel. The so-called Press Bar, opposite the *Star*. But I ran into him in several other places too.'

'The Press Bar. So he was looking for a job as a writer?'

'Yes. He said he'd done some writing – freelance. Recently arrived in Jo'burg. Been all over the world.' He added: 'Told me he had this cute cottage, but he really wanted a place in town.'

'I *see*. A globe-trotter, hey. Very hard to find him. Pity. An' what other friends did this friendly Mac have?'

'I don't know. I only ever bumped into him alone.'

'So who told you he'd left the country?'

'*He* told me he was thinking of leaving last time I saw him.'

'An' what arrangements did you make about the cottage?'

'None. He'd only said he was *thinking* of leaving soon. No job. I presumed he would tell me about that when he left.'

'And *Miss* Gandhi? She never went to the cottage?'

Oh Jesus, had they found any of her fingerprints? 'Only once.'

'*Once*? And why?'

He waved a shaky hand. 'Just to . . . show it to her. We're friends. We went for a picnic there one Sunday.'

'A *picnic*? Agh, how nice.' Colonel Krombrink shook his head. '*Not* for the purposes of sexual intercourse, of course.'

Oh God, why not admit it for the sake of credibility, the Immorality Act was peanuts compared to treason. He heard himself say: 'Perhaps that was *my* purpose. Even you will admit that Miss Gandhi is extremely attractive. But unfortunately it never happened.'

Colonel Krombrink burst into a wide grin. 'Mr Mahoney, I like your cheek, hey. You expect us to believe that?'

And suddenly Mahoney had had enough of terror. He crashed his hand on the desk. *'I don't give a shit if you don't believe me – it's the truth! Now, are you charging me under the Immorality Act or not? If not, I'm going home!'*

The colonel grinned. 'Mr Mahoney, we've got a very nice cell for you, provisionally booked for ninety days. In fact, we took the precaution of putting your name down for the following ninety days too, so don't worry about accommodation, hey.'

Mahoney stared at him, unnerved. 'Provisionally'? And, oh God, he wanted to say something, to *do* something to ingratiate himself.

Colonel Krombrink said: 'An' tell me, Mr Mahoney, as neither you nor Miss Gandhi knew anything about the farm, how come we found your story – *her* story – buried on the farm?'

Oh Jesus, Jesus . . . Then he heard himself say: 'It was stolen.'

'*Stolen*?' Colonel Krombrink looked taken aback for a moment.

Why hadn't he thought of it before? 'Yes. When I finally finished the job I put the story in my briefcase. I drove back to town. I stopped to buy milk. I thought I'd locked all the car doors. But when I came out – the briefcase was gone!'

Colonel Krombrink made big eyes. '*Got*, man, you must have been *horrified*, hey!'

'Yes. And so was Miss Gandhi. Imagine – the whole story and those pictures of her falling into . . . wrong hands.'

'*Got*, yes, man. How *embarrassing*! An' you rewrote the story?'

Mahoney had stumbled ahead to this one. 'No. Miss Gandhi was so horrified she just wanted to forget the whole thing. And the story was no good without the photographs to prove it was true.'

Colonel Krombrink nodded deeply. 'And, of course, she had destroyed all the negatives?' The detective snickered. Colonel Krombrink sat back. 'Mr Mahoney, you expect us to believe all this crap?' He shook his head, then looked at his watch. 'Well, I must go, but we've got plenty of time to get to the truth in the next ninety days. Mr Mahoney, we hoped this wouldn't be necessary.' He turned to the detective. 'Put him in the cells.'

Mahoney was aghast. The colonel stood up and straightened his jacket. He put his pen in his pocket, then paused, as if remembering something.

'Mr Mahoney, do you know who that Indian girl is sleeping with on the nights you don't visit her for the purposes of contravening the Immorality Act?'

Mahoney stared, his mind stuttering. Colonel Krombrink looked at him over the top of his spectacles, then opened the file again and ran his finger down a page. He shook his head. '*Got . . .* ' He took off his spectacles. He said sadly: 'Amazing – that you're prepared to go to the gallows for a coolie woman like that . . .'

Mahoney's mind reeled. He bellowed: '*Lies!*' The detective grabbed him by the wrist and the colonel walked out of the door.

19

The worst thing was the not knowing.

Not knowing what's going on out there, what they're doing, what they're thinking, what evidence they're fabricating, what they're doing with *her*. Oh god, what are they doing to her? What is she going to say? Is she going to hang herself with her answers – and you with her? The helplessness, being unable to warn her, to tell her what to say, to tell her to run for her life . . . And, oh God, the not knowing how long. How long are they going to keep me in this cell? Days? Weeks? Months? When they lock you up you are panic-stricken by the not knowing, frantic, you want to bellow and shake the bars and pound the walls, roar to the sky that they can't do this to you.

He did not bellow and shake the bars, though he wanted to: he sat on the bunk and clutched his face, desperately fighting panic, taking deep breaths and trying to calm himself. It took a long time for the screaming despair to subside; and then the cold, solid fear set in. The fear of that courtroom, that judge, those gallows. It took a long time for the dread to subside sufficiently to be able to think. He began to pace up and down.

Think . . . They hadn't charged him with anything, not even under the Immorality Act – they'd only detained him. Surely to God, if they thought they could hang him they would gleefully add him to their bag

174

of traitors. 'We hoped this wouldn't be necessary,' Krombrink had said. So they were only trying to squeeze more information out of him with talk of ninety days and the gallows. Bullying him for information about Patti – they'd tried to poison his mind against her. So the way out was to play the bastards at their own bloody game, and agree to become an informer – like Patti had said. Agree to any fucking thing, then get the hell out of South Africa. *Grab Patti and run like hell, run right off this continent.*

In an hour or so they would come for him. Play it cool. Play them at their own bloody game . . . and say what?

How much are you going to admit?

But they did not come for him in an hour or so.

The sun went down, gleaming on the bars of the small high window, and the panic began to rise up, and he had to fight fiercely to keep it at bay. *Think . . . Think about anything except this cell. Think about what you're going to say to Krombrink. Think about how you're going to get the hell out of this country.*

Without a passport? Surely they would give him back his passport if he said he was going to be an informer?

And if they didn't?

Now think calmly. Be calm. They'll come for you tonight and you've got to have thought of everything.

But they did not come for him that night. A black constable brought him some food.

'I want to see Colonel Krombrink!'

'Yes, sah.'

As he waited into the night, the sounds of traffic grew less. Occasionally there were shouts from the courtyard below, the slam of a vehicle door, an engine revving. Every time he heard a car's noise he desperately wanted it to be Colonel Krombrink. *Wanted Krombrink to come so he could throw himself on his mercy and beg to be an informer?*

He pressed his forehead to the brick wall and tried to get the calm back. No, not mercy! Admit nothing! Play it cool, man. Remember they want you to be an informer, they're just softening you up in this cell . . .

Finally nervous tension turned to exhaustion and he threw himself on the bunk. *Sleep so you're on the ball tomorrow* . . . But he could not sleep, his mind a turmoil of screaming claustrophobia and fear and frustration. And through the turmoil there seethed the black poison they had injected, the image of Patti screwing around. *He did not believe them, it was just to make him inform on her, to soften him, like this cell.* But, oh

God, in the long hours of that night there were many times when he did not know what to believe and his heart turned black with jealousy, as it was meant to, and he had to hang on tight.

In the small hours of the morning he fell into an exhausted sleep and woke up gasping, rasping, scrambled up off the bunk and into the wall; for he was standing on the gallows with a row of faceless men, the noose around his neck, then the sudden horrific plunging, the screaming, choking . . . He leant against the wall, taking deep shuddering breaths, his mind reeling in horror.

He stared at the first light penetrating the high window, trying to remember all the things he had thought and decided, but he felt the panic of not knowing come back and he had to press his forehead against the wall again to control it.

Get the calm back . . . They'll come for you soon. You've got to be calm.

But they did not come for him. At six o'clock footsteps approached, but it was only a white policeman ordering him to shower. He was led into a bleak ablution section. He let the cold water beat down on his head. He took it as a good sign that he was not given any kind of prison garb.

'I've got clean clothes in my car downstairs.'

'Your car's in Pretoria.'

'In *Pretoria*? What *for*?'

'Forensic tests.' The door clanged shut.

Forensic tests? But what the hell were they looking for? Explosives? Drugs? Well, they'd find nothing!

And suddenly he felt relieved – the tests on his car accounted for the delay. The tests were done yesterday, the results would be reported this morning. Krombrink would soon send for him to bully him into making a deal. And he would play it cool and finally let himself be bullied, and this afternoon he would be out and tomorrow he would be gone, gone . . .

But Colonel Krombrink did not send for him that morning. He could hear the Sunday traffic outside. Out there people were with their families and he wanted to cry out, and he wanted to sob in self pity. He had to restrain himself from beating on the door and bellowing: '*Colonel Krombrink, where are you?!*' As the long African afternoon wore on, his nerves stretched tighter and tighter. He paced up and down the small cell: three paces up, wall, turn, three paces down, door, turn. Finally the sun began to go down, glinting on the window, and he had to press his forehead against the wall again to stop him bellowing his dread. And, oh God, Colonel Krombrink was the only man who could get him out of here, *Colonel Krombrink was his saviour* . . .

He threw himself down on the bunk and held his face.

Get the calm back. Krombrink needs you as much as you need him, remember – you're no use to him standing on the gallows. He knows he'd be hanging an innocent man, *he wants you as an informer* . . . *Krombrink will come for you tonight* . . .

But Krombrink did not send for him that night. Mahoney fell into an exhausted, troubled sleep. Monday dawned brilliant red and gold through the high barred window and the world began to come to life out there, and he clutched his face to stop himself bellowing out loud. But he was sure Krombrink would send for him this morning – he wanted him as an informer and the sooner he was sent out into the world the better. But Krombrink did not send for him that Monday, and he thought he would go mad. Tuesday dawned. At midday the policeman brought him the clothes from his bag and Mahoney wanted to shout for joy: his car was back from Pretoria! They were giving him clean clothes to go home in.

'Now come to the ablutions and wash your old clothes.'

'When am I seeing Colonel Krombrink?'

No answer. Mahoney wanted to seize the man. Tuesday dragged by and darkness fell and he had to clutch his face to stop himself weeping. He knew what game Krombrink was playing – Krombrink was brain-beating him with fear, with the horror of indefinite incarceration, soft-ening him up so that he would do anything to get out of here. And, oh God, it was working. When he shaved on Wednesday morning his hand trembled so much he cut himself. His eyes were gaunt, with dark shad-ows. He had to clench his fist to stop himself saying to the policeman, 'Tell Colonel Krombrink I have a statement to make.' No, that's not the way to be cool. Give it one more day. He'll send for you tomorrow.

But Colonel Krombrink did not send for him on Thursday. Or on Friday. On Saturday, listening to the midday traffic, Mahoney was ready to crack.

It was mid-afternoon when Colonel Krombrink sent for him.

He was bordering on euphoria, bordering on gratitude – as he was meant to feel. He tried to play it cool.

'Good afternoon, Mr Mahoney, have you had a good rest?'

'Sure. Not that I needed it.' He sat and crossed his legs.

'You look tired. Haven't you been sleeping?'

'Like a baby, Colonel. Maybe I've been overdoing it on the exercise. Jogging on the spot, press-ups.'

'I hope you thought while you did it. That bullshit about Mac and the cottage and your briefcase being stolen.'

He managed a frown. 'It's the truth!'

The colonel opened a file and withdrew a typewritten sheet. He put on his spectacles and said: 'Mr Mahoney, we have a new charge against you. The same charge the others face.'

'What bullshit – '

'Forensic tests were done on your car. And under the back seat – ' he consulted the report – 'were found numerous particles of explosives, identical to those found on Lilliesleaf Farm.' He sat back and took off his spectacles.

Mahoney stared at him, aghast, his heart pounding. Krombrink went on: 'The evidence at your trial will be that these explosives from Russia usually come wrapped in cheap plastic which often cracks and small crumbs fall out, hey.' He smiled. 'The evidence against you now is: one, that you used the cottage on Lilliesleaf Farm; two, that you wrote a story to try to blackmail the police force on a typewriter found on the farm; three, that said story was found buried on the farm which was clearly the underground headquarters of the ANC; four, that Russian-made explosives were found in and around that farmhouse; five, that traces of identical explosives were found in your car.' He raised his eyebrows, then spread his hands. 'And, six, that you regularly went to Swaziland and Botswana where we *know* there are ANC bases with supplies of explosives.'

Mahoney stared, his mind fumbling, his heart white with fear. 'You're lying!' He scrambled to his feet and smashed his fist down on the desk. 'Ridiculous! You're lying . . . '

Colonel Krombrink said quietly: 'And point number seven: you're the lover of the notorious Patti Gandhi.' He raised his eyebrows again. 'Who is well known to us as an ANC operative.'

Mahoney's mouth was dry. He smashed his hand down on the desk again and cried: '*You're lying! You didn't find explosives in my car! I've never touched explosives in my life!*'

The colonel smirked: 'The gallows, Mr Mahoney . . . '

'*You bastards put the explosives in my car!*'

The colonel had not moved. 'Why would we want to hang an innocent man? That doesn't suppress terrorism, does it?' He sighed, then sat up. 'Mr Mahoney, either *you* put those explosives in your car on one of your trips with Miss Gandhi, or *she* did.' He added: 'With or without your knowledge.'

Mahoney stared. And, Jesus Christ, the bastard was trying to make him pin the explosives on her, to hang her! He rasped: 'Patti wouldn't have anything to do with explosives!'

'Then *you* put them in your car?'

'No! *You* did!'

'Why should we waste our time framing people when we've got our hands full catching real terrorists – like Miss Gandhi?'

'To blackmail me into giving information about her! And she's not a fucking terrorist!'

Krombrink smirked. 'There're easier ways of getting information without resorting to the dangerous crime of blackmail. Mr Mahoney, your car was never searched at the borders, was it?' He tapped the file. 'They keep records at the borders of cars searched.'

'No! And if they had they'd have found nothing!'

'*But*,' Krombrink said significantly, 'they usually search an Indian's car. Because you know what bladdy crooks they are.'

'And they never found anything in her car either! Or you'd have hanged her long ago!'

'Right,' the colonel said. 'They only ever found merchandise samples.' He spread his hands. 'If we were going to frame somebody, surely we would frame Miss Gandhi, who we know is ANC.'

Mahoney stared, his mind fumbling, an awful thought dawning on him that perhaps the bastard was telling the truth. He looked so convincing.

The colonel said: 'So, who put the explosives in your car? Miss Gandhi, who knew she was likely to be searched on the border? Or you? Or both?'

Mahoney rasped desperately: 'Neither of us!'

The colonel sat back. Then he said thoughtfully: 'When you went on these lovers' jaunts, were both your cars parked in the same place?'

Lovers' jaunts. 'Yes.'

'But Miss Gandhi wasn't in your company the *whole* time?'

'You're suggesting that she sneaked out and put the explosives in my car? Bullshit. *You* put them in my car!'

'But she had the opportunity to instruct her ANC friends to hide explosives in your car while your back was turned?'

Mahoney glared at him. The man was offering him an escape route. And, oh God, the cleverness of the swine, planting the doubt in his mind! All he wanted was to get out of there and find out the truth. Yes, he was prepared to make bargains. *But play it cool . . .* 'I don't believe she did it.'

'You don't believe she would expose you to the death penalty?'

The words struck dread in his breast. No, he did not believe Patti would do that, but they had planted the doubt and, oh God, he would do anything to get out of there, out of South Africa. 'That's right, I don't.'

'So *you* did it?' He suddenly became angry: '*Got*, man, admit it!'

It shocked him all over again – the suspicion was suddenly back on him. '*I deny it! You planted that stuff on me!*'

The colonel sneered. 'Why d'you think she wouldn't do that? Because she loves you? And, are you in love with her?'

Relief that the suspicion was shifting back to her. What did they want to hear? *Yes*, so he wouldn't betray her and hang himself. *No*, so he would betray her? He tried to think fast. 'I don't know now.' *Doubt was what the bastard wanted to hear.*

Krombrink took a breath of satisfaction. And proceeded to poison the hook. 'Do you know what Miss Gandhi does on the nights you don't visit her for the purpose of contravening the Immorality Act?' He studied a typewritten page.

Mahoney's heart gave a pump of black jealousy. Oh, that poisonous doubt again. 'She has numerous business meetings.'

The colonel nodded over his file, reading. 'Ja, some business meetings also . . . and other types of meetings?'

Mahoney wanted to snatch the page from him. He said grimly: 'Friends.'

Colonel Krombrink did not look up, running his finger down the page. 'Friends, ja . . . boyfriends?'

Oh Jesus . . . 'I don't know. You tell me.'

'Would you be angry if you found out she was sleeping around?'

'Yes.' That's what the bastard wanted to hear. And he was jealous already.

'And you would be *disgusted* if in addition she placed those explosives in your car so you unwittingly took the risk of smuggling them across the border on her behalf?' He added: 'Exposing you to the gallows.'

Mahoney closed his eyes. He almost believed the bastard now. 'Yes.'

'Yes.' The colonel nodded. 'And what would you do about it?'

Thank God the man was at last getting to the point of this torture. 'I'm not sure, I've never been in this position.'

The colonel leant forward and said softly: 'Mr Mahoney, that girl is sleeping with two men apart from you.'

It was a shock, even though he had known it was coming, even though he didn't believe it. He stared; the colonel went on: 'And one of them, Mr Mahoney, is a kaffir, hey.'

Mahoney blinked. It was intended as a sickening blow, and it was. He had to bite his tongue to remind himself it was lies. The colonel looked at him:

'The kaffir is called Amos. The other is a white called Michael. Both are ANC. Communists. And terrorists. Mr Mahoney, the explosives in your car ended up on Lilliesleaf Farm. And we're sure that these two men used them. To blow up Johannesburg station. And other jobs.' He paused. 'The men who're screwing Miss Gandhi, for whom you now stand in risk of the gallows.'

If this was for real it was mind-blowing. *This wasn't true!* 'Have you arrested these two guys?'

'They weren't on the farm when we raided. But we're working on it.' He paused. '*Evidence*, Mr Mahoney. We need evidence, and I do not fabricate evidence, contrary to what you think. *Remember* that, when you accuse me of planting traces of explosives in your car.'

Oh God, God.

'Do you *see*,' Krombrink demanded gently, 'that you were *used*? As an expendable pawn – to be hanged if you were caught.'

It was mind-blowing. He did not believe it. And he did not know what to believe.

Krombrink continued: 'Doing the dangerous dirty work for Miss Gandhi's other lovers? The men she fucks.' The colonel went on softly: 'Mr Mahoney, we have enough evidence to hang you . . . '

Mind-blowing . . . He hung on his words, like he was meant to, desperate for reprieve.

Krombrink said quietly: 'Are you going to go to the gallows for those two guys? And for Miss Gandhi?'

Oh God, of course not. And he wanted to roar with outrage that the bastard was terrifying him. He rasped: 'No.'

'But how're you going to escape those gallows?'

Oh, he knew how he was going to escape them – get to the border and run like hell! And he didn't care that the man was lying – run like hell and never come back!

Krombrink sat back again, in deep thought. Then he said: 'Mr Mahoney, speaking *per*sonally – and not for my superiors – I do not believe you are a terrorist. An ANC sympathizer, definitely. But not a terrorist, in the normal sense of the word.' (Oh God, the relief. The veritable rush of gratitude. Just like he was meant to feel.) '*But* we have this evidence. And I can assure you that any court will convict you on this evidence.'

Mahoney stared at him, desperate for his deal, his mercy.

'Mr Mahoney, the only way to escape evidence like this – ' he tapped the file – 'is to *prove* that you're the victim of a terrible, *cynical* plot by these people.' He held his eye. 'I am prepared to give you a chance to do that.'

Mahoney closed his eyes in relief. He wanted to gush his gratitude. 'And how do I do that?'

Colonel Krombrink nodded solemnly. 'Only by cooperating *completely* with us. Doing exactly as we say. Reporting absolutely *every*-thing to us.' Then his eyes took on a steely glare. 'And not only will you prove your innocence but we will make a break into these communist cells. Do you agree to cooperate?'

Oh yes, yes, he agreed. 'Okay,' he said.

Colonel Krombrink studied him, assessing. Then gave a judgement: 'Okay.' He sat up. 'We'll get you to sign a statement to that effect.' (Mahoney wanted to whoop for joy.) 'And another statement. Our insurance, hey, that you don't cheat us.' He shrugged. 'Not important to you, really, in your circumstances, just a Cautioned Statement admitting to contravening the Immorality Act on various occasions with Patti Gandhi.'

The Immorality Act was peanuts compared to that cell for ninety days! Absolutely nothing compared to those gallows!

'And a third statement. Summarising how you wrote the story for this Gandhi woman at Lilliesleaf Farm, how you often went to neighbouring countries together, et cetera.'

'And that I knew nothing about the farm being an ANC base? Nor about explosives? Nor did Miss Gandhi?'

'Not to your knowledge, no.'

'And if I refuse to sign?'

Krombrink sighed. 'Mr Mahoney, everything you've said has been tape-recorded, we've got the evidence against you if we want to use it. But you're much more valuable working with us than hanging by your neck until SAFFAS – they're the prison's contract undertakers – take you away to an unmarked grave.'

Mahoney's face was ashen, his heart knocking.

'Okay, I'll sign.'

Krombrink gave him a small reasonable smile; then clasped his hands together. 'I personally will be your handler – you will report to me. You will receive all reasonable expenses incurred. Of course, we will retain your passport. But, of course, you will be given it back if and when you need it to travel with Miss Gandhi to somewhere like Swaziland again, provided I approve.'

He heard himself blurt: 'Why can't I have it back now?!'

Krombrink smiled. 'We're not fools, Mr Mahoney. You must realize you're on a kind of unofficial bail. Now,' he hunched forward, 'remember I explained to you about the snake that laid the eggs? It's those *eggs* you're going to help us find . . .'

182

20

It was unreal. The joy of walking back down the long corridor, his car keys in his hand, Colonel Krombrink escorting him to the security grille, shaking his hand . . . It was unreal that he even felt grateful to the man – he even almost *liked* Colonel Krombrink, for Christ's sake . . . Then walking out of that dread-filled building into God's own sweet fresh sunset – and, oh, he loved the world with his whole heart. Driving away up the empty streets was a wonderful feeling. Look at those shop windows, look at the lights . . .

And it was unreal that he could now drive to her shop without worrying about being seen, could spend the whole night with her now without being arrested: Krombrink had *ordered* him to get back together with her – Krombrink would be *expecting* him to go to her immediately. No car was following him. He drove down Pritchard Street, turned left into Diagonal Street. Carmel Building, the row of Indian shops underneath, the apartments above – it seemed a long, long time since he had been here. And, *yes*, there were lights in her window! He parked. He went through the big front archway, for all the world to see. He entered the yard, then climbed the staircase onto the access verandah. He rang her bell.

The door opened. She stared at him, amazed.

He put his finger to his lips, then took her in his arms. And, oh, the wonderful feel of her again! He was trembling. And, oh God, he could not bear to believe what Krombrink had told him about her.

It was likely that her apartment was bugged with a listening device. As he told her his story, they sat in the courtyard, outside the back door of her shop. She listened without interruption, her face grim.

'And you signed those statements? So they've got you nailed down. If you don't cooperate they charge you on those confessions.'

'If I didn't agree to cooperate they'd have pulled you in and put you through the wringer.' He looked at her shakily. 'How *did* those traces of explosives get in my car, Patti?'

She closed her eyes. 'There never *were* any explosives in your car, don't you see? They're framing you.'

'Then why not make a good job of it and plant a whole bag?'

She held her face. 'For credibility. It sounds so convincing, mere traces, whereas a whole bag may sound like a plant.'

'But they're after *you*; you're the ANC member. If they were going to frame somebody, why didn't they plant explosives in *your* car?'

'Because they don't *want* to arrest me yet – they want *you* to find out what I'm up to, what the ANC cells are doing.'

He took her hands from her face. He looked into her beautiful brown eyes. 'Patti, the time for need-to-know crap is passed. We're both in very big shit and I *do* need to know. The truth! Now, did you or did you not ever smuggle explosives?'

She stared at him, eyes gaunt. 'You've swallowed their poison, haven't you? You think I really might have hidden explosives in your car, so that you would take the risk instead of me!'

Mahoney closed his eyes. Oh God, he wanted her to say the right thing, to *stop* their poison working. 'Did you?'

She hissed: 'I swear to God I didn't do that! I would never expose you to that risk – I *love* you!' She glared, then sighed feverishly. '*Oh*, what's the use – you need to know . . . ' She looked at him. '*Yes*, I smuggled explosives. But I *never* did so in your car, *always* in my own. But on one occasion the fools in Swaziland put the stuff in your car instead of mine – the guy got his instructions mixed up. I discovered the mistake – I looked under my back seat, they weren't there. I guessed what had happened, looked under the back seat of your car and there they were. I transferred them to my car. That's how the traces got into yours.'

Mahoney sighed in relief. Thank God she admitted it. Or the poison may have worked. But Jesus, smuggling *explosives* . . .

'And did you know what they were going to be used for?'

'Yes.' She jabbed her finger at him. '*Military* targets. *Not* blowing up women and children on Johannesburg Station.'

'How could you be sure of that?'

'Because that was ANC policy! Military targets only.'

He said: 'Krombrink told me that when they raided the farm the ANC boys were sitting around a table covered with documents about hitting soft targets.'

She glared at him. She said slowly: '*If* that is true, I know nothing about it. I am *not* a member of the executive. I simply did as I was told. And I was told that only military targets were legitimate.' She narrowed her eyes. 'Do you believe me?'

He sighed. 'Yes. Thank God.'

'If I was using you to smuggle my explosives, why did I tell you last week that I was never seeing you again?'

Right. Which brought him to the next bit of poison. And he desperately wanted to believe her on this one. 'Do you know a man called Michael? And a black called Amos?'

She looked at him steadily. 'What about them?'

He took a deep breath. 'Krombrink says you're screwing both of them.'

Her expression did not change. She looked at him a long moment, then said quietly: 'That's an absolute lie. To poison you against me.'

Oh God, he wanted to believe that. 'But you do know them?'

'Obviously,' she said grimly.

'You've never screwed either of them?'

'No. On two occasions recently I have hidden them in my apartment for the night. That's all. Obviously the police know about it.'

Oh, thank God. 'And are they saboteurs?'

She said quietly, 'No.'

He did not believe that. 'Did they blow up Johannesburg Station and kill those people?'

She hissed: '*No.* I've told you – that was *not* an ANC bomb! It must have been a bloody Poqo bomb – or those African Resistance Movement guys! No loss of life is our policy!'

'But lives have been lost, apart from Jo'burg Station. How do you know Michael and Amos didn't plant that bomb?'

'Because I would know what's going on in my cell!'

'They're in your cell?'

She closed her eyes. 'I'm not going to answer that.'

She already had. 'But it's possible they did it without your knowledge.'

Her hands were shaking. 'Anything is possible.'

'How do you know your smuggled explosives weren't used in that station bomb? Who did you give them to?'

She looked at him fiercely, tremulously. 'I wouldn't answer that question if I knew. But I *don't* know. The procedure is secret, so I *can't* know, so I *can't* tell the police if I'm caught. I simply park my car in an appointed place, and walk away. Somebody comes and collects the stuff.' She added: 'For use against *military* targets.'

Mahoney took a deep breath, and massaged his eyes. Okay, he believed her. Thank God. He sighed. 'Smuggling explosives . . . is that the reason you weren't going to see me again?'

Her eyes moistened, and she wanted to cry, *I'm pregnant, that's why I can't see you again!* She blinked back the burn and told half of it: 'The reason is that there's no future in our relationship. Because I will not leave this country. And I don't want to break my heart further. Or yours. And because it's too dangerous now that Lilliesleaf's been raided. On the day of the raid Krombrink put the screws on you to be an informer, and I refused to let you be a double-agent, expose you to those risks. And anyway you're not the type.' She tried to glare, to smother the tears. 'And if you don't believe that you can go to hell.'

Mahoney sighed. 'Well, I was coming back to tell you, before I was so rudely interrupted by Krombrink, that I'd decided I *am* the type. If you can be, so can I. That you're right, we can't take this government lying down.' He added: 'And that's the only way we can be together.'

She was staring at him. Taken aback. She began to argue but he continued grimly: 'However, I didn't know you were involved in bombs – even indirectly.' He looked at her. 'I'm not prepared to be involved – even indirectly – in things like that, Patti. In murder. Nor am I prepared to let you be.'

'Are you saying you're prepared to be a double – work for the ANC and feed Krombrink disinformation?'

He said quietly: 'That's what I was coming back to tell you, yes. But that's before I learnt about the explosives. However, that's all academic now. Because we've got to leave the country. Fast. And never come back until this government's fallen.'

'But are you still prepared to work for the ANC?'

He took a deep breath. 'That very much depends. On a whole lot of things: where we are, what kind of work. Give them free legal advice when I'm qualified? Sure. Do some writing for them? Sure, as long as it's not Marxist crap. Write about apartheid? I already do that. Do some administrative work? Yes, as long as it's honest – and nothing to do with bombs. And that kind of thing –' he jabbed a finger at her – 'is the only sort of work *you* are going to do for them in future too!'

There was a pause. Then she said: 'You're only doing this to be with me.'

He said impatiently: 'Of course that's the main reason. But I'm also doing it for the other goddamn reasons. But right now that's all on hold – we've got to get out of the country. And right now we have to do something about your car. Clean it up, or get it out of the country. Because if there are traces of explosives in my car, there're plenty in yours. And they want me to deliver it to them for forensic examination.'

'*Bring* it to them?'

'My first job as informer,' he said. 'I pretend to borrow your car and they examine it for evidence to be used at a future date.' He squeezed her hand. 'Before we go anywhere you've got to get that car vacuum-cleaned from top to bottom, even tonight.' He rubbed his chin feverishly. 'The only hard evidence they've got against you is that you were my "guest" once on Lilliesleaf Farm, for a picnic. And that the story I wrote for you was found buried on the property. That's not enough to hang you. But if they find traces of explosives . . . ?' He looked at her. 'We've got to get out of this country, fast, Patti.'

She stood up and began to pace across the courtyard. She turned to him, eyes gaunt.

'Tomorrow night. They won't be expecting you to move so fast.'

He sighed with relief that she didn't argue. 'Okay, how? What do I do for a passport?'

'You couldn't use your passport even if you had one because they'll be watching for you at all border posts. And for me. We'll have to cross on foot.'

'On *foot?* Where?'

'Leave that to me. There're procedures for this situation.'

'So the ANC will get us out?'

'Of course.'

So he was on the bandwagon already. In their clutches. But thank God. 'But once we're over the border I'll need a passport to travel elsewhere.'

'Leave that to me too.'

'But we can't leave till the banks open on Monday, I've only got about a hundred rand on me.'

'I've got some money in my safe. And I can pick up some outside the country. We daren't wait till Monday.'

He sighed tensely. God, he just wanted to get going. 'Can't you organize all this tonight?'

'I can't organize the border crossing that fast. You don't make arrangements like that by telephone, you use a messenger. And I've got to find him. Organize a vehicle, and so forth.'

He didn't want to let her out of his sight. 'We'll go in my car and abandon it in the bush.'

'The *last* vehicle we should use is yours. Or mine. We've got "safe" cars that'll get us to the border. Now, I've got work to do. You go home to pack and stay there until I send a car for you tomorrow.'

Mahoney's nerves stretched tighter. 'You don't understand that we've got *carte blanche* now – and Krombrink certainly expects me to be with you tonight after a week in a fucking cell. And I've hardly slept, and if I don't sleep in your arms tonight I'll fucking burst. And – ' he jabbed his finger – 'I'm fucking *going* to sleep with you!'

21

Krombrink had explained it to him: he had drawn a triangle, then divided it into blocks, like bricks in a wall.

'Mandela's M-Plan is based on the Zionist Irgun method used in Palestine during the British occupation. Each of the blocks in this triangle represents a cell. No member of any cell knows the identity of any other member of another cell on the horizontal level. The leader of each cell knows only the other cell *leaders* on his level, and knows only the leader of the cell immediately *above* him. And so on, up to the apex: the regional commander. In this way, orders are passed down to each cell-leader, who passes them on to the leader below him.

'The regional commander receives orders from the ANC's national executives – some of whom we arrested at Lilliesleaf Farm. The rest are in London and elsewhere, living on the money the Russians give them, hey. Anyway this is how they maintain security. No member of any of the cells knows more than about ten members in the whole set-up. So if one member talks, most of the network is still intact. But they must be in a mess now – their safe houses must be pretty busy, and they'll want all the help they can get. An' that's where you come in, Mr Mahoney. You're going to penetrate this triangle, through your Miss Gandhi. We believe she's just below regional commander level. This is the ideal time for *you*, sir, to join the underground ANC and "help" them. An' report back to us.'

That Sunday was long, and unreal. It was unreal walking brazenly out of Carmel Building that morning, for all the cops in the world to see, as if he had just left a white girl's apartment. It was impossible to grasp that tonight he was leaving this town forever, only to return if and when the fucking Afrikaners were driven out of power, that he felt no sadness, only a hate-filled calm. Back at The Parsonage, it was unreal that he felt no affection for the nice old apartment block. The flat was quiet, the boys either still asleep or sleeping out, and it was unreal that he probably would never see them again.

He began to pack. His law lectures and the typed copies of the family journals took up his briefcase and most of his big haversack. He stuffed in three shirts, three pairs of underpants and socks, two pairs of shorts, one pair of slacks, one towel, one tie, his toilet bag. He would carry his blazer. He had to leave everything else: the rest of his clothes, all his other books, his portable typewriter. That was it – all he had to show for his life so far. And how did he feel? Not sadness, only reckless calm, and hate for the system that had forced him to do this to save his life, and hers. And, yes, there was fear.

Now cut out the fear. Get back the anger!

It was noon. He had six hours to wait before the safe car fetched him in the underground garage below. What was he going to do? He had letters to write: to *Drum*, to his parents, to his sister, to his bank; but Patti had told him not to write anything until he was outside the country. 'Not even a cheque to pay your Parsonage bills.'

He sat down at his table. He pulled out the first typed volume of the family journals. He opened it at random. He read his great great grand-father's words, written the night before he trekked out of Natal with his beloved Sarie:

> *I have supped full of horrors in this benighted land, under this misguided British government, and now I must leave before it takes my life as it has taken so many others. And I leave without sadness, for who can regret turning his back on injustice? And there must forever be injustice where white and black meet, for each will fear and seek to overwhelm the other.*

Then he opened the latest volume, near the end. He read his own father's last entry; written in 1948 on the day the National Party won the elections:

> *And so, after 150 years of struggle, which began on the bloody eastern frontier, the Afrikaner has won his battle. Alas, I have no hope for this country now.*

Luke Mahoney stared at the words. Then he turned to his own, current volume, and wrote at the top of a new page:

> *The Story of Apartheid Continued: 1960 Onwards.*

The safe car was driven by a young white man Mahoney had never seen before. His name was Michael Sullivan, the man who had planted the bomb on Johannesburg Station. Even though Patti had warned Mahoney that she would probably be travelling in a separate vehicle, he demanded: 'Where's Miss Gandhi?'

'I'm just the driver around here, I don't know a thing.'

'Am I allowed to know your name?'

'Tom. And you're Luke. We can talk about anything you like, horse racing, women, but not politics or who I am or who you are.'

It was mostly silence after that. They drove out of Johannesburg in the sunset, onto the Pretoria Road. 'Where're we going?'

'You'll know when we get there.'

And it was all unreal that he was leaving, that he was trusting his life to this driver. They by-passed Pretoria and entered the heartland of Afrikanerdom. At Potgietersrus they stopped for petrol. Then they turned west, into the bush, and Mahoney knew where they were going. 'Botswana.'

The bush flashed by in the headlights, ploughed fields carved into scrub, cattle, maize, grain silos, the distant twinkle of farmhouses, tall yellow grass by the roadside. Then the tarred road ended and they were on corrugated dirt. Three hours later they were near the Limpopo and the border post of Grobbelaar's Drift. The driver switched off the lights and turned down a dirt track. They ground through the featureless bush for five kilometres, then a black man stepped out of the darkness. The driver stopped. 'Here we are.'

Mahoney peered at the featureless bush. 'Miss Gandhi here?'

'Follow that man.'

Mahoney climbed out of the vehicle. He shouldered his haversack and gripped his briefcase. The car immediately reversed, swung around and went grinding off into the night. The black man was already walking off into the darkness. Mahoney followed.

It was then that the reality hit. Walking through the darkness of Africa, following a black man without a name, into the unknown, having to trust him with his life . . . And suddenly he did not want to leave South Africa and everything he knew, following a black man. This is it, he said to himself: You're a refugee . . .

He trudged through the starlit bush, desperately trying to keep his mind straight: *You have to do this, just think of those gallows, just think of her*. After about an hour he saw the Limpopo ahead in the starlight. It was almost dry. The guide cupped his hands to his mouth and made the low sound of an owl. After a moment there was an answering hoot. The guide pointed across the river.

'*Hamba gashle, Nkosi.*' Go carefully, Lord.

Go carefully, Lord. Oh God, this is Africa. He shook the man's hand briefly, turned and clambered down the bank.

He hurried across the starlit riverbed, jumped across the water. He ran across the other side and scrambled up the dark bank, into Botswana. He looked around, waiting.

After half a minute he heard a rustle. He jerked and a dark form materialized. It beckoned. Mahoney whispered: *'Upi lo umfazi kamina?'* Where is my woman?

'Mina kona nikis.' I know nothing.

The man turned and led the way off into the bush.

It was just before dawn when the bush parted and there was the road that led from Grobbelaar's Drift. The guide retraced his steps half a mile into the bush, to a large thorn tree; he placed both hands beside his face. Mahoney slung off his haversack, slumped down; in a moment he was asleep.

He was woken an hour later by the guide shaking him. He sat up, expecting disaster. Two black men were towering over him, unsmiling. One had a beard. Mahoney clambered to his feet. 'Good morning.'

They did not answer. They scrutinized him from head to foot; then one beckoned and turned. And, oh God, Mahoney hated this.

He trudged after them, his body crying out for sleep, his heart yearning for the life he had left behind. *Think of those gallows . . .* They came to a Land-Rover. The man pointed to the back seat. Mahoney slipped off his haversack. *'Upi lo umfazi kamina?'*

The bearded man replied in English: 'Ask no questions. Get in.'

Jesus. Nice guys. He got in. The man produced a black cloth from his pocket. 'Blindfold. Sit still.'

He let him place the cloth over his eyes and knot it at the back of his head. 'Is this necessary?'

'When I tell you to lie down, you lie down.'

'Mind if I go to sleep?'

The doors slammed. The vehicle rumbled off through the bush.

It turned onto the major dirt road and drove off at speed. Mahoney sat in total darkness, his nerves stretched tight.

An hour later the vehicle drove onto the tarred road that runs from Gaborone to the north. The Missionary Road . . . The vehicle swung right. To Francistown, he thought – any fool can work that out so far, so why the fucking blindfold?

A couple of hours later, the sounds of other vehicles became more frequent. 'Lie down.'

He obeyed. He lay, feeling the vehicle turn left and right, now leaving tar and going on up dirt roads. Then it slowed, ground forward, then stopped. He heard iron garage doors clanging closed. 'Get up.' He sat up. A hand gripped his biceps unnecessarily hard.

He clambered out. The hand led him up a step. Through a doorway. Fingers undid the knot at the back of his head. The blindfold was pulled off.

Mahoney blinked around. He was in a kitchen. Heavy curtains

covered the window. A bright angle-poise lamp stood on a wooden table. Two men sat behind the glaring lamp, their faces in shadow. Mahoney could only make out that one was white, the other black.

The shadowy black man said quietly: 'So you want to join the ANC?' His voice was rich and dangerous.

Mahoney raised his hand to shield his eyes. 'Will somebody tell me where Miss Gandhi is?'

The white man said: 'We will ask the questions.' He had a guttural, foreign accent. 'What has Miss Gandhi got to do with whether you join the ANC? If she is not here, you won't join?'

Mahoney closed his eyes, because of the bright light and in exasperation. 'For Christ's sake, man, I've been walking through the bush all night, I haven't slept and I haven't had anything to eat! I expected my woman to be with me and she isn't! Now will somebody for Christ's sake tell me what's happened to her!'

The black man said: 'Answer the question. What's Miss Gandhi got to do with it?'

Mahoney closed his eyes again. And by Christ he didn't care anymore, all he wanted was his woman. He rasped: 'Yes, I want to join the ANC. Though you're not making it very attractive. I don't give a shit what you've done with Miss Gandhi! Oh no, my love is only for the ANC! The fact that Miss Gandhi is my lover is totally irrelevant! Just show me where to sign up!'

'So, we have a humorist,' the white man said.

'Oh sure, I feel a laugh-a-minute after eight days in solitary confinement and no sleep!'

The black man said: 'And you want to join because you need a passport.'

Oh, they could stick their passport right up their arses. But, yes, he needed their fucking passport. He took a grip on his nerves. 'My passport has been confiscated, yes. But I also want to join the ANC for ideological reasons. I disapprove of the government. Apartheid stinks.'

'Why?'

Mahoney frowned into the light. 'I would have thought that was obvious! Do you mind turning that bloody lamp aside?'

'Yes, we mind. You "disapprove" of the South African government. Strong language. Sufficient to commit treason?'

'Joining the ANC is almost treason in itself, isn't it? But to answer your question, I am not a killer. I would not plant bombs.'

'Why not?'

'Soldiers should kill other soldiers.'

'And are you prepared to be a soldier? You've been trained.'

192

'I did my national service, yes. That's the law.'

'The ANC also has laws.'

Mahoney sighed. 'Look, I'm a journalist – that's my speciality.'

'What will you write about us? The ANC? The Struggle.'

He said: 'The truth. That it is just.'

'And if we happen to do some – ' he waggled his hand – 'things your exquisite South African judgement does not consider entirely *just*?'

Mahoney forced a smile at the shadowy face. 'If you mean will I write propaganda, the answer is yes. If you mean will I write shit, will I twist facts, will I deny the obvious, will I make a laughing stock of myself by so doing, the answer is no.'

'Why not?'

'Because I'm not a fool. Fools do a disservice. Fools only fool other fools and not the people that matter. Give those jobs to somebody else if you insist on foolishness.'

'The masses are fools?'

Mahoney sighed. 'I didn't say that.'

The white man smiled. 'But the masses *are* fools, don't you agree? Important fools, *powerful* fools, but fools nonetheless, who need to be told what to think, for the good of the state.'

Mahoney closed his eyes. Of course they were fools. 'As you say. And can you please turn that lamp?'

'So what is wrong with giving them the right medicine?'

'As you say. Will you please move that light?'

The two men looked at each other, then the white man said: 'Mr Mahoney, your manner is very dangerous. You do not seem to realize that you are on trial. For your life.'

Mahoney stared at the shadowy forms. Jesus Christ . . . On *trial*? *Who did these bastards think they were?* Before he could say anything, the bastard went on: 'For your *life*. To determine whether or not you are a spy. *And*, if we decide that you *are* a spy – or that you *may* be a spy – the sentence will be *death*.'

Mahoney stared through the glare, his heart knocking with fear and outrage. He wanted to lunge across the table and seize the bastard by his throat. Before he could marshal any words the other man went on:

'Or you may be a double agent, Mr Mahoney, who pretends to each side that he is spying only for them, but who in reality is working for both sides – and getting money from both, *cheating* both. Passing on *dis*information to both sides as it suits him.' He smiled dangerously. 'You know what happens to double agents when they are found out?'

193

Mahoney wanted to bellow his outrage. And he felt the same terror as Krombrink had evoked, felt the same desperation to plead, to ingratiate himself. And, oh God, he wanted to grab Patti and get out of all this. He clenched his teeth against his dread. He took a deep breath. 'Sure, I know.'

The man smirked. 'Sure? You realize they get no mercy? That they are ruthlessly debriefed, to find out how much damage they have done? Then tortured, to double-check their stories? Then, when we're satisfied . . . ' He cocked his finger to his head like a pistol.

Jesus, he hated the bastard. And feared him. 'Yes.'

'How do we know you're not a spy, Mr Mahoney? Or a double?'

'You know that they found traces of your explosives in my car. That they kept me in the cells for eight days. That they took my passport and told me to penetrate the ANC through Miss Gandhi.'

'Which you are now trying to do.'

He rasped furiously, 'But I told Patti, who told you! If I were a spy I wouldn't have told her or you, would I?'

'Or you could be a clever spy – who *pretends* to have made a clean breast.'

He shouted: 'I'm not a fucking spy at all! I'm a journalist! I know nothing about the cloak and dagger business!'

The black man said: 'You realize that if we accept you we will expect you to be *very* useful. And if you let us down it will reflect *very* badly on Miss Gandhi. On her *health*.'

Jesus, he hated the threat to her. 'I do.'

The white man studied him expressionlessly, then he sat forward. 'So start from the beginning. Why apartheid *"stinks"*. Why you're a so-called *liberal*. What happened with BOSS. Everything you said, everything they said. You will be cross-examined. At the end, if we are not completely satisfied you are telling the truth, if there is the *slightest* suspicion that you are hiding anything, you will be dealt with as a spy . . . '

22

It was like a nightmare. His body crying out for sleep, his nerves stretched tight, the light glaring, the emotional exhaustion, and all the time the fear and the anger. Desperately answering, desperately trying to think, to remember, mouth dry, fumbling facts, voice rasping. '*Jesus, is this how you treat all your members?*'

'You're not one of our members, you're a spy, sent by BOSS.'

'Oh, sweet suffering Jesus . . .'

Another time he leapt to his feet and crashed his hand down on the table. *'Then take me out and shoot me! Anything for a quiet life! But I tell you what, big-mouth, before you get me out there you're going to lose all your fucking teeth!'*

The white man replied softly: 'We'll shoot you right in this kitchen.' He patted a holster. 'And I assure you my teeth will remain intact.'

'Don't bank on it, your mouth's so big I couldn't miss!'

The black man said: 'Sit down. And try to save your life.'

And try to save your life . . . Oh God, he hated them. He sat. The black man said: 'Do you know what a white South African calls a cheeky bloody kaffir who is sitting in judgement on him?'

Mahoney massaged his eyelids. 'No. But give me a laugh.'

The black man bellowed: *'Sir!'*

Mahoney jerked. *'Stand up!'* the black man roared. *'Stand up and call me sir!'*

Mahoney frowned into the light. 'Do tell me you're joking.'

The black man hissed from the gloom, teeth clenched: *'Get to your feet, white boy, and call me sir.'*

Mahoney controlled his exhausted fury, and closed his eyes. He shook his head and said softly: 'No. You're not my boss yet. Even my editor and Colonel Krombrink combined didn't require that.'

The whites of the black man's eyes bulged. *'Stand up, white boy, when you speak to me!'*

Mahoney flinched, nerves stretched to snapping. 'If this is how the ANC tests their recruits, count me out.'

The white man leaned forward furiously, his face entering the light for the first time. 'Because you're a white supremacist! Because you're a typical South African who cannot bring himself to stand up and call a black man sir! Because you cannot believe that a black man can rule South Africa! Which shows you are a spy sent by BOSS to infiltrate the ANC!'

Mahoney tried to smile. 'Is *this* ANC logic?'

The white man lunged for his holster and wrenched out the gun. He levelled it at Mahoney's nose. *'Stand up,'* he hissed.

Mahoney stared at the gun, too astonished to be terrified. He couldn't believe this. 'Jesus Christ . . . ' But he got to his feet.

The white man held the gun on him. He whispered: 'What do you call a black man who's sitting in judgement on your life?'

Mahoney stared, incredulous. 'I don't believe this.'

There was a sharp popping noise as the man pulled the trigger. The bullet smashed into the wall behind Mahoney. He lurched, absolutely horrified, then his head reeled. He clutched the table, head down, trying to recover. The white man hissed: 'What do you call him?'

Mahoney whispered: 'Sir.'

It was mid-afternoon when he was dismissed and locked in a bedroom, 'to await our decision'.

He threw himself on the bed, trembling, exhausted, his mind bludgeoned. And, oh God, he knew what he was going to do if he got out of this house alive. His body wanted to collapse in sleep but his mind was in turmoil. Who can sleep when his immediate execution is being considered? He still could not believe this was happening.

It was late afternoon when the door was thrown open. Two black men with pistols beckoned. 'Come!' He heaved himself up, his heart knocking. They escorted him into the kitchen.

Mahoney stood in front of the glaring lamp, forced to screw up his eyes, his nerves screaming.

The white man said quietly: 'Have you anything else to tell us that may affect our decision?'

Affect their decision?! What was the decision? He cried: 'What do you want to hear?! I've told you everything! Ask me!'

The two men staring at him. 'Well? Anything else?'

Mahoney shouted: *'I've told you everything! What do you want to know? I'm not a fucking mind-reader!'*

The white man glanced at the black. Both nodded briefly. The white man sighed, then said: 'I'm afraid we do not believe you. We think that you are a spy – a BOSS agent. Anyway, we cannot take any risks.'

Mahoney stared, his ears ringing. He cried desperately: *'Bullshit! Ask Patti Gandhi! She'll vouch for me! Where's Patti!?'*

'We have questioned Miss Gandhi this afternoon. She cannot throw any more light on the matter.'

His desperate mind fumbled. *'Why wasn't I present? I could have proved my innocence to you by asking her questions!'*

The white man said: 'I'm afraid not. We're not sure Miss Gandhi is a reliable witness.'

Mahoney's ears were ringing. *'She's absolutely reliable! Totally ANC!'*

The white man said quietly. 'You went into this with your eyes open. You know what the sentence is.' He nodded to the two guards; they both grabbed Mahoney's elbows, and he lashed out.

With a desperate roar he lashed his elbow backwards into the guard's guts, then he whirled on the other one and drove his fist into his face.

The man staggered backwards, still clutching Mahoney's elbow, and they both sprawled. Mahoney crashed on top and he hit him with all his might again, then his head seemed to explode as the other man kicked him. He rolled and grabbed the man's boot and tried to fling him. The man lurched and Mahoney scrambled up and hit him with all his might in the guts, and a pistol butt hit him on the head with an explosion of red-black stars.

He came to, rasping, sitting in a chair, his hands cuffed to the legs. His head was pounding, his guts heaving. The two black guards stood over him, bloody, battered, pistols drawn. The white man said softly: 'Anything else to tell us, Mr Mahoney?'

Mahoney rasped: 'Call Patti . . . you murdering bastards.'

The white man stood up. So did his black companion. 'Give him a minute to say any prayers.' He turned for the door. Mahoney roared to the sky: *'Bring Patti Gandhi!'*

The two interrogators walked to the door. Mahoney bellowed: *'Bring Patti Gandhi!'*

The door closed with a slight bang.

And Mahoney broke down. He dropped his head and sobbed.

He felt the hard muzzle of the pistol against his head. He screwed up his eyes and gasped, 'Dear God, help me now.'

The trigger clicked. He fainted.

He came to sprawled on the chair, his hands free, smelling salts being waved under his nose. He lurched upright, gasping for breath. Hands steadied him as he began to fall. He shook his head and tried to focus. And he couldn't believe what he saw. Both interrogators were smiling at him. The light was turned aside.

The white man said: 'Okay, it's all over. We believe you. Congratulations.'

Mahoney's splitting head was reeling. The black interrogator leant across the desk, his hand extended: 'Welcome to the ANC.'

Mahoney stared at them; then he felt faint, and overwhelmed with joy. *Joy to be alive*, and he wanted to laugh and seize the man's hand in both of his and gush his thanks and swear eternal loyalty. With a supreme effort he retained his dignity and took the hand without a smile. He turned and shook the white man's hand too.

'Sit down. And we'll outline your duties.'

Mahoney slumped. He just wanted to hang his head and laugh his relief. 'Can I finally be told where Patti is?'

'She's safe, here in Francistown. You'll be with her tonight.'

Mahoney wanted to sob with relief. The white man said: 'And she did vouch for you. Sorry about the ordeal. But it was necessary.'

Oh God, all Mahoney cared about was that he was alive. The white man continued: 'Tomorrow you two can have a good rest, you both need it. Then tomorrow night we'll get you back to Johannesburg.'

It was like a blow. Mahoney's mind fumbled.

'To *Johannesburg*? But Jo'burg's where BOSS is expecting me to work for them. To join the ANC and feed them information, on pain of death on the gallows.'

The white man smiled. 'And that's exactly what you're going to do. We'll do our best to see you don't end up on the gallows – you're far too valuable. You will feed BOSS information – but disinformation. And you'll feed us correct information about BOSS.'

Mahoney couldn't believe this.

'But,' he protested, 'I've just escaped from their clutches . . . ' He waved a hand. 'If they find out that I've told you everything, that I'm working for you, they'll fucking hang me!'

The black man said: 'But the name of the game is not to get found out. That's espionage. And we'll be careful about your instructions, so that you don't give the game away.'

Mahoney stared, disbelieving. And, oh God, he knew what he was going to do about *this*. He said: 'But Patti? They know she's smuggled explosives. If I put a foot wrong they'll grab both of us and fucking hang her too!'

The white man smiled reassuringly. 'But Miss Gandhi is vital to the plan. She *is* the plan. If she doesn't go back – if BOSS finds out she's fled the country – then you've got no credible connection to the ANC. And they'll certainly guess what's happened. And, as you say, hang you . . . '

23

Patti had been telephoned, and the message had been 'Green light'.

It was ten o'clock that Monday night when Mahoney arrived at her cousin's house in Francistown. He had been blindfolded again before leaving the ANC house, so that he could never be forced to tell anybody where it was. The driver stopped and undid the blindfold. Mahoney felt feverish. He hefted out his baggage. He rang the bell in the garden wall.

The iron door opened; there stood Patti, eyes gaunt. 'Darling!' she whispered. She led him up the path into the guest wing, where they had stayed occasionally. She turned to him, saw the bruise on his face. 'Oh God. Are you all right?'

'Have you got a brandy?'

'Yes.' She went to a cabinet.

He took a big sip, eyes closed. 'The bastards put me through a mock execution.'

She was aghast. She had not expected that. 'Oh God, how awful . . . '

'And I'm quite sure that if they hadn't been satisfied they'd have given me the real thing.'

She closed her eyes. 'I thought I'd convinced them about you.'

He tossed back the brandy and sloshed more into the glass. Exhausted. 'We've got to get out of here, Patti. Immediately. They intend sending us back to Johannesburg tomorrow night. I'm not exposing you or me to BOSS. And the only way is to get the hell out of here.'

She had been expecting it. She had been certain what he would do when confronted with the plan, but it was like a blow nonetheless; in a corner of her heart there had lingered hope. Now came the inevitable. And it felt as if her heart would break. But at least she had got him safely out of South Africa. All she could do for him now was get him away. And forget. 'Yes.'

'We have no option, Patti. The only reason BOSS hasn't arrested you already is because you're more useful to them alive as my connection with the ANC. With me gone, they've no reason not to add you to their bag. And if I go back with you, we'll both end up on the gallows.' He took a deep exhausted breath. 'Get it into your head that neither of us can go back, Patti.'

She sat at the table, her brow propped on her fingertips. She nodded. 'Yes.'

'And we can't stay here either, Patti. Nor in any other part of Africa where the ANC is. Because if I refuse to do their bidding there's every likelihood they'll change their mind about me being a spy. They made it clear that I was very much on probation.' He raised his fingers in the shape of a pistol and pointed it at her forehead. 'Can you imagine what that felt like?'

She closed her eyes. 'I apologize. I'm deeply sorry. But in their defence I must say that you can't blame their suspicion, knowing you'd just been enlisted by BOSS.'

'Boy, did they make me understand that. But you must please understand that I'm not going to stick around to find out how suspicious they can get when I refuse to return to South Africa to find out how suspicious *BOSS* can get.'

199

She put her fingertips to her eyes. 'Yes, I understand.'

'Nor am I going to let *you* stick around to find out how suspicious they can get about *you* when *I* defect.'

She sighed wearily. 'I understand.'

Mahoney looked at her. 'So we're getting the hell out of here tonight, Patti. *Tonight*. So, can we borrow your cousin's car? You drive over the Rhodesian border, with your passport, I walk around the border post through the bush, we meet up on the other side. Tomorrow morning we're in Bulawayo. We leave the car with your relatives. Then we figure out what to do from there.'

Her heart was breaking. And, oh, she wanted to tell him honestly what she was going to do, what she *had* to do, surely he deserved that honesty? But she simply could not bear the argument that would have ensued, the anger, the fear, the anguish – he was in no shape to endure that after what he had been through these last ten days. And it might well have not worked: it hadn't worked in Swaziland. And that would have been fatal. It might even have been better to lie completely and tell him that she didn't really love him, that he must go, forget about her – but she simply could not bear the anguish of that lie, and he would refuse to believe that too, he would refuse to leave. And so there was only one thing to do.

'We can't take my cousin's car, it's the only one she's got. We'll take the train, it passes through at eleven.'

'But I haven't got a passport.'

'When the train stops at the border, you get off. I carry on to Bulawayo, then Salisbury. You walk through the bush, over the border, then rejoin the road and walk to Plumtree. From Plumtree you take a bus to Bulawayo. Then the night train to Salisbury. I'll be at my friend Jennifer's flat, I'll give you the number.'

His bludgeoned mind was trying to work. 'But the ANC may be watching the railway station.'

She had to stifle the sob in her voice. 'They know you're with me. They don't suspect me.'

Mahoney was trying to find a snag with the plan, but he was too tired to think. It seemed too simple. 'Are you sure?'

'Quite sure. Or you'd be in a cell right now.'

Mahoney put his hands to his exhausted face. Thank God she wasn't arguing, thank God he was getting her out of this mess. And all he wanted was to collapse in her arms on the bed and sleep, sleep. He took a deep breath. 'I love you.'

She whispered: 'I love you too.'

The best words in the world, nothing else mattered, all he had to do now was get them out and face tomorrow tomorrow, one way or another they would make it and live happily ever after somewhere. He looked at his watch. They had three hours. He heaved himself to his feet.

'Pack, Patti. I'm walking up to the railway station. We'd better not be seen arriving there together. We'll buy our tickets on the train. I'll wait in the shadows somewhere. You get there just before the train comes in, park in the dark. Just walk to the nearest coach. Ignore everybody, get on and go into the nearest toilet. When the train's moving, look for the conductor and buy a ticket. Got that?'

Tears were glistening. 'Yes. Got it.'

His heart went out to her. He held her tight, and whispered: 'I'm truly sorry, but it's got to be this way. I'll make it up to you. We'll have a wonderful life, I promise you.'

She looked up at him, her eyes full of tears. She said: 'There's one thing I want to do before we leave. We've got time, it'll only take about quarter of an hour.'

'What's that?'

She took a deep, tearful breath. 'Get married. By Hindu custom. In the temple down the road.' Her eyes were brimming: 'It's not legally binding. But in the eyes of Indians it's very important. To people like my parents.'

And that was unreal too. The dim temple, the candle light, the smell of incense, the altar with wilting garlands. Mahoney sat cross-legged beside Patti, the priest's face flickering in the candle light, hearing the droning sing-sing as he intoned from the holy work, and he could not truly grasp that this was happening.

Then the priest said: 'Do you truly take this woman as your wife?'

Mahoney's ears were ringing. 'Yes, sir.'

The priest turned to Patti. 'Do you truly take this man as your husband?'

'Yes.'

The priest read aloud again. Then he looked up and said: 'In the eyes of God you are married. Go together in peace.' He dipped his finger into some paste, and placed a red dot on Patti's forehead.

And suddenly, Mahoney recalled the words of the witch doctor to whom Justin Nkomo had taken him the night before he left Umtata in disgrace: 'Beware the woman with the red forehead . . .'

24

It took him an hour to reach the station via deserted suburban roads. He stopped in darkness a hundred yards from it.

There was only one platform. The small station building had one light burning inside. A dozen Africans were waiting with bundles and baggage; a truck was unloading cargo. Several taxis. A woman was selling roasted mielie cobs at a charcoal brazier, her baby asleep on her back. Some youths were setting out rows of wooden carvings. A transistor radio blaring African music. The car park was in darkness. On the other side of the tracks, where Mahoney was, there were goods sheds and a cattle pen. He found a dark place between the sheds and sat down.

He hung his head. He was numb, feverish, exhausted, euphoric. *He had done all the right things and tomorrow everything would be safe, tomorrow would look after itself* . . . And he was happy that he had married Patti by Hindu custom, even if it didn't have the force of law, he was glad that he had given her that . . .

More people began to arrive, straggling down the road. Several cars drew up. At five minutes to eleven he saw Patti's car drive into the car park, and he gave a sigh of relief. A few minutes later he heard the train whistle, and saw the distant headlight coming down the track. The big engine hissed to a halt, the line of coaches obscuring the platform. Mahoney strode out of the shadows.

All the activity was on the other side of the train. Passengers milling, vendors crying their wares. Mahoney hurried across the tracks to the nearest coach and swung himself up. Now he could see the mêlée on the platform. The toilet was in front of him, he grabbed the door handle. What a relief that it was unoccupied. He slung his baggage inside, stepped in and shot the bolt. He leant back against the door, getting the knocking out of his heart. Then he went to the window and lowered it an inch.

The platform was swarming with people, all black. He could see part of the car park. He could just see part of the windscreen of her car, but not inside. He squeezed himself into the opposite corner, to see more of the platform. He could not make out anybody who looked ominous. He slumped down and held his face.

The engine gave a warning whistle. He scrambled up and peered. The platform had many fewer people on it but it was still clamorous with vendors. She must surely be aboard by now. Then the train gave a lurch, and it began to ease forward.

He slumped against the window in relief. His heart singing an exhausted hallelujah. The train eased forward, and the rest of the car park eased into view. And his heart lurched.

He saw a woman climb out of the driver's seat, and stand beside the car. Mahoney could not make out her face. His mouth opened, to bellow her name to the skies – then he slumped against the corner, eyes closed, thanking God. The figure he had glimpsed was Patti's cousin. And he felt the bile of tension come erupting up his throat, and he lurched over the lavatory bowl, his stomach heaved and up it erupted. He retched and retched, the railway ties flashing by beneath, vomiting up his exhaustion and fear and relief.

Finally he clambered up. He turned to the basin, still shuddering. He opened his haversack and found his toilet bag. He fumbled for his toothbrush and paste.

Patti Gandhi stood beside the car, her knuckles to her mouth, the tears running down her face. She watched the train lights slide out past the station building. They got smaller and smaller, disappearing down the track. Then they were gone into the night; and she dropped her face into her hands and she sobbed, and sobbed.

Her cousin put her arm on her shoulder.

'Don't cry. It was bound to turn out this way, you knew it long ago. And so did I. So, let him go, no harm's been done, he doesn't know anything the police don't know already. Forget him.'

Patti held her face and sobbed, her shoulders jerking. Her cousin said: 'The Struggle is much more important than personal pain. He was a good young man, but his heart was not with us, he's a typical South African. He was no good for you.'

Patti lowered her hands and slowly turned, her eyes bright. '*Don't,*' she whispered fiercely, '*ever* say that again.'

About an hour later the train stopped at the border. As it eased to a halt, Mahoney climbed down on the dark side of the tracks. Other passengers were disembarking on the other side, into the patchy lamplight. He shouldered his haversack and walked off into the darkness, trying not to look as if he was hurrying.

He walked five hundred yards before glancing back. The train was a long glimmer of lights through the bush. Then it gave a short whistle and it lurched forward. Mahoney looked at the African sky for two big stars to take a bearing by.

He walked until he reckoned he had covered a mile. Then he turned at right angles to the line between his stars, selected two more, to the north. He set off through the starlit bush.

When he reckoned he had covered three miles, he took a new bearing and turned west. Half an hour later the bush parted and before him lay the road again. Plumtree lay a mile away.

He walked two hundred yards back into the bush, then slumped down on the grey brown earth beneath a thorn tree. He laid his brief-case flat, slumped his head down on it, thanking God.

In an instant he was asleep.

It was early afternoon when the bus dropped him in the middle of Bulawayo. He asked directions, then he set off trudging across town.

The Railway Hotel was an old Victorian building, once grand, now the hangout of white railway workers. He had four hours before the train left for Salisbury. He sat in the bar, drinking a row of cold Lions, letting it flood his jagged system. There was a bunch of noisy young men waiting for the train to Lusaka: they were going to enlist in Tshombe's army in the Congo. As a journalist he should have got talking to them but he was too tired, he just thanked God it wasn't his problem, that he was getting off this godforsaken continent. At seven o'clock he boarded the train, found his compartment and climbed up onto the topmost bunk.

It was a beautiful day when he arrived in Salisbury at eight o'clock the next morning. He found a public telephone and dialled Patti's friend. 'This is Luke Mahoney; may I speak to Patti, please.'

Jennifer said: 'I've got a message for you. I received a phone call last night, from Patti. She's returned to South Africa. "As scheduled", she said. She said you would understand what that meant.'

Mahoney stared. He couldn't believe this. *'She called from South Africa?'*

Jennifer went on: 'And the message was, "Goodbye and good luck".'
He could not believe this.

'But . . . did she explain *why?*'

'She simply said you'd understand what "as scheduled" meant.'

As scheduled. Returning to underground as scheduled . . . Oh God! He slammed down the telephone and hung his head.

He hurried to the ticket office and got some change. He dashed back to the telephone and feverishly dialled the international operator. He booked a call to Gandhi Garments in Johannesburg. It was answered immediately. 'Can I speak to Miss Gandhi?'

The girl recognized Mahoney's voice. She hesitated then said: 'Miss Gandhi is at the police station, sir.' She hung up.

Mahoney stared, his heart pounding. *At the police station?* Oh Jesus! He hung up, his ears ringing. *At the police station? Under arrest . . . oh God!*

He stood there, staring at the wall, sick in his guts, frantically trying to think. Then he dialled the operator again. He booked at call to the *Star*. He asked for Gloria Naidoo.

'Where are you?' Gloria demanded.

'In Rhodesia. For Christ's sake tell me what's happened!'

'Stay there. All I know is that the cops arrived when the shop opened and took Patti away. Under the Internal Security Act.'

The Internal Security Act. Ninety days' detention without trial . . . and ninety and ninety, to the far side of eternity. He knew all about that.

Gloria said: 'I phoned your flat to tell you, and Splinter Woodcock told me the cops had been there this morning too. Looking for you. So stay in Rhodesia, pal, don't come back. I suggest you phone her lawyer, Mr Rubenstein. Here's his number . . . '

He was stunned. He numbly hurried back to the ticket office. But the clerk did not have enough change. He shouldered his haversack and feverishly set off uptown to find a bank. He got his coins and hurried across the square to Meikles Hotel. He shut himself in the telephone kiosk and put a call through to Rubenstein.

The lawyer said: 'Yes, I'm familiar with your name. And please be circumspect in what you say, because my telephone may be tapped. Got that? Now, although you're not a client of mine, I must advise you not to return. Have you heard that?'

Mahoney's ears were ringing. 'Yes.'

'Very well. Now, my client is in police custody under the Internal Security Act. That means she can be detained indefinitely, without access to her lawyer, or anybody else. However, I have managed to speak to a certain Colonel Krombrink of BOSS and he told me that in all likelihood she will be charged with treason.' He paused. 'Did you hear that?'

He couldn't believe this was happening. 'Yes.'

'I don't know what evidence they've got against her. I suspect there's a warrant for your arrest too. They may intend to use you as a witness against my client. However, they may well join you as a co-accused with her. So I advise you not to return, for your sake *and* my client's. Now, they may try to extradite you. That means they may apply to whatever foreign country you're in to have you arrested and returned to South Africa to face trial. Very few countries would cooperate with them, because of apartheid, but Southern Rhodesia might. Without doubt Britain would be the safest place for you, but at least make sure you get across the Zambesi into Northern Rhodesia.'

'But I can't just leave her to her fate!'

'There is nothing you can do to help if you're in jail yourself. Or forced to give evidence against her. I hope I make myself clear.'

Mahoney hung up, numbly. He stared at the telephone: he just wanted to fill his lungs and bellow in outrage.

He walked in a daze out of the hotel, into Cecil Square. He went to a park bench and sat down in a heap. He hung his head, trying to grapple with what had happened. Then up it came from his heart and loins, his overwhelming grief, and he wept.

PART IV

1963–1964

CONGO WAR INTENSIFIES –
TSHOMBE ELECTED PRIME MINISTER

LILLIESLEAF FARM TRIAL COMMENCES

MISS SOUTH AFRICA CONTENDER

ON TRIAL FOR HER LIFE

FEDERATION OF RHODESIA AND
NYASALAND BREAKS UP

25

There is only one thing to do when you're on the run and have no money, and that is to hitch-hike. Walk, walk, walk, and when a car comes along you desperately thumb it, and if it doesn't stop you keep on walking. You dare not sit and wait for the next car, you keep walking, to put as much distance as possible between you and that South African border; but no matter how far and hard you keep going, you cannot walk away from your grief. And your horror. Your utter horror of what's happening back there, to her . . . And your helplessness. Your sheer utter impotence to do anything to help her. And your outrage, that they're doing this to *her* . . . that she was driven to do it by the law of the land. And your weeping outrage that she had been such a fool as to go back! 'As scheduled'! 'Scheduled' to go back to do the job, to risk her life, scheduled to be a martyr to the cause. Your outrage that *as scheduled* she had been sent back into the lions' den. And, oh God, I hated the bastards. And, oh God, I admired her, her courage . . .

And there is only one thing to do when you've got no money, and that is to get a job in a hurry. And the only job that I knew about was in the Congo, fighting under Mad Mike Hoare for Moise Tshombe. I had a cousin in Salisbury, Joe Mahoney, a government lawyer, who would probably have lent me a bit of money – but I hardly knew him and how would I repay him?

So I walked. I walked out of Salisbury onto the Great North Road, heading for the Zambesi River and Northern Rhodesia. Ten miles out of town I got a lift with a commercial traveller. The man was a talker and I was in no mood for that. 'Are you feeling all right?'

'I'm fine,' I said.

'You look uptight.'

'I'm just tired.'

'Are you in some kind of trouble?'

I'm in more trouble than you can imagine. 'I've just broken up with my girlfriend, that's all.' It helped to say that much.

'Oh. Oh dear. Want to talk about it?'

Yes I wanted to talk about it. Talk and talk and cry about it. 'No, thanks. Tell me about you. How's business?'

And he sighed and told me about business. Business was terrible. All Britain's fault, for breaking up the Rhodesia Federation, for refusing Southern Rhodesia independence, for siding with the blacks. For the Wind of Change. Britain's granting independence to Northern Rhodesia and Nyasaland, so why not to us? Because we're white – wrong colour for Africa these days. NIBMAR is the rage these days – No Independence Before Majority Rule. And they know the blacks can't rule – look at the Congo. Look at Ghana. Look at Tanganyika. All Britain's fault. People leaving the country in droves. Business gone to hell, and it's all Britain's fault.

'So we must declare ourselves independent,' he said.

Declare independence unilaterally like the United States did two hundred years ago – and if Britain imposes economic sanctions they're the lesser of two evils, less evil than black rule, less evil than uncertainty which is driving business to hell and ratshit. We'll get around sanctions – Portugal and South Africa will trade with us and the world needs our tobacco and gold and chrome and beef and maize and coal.

'And what about the terrorists?' I said. 'ZAPU and ZANU?'

'We'll just have to fight,' he said. 'One white soldier is worth a hundred of them, Mad Mike Hoare has proved that in the Congo.'

In the late afternoon he dropped me at the top of the Zambezi escarpment, by the turn-off to Kariba. It was hot as hell and my nerves were stretched tight. There is a hotel at the turn-off, and I badly needed a beer but I couldn't afford it. Keep moving. I looked down on the vast mauve Zambezi Valley down there, and I knew it was unwise to walk through it alone at night unarmed, but I wanted to get the hell out of Southern Rhodesia. I shouldered my haversack and started walking, trying not to think.

The sun was beginning to set in a blaze of pink and gold, casting long mauve shadows down the vast valley, when the police Land-Rover appeared round the bend and my heart missed a beat. 'For Christ's sake,' the policeman said, 'you're asking for trouble.'

'Lions don't take people as a rule.'

'No? And what about the terrorists?'

Trouble, everybody talking about trouble. All along the Zambezi were the terrorists' crossing points when they came back from their training in Moscow, their heads stuffed with Marxism and their bags bulging with hand grenades and land mines. They aren't much trouble yet because we usually catch them before they reach the escarpment.

They aren't much trouble because they're incompetent, they leave tracks for us to follow and we usually catch up with them, and they usually give up without a fight. They're not much trouble yet because they're badly trained, and they're too weighted down with gear to move fast enough and they're not fit enough to climb up those water-less escarpments fast. They're not much trouble yet because they're piss-poor terrorists. 'But that'll change, and then they'll be big trouble.'

We came down to Chirundu, at the bridge over the mighty Zambezi. He dropped me off at the gate to the police station. Nearby was the old Chirundu Hotel.

'Thanks for the lift,' I said.

'Maybe see you in the bar for a drink later,' he said.

The hotel lights were twinkling amongst the riverine trees, and, oh God, I needed a beer, six beers, and a gutful of food, but not only could I not afford it, I did not want to be remembered if the South African police ever tried to extradite me. I walked past the twinkling hotel. And there before me was the great expanse of the Zambezi, the clear water slowly swirling and turning mauve in the sunset, the sandbanks golden, the tips of the distant northern escarpment just catching the last of the sun.

I walked out onto the bridge, just the sound of my shoes on the road, and it was unreal that I was leaving southern Africa behind for ever, that I was on the run; unreal that with this river I was leaving Patti behind forever unless a miracle happened: it felt that if I just kept walk-ing I would find that everything was all right, that she was waiting for me somewhere up north, that she had not been so foolish as to return to South Africa, the ANC had not been such bastards as to send her back to do their dirty work . . .

I walked across that unreal bridge trying to tell myself that there was hope that Patti would pull through. When I got to the other side, I looked back at the vast mauveness behind me, and she was a thousand miles over there beyond that darkening horizon, in a cell in Marshall Square, and here I was on the north side of the Zambesi . . . And suddenly it was all too real again, Marshall Square was real, Patti in that cell was real. I slumped down on the riverbank in the dusk, and I held my head and I wept.

That night I slept under a mopane tree out of sight of the bridge. I did not build a fire, because of the terrorists: it was highly unlikely that they would cross the Zambezi near the bridge but I didn't feel up to finding out. I had a quick bath in the Zambezi, rubbing off the sweat with river-sand because I had no soap in my toilet bag, then I dunked my clothes. I opened a can of bully beef I had bought in Salisbury and tore off a hunk of bread and sat staring at the moonlight on the Zambezi, hearing the grunting of hippo and the distant squeal of elephant.

That night was very bad. I could not sleep. I had made it across the Zambezi, as Rubenstein had advised; the only people who could trouble me now were the Northern Rhodesian police, but they were British and would not send me back to face trial in South Africa. That crisis, that panic, was over, and now I had time to sit still and think. To feel, to grieve, to weep, to punish myself, time to crash back on the sand and cry up at the stars . . . The first light was coming into the sky before I fell into an exhausted, anguished sleep.

And the next day was worse. I awoke with the sun on my face, my nerves crying out for more sleep. And any sense of relief had vanished: there was only the anguish – of deserting her, of leaving her to her fate. Intellectually I knew I had no options, Rubenstein had told me loud and clear. I knew I could do nothing to help her, knew I could not go back. I knew that I had to keep going – but I could not make it. I could not bring myself to leave that place, to turn my back any further on her. All I wanted to do was walk back across that bridge, back into Southern Rhodesia, and keep going, back across the Limpopo and somehow get her out of that cell and make her run with me.

I spent the whole morning under my mopane tree, just staring at the Zambezi, and my heart was breaking. A few cars passed, heading north, but I could not bring myself to go and thumb them. It was late afternoon before I trudged back to the road and started walking, heading for those northern escarpments, and Lusaka beyond, to join Mad Mike Hoare's army in the Congo.

This is it, I said: not only are you a wanted man, a stateless person, you're a hired gun.

26

No, not a hired gun. Not a soldier of fortune. Moise Tshombe was no longer the outlawed president of secessionist Katanga, he was now the lawfully elected prime minister of the entire Congo federation, invited back from exile to crush the other numerous rebels, particularly the crazed pro-Lumumba communists, supported by China. Hadn't Chou En-lai, the prime minister of China, recently said: 'An excellent revolutionary situation exists in Africa'? Hadn't Mao Tse-tung recently said: 'If we control the Congo we control Africa'? Hadn't both Russia and China just rushed arms and aid into Oriental

Province of the Congo to support that rebel butcher Gbenye and his Simbas? Hadn't the Cold War come to the Congo now the United Nations troops had left? And weren't the American CIA and Belgium supporting Tshombe with airlifts and paratroops? So wasn't I fighting in an honourable war? Ah yes, all that was true, but when I stood before the recruitment officers in that seedy Lusaka hotel commending myself to them as a trained rifleman from the South African army, I did think of myself as a hired gun and I did not feel good about it. I needed the fucking job, that's why I was there. And I didn't want to leave Africa, where *she* was.

But five days later, when I went into my first battle, and saw those Simbas, I did not feel bad anymore. Shit-scared, yes, but bad, no. Those Simbas. They were crazed with drugs, and the communists had told them that the white man's bullets would turn to water because they had the 'golden book of Lumumba' and they just kept coming at you. But it wasn't being shot that I was so shit-scared about – it was being taken alive and eaten. The Simbas used their prisoners as walking larders, cutting chunks off them, eating the flesh raw.

'You fight to your second-last bullet,' the sergeant said. 'The last one is for you. Like this.' He put the muzzle of his rifle in his mouth. 'Bang. They'll still eat you but at least you won't feel it. Now look at this map . . . '

The Catholic Mission was on the banks of a river. It had a school building, a hospital, a church, a workshop, barns and farmlands, and there were twenty-two Belgian nuns and five priests running it. Nearby was an African village of about two hundred huts. Beyond was a bridge, at both ends of which were clusters of white habitations, maybe a dozen on each side, a railway siding, a goods shed, a petrol station, a police post, a hotel.

The sergeant said: 'The Simbas are attacking the mission on the far side of the river, and they're trying to cross the bridge. The police are trying to defend it – if the Simbas take that bridge we're fucked, they'll have a clear run to Morubu.'

By the time we got there the Simbas already had the bridge and they were overrunning the houses on this side. As we came over the rise, the smoke was barrelling up on both sides of the river, Simbas swarming everywhere. '*Out!*' the sergeant yelled. '*Fight your way down to that bridge and hold it!*'

I ran flat out through the bush beside the road, jumping over logs, following the sergeant and the other guys in my squad. Blacks were fleeing from the Simbas towards us, crying, carrying babies, possessions. All the time the gunfire from the bridge and the stink of smoke.

We ran about two hundred yards, then came to the first house. The sergeant threw himself at a corner of it. The bridge was about two hundred yards ahead. People were swarming everywhere through the trees and smoke, fleeing, crying midst the gunfire. On the other side of the road were more houses, more chaos. The sergeant rasped: *'Go! Get to that bridge!'*

I ran and hurled myself against the wall of the river-front house, gasping. Across the road I saw a man drag a white woman out of a house by her hair and hurl her on the ground. He had a gun in one hand and with the other he ripped open his fly. I stared, heart pounding. I raised my rifle, sick in my guts: *I was about to shoot a human being.* The woman tried to get up, and he kicked her. His face was mad. He dropped his gun and jumped on top of her. I had his head in my sights. I fired. He sprawled sideways. I stared, and the woman scrambled up, screaming in French, her eyes wild, her hair awry. She reeled back into the house.

I closed my eyes. I had just killed my first Simba. And I felt the vomit coming up my throat. There was a slap on my shoulder and the sergeant was rasping: *'I said attack the fucking bridge!'* I crouched behind the garden wall, mouth dry, heart pounding midst the cacophony of gunfire, and attacked the fucking bridge.

The Simbas were charging across it, pangas on high, eyes wild. Some had blood on their mouths. I aimed desperately into their midst and fired. My rifle juddered and all I saw was wild men crashing and sprawling, but more were barrelling over behind them. Then some bastards were firing at me from the direction of the corner store and I swung my gun and fired blindly until my ammunition clip was empty. I fumbled for a new one, rammed it in, then swung the gun back on the bridge. Simbas were pouring across it, trampling over their dead, eyes rolling wildly, running straight into the gunfire, drunk on bloodlust and witchcraft and belief that the bullets would turn to water, all around me was gunfire and they were falling like flies, but still they kept coming. I pulled the trigger and there was nothing in the world but the clatter of the guns and the stink of cordite and sprawling black bodies.

Then suddenly there were no more Simbas running onto the bridge on the far side, and the sergeant yelled *'Come on!'* He leapt over the wall and ran. He skidded to a stop behind the parapet at the start of the bridge. We all did the same. It was very crowded and I was out in the cold. Down the road, on this side of the river, B and C squads were working the houses, cleaning up Simbas. On the far bank there was smoke and flames, and downriver at the mission there was gunfire.

The sergeant spoke into his walkie-talkie radio then he yelled at us: *'Across the bridge! When we get to the other side shoot the shit out of everybody and fight your way downriver to the mission!'*

We ran flat out across the bridge, doubled up, leaping over bodies, trampling on them, trying to dodge behind the girders, trying not to trip. B and C squads behind us were blasting the far bank, giving us cover. The sergeant in front, blasting from the hip as he ran, half a dozen guys behind him, then me, another five behind me. We ran and leapt and ran and ran, the longest hundred yards in the world, every instant expecting a bullet through the chest. Then the end of the bridge was there, the flaming houses beyond. The sergeant burst off the bridge and raced for the hotel and flung himself against the wall. I raced after him. He peered into the bar. It was a shambles, the shelves looted, windows and stools smashed, two white bodies on the floor, blood everywhere. Gunfire was coming from the railway siding, screams were coming from the backyard. *'Come on!'* The sergeant burst into the bar and ran at the back windows.

There were bodies everywhere, black and white. Heads blasted open, chests pulverised. A white woman was sprawled, her dress over her head, her vagina and breasts mutilated, muddy blood all around her. A white boy lay on his belly, his back slashed open, his liver cut out.

The sergeant shouted out orders: *'We sweep in a line downriver towards the mission. Then regroup and recce before we go in. Go!'*

He plunged out of the back door, and ran for the black village beyond. We ran through the village, dodging from hut to hut. Many huts were on fire. Bodies and blood everywhere, shot, butchered, hacked. All the survivors had fled to the mission. There were many dead babies. I ran from hut to hut, peered, then ran to the next. I kept the sergeant in sight – Harry knew what he was doing. Nobody was firing. We ran and ran, stopping and starting. The gunfire from the mission was getting closer, only about four hundred yards ahead now.

The sergeant was a hundred yards ahead. I couldn't see the others. I ran after him, trying to keep in the cover of the huts. The mission was only three hundred yards ahead now, the gunfire over there getting louder. Then ahead was a pole fence, a cattle kraal. The sergeant was running for it, crouched double. I could hear shouting and singing above the distant gunfire. The sergeant was beckoning. I stumbled to a crouch beside him. The other guys were spread along the kraal. The sergeant panted: *'About thirty yards ahead – about ten of the bastards. You, you and you – keep us covered. The rest come with me.'*

We crept through the undergrowth, spread out. I kept myself next to the sergeant. I could hear the bastards singing and ululating above the rattle of gunfire from the mission. I crept and crouched and crept, desperately trying to peer ahead through the foliage. Then I saw the bastards.

There were about a dozen, clutching bottles, staggering about, laughing: on the ground in the midst of them was a writhing mass. It was a black man grinding on top of someone. Then I saw a flash of white leg kicking and I realised it was a white woman, wearing a nun's habit. Her face was contorted, her cries drowned by the laughter. Now the man was clambering up off her, his penis hanging out of his trousers, and the woman tried to get to her knees and a Simba kicked her and she sprawled again. Another Simba was collapsing on top of her. The sergeant was crawling over to me: *'Everybody except the one raping the nun – leave him to me.'*

I nodded desperately, and crawled over to Potgieter to repeat the instructions. I desperately checked my magazine clip. Then the sergeant scrambled up onto one knee, and he fired. And I desperately scrambled up, and there was nothing in the world but the clatter of gunfire and the black bodies jerking and contorting and sprawling. I fired on automatic, my rifle sweeping, and all I saw was Simbas lurching and crashing, then the sergeant was running down the slope, and I ran after him. The man raping the nun was still humping away on top of her, he hadn't noticed a thing. The nun was weakly writhing, beating his back with her fists, her head tossing from side to side – she hadn't heard the massacre either. The sergeant swung his boot with all his might. It connected with the man's cheek, and he sprawled sideways. The nun continued to writhe, eyes fiercely closed, her fists flailing. The sergeant bounded and kicked the Simba again. The nun still fought, her legs kicking wildly. Her stomach and thighs were smeared with blood, blood on her battered face. I crouched and put my hand on her head. *'It's all right,'* and she opened her mouth wide and sank her teeth into my wrist. I yelled and she clung on, biting and shaking her head like a dog. The Simba was clambering up and the sergeant kicked him again, and he sprawled again. The nun clambered to her feet, still biting my wrist wildly, then she tried to run. She lurched away wildly, stumbling towards the mission. The Simba was clambering up, his eyes wild, and the sergeant shot him in the guts. There was a sudden clatter of guns, and I looked around wildly and saw Potgieter crash and the sergeant reeling, clutching his arm. I could not see the gunman but I swung my rifle in an arc and blasted the bushes, and I ran.

I blundered through the dense bush, doubled up, rasping. The sergeant came crashing through the foliage, gasping, clutching his arm. *'There must be some Simbas coming down from the road. Where's the nun?'*

'She ran this way.'

I desperately followed the sergeant through the bush. The smoke from the mission was wafting thickly. Then suddenly there was a corn field; beyond the mission. The nun had blundered a path through the corn. We ran through the field for fifty yards, then ahead was the mission. I crouched beside the sergeant, my heart hammering. Across open ground was a row of buildings, their thatch roofs already burned out, rafters smoking. On the far side was a large church, with a galvanized iron roof. The sergeant began crouching through the corn towards the riverbank.

We ran along a path by the river, ducking under branches. We could not see the mission buildings from down here but the gunfire was louder. We ran for about two hundred yards, then ahead was a small boathouse. But there was no boat. The sergeant scrambled up the bank and peered over the top.

A hundred yards ahead was a quadrangle of buildings, the church forming one side, numerous smaller buildings forming the other three. Some had iron roofs. The spaces between the buildings were barricaded with furniture and vehicles and barrels. A hundred black bodies were sprawled across the lawns and flowerbeds. In the church doorway were sandbags. From behind all the barricades poked guns. But all the gunfire was coming from the far end of the quadrangle. The sergeant pulled out a white handkerchief, grabbed his walkie-talkie and rasped into it in French. Then he waved the white handkerchief. *'Come!'*

We ran flat out across the garden for the church door, doubled up, leaping over bodies; then there was a burst of gunfire and I threw myself flat, but the sergeant kept running. He ran flat out for the doorway, leapt, and disappeared beyond. I tried to scramble on my elbows and knees, desperately shoving my gun in front of me, trying to keep behind the cover of bodies. I crawled and wriggled flat out, the bullets flying all about, then I took a terrified breath and scrambled up and I raced at the church door gabbling, *Please God! Please God! Please God!* I went flying through the air, like a man throwing himself into a river, and I hit the cement floor beyond.

The sun was going down. The quadrangle was a shambles of black bodies, lying, sitting, blood everywhere. Women, men, children, babies, a dozen nuns hurrying amongst them, ministering, consoling. Spasmodic gunfire was mostly coming from the front of the quadrangle. The sergeant consulted urgently with the chief gendarme in French, then we followed him around the defences, peering through the barricades. The mission's farmlands gave us a clear field of fire for a hundred yards, up to the road where the thick bush began. The ground was littered with dead Simbas. All the scattered outbuildings were burnt out.

The gendarme said: 'They're drunk on the hotel's booze and on muti – yesterday they caught a party of nuns about five miles away and ate them for muti, they've been attacking like zombies, running straight into the gunfire. But there're plenty more where they came from. They're regrouping in the forest now, doing their mumbo-jumbo.'

'What weapons have they got?'

'Stolen automatic weapons, home-made guns, blow-pipes, spears, axes – the usual. They've also got two mortars but haven't scored a hit yet.'

'Have we got any boats?' I asked hopefully.

'No, the mission's boat was stolen, the police launch is broken down.'

Harry said to me: 'Stay at this window, shoot the shit out of anything that moves.'

He went off with the gendarme to inspect the rest of the defences. I propped myself against the corner of the window, peered out, gun up: nothing moved. Singing came from the forest beyond the road, smoke from the outbuildings. And the buzzing of flies on the corpses. *Oh Jesus* . . . We were supposed to rescue these guys and now we were locked in with them, zombies on three sides and crocodiles on the fourth.

Five minutes later Harry came back. 'We hold 'em off till nightfall. B squad holds the bridge and C is going to hold the cornfield, cleaning out any Simbas in the way. When darkness comes we all break out along the riverbank, back to the bridge – '

Just then there was a thud from the forest, a thin trail of smoke arced through the sky towards us. Harry roared: '*Down!*' There was a shocking explosion in the quadrangle as the mortar shell hit and the shrapnel flew midst the screams and scrambling; then there was another thud, another trail of smoke rose up, and there was another terrible explosion; then out of the forest came the Simbas.

They erupted out of the forest a hundred yards away, a great black mass suddenly barrelling across the road, eyes wild, faces contorted, yelling, ululating. They came swarming across the fields, hundreds of them, guns stuttering and spears and axes on high, trampling over the corpses, and Harry yelled '*Hold your fire!*' I crouched at my window, heart pounding, and on they came in a great black ragged yelling line, and now I could see the whites of their rolling eyes, the rolling eyes of madmen, and now I could see the blood on their faces from their feasting – and the gendarme yelled: '*Fire*!' And there was nothing in the world but the da da da da coming from everywhere, the stink of cordite and the juddering of the butt against my shoulder, black bodies sprawling, trampled underfoot, the screaming black mass bulldozing on at us. All I knew was my terrified determination to kill the bastards before they hit the wall and killed me. I fired and fired and reloaded and fired, now firing point blank into the mass of black flesh, blood and guts and weapons flying, firing right into their rolling eyes, the rifle juddering. Then suddenly I could see the forest again – and the whole lot of them were gone, sprawled on the blood-stained ground, and the clatter of guns died down. And for the second time that day I felt the vomit rising in my throat and I retched. Then there was another thud, another trail of smoke rising up, and there was an explosion in the next room and the world shook, and the next mass of black flesh came erupting out of the dark forest.

They came from all sides in the dusk, screaming, firing, hurling, mobbing the barricades, scrambling through the windows, smashing down the doors. I desperately retreated across the quadrangle, firing wildly from the hip, lurching over bodies, making for the church's side-door, following the fleeing nuns and gendarmes. I lurched through it backwards, then ran down the aisle towards the main door as the last survivors scrambled over the corn bags. I leapt over them. The nuns were running for the riverbank, Harry covering their retreat. I looked back and saw the Simbas running down the aisle. I ran for the bank and leapt down into the bushes. The nuns were fleeing down the riverine path fifty yards ahead. I swung my gun on the church door and fired wildly, then I lost my footing and fell backwards. I went crashing down the bank and sprawled on the path. I scrambled up wildly and started to run. Simbas were running along the top of the bank to overtake the nuns. There was crashing of foliage behind me and all I saw was a dozen Simbas leaping down onto the path, and I gargled in horror and swung my gun on them blindly as I tried to run backwards, my gun clattering in a stink of cordite, yelling Simbas jerking, reeling, sprawling in the half darkness – then suddenly my gunfire stopped. I wrenched wildly on the trigger before I realized my magazine was empty. I groped desperately for another one and my pocket was empty – and my heart lurched and I turned and ran flat out down the path, terrified. I looked frantically over my shoulder, and I sprawled. I scrambled up and wildly groped for my last personal bullet and rammed it into the breach as I fled.

I ran and I ran, stumbling, fleeing for my life. I ran through the dark riverine trees after the nuns, then there was a crashing in the bushes ahead and Simbas burst down the bank, axes, pangas, spears on high. I skidded to a heart-pounding halt, looked wildly behind me, and thundering along the path fifty yards away were more Simbas, and I cried in horror and scrambled up the bank, burst out into the open, and there were Simbas everywhere. Simbas storming the mission, Simbas running towards the bridge, and I gargled in horror and threw myself flat. I looked desperately behind me – I had about three seconds to decide whether to blow my own head off as Harry had said or be eaten alive. I desperately faced down the bank, and the first Simba gave a bloodcurdling scream and came charging up the slope at me, panga on high, bushes crashing, more yelling Simbas behind him, and I roared in terror and I fired my last shot into his face. And I gave another terrified roar and I grabbed the muzzle and I swung the gun with all my might and there was the thud of wood on bone, and I hurled myself down the bank. I plunged through the foliage trying to swing my rifle, crashing over bushes, running for my life from the screaming horde. I ran and leapt and stumbled down the bank, branches tearing at me, and there was the river and I cried: *Please God*, and I dived.

I dived through the reeds, terrified, gabbling prayers, and I hit the water. I desperately kicked and kicked, trying to get away under the water. I swam and desperately swam, trying to get as far as possible from those terrifying Simbas, kicking and kicking with all my desperate might, then I could hold my breath no more and I broke surface and gasped and plunged under again – and my boots were dragging my feet down and I gargled in furious terror and ripped at the laces, wrenched and got one boot off, desperately gasped another lungful of air and plunged under again and wrenched the other boot off. I swam and swam, getting the hell away from the bank. Then I came up for air again and swam flat out on the surface, arms and feet thrashing. And then, when I was lost in the darkness, came the dread of the crocodiles.

And, oh God, I was frightened. I desperately wanted to swim flat out, making as much disturbance as possible in the hope of intimidating the crocodiles, but the decision was made for me by the exhaustion grabbing at my guts and legs and heart. I slowed to a breast-stroke. I swam and I swam, spluttering, sobbing, terrified witless, every moment expecting the dreadful clamp of mighty jaws and the dreadful thrash of the scaly beast as it dragged me down to the muddy depths to drown me. The opposite bank was a hundred yards ahead, and I could see the silhouette of the bridge half a mile upriver: *please God, look after me for only one hundred yards*. I swam and I swam, and, oh God, that bank did not get any closer – and suddenly there was a dreadful bump against me, and I cried out in horror. I had hit a body. I tried to thrash away from it, and I hit another one. I was in the middle of a clutch of floating dead Simbas, wherever I tried to thrash I hit another mass of soggy flesh. I cried out and plunged my head under water and swam and swam again, trying to get the hell away from those dreadful corpses; then I came up for air and I banged into another one and I dived again. I broke surface, gasping, horrified, then there was a thrashing in front of me and my hand hit something hard and I realized in terror that I'd hit a crocodile. And I gargled in horror and lunged sideways and I saw a pair of great jaws snap down on a body and wrench it underwater. I strangled a scream and plunged the other way and I kicked with all my might. I swam and swam, my arms flailing the water, thrashing my way out of that mass of flesh and beasts, and my hand hit another solid back and I screamed into the water and just kept thrashing. Head down, arms flailing, feet kicking, horrified, terrified, screaming prayers to the Lord. I swam and thrashed and flailed and swam, sobbing, gasping. Suddenly there were no more bodies. The bank was thirty yards away. I gasped a big lungful of air and screwed up all my strength for one last dash. I thrashed and thrashed with the last of my might, crying, 'Please God,' and now the bank was ten yards off, now seven, now six, now five – *Please God, not one on the bank* – and I thrashed and I thrashed, and my hand hit the reeds. I grabbed them and heaved with all my might and I floundered up onto the soggy bank, slipping, sliding, my legs buckling, gasping tears of joy. I kept going, getting away from that dreadful bank, staggering and reeling into the bush, then I crashed onto my side. I rolled over onto my back, sobbing my thanks up to the Lord.

A thousand yards upriver B and C squads were holding the bridge.

I had eleven months and twenty-five days to go on my contract.

27

Nobody seemed to know which way the war was going, except that it was chaos. Sometimes a foreign correspondent showed up and gave us some news: a quarter of the Congo was overrun by Simbas and other rebels. The United States was sending in troops again, now that L.B. Johnson had taken over the presidency after Kennedy's assassination. Sometimes we got some international news on somebody's portable radio. I heard that the Rivonia Trial had started in Johannesburg, of the people arrested at Lilliesleaf Farm, plus Nelson Mandela, all charged with treason, but there was no news of Patti Gandhi. I asked every foreign correspondent we encountered but none of them knew anything about her case, though most of them had heard of her. I wrote letters to my sister, to Splinter Woodcock, and to my father, which I tried to send back to Leopoldville for posting, but I never got any reply: I didn't know if they ever got out of the Congo. None of the telephones we came across ever worked. About once a month we got back to Pierreville for a couple of days, where our barracks were supposed to be, and the Bar Pigalle was where you sometimes met foreign correspondents, but none of them knew anything about Patti Gandhi's case.

Then one night the man from the *Telegraph* said: 'She's that beautiful Indian woman who made such a stink over the Miss South Africa contest?'

'*Right.*'

'No, she hasn't been tried yet, they're holding her on the ninety-day law.'

Hope . . . 'Can you find out?'

'When I get back to Leopoldville – *if* I get back – I can ask our man in Jo'burg, but he won't know anything if she's on ninety days. Where do I contact you?'

'Right here, Bar Pigalle, Luis looks after any mail. Listen, will you post some letters for me?'

Another time I met the man from the *Guardian*. 'You saw all the accused in the Rivonia Trial dock? You sure Patti Gandhi wasn't one of them?'

'Quite sure.'

I sighed, thanking God. 'Can you find out what's happening to her when you go back? And wire me here, Bar Pigalle.'

'I'll try, but the wires are always down. If it's not the Simbas it's the fucking elephants.'

Another time I met the guy from *The Times*, who had been at the opening day of the Rivonia Trial. 'What was it like?'

The *Times* man described the crowds outside the big old Supreme Court, blocking the street, the public gallery packed with black faces, the press-tables with journalists from around the world to report the trial of the State versus Nelson Mandela and Others. At half past nine the yellow prison truck arriving, carrying the accused, the roar going up and the people surging. '*Amandla!*' they roared, clenched fists aloft. '*Amandla!' Power!*, and back through the mesh of the Prison truck came the cry '*Amandla!*' He described the truck grinding through the avenue of policemen holding back the people, disappearing behind the courthouse. The accused coming up the stairs into the big dock of the court, the gallery rising to its feet and the clenched fists shooting up, '*Amandla!*' rising up again, Nelson Mandela and his co-accused raising their fists and crying back '*Amandla!*' The loud rap on the oaken door, the Honourable Mr Justice de Wet entering in his scarlet robes, the hushed silence.

Mahoney said: 'Will you post some letters for me from London? And try to find out about Patti Gandhi, and write to me here at Bar Pigalle?'

'Certainly, old chap,' the *Times* man said. 'But when are you going back into the bush?'

'I don't know. This *is* the fucking bush.'

'But when are you going back to the front again?'

'This *is* the fucking front; can't you hear the gunfire?'

'But where are you going from here?'

'I go where I'm sent. When are you going back to London?'

'I don't know, old man. Like you, I go where I'm sent. *When* I can get some instructions from head office. Do you think I can get a ride to the front with you chaps?'

'Sure, ask my sergeant over there, Harry. He's a good guy.'

'Jolly good,' said the man from *The Times*. 'So, shall we have a bit of fun in Bar Pigalle? Tomorrow we may be dead . . . '

Yes, it was fun in the Bar Pigalle. Pierreville was a shambles, no electricity, no telephone, no water, no post office, sometimes no beer, but the old Hotel Pierre and its Bar Pigalle had its own generator, its own rain-water tanks, it even had a swimming pool, and if there was no beer Luis always had a stock of native beer which his whores brewed up in forty-four-gallon drums in the backyard, which had the kick of a mule. When you came back from the bush you went straight to Bar Pigalle and had a shower and if you bought one of the whores for the whole night you only had to pay half price for an air-conditioned room. The bar had a horseshoe counter and at about two a.m. the whores who had not been spoken for all jumped into the swimming pool and swam around naked for a bit to show themselves, then they all got up onto the bar to dance to the jukebox, while Luis tried to auction them off at knock-down prices. If you could wait that long, and drink that long, it was worth waiting for the auction because you could get two for the price of one, and sometimes even three if the bidding was slack, and you were allowed to feel them before deciding on your bid. '*And now we come to Imelda,*' Luis would shout in a mixture of French and English, '*who takes it up the arse as well as other ways – show 'em, Imelda –* '

223

Imelda's trick was two candles, both lit, one in her pussy, the other up her arse as she did the Charleston without burning herself. She was very pretty. Mini, who was Vietnamese, could inhale a cigarette through her pussy and blow perfect smoke rings, the most impressive performance of all, but she was the plainest. Almost as impressive was Suzie, a big Congolese, who, from a prone position, could eject a banana from her vagina and catch it in her hand behind her head.

'Wonderful muscular control! Pure bliss for the bidder!'

Most agreed that Suzie's muscular control was very good news, but she ate garlic which made the rest of her difficult work. Another of Luis's party tricks, at about two a.m., if the going was slow, was oil wrestling: a large foam-rubber mattress was placed on the bar's floor, covered with a sheet of plastic, which was then soaked in vegetable oil. You could bet on which whore would triumph in the wrestling match, and the punters could grease them up in their corners before they got stuck into each other in a mass of thrashing arms, tits and arses whilst the boys cheered and placed more bets: and then the punters could front up and wrestle the winners. That usually sold the remaining whores. Luis was a good showman, and he was a kind man who had our interests, and his own, constantly in mind.

The other thing that Luis was good about was the mail. Luis collected it each day from the remnants of the post office, and kept it in a fruit box until you came back from the bush. I never got any letters, not even from all the foreign correspondents who promised to write about Patti, nor had I ever been able to get a telephone connection to her lawyer, Rubenstein, nor to my father, until the fifth month of my contract. I had come out of the bush and gone straight to Bar Pigalle for some serious Rest and Recreation. The leftover girls were on the bar doing their numbers; I made my bid and off to bed upstairs we went. The air-conditioning was like silk on my skin, Imelda turned on the shower while Suzie began to undress me – then came a knock on the door. And there was Luis with my first ever letter.

I stared at it. It was the handwriting I had so often copied from my classroom's blackboard. It was Lisa Rousseau's.

I ripped it open and slumped down on the bed.

> *My dear Luke*
> *Perhaps this will never find you – your sister tells me she has received one letter from you but no replies to her numerous letters. She begs you to write: she sends her best love. I have also taken my courage, as the Scarlet Woman, in both hands and telephoned your dear father: he is frantic to hear from you – vide infra. As for*

myself, I am now unbanned, happily married, and teaching at the University of the Witwatersrand. I often think of those wonderful family journals of yours, and I sincerely hope that you are making your own additions, chronicling the harsh, dramatic times we live in. However, it is about your friend, Patti Gandhi, that I am writing.

Her trial has attracted a great deal of publicity. She really is a beautiful young woman. Your name has come up frequently during the trial, as her alleged paramour and accomplice – both of which details she stoutly denies. I am terribly sad to tell you that yesterday she was convicted of importation of explosives, which carries the mandatory death sentence, but the wonderful news is that she was not so sentenced. When she was asked whether there was any reason why such sentence should not be passed, her counsel announced that she was 'with child of a quick child'. As she cannot be executed until after she's given birth, the judge is empowered to pass another sentence. This he mercifully did. But I'm afraid it was life imprisonment. Her trial, despite the on-going Rivonia Trial of Nelson Mandela et al, has attracted a great deal of media attention. It was a moment of high drama in the courtroom and there was hardly a dry eye. As she was led out of the dock she gave the black power salute and shouted Amandla!

My dear Luke, I earnestly warn you not to return to this country. Not only is a warrant doubtless out for your arrest, there is nothing that you can do to help her now, nor, her lawyer assures me, is there anything you could have done – indeed your presence, either as a defence witness or in the dock beside her, could only have harmed her case. It has happened, Luke; it is irreversible. You can only pray for her sanity and strength. You should not write to her. I'm afraid that her counsel told me that in her case life imprisonment means life, as long as this government is in power.

Yesterday, I again telephoned your dear father in Umtata and discussed this with him: he agrees – and he is desperate to contact you to confirm this advice. Like your sister, he has written often, but received no reply. Please do your best to get through to him. Your mother is well, if very worried about her son.

There remains the question of Patti's child. She refused to tell the court who the father is – or, rather, she blandly told the court she didn't know. Doubtless this was to protect you. As you are my 'special' friend, for whom I have high regard, I take the liberty of suggesting you lay no claim to the child, even if you are convinced it is yours. I say this for the child's sake, and for Patti's. You are not a suitable candidate for parenthood, Luke. Much better that it be brought up by Patti's close-knit Indian family. You must now live your life to the full – and so must the child. Got that, my friend?

In closing, I offer another bit of advice, dearest Luke: get out of Africa altogether. And get out of journalism. It has served you well – you have a gift for it – I have followed your pieces in Drum *with pleasure – but I am sure you have a far, far greater gift for the larger intellectual life of an historian. Please do not waste such talent. I want, dear friend, to watch your progress with the pride of a teacher who says: 'I taught him first.' Above all, you must keep up those family journals. Now you are fighting in the Congo, as your ancestors did at the Battle of Blood River, and in the Boer War and in the 1914 Rebellion, and as your own father did in World War II – and in Parliament. Okay, you are fighting a just war, you probably joined Mad Mike Hoare's army in a time of desperation, and I admire your courage – but I beg you to get out when your contract is finished, to pursue your promising life . . .*

I close on those dots. I remain your good friend who thanks you for many happy memories, who is full of fervent hope for your future.

> *Love*
> *Lisa*

The rest is confused in my memory. I remember I wanted to bellow my anguish to the skies: *Her whole life in prison . . . And, my child . . . I had a child – Patti's child. And thank God that my child saved Patti from the hangman's noose! But what the hell can I do about all this?* I remember Imelda saying, 'Hey, *cheri*, we fuck now?', I remember her white nakedness beside Suzie's big black nakedness, I remember throwing a fistful of francs on the bed, I remember clattering down the staircase, to look for Luis, frantically beating on his door.

'Luis, I've got to try the telephone!'

And, miracles of miracles, the telephone finally worked. Luis re-opened the bar for me. I sat in the dark drinking whisky, desperately trying again and again to get through to Lusaka to tell the operator to get me through to Johannesburg. By dawn I was very drunk and had figured out what I was going to do: I was going to instruct attorneys to apply for custody of my child, and if that didn't fucking work I was going to cross the border back into South Africa by hook or by crook and grab my child and run for it. Run like hell back across the border, leave it somewhere safe then get together a bunch of the boys and make a plan to break Patti out of that fucking prison – there were guys in Mike Hoare's outfit who would think that was all in a day's fucking work!

The sun was coming up when the telephone suddenly rang and I found I was speaking to Arnie Rubenstein, the lawyer. He listened in stony silence to how I was going hire the best fucking lawyers in Johannesburg to get hold of my child, then he said: 'First of all, Mr Mahoney, disabuse your mind of the notion that the child is yours. *Listen to me!* You can rant and rave but it will avail you nothing against Patti Gandhi's simple affidavit that you are *not* the father, because she is presumed in law to know who the father is – '

'*But I am the fucking father!*'

'Secondly, even if she admitted you are the father – which she does not – no South African court would give the custody of a half-Indian child to a white person – '

'*But I won't be living in South Africa – *'

'And thirdly, I can assure you that no South African court – indeed no court in the world – would give custody of a new-born child to a young bachelor with your track record of being a soldier of fortune, a sometime journalist, and a fugitive from the law of the land – such as it is.'

'*I'll be employed! I'll get a proper job when my contract's over – *'

'Not in South Africa: don't dream of coming back here.'

'*In Rhodesia! Or Swaziland, or Botswana!*'

'Rhodesia and Swaziland and Botswana are too close to South Africa for comfort in your situation – the South African police can cross the border with impunity to get somebody they want.'

'*Then I'll be a fucking lawyer in England!*'

Rubenstein sighed. 'It doesn't matter if you become the Lord Chief Justice – she says the child isn't *yours*! Mr Mahoney, I earnestly advise you, in the interests of both my client and yourself, not to waste your money, or Patti's, on hopeless legal actions. And now, if you'll excuse me, I must have my bath – '

'*Mr Rubenstein!*' My eyes filled with desperate tears. '*You're not going to have your fucking bath! I'm in the fucking Congo and it's taken me five fucking months to get hold of you! You're going to stand right there and listen to me, in the name of pity!*'

There was a pause. 'Very well, I'm listening.'

I choked back the tears. I whispered: 'Is there any hope?'

'On appeal? In my view, none. The evidence against her is strong. As regards the paternity of her child, no hope, Mr Mahoney. So I advise you to forget it. And don't under any circumstances take it into your head to return to South Africa. And now if you'll excuse me – '

'*Mr Rubenstein?*' The tears were running down my face. '*Please tell her I love her.*'

There was a pause. 'I doubt it's in my client's interests to be thus informed, but if I consider it appropriate I'll pass that on when next I visit her – '

I roared, *'You'll fucking thus inform her! And I'll see you in court!'*

I slammed down the phone and I held my head and wept. Then I snatched up the phone again and tried to reach my father but the line was dead again. I filled my lungs and bellowed to the dawn: *'Oh, you stupid bitch!'*

The rest was more confused. I had drunk a whole bottle of Luis's whisky when the boys and girls came into the Pigalle at breakfast time, all hungover and horrible. I was fighting drunk and all I wanted to do was cry and brawl. I remember telling Pottie Potgieter and the others that I had this problem, this job they had to help me with, how we had to make a plan to hit Diepkloof Prison and break my pregnant woman out, blast our way in and blast our way out and run like hell for the getaway cars and drive like hell to this place where we would have a helicopter standing by and then fly like hell for Swaziland. All we needed was the helicopter and we could steal one from the Congo, and we needed a map of Diepkloof and the surrounding roads, we could hire the getaway cars from Avis, and a few more guys to throw up road-blocks on our escape route to the helicopter. *Shit, yes it could be done*, and Steve just happened to have a Johannesburg road map, and Pete had done time in Diepkloof so knew the layout of the fucking joint and Mike knew a farm just outside Johannesburg where we could land the helicopter, and Ivan was our demolition expert who could plant the plastic explosives at the right places to blast our way into the fucking joint, and one way or another, mostly the other, the whole fucking plan was coming together and we were all full of fight – and then a mortar exploded in the street, and the Pigalle's windows shattered, and the Simbas were hitting Pierreville.

28

The day my contract ended I was flown back to my recruitment point, Lusaka in Northern Rhodesia, where telephones still worked; I got through to my parents and they were overjoyed that I was out alive, my mother sobbing. Then my father said uncomfortably: 'Did you get my letter about Patti Gandhi, son?'

'No!' My heart leapt.

'I'm terribly sorry to have to tell you, but her child died. I wrote as soon as Mr Gandhi told me.' He went on hastily: 'But I beg you to remember, son, that Patti denies the child is yours – I phoned her lawyer and he confirmed that she still sticks to that, I beg you to bear that in mind.'

My ears were ringing.

'Did you hear that, son?'

'Yes.'

My father's voice was thick. 'Son – *please* put all that behind you now. *Finish* that law degree. Please catch the first plane to England, even tomorrow – don't *dream* of coming back here, there's nothing you can do, and you'll be arrested at the border. I'll pay your airfare.'

From a distance, I heard myself say: 'I've got a year's pay; I've got plenty of money.'

'Just get to England, son. I've been in touch with a good lawyer over there who thinks he can get you a British passport because your mother's father was born in England. He's standing by to help you with the immigration authorities the moment you land; I'll give you his number. Just get to England immediately . . . Son?'

'What was it? The child.'

'A girl. The cause of death was meningitis. Mr Gandhi says the doctors did everything.'

I sobbed. 'And . . . how did Patti take it?'

'Rubenstein told me she took it with great fortitude, he says she's handling prison life with tremendous courage, Luke. So I beg you to put all that behind you now. And just get out of Africa. Luke?' His voice caught.

'Father?' I sobbed.

He sobbed: 'I just want to hold you . . . and so does your mother . . .'

And the emotion welled up, and up it burst, the grief.

I'd got a passport off a Belgian corpse about my age. Lennie, who'd done time in the States for forgery, had changed the details. The motor-bike I bought second-hand in Lusaka.

A motorbike is one of the best ways to go when you're on the run from yourself, and your grief. A plane does not offer the same catharsis: on a plane you're strapped into a kind of time capsule, you get on and twenty-four hours later you land up in some strange, cold country, and you don't know where to go from here and all your troubles are still there, fresh and painful, you've had no time to adjust, to physically sweat them out. But you don't have much time to think about your grief when you're astride this bloody great machine, struggling to hold the bloody thing down on the rough highways and byways of the real big bad world, bouncing, jolting, swerving, with the sun and wind battering you; most of the time all you can think about is missing potholes and avoiding the treacherous bits, and all the time the bush is juddering by; you don't have much time to think about your grief on your motorbike. And when you stop for the night to camp you are so relieved to be off that fucking machine, and it is so nice for your body to stop vibrating and the roaring to go out of your ears that all you want to do is collapse. You unpack your saddlebag and build your fire and open your bottle of brandy, and you're so fucked up by the last twelve hours that you do not have the energy to think about much more than eating something and zonking out, which is better than sitting in some miserable London bedsitter grieving about her. When you ride a motorbike you are battling your body forward, forcing yourself to move, *move* to get on, get away, leave the past behind, and every shuddering, juddering minute is taking you further and further away from the horror that lies behind.

I rode through Northern Rhodesia, which was soon to become Zambia, onto the Great North Road towards Tanzania. I rode and I rode, bouncing over the corrugations, grimly riding, getting the hell away from South Africa. On the third day I got near the border post of Tunduma. I had to presume that the immigration authorities of all neighbouring countries would have been alerted to the fact that if a Luke Mahoney showed up he was using a forged passport. I stopped two miles before the border and wheeled my bike off into the bush. I parked it against a tree and began to plod towards the border, to scout out the land.

The sun was getting low when I got back. I had met no natives. The border post would be closing for the night soon. I ate a can of bully beef, then I lay back on the ground and stared up at the sky and tried not to think about leaving my part of Africa. And I couldn't make it, all I wanted to do was turn my bike around and ride, *ride* back, to *her*. I made myself think of what my father had said: '*Don't dream of coming back, son – just get to England and finish that law degree.*' I screwed up my eyes and made myself think of that prison cell she was in, those bars and those walls, tried to make myself accept there was nothing to go back to, nothing I could do to help her. I forced myself to think of Krombrink waiting for me, that dock in the Supreme Court. But those things didn't seem real: I had just come out of a war and now I wanted to go home, to my woman, and my child was dead, and it felt that if I just turned the bike around everything would be waiting for me.

When darkness fell I heaved myself up. I loaded my saddlebags, took a bearing on the stars, and began to wheel my heavy bike through the bush towards Tanzania, and my heart was breaking.

PART V

1965–1976

RHODESIA DECLARES INDEPENDENCE

VERWOERD MURDERED IN PARLIAMENT

NKRUMAH OVERTHROWN IN GHANA

PORTUGAL'S COLONIAL WARS START IN
MOZAMBIQUE AND ANGOLA

BLACK CONSCIOUSNESS MOVEMENT
APPEARS IN SOUTH AFRICA

IDI AMIN SEIZES POWER IN UGANDA

RHODESIA WAR STARTS

ZULUS FORM INKATHA –
INTERNAL WING OF ANC

RIGHT-WING AFRIKANERS FORM AWB

RIOTS IN SOWETO

29

In London I got a job as a reporter on the *Globe*. The year I got my LLB degree the editor made me a 'fireman'.

'Listen, son,' my father cried on the telephone, 'congratulations on your degree, it was a stout effort doing it part-time – now chuck in this newspaper lark, get called to the English bar and get a job as a public prosecutor somewhere, to get some experience.'

'Father,' I said, 'I'm not going to be a lawyer. If I stick with the *Globe* as a fireman, I have the chance of becoming a foreign correspondent in a few years and they'll probably send me out to Africa where I want to be – '

'Don't,' my father pleaded, '*dream* of returning to *South* Africa!'

'Dad, have you any news of Patti Gandhi?'

'No, Luke,' my father sighed. 'Please, you must forget about her, son. Get yourself a nice English girl. Better still, get a dozen, you're far too young to get married. And, if you don't mind my saying so, you have a knack of falling for the wrong ones. Okay – I'm sorry I said that – '

'How's my sister?' I said.

'I said I'm sorry, Luke. Okay? Jill's fine. Spoke to her last week, sends her love. Her marriage seems fine, she's still head over heels in love with long-haired Leonard. . . Here's your mother – '

'Hullo darling!' my mother cried. 'Congratulations! But what on earth is a *"fireman"* . . . ?'

A fireman is a young journalist who is sent by his editor at a moment's notice to cover a 'fire', a sudden crisis like a rebellion in some faraway land where the newspaper has not got a stringer. Becoming a fireman is the first step to becoming a foreign correspondent. There is a lot of luck in being sent to your first fire. First you must have impressed the boss that you're a good scribe: I was lucky because the *Globe* had published some of my articles way back when I worked for *Drum*. Secondly, there is favouritism in the newspaper game: and here I was lucky too, because my boss liked me. Thirdly, you must happen to be in the office when the fire breaks out and the foreign desk editor hollers.

'Mahoney,' he hollered, 'have you got your passport on you?'

'Yes, *sir*.'

'All your inoculations up to date?'

'Yes, *sir*.'

'You up to date on the Congo situation? You know that Moise Tshombe has just been fired as prime minister and a new civil war's just broken out?'

'Yes, *sir*.'

'Then grab some traveller's cheques from Accounts and get your arse out there. I want a full update, which even I can understand, special reference to the significance it has on the Rhodesian political situation. And I want it yesterday!'

'Yes, *sir*.'

I hurried to Accounts, on air – *I was a fireman at last*. Then I hurried to the newsroom library and pulled out the Congo file. I had three hours before my plane left. I feverishly began to make notes for an update.

The Congo was chaotic. After the battle for Stanleyville, in which I had fought in the last week of my contract, after the rebel Gbenye had fled with his gold, Tshombe's white mercenaries had pursued the Simbas, liberating other towns, rescuing another 1300 white hostages. Enraged, the fleeing Simbas slaughtered all before them – the Red Cross estimated they killed 12,000 people in their retreat. Meanwhile, the communist bloc were rushing more arms and aid to rebel strongholds. Meanwhile, back in Stanleyville, Tshombe's victorious Congolese National Army outdid the Simbas in their bloodletting: they tried 20,000 prisoners by public acclaim and executed them on the spot in the public square. Meanwhile, in the United Nations in New York, the Soviets were furiously denouncing the American and Belgian intervention as a shameless capitalist plot to exploit the downtrodden natives, 'dragging innocent people into the Cold War', and the United States Information Office in New York was smashed up by an international mob. Meanwhile, Tshombe was busy recruiting a bigger and better mercenary army, to wipe out the rebel strongholds and drive back the communist bloc. Shit and blood hitting the fan everywhere. And then last night President Kasavubu had evidently decided that Tshombe was getting too powerful and had fired him as prime minister. And Tshombe had refused to budge, he was holed up in the palace, and new civil war had broken out.

The story thus far. Situation normal. I gathered my notes and rushed out into Fleet Street. I flagged a taxi to take me to the airport. With a hey-nonny-nonny and hot cha-cha! *I was a fireman*.

When I got to the check-in desk there was a message from the boss to telephone him urgently.

'You called, sir?' I said anxiously.

'Scrub the Congo,' the boss said, 'and get your arse to Rhodesia. Rumour has it the prime minister is going to declare independence from Britain any minute. I want the full historical background, the Wind of Change, how that affects Rhodesian thinking, the situation in South Africa, the Congo crisis, the works.'

'Yes, *sir!*'

'And I want it yesterday. God help you if Ian Smith declares Rhodesian independence before you've got there. Got that?'

'Got it, sir! How long can I be away?'

'As long as it takes. Provided you're back last night. And take it easy on the traveller's cheques, they're only meant to keep you in bread and water, and water's free.'

30

It took a long time. Almost ten years.

'*Ex Africa semper aliquid novi*', Pliny wrote two thousand years ago: From Africa there is always something new. True. Always a new revolution, war, bloodbath. Always something new, but as old as Africa, always more of the same. Sitting in England it seems hard to understand until you grasp, admit to yourself, that Africans are not black Englishmen. Africa has not yet learned the thin veneer of civilization that it took Europe two thousand turbulent, bloody, undemocratic years to learn.

'Don't talk to me about witchcraft and human rights,' said Hastings Banda, the new prime minister of newly independent Malawi, formerly Nyasaland, 'you people burned Joan of Arc!'

True. So what was all the incomprehension, the breast-beating and hair-tearing about? What else do you expect, for Christ's sake? Look at Attila the Hun. Look at the Dark Ages. Look at the Inquisition. Look at slavery. Look at the Soviet Union. Look at Hitler. If we made such a mess of it why should we expect these guys to be any different when we thrust our slender two-thousand-year-old institutions on them overnight and hightail it back to Europe, dusting our hands? Add to that the Cold War. For Christ's sake.

Ah, the Cold War. Now you're beginning to get the big picture. The whole shooting-match started with Karl Marx, then Lenin, then Stalin. The whole colonial era was getting along just fine until Stalin, having killed off all his opposition in Russia, having grabbed Eastern Europe in

World War II, having promoted Mao Tse-tung's conquest of China, having launched the Korean War and the Vietnam War, turned his attention to Africa in furtherance of Marx's grand design of liberating the whole world from the capitalist yoke. Harold Macmillan would not have made his Wind of Change speech if the Russians hadn't been stirring the black pot of Africa. So the colonial powers pulled out and the communists stepped into the power vacuum left behind. The Cold War had come to Africa, and the communists were winning by the West's default. The domino principle: one after the other the dominoes fall, become revolutionary stepping stones in the communists' march down to South Africa, to the gold fields, the diamond fields, the Cape Sea Route. Ghana gone. Kenya gone. Uganda, Tanzania, Nigeria, the Congo, Zambia, Malawi, all given their independence, all gone to hell, the sewers breaking down and the roads breaking up, all gone to the communists. And the Rhodesians were determined it was not going to happen to them.

The Rhodesians were also demanding their independence from Britain now. But NIBMAR was the British policy now, for Rhodesia, the new buzz-word in Westminster: No Independence Before Majority Rule.

'Make that NIBMARR, with a double R,' the police officer said. 'No Independence Before Majority *Red* Rule. We mustn't upset Russia and Red China.'

Out there in the western Rhodesian bush there were the political ones who had been trained in Moscow, going from kraal to kraal, telling the Matabele people they must join ZAPU, the Zimbabwe African People's Union – '*Anybody who does not join is a sell-out, everybody must take action, anybody who does not take action is a Tshombe and must be killed, find out who are the Tshombes and kill them! Action, boys, action!*' And in the vast eastern bush there were the political ones who had been trained in Peking, going from kraal to kraal telling the Mashona people they must join ZANU, the Zimbabwe African National Union, '*Anybody who does not join ZANU is a sell-out, everybody must take action, anybody who does not take action is a Tshombe and must be killed, anybody who joins ZAPU instead of ZANU is a Tshombe and must be killed, find out who are the Tshombes and kill them. Action, boys, action!*' Burn, kill, throw petrol bombs! Burn the schools, burn the dip tanks where the government makes us dip our cattle, burn the clinics, burn the mission stations, burn the buses, burn the white farms, burn the Tshombes! And in the midlands where Matabele met Mashona, ZAPU burned ZANU, ZANU burned ZAPU, Tshombe burned Tshombe.

'*Black*s killing other blacks, note,' the police officer said, 'make sure your readers in England grasp that. That's African democracy for you. That's what One Man One Vote will bring – Look at the Congo.'

Look at Ghana. The showcase of Africa. Kwame Nkrumah, The Great Redeemer, the Pan-Africanist visionary who was going to lead the continent into greatness, President-for-life, his opposition in jail. Look at Kenya, a one-party state. Look at Uganda: one-party state. Look at Tanzania, communist one-party state. Look at Malawi, one-party state with Hastings Banda president-for-life. Look at Zambia. All one-party states. 'One Man One Vote *Once* . . . Try to make your readers understand that. Make them understand that NIBMAR is Russian for Beautiful Bullshit.'

Yes, I understood that. Even the foreign correspondents from the left-wing papers understood that after a few weeks in Africa – it doesn't take long to get the big picture, with the horror stories of Africa humming in every day over the Reuters and UPI wires into Frankel House where we all hung out. Even the mandarins in Westminster understood it. But NIBMAR was the pious cry.

'For Christ's sake, Luke,' the boss shouted over the telephone from six thousand miles, 'it's good stuff, but I suspect you're becoming prejudiced out there!'

'I'm not prejudiced; I like Africans, grew up amongst them. I'm only a *realist.* You should see the blood.'

'I can *smell* the blood in your dispatches. Now, I want a full-length piece comparing the Rhodesians with the South Africans. How there's no apartheid in Rhodesia, et cetera.'

No, there was no apartheid in Rhodesia. Not really. Equal Rights for all Civilized Men, Cecil John Rhodes had said, and that was still the idea. There was no Immorality Act. A black man could sit beside you on the bus if he insisted, go into a bar and drink beside you if he dared – but there were a lot of bars where he wouldn't dare. 'The Management may reserve the right of Admission', the Liquor Act said, and the management usually did, if he wanted to keep his white clientele. There was legally nothing to stop a black man from joining the country club, but the membership would have had a lot to say about it. A black man could practise a profession anywhere he liked, but he would have had very few white clients, and there were very, very few black professionals. A black shopkeeper could trade anywhere he liked, but there were very few black shopkeepers. True a black man could not buy a house in a white residential area; but that was academic, because there were very, very few blacks who could afford to live in white areas. True, a black child could not attend a white school, nor a black patient be put to bed in a white ward in a hospital, but there were adequate black schools and black wards.

'But there the similarities with South Africa end,' I wrote. 'There is not the same racism here as in South Africa. "Lordism" yes, a white superiority complex which has characterized the white man through-out the colonial era, but nothing like as rigid as in South Africa. But, having said that much for the Rhodesians, why oh *why* are they so stupid as to have any segregation at all at this emotionally charged time when they are demanding their independence, when the rest of Africa is so swaggering, so full of angry pride, when Britain is wringing its hands trying to win hearts and minds away from the communists? Why doesn't the Rhodesian government show what nice chaps they are by passing legislation that *prohibits* discrimination on the grounds of colour? *Why,* for Christ's sake, when they are angrily trying to negotiate their independence from worried Britain, do the Rhodesians not rid themselves of this garbage can of segregationist legislation that smells of apartheid? Why not repeal it all with great fanfare so they can claim they have a truly non-racist society?

'The answer is they don't want to. The Rhodesians are not nasty colonialists, indeed most consider apartheid a cruel system, but they consider that such segregation as exists in Rhodesia is natural and proper, and they would like to keep it that way, thank you.'

And the black man could vote: of the sixty-five seats in the Rhodesian parliament, sixteen were reserved for black members, elected by blacks. 'Not bad,' I wrote. 'Not true democracy yet, but not bad in a continent where there is no democracy at all, where one-party states are the rule, where the democratic constitution bequeathed by Britain on independence has been thrown out the window and any opposition thrown in jail. Sixteen guaranteed black seats, twenty-five per cent of the total, constitute a significant opposition, give a substantial voice to the black people. Not bad in a continent where the opposition has no voice at all. where the opposition, languishing in jail, would be green with envy – they'd shout Hallelujah. And if the black Rhodesian parliamentarians find common ground with other white parliamentarians they could find themselves forming a coalition government. Unlikely, given Rhodesia's present political temperature, but perfectly legally possible and a hell of a lot more than you can say for the rest of Africa. So twenty-five per cent isn't a bad start – provided the purpose of the caution is a gradual extension of the franchise to majority rule in, say, 1985. That should be long enough for the blacks to learn about democracy, to allay white fears, and that should be short enough for the British to buy and re-sell to the United Nations. But is that the Rhodesians' strategy and purpose? Is it Hell. What did Ian Smith, the Rhodesian prime minister, say last week after another row with the British, when asked by the press when there would be major-ity rule? *"Not in a thousand years!"* . . . '

My boss said: 'Okay, great stuff, Luke, but will you please, for Christ's sake, cut out the blasphemy and four-letter words? All very Damon Runyon, but sometimes I've got to re-write a whole paragraph, and one day I'm going to overlook something and there'll be hell to pay. Got that?'

'Got it, sir.'

'Wish I believed that. So what's going to happen?'

'It's a stand-off, a deadlock. So the Rhodesian government will declare UDI soon. They have to, they've threatened it for so long their voters expect it of them, and the blacks will take it as a sign of weakness if they don't.'

'And the likely consequences of UDI? I want a full piece.'

And the likely consequences of the Unilateral Declaration of Independence were war, economic decline and collapse. You didn't have to be a whiz-kid fireman to see it coming, but the Rhodesians couldn't see it, didn't believe it would happen. Harold Wilson, the British prime minister, had told the Rhodesians in no uncertain terms that most of the world would impose economic sanctions: no more Rhodesian tobacco, no more beef, chrome, copper, emeralds, coal, would find a market. But the Rhodesians thought Harold Wilson was bluffing because surely the world simply could not do without their fine products and, anyway, they could export, in disguise, via South Africa. 'The South Africans will be on our side.' Okay, but they forgot about the middle-man and his ten per cent. Ten per cent of Gross Domestic Product is, as any undergraduate will tell you, very serious money indeed. And the Rhodesians did not believe there would be a war that their soldiers could not handle. Okay, but they overlooked the inexhaustible reservoir of potential black soldiers, and Russia's and China's readiness to train and equip them. And they overlooked the age-old military maxim that Fidel Castro and Mao Tse-tung proved, that the guerrilla almost always wins in the end. Maybe South Africa would support them for a while, but they overlooked that South Africa had its own international troubles as a pariah and would not want to get its hands much dirtier.

'In short,' I wrote, 'the average Rhodesian, nice guy, with a lot of balls, believes his politicians when they tell him that the world will soon accept UDI as a fait accompli. Then, they believe, with the uncertainty passed, they will be able to deal with their terrorists without fear of interference, foreign investment will flood in, everything will be hunky-dory: the chaos that is Africa will be stopped at the Zambezi.

'They're dead wrong. There *will* be sanctions, and it will be costly to get around them. UDI will not be a nine-day wonder – the communist bloc, and the rest of black Africa, now vociferous in the United Nations, will see to that. Foreign investors, because their products will be subject to sanctions, will stay away in droves. And because the Rhodesians will legally be outlaws, the terrorists will be legally *justified* by international laws. All this will become an unbearable strain on the stagnant Rhodesian economy and white manpower resources as young men are drafted into the army. Eventually Rhodesia will have to surrender to avoid terminal economic exhaustion.

'The Rhodesians don't believe it, but UDI is suicidal, and very dumb politics. *Why* make themselves outlaws by declaring UDI and thereby legitimizing the terrorists? Why declare UDI, thus attract sanctions and make it harder to fight?'

The big farmer in the Quill Bar demanded: 'So what's the fucking alternative, wise guy?'

Journalists are supposed to observe, digest and report, not argue. But I said: 'The alternative is to fight your battles the way you are, not give yourselves the additional handicaps of being outlaws while you fight. Rhodesia has been a *self-governing* colony since 1923, the only way Britain can interfere is to suspend your constitution entirely and rule by decree from Westminster. But she can't do that unless she sends troops to enforce the suspension and she won't do that because, firstly, it would be too expensive, and secondly the British troops would be unwilling to fight their Rhodesian kith and kin – Mr Wilson wishes to remain popular in Britain. So it's a sure bet Britain won't do that, she'll try to bully you but you're *safe* from interference *provided* you stay legal. You'll still have to fight a guerrilla war but at least you'll be doing so legitimately, instead of as outlaws, with the whole world against you and sanctions sapping the economy.' I ended: 'UDI would be dumb, cowboy politics. You'll be playing right into the terrorists' hands, and Russia's.'

The farmer flared. '*Are you saying Ian Smith is a dumb cowboy*?' I saw his big fist coming from way behind his shoulder, and the next thing I was involuntarily cutting a swathe through tables and plastered against the far wall. The rest was costly.

'For Christ's sake!' the boss shouted from six thousand miles. 'Have you gone troppo? Firemen are supposed to *report* on international fires, not *provoke* them! You not only represent your fine newspaper, you're also supposed to represent your fine country! Pub brawls?! Smashed furniture?! The cops?! The night in jail?! After he hit you why didn't you cool it?'

'I know, sir, and I pleaded guilty in front of the magistrate. But he did hit me first, and that made me cross.'

'So cross he ended up in hospital! And the bar ended up a wreck! And you're the pious scribe who writes how violent the Africans are!'

'I'm also a bit of a wreck, sir. I lost some teeth. Two broken ribs. He was a big farmer.'

'*Two hundred pounds' worth of damage to bar furniture!*' the boss said. 'Well, I tell you, Luke, you're paying for that, not the *Globe*! And you're going to pack your bags and catch tomorrow's flight to London!'

I had checked through the immigration gate, waiting in the departure lounge when I heard the special announcement on my portable radio: the prime minister requested all people of Rhodesia to listen at one o'clock when he would make an important speech to the nation.

I turned and jostled my way back through the immigration gates. I grabbed a taxi back into Salisbury, to the Quill Bar.

My luggage had been airborne for half an hour when I burst into the bar. It was crowded with journalists, and there was not a sound from anybody: the radio announcer was saying: ' . . . the Honourable Ian Douglas Smith.' There was a moment's silence, then came the familiar voice of the prime minister, announcing that Rhodesia had declared itself independent of Great Britain.

31

The parliament of South Africa stands at the foot of Table Mountain. It is a grand old colonial building, built during the British reign, and the legislative chamber is modelled on its Westminster parent, panelled walls, a high speaker's throne of ornate carved oak, a dais for the mace, long rows of leather benches facing each other, all overlooked by the stranger's gallery. Above and around the big chamber is a maze of offices for parliamentarians, conference rooms, committee rooms, a vast library, lounges, dining-rooms, bars. Secretarial staff bustle, messengers deliver notes, parliamentary papers, instructions.

Demetrio Tsafendas was one of those messengers, dressed in traditional eighteenth-century livery. He was Portuguese, from Mozambique, and a practised South African eye may have suspected, rightly, that he was a half-caste, but the Portuguese are a swarthy race. When he came to South Africa and applied for his identity card, through the mail, he was not summoned to an interview because his Portuguese name and his photograph were sufficiently reassuring and he was classified, unseen, as white. When he applied for a post as a messenger in parliament he was accepted because, under apartheid laws, a messenger's job was reserved for whites. His colleagues muttered amongst themselves and some legislative eyebrows were raised, but the authenticity of his plastic identity card was beyond question. He was quiet, a loner, and did his work satisfactorily. He did not discuss politics. Demetrio Tsafendas was a low-paid nobody in the beating heart of South Africa's house of power.

'But you will be famous,' the husky voice said. 'You will be in the history books. You will forever be remembered as the man who struck a mighty blow for freedom, who lit the torch. You will become a legend. And in the dock at your trial you will stand tall and handsome and dramatic, a beacon to inspire others, every newspaper will publish your name, your photograph, your great deed. And the people will rise up and the great revolution will follow.'

'But they will hang me.'

'No, the crowds outside the courthouse will be howling for your release, you will be carried shoulder high from the court to a great celebration, where she will be, applauding you with shining eyes. They will not dare to hang such a hero, because the people will storm the prison and carry you out.'

'But nonetheless they may hang me.'

'Then what a glorious death! What glory to stand upon those gallows for such a noble cause, what martyrdom, how glorious to know that the whole world is thinking of you at that moment, praying for you, lighting candles for you. And she will be in church praying for you, her broken heart full of glorious admiration, and she will remember you forever. You love her, don't you?'

'Yes, I love her.'

'And she is beautiful. But you can never have her. You see her every day going to work, but you can never make love to her, you cannot even invite her to drink coffee with you, because you are a white man, and she is a Coloured. You can never have her, whether you do nothing or whether you stand on the gallows. But if you do it you will be famous, having struck a glorious blow for freedom, for her, you have nothing to lose. So you must be ready in your heart and soul, ready to do it when the time is right, always ready.'

On the morning of 6th September, 1966, the prime minister of South Africa, the Honourable Hendrik Verwoerd, entered the legislative chamber of parliament to start a new day's business. The benches were filling up. Messengers were delivering notes across the floor. Demetrio Tsafendas was in his customary position. The prime minister walked across the floor to the centre of the front bench, acknowledging greetings. As he sat down he began to speak to the cabinet minister next to him. Nobody paid any attention to Demetrio Tsafendas as he walked towards the prime minister, his hand inside his tunic. The prime minister looked up, expecting to receive a note, and for an instant his blue Dutch eyes looked into Demetrio's brown eyes, then Demetrio pulled out his hand and clutched in it was a kitchen knife. For an instant it flashed on high, the prime minister's eyes widened in shock, he instinctively flung up an arm, then the knife sank deep into his chest. The prime minister crashed backwards, blood spreading across his chest, eyes wide, and all about him parliamentarians were gasping; and Demetrio wrenched the knife out and wielded it again, and plunged it into the prime minister's neck. It sank to the hilt, and Demetrio wrenched it out again, and the shocked parliamentarians scrambled to their feet, crying out. Demetrio wielded the knife again, his face contorted, and he lunged and plunged it into the prime minister's chest. Hendrik Verwoerd, the architect of apartheid, sprawled on his bench, dying, clutching his throat, blood spouting between his fingers. The knife clattered to the floor as Demetrio Tsafendas was grabbed, then half a dozen people pinned him down.

That was the same year, 1966, that Kenneth Kaunda, President of Zambia, formerly Northern Rhodesia, sent his troops to open fire on the religious sect of Alice Lenshina for failing to salute the Zambian flag. The same year that Kwame Nkrumah was turfed out of his solid-gold bed by his army. It happened when he was en route to the Far East to offer his services as mediator to the USSR and the United States in the Vietnam War. His friend and neighbour took the Great Redeemer in and made him co-president of Ivory Coast. 'So who says there isn't democracy in Africa?' quipped Chris Munnion, foreign correspondent of the *Telegraph*. It was the latest proof of Britain's folly, and it raised a horse-laugh in El Vino's, the wine-bar where the firemen and foreign correspondents of Fleet Street foregathered to solve the problems of the world, but it didn't stop Britain trying to foist the same fate on Rhodesia.

That was in the third year of Patti Gandhi's life sentence. I had written her many love-letters, but she did not respond. Lisa Rousseau did, however:

> . . . *I understand your suffering, dearest Luke, but I must advise you, for Patti's sake, to stop writing. She occasionally replies to my letters, and indeed in her last one she asks me to tell you to stop. She says that she is 'building a wall of defences' against her*

emotions, that she is slowly succeeding and your letters are an attack on that wall. For days they lie unopened as she wills herself to resist them, then she succumbs and for days thereafter she is in deep depression, weepy, 'wanting to scream and shake the bars'. Luke, the only way she can remain sane is if she adjusts to prison, learns to live without love, steels her heart, forgets about you. Indeed, the best medicine would be to hear that you have married somebody else – she said that herself. She wants to forget about you, Luke, so help her. Remember, too, that one day you will fall in love with somebody else: it would be terribly cruel to Patti if you have kept her love for you alive.

And for your own sake you must forget. She is gone, Luke, forever. Only a revolution will get her out, and that is highly unlikely – the ANC seems to be a very lame duck, wherever they are. You owe it to yourself to enjoy your life to the full and marry some lucky girl. Realize, too, that however liberal you may count yourself, mixed marriages seldom work: try to console yourself with the fact. And for God's sake put the child out of your mind. Patti is adamant that you were not the father, and I too am convinced. Enough said on that touchy subject. Patti is progressing well with her degree through the University of South Africa: she writes her finals next year. Meanwhile she is in charge of the garment work-shop in the prison, making uniforms for the police and armed services. She doesn't relish that, but a friend of mine in the prison service reports that she is well thought of by the warders, and is no longer a troublemaker. She is adjusting, Luke – do not disturb that process. Your compassion is destructive, your sense of guilt quite irrational: she did what she did without your complicity, and nothing would have dissuaded her. Get that into that intelligent head of yours.

Speaking of intelligence, I read the overseas edition of the Globe *regularly and often see your by-line. You seem to be sent to all the trouble spots. You have matured. I do hope you are also keeping up those family journals. Dear Luke, do write to me but, please, not about Patti. For both your sakes, forget about her . . .*

Forget? How could I, when I so often dreamed about her?

Sometimes it seemed I was beginning to get over her, when I was on the move, rushing to the airport to catch yet another plane to yet another firespot, to Accra, to Addis Ababa, to Aden, to Khartoum, to Kampala, to Saigon, when I was holed up in some beat-up far-flung hotel with the foreign correspondents, hungover, hot, dirty, trying to get the story, trying to sift the wheat from the chaff, the bullshit from the real shit, the propaganda from the propergoose, the half-truths from the half-lies, then trying to bash out a story before filing time, before the *Globe* went to print in the middle of the London night.

God help you if the other scribes bashed their stories through in time for the morning edition and you didn't. The code was that you all helped each other, shared a new story, unless you had an exclusive, a story only you knew about. The code allowed you to keep it to yourself until the morning editions had gone to print in London, then you had to share it with the others. But if you didn't have an exclusive you all pooled your facts, chewed them over in the bar for Joe Public's edification before you hurried back to your portable typewriter, then tried to bash it through to London. *Bash* being the appropriate verb. *Trying* to bash your story through on telephones that only work sometimes, on telex machines that break down, trying to bribe switchboard operators to give you priority on lines that go dead in mid-sentence, trying to out-bribe the other scribes. And then, when you finally got through, the bored copy-taker in head office with his jaunty earphones saying:

'Oh, it's you at last, Luke, where've you been, the boss is pissed off, he didn't think much of your last story . . . '

Or: 'I hope you're not going to take up *too* much time, it is my teatime, you know the union rules, couldn't you have rung earlier?'

Or: 'Don't expect any sympathy just because you're being shot at, Luke, it's pissing with rain here and *there* you are, having a wonderful time with all those *sweaty*-thighed *dusky* wenches . . . '

Or: 'Is there *very* much more of this crap, Luke?'

Yes, in that kind of hurly-burly, in all the flea-bitten hotels that once were grand, with the plumbing that didn't work, the food that was dangerous, the information that was dangerous, the whores that were very dangerous, the bullets which were extremely dangerous, it got easier and slowly easier to get over Patti Gandhi. The image of her in that prison cell, in that workshop making security-force uniforms, grew a little more faded with each fire, a little more jaded. The proliferation of whores also made it easier: when you're grunting and rumbling over a good-looking whore – or two, or more, at once – before collapsing into half-drunken sleep, then waking up all hungover and horrible and worried about having got the clap while you rush back to trying to get today's story, and the shit's hitting the fan everywhere, it gets easier to forget. But then come the dreams.

The dreams. The awful thing was, they were always happy dreams. Of open places, of towering forests and wide open valleys, of tumbling waterfalls, and there she stood at the top, her glistening body naked and joyful for all the world to see, smiling, her long black hair hanging in wild tresses. Then she was launching herself, arms wide, her whole body taut, and she hit the water in a silent splash. That was a frequent dream. And I dreamed of the Okavango delta, those clear waters meandering over that white sand, the reeds towering up, the fish darting, and there she was swimming amongst them fearlessly, her long legs flipping as she peered, marvelling, quite unafraid and free. And I remember a dream – it must have been England – where she was at a ball, in a gorgeous white gown, her long black locks swinging and her wide smile flashing and her big eyes laughing as she waltzed around, and then it was me waltzing with her, I could feel her in my arms.

I would wake up, wherever I was, in a hotel in Africa or Asia or back in my digs in London, and I would be full of joy because I was with her: until I realized it was a dream, and I would try desperately to go back to sleep so I could be with her again. Yearning for what might have been, my heart breaking, I would swing out of bed and shower, trying to scrub her out of my hair, and head, and heart, and plunge myself back into the new day, wherever it was, trying to go about my employer's fine business of informing the world. For days the sadness, that yearning, would stay with me, I could not shake it off, and the terrible truth is that I did not want it to go away; I wanted to live with it, to somehow be near her.

Then there were the other dreams, the terrible ones, where she was in the cell, the walls towering up about her, and she was shaking the bars and letting out a long animal wail of anguish. Then I would wake up, sitting bolt upright, staring, heart pounding, before collapsing back onto my pillow, my heart breaking, the tears running down my face. Oh God, I would give anything to free her from that anguish, from that howl rising up from her breast, that howl of my woman; and I wept all over again.

32

The following year the *Globe* made me their fully fledged foreign correspondent for Africa: no more flying back to London when the shit had finished hitting the fan. Now they rented a house in Salisbury for me, with a swimming pool and servants, a car and a full-time expense account. Now trouble was my full-time business. And there was plenty of it. That year Frelimo started their war of liberation in Mozambique, the Portuguese colony on Rhodesia's eastern border. Frelimo was trained and equipped by China, and soon thousands of soldiers were being shipped out from Portugal to fight them. It was bad news for Rhodesia because its eastern flank was now a war zone. How long could Portugal afford to fight an expensive, distant guerrilla war, how long before they too decided to throw independence at their African colonies? Then Rhodesia would have a hostile communist neighbour which would provide bases for guerrillas attacking her. You did not have to be a military genius to see it coming, but it amazed me that the Rhodesians didn't seem worried. They were cock-a-hoop with their unilateral independence, delighted with the black eye they had dealt Harold Wilson. His sanctions were not working, oil was coming in from South Africa, Rhodesian exports were going out via South Africa and the British regiments Horrible Harold had flown out to Zambia refused to attack their kith and kin across the Zambezi. '*Kith my arthe, Harold,*' said the Rhodesian bumper stickers. And the Portuguese would never give up Africa, the Portuguese had been in Africa over four hundred years.

'And those guys don't fuck about, they shoot first and ask questions afterwards; they wipe out a whole village if it's harbouring one guerrilla.'

'But Portugal's poor. And wars are expensive.'

'She'll be a damn sight poorer if she gives up her colonies: that's where all her oil and diamonds come from.'

The following year war broke out in Angola, with three rival liberation armies all fighting the Portuguese, all sponsored by Russia, and many more thousands of troops had to be shipped out from Portugal. This was more bad news for Rhodesia, but still they didn't seem to see it. In fact Rhodesia seemed to be booming: real estate prices were rising, houses were being built everywhere, swimming pools installed, industrialists were making lots of money manufacturing products that the country used to import.

'But it's an artificial boom,' I said. 'Money is dammed up inside the country by exchange control, people can't go on holidays, they can't emigrate because they can't take their money with them so they think they might as well spend it.'

'Listen, mate,' my Special Branch policeman said, only half in jest – each foreign correspondent had his own Special Branch tail to see he didn't get up to subversive nonsense – 'if you spread alarm and despondency by writing crap like that you'll find yourself deported.'

Even when the first shots in their own real war were exchanged the Rhodesians weren't worried: the guerrillas were half-baked Russian-trained ZAPU boys, and the army patrols could clean them up easily. But the average Rhodesian didn't seem perturbed that there were plenty more where they came from.

'They'll have to improve a hell of a lot before they frighten us, mate. And anyway, South Africa will send us troops.'

'Don't bank on it,' I said. 'South Africa knows it's unpopular enough without getting its hands dirtier fighting on the side of Britain's outlaws. She's South Africa's biggest trading partner, remember, so Rhodesia is expendable.'

But the guerrillas did improve, and the battles in the bush grew longer and tougher. South Africa did send some troops, but not very many and not for very long because Britain soon protested about South Africa 'giving succour to rebels against the Crown'. The wars in Mozambique, Rhodesia and Angola were bad news for South Africa, because sooner or later the white man would lose those wars because of sheer weight of numbers, and then South Africa would have hostile communist neighbours all along her northern borders. Then the war of liberation would start in South Africa.

'And that,' I wrote in the *Globe*, 'will be bad news for everybody. Bad news for the black man because there'll be a bloodbath as the white man gallops forth from his laager. Bad news for the white man because plenty of his blood will be spilt too, despite the ring of steel with which he'll reinforce that expensive laager. Bad news for the Western world because the white man will eventually lose, and the communist bloc will control the whole of Africa, and the Cape Sea Route. Suez gone. The Cape gone. The Mediterranean a Russian lake. That only leaves Panama, and the Reds will have the world sewn up.'

Trouble was my business, all of Africa was in trouble, but Uganda, that 'pearl of the British Empire', as Winston Churchill described it, was in very big trouble indeed. President Milton Obote had sent his army, under General Idi Amin, to storm the palace of the King of Buganda, and then, having declared a one-party state, had really fucked up the economy by turning it into a Marxist paradise, having first opened several Swiss bank accounts. Then, when everything was going so swimmingly, from his and Moscow's point of view, he had made the same boo-boo as Kwame Nkrumah a few years earlier. He had left town to attend a Commonwealth Conference ('*When*,' I asked my readers, 'will these British-made presidents-for-life ever learn not to turn their backs?') but no sooner was Obote shaking hands with his fellow potentates when General Idi Amin kicked the chair out from under his arse by seizing power and taking the title His Excellency President-for-Life Field Marshal Al Hadji Dr Idi Amin Dada, VC, DSO, MC, Lord of All the Beasts of the Earth and Fishes of the Sea,

Conqueror of the British Empire in Africa in General and Uganda in Particular.

'Luke,' the boss sighed on the telephone from London, 'cut out the racist crap, I had to rewrite that whole paragraph.'

'Can't you guys in Britain distinguish between a racist and a purveyor of the truth? I'm just telling you how it is, warts and all, and the truth is that the British Commonwealth, which was created on democratic principles, is now a farcical club of dictators, sir.'

'But you can't say it like that. You must let the public read between the lines. Now get your arse over to Uganda and tell us what's happening there . . . '

Obote had been such a bastard that, at first, big, bluff, colourful Idi Amin was popular, even with the British government: he was a jolly sergeant-major who had fought for the British in Burma, a spit-and-polish showman who made great copy for us foreign correspondents. Then he began his house-cleaning, getting rid of his enemies. He started by slaughtering Obote's tribesmen, and the terror began.

The terror: the systematic slaughter, the clatter of guns, flames and smoke barrelling up, villages destroyed, men, women and children gunned down, the Nile clogged with bodies, the crocodiles getting fat, the stink of death everywhere, the earth muddy with blood. In Kampala squads of soldiers went on the rampage, searching for Idi's enemies, crashing down doors, smashing windows, raping, looting. People were dragged away, thrown into cars, executed in the streets, the air pierced by the screams from the torture chambers in the basement of Idi's palace.

The foreign correspondents were prime suspects as enemies: we were followed everywhere by 'VIP Protection Squads', big grim guys in dark glasses. One unwise word and you would be grabbed, thrown into the boot of a car, never to be seen again. All the foreign correspondents stayed in the Apollo Hotel, from where we telephoned our day's story to Europe, and the goons camped in the switchboard room, listening in to every call. If you did not want to disappear, you had to be fulsome in your praise of Idi: you used code words, opposites and exaggerations and your editor rewrote it.

'Kampala, Wednesday,' I said on the telephone. 'Today, as order, milk and honey and goodwill continue to reign supreme, His Excellency, Idi Amin, has announced that the Asian population of Uganda have decided to donate their houses, businesses and bank accounts to the government as a token of their esteem, and in exchange will be assisted to emigrate as soon as possible. All over Kampala, grateful soldiers are politely visiting Asian shops, congratulating the donors, brightening their windows, remodelling their doors, helping relocate their goods, helping remove the money in the tills, being gallant to their women. Laughter and celebratory gunfire abound, and there have been not a few unfortunate fatal accidents: this reporter counted twenty-three Asian stretcher-cases in one hour whilst respectfully accompanying His Excellency's entourage through the well-ordered town as he graciously allocated the Asians' shops and enterprises to their new indigenous owners without favouritism.

'This latest move by the benevolent Conqueror of the British Empire will greatly improve Uganda's prosperity, which had declined seriously under the socialist measures of the former president: the Asians were wrongly perceived as the backbone of the country, but their alleged brainpower, skills and commercial know-how will easily be replaced by indigenous people. The economy will now boom.

'Meanwhile, in their thousands, Asians are flocking happily to the airport, gratefully accepting His Excellency's assistance to emigrate. Most have already donated their cars, so many are enthusiastically walking, enjoying the carnival atmosphere en route, accepting the well-wishes of the soldiery and the indigenous population, making more donations: battered buses and taxis are jam-packed with jolly Asians confidently contemplating the stimulating challenge of starting life anew without material encumbrances. As they have made their donations none of them has money for air tickets but Britain has shown her appreciation of their generosity by sending aircraft. At the airport they are greeted by more helpful soldiers. A noisy, jolly atmosphere reigns as soldiers politely assist them in making last-minute donations of jewellery and money from their underwear and vaginas, the ladies laughing girlishly – '

The copy-taker in London said: 'Is there much more of this bullshit, old chap?'

Jesus, the goons were listening! 'It's the honest-to-God truth!'

'Don't get touchy with me; spare a thought for us here in the pissing rain while you're enjoying yourself . . .'

The next day came the dreaded bang on my door. The two big goons in their dark glasses. 'His Excellency wants you!'

My heart was knocking as we drove to the palace. None of my colleagues had seen me leave, nobody would warn the British High Commission until it was too late. The bodies lying in the streets, the bullet holes in the walls, the smashed windows. I was shaky as I mounted the palace steps. Goons everywhere. Into the hall, down marbled passages, more goons. Into a big room. And there was the enormous dreaded man, resplendent in his field marshal's uniform, beaming from ear to ear.

'Mr Mahoney, you good man!'

I felt faint with relief. I shook his huge limp hand shakily. 'Thank you, Your Excellency, you're a good man too.'

'You write good newspapers about me!' He held up a reel of tape that must have been recorded last night in the switchboard room. 'Very nice story about the Indians.'

'Thank you, Your Excellency.'

'True story!'

'Yes, true.'

Idi Amin, Lord of All the Beasts of the Earth, looked at me, then his big face creased into a scowl and he roared: *'But your boss in London says it is bullshit!'*

Oh Jesus . . . I felt myself go white. 'That wasn't my boss, Your Excellency, that was just the silly man who types the reports when I dictate them. He was joking.'

'Why he joke about me?!' He had froth in the corner of his mouth and his eyes bulged wild.

Oh, Jesus Christ . . . 'Just because he is bored, Your Excellency; all night he sits in his little office typing reports that journalists telephone through from all over the world.' I elaborated: 'About kings and queens and prime ministers and important leaders like you, so he tried to be funny – '

'He thinks I am funny?!'

'No, no, no, Your Excellency! He thinks *he* is being funny, trying to make fun of *me*! But really he is stupid no-good arsehole.' (I sincerely meant that.)

The president glowered. Then he held up the tape again and shook it at me. 'He must put this story in the newspaper! Good story about Idi Amin! Not bullshit! Otherwise – ' he drew his finger across his throat and made a long guttural noise – 'understand?'

Oh Jesus, yes, I understood. And the true version of the story was on the streets in London, this time tomorrow a copy may be on his desk. 'Yes, I understand, Your Excellency.'

'You understand good?!' he roared.

I closed my eyes. 'Yes, I understand good.'

'Your friends understand good?!'

'I'm sure they do, Your Excellency.'

'I make you understand!' He grabbed my arm. The goons stepped aside as he hauled me out of the gilded room, down the wide corridor towards the rear of the palace. We burst into the palace kitchens. A woman, stirring a big pot of porridge, cowered. Idi Amin hauled me to the refrigerator and wrenched the door open. He roared: *'You understand?'*

I stared. And I felt my legs weaken and the vomit begin to rise in my guts.

Four human heads stared back at me, their glassy eyes propped open with match sticks, their ragged bloody necks dripping, their broken faces encrusted with congealed blood. Two were the heads of black men, one was Asian, the fourth was a white man with blue eyes. '*You understand?!*' Then he began shouting at the heads furiously. I lurched from the refrigerator, and up it welled from my guts, the vomit.

And there was nothing in the world but those ghastly heads and Idi Amin shouting at them and my retching and retching, all over his kitchen table; then his big hand was slapping me on the back of the head as he laughed: '*You good man, you understand, you tell your friends write good stories about Idi . . . !*'

33

So what does a man do? By which I mean a newsman, not the sensible man on the street who reads the newspaper and tomorrow uses it to line the bottom of the budgie's cage.

'He gets the hell out,' Bill Dobson, my Special Branch sleuth, said, 'tells his buddies in the hotel and makes himself scarce, pronto.'

'But what did he do?' Charlie-girl McAdam, my distant cousin, enquired of the assembly in her southern drawl, she of the big blue eyes and the magnificent tits, whose daddy was a big-wheel lawyer in New Orleans. 'He was a hero.'

'No hero,' I said, 'I was shit scared. The boys were all terrified what would happen if our newspapers reached Uganda, but the Asian story was too big to run away from just because one didn't want to end up in Idi's refrigerator with a Ugandan haircut. And anyway, could Idi *read*? But after a few more days most of us got the hell out across the border into Kenya before Idi refrigerated us.'

'And now you daren't go back to Uganda?' somebody asked. We were sitting round my pool in Salisbury on a Sunday, all the foreign correspondents and our women and our Special Branch sleuths.

'Oh, he'll go back next time there's a story,' Charlie-girl said. 'He's a *newspaper* man, not a *reasonable* one!'

This girl, Charlie-girl, real name, Charlotte: she wasn't really a cousin, except by very distant marriage, and I was in lust with her. Find somebody to love, Lisa Rousseau had said, and, yes, I could have loved Charlie-girl, a forthright Louisiana wench with long legs and as lovely an ass as you ever saw around the Mississippi, and a ready smile to melt your heart. And she was rich. She was one of the American McAdams, one of the old HM shipping line clan. She had visited my parents in South Africa, and they had told her to look me up in Rhodesia, in the hopes that I would marry her, I think. 'She's a stunner, son,' my father had said on the telephone. She had come out to Africa to produce wildlife movies 'and gotten involved with these no-good newspaper types, like *him*. *When* he's in town, not getting his ass shot off in Bongo-Bongo land, the ass-*hole*.' Charlie-girl was in love with me. Or thought she was. 'He's not *really* my cousin, there ain't no common *blood*, it's not *incest*.' Each time I came back from an assignment I expected her to be in love with somebody else, but she wasn't.

'And so do you love me,' she drawled, 'deep down, or almost, or sort of, and one day you will com*plete*ly when you stop thinking about her. So tell me about her – talk it out!'

Patti. It seemed each day I thought about her a little less. And that was the tragedy, the injustice.

'Injustice?' Charlie-girl said. 'Okay, because apartheid is unjust. But *you* did nothin' unjust. And it was years ago, for Christ's sake . . .'

'Call me Hank, Luke,' her father said on the phone from New Orleans. 'Now, my lovely daughter tells me that you've got a law degree. Well, I don't want to interfere with you two young people's decisions, but I just want you to know, Luke, that we could always find a good place for you in the old firm. You'd have to do our Louisiana bar exams, of course, but they'd be no trouble for a bright guy like you, and we'd sure pay you a living wage while you tackled it, and as soon as you got those exams we'd put you on, oh, fifty thousand dollars a year? After all, the Mahoneys are sort of family, we do most of HM's legal business too. Now, fifty thousand's pretty good potatoes, Luke, and I sure would like to see our li'l gal come home. So all I'm saying, Luke, is *think* about it . . .'

Fifty thousand bucks a year. I hadn't earned fifty thousand bucks in ten years. 'Just *think* about it, honey,' Charlie-girl said, 'and stop thinking about your irrational guilt. Or, if you don't want to go to New Orleans and be the youngest partner in the best firm in town, we can stay right here. I'd muddle along makin' my movies and we'll still be rich, because my daddy is *very* rich. Do you love me a little?'

'Yes.' That was true. She was very easy to love.

'Do you love me *quite* a lot?'

'Yes.' Also true.

'D'you think you could love me *lots* if you got her out of your system?'

'Yes.' Not untrue. But this was getting tricky. Did I want to get married yet?

'Do I give as good head as she did?'

I grinned. 'Yes.' Absolutely true, Charlie-girl really worked when she gave head.

'Is my ass as sweet?'

'I am particularly impressed with your sweet ass.'

'Then *that*,' she said, 'is good enough for li'l ole me. I'm stickin' around, honey-chil'. . . '.

We had a good time. '*Marry* her, for God's sake,' Bill Dobson said. 'She's beautiful and she's rich – do you want to spend the rest of your life writing about black mischief and getting your arse shot off? Journalists never get rich.'

Indeed, what more did I want? No, journalists never get rich. And yes, I was getting sick of getting my arse shot off, it seemed I had been wading through blood ever since I left school. And, yes, she was beautiful, and I did love her, sort of, and, yes, it would be nice to be a rich lawyer in New Orleans. But I did not want to leave Africa. I was heartily sick of the fuck-up of Africa, sick unto death of her wars and brutality, but I did not want to leave it even if I was going to make fifty thousand in my first year.

'Okay, so practise law right here in Rhodesia,' Charlie-girl said.

'There's no future in Rhodesia, darling,' I said.

'There is if you've got a wealthy wife, with all her money safely in the US of A. I *love* Africa.'

'Charlie, I'm not going to live on your money.'

'Of course *not* – you're going to make plenty of your own. But my money will be the cream on top of the cake, honey, the yacht in the Caribbean, the holiday home in London, the air tickets and nice hotels, all that shit most lawyers cain't afford. I cain't possibly spend it all myself. You know how much I got right now? Over a million bucks. My daddy gave me that for my twenty-first birthday present.'

Jesus, I'd had no idea. I said: 'Practise law here? When these guys take over a colony, first thing is most of the whites leave, so everything breaks down. Including the white police. Then they get rid of the judges and magistrates and shove inexperienced blacks on the bench and the judicial system goes to ratshit. The police and the courts are the cornerstones of a good society, if they become unreliable you can't rely on anything.' I shook my head. 'I don't want to practise law in an environment like that.'

'So you wanna to go to South Africa? – that's fine with me.'

Yes, I wanted to go home to South Africa. I longed to go home, to my own people, where I came from, I had been on the bloody road too bloody long. I wanted to go home where things worked; I'd had enough. But no way could I go back: even if Patti Gandhi had cleared me of the capital charge of smuggling explosives, there was still the crime of leaving South Africa without a passport, there was still Colonel Krombrink and all his BOSS men to watch over me, there was still the offensiveness of apartheid. And there would always, *always* be Patti Gandhi, the impossible love of my life, just fifty kilometres up the road, withering in Diepkloof Prison for the rest of her life, to haunt me. I simply could not bear that.

'I couldn't live under apartheid, Charlotte.'

She said quietly: 'Luke, you've got to forget about *her*. And apartheid cain't last forever, it'll collapse.'

Apartheid collapse? No, the Boer does not *collapse*, he fights to the bitter end. Like he did in the Boer War. Maybe he would be forced to change little by little, but a sudden collapse? Never. Christ, already the right wing of Afrikanerdom was up in arms because Prime Minister Vorster was considering – only *considering* – a proposal that the Indians and Coloureds be granted some kind of legislative council to govern their 'own affairs'. Up in arms because New Zealand might be allowed to send a rugby team including some Maoris to play in South Africa. The prime minister had been forced to cancel an English cricket tour because their side had one Coloured in it. Afrikanerdom had been outraged by the prime minister's suggestion that South Africa might one day have to admit black ambassadors. Afrikanerdom had been so incensed by these flirtations with heresy that the ruling National Party had split, a *Reformed* National Party had been created. And now the Afrikaner Resistance Movement, the AWB, had been formed, with a swastika-like emblem, to fight any governmental changes to pure Verwoerdian apartheid.

And pure Verwoerdian apartheid was in full heartless swing. The forced removals, the uprooting of unwanted people back to the crowded homelands under the Promotion of Bantu Self-Government Act: all that heartbreaking shit was still going on harder than ever. And the Coloureds and Indians were bearing the brunt too.

District Six, the sprawling, colourful area on the slopes of Table Mountain with its magnificent view of Table Bay, had been the home of Coloureds, Malays, Indians and Chinese since the days of the Dutch East India Company. Old Dutch architecture, old Victorian houses and shops, cobbled streets, winding lanes, mosques, bazaars – District Six had been re-zoned a white area and bulldozed down for white development, the people moved to joyless little concrete houses on the sandy Cape Flats. For weeks the heartless dust of District Six rose up as the government bulldozers rumbled. Simonstown and Kalk Bay, the homes of the Coloured fishing community for centuries, had also been re-zoned white, the fishermen moved many miles inland. The Indians had been cleared out of Durban to the new township of Westville. There were many more non-white people to go before the paradise of apartheid was completed. True, there was now a Coloured Representative Council, but it was a government puppet and never accepted. But there was no Indian council.

'But the South African government *has* kept its promise about self-government in the black homelands,' Charlie-girl said.

True. The Transkei, where I came from, was now the independent Republic of Transkei: the Xhosa people had been offered a referendum on whether or not they wanted independence from South Africa and they had responded with a resounding yes. It was, after all, a country almost the size of Scotland. Similarly the Xhosa of the Eastern Cape had voted yes for independence, and they were now citizens of the Republic of Ciskei. The Tswana people had been granted independence as the Republic of Bophuthatswana. Venda had become the Republic of Venda, half the size of Northern Ireland. Zululand had become the 'self-governing territory' of KwaZulu – but Chief Buthelezi had refused to accept full independence, insisting that his people remain South Africans. And the same decision had been taken by the newly 'self-governing territories' of QwaQwa, KwaNdebele and Lebowa. Now there were eight black self-governing territories, four of them totally and legally independent of the whites, with their own parliaments and civil services. It all looked fine on paper: in theory the science of apartheid, keeping people separate, had attained its promised moral high ground of giving each people self-determination without interference from others.

'Bull*shit*,' my father said on the telephone. 'In fact it's a cruel shambles, a hollow *sham* of self-government. Because these so-called independent republics and self-governing territories are poor, overcrowded *dumping* grounds of apartheid's unwanted people. With no hope of prospering economically. And it's a profligate waste of the white South African taxpayer's money because we'll have to support these tinpot republics, support the inefficient civil service and guaranteed-corrupt-upstart presidents. And it's a profligate waste of a precious opportunity! We complain bitterly about Britain not teaching the blacks about democracy *before* they granted them independence – *that's* the cause of the chaos of Africa today! And that chaos is half of the government's justification for apartheid. But when the *South African* government grants its blacks independence, does it learn the lesson from Britain's mistakes? Does it hell! Instead of using its power under apartheid to *impose* a learning process on these people, it *throws* independence at them, just like Britain, to get rid of them! The government should be *using* this precious time to *teach* the blacks democracy *gradually*, with *supervised* local self-government, spending the money on training a black civil service, spending it on black *betterment*, not throwing independence at them to get rid of them . . . '

And all the time the forced removals, the upheavals, the pass laws, the Separate Amenities Act, the heartbreak and shame of the Immorality Act, the inferior education under the Bantu Education Act, and all the time the *kragdadigheid* of the Internal Security Act and the Suppression of Communism Act: the dreaded ninety-day detention law had been beefed up to successive periods of a hundred and eighty days now.

'No,' I said to Charlie-girl, 'I couldn't live under laws like theirs.'

'So that leaves New Orleans,' Charlotte said. 'It's lovely there. And our blacks are civilized.'

But I didn't want to live in America either. Who was it who said, 'America is the only country which has gone from barbarism to decadence without the usual intervening period of civilization'?

So what the hell did I want to do?

Then the decision was made for me, because ex-President Obote invaded Uganda to conquer Idi Amin, Lord of All the Beasts of the Earth, Conqueror of the British Empire in General.

34

The invasion was a failure, but there was plenty of other news: Idi Amin was purging his populace again.

'For Heaven's sake be careful how you dictate your stories on the telephone,' the British information attaché told us. 'The Chief Justice was last seen being dragged out of court. The vice-chancellor of Makerere University likewise. The Governor of the Reserve Bank. It's an absolute reign of terror. Up in Lango and Acholi districts it's mass murder, don't go *anywhere* near there. In fact I'm surprised to see you gentlemen back here. Particularly you, Mr Mahoney – didn't you break that story about the heads in the refrigerator?'

'Yes,' I said, 'but I shared it, we all published it.'

'Well, Amin was enraged, your head would have been in the icebox had you been in town. I advise you all to get out of Uganda. Or make a deal amongst yourselves that only one stays and telephones the stories to the others in Kenya.'

But the shit-hot newspaperman always gets his story, and Idi Amin's pogrom was too big to run away from.

The next night the goons came for us. But they only found the *Washington Post* man, Chris Pauling, and myself. They threw us on a truck and carted us off to Makindye Prison.

We knew about Makindye. It was a military prison, where Idi Amin did most of his killing.

The soldiers who beat us up did not say anything about our stories, I don't think they even knew who we were, they only knew we had to have the living shit knocked out of us. As I got off the truck I was seized from behind, and all I knew was a black fist coming at me and my head exploded, then a blow at the guts and I doubled over in agony, then an uppercut smashed me upright again. All I knew was two bastards raining blows on me, my flesh splitting, the taste of blood, the crack of my teeth, until I couldn't see for blood, then I was on the ground and they were kicking me, and there was nothing in the world but the thudding and the jolting and the red-black stars, the gasping for air and the pain. I tried to fight my way up, and a rifle butt smashed down on my head and I sprawled again and they were kicking me again, until the world went black.

I came to in the cell, sprawled on a stone floor, my head splitting, my swollen eyes sodden with blood. I slowly raised my head. Chris Pauling was sprawled beside me, covered in blood. About forty black frightened faces lined the cell walls. One had an eyeball hanging down his cheek. In the corner was a latrine bucket with shit to the brim, dribbling down the sides. The place reeked of shit and blood and sweat.

There was a clang of the big iron door. Three soldiers sauntered into the cell. One was carrying a sledgehammer. The head was shiny with blood. They were grinning. They looked around. The blacks stared away from them, terrified. The soldiers leered from face to face, considering. One said something and they both frowned at a black, considering, and the man began to gabble. Yes, the soldiers said, *him*. Who else? They looked around some more. Blacks were cringing, hanging their heads. I desperately muttered prayers. *Him!* Yes, him! said the sledgehammer man. And they sauntered across the cell to the man, and he cowered and tried to scramble away, and they grabbed him. They wrenched him up from the mass of cowering blacks and dragged him to the door. They flung him in the corridor, then they returned and bounded at the first man they had chosen. He was crying out, his hands curled over his head. They wrenched him up, and dragged him out, screaming. The sledgehammer man followed importantly. The door clanged shut.

We heard the condemned men gabbling, begging. Laughter, shouts, goading, kicks. Then the crunching thud of the sledgehammer. Two, three more crunching thuds. Then laughter. Then more pleading from the other guy. Then another thud of the sledgehammer. And another, and another. Then laughter again. Then talk.

The executions took place throughout the night. We could hear the sledgehammer men laughing between jobs. Then, every half hour or so, the door would clang open and in they came to take out two more. They always made a great show of deciding who was to die next, discussing, pointing. They spoke in English, for our terrified benefit. 'What about this one, sergeant?'

Every time the cringing, the scrambling away, the begging for mercy, then the door clanging, and the sickening crunch of the sledgehammer. Then the chatting and laughter out there again. And you knew that you had about half an hour before they came back, maybe for you this time. Half an hour to pray. The blacks prayed, taking it in turns to lead the whispered prayers, to sing hymns softly. They were all policemen or soldiers, in uniform. 'Why are you here?' I whispered to the man next to me.

He whispered: 'We are from Obote's tribe.'

'How long have you been here?'

'Twelve days.'

He'd lasted twelve days? 'Have they been killing all the time?'

'We were ninety-two. Many more have come in.'

The door clanging open again. Enter the executioners. The sledge-hammer dripping blood and slimy grey matter. Everybody cringing, averting their eyes. I also averted my eyes, the instinctive cowardice of a man desperately hoping, trying not to antagonise by locking eyes with the Almighty – I hated myself but I was too terrified to be dignified.

'I like a white one!' the corporal cried.

My heart was pounding, my ears ringing. Chris and I had desperately rehearsed what to say, to try to bullshit our way out of death. I opened my mouth but no words came.

The sergeant laughed and said: 'Yes, but this time I think I like black one!'

I felt the vomit turn in my guts. The struggle, the pleading, the drag-ging went on without me. The door clanged shut. The thud of the sledgehammer.

'What are we you going to do?' Chris whispered.

'Fight,' I whispered. 'First we try to bullshit them that the British High Commissioner is coming, then we go down fighting.'

Chris's bloody black eyes were just slits. He whispered: 'I can't fight, I'm fucked.'

'So am I, but we'll give it a go. Try to get that sledgehammer. One of their guns. Then we shoot our way out of here.'

Chris took a deep breath. 'But they'll catch us and cut our balls off and pull our fingernails out and gouge our eyes out like that guy over there. I'd rather have the sledgehammer.'

I held my bloody brow. Oh God yes, I was terrified of what they could do to me: the same cringing cowardice as averting my eyes, trying to be insignificant, trying to ingratiate myself with my executioners. I hissed: *'You can still fight! Remember these poor bastards here will be on our side once we start.'*

Chris tilted his bloody head back against the wall. He breathed softly: 'Then we've got to jump on them the next time they come in.'

'No,' I whispered, 'the High Commissioner *may* come! The boys will report we're missing! There's no sense in starting a fight while he's looking for us! He could come through that door any moment!'

'And our executioners could be coming through that door any moment . . . '

All night the killing went on, all night the terror, the prayers, the stink of blood and shit and fear. Sweat glistening, blood congealing. Bodies aching. Then the first light came through the small barred window, and the killing stopped. We heard the executioners go off duty, laughing. We waited in dread for the new shift. In the prison yard there was shouting and gunfire, but no fresh executioners came. In the middle of that dread-filled morning I fell into a nerve-shattered sleep.

I woke up in the afternoon when more prisoners were thrown into the cell. I could not open my eyes for the congealed blood. I prised the lids open. I got painfully to my feet. The blood throbbing back to my cuts and bruises. 'Stand up. Loosen up, you must be ready to fight.'

'Please God, the Commissioner comes this afternoon . . . '

But he did not come. The dread-filled afternoon ground on midst the feverish prayers and the hymns. I went to the prayer-group, knelt and prayed with them. So did Chris. At sunset the executioners came back, and the killing resumed. The crying, the cringing, the pleading, the scrambling, the struggles, the door clanging shut again, the dreadful sounds of the sledgehammer.

'If we get out of this,' Chris whispered, 'I'm finished with Africa. I'm finished with journalism.'

Oh God, yes: I was finished with Africa. I hated Africa. I hated journalism. 'What'll you do?'

'Anything. Write a book. Be a teacher. What'll you do?'

'Get very drunk.'

'Me too, but after that? You've got an LLB.'

I didn't know. I didn't know anything. All I knew was I wanted to get out of dreadful Africa.

It was about midnight when the executioners came for us. The door clanged open and the three walked in with the bloody sledgehammer. *'You!'* the sergeant cried. *'Now it is your time!'*

'Get up,' I hissed to Chris. I got to my feet shakily. 'Not us, sergeant.' My whole body was trembling. 'The British High Commissioner is coming for us in the morning, the message arrived today when you were off duty.'

He screamed: *'What is message?!'*

My voice quavered. 'This is all a mistake, the British High Commissioner explained to His Excellency the President and the President gave him a paper for our release.'

'Where is the paper?!'

'He is bringing it in the morning.'

I saw indecision cross his furious face and I closed my eyes in prayer. When I opened them the sergeant was pointing at somebody else. *'Him!'*

I turned and clutched my guts and slumped back in my corner, thanking God.

All night the killing went on.

Chris whispered: 'God help us tomorrow if he finds us still here.'

I held my head and whispered fiercely: *'Somebody will come in the morning! Think positively . . . !'*

But the High Commissioner did not come in the morning after the executioners went off duty. He did not come that whole long dreadful day. And the sun began to get low, and I was faint with dread. We heard the executioners come back. The heavy tread of boots, the jabbering. 'This is it,' I whispered. 'Be ready . . . ' I closed my eyes in terrified prayer. The cell door clanged open.

'You!'

I scrambled up, trembling. *'There's been a mistake – '* The corporal bounded at me, and I roared in terror and swung my fist with all my horrified might and he lurched, I swung wildly again, I saw the sergeant's baton coming at me, my head exploded and the world went black.

I came to in the corridor. I was being dragged by my feet by two executioners. Chris was stumbling along behind me. Then the door at the end was clanging open and I was being thrown out into the yard.

I landed with a crash, on my back, and scrambled up desperately, to fight, to plead, a hand grabbed my shoulder and a voice was saying: *'Take it easy. Are you okay?'*

I stared at him, chest heaving. A collar and tie came into focus, then a face. It was white.

'Are you the High Commissioner?'

'The American chargé d'affaires. I'm getting you out; you're being deported. Are you all right?'

I looked at him incredulously, then my battered face crumpled and I just wanted to howl.

'I'm beautiful. Just fucking beautiful . . .'

35

When you're sitting in a condemned cell waiting for your turn with the sledgehammer it's very easy indeed to say I'm finished with Africa, finished with this job, finished with blood, all I want to be is a nice lawyer like my father said, all I want is a nice safe house in a nice safe white country where savages don't run the place, all I want is a nice wife and nice children and I swear that if I get out of here alive I'm going to quit this fucking job and quit fucking Africa and marry Charlie-girl and become the youngest partner in the best law-firm in New Orleans and live happily ever fucking after.

It takes about a year to prepare for your English bar examinations after you've got the LLB. It was a humdinger of a year. My boss was at London airport to meet me when I arrived from Uganda, to keep me away from all the pressmen clamouring for my story – the boss wanted an exclusive. The next day Charlie-girl arrived, rushing into my arms, and it was so wonderful to see her, to be alive, that we got engaged that very night, and when we telephoned the news to her father he was so thrilled he sent us two air tickets to go to New Orleans for the party. And my parents were so thrilled that they flew over to New Orleans too.

It was a helluva party. The McAdam house was a magnificent, Deep South mansion, and there were so many black servants I felt at home. Equally impressive were the McAdam law offices: he introduced me, still with my black eyes, to his staff as his future son-in-law and future partner, and it really came home to me how much money I was going to make. Even if I turned out to be a bum lawyer I was going to be extremely rich. Even if I decided not to become a lawyer, I was going to be very rich through marriage to his gorgeous daughter.

'You must pay a huge rent on these offices,' I said. They were a far cry from my father's offices in Main Street, Umtata.

'Nothin'. We own the whole goddamn building, Luke.'

Jesus. It was a towering modern block, with magnificent views of the Gulf of Mexico. 'We do a lot of shipping work,' Hank said. 'How's your maritime law?'

I knew fuck-all maritime law; I'd forgotten it all. *Mare liberum*, maritime belts the range of a cannon, that was about it. 'Not bad.'

'Good, and private international law?'

Fuck-all. Renvoi's Doctrine, the seat-of-contract rule, that was about it. 'I like private international law.'

'We do a lot of that, especially for HM. Contract law?'

'Good,' I lied. 'But do you do much crime?'

'We've got a couple of guys who specialise. You like the courtroom, huh? That's fine.'

Yes, if I was going to be a lawyer I wanted the courtroom. The drama. 'Yes.'

'Well, I sure hope you join us. But whatever you decide to do, you must write those English bar exams. As insurance. Then the Louisiana exams are a piece of cake. That gives you a year to make up your mind whether you want to give up this dangerous writing game.'

'He's giving it up, Hank,' my father promised.

Yes, I was giving it up. I was going to be a rich lawyer.

'You've fallen with your bum in the butter, son,' my father whispered. 'Go for it.'

'And she's such a lovely girl,' my mother said.

Yes, I was going for it.

The next week Charlie-girl and I flew back to Rhodesia. We set up home together in Salisbury. And for twelve months I had the best of both worlds: big wheel foreign correspondent, or big wheel lawyer, whichever I chose. We flew to London twice so that I could eat the required number of dinners at my Inn of Court to satisfy the dining terms for a candidate for the bar. We made a lovely holiday out of it: my future father-in-law arranged for us to have the HM executive suite in Mayfair – white butler, the works. We were invited to the country by the HM Mahoneys and went huntin', shootin', fishin'. It was a wonderful year: Luke Mahoney had struck lucky at last. And with such a lovely girl. At the end of that year I wrote the bar examinations, and passed. The next month the wedding invitations went out. And then my cock got in the way, just like the witch doctor said it would.

Suzette Donovan, the best lay in British Airways, with whom I frequently flew when about my employer's business, sent me a telex in Rhodesia saying: '*Got three days stop-over in Mauritius starting Wednesday night. How about it?*'

How about it? Maybe if I hadn't been getting married soon my cock wouldn't have ruled my head. But impending marriage does funny things to a sensitive young man like me.

I said to Charlie-girl that night: 'Got to go to Nairobi tomorrow for about three days, the boss says, some United Nations conference or other.'

'*Please* be careful,' Charlie-girl said.

It was a great three days in Mauritius with Suzette, just like it always was. Until the third day. I was leaving that night, back to Rhodesia. In the bar I saw a newspaper, three days old: it was one of the opposition's and the front page headline read:

MILITARY COUP IN PORTUGAL —
MOZAMBIQUE, ANGOLA TO GET INDEPENDENCE.

I stared, my heart sinking. I speed-read the story. Then I closed my eyes in dread.

It took me half an hour to summon the courage to telephone my boss in London.

'*Where the fuck were you when the shit hit the fan? Sent you to Nairobi, did we . . . ? The most significant story to hit Africa in years, and where are you? You realize what this story means for Rhodesia and South Africa? It means the beginning of the end for both of them! And where are you? We telephone and your fiancée says we sent you to Nairobi! But where are you? Screwing your cock off in Mauritius!*' There was an ominous pause, then he roared: '*You're fired, Mahoney!*'

It took me another half hour to figure out what I was going to say to Charlotte. Then I took a deep breath and placed the call.

'*Nairobi*, huh!' Charlie-girl hissed. '*Boss's* orders, huh?! Meanwhile you're screwing yourself black and blue in Mauritius! Well, now he's *fired* you! And *Daddy* says if you ever come near me again he's personally *suing* you . . . !'

PART VI

1975–1985

ANGOLA COLLAPSES IN CHAOS AS PORTUGUESE
PULL OUT – COMMUNISTS SEIZE CONTROL

MOZAMBIQUE COLLAPSES IN CHAOS
AS PORTUGUESE PULL OUT –
COMMUNISTS SEIZE CONTROL

RHODESIAN WAR INTENSIFIES AS ANGOLA
AND MOZAMBIQUE COLLAPSE

RHODESIA SPONSORS
RENAMO REBELS IN MOZAMBIQUE

SOUTH AFRICA SPONSORS
UNITA REBELS IN ANGOLA

RIOTS IN SOWETO

36

When you're sitting in a condemned cell it's very easy to say I never want to see Africa again, to hell with Africa and all her dreadful works, I'm going to be a lawyer and live happily ever after. When your future father-in-law is showing you round your future offices, and out there is the sparkling Gulf of Mexico, and you're going to be a millionaire, it's easy to say to yourself: home was never like this. When you've got the best of both worlds to choose from it's easy to say I'm bored with writing, I think I'll be a rich lawyer instead. But when you've fucked up and the chair's been kicked out from under your arse and you've *got* to be a fucking lawyer whether you like it or not, and you've *got* to leave Africa because the only place you can get a job is the British foreign service, and you're stuck in the Falkland Islands as your first tour of duty (nobody wants to go to the Falklands), Africa gets you right here, right here in the heart. And, as Mahoney wrote in his journal, 'Once a newsman, always a newsman, you can't expect too much of us.'

Once a month the mail-ship brought him the English and South African newspapers. Every day he listened to the BBC and the South African Broadcasting Corporation. Every night there was nothing to do but write up his family journal. He wrote:

> The collapse of Portugal is bad news for Rhodesia and South Africa, but for the blacks in Mozambique and Angola it is very bad news.
>
> The Portuguese handover in Mozambique was chaotic. No elections were held. On independence day 'Comrade President' Samora Machel simply declared that 'the new government will be Frelimo', and announced his Revolutionary Socialist Programme whereby all industry, business and professions would be nationalized, all farming collectivized, all media governmentized, all intellectuals, schools, churches and reactionaries 'revolutionized' – and Mozambique would 'fight for the liberation' of Rhodesia and South Africa. The economy collapsed, and Rhodesia organised a rebel army called Renamo to stop this new government providing bases for guerrillas fighting the Rhodesians. And the mayhem began.

It was worse in Angola, where three rival liberation armies had been fighting Portugal. On independence day the Portuguese simply vested power in 'the people of Angola'; immediately the communist MPLA seized power, simultaneously anti-communist UNITA declared itself the government, and the civil war began.

The Afrikaners' belief that apartheid is the will of God, necessary to save the nation from such Darkness of Beelzebub, is constantly reinforced by the chaos that is the rest of Africa: the coups, the tyranny of one-party dictatorships, the corruption of officials, the chaos of economies bankrupted by incompetence, of bloated bureaucracies that don't work, of technicians who don't understand, telephones that don't work anymore, of sewers breaking down and roads breaking up, of hospitals and schools that don't function anymore, of harbours and railways that don't run anymore, the tragedy of forests cut down for firewood, of farms that aren't farmed anymore, of wildlife shot out by people for whom the word for game is 'nyama', the same as the word for 'meat'.

But the African is not to blame. An uneducated nation simply cannot produce the legislators, professionals and technicians to run a modern country, nor can an uneducated electorate vote in a sophisticated way. The African chaos is the white man's fault, for thrusting such responsibilities on uneducated peoples prematurely. And deplorably the white man did this to save himself the expense of educating them. The colonial powers cut their losses when there was trouble from black politicians. The Belgian government was recklessly irresponsible in giving independence overnight to the Congo. But even more irresponsible was the British government which, seeing the Congo chaos and knowing the despotic excesses of Kwame Nkrumah in Ghana, nonetheless proceeded, with indecent haste, to give independence to Nigeria, Kenya, Uganda, Tanganyika, then Northern Rhodesia, then Malawi. In each case a dictatorship immediately came about, one-party rule, the opposition crushed, the economy plundered. The British government now knows this was folly, yet it wages economic warfare against Rhodesia to force it to accept the same mad fate, while continuing to support the tyrants. And the South Africans behold all this madness and their resolve is stiffened. The madness of the West begets the madness of Africa, begets the madness of apartheid.

Why does Britain and the West continue to throw money at corrupt African dictators? The answer is: the Cold War. 'Liberating the world from the capitalist yoke' is the cornerstone of communist theory. The communists intend to crush the capitalist West; they do not intend a 'peaceful co-existence'. Their Warsaw Pact already out-guns Nato in Europe, their nuclear arsenal is probably as powerful as America's. Part *of their strategy was destabilization of the colonial empires, to make the colonial powers quit. The communists stepped into the vacuum left behind. Their purpose is the domination of the whole of Africa and its Cape sea-route. Because they already dominate the Suez Canal, they will then be in an excellent position to overrun western Europe in a blitzkrieg.*

That is what the West is terrified of. So they appease the African dictators to win back the influence they recklessly abandoned when they granted independence. And it is to appease these dictators that they wage economic warfare against Rhodesia whilst Rhodesia fights Russia's and China's protégés: Rhodesia is expendable.

The South Africans look at this successful communist strategy, and their apartheid and kragdadigheid seem vindicated – and they know that, unlike Rhodesia, they are not expendable. They know South Africa is important to the West as the last bulwark against communism in Africa – besides, the West has too much capital invested there. And they know they can beat the ANC.

The ANC is piss-weak. As a liberation movement it must surely be one of the most ineffectual ever. With Mandela and others in prison, the leadership under Oliver Tambo seem to have settled down to a soft life funded by donors, and doing very little. The PAC is doing even less. Admittedly the ANC originally had only Tanzania as a 'sanctuary state' in which to place military bases – the 'front-line states' that border South Africa still then being under colonial rule. But Zambia got independence and became a 'sanctuary state', and now Mozambique and Angola. Why has the ANC failed to establish effective military bases? What MK has achieved is minimal: a few bombs. It is hard not to suspect that the ANC, too, are incompetent. Are all those underground cells of Mandela's M-Plan still active, scheming away courageously, ready when the trumpet sounds? No, I think you can write off the ANC, they've gone soft, there is no chance of them beating South African kragdadigheid, and they know it. (I wonder if Patti knows it, languishing in her prison cell – I pray, for her sake, that she does not.) Now a new liberation movement has appeared – BC, the Black Consciousness movement.

I fear they are black racists. They are inspired by the Black Power movement in America, by Martin Luther King and Malcolm X. South Africa's Black Consciousness is led by Steve Biko, a charismatic young man, but a firebrand who believes the blacks must have nothing to do with whites: they reject even liberal white organizations who champion their cause. They say that psychological liberation is necessary: their second-class citizenship and education has given them an inferiority complex which must be purged – 'Black is Beautiful!', 'Black Culture is as good as Europe's!' They reject multi-racialism, reject the ANC because it is multi-racial – so that they harden themselves to fight from a position of proud black strength.

Black Consciousness spells Blood. The Financial Mail *says 'A new generation of blacks has grown up. Unlike their parents who fatalistically accept second-class citizenship, these younger men are impatient, radical, militant, brave, and proud . . . ' Good stuff, and understandable after the shitty deal blacks have had, but BC does not spell a bloodless solution to South Africa's problem. The government denounces them as 'Black Nazis'. I fear them.*

That leaves Inkatha, the Zulu political movement. And I'm not sure what to make of these guys. But the white man and the Zulus have always had a grudging respect for each other, ever since Shaka.

Only recently has Chief Buthelezi, a direct descendant of Shaka, welded the Inkatha cultural organization into a tough political party. Buthelezi supported the ANC's freedom struggle: when the ANC fled into exile, Inkatha became their internal wing: but then Buthelezi began to go his own way. The ANC demands world economic sanctions against South Africa; Buthelezi rejects this, saying the blacks will be the ones to suffer. The ANC flatly rejects the government's policy of granting independence to the black homelands; Buthelezi has accepted self-government for Zululand but refuses independence. He wants one-man-one-vote, but he wants a federation of states, each tribal group governing itself at local level; the ANC wants tight unitary government by one central parliament. The ANC wants a socialist state; Buthelezi wants a capitalist one. Buthelezi is carrying the torch of freedom, but he has political ambitions of his own, he is building a strong power-base in Zululand, and the ANC is nervous about him. And the Xhosa, who dominate the ANC, have always been frightened of the Zulus.

I think we can forget about the ANC. If reform is ever to come to South Africa, the driving force will be Buthelezi and his Zulus . . .

But Luke Mahoney, sitting in the windswept Falkland Islands, licking his wounds and yearning for his good old days as a journalist, got it wrong in that last paragraph. The next month something happened which was to change the ANC's lacklustre fortunes, change the course of South Africa's history. And the driving force was the Black Consciousness movement, not Inkatha. That month the government announced that black children must receive their education in the Afrikaans language.

First there was the outcry from the English-speaking press denouncing the heartlessness of forcing greater difficulties on underprivileged children, denouncing the impracticality of it because very few black teachers were competent to teach in Afrikaans, denouncing the cruelty of forcing poor people to buy new textbooks, denouncing the stupidity of forcing people to be taught 'in the language of the oppressor'. Then came the anger on the street corners of the black townships. Then the Soweto Riots.

37

Justin Nkomo didn't much like it in the United States of America.

Oh, he liked the University of Miami well enough, and the students were pleasant, if naive. ('Hey Zulu-boy, where's your *ass*-e-gai?') They couldn't grasp the difference between a Zulu and a Xhosa – when he explained, they pronounced it *Ex-hose-a* or, the brighter ones, *Ikoza*; not one of them could do the click, even the drama students. Most thought Nelson Mandela was a warrior in a leopard-skin, something like Chief Sitting Bull. None of them had heard of Chief Buthelezi, nor could they understand why he was a traitor to the ANC ('shee-it, if he's a capitalist he's okay!'). Most of them were antagonistic to apartheid because it was so un-American: niggers still sat in the back of the bus but, yes, they had the vote in the US of A. The South Africans were up-to-shit because they whipped their niggers all day and didn't give them hardly nothin' to eat, did they? (And all those lions an' tigers roaming around Johannesburg must be another serious problem.) Prime Minister Vorster sounded like another jerk, too. ('But does he sound just like you, Zulu-boy, that zany accent; everything you say sounds so *intelligent* . . . ') Oh, Americans were nice people, by and large, and he enjoyed their women, and when the crowd rose to their feet when he hit another home run and chanted: '*Five, six, seven, eight – who do we appreciate? ZULU-BOY! ZULU-BOY!*' he loved them, and he even felt patriotic. He confided to Luke Mahoney in one of his spasmodic rambling letters:

> *I spent my entire life in South Africa being called 'boy' and I*
> *hoped to escape the word when I came to these democratic shores,*
> *but no such luck. However, the Yanks use it affectionately, and I am*
> *quite proud of my nickname in a perverse 'patriotic' way. Oh, how*
> *I long to return to South Africa and my own people, as you say you*
> *do. (I hope your next posting is more congenial – I found the*
> *Falkland Islands in an atlas, they look so lonely). But what hope is*
> *there for us in South Africa, friend? Zilch. My only hope, when I*

*finish my Master of Economics thesis, is to take a doctorate. That'll
give me a reprieve from repatriation for another few years (especially if I change my subject when I look like finishing). But I am
over thirty, and the only money I have earned is working in the
campus library, and as a waiter. I want a proper job, but when my
student visa expires I must leave America – and go where? What
country wants a black South African (Marxist?) economist? If I
were a Jamaican I could go home. But what home is there for a
Xhosa-boy, locked up in that toytown 'Republic of Transkei' where
'prime minister' Matanzima throws his opposition into jail, and
sends the taxpayers' money to his bank account in Switzerland?
And the 'Republic of Ciskei' is even more pathetic. And even the
other pisspot 'Bantustans' are closed to me now that we're all
'foreigners'. Count your blessings that you are white and able to
make a career in the British foreign service . . .*

Oh, Justin liked Americans, but their ignorance about Africa was
bottomless. He knew American history because he had taken the trouble
to read it, he knew they had slaughtered the Red Indians, he knew their
history of slavery, so why weren't *they* prostrate with guilt? He knew
about the Australians butchering the Aborigines, the New Zealanders
butchering the Maoris, he knew about the English and Americans
waging the nefarious Opium War in China – so why didn't these so-
called educated Americans? *He* knew about world affairs, why didn't
they? *Oh*, Americans were so insular. And he disliked their materialism,
their blind dedication to the 'Pursuit of Happiness' when three-quarters
of the world lived in *un*happiness. He had a degree in economics and it
seemed that all he'd heard about was 'the failures inherent in communism'. That was bullshit. Capitalism would probably fail because of the
inherent contradictions in it – because it had no ideology above selfish-
ness, whereas Marxism had the noble ideal of *selflessness*.

'*I have a dream . . .*' Martin Luther King had cried shortly before the
assassin's bullet pulled him down. '*I have a dream . . .*' Justin repeated to
himself. A dream of an unselfish South Africa. But there was nothing he
could do about his dream. In America black men could mount a podium
and bellow, but what hope did Justin Nkomo have of doing that in South
Africa? He wouldn't last five minutes before he was slammed inside
under the 180 Days law. And he could not envisage that situation changing now the ANC had fled into exile. There was no hope.

Then, in his first year of writing his thesis, he had heard about Steve
Biko and Black Consciousness. 'Hey, Zulu-boy, instead of mopin'
around, saying there's no hope, why ain't you out there with Steve

Biko a-rattlin' those pots an' pans?' Sally Freeman said.

Justin had recently attended his first meeting of the NAACP, the National Association for the Advancement of Colored People. Sally was a pretty, bouncy, caramel brown. She'd had her hair straightened and wore a saucy fringe. In South Africa she might have passed as Coloured instead of black, Justin thought. 'Steve Biko?' he asked. The Miami newspapers carried very little South African news.

'Man, Zulu-boy, he's all the rage. Forget about your half-assed ANC.' She opened a file and began to quote from her notes: 'Born in King William's Town, 1946 . . . attended Catholic mission schools et cetera, before devoting himself full-time to politics. A man of refreshing candour, real leadership qualities . . . Biko sees the need for the black man to win psychological emancipation after generations of conditioning as the underdog. This means freeing himself from the tutelage of white liberals and a social system dominated by white cultural values. Biko's vision includes all the oppressed races, the Coloureds and Asians, not just the blacks.' She looked up. 'But, of course, he rejects the government's homeland-independence policy, even though it would seem to suit his ideology, because of the inherent economic injustice, and because it would be collaborationist.' She reverted to her file. 'His Black Consciousness movement is inspired by the ideology of Black Theology and Black Power in America, though its aim is *not* to trigger a spontaneous eruption in violent action, as happened in Algeria, but to rebuild the mind of the oppressed so they can forcefully demand what is rightfully theirs.' She looked up. 'That's for me, Zulu-boy!'

She read on in silence for a moment, then continued: 'A number of new organizations have sprung up in South Africa as a consequence. SASO – the black South African Students Organization – broke away from the white student body NUSAS. The Black Peoples Convention has been formed to operate on the political level, and on black health and welfare services, et cetera.' She looked up at him. '*That's* what you should be doin', Zulu-boy, instead of mopin'.' She turned back to her file. 'At first, Black Consciousness enjoyed some support in government circles because it appeared compatible with apartheid's notions of separate development – blacks were *supposed* to develop their own organizations. But then, predictably, when it got too strong, the government clamped down. Steve Biko and other leaders got banned.' She looked up. 'But he's still operating underground. So how can you say there's no *hope*?'

He was amazed that an American knew so much about his country. 'How do you know all this?'

'If you buy me a coffee I'll tell you more. About *my* plans . . .'

They went to a pizza joint. Leaning intently over the formica table, she said: 'Know what you should do? You should go back to South Africa when you've got your MA and work with Steve Biko – underground. That's what *I* intend to do when I've got my degree. I'm the right colour.'

Justin grinned. This was fanciful – typical American, they imagined all blacks were like themselves. 'But you couldn't pass yourself off as a South African black.'

'Sure I could, Zulu-boy: I've taken Drama.'

He smiled. 'There's your first mistake. I'm not a Zulu.'

'Sure: you're a Xhosa.' He was amazed that she got the click right. 'And so,' she added, 'am I. I'm one-sixteenth Xhosa!'

Justin was astounded. 'You're *what*?'

She grinned. 'Thought that would throw you. But all blacks in America come from some tribe or other in Africa. I happen to be one-sixteenth Xhosa. The rest is hodgepodge, I've never been able to find out, but doubtless mostly West African. And, alas, I'm one-eighth Irish. A randy great grandfather.'

Justin grinned. 'But no Xhosa slaves were ever imported into America, were they?'

'But remember the Xhosa national suicide? When they slaughtered all their cattle and ate all their crops so the dead ancestors would arise and they'd drive the white man into the sea?'

Justin was amazed at her knowledge. 'Of course.'

'Well, my great *great* grandfather was a little Xhosa boy at the time and when the dead didn't arise and the blacks streamed into white man's land begging for food, his mother put him in a tree. A frontiersman called McPherson found him, and brought him up. They called him Steven. Then Mr McPherson decided to become a Mormon, and emigrated to America with his family. He intended leaving Steven behind but he cried so much they relented. So this Xhosa boy grew up in America! He was shot in a gunfight when he was twenty-two. But not before he'd sired offspring with an emancipated slave girl.' She grinned. 'So, Zulu-boy, ah's one of you *muntus*!'

Muntu means 'person'. '*How* do you know that word?'

'I read. I love social anthropology. And I *love* my African roots. I've even learned a bit of Swahili.'

Justin smiled. 'We don't speak Swahili in South Africa. And your American accent would give you away.'

'You can coach me in the accent. So, what do you think? Wouldn't that be a wonderful thing to do, to go and work underground with Steve Biko?'

Justin smiled widely. He said: 'The South African government would never give you a visa. They're scared of foreign blacks.'

'I've got relatives in the US diplomatic corps.' Then she grinned and hunched forward. 'Tell me, Zulu-boy, do you guys really get circumcised in cold blood with a sharp spear?'

Justin grinned. 'Yes.'

'*Jesus*. Didn't it hurt?'

'Agony.'

'I bet. Did you holler?'

Justin grinned. 'No. If you cry out you're not a man.'

'*Je-sus*,' Sally said in admiration. 'You just sort of queue up bare-assed, whack your dick on the block and there's the mumbo-jumbo man with his blood-stained spear?'

'Something like that,' Justin grinned.

'Weren't you shit-scared?'

'Terrified. But you couldn't show it.'

Sally shook her head. 'If somebody wanted to lop off my clitty I'd sure have something to say about it!'

Justin laughed. 'The Xhosa don't circumcise girls. The Zulus used to. The Kikuyu do, in Kenya. Many African tribes do.'

'Jesus. Yeah, I've read about it. Just spread the girl's legs and *whop*, off comes her clitoris?'

'Uh-huh.'

'But the clitty's the best *part* . . . '

He spent the night in her studio apartment. The walls were draped in bright African rugs, festooned with African masks, shields, spears, axes, totems, fly whisks, musical instruments. In the centre of the room was a black three-legged African cooking pot holding African charms, trinkets, Oriental joss sticks. She had expensive hi-fi equipment with stacks of African music. There were photographs of Martin Luther King, Malcolm X, Jesse Jackson, Nelson Mandela, Winnie Mandela, Patrice Lumumba, Emperor Haile Selassie. Her bed was a mattress on the floor, covered in brightly coloured African blankets.

'You make me homesick,' Justin said.

She giggled. '*Voetsak, you bladdy kaffir!* Doesn't that make you nostalgic for the dear old Afrikaner?!'

She made him teach her Xhosa. Through far-flung bookshops she bought a Xhosa–English dictionary and grammar books. Each day she learned thirty new words, and she insisted they speak Xhosa in the apartment. At home she swanned around in traditional African garb. She made him coach her in the peculiar accent of Africans when they speak English. ('Man, it's so *cute*.') At the university she changed her major to African history and culture. '*Man*, I really dig this Africa shit. Ole Steve Biko's gonna go a bundle on me, Zulu-boy!'

Alex Hailey had recently published his bestseller, *Roots*, and there was a constant trickle of black students through the apartment who were busy discovering theirs.

Justin found it all charming, but it was pie-in-the-sky: no way would she get to South Africa, let alone to Steve Biko. Oh, he would love to go home: he had had a gutful of America. But there was no hope in South Africa. And there was no hope for him in America either: when he finished his doctorate his student visa would expire and he would have to leave.

Unless he married an American citizen.

Justin didn't want to marry anybody yet, let alone an American. When he did marry, he wanted his wives to be full-blooded Xhosa girls, who knew their place – not a gum-chewing American girl who thought she wore the trousers. But South Africa was not to be. So, what *was* to be? He was fond of Sally, she was amusing and intelligent, and she adored her Zulu-boy; but did he love her enough to marry her and live in goddamn America forever? No . . .

The wedding took place the day before his visa expired, six days after being awarded his doctorate. The marriage was performed by a black Pentecostal preacher and the only guests were immediate black friends. The bride wore a traditional red Xhosa blanket with a fetching red turban. She was barefoot, wore many brass bangles, and her face was painted with red ochre. She looked very pretty. She had pretended to insist on ten head of cattle as *lobola*, bridal price, but she settled for ten chickens instead. They barbecued them for a wedding feast in the back-yard behind her apartment: Justin had to slaughter them but the bride insisted she personally gut and pluck them, 'as befits a Xhosa *umfazi*.' There was blood everywhere, but she had a barrel of fun.

But Justin Nkomo did not have a barrel of fun as a legal American resident. He got a job at the technical college teaching commercial subjects, while Sally continued her studies at the university, and he was bored. The students bored him, the American lifestyle bored him. And, alas, Sally bored him: her hodgepodge Afro-American lifestyle was endearing, but it was a hollow reflection of the real thing, the real Africa, he longed for.

'Quit mopin', we're goin' to South Africa to be revolutionaries when I've got my degree, honey-chil'.'

But that was pie-in-the-sky too. There was no hope of revolution in South Africa for a long, long time.

But then came the Soweto riots.

Soweto. Bureaucratic acronym for South Western Townships, the sprawling black city sited over the horizon so the whites could not see it, like many other joyless shanty cities surrounding eGoli, the golden city of Johannesburg. Long before dawn the cooking fires send smoke up, and the rivers of black people set out for the bus and railway stations. In the cold winter sunrise of 16th June 1976, when most workers had left, twenty thousand youths began to assemble at their schools across Soweto to protest against the government's recent edict that they should receive their tuition in Afrikaans.

Most were in school uniform. They were excited but disciplined – their Action Committee had seen to that. At seven o'clock they began to march towards the main Soweto school. They marched by a dozen different routes, to confuse and stretch the police. As they did so they chanted freedom songs and held aloft placards reading *'We are not Boers'*, *'We don't like Afrikaans'*, *'Blacks are not whites'*.

A police vehicle encountered a column. An officer lobbed a tear-gas canister. The youths scattered from the stinging smoke, then retaliated with stones. The police vehicle sped away, its radio crackling. Another column met a black police foot-patrol. *'Sell-outs! Sell-outs!'* the youths chanted, and the black policemen beat a retreat. The columns began to converge, a great swarm of chanting, singing, excited humanity. Then police vehicles came speeding towards them.

There were half a dozen. They slammed to a halt and forty white policemen ran to form a line across Vilakazi Street. The commanding officer strode towards the chanting mass, ordered them to disperse, then lobbed a tear-gas canister. The mob of youngsters surged backwards, yelling, coughing, until out of tear-gas range, then they began to regroup, yelling, taunting, throwing stones. And the commanding officer dramatically pulled out his pistol, and fired.

There was the shocking *crack*, and screams as youngsters fled in all directions, barging into each other; then there were more shots and four children crashed, wounded. Many started hurling stones, more shots rang out and a black boy called Hector Petersen hit the road, dead. And there was pandemonium: screams and yelling and stones flying, black youths running everywhere, leaping over fences and through backyards.

The police radioed for reinforcements. And the youths began to rampage through Soweto.

* * *

Dr Dick Wallenstein was a social welfare officer employed by the West Rand Administration Board, the governmental department that ran Soweto, and he was dedicated. He had chosen to work in Soweto because of the immense scope for his science there. That morning he was writing a caustic report on the adverse social conditions of Soweto:

> ... *conditions absolutely calculated to breed insecurity, and therefore recklessness: conditions guaranteed to breed breakdown in family authority, normally so strong in African society, calculated to lead to youthful rebellion, truancy from school, gang mentality, hostility towards all authority, amorality if not immorality, crime, volatility and downright subversion ...*

Dr Wallenstein heard the mob coming down the road. He got up and looked out of the window, but the part of the street he could see was empty. Then he heard the anxious cries of his co-workers, running feet, cars starting. He hurried to his door. The corridor was empty. The far door leading into the yard was open. He looked into the main office – it was abandoned. He ran down the corridor and peered out into the yard – most of the cars had disappeared. He ran to the gate, and he saw the mob roaring down the road. He stared. In the front ranks he recognised half a dozen youths whom he had counselled. He walked out into the road to confront them – they were his wards, he *understood* them, they were up to no good and it was his duty to intervene. He was perturbed as he stepped out to reason with them, but not actually afraid. He held his palms aloft in peace, smiling: and a roar went up and the first stones flew, and Dr Wallenstein turned and ran.

He ran back across the yard and flung himself in the side door. He locked it, ran down the corridor to the back door and bolted it. He heard the front doors crash open. He ran to his office. He slammed the door and locked it. The window had bars. He could hear the mob smashing up the general office. He feverishly shoved his desk up against the door. The bangs and crashing in the general office were louder. He snatched up the telephone, but his line worked through a switchboard in the general office and it was dead. Then there was an explosion as his windows shattered. He threw his arms over his head and ducked under his desk.

And down the corridor all hell was breaking loose. The smashing, crashing as the mob tore apart the property of the hated landlord, overturning the furniture, hurling files in a storm of papers, smashing typewriters, telephones, windows. They rampaged down the corridors wrecking all the offices. They crashed down the door of the store room and looted it; they looted the petrol stores and set fire to the cars, flames whooshing and black smoke barrelling up. And inside the building they beat on Dr Wallenstein's door.

Dr Wallenstein crouched under his desk, desperately trying to hold it against the door with his back, and the door shook as the youths furiously kicked it, yelling and screaming. Dr Wallenstein screwed up his eyes and prayed with each kick. Then came the crash of an axe, and the gleaming blade burst through. Dr Wallenstein thrust against the desk with all his might and cried: '*I'm a social welfare officer!*'

The axe smashed and crashed frenziedly. Dr Wallenstein gargled in terror and scrambled out wildly from under the desk, he flung himself at the shattered window and shook the bars, and the axe smashed the door panel wide open and he saw the mass of gleeful black faces and he bellowed: '*I'm your social welfare officer!*'

He lunged desperately at his bookshelf and snatched up two stout volumes. He turned wildly towards the door, books on high, ready to sell his life dearly. The door burst open and Dr Wallenstein hurled his sociology textbooks with all his frantic might in a great flapping of pages, and he screamed, '*I'm on your side –* ' and he snatched two more books and hurled them at the youths bursting into the office, axes and sticks on high, shouting and swiping, and the first stick got him. It swiped him across the head and he reeled, stunned, and they hit him again and again, heavy sticks thudding, and Dr Wallenstein went down. He crashed to the floor, gasping, and they grabbed his ankles and dragged him.

Dr Wallenstein kicked and struggled, crying: '*I'm on your side – I try to help you!*' They dragged him down the corridor, out into the yard where the cars were burning. They slung him down on the gravel, and formed a prancing ring around him, kicking him and swiping him, yelling at him to stand up. Dr Wallenstein staggered to his feet, and he cried out: '*I'm your friend – I'm the social welfare officer!*' Then the first stone smashed into his chest, knocking him back against the wall, wild-eyed, and through his terror he recognised one of the mob and he cried: '*Amos! I am Dr Wallenstein who helped you!*' and another stone cracked into his mouth and he reeled, clutching his face, and sprawled. And the mob proceeded to stone him.

Fifty youngsters hurling stones, leaping and cavorting in a big ragged circle, throwing stones with all their might, and Dr Wallenstein crawled and sprawled and crawled, and sprawled again, desperately trying to escape, gasping, sobbing: '*I'm your friend . . . !*' Youngsters danced forward and kicked him and shrieked in glee as he writhed and cried out for mercy. And all the time the flames and smoke barrelling up from the burning vehicles midst the yelling from the road. Dr Wallenstein crawled, lurching and gasping under the blows, his head a mass of blood, his teeth broken, his ribs broken, trying to get to the gate, and the circle of tormentors pranced with him, kicking and hurling, giving way for him so their sport could continue. Out in the streets the mob was ransacking the shops and liquor stores. Dr Wallenstein crawled and sprawled and crawled again, trying desperately to get to God knows where out there amongst the screaming, smashing, crashing, grabbing masses – then the big stone hit him, he sprawled for the last time, and they proceeded to kill him.

Constable Phineas was, according to his station commander, the stupidest bladdy kaffir on the police force, hey. His fellow black policemen said so too. He was a Zulu, and while any Xhosa will tell you Zulus are stupid, in Phineas's case they were right. On two occasions he locked up the witness in the cells and let the accused go home. Another time a packet of peanuts was a vital exhibit in a murder case, and Constable Phineas ate them. He was of an amiable disposition and, though a big man, he was not much cop in a riot squad, and he wasn't fleet of foot because he had shot his own big toe off when practising his draw. He was frequently late for duty, and if sent on an errand it took him twice as long as anyone else. He had been warned that the next time he was late it would cost him his job. He was late this morning, returning from HQ, where he had delivered a docket, and it was to cost him his life.

Because it was winter his vehicle's windows were closed so he did not hear the noise coming from the administration building. He had forgotten to switch on the two-way radio so he did not know about the riots. He took a circuitous route back towards his station because he enjoyed driving. As he approached an intersection he saw children running past, and he decided to follow them, not as a policeman investigating something suspicious but in the hope of excitement. As he rounded the corner he saw the mob outside the administration building ahead, and saw the smoke, but his suspicions were still not aroused: those people were watching a fire and fires excited Constable Phineas as much as anybody. It did not occur to him to report it on the radio because fires were the job of the fire brigade, whom he presumed were on their way. It was not until he was thirty yards from the building, admiring the smoke barrelling skywards, that he noticed anything untoward. It was a brick smashing his windscreen that aroused his suspicions, which were reinforced by a section of the mob running towards him with hostile intent, manifested by the hurling of more missiles. Constable Phineas slammed on his brakes, more by way of reflex than strategy, made a conscious decision not to arrest the culprits, tried to ram the vehicle into reverse but got it into top gear instead, and stalled. He restarted the engine, found reverse, roared backwards under a hail of stones, and crashed into a telephone pole.

Constable Phineas entertained a flash of anxiety about what the station commander would say about that, then the mob was onto him with the smashing and crashing and bashing of stones and bricks and sticks, rocking and jolting the vehicle, shattering the windows. Constable Phineas was bounced around inside, shouting at them to please stop this nonsense. He did not use his pistol because he might kill somebody and he was in enough trouble with his station commander without an inquest to worry about, but it did occur to him to grab the radio to try to report his unhappy circumstances. As he was fumbling with the transmitter a can of petrol was hurled through the windscreen, and he shrieked in terror. He wrenched the door handle but he had locked himself in; he gabbled in terror, fumbled frantically for the lock, flung the door open and the safety strap wrenched him back. He shrieked in terror and lunged at the buckle but it didn't come undone, and the match flew through the windscreen and there was an explosion all about him.

The flames leapt about his screaming head; then the petrol tank exploded in a great eruption of flame. Constable Phineas screamed and clawed at the buckle of his safety strap and wrenched on the door handle as the flames leapt up around his wild-eyed face, his chest and arms and hair on fire; his burning hands clawed at his flaming hair and beat at his flaming uniform as he bellowed his agony to the skies. And all the time the shrieking, prancing toyi-toying of the mob.

They petrol-bombed post offices and government beer halls, they looted the government liquor stores before burning them, they petrol-bombed the shops belonging to black businessmen, smashing, looting, burning, attacking anything associated with the hated government, attacking any black person who failed to give the Black Power salute. Then the riot police arrived, and the real bloodshed began.

There were running battles through the rutted roads and lanes and backyards of Soweto: gunfire and tear-gas and baton charges midst the hail of stones and the flying petrol bombs, the whooshing flames and clouds of smoke. Twenty thousand yelling, taunting, running, smashing youths against thousands of Afrikaner policemen. Then began wild and indiscriminate shooting, policemen firing into the mobs and not just at the ringleaders.

Hundreds fell that dreadful afternoon. In the evening it was even worse as the people returning from work joined the rioters, the running battles redoubled, and police stations were besieged by riotous mobs. The army arrived to break the sieges of police stations, and the fighting grew fiercer: and all the time the cacophony of the gunfire and the yelling and the explosions, the leaping flames and the stink of tear-gas, and the blood. Baragwanath Hospital was inundated with the wounded, and the dead lay all over Soweto.

That was the first day of the Soweto riots.

The next morning the mobs began to re-form, and now many were inflamed by booze they had looted from ninety-four liquor stores. The rampage resumed: thirty-one Administration Board offices set on fire, clinics, schools, more bottle stores, more beer halls, over a hundred vehicles – all set on fire. And all the time the running battles, policemen firing from pursuing cars, once again filling Baragwanath Hospital with the wounded and the dying.

In Johannesburg three hundred white students from Witwaters-rand University marched in protest at the killing of children in Soweto. They were joined by a big crowd of blacks and then were attacked by a mob of whites. There was another running battle before the riot police arrived with dogs and baton-charged the protesters. In Cape Town there was uproar in parliament but the Minister of Law and Order angrily insisted his police had acted with admirable restraint, and the prime minister promised the nation that 'Law and order *will* be maintained'. Out there in Soweto the police had a free hand and the *crack-crack-crack* of their gunfire filled the afternoon. By nightfall they were at last able to announce that they had Soweto under control.

And it was, more or less. But underneath, Soweto simmered, and in the black shanty-township of Alexandra, on the other side of Johannesburg, the youths took to the streets denouncing the shootings in Soweto. Stones were thrown, they refused to disperse, the police opened fire, four children fell dead, and Alexandra erupted in fury. Up went the barricades of rocks and burning tyres, and the people rampaged, and the armoured vehicles poured into battle through the smoke and flames and stones. Twenty policemen were killed with sticks and stones, and the war spread to the black townships of Alberton and Vosloorus and Germiston. Down south in Natal and up north in Venda the black university students went on the rampage in sympathy, burning, smashing, looting. The next day rioting broke out in the Cape, in the black townships of Langa and Crossroads, and then the Coloureds of Mitchell's Plain and the University of Western Cape rioted: flames were roaring up all over South Africa midst the stink of cordite and tear-gas and blood.

A thousand miles away, in the windswept Falkland Islands, Luke Mahoney pieced the picture together from the radio and newspapers. And, oh God, he fretted for Africa; he longed to be back there witnessing all this, witnessing this rebellion against the South African government, against the mad science of apartheid. He yearned for Patti Gandhi and hoped with all his heart she was heartened by this, for Mahoney saw this as the beginning of the end of apartheid. He wrote in his journal:

> The Afrikaner government has in its ranks some of the best intellects, yet their conviction in the righteousness of their dream-state, their belief in the inferiority of blacks and in the holy mission of their white tribe to bring to fruition the Divine Will of the Separation of the Races, is so pigheadedly profound that it does not occur to them that the riots are due to human resentment at inhuman living conditions inflicted in the name of Influx Control, at the concomitant poverty, at the hatred of the inferior education forced upon them under the Bantu Education Act, the humiliations of the Separate Amenities Act, the terror of the Suppression of Communism Act. All this seems perfectly necessary to the government intellectuals, and the riots are seen simply as the forces of darkness at work, the godlessness of communism which must be crushed. The stupidity of ramming the language of the master race onto the oppressed does not occur to them. And now, to add insult to injury, the government scornfully rejects the Erika Theron Commission's recommendations that the Coloureds and the Indians be given a share of power in the form of their 'own affairs' mini-parliament – yet it is the government itself which appointed this commission! And now, to add further heartless insult to injury, the mass funeral which has been planned for the Soweto dead has been banned by the government. Jesus . . .
>
> As the riots spread across the country, I have no doubt that something very dramatic is going to happen.

Mahoney got it right on that one. And, when it happened, it marked the beginning of the end of the old South Africa, and the birth of the lost generation. The mechanics of it were extraordinary: for the next year the youths, the 'Soweto Students' Representative Council', became the de facto rulers of their vast township. And they ruled with the weapons of Steve Biko's Black Consciousness.

It was during this bloody time that Justin Nkomo returned to South Africa. One day, when Sally was at university, he packed a bag, drew exactly half their money out of the bank, opened a new account for himself and withdrew one thousand dollars in traveller's cheques. He bought an air ticket to Lusaka, Zambia.

He left Sally an apologetic letter, which ended: ' . . . *I'm truly sorry, honey, but America just ain't the place for a real nigger.*'

39

Albert Mpofu was a leader of the Soweto Students' Representative Council.

It was extraordinary power for anybody to have, let alone a black schoolboy born of semi-detribalized parents, humble factory workers. The power was born of righteous anger at the whole mad badness of apartheid and the hopelessness it created; but the power was also delicious. The power of commanding adults was very heady wine; the power of disrupting the white man's state made Albert feel a giant; and being on the run, being *hunted* by the police, made him feel a swash-buckling figure. Albert Mpofu, sixteen years old, in the extraordinary position of being one of the de facto rulers of the sprawling black city of Soweto, considered himself a man of destiny, and maybe correctly so. And the power was great fun: Albert had no intention of stopping.

'*Liberation before education!*' Albert cried. And the slogan reverberated across Soweto.

Albert's first decree was that all children must return to their school – but not to learn. The schools became the cells from which the Council's insurrectionist activities were coordinated.

'There must be a strike!' were Albert's orders, delivered from school to school, whispered in classrooms. 'Everybody must tell their parents to go on strike for the first week of August! Anybody who does not strike is a sell-out! On the first of August we must make roadblocks and stone the buses!'

A 'sell-out' – everybody knew what that meant: sell-outs are beaten to death, sell-outs have their houses petrol-bombed, sell-outs have their families killed. It is a dreaded threat in Africa. However, an African adult does not take kindly to orders from juveniles: jobs were precious, and on the first day of August most people of Soweto set off to work. But before dawn roadblocks had been thrown up on strategic routes and the buses and taxis were heavily stoned. Children taunted workers, and many turned back. The police arrived and the running battles resumed, the stones flying midst the stink of tear-gas and clatter of gunfire. The next day it was the same, but by now many workers were angry about being bullied; they carried sticks and got stuck into the juveniles obstructing them. For the next two days the battles with the police continued until Albert and his Council called off the strike without admitting defeat.

'It was a success!' was Albert's message, carried to the schools. 'Now everybody must tell their parents to strike in the last week of August! Everybody must make leaflets!'

The police were out in force for this strike, guarding the bus stops and taxi-ranks and train stations, but the pupils had distributed leaflets saying, *Azikkwela*, 'We don't ride', and seventy per cent of the workers obeyed. Those that did not were stoned, and the battles resumed. That night the Zulus decided they had had enough of intimidation by Xhosa juveniles, and they went on the warpath.

Mzinhlope Hostel was a squalid place. It was like a barracks, a quadrangle of single-storey red-brick buildings divided into small rooms with eight bunks in each. Communal kitchens and latrines at each corner were dirty, unpainted, unhygienic and malodorous. The West Rand Administration Board was the landlord who rented bunk space to workers who had valid passes. No women were allowed on the premises. The hostel was designed to house four hundred single men but at any time hundreds more were squatting there illegally. Regularly the police raided all the many hostels like Mzinhlope to arrest the squatters and pass-offenders and women sleeping there. As Dr Wallenstein had said, the hostels were degrading, dangerous places, fertile breeding grounds for trouble from men forced by Influx Control to live far from home without the bonds of family. The hostel-dwellers were regarded as dangerous people, looked down upon by the Sowetans who qualified under Section 10 of the Group Areas Act to rent the cottages. To be a 'Section 10 Resident' was a big deal: it meant you had worked for the same employer in this part of white South Africa for ten years, and thus qualified to have your family living with you, until your employment ceased.

Isaiah Ndhlovu was a Zulu who lived in Mzinhlope Hostel. His great great grandfather had been one of Dingaan's indunas who fought at the

Battle of Blood River, his great grandfather had been one of Cetshwayo's indunas who defeated the British at the Battle of Isandhlwana before falling at the Battle of Ulundi. In those days a man had to be a seasoned warrior before he became an induna, at about age forty, whereupon he was allowed to marry. Isaiah guessed his age at about thirty, but he considered himself an induna: he had two wives and seven children, and he had acquitted himself well in many bloody stick-fights back in KwaZulu. In his kraal he had the full regalia of a warrior, the big oxhide shield, the skirt of civet tails, the leggings, the stabbing spears and knobkerries. Up here in eGoli, he was just an unskilled factory worker who set off before dawn to get a bus, and the whites called him 'boy', which he deeply resented, but back in KwaZulu he sat in the shade and drank beer with the other indunas, watched his wives hoeing the fields and his cattle grow fat, which was the correct way for a Zulu gentleman to live. Ndhlovu, his totem or surname, means elephant, and it was apt, for Isaiah was a big man.

And tonight Isaiah was an induna to be reckoned with, and so were his fellow Zulus in Mzinhlope Hostel. Jobs were scarce, they had acquired their passes the hard way, now all Isaiah and his compatriots wanted was to get on with their jobs, save their money, then go home to KwaZulu and watch their wives and cattle grow fat. Today, for the second consecutive day, they had been taunted by Xhosa juveniles, their buses and taxis stoned. As a result, they had been late for work, and the same nonsense had made them late getting home. The hostel was resounding with war-talk when Isaiah reached it. Traditional weapons were everywhere, plans were being loudly discussed. A room-mate handed him a strip of red cloth. 'Sleep early tonight, kinsman! Tomorrow wrap this around your forehead when we teach the Xhosa puppies a lesson!'

'What about the police?'

'The police will be happy that we do their work for them!'

Before dawn four hundred Zulus set out from the hostel into the areas of Soweto called Meadowlands and Orlando, armed with sticks and spears and axes and pangas. Before dawn the juveniles were out in their thousands, rebuilding their roadblocks, taking up positions near the bus stations and along the railway line. Before dawn the first stones started flying. The Zulu impis pulled out their red rags, wrapped them around their heads and they struck.

Suddenly there seemed to be Zulus everywhere, charging and yelling and swiping midst the hail of stones; Zulus beating and swiping and chasing fleeing youths; Zulus leaping over fences and charging through back yards and pounding down lanes in pursuit of Xhosa juveniles, swiping, hacking; Zulus breaking up the roadblocks under hailstorms of stones; Zulus leaping from buses and taxis and laying about with sticks and pangas and axes midst the screaming of the passengers.

Isaiah Ndhlovu was one of those from Mzinhlope detailed to ride shotgun on the buses. At the first barricade, when the stones rained down, he burst onto the road, a Zulu war cry in his throat, and he charged.

He charged into the dawn, his stick on high, leapt over the barricade and the mass of juveniles scattered before him. Isaiah's stick connected with the head of the nearest one and, as he sprawled, bounded after the next one and smote him on the head with all his might. All about him Zulus were lashing out with their knobsticks at the fleeing students, the thud and crack of stick on skull and flesh. Isaiah and his men went lashing, swiping, thrashing through the mob of Xhosa juveniles, roaring *Ndipuza!* – I have eaten! – chasing them down the lanes and through backyards. But there were only a few Zulus against hundreds of students and while the fighting was going on here the roadblocks were being rebuilt there. And all the time the stones were flying.

Isaiah did not get to work that day. By mid-morning he was exhausted, left the fighting and made his way back to Mzinhlope Hostel. He had been hit by many stones; his face was a mass of blood and bruises. He had thrashed many youngsters, left a good few unconscious, but he did not think he had killed anyone. Many of the Zulus were still out fighting but the hostel was a hive of bloodstained happy warriors loudly recounting details of battles, dressing their wounds. There were reports of the police battling in other parts of Soweto, many reports that the police had done nothing to stop Zulu warriors, even reports of police vehicles giving warriors lifts to battle-zones. And then they got the news on the radio that the Minister of Law and Order, in Parliament, had applauded the Zulu backlash, saying: 'Responsible workers are sick and tired of being bullied by juvenile upstarts.' And there was cheering and congratulations in Mzinhlope Hostel, and zealous preparations for more bloody war.

The battles lasted two weeks. Thousands were injured, many killed. For two weeks the Zulu impis raged through Soweto, in running fights and going from house to house, smashing down doors, hacking, beating with sticks, spears, axes, pangas. For two weeks the juveniles fought back with stones and sticks and spears and axes and pangas. For two weeks the carnage of Soweto was on the front pages of the world's newspapers. Now it was doubtful whether the police could put a stop to it even if they wanted to, which was more doubtful.

The bloodshed only stopped when Chief Buthelezi flew up from KwaZulu and called a peace conference with the Soweto Students' Representative Council at a secret venue. It is not known what was said at that meeting, but a brittle peace descended on Soweto.

When a third strike was called by the students two weeks later it was a complete success, with no Zulu backlash. For three days no buses ran in Soweto, no taxis, the trains almost unused, the streets empty. A triumphant, ominous quiet reigned over vast Soweto. In Johannesburg, the shops were almost empty, the streets almost deserted. In the industrial areas the factories were almost at a standstill. In those three days billions of rand were lost.

Sitting thousands of miles away in the Falkland Islands, with his notes of radio broadcasts, Mahoney rejoiced, and wrote in his journal:

> South Africa flinched. It is a dramatic exhibition of People Power, the power of withholding labour; it is a dramatic indication of the things to come. Black labour is our Achilles' heel and it is this matter of Labour which has dominated South African political thinking since the days of the Trekboers: labour of those slaves for those herds, labour for those farms of the Eastern Frontier, labour for those Boer republics, labour for those mines and farms and factories of the Lekker Lewe of the modern South Africa. This Achilles' heel has been struck.
>
> But the most significant aspect is that it was the new generation who struck the blow – the youth, not their browbeaten parents. This rebellious youth is the predictable product of apartheid, of the Afrikaners' self-destructive formula. It is the spirit of Black Consciousness and Black Power of America – and I am sure we will see much more of this muscle . . .

And, oh God, he hoped it would come soon, and bring apartheid down. And get Patti Gandhi out of prison. Oh God, he yearned to write to her, to talk to her, to give her hope. To hold her in his arms.

As Albert Mpofu explained to his Council, 'we have to prove Black Consciousness power to our own people, not only to the white "baas"! Our parents are fools! They are the donkeys who obey the baas and they do not understand that they are stronger than the man who tells them to work. The donkey is stronger than the man, he can kick the man, he can run faster than the man, but he obeys the man, because he is stupid. All the donkey cares about is food and water – then he is willing to work. It is the same with our parents – they are donkeys. And they are *drunken* donkeys.'

So the decree went out that all the shebeens must close for two weeks' mourning for the dead, on pain of being petrol-bombed. Even the bootleggers who supplied the shebeens with illegal liquor obeyed. When the shebeen-owners applied to Albert for permission to reopen he refused: three owners defied and the Council petrol-bombed them. It was a spectacular discipline, the flames exploding, the boozers fleeing out into the night, their flesh on fire. It was a sobering experience and there was no more trouble from the shebeens after that.

Flushed with this success Albert told his Council: 'Football distracts the people, it makes them forget their troubles. So all football matches must be cancelled!'

The decree went out, and there were no more football games on the dusty vacant spaces, and even the National Professional Soccer League obeyed, and placed this advertisement in the press: *'The League salutes the Soweto Students' Representative Council and supports them in their struggle. However, because the League is made up of professional footballers, we request permission to play our last two fixtures of the season.'*

It was extraordinary public recognition from local sports heroes. Flushed with success Albert decreed that all shops in Soweto must close at noon as a sign of mourning, and this too was obeyed. Then Albert summoned all shopkeepers to a big meeting where he, in disguise, told them they had to have clean premises, give good service, and sell at reasonable prices: the shopkeepers, mindful of what had happened to the shebeen-owners, obeyed and the next day an advertisement appeared in the press: *'The African Chamber of Commerce will encourage traders to live up to the requirements set . . . '*

Heady stuff indeed from the captains of black commerce. Then the Black Taxi-owners Association announced through the press that they supported the students, and their taxis drove them around free on their secret business. Then the Black Priests Solidarity Group announced that they supported the students, and the Coloured and African branches of the Dutch Reformed Church did the same.

Heady, *heady* stuff indeed, but there was no denying that the people were supporting them. Then Albert and his Council decreed there must be no Christmas shopping; returning workers were searched, their purchases confiscated, and Johannesburg shopkeepers reported a huge drop in business. Albert and his Council were calling the shots, and there wasn't a thing the police could do except raid the schools; hundreds were arrested but they could not catch that little bastard, Albert Mpofu.

And hundreds, then thousands of students fled across the borders, to join the ANC and the PAC. When the school year re-opened in 1977 there were twenty thousand students fewer. The government rescinded the edict that black education must be in Afrikaans, and it offered amnesty to those who had fled the country illegally. But only two came back. Mahoney wrote:

> This is the turning point in the lacklustre fortunes of the ANC. They will finally have to get off their arses and do something with these thousands of barefoot recruits who have risked life and limb travelling thousands of miles to reach them – if they don't, the opposition PAC will get 'em. They'll have to set up bases for them in the sanctuary states of Zambia, Angola and Mozambique. And sure as God made little green apples South African *kragdadigheid* will hit those bases, the theatre of conflict is going to spread, and the shit is really going to hit the fan: there will be a world outcry, sanctions are likely to be imposed, and that is what will finally make the apartheid government change its ways.
>
> But meanwhile the youth have tasted power and it is sweet: the Afrikaans edict has been repealed, but they are not going back to school. They have boycotted the end-of-year examinations, rioting, burning books and examination papers, thousands have been arrested, now they are boycotting schools to topple the whole Bantu Education system. Five hundred black teachers have resigned. And when the government drastically increased rents to compensate for the lost revenue from their liquor stores and beer halls, the students successfully organized rent-boycotts. And all the time there are the battles with the police. There has been a six hundred per cent increase in the purchase of guns by whites. South Africa has become the most heavily armed nation in the world and emigration has increased dramatically . . .

And, oh God, he hoped Patti knew all about this. And he yearned to contact her.

Then, in October 1977, came 'Black Wednesday'. The police swooped in massive pre-dawn raids, and they finally arrested most of the student leaders. That day the government banned another eighteen organizations including the Soweto Students' Representative Council, the Black Parents Association, the South African Students Organization, the Black Peoples Convention, the Black Women's Federation, Urban Black Justice, the Christian Institute.

But the police did not catch Albert Mpofu.

Albert never slept at his parents' home; he seldom slept in the same place for two nights. He had a number of disguises: as a schoolgirl, a female domestic worker, a nurse, an office-girl. He carried the disguises in a small hold-all wherever he went. Albert was a natural actor and could change mannerisms and voice. He had never been challenged by the police in his disguises and he had even fooled his own mother.

Albert was asleep in a safe shebeen when word reached him about the police raids. He scrambled into the office-girl's disguise. He wrenched on his knickers and bra, stuffed in cotton wool, pulled on his dress, rammed on his chic wig, tucked his handbag under his arm and minced out.

There were policemen everywhere, banging on doors, marching off suspects. Albert's feminine gait did not falter as he feigned great surprise at the goings-on, while working out his escape routes in case he had to kick off his high-heels and run for it. He tried to avoid uneven bits with his high-heels. He was halfway down the block when the white policeman barked: '*Iwe!*' You!'

'*Ek?*' Albert said in Afrikaans, looking startled.

'Yes, you! Where do you live?'

Albert's heart was thumping. 'My name is Elizabeth, baas. I live at number ninety-eight.' He pointed up the road delicately.

'Where is your pass?'

Albert fumbled in his handbag. The policeman snatched the forged document. 'It says you live in the other side of Soweto!'

Albert shuffled his high-heels coyly. 'I sometimes sleep at my boyfriend's house, baas.'

'Do you know any of these people?' the policeman demanded. He produced a list and began to read off the names. Albert listened earnestly. His name was first. He shook his head coyly after each. The policeman snapped: 'Just sleep in your own pondoki next time, hey!'

'Yes, baas,' Albert said.

Policemen were stopping people at checkpoints. But they were searching for certain youths, not office girls. Albert reached the crowded bus station. Policemen were questioning youths, demanding their passes, checking them against their lists. Albert shuffled onto a bus. A middle-aged man took the seat beside him.

'Children,' he sighed. 'They make trouble for all of us.'

'They have no respect,' Albert murmured demurely.

The jam-packed bus rumbled off into the bleak, swarming, early-morning Soweto, streams of people hurrying to work, buses and taxis grinding and hooting. And policemen all over the place, looking for Albert Mpofu.

Albert left the bus at the teeming municipal market, near the Indian quarter where Patti Gandhi used to live. He walked to the station for buses departing for the eastern Transvaal. In the late afternoon he arrived at the pretty town of Barberton near the Swaziland border. He took off his high-heels and started walking. In the small hours of the morning he crept over the border into the former British Protectorate of Swaziland. It was late afternoon when he found the road that led him into the village of Pigg's Peak, and found the Anglican church.

It is an indictment of the ANC that Albert knew almost nothing about them. Nor about their rivals, the PAC. Both had been in exile since Sharpeville, in 1960, both had been massively funded by Moscow, Peking and numerous organizations like the World Council of Churches and the Anti-Apartheid movement, but both had been so ineffective that Albert and millions like him knew nothing. Nelson Mandela was a name vaguely known as a martyr on Robben Island, and Winnie Mandela, his wife, was also a martyr but nobody knew why or where she was.

'Who do you want to join?' the young English priest asked.

'Black Consciousness.' Albert added: 'Steve Biko.'

'Steve Biko?' the priest said. 'Can't say I know him.'

He took Albert to the ANC office. Albert wanted to be a soldier. But it was a year before he was sent on with others from Swaziland to Zambia for training.

40

Justin Nkomo broke his journey in London and visited the ANC offices. As he entered the building he was photographed with a telescopic lens from across the road by a member of BOSS, the South African Bureau of State Security. 'Never seen *him* before,' the officer said in Afrikaans.

'Put a tail on him when he comes out.'

Justin had expected a warm welcome from the ANC: he was, after all, a highly qualified economist and he wanted to be of service. The black girl in the reception room with its posters and pamphlets about the Struggle was polite, but the official who interviewed him thereafter was suspicious. 'I am a member of *Mbokodo*,' he said in English. 'You know what that is-i?' He spoke with a strong accent.

'Mbokodo? That means the Boulder that Crushes.'

'Yes. We are the ANC's security department, worldwide. We are the boulder that crushes *spies*. Are you a spy?'

Justin suppressed a smile. 'If I were I would not admit it, would I? But I am not a spy.'

'Why did you spend so many years in America? Why didn't you return to South Africa and do your duty to the Struggle?'

'Because,' Justin said, 'there did not seem to be any struggle going on. Nothing was happening. And, I got married.'

'Nothing going on?' The Mbokodo man smirked. 'We have been working underground! At great risk!'

'Good,' Justin said. 'Look, all I want to do is find out if there's a job I can do to help.'

'So you married an *American*. A white liberal?'

'Actually,' Justin said, 'she is black.' He decided not to elaborate on Sally being one-sixteenth Xhosa.

'And she is still in America. Waiting for your letters? Giving her information about the ANC, to tell the CIA?' Before Justin could respond, the Mbokodo man said: 'America does not impose sanctions against South Africa! America is our enemy! America is helping UNITA fight the government in Angola! America is against Cuba! Cuba is our friend. America is against Russia and Russia is our friend! And your wife is waiting for your letters in America! And you say you are not a *spy*?'

Justin wanted to laugh. And Miami did not look so bad. Before he could muster a retort, the Mbokodo man said: 'So you're an economist. Tell me, doctor, are you a Marxist?'

Justin sighed and concealed his impatience with this fool. 'No. But I belong to a moderate school of economic thought that considers there should be a measure of socialism and state planning of the economy, particularly in Africa where massive problems bequeathed by colonialism have to be redressed.'

The Mbokodo man had not followed all that. He rasped: 'Must there be land re-distribution when the ANC rules South Africa?'

Justin had no doubts about that one: 'Yes.'

'Must we nationalize the Commanding Heights of Industry?'

Justin was getting fed up with this guy. He was going to say 'That very much depends on which heights, why, whose, what the graphs and projections show, viability, et cetera,' but the fool wouldn't understand. He said, for peace: 'Yes.'

It seemed to deflate the man. 'If you are not a spy, why you ask about Steve Biko and AZAPO, *hmmm*?'

Justin was taken aback. 'But Steve Biko and AZAPO, the whole Black Consciousness movement, they're your allies, surely, aren't they?'

The Mbokodo man looked triumphant. 'No! No, *no*! They say they are better than ANC! They are troublemakers for us, they try to divide the people! Same like the Zulus, Chief Buthelezi! *Maningi indaba!* Too much trouble! Buthelezi like to think he famous like Nelson Mandela, maybe one day president of Sout' Africa!' He glared: 'You like Chief Buthelezi, *hmmm*?'

Justin had had enough of this bullshit. If this was the ANC, forget it – but maybe he was just having an unfortunate exposure. (If Justin ever got any rank in the ANC guys like this would be kicked in the butt.) For peace he said: 'I think all black South Africans should pull together for the greatest good of the greatest number, whether you're Xhosa, Zulu, Tswana, Sotho, Ndebele, Coloured, Asian – and even *white*. We should all *work* together to fight the Boer enemy.'

This appeared to deflate the Mbokodo man again. Then he rallied: 'You willing to go Cuba? Russia? And join MK?'

Justin had to suppress a smile. MK, in the final result, had *been* his patriotic notion until meeting this jerk. *Cuba?* He had just come from that neck of the woods, Miami had been full of Cubans telling the world what a disaster Castro and communism was. And Russia? But beggars couldn't be choosers. He began: 'Okay, but I *am* an economist and I thought I might be of greater service elsewhere – '

The Mbokodo man pounced triumphantly: 'You capitalist! You no like Castro! You no like Russia! You like the Boer! You spy!'

Justin wanted to excuse himself and walk out. At that moment the door opened and a grey head appeared. The face was chubby and avuncular, and Justin was taken aback to recognize Joe Slovo, the Secretary General of the South African Communist Party. He flashed Justin a smile. 'Excuse me, but can you please see me when you've got a moment, Sam?' He turned to Justin, hand extended. 'Hi. Joe Slovo.'

The Mbokodo man had leapt to his feet. Justin took the hand. 'How d'you do?'

Joe Slovo began to disappear, bumping into a black man behind him who now stuck his head around the door: 'Sam – want to have a talk about those figures. *Hullo* – ' he smiled at Justin, and Justin recognized Chris Hani from the photographs on Sally's walls. He was handsome, young and jolly.

The Mbokodo man said stiffly: 'Dr Justin Nkomo, sir.'

'Doctor, huh?' Chris Hani said brightly. 'We need doctors!'

'Of economics,' Justin grinned apologetically.

'Well,' Chris Hani grinned, 'we sure need them too!' He winked. 'Don't let this guy – ' he jerked a thumb – 'give you too much of a hard time.' He disappeared.

Justin Nkomo emerged from the ANC offices half an hour later, into the cold London drizzle, confused. He had brusque instructions from

Sam to write his biography and to present it the next morning. He wasn't going to do it. He didn't like that Mbokodo bastard – no American cop had treated him like that. He did not want to go to Cuba or Russia for military training, he wanted to work with Steve Biko's Black Consciousness. If that didn't come off he would do military training, but he wasn't going to take shit like that from an uneducated jerk. He saw a bus coming, and he ran for it.

By running for the bus he shook off the tail which Sam had set following him. But he did not shake off the BOSS tail until his flight left London the next day.

He had routed himself via Lusaka, Zambia, in the hopes of consulting the ANC people there about Steve Biko, but he decided to give them a miss. When he arrived, he was taken aback. He was used to slick, efficient America; he was amazed, and depressed, by the run-down condition of Lusaka. The immigration officials at the airport were shabby and tried to cadge cigarettes off him. There was a beat-up bus outside but it had broken down. Justin gave up and looked for a taxi. The tyres were bald, the windscreen shattered, the meter did not work. The suburbs, which once were white, judging by the middle-class architecture, were dusty and dry, with goats and cattle grazing in the gardens. But the real surprise was the main street, called Kenneth Kaunda Way. It was obviously once well ordered, for the Victorian shopfronts were solid and there were a few tall office-blocks, and there were traffic lights: but there was almost no traffic, and the lights were not working. Goats grubbed on the traffic islands and roundabouts. The street was full, but they were not people going about their business; they were idle, sitting on the sidewalks, poor people with nothing to do. Justin was astonished at the shop windows: he was accustomed to shops jam-packed with goods: but here there was almost nothing to buy.

Justin walked down Kenneth Kaunda Way, inspecting the shops with his economist's eye: this was an African economy? He knew that Africa was in economic trouble, that experiments in socialism had resulted in problems, but no contemporary accounts had prepared him for this degeneration. He passed a butcher's shop. There were only three dismembered chickens and a piece of goat; flies buzzed and crawled busily. He looked around for a supermarket. There was none. But further down the pot-holed street he saw the Russian flag flying over a building. He walked down to it. He looked in the big display windows.

And, ah yes, all was milk and honey in Russia. Big Technicolor photographs showed rolling Russian fields burdened with crops, robust

Russian maidens and strapping Russian lads in love with their combine harvesters. Jolly workers saluting the hammer and sickle, jolly Russian housewives presiding over tables groaning with goodies, avenues of rumbling tanks on May Day parades. Ah, yes, it was the workers' paradise in Russia.

Justin Nkomo knew that the pictures were propaganda bullshit. He knew all the graphs and analyses of Russia's Gross Domestic Product for the last fifty years, and China's. And Hong Kong's, America's, Germany's. Communism, worldwide, was in deep shit. *It had not worked*, that was irrefutable, to argue would be as futile as arguing with Pythagoras' Theorem. What he argued for, idealistically, was the possibility of the Conscientious Man, the *Good* Man who worked hard both for his own benefit and the greater good of the masses. *If only everybody thought like that*. And this was where Steve Biko's Black Consciousness came in.

Justin saw a statue, in the middle of a traffic island. He walked down to it. It was a glorious bronze statue of a muscled black man rising up, and above his angry head he clutched the heavy links of a chain. He had triumphantly snapped the chain with his strong arms. The inscription beneath commemorated the independence of Zambia. A goat was chewing a plastic bag beneath it. Somebody had written on the stonework with spray-paint. The authorities had tried to scrub it off but the faint words were still legible: *A kaffir will break anything*.

'*Fuck you, white man!*' he whispered. '*We'll show you!*'

He walked away up Kenneth Kaunda Way, angry. But he had to admit that the Zambians hadn't made a very good job of scrubbing the racist libel off.

He arrived in Salisbury, Rhodesia, in the early afternoon, to hook up with his connection to Johannesburg. There were sandbagged military emplacements around the airport. There were lots of jolly English-sounding Rhodesians drinking at the bar. There was much talk about the war. From the windows, Justin could see into the parking area. Almost everybody was carrying a rifle, even the women, and pistols swung from hips conspicuously.

When the South African Airways flight arrived, he was put next to two elderly Indian businessmen at the very back. When the steward eventually reached them he said in a heavy Afrikaans accent: 'You chaps want something to drink, hey?'

It was late afternoon when his aircraft circled over Johannesburg and the sprawling black townships around it. Smoke was rising from burning shacks. The Afrikaner immigration officer examined Justin's South African passport as if he had made it himself, then summoned a BOSS officer. Justin was taken into an office and questioned. 'I've come back to seek employment,' he answered.

'Well,' the BOSS officer said, 'you can get a job in your Republic of Transkei, they need chaps like you with degrees, hey.'

'But I'd like to work in Johannesburg.'

'*Every*body,' the officer said, 'would *like* to work in Jo'burg, that's the bladdy trouble. You're a citizen of the Republic of Transkei and that's where you'll bladdy-well work, hey.'

'But I'm a South African citizen,' Justin said, 'I've got a South African passport – '

'Not any more – you're a foreigner. This passport is issued in the old days. You're surrendering it an' applying to the Transkei government for a Transkei passport, hey.'

'But, they're not recognized anywhere in the world!'

'An' where do you think you're going, hey? Russia perhaps? Zambia, to join your ANC pals? Now I'm giving you a three-day pass to get to the Transkei border. There's a train, or a plane. An' don't let us catch you in South Africa, hey, with your fancy American ideas.'

Justin emerged into the concourse seething with anger. And shock. He felt naked, bereft, defenceless. Literally stripped, of his citizenship. In America some of those redneck cops were hard bastards but he'd always had confidence in the law. Here the law stripped him. And, yes, he was frightened of the bastards. And, yes, he hated them. Suddenly Miami did not look so bad at all. And now he didn't even have a passport to get back . . . But no way was he going to give up. And no way was he going to be exiled to the Transkei.

Now where to go? If he were a white man he would catch a bus into the city and look for a cheap hotel. But there were no hotels for blacks in this city. Soweto was in chaos, with the riots. He looked for a bank. He joined a short queue. The teller said: 'Go to the Non-European counter, please.'

'But there's no teller there.'

'Just go to that counter, hey!'

Jesus. Justin walked to the counter. And waited. The teller did some paperwork. After five minutes he came to the Non-European section. 'Ja?' He was surprised to see Justin's American Express traveller's cheques. 'Where did you get these?'

'In Miami.'

'Where's that, hey?'

'In America.'

'You mean Miami, *America*?! Don't make me laugh. Show me your passport, hey!'

He explained about his passport. He produced his new pass, his American driver's licence. No good. He didn't have a South African reference book – why not? With great reluctance the teller agreed to change some English bank notes. Justin walked away, seething, looking for a public telephone. He saw a row of them, one marked Non-Europeans. He dialled *Drum* magazine.

'Well goodness me,' the boss said. 'Come into the office! We're just starting the editorial booze-up!'

Justin's eyes burned in gratitude. He went outside to look for a bus. He joined a queue of passengers, but a policeman told him to go over there and wait for the Non-European bus. He waited an hour. He was the only passenger into the city.

It was midnight when the editorial meeting broke up. Willie Thembu was going to put Justin up for a couple of nights in Soweto. The boss said: 'You could sleep in my servants' quarters for a few nights but the cops are watching my place. And I don't think a doctor of economics could credibly pass as my garden-boy, you'd be in jail. *And* me. Now as regards your deportation to the Transkei – leave that to me. Tomorrow I'll tell the Department of Bantu Affairs that I've hired you and that you're indispensable. That'll give you a work permit. But we can't pay you much until you've proved you can write good copy. And the first copy I want from *you* – ' he jabbed a finger – 'is how it feels for a Xhosa-boy to return from years in America to apartheid. Sparing no gory details. Starting at the airport. Life in Soweto, compared with life in Miami. Go and visit your parents in the Transkei – life in the kraal compared with your life in America. And so on. If you do that story right, you're a full-time Mister *Drum*. With all the liabilities attached thereto.'

'And what about the Black Consciousness business?' Willie said.

The boss took a semi-final slug of whisky. '*Drum* is a law-abiding magazine. Steve Biko is a Banned Person, he may not be interviewed by the vulgar press, nor have anything written about him. Sorry, Justin, but if you want to do your Black Consciousness thing – and I would applaud – you're on your own. And probably in jail. Same applies to Winnie Mandela. Wonderful woman, wonderful story about how she's suffering under apartheid in exile, but we can't publish a word because she's a Banned Person. Nor about Nelson. What a story that would be, imprisoned now for how many years on Robben Island – fifteen? Like Napoleon on Elba. What is his prison like? What does he do all day long – break rocks? How do the warders treat him?' He spread his hands. 'But we cannot write anything. If you want to write it for overseas newspapers, fine – but *Drum* can't publish it. Okay?'

'Okay,' Justin said. He had not intended to be a writer at all until he'd walked into these exciting offices. He was very grateful.

The boss continued: 'Like that beautiful Patti Gandhi. Luke Mahoney's girl. In prison for the rest of her life. What a story that would make. But *Drum* can't write it. You ever hear from Luke?'

'We write to each other occasionally.'

'And how is the old sumbitch? We get a Christmas card every year but that's it. Still wandering the globe as a lawyer?'

'Yes. I think he's in Hong Kong now.'

The boss snorted. 'What a waste of writing talent. How,' he appealed, 'can anybody have the chance to be a *writer* and turn it down for being a lawyer? *Writing* – ' he spread his hands – 'is a gift from the gods. Sure, lawyers make more money, but what about the sheer *fun*?' He looked at Justin. 'I'm giving you a break, doc, because *Drum* put you on the road. You want to go'n play with Steve Biko, good luck to you. But *Drum* won't be able to get you out of jail.'

41

'Compare Soweto with your life in Miami,' the boss had said. Jesus, Soweto was a culture shock. A shattering difference.

Soweto was still in the grip of the Students' Representative Council. Albert Mpofu's successor had also fled the country to join the ANC: now the third chairman ruled Soweto. Police everywhere, checking passes, guarding bus and taxi ranks, clearing roadblocks. Schools burnt out, windows smashed.

'The students go quiet for a bit, then the word goes out, and out they come,' Willie Thembu said. 'But the police are getting the upper hand. And the adults are getting fed up with being pushed around.'

'But are they back at school?'

'Some; most aren't. It's a tragedy, this Liberation Before Education slogan of the ANC's. It's going to result in a lost generation of uneducated kids – *defiant* kids. Pure trouble. For this government *and* the ANC when they come to power.'

Justin snorted. 'And when's that going to be?'

'I lose hope. Thousands have run away across the border to join them. But we haven't seen any evidence of MK yet.'

Willie was driving a circuitous route through Soweto to familiarize

Justin with his new town. Jesus, it depressed him. Miles of little concrete cottages between pockets of squatter shacks, then more cottages. Clusters of grubby shops, some burnt out, some boarded up. The joyless terrain undulated, the cottages and shacks extending over the horizon in all directions. They passed a burnt-out beer hall. Willie pointed to another gutted building, which was being restored. 'West Rand Administration Board, which runs Soweto. That's where you go to-morrow to apply for a bed in a hostel.'

Jesus, it was depressing. Willie drove along a lane at the foot of a rocky ridge. He stopped and pointed: 'Nelson Mandela's house, before he was sent to jail.'

It was a grubby cottage in a bare-earth yard. A few plots away stood a small church. 'Who lives in it now?'

'Nobody. Winnie's in exile in Brandfort.' He snorted. 'One day that'll be a national monument.'

Jesus, Justin thought. Nelson Mandela, qualified lawyer, president of a political organization, and he had to live in a dump like this? In a *slum* like Soweto? That's all apartheid allowed him?

Willie's cottage was a similar shock. It was a small concrete oblong, divided into four without corridors: a small living room, two small bedrooms, a small kitchen. There was an outdoor toilet and shower. The cottage was whitewashed, and Mrs Thembu had made a garden. A neat cement path from the front gate divided tiny flowerbeds; in the backyard was a vegetable patch. The furniture was good, the radiogram was modern, the little kitchen had all the modern appliances – but, *Jesus*, this is how Willie had to live? This was the best he could expect? Anywhere in America this would be a poor-black's house. A cotton-picker's shack. But Willie was a middle-class, veteran journalist on a respectable magazine with a respectable salary and a respectable wife – Mrs Clara Thembu was a teacher – but they had to live cooped up like this?

Justin tried to conceal his dismay, but Willie smiled as he passed him a bottle of beer: 'Pretty shitty, huh, compared with Miami. But I'm lucky: I'm a Section 10 Resident. Know what that means?'

'No.' Justin took out his new notebook.

'I've worked for *Drum* for more than ten years, I've got a valid work permit, so I qualify under Section 10 of the Group Areas Act to rent this *family* dwelling from the government and have my family *living* with me. Until I die, or retire, or I'm fired. When that happens the whole family has to return to our homeland and settle down on the kraal. If I *weren't* lucky enough to qualify, I'd have to live here as a bachelor, in a hostel – like you're going to do. I'm a "foreigner" now, just like you.

Used to be a South African, but now I'm a citizen of the Republic of Bophuthatswana, that itty-bitty patchwork over there in the western Transvaal. Surrounded by Boers.'

'So you could be deported?'

'Anytime I put a foot wrong. Deported as an Undesirable.'

It made Justin angry. 'You're a Tswana? I thought you were a Zulu.'

'No, my wife's Zulu. Which raises another problem. When I die, where does my wife live? She doesn't speak Tswana. And the Tswanas don't like Zulus. Shit-scared of them, ever since Mzilikazi wandered through on the warpath.' He winked. 'And so am I.'

'I heard that,' Clara shouted from the kitchen. She appeared in the doorway and threw a carrot at her husband. 'I'll Zulu you!'

'See?' Willie grinned at Justin. 'No respect. So war-like.'

It seemed the first time Justin had laughed in months. Willie continued: 'So all of us are now "foreigners" in white South Africa. Tolerated only to the extent our labour is required. After that we're deported. With no redress – not even for any improvements we've made on these miserable cottages, like adding on a proper bathroom. And of course we've got no political representation, except our new republican "consulates" – ' he made quotation marks with his fingers – 'in Pretoria, and they're useless because they're shit-scared because the government pays their salaries through subsidies.' He shook his head. 'The only voice we have is through the so-called "Urban Bantu Council", like a municipal council, which is under the supervision of the West Rand Administration Board. But the UBC councillors are mostly government-appointees. The students call them the Useless Boys Club. Because they're corrupt. And the chairman of the council is a white official. The UBC is bankrupt because of non-payment of rents, and because of the riots, so now they've *increased* rents, to compensate, and so people are building more squatter shacks to escape rent. So the UBC has now put a tax on squatter shacks, and if you don't pay they send in a bulldozer. And so people build another shack somewhere, and the UBC – on government orders – sends in another bulldozer. And so on.' He shook his head. 'It's fucking terrible. Where is your kraal, by the way?'

'About forty miles outside Umtata, on the way down to the Wild Coast. It's pretty country.'

'Not anymore, I bet. Bet it's overpopulated. Soil erosion. Thanks to apartheid. Have you got any cattle?'

'My father gave me a cow when I was circumcised. She must be dead now, but I suppose she multiplied.'

'Haven't you written?'

'My parents are illiterate. I have written a few letters but I've had no reply. Of course, there is no postal delivery there. I had to write care of the trader's store.'

Willie snorted. 'Well, buy some cows when you're there. What else is there for a black man to invest in?'

'Have you got cattle back in Bophuthatswana?'

'About twenty, at last count.'

'You father looks after them?'

'My other wife.' Willie put his finger to his lips. 'Shh. Sore point with the Zulu warrior in the kitchen.'

The next day Justin went to the Bantu Affairs Department, armed with a letter certifying that *Drum* magazine had employed him. He stood in a queue all day, and eventually was given a work permit. The following day he went to the Urban Bantu Council office, and queued all day to apply for bunk space. He was assigned to Nkosana Hostel. He returned to Willie's cottage to collect his belongings. Mrs Thembu was home from school and she drove him to his new abode. En route they stopped at a store to equip Justin for his new life as a bachelor. The store was called *Kona-zonke*, which means Got Everything: it sold cheap blankets, bicycles, guitars, clothing, cooking utensils, foodstuffs.

'Isn't there a real department store?' Justin said.

'This is it,' Mrs Thembu said. 'Unless you go into Jo'burg.'

He bought two blankets, two enamel pots, a tin mug, cutlery, a padlock. 'Is there a supermarket near here?'

'In Jo'burg. But you won't have a fridge where you're going.'

He bought mielie-meal, powdered milk, tea, sugar, bully-beef. Mrs Thembu dropped him at the hostel. 'Good luck.'

It was a single-storey quadrangle. Weeds grew around it, festooned with plastic bags. Adjacent was a squatter area: about five hundred shacks of tin and cardboard. On the other three sides rows of cottages stretched away down dirt roads. People were streaming home from work. Justin walked in.

The quadrangle within was bare earth. It was littered with rubbish. Men squatted around small cooking fires, eating. Justin consulted his receipt and walked down the inner verandah, looking for room 38. Radios gabbled. Nobody took any interest in him.

Room 38 was much smaller than Sally's studio, and it held eight bunks. Four window panes were broken, patched with cardboard. A row of eight battered metal lockers lined one wall. They were plastered with photographs of semi-naked women, mostly white. The brick walls were similarly decorated, between nails holding clothing, cooking utensils. *Death to Buthelezi* had been spray-painted across a section. The floor was raw cement.

Justin's sunken heart sank further. He had forgotten how awful the townships were. He whispered to himself: 'Steve Biko.' He found bunk 38G. It was three foot wide, bare wood. No pillow. He opened locker 38G. He unpacked and hung up his clothes. He spread his new blankets and lay down on his bunk.

'*I'm just a tourist,*' he whispered to himself.

His room-mates started arriving. They were all Xhosa peasants. They mostly ignored him. Justin wondered where they worked, but he did not ask. He got up, got his food from his locker and walked down the verandah to the communal kitchen. It was crowded with men cooking over wood fires. He gave up. Next door was one of the ablution rooms. He looked inside. There were rows of exposed lavatories against one wall, shower pipes on the other. The lavatories had no seats and the bowls were foul with old excrement. The floor was sodden, pieces of sodden newspaper everywhere. The place stank of shit.

Justin sat down on the verandah, by himself, opened a can of bully beef. The quadrangle was filling up. More cooking fires started. A man arrived with an emery wheel. He set it up and started receiving customers who wanted their spears and axes sharpened, to be ready for the Zulus.

'Jesus,' Justin thought. 'I'm a doctor of economics, and this is all I can look forward to for ten years, until I qualify as a Section 10 Resident?'

He went to his bunk early, to block out the misery in sleep. People were streaming down the road to the cottages, pouring into the hostel. It was noisy. There was distant gunfire and police sirens. Sounds of running feet in the road. The clatter of rocks on rooftops, the smash of glass. The naked overhead light kept him awake: he pulled his blanket over his head. His room-mates came in one by one. Fifteen people finally went to bed. One man crawled under Justin's bunk: that was his space.

That night there was a police raid. Justin woke up to shouts, thuds, a white constable ripping the blanket off him and demanding his pass and hostel permit. Justin groggily pulled them out of his pocket. Two naked women were scrambling out of bunks, pulling on dresses while constables harangued them. They were jostled outside. So were their boyfriends. The man under Justin's bunk escaped detection.

Justin lay in his bunk, a sob in his throat. And Willie Thembu's shitty little crowded cottage seemed wonderful. And Sally's silly little apartment with its hodgepodge of African trinkets was luxurious. And, oh God, he couldn't wait to get out of here, and find Steve Biko.

42

Steve Biko, being a Banned Person, was confined to his native township outside King William's Town, a thousand kilometres south of Johannesburg. His black township was a smaller version of Soweto, but poorer, more disorganized. But Steve Biko's Zanenepilo Black Community Programme Centre was impressive: clean grounds, white-washed walls, flower beds. There were workshops, a lecture room, a medical clinic, an bare-earth football field with whitened lines, a church.

'I'm not allowed to speak to the press,' he said to Justin. 'So if the cops burst in you're just a visiting academic interested in my Black Community Programme, okay? Did any cops see you arrive?'

'I don't know. I just got off the bus, asked the way and started walking.' He added, 'I've got an onward ticket to Umtata, where my parents live.'

'Not much of an alibi.' Biko spoke perfect English. He was a charming young man, emanating self-confidence. He was wearing football kit, having come off the field to talk to Justin. 'You'd better be on that bus this afternoon because the cops will know by tonight you've been here. But I've had a number of academics visit my centre, even a few foreign diplomats and correspondents; they know Black Consciousness is the future. Come into the workshop.'

It was a big, long room. Rows of African women and girls sat at tables and on the floor making dresses and handicrafts. Biko said: 'We sell our products. Next door is a carpentry shop. That building – ' he pointed through the window – 'is our lecture room where we hold leadership classes. And literary classes and so on.'

'But, I thought a Banned Person could not be in the company of more than two other people. What about all these people working here?'

'Depends on the terms of the banning order. When I'm *off-duty* I cannot be with more than two other people. Confined to my cottage. But even this government doesn't stop me working – unless they put me in detention. Black Consciousness is not banned – *yet*. And my Black Community Programmes are legitimate work; they can't deny that. It's even theoretically compatible with apartheid, isn't it? Blacks working together for self-betterment without white "help" – that's what apartheid is supposed to *achieve*. So they can't complain.'

'So why did they ban you?'

Biko snorted. 'Long story. But I was involved in some successful strike action in Durban. And Black Consciousness was getting too strong for the government's liking. And of course BC is only compatible with apartheid up to a *point*: our purpose is to liberate the black *psychologically* from his inferiority complex so that he gets the self-confidence to claim what is rightfully his. And, of course, *that* notion doesn't suit apartheid.' He waved a hand. 'It started when I formed the black student representative body called SASO and we split away from NUSAS, the multi-racial National Union of South African Students. Theoretically the government had to approve of that too, black students representing themselves. But we made ourselves unpopular by publicly applauding when the new communist government took over in Mozambique. Then we formed the Black Peoples' Convention, to unite the black community into a political organization, with Black Consciousness as our creed – and the government did not like that, although we are making no specific political demands at this stage. We are just preparing ourselves *psychologically*. But, of course, we excluded the so-called Homeland leaders because they're collaborating with the apartheid system – we even excluded Chief Buthelezi. And that made us unpopular.' He grinned. 'That, in a nutshell, is why I'm banned. Now – in case you're a cop – that wasn't a political discussion.'

'I'm not a cop,' Justin grinned. 'Tell me about Chief Buthelezi?'

Biko stared out the window at the football field. The game was still in progress. 'I like him personally. He's a good politician. We used to be allies. But he says our Black Peoples' Convention is unnecessary, we should support existing leaders, like himself. So we've come to the parting of the ways.'

'But he's not collaborating with the government, is he?'

Biko sighed. 'No. He's refused to accept independence for KwaZulu – because he insists the Zulus are South Africans, not "foreigners" – and intends to remain part of South Africa. So that he can be prime minister one day? But he *has* accepted "self-government", with himself as chief minister. Thereby getting all the perks – a fat salary, a fat budget subsidised by the South African government, a nice purpose-built capital of Ulundi, a nice palace, a nice fleet of cars, his own police force, his own tame parliament of Inkatha members.'

That sounded sensible enough to Justin – take the government's money. 'But he is *arguing* with the South African government for the abolition of apartheid, and democracy for all?'

'Yes.'

'So he's only taking advantage of apartheid, to suit his democratic purposes. He's not *collaborating* like the puppet republics of Transkei and the rest?'

'True. But in our view he's selfish – he's looking for his own future power, and that's divisive. He's also indirectly supporting the government's policy of tribalism – he's building up the Zulus' future, and the Zulus have always considered themselves the master race. Ever since Shaka. Whereas we in Black Consciousness say all the black peoples must be united, we must forget tribalism, we must unite to throw off our yoke of the underdog.' He gave Justin a brilliant smile. 'Unity in our black power, in our black pride. Black Consciousness is the only future, my friend.'

Oh yes, Justin agreed with that. And this man radiated all he stood for. 'And the ANC? How do you rate them?'

Steve Biko turned and strolled through the workshop. He spread his hands theatrically. 'The ANC – where are they? I don't see them. Okay, they're banned, but where is their *organization*? Their cell-structure. I am also banned, but here I am, large as life, in my Centre, *working*. Where is the ANC? Sitting in exile. Comfortable.' He spread his hands again. 'Where is MK? All gone to bed since Nelson Mandela was put away?' He snorted. 'At least Buthelezi is tackling the apartheid regime from *inside* the country, not sitting on his arse in London. Don't get me wrong – I applaud any respectable liberation movement. But the ANC's barking up the wrong tree – they're a *multi*-racial organization. They look for support from white liberals. They espouse liberal white standards. They mimic whites. That's wrong. We don't want to become black white men. Black Consciousness teaches blacks to stand on their own two feet without white help. That's the only way blacks will become truly liberated.'

'And how do you rate the Pan Africanist Congress?' Justin asked.

'Now, *they're* more akin to my philosophy, they're *Africanists* – "Africa for the Africans", "All the land must be returned to the Africans". Not milk-and-water multi-racialists who rely on white men, like the ANC. But where is the PAC?' He spread his hands. 'Also in exile. What good can they do in exile except train another little army to try to take on the great big South African army? Where is their underground organization? Hiding in fear?' He shook his head. 'And they've got this stupid slogan, "One Settler One Bullet".'

'You don't approve of violence?'

Biko grinned. 'You sure you're not a cop?'

Justin smiled. 'Quite sure. But as a result of these student riots in Soweto thousands have fled to join the ANC and PAC. How do you feel about that? You're losing supporters.'

Biko nodded. 'But it was the spirit of Black Consciousness which ignited the riots, they're carrying the torch of BC with them. That's good. I hope they teach the ANC and PAC a thing or two. And their parents are still here, keeping a light in the window for them.' He sighed. 'Look, violence is inevitable. This is a violent, repressive government, and it will evoke counter-violence. And one day this government will give in, and it will be because of the just demands of Black Consciousness. But when that happens, and the black people take back what is rightfully theirs, they must have the self-confidence, the pride and the ability to run South Africa properly, justly, the African way, not make a hybrid mess of it. And that is what Black Consciousness is all about. We hope Black Consciousness will do it without violence, but I suspect violence is inevitable.'

'But when?'

'It's already started, with the Soweto riots. These riots will continue because suddenly blacks have some reason for hope. There were the successful strikes in 1972, during which I got banned. And then along all our borders there are wars, in which South Africa is directly or indirectly involved, exhausting itself, and making it easier for our freedom fighters to cross. South Africa lost a buffer state when the Portuguese collapsed in Mozambique in 1974. Same in Angola – the Marxists have taken over and South Africa is engaged in helping UNITA fight them. The war in Rhodesia has intensified, and Henry Kissinger and even South Africa's prime minister are pressurising Ian Smith to negotiate a settlement, so soon we'll have a black government in Rhodesia too. And remember that all these wars, all these liberation movements, have Russia and China behind them – there are thousands of Cuban troops fighting in Angola against the South Africans and UNITA, the Russians and Chinese are supplying the freedom fighters in Rhodesia. So South Africa's back is getting closer to the wall. So, when?' He nodded. 'Soon. Though it may be some years yet, the Boer does not give up easily.'

Justin sighed tensely. He could not wait for it to happen. 'Are you – is Black Consciousness communist?'

Steve Biko smiled. 'Let me say this: there was *no* poverty in Africa until the white man arrived. Why? Because the *land* was the only source of wealth, for grazing, and the land belonged to the whole *tribe*. True, a man owned his own cattle, but cattle are no good without grazing land, and that land was *communal*. And the land must become communal again.' He added: 'And remember that the whites, who are only twenty per cent of the total population in this bloody country, own *eighty-seven* per cent of the land.'

Justin sighed. He was no communist, but what Biko had said about land was so true.

'So, having told you all that, what can I do for you? As you can't publish it.'

'I want,' Justin said, with a smile, 'to work with you.'

Biko turned pensively. He led him back through the workshop, into his little office. He waved to a chair, sat and put his feet up on the desk.

'We could use an economist. To keep our account books, hold literacy classes, administration and so forth.'

'I'd like to be involved in extending your cell structure. In *policy*. Underground work.'

Biko smiled. 'How do you know whether we've got an *underground* cell-structure?' He sat up straight. 'I'll have to check you out, Dr Nkomo, but in principle we'd be delighted to have you – though we can only pay you pocket-money. You go home to the Transkei to see your parents, then come back to me in about a month. Don't telephone me, or write, because the police will intercept all that. And now,' he picked up a pen, 'start telling me your history. All about yourself.'

43

Living in Miami all those years in small apartments, Justin had yearned for the wide open spaces he grew up in, and romanticised his home country, its spaciousness, its rolling greenness, its simplicity. Being with Sally and all her 'African' silliness, socialising with her black friends endlessly going on about their African 'roots', he had longed for the real thing. Now here was Transkei, the real thing, and it was a terrible shock.

Where were the rolling green hills with their fat cattle? Where were the neat thatched huts? Where were the handsome people in their red blankets? The rolling hills were cropped to stubble, the cattle were scrawny. And soil erosion was everywhere: great jagged dongas running between the hills. There were many, many more huts than he remembered and they were no longer clustered in isolated family kraals. Many were not even thatched, they had corrugated iron roofs; in fact most of them were not round anymore, they were square, for it is easier to build a flat roof than a conical one. The huts were not decorated with patterns as they used to be. There were many, many more people, and they wore old white man's clothes now. And everywhere, along the roadsides, clinging to kraal fences and bushes, were the plastic bags.

The Transkei of Justin's boyhood was degraded. It was apartheid that had done it. There were too many people trying to live off the land, and apartheid's forced removals had put them there. Because there were too many people there were too many cattle, and because there were too many cattle the grass was cropped down, and because the grass was cropped down there was no retention of rainwater so there was soil erosion. And because of the soil erosion the fields were infertile and the crops were stunted, and there was no long grass for thatching. The very earth of the Republic of Transkei was exhausted because that was the only economy there, and it was the only economy because apartheid had created the republic there. And far too many people were far too under-educated for any other type of economy, and apartheid had under-educated them. So the only other asset they had was their labour and when they left the impoverished land to sell their labour they had to have a pass from the white man, sell their labour within fourteen days or return to their impoverished land. And if they did not return they were put in jail.

And because they were under-educated and poor they did not see anything offensive in all this litter, they simply did not know better . . .

It was a sick economy, doomed to failure, and Justin was amazed that any government had ever imagined it could be anything else. Oh yes, he wanted to work with Steve Biko . . .

The capital Umtata was even more infuriating to him as an economist. It was not the thousands of Xhosa aimlessly wandering the streets – his long bus journey from the River Kei border had prepared him for that — it was the appalling waste of money. Jesus, out there in the hills the people were impoverished, the land ravaged by unchecked soil erosion and over-grazing and over-population by under-educated peasants; the country cried out for socio-economic development, but what did Justin see? Towering, grandiose, ugly buildings dominating the single-storey Victorian shopfronts of Main Street; the simple municipal recreation field replaced with the ostentatious Independence Stadium; the outskirts of Umtata smothered by the villas of government ministers. It made Justin Nkomo's blood boil.

It was four o'clock in the afternoon when he arrived at the Mahoneys' house, to pay his respects and ask after Luke. He approached the front door; then he hesitated, and walked around the house to the kitchen door.

'Goodness me – *Justin*!' Mrs Mahoney exclaimed when the housemaid summoned her to the back door. 'How you've grown!'

Mrs Mahoney entertained Dr Justin Nkomo in the kitchen. They drank tea at the big scrubbed table where Justin had laboured over his homework many years ago.

'Oh, Master Luke – or maybe *Mister* Luke is more appropriate now – seems to be doing *very* well,' Mrs Mahoney said. '*When* he writes to tell us. He's a government lawyer and magistrate in all kinds of funny places, but now he's back in Hong Kong, which seems to be the headquarters of the remnants of the empire. Hasn't married yet, though from time to time we hear about this girl or that. I *do* wish he'd marry and settle down. And you, Justin? By the way I must congratulate you on your English, you're absolutely idiomatic.'

Justin grinned. 'Thank you. And Miss Jill?'

'Miss Jill is now *Mrs* Jill, married to the *Reverend* Leonard Dawson of the American Mission, in KwaZulu. She seems very happy, three lovely children – but growing up in that *wilderness* . . . I shudder. They've got a very nice little mission, a beautiful little church, and a clinic and workshops and things, but, my goodness, the *trouble* she has to put up with – all those Zulu faction fights and clan grudges. She seems to spend most of her time stitching up split heads. Mister Luke offered her a holiday, sent them the airfares to visit him in Hong Kong, but they simply couldn't afford the *time*. So Mister Mahoney and I went. And, I must say, Mister Luke has a very comfortable life. He's got a lovely apartment, and he's got a very nice elderly Chinese house-girl called Ah Chan who cooks marvellous meals. He showed us round his clubs, the Yacht Club and the Hong Kong Club and the Foreign Correspondents' Club – though he's not writing for newspapers anymore, thank God. But he *is* writing a book. Won't tell us what it's about. Anyway, he says he *hankers* so for Africa – '

'Justin!' George Mahoney exclaimed, striding into the kitchen. 'How good to see you!'

They had adjourned to the living room. 'No,' George said, 'I lost my seat in Parliament when the Transkei got independence thrown at it – my seat ceased to exist. And what a shambles this Transkei is now. And *corrupt*? The damn-fool South African government pours millions of rands into us every year to try to make the place work as a model of apartheid, and most of the money disappears into our politicians' pockets. And of course our opposition party is muzzled.'

'Yes, I saw the big new government offices,' Justin said.

'Madness,' George said. 'As well as an eyesore. And all those palatial houses for cabinet ministers. Same in the so-called Republic of Ciskei – the South African government paid for a whole new *city*, called Bisho, starting from scratch. Madness. And the first thing the new prime minister of Ciskei does is proclaim himself Life President!' He snorted. 'On Independence Day, the pole fell down as they were hoisting the new flag!'

Justin smiled. Embarrassed. These were Xhosa people the old man was disparaging. And it made him angry that his people were making fools of themselves.

George Mahoney continued: 'Same in the Republic of Bophutha-tswana. Whole new grandiose capital of Mmabatho has been built by the South African government, slap-bang next door to Mafikeng. *Madness*. And where is all the money coming from? The white South African taxpayer! *Billions* spent every year to sustain the *fiction* of these little black "republics" so the South Africans can try to claim that apartheid is working. The money should have been spent on black betterment schemes. Agriculture! Dams! Technical colleges!'

Justin said: 'Yes, I saw terrible soil erosion.'

'Terrible. And we need to get rid of these scrawny cattle and import some decent breeding stock. It's the same in all these homeland-republics the government's created. Poverty and corruption. It's not only a terrible waste of money, it's such a criminal waste of precious time. The government should be using its advantage of being its own boss, using the time and money to uplift the African and teach him about democracy, instead of thrusting "independence" at him to get rid of him.'

Mrs Mahoney said: 'To be fair, the government did hold a referendum in each homeland to ask the people if they wanted independence.'

'Big deal. What do tribesmen know about independence? Their own corrupt politicians told them the skies would rain bicycles and transistor radios if they voted yes.'

Justin felt resentment again at the disparagement. But he had to admit it was true – and that was what Steve Biko was all about. He said: 'And what do you think of KwaZulu and Chief Buthelezi, sir?'

George Mahoney nodded. 'I like Buthelezi. Oh, I like the Xhosa people too, that's why I live here, it's their damn corrupt politicians I can't stomach – apartheid's puppets. But Buthelezi is no puppet, he's a sensible man, and he's a capitalist. He's against these economic sanctions the ANC is calling for. He says the blacks will be the ones to suffer most, and he's right. He's stoutly refused independence but accepted self-government, and that's smart – he's his own boss but he's still a South African, and he's doing a good job arguing with the government.'

'Is his KwaZulu government democratic?'

George sighed. 'He held proper elections, but his Inkatha Freedom Party won all the seats. There's always intimidation in Africa but how much in KwaZulu, I don't know. There's no opposition party in the legislature, and that's not healthy. Democratic?' He shrugged. 'Buthelezi is a strong personality. And he's got the Zulu monarch, King Goodwill, on his side. And the Zulus adore their king. So Buthelezi has things pretty much his way in KwaZulu.'

'Is there corruption in KwaZulu, sir?'

George sighed. 'I don't know. But is there a government in Africa that isn't corrupt?' Justin winced inwardly, but George mollified him by declaring: 'Including the South African government! *God*, it's a pork-barrel government! Jobs for the boys – white Afrikaners, of course. Do you know that forty per cent of the white working population work for the government? Is that a healthy economy? And almost all Afrikaners. Fat salaries – and enormous pensions. This government has solved the poor-white problem by employing them all in the civil service! How can the economy stand it? Only because we've got a vast reservoir of cheap black labour – a poor-black problem! Jobs for pals – just like in the rest of Africa? So the Afrikaner is a typical African! And apartheid itself – isn't that the biggest corruption of all? The whites having eighty-seven per cent of the land! Isn't that *gross* corruption?'

Exactly as Steve Biko had said. 'Yes.'

'And,' George Mahoney said, 'there're all kinds of ugly rumours. I may be out of politics but I've got a lot of friends in the game. This security-mad government has got a huge secret fund called the Security Services Special Account which is not subject to public audit. *Billions* go into this account, and the money is supposed to be used for *external* security measures. Whatever that means. Dirty Tricks Departments is my guess. But the money has been slipping into other *internal* departments, like the Department of Information – or should I say "propaganda"? The rumour is that the department is spending the secret funds to stay in power by buying influence overseas, buying controlling interests in left-wing newspapers in this country, and even starting up a pro-government English-language newspaper to be called *The Citizen*.' He snorted. 'How do you like *that*? Taxpayers' money being spent to keep this Afrikaner government in power! Is that any different to what these one-party dictatorships are doing in the rest of Africa?'

Justin was delighted with this government-bashing. He wondered if Steve Biko knew this. 'No. And do you have an opinion about Black Consciousness, sir?'

George's old eyebrows went up. 'This chap Steve Biko? Good man. Exactly what the black man needs – pride, self-confidence. Black Community programmes are starting up all over the country thanks to him. What Biko's doing is what the *government* should be doing to prepare the poor old black man for democracy. The government should have been doing that for the last twenty years!' George raised a finger.

'Steve Biko is a born leader, by all accounts. He could have the stature of Nelson Mandela. So what happens to him?' He spread his hands. 'The bloody government *bans* him. *Typical* bully-boy politics. I tell you, Justin, the Afrikaner is more African than the African . . .'

44

The peasant-laden bus took Justin as far as the grubby hamlet of Ngqeleni, grinding over dirt roads through the rolling hills, towards the distant sea. Justin bought half a loaf of bread and a Coca-Cola, then hefted his bag and started walking.

The sky was grey with thunderclouds. He was wearing a black blazer, fawn slacks and loafers. He trudged towards the hut-studded horizon. As he walked, women looked up from hoeing their patches, children came running to skip beside him and ask him his name. And, God, their poverty was depressing. But after about an hour he began to see some red blankets again, and some women were wearing the elaborate turban. He lost his way several times because old landmarks were gone, and it was late afternoon when he identified his father's kraal on the distant hilltop.

Justin frowned. That must be his father's kraal, that was definitely the hill. But so many huts? There had been only four when last he saw it: a communal hut, his father's bachelor hut, and one hut for each of his wives. Now there were a dozen scattered over the hill.

The sun was setting behind thunderclouds when Justin toiled up the slope to his ancestral seat. Old women in red blankets stared, children came running to look. An old man in white man's clothes emerged from the bachelor hut.

'Ba-ba!' Justin strode up to the astonished old man, beaming, then dropped to his knee. 'It is I, Justin, your son, who has returned from beyond the seas . . .'

That night there was a feast. A goat was slaughtered and many calabashes of corn-beer came out of the bachelor hut. A big black pot of maize porridge was cooked.

Justin's own mother had died years ago. Of his father's three wives he knew only the eldest: the old man had married the other two after Justin left school. Both of them were younger than himself. One was a comely lass of about twenty; the other about Sally's age. Justin did not know any of his eight half-brothers and sisters gathered around the fire; they ranged from infancy to fourteen, and they all stared at him with big eyes. The youngest wife suckled a babe at her breast whilst they feasted. It was an enormous treat for them to eat a whole goat. All three wives wore their best blankets for the occasion, and their best head scarves and bangles. The children had put on their best clothes, and his father had even put on his jacket. He and Justin sat on hand-hewn stools, while everybody else sat on the ground. Justin looked at his family, and his eyes burned with love for them all.

The old man said: 'My heart aches that your mother is not here to see her first-born, Justin.'

'My heart aches also,' Justin said; and the other three wives and all the children nodded solemnly and said 'Eh-we . . .'

'And my heart aches that your three other brothers are not here also,' the old man said.

'My heart aches also,' Justin replied.

'But they are far away. Gideon and Moses are working on the mines, under the earth.'

'Do they send you money?'

'They are dutiful and send me money – do they not?' he enquired of his family, and they chorused 'Eh-we . . .'

'And your third brother is a teacher and he too is dutiful and sends me money,' the old man said. 'Does he not?'

'Eh-we . . .'

The old man took a deep draught from the calabash of beer, then passed it to Justin. He pointed at his second wife and said: 'And your second-mother's first-born is not here. But he is an Abakweta, living in the hills until he is circumcised.'

'When will that be?' Justin asked.

'In seven days. You shall accompany me to the ceremony.'

'I shall accompany you, to greet my second-mother's first-born and welcome him into manhood.' Justin said, and he drank deeply from the calabash. And, oh yes, the soupy maize beer was so much better than Budweiser.

'And next year,' the old man exclaimed jovially, pointing at the eldest youth present, 'your second-mother's second-born becomes an Abakweta! Then I will have *two* more men to send me money!' Everybody laughed politely with him.

Justin said to the lad: 'Are you excited?'

'I am excited.'

'You are not afraid?'

The lad cast his eyes downwards. 'I am not afraid.'

Jesus, Justin thought. About to have the foreskin cut off his dick with a spear and he's not afraid? It said a lot for the African. Was I afraid? No, until the dreadful day dawned, I wasn't either, it was something I just had to do, I was *proud*. He said: 'And I see I have four sisters now, father.'

'Yes!' The old man pointed teasingly at his two junior wives. 'Those two mothers are no good! They bring forth only girl children! I think I must send them back to their fathers and demand my cattle back!' He burst into giggles.

Everybody laughed. Then the old man sat back on his stool and put his hand on Justin's shoulder and said: 'All your mothers are good women, my son. They are dutiful and thanks to them all I am rich. I have thirty-seven cattle and when my daughters grow up I shall have many more cattle from their bridal prices. I am content. But *you*, my son? You have not taken a wife, yet all your brothers have wives. Moses is much younger than you but he has two. Five fine children already. My son, there are many pretty maidens in these hills for you to choose. Is it true?' he demanded of his family.

'Eh . . . ' his family chorused.

Justin decided to change the subject. 'And what do you think of the politics here nowadays, father?'

The old man said. 'I do not like politics. Strange men come here and say we must vote for Matanzima. If we vote for him we will be given many things, but if we do not we will be beaten. Matanzima is not my chief, but I voted for him because I do not like to be beaten, but nobody gave me anything. It is not the way to make laws. In the old days the chief and elders made the laws and they were sensible. Even the white man was more sensible than these new politicians.'

One of the boys said: 'Is it true that when the sun is shining here it is dark in i-America?'

'It is true,' Justin said, 'because the world is round. Like a football.'

'No,' the old man said. 'I was also told that the world is round, but the teacher meant round like a penny. If it is round like a football the sea would fall off, it is obvious.'

'Eh . . . '

It was three weeks later when Justin arrived back in King William's Town to keep his appointment with Steve Biko. He walked from the bus station out to the Centre. He looked over his shoulder to check whether he was being followed, but it was impossible to tell. The office door was open.

'I have an appointment with Steve Biko,' he said to the woman.

The woman looked at him.

'Steve Biko is dead.' She burst into tears.

Steve Biko had broken the terms of his Banning Order by driving beyond the magisterial district of King William's Town on Black Consciousness business. It was just the excuse the police had been waiting for. They were waiting for him when he crossed the Fish River bridge. He was taken to the offices of BOSS in Port Elizabeth.

Exactly what happened to Steve Biko from this point is not known. The many journalists, including Justin Nkomo, who attended the inquest, agreed that the police witnesses were lying; but they never got to the truth. All that is known is that Steve Biko suffered such severe injuries while under interrogation in police custody that he entered a coma. He was rushed through the night to Pretoria, naked in the back of a police vehicle. He died without regaining consciousness.

The next month the government banned Black Consciousness. It also banned eighteen other black organizations.

Kragdadigheid had done it again. As George Mahoney had said, the Afrikaner was as African as the African.

A number of other things happened in the months that followed.

The scandal broke about the government's misspending of funds in the Department of Information, a number of important heads rolled and Mr PW Botha became the new prime minister of South Africa.

A general election was held and the government won with a bigger majority than ever because *kragdadigheid* had put the lid back on the black boiling pot.

Justin Nkomo left the country to take up arms.

Luke Mahoney's book was published. It was called *Alms for Oblivion* – a passionate, tragic love story, based on his affair with Patti Gandhi. It was an immediate bestseller, received with international acclaim, but it was immediately banned in South Africa.

PART VII

RHODESIAN WAR ENDS IN WHITES' DEFEAT

ANC BOMBS START ROCKING SOUTH AFRICA

ERA OF TOTAL ONSLAUGHT–
TOTAL STRATEGY EMERGES

BLACK SCHOOLS ERUPT AGAIN

PW BOTHA PROPOSES 'HEALTHY POWER-
SHARING', TRI-CAMERAL PARLIAMENT

NEW CONSERVATIVE PARTY SPLITS FROM
GOVERNMENT

UNITED DEMOCRATIC FRONT EMERGES –
BLACK CIVIL WAR IN NATAL

VAAL UPRISING

45

'You don't know me but . . . '

When you live in Hong Kong many telephone conversations begin that way. 'You don't know me but . . . I'm a friend of so-and-so and he/she said that when I was in Hong Kong I should look you up.' 'Oh,' you say, your heart sinking, and if you've got your wits about you you have an excuse to hand. What they want is to be shown the town and given accommodation for a week. If you have your wits about you, you meet them for a drink, make polite noises, tell them about the best shops and tailors, and take a powder.

Mahoney had had his wits about him last night when the telephone rang, but his excuse had gone right out the window when the female American voice said: 'You don't know me but I'm a friend of Lisa Rousseau.'

Lisa Rousseau . . . Mahoney would go on his hands and knees to be nice to Lisa Rousseau. 'How lovely,' he had said. 'Where can I meet you? Do you need a bed for a few days?' he had said. Which accounted for the black woman beside him in his bed this hungover Saturday morning when the telephone's ring dragged him abrasively from sodden sleep.

'You don't know me but,' the male voice said, 'I'm notionally your boss – you'll probably remember me, the Director of Public Prosecutions, yes? Anyway, you may remember that I'm proceeding on overseas leave today and I'm waiting here to hand over my responsibilities to you before so doing. Whilst you, no doubt, are screwing that dusky American lady who was dragging you so willingly around Wan Chai last night. Your rickshaw race has resulted in a summons under the Road Traffic Ordinance, but so what, it was fun. But Mini Ho-Ho is setting the triads onto you for breach of promise. And, the Chief Justice wants to see you.'

'All very funny,' Mahoney said.

'The Chief Justice *does* want to see you. Give him a call now.'

'What the hell for?'

'When I return from leave, you're going to Borneo for two months as acting judge while their judge goes on home-leave.'

Mahoney groaned. *'Why me?'*

'The CJ asked who I could spare and your name immediately sprang to mind.'

Mahoney held his aching head. 'Why the hell doesn't he send one of his own guys? And I don't want to go to fucking Borneo.'

'Nor does anybody else, but you're the only bachelor with the required seniority. Try to think of it as a feather in your cap!' Max hung up, laughing.

Mahoney slumped, trying to soothe his throbbing head. Then the telephone shrilled again. Oh God. 'Hullo?'

'You don't know me but!' the Flower of the Orient snapped.

Oh Jesus. 'Hullo, Mini.'

'Why you no come see me last night, *hah*?!' Mini Ho-Ho shouted. 'Friday night my night! But you get phone call say "You don't know me but," *hah*? You no-good number ten butterfly man! I never see you again!' She slammed down the phone.

Mahoney replaced the telephone gratefully. Well, that was the end of that little romance. He was still trying to hold his scalp down. Trying not to grapple with the problem of the black girl yet. How long was she staying? Then he noticed her shoulders shaking – she was giggling.

She raised her head. 'One of those days, huh?'

'Good morning, Susan.' He swung carefully off the bed.

'Sally,' she giggled.

Well, he'd known it began with an S. 'That's what I meant. What did we drink last night?'

'Everything!'

He went through to the kitchen and switched on the kettle, trying to remember last night. Max's farewell party starting at lunchtime at the Foreign Correspondents' Club. Adjourning to the Yacht Club. Adjourning back to the office. The telephone ringing: 'You don't know me but.' To the Hilton to meet Lisa Rousseau's friend, then to the Floating Restaurant for dinner. Moving on to Wan Chai . . . Well, there was only one way to treat a hangover like this: he went to the refrigerator and got out a beer. It glugged down into his jagged system like a balm. Just then there was a loud bang on the front door. He peered through the spyhole, and there stood the Flower of the Orient.

'I know you there, butterfly man, your car downstairs!' Bang! Bang! Bang!

Oh Jesus. He hurried down the corridor, into the bedroom. Sally was looking alarmed. 'Quick – into the other bedroom!' He snatched up her clothes. She ran naked across the room, laughing, across the passage into the spare bedroom.

Bang! Bang! Bang! went the Flower of the Orient, *'Hey, you butterfly man!*

'Into that bathroom.' Sally disappeared inside and locked the door. Mahoney turned shakily back to the living room. The bangs were going straight through him. *'Okay!'* he shouted. *'Okay!'*

He unlocked the front door just as the Flower of the Orient kicked it, and it burst open. Mahoney reeled backwards, clutching his brow. The Flower of the Orient marched into the room, breathing fire. *'Where is she, hah*?!'

'Who? And stop shouting!'

'The you-don't-know-me-but girl!' She stomped off down the passage purposefully. Mahoney followed, holding his brow. She burst into the bedroom and glared. She wrenched back the bed covers, looking for evidence of female occupation. She peered underneath. She flung the wardrobe doors open. She strode for the spare bedroom.

Mahoney grabbed her arm in the passage. 'For Christ's sake there's nobody here!'

She wrenched her arm free and strode for the bathroom door and grabbed the handle. And to his horror the door opened. He blundered after her to try to stem the bloodshed. And Sally was nowhere to be seen.

'See?!' Mahoney rasped, astonished. Where the fuck had she gone? He hurried back into the corridor and saw Sally dart out of the kitchen into the living room. He spun around and blocked the doorway, colliding with the Flower of the Orient. *'Now* will you believe me?' He heard the front door click and he closed his bloodshot eyes in relief. 'And *now,*' he said, jabbing his finger aloft, 'I'm going to have my shower!'

'No!' The Flower of the Orient shoved past him, threw herself onto the bed, hoicked up her dress and spread her Shantung thighs.

'You fuck me now, butterfly! Friday night my night!'

Mahoney looked at those magnificent loins, and he couldn't face the effort. He turned into the bathroom righteously and locked the door behind him with an elaborate bang.

He took his time in the shower, in no hurry to face the injustices of the Flower of the Orient. Letting her sweat it out a little. He brushed his teeth elaborately. Then had a shave, with great care. He combed his hair carefully. Now he was beginning to feel some interest in those Shantung thighs. And, when all's said and done, who am I to spurn the best lay in the Orient? (But what about the Chief Justice?) He looked at himself in the mirror and decided: *fuck the Chief Justice.* He flung open the door. And stared.

The Flower of the Orient was gone. His bedding lay in shreds, slashed down to Her Majesty's mattress. The pillows in tatters. The wardrobe doors stood agape; from the rail hung all his jackets and suits, slashed to ribbons. Mahoney stared, then bellowed: '*Bitch!*'

So it really was one of those days. Now what the hell was he going to do? How could he see the Chief Justice? He held his head, trying to think; then he shuffled to the telephone. He dialled Mr Wong, his tailor, and told him to sent his foki up with a suit off the peg, chop-chop. He went back to the kitchen to get another beer. He drank it down, took the cap off another bottle, went back to the bedroom, and dialled the Chief Justice. He was immensely relieved to be told that the old boy had gone to play golf. Thank God for that. He returned the telephone to its cradle and immediately it rang again. Oh *Christ*. '*Hullo?*' he barked.

'You don't know me but,' the female African accent giggled, 'I accept your proposal last night of immediate marriage, boss!'

Oh, Sally. He managed a smile. 'That was a very good impersonation. And a very good escape-job. Where are you?'

'At my hotel. I'm taking you to lunch, remember?' She giggled again, 'So what time can a darky expect her honky to show up? And to make the prospect less fearful I hasten to add that you are not going to be a father. You fell asleep before we got it up. Though I did my damnedest!' She burst into giggles again. 'What a performance! Such a pity you missed it.' She went into hysterics.

'So how long have you lived in Hong Kong, lover-boy?'

Why does every conversation in Hong Kong start like that (apart from the lover-boy bit)? Because everybody has come from somewhere else. Borrowed place, borrowed time. 'Too long.'

'You don't like Hong Kong?'

'I'm really a newspaper man and nothing new is going to happen in China until communism collapses.'

'And *is* communism going to collapse?'

'One day. It's called bankruptcy. No bankrupt economy can function indefinitely. Russia's coming apart at the seams.'

'And is apartheid going to collapse too? Is there hope?' She added: 'Would you like to go back there?'

There is definitely no such thing as a free lunch is there? But Mahoney tried to be polite: 'Yes, apartheid is going to collapse. And no, there is no hope. And yes, I would love to go back there. Once a South African, always a South African, you can't expect too much of us.' He tried to change the subject: 'So tell me about Lisa.' He added: 'You probably did last night.'

'I did. She was a visiting professor at my university, teaching a post-graduate semester on African history. We got friendly. I thought all South Africans were monsters, but she's nice. She introduced me to your books.' She added: 'I'm going to South Africa next year. I'm related to an officer in the American embassy there. Did you know that even the American ambassador in Pretoria is black?'

Mahoney did. The first black man as ambassador in South Africa, part of President Reagan's carrot-and-stick programme of Constructive Engagement – a black ambassador, with all ambassadorial privileges, in pure-white Pretoria. Brilliant idea. 'Well, well. You'll have an interesting time.'

'But Lisa isn't the only reason I looked you up.' She smiled impishly. 'I was married to your friend, Justin Nkomo. He told me all about you.'

Mahoney stared. *Justin's wife!* (Thank God he hadn't managed anything last night.) 'Good God. I didn't know Justin had married an American. Though I haven't heard from him for ages.' He added: 'He visited my parents in South Africa some years ago, but didn't tell them that.'

She said grimly: 'Because he'd deserted me, the bastard. Came home from university one fine day and there's this letter: "Got to go and do my duty. P.S. Don't call me, I'll call you".' She snorted. 'I'm divorcing the sonofabitch. See what that does to his American work permit. Think that's the only reason the bastard married me.'

'I'm sorry,' Mahoney murmured.

'Don't be, I'm over the sumbitch. Though if I find him I'll kick his pretty black ass all the way to Pretoria.'

'You haven't heard from him since he left?'

She snorted. 'Got a lovey-dovey letter about three years later, written in Angola. Said he was an officer in MK, the ANC's army. He'd escaped South Africa via Mozambique. Hell of a journey. Hell of a hero. Said the ANC was chaotic with all the youngsters who'd fled South Africa after the Soweto riots. He was eventually sent to Cuba for military training.' She clenched her fist. 'The sumbitch was in *Cuba* for a whole year! Just ninety miles from Miami! And he didn't even call! I could have visited the sumbitch!'

Mahoney suppressed a grin. 'I'm sorry,' he murmured again.

'Don't be. I'm over the no-good cotton-pickin' motherfucker.' She flashed a brilliant smile. 'Can't you tell?'

Mahoney grinned. 'But perhaps he's in the bush now and can't write. Or underground. There's been a lot of ANC sabotage in South Africa over recent years, bombs and so forth.'

'*Sure*, let's give the motherfucker the benefit of the doubt, huh?'

'Is that why you're going to South Africa, to look for Justin?'

'Hell, *no*. Ah's goin' back to discover my *roots*, boss. So.' She hunched forward. 'So tell me, Mr Bestselling Writer, what's happening in your benighted country which Mr Shit-face Nkomo is so busy liberating? What's this gent PW Botha up to? He's some kind of reformer?'

In his youth PW Botha had been one of those Ossewa Brandwag Afrikaner stormtroopers who burst into opposition parties' political meetings and broke them up. As Minister of Defence he had presided over the massive expansion of the armed forces and the wars in Angola and South West Africa. As Prime Minister he had centralized power in himself, brought the army chief into the cabinet as Minister of Defence, and devised a 'Total Strategy' to combat the 'Total Onslaught' he saw confronting South Africa. There was no reason, therefore, to expect him to be a reformer.

'Yet that's what he is,' Mahoney said. 'Or seems to be. Soon after becoming prime minister he told a conference of businessmen: "Apartheid is a recipe for permanent conflict." Addressing his own party congress he told them they had to "adapt or die". Later he spoke publicly about "healthy power-sharing". And he's announced he's going to repeal the Mixed Marriages Act and the Immorality Act. That means that a lot of other petty apartheid will go by the board. All this is absolute *heresy* in apartheid's thinking. So much so that it's caused a split in his party – numerous parliamentarians have deserted him and set up the Conservative Party under Dr Treurnicht – the cabinet minister who caused the Soweto riots by decreeing that education for blacks must be in the Afrikaans language. There's been a backlash from conservative whites across the land – the AWB have been greatly strengthened. You know about them?'

'They're the neo-Nazi guys with the swastika-like badge.'

'Right. They're very militarized, and they intend to maintain pure apartheid at all costs. They say they're going to "restore law and order" because the government is going to plunge the country into chaos with their reforms. And there's plenty of chaos for them to point to: the school riots in Soweto simmered on and then in 1980 there was another massive eruption. Started in Soweto again, then spread across the country – non-stop demonstrations, stop-outs, burning schools down. There was almost no education the whole year.'

'What were they protesting about?'

'Grievances varied from place to place – that the education was inferior to white education, insufficient textbooks, unqualified teachers, school uniforms were expensive, inferior buildings, et cetera. But the basic demand was for an integrated Department of Education – instead of separate departments for blacks and whites. But PW Botha has flatly rejected that. However – ' he held up a finger – 'it's significant that there was no demand for racial integration in the *classroom*. Why? Because the children are still inspired by Steve Biko's Black Consciousness.'

Sally glowed. 'And so am I.' She grinned. 'Notwithstanding ending up in your bed last night.'

Mahoney smiled. He would rather not talk about that. He continued: 'The ANC takes credit for the new school riots, but it was Black Consciousness. It's taken hold. Since the movement has been banned, they've formed a new party called AZAPO, the Azanian People's Organization, which is rigidly Africanist – '

'What's wrong with that? It's *their* country.'

Mahoney sighed. 'That's a recipe for trouble. For black racism. They reject any form of white participation. And, unfortunately, they're communist – or very nearly so. They've tied themselves into the trade unions and they talk about a "black workers' republic where workers will be paramount through worker control of the means of production".' He shook his head. 'Communism has failed throughout the world, but it's done so *spectacularly* in Africa.'

Sally pursed her lips. She waved a hand. 'Carry on. About poor Mr Botha's bi-i-g troubles as a "reformer".'

Mahoney ignored the hint of aggression. 'Well, there's trouble everywhere. The schools. The riots. The bombs. AZAPO. The strikes. The white backlash. And in the midst of all this there's the worst drought in history, maize production plummets, there's a food crisis, destitution – and the price of gold plummets too, from eight hundred dollars an ounce to under three hundred, so government has a revenue crisis. Meanwhile the army is fighting an exhausting and expensive war in Angola against the Cubans and SWAPO – the South West Africa People's Organization. Meanwhile the government's got to spend billions on forced removals to these tin-pot homelands and republics it's created. Financing them. Meanwhile the black population is soaring and you haven't got to be a mathematician to figure out that there's going to be no work for them in ten years' time unless the economy *booms* – '

Sally interrupted: 'How do you know all this, living a million miles from South Africa? You seem to know more than Lisa.'

Mahoney smiled. 'I'm flattered. I'm writing a book about it. I get all the leading South African newspapers and journals.' He continued: 'Meanwhile, in the midst of all this trouble, old PW Botha was pushing ahead with "power-sharing", appoints a Minister of Constitutional

Development, and people were optimistic that real reform was going to come at last – the right wing was up in arms – and then it became clear what he really meant by "power-sharing". And there was massive anger.'

'What did he mean?' Sally demanded.

Mahoney said: '*Limited* power-sharing with the Coloureds and Indians *only* – they were to be given their own mini-parliaments, but the blacks were excluded. The reason given was that under apartheid the blacks had their democratic rights in their homelands and republics. So the government isn't giving up apartheid, as we hoped. And there was a massive outcry and more riots. A new movement called the United Democratic Front was formed to protest against the exclusion of blacks. The UDF is a huge umbrella outfit representing about six hundred organizations like trade unions, churches, student bodies, academics, professional associations and social clubs – it has millions of members. But old PW Botha stuck to his guns, held a whites-only referendum on his "power-sharing" proposals, and rammed the new constitution through parliament. And,' he sat back, 'it's been a disaster. Satisfied nobody. Angered almost everybody, left and right.'

'So exactly what is your constitution now?' Sally demanded.

'Now South Africa has three parliaments. One for Whites, one for Coloureds, one for Indians. Each parliament has exclusive legislative power over "Own Affairs", meaning matters that affect them as a racial community. When legislation is required for certain *national* affairs which affect all three communities, the three parliaments sit together, and vote together, but the numbers are such that the white parliament dominates the other two and remains firmly in control. So, the other two are more like municipal councils. But the Coloured leader and the Indian leader do have a seat each on the President's Cabinet. But most Coloureds and Indians reject it and don't vote. So, the power-sharing is really little more than window-dressing on the edifice of apartheid.'

Sally sat back angrily. 'And the blacks get nothing.'

'Well, the only concession PW Botha gave them was to replace the Urban Bantu Councils, which ran the townships under a white administrator, with "Black Local Authorities", which are now entirely elected and function independently of the government. But that's been a disaster too. Because the black councillors are corrupt and inefficient, and because they have to be self-financing they raised rents, and there've been new massive riots about *that*. On top of the renewed student riots and the "non-power-sharing" riots – the government had to send in the army to support the police.' He raised his eyebrows. 'And this is on top of the *economic* crisis. And on top of the ANC's bombs. Now the Rhodesians have lost the war our whole northern border is vulnerable to guerrillas. And that's on top of the war South Africa is fighting in Angola, against the Cubans and SWAPO, who're fighting for the liberation of Namibia from South African rule.' Mahoney shook his head. 'South Africa's in big trouble.'

Sally sat back. 'Good. So why d'you say there's no hope?'

Mahoney sighed. This could be tricky. He said: 'The question is, what kind of government is going to follow apartheid?' He took a sip of wine. 'African government.' (He was going to say Black and managed to change it in his mouth.) 'And what has happened in the rest of Africa?'

She frowned indignantly: 'You mean – '

Mahoney held up an apologetic finger. 'Do I think apartheid is right? The answer is a resounding no. However, do I think the South African blacks are capable of governing a complex country like South Africa? The answer is also no.' He shook his head earnestly. 'This has got nothing to do with racism, Sally, it's to do with *facts*. With *history*.' He shook his head again. 'I've spent God knows how many years working in Africa. And the overall inefficiency and corruption has been mind-blowing. And the politics have been terrifying. *Crush* the opposition . . .' He shook his head. 'There's no democracy in Africa, Sally. And I'm afraid that it will be the same in South Africa.'

She said archly: 'So you don't think they should be given the vote?'

Mahoney raised his palms. '*No*, the South African drama has been waged too long to deny them that, now that the end of apartheid is nigh. What I'm saying is that, nobody, *anywhere*, should have the vote until they understand democracy. And that means education. And that is the responsibility the British shirked when they folded their colonial tents and granted independence overnight because it was a cheap way out. And so the new African states went to ratshit. One-party dictatorships. An uneducated electorate and an uneducated civil service. And a Marxist economy. It hasn't worked anywhere in the world, it's *guaranteed* to fail in Africa.'

She said: 'And if South Africa went democratic the blacks would fight each other? Well I think they'll be so overjoyed that apartheid's gone that they'll *embrace* each other!'

He sighed. 'Jesus, they're doing it right now, in Natal. Inkatha and the United Democratic Front are knocking the living shit out of each other. Civil war, fighting about which of them is going to be the next government in the new South Africa. Inkatha is the traditional Zulu party. And then the United Democratic Front was formed and became the internal front for the ANC, who've declared war on Inkatha on

Freedom Radio – "the Buthelezi snake must have its head chopped off", et cetera. Called for making the country ungovernable. And Inkatha responded with a vengeance. And they've been butchering each other ever since.' He shook his head. 'And it will go on.' He ended apologetically: 'That's the African way, Sally.'

She said, archly: 'Or until the police put a *stop* to the fighting. Why the hell don't they? Or don't they *want* to? Let them destroy each other?'

'Is that what Lisa thinks?'

Sally subsided sulkily. 'No, I've made a study of South Africa. But Lisa taught me a lot. And she's my accomplice.'

'Your *accomplice*? In what?'

She hesitated, then said defiantly: 'I'm going to South Africa next year and I'm going to pretend I'm an ordinary black. I'm going to stay in black townships, pretend to look for work, all that shit. And then tell the world about it.'

Mahoney looked at this lady in a new light. So maybe she wasn't just an all-American bimbo.

'What a brilliant idea.' (*And God he wanted to go back there and write.*) He added: 'I hope you don't spend too much time in jail.'

'Jail would be the best part. I want to *suffer*.'

Mahoney smiled. 'Will you have any difficulty getting a visa?'

'Being black?' She snorted belligerently. 'Officially, I'll be visiting my ambassadorial relative, even the fucking South Africans can't stop *that*.'

'But you'll be very conspicuous with your American accent in the townships.'

'Justin Shithouse Nkomo coached me. How's this? Please, seh, can I catch-i this bus-i to Jobek?'

It was a creditable black South African accent. Mahoney grinned. 'And when they speak to you in Xhosa?'

'I speak passable Xhosa.'

Mahoney was amazed. 'Justin Shithouse Nkomo teach you?'

'Yes. But I'll pretend to be from another tribe, to cover my deficiencies. And there's always pidgin – Fanagalo, Lisa gave me a book on it, it's easy.'

Mahoney was vastly impressed. 'Well, good for you, lady. But why exactly is Lisa encouraging you in all this?'

'Working with Steve Biko was my own dream for a long time. Then he was murdered. Then I met Lisa. She thought it was a brilliant idea for a sociological study, said she'd do it if she was an American black. She's very anti-apartheid, you know.'

'I know.' He added: 'So am I.'

Sally snorted. 'I think,' she smiled sweetly, 'you're a racist.'

Mahoney groaned. '*Me* racist? Anybody who's read *Alms for Oblivion* or *Not Enough Tears* knows I detest apartheid.'

'You say in *both* those books – and you've said it again today – that blacks can't govern themselves.'

Mahoney sat back. He smiled. He shook his head.

'Why is it that anybody who suggests that Africans have made mistakes – that not *everything* they do is wondrous – is branded a racist?' He leant forward. 'I said that the *Africans* have *mis*governed their countries because of lack of education, expertise and democratic traditions. That is not a racist *opinion*, it is historical *fact*. Anybody who denies those facts is exhibiting their ignorance of *history*. However, *when* the Africans have sufficient education, expertise and democratic traditions, they will be quite capable of governing themselves.'

She glared. 'So the blacks in South Africa should not have the vote until they're educated?'

Mahoney sighed and shook his head. 'Too late for that. The die is cast. Neither the blacks nor the world would wait. South Africa had its opportunity to educate them in the last forty years and we wasted it. One of apartheid's many sins. The Afrikaner fucked up the country, now it's the Africans' turn to fuck it up.'

She said sweetly: 'Tell me, Mr Mahoney, have you ever fucked a black girl? I mean a *real* black – not your tragic, exotic Indian heroine in *Alms for Oblivion*.'

Mahoney was taken aback. As a matter of fact, he had. Plenty, in the Congo. 'Sure. But what's this got to do with anything?'

She said: 'You're a liar. I bet you ain't screwed a darky. And it's got plenty to do with it. Because I invited you to lunch today specifically to screw you.'

Mahoney was taken aback. 'Well,' he grinned, 'you won't have to try very hard.'

Sally stood up abruptly. She glared down at him.

'*You*,' she said, 'can go fuck your*self*. Because, for all your fine words, you're a *racist* in your nasty, secret South African heart! Excuse *me* – and good*bye*.'

She turned and stomped elegantly out of the restaurant, her pretty ass swinging indignantly.

46

BIG TROUBLE. THE VAAL UPRISING.

Mahoney typed the headline at the top of his page. Then stared at it, thinking. He ran his eye down the wads of notes he had extracted from the piles of South African newspapers over the last year. Then took a deep breath, stood up and began to pace. Frowning, thinking. Then he stomped through his apartment to his bar and poured himself another big shot of whisky. He stomped back to his word processor, and glared at it. Then he sat down and began to type.

Apartheid's poisonous fruits are dropping heavily, splitting open, splatting their seeds of outrage in all directions.

Apartheid's chickens are coming home to roost. The theory always was that the towns were the white man's creation, that the black man was only tolerated there in so far as he served the interests of the white man. This was achieved by Influx Control's pass laws, by keeping black housing in short supply to discourage notions of permanence. By keeping the black man in a state of impermanence for decades an enormous sociological crisis has developed: so now the government has tried to pass the buck to the blacks themselves by creating Black Local Authorities – making them responsible for resolving the crisis. But the infrastructure is too rotten, rent increases have led to massive rioting, and the Vaal Uprising of 1984 began. Seven thousand troops have been sent into the townships, over one thousand people have died, and still the rioting goes on.

The Soweto Riots of 1976 spelt the beginning of the beginning of the end of apartheid; this Vaal Uprising spells the real beginning of the end. It has unified blacks, interweaving their outrage over the Tri-Cameral Parliament which excludes them, Bantu education which under-educates them, rent increases which impoverish them, evictions and bulldozings which destitute them, township conditions which dehumanise them, corruption and inefficiency of black quisling councillors which insults them as the most democracy they can expect. All these grievances have come together in the fundamental cry for the vote. Bloody though it is as the government responds with repression, history will view it as good news for South Africa.

Out there in the black townships there were the running battles, the armoured vehicles roaring, the policemen charging midst the hail of stones, the stink of tear-gas, the screaming and the blood and the stink of sweat midst the dust and the crack of guns, the taunting and the prancing, the flames leaping up. It was the worst unrest in white man's history. Chief Buthelezi warned that a 'Beirut situation' was developing. On Radio Freedom the ANC president, Oliver Tambo, declared that they would make South Africa ungovernable, and 'take the violence into the white areas', urging the people to 'arm themselves with home-made weapons, to ambush security forces, to destroy communications, to sabotage industry, to attack "soft targets" – the People's War is entering a new phase, intensively training people to use petrol bombs and hand grenades for attacks on whites.'

That year there were numerous attacks with hand grenades, land mines, car bombs. Over eight hundred houses belonging to black policemen were destroyed, many black councillors were killed, many resigned in terror. Then there were the consumer boycotts: gangs of youths stopping the people coming home from work, searching their bags, beating them up, forcing them to eat their purchases, raw meat, soap powder, liquid detergent, cooking oil, toilet paper. Old women and grown men beaten and kicked as they staggered about retching and gagging.

But it worked. The police raided and arrested but the boycotts went on midst the running battles, and the businessmen were prised out of their tacit complicity with the apartheid system. Within weeks the Port Elizabeth Chamber of Commerce issued a manifesto calling for the removal of all discriminatory legislation, to encourage a black middle-class, to grant blacks a share in decision-making. Then all over the land business leaders discovered the courage to speak up. The American Chamber of Commerce sent a delegation urging the South African government to reform the constitution, to end removals, to grant freehold rights to blacks in the townships, to end Influx Control, to end the inhumane theory that blacks don't belong in white South Africa. The chairmen of the mighty Anglo-American Corporation and Barclays Bank plus the editors of six influential newspapers made a pilgrimage to the ANC in Zambia to talk about the reforms. On their return they were met at the airport by a howling mob of AWB supporters and a cheering mob of university students, and a fight broke out. Ninety leading businessmen published a full page advertisement titled *There Is A Better Way*, calling for the abolition of racial discrimination. Then 186 American companies petitioned the government to do the same; then the governor of the Reserve Bank did the same. The Dutch Reformed Church called for a Declaration of Human Rights, then hundreds of church leaders marched on Parliament in Cape

Town. The police arrested 240 of them. And in the townships the rioting went on.

Then, in the midst of this chaos and clamour, came the news that President PW Botha would make a landmark speech

Excitement was high. Speculation was rife that in this speech President Botha would cross the political Rubicon, announce the repeal of apartheid laws, announce a new constitutional dispensation. The eyes of the world were on Durban on the night of 15th August 1985, as President Botha arrived at the City Hall.

Ten thousand miles away in Hong Kong, Mahoney sat in front of his television with a notebook. On the screen were the huge crowds, the policemen, the placards, the banners, the red carpet, and, oh God, he ached to be there. Once a newsman, always a newsman. And, oh God, what this speech could mean to Patti Gandhi . . .

A television journalist stood in front of his camera and said: 'The excitement is electric as we await the President's arrival – and tempers are high. Large numbers of AWB members are here in their khaki uniforms with their swastika badges, chanting. There have been several fights. Meanwhile, war rages in the rolling hills of this beautiful province between Inkatha and the UDF, the ANC's internal wing – their call to make the country ungovernable is succeeding and this is a major factor in bringing about this much-awaited speech tonight. Meanwhile, of course, the government also has its hands full fighting the "border war" in Angola. *And now here comes the President's motorcade – listen to that roar . . .* '

The cheers and the boos and the chants of *Ah Wey Bey,* the placards waving, the cameras flashing, the television crews scurrying. The President climbed out of his limousine, waving and smiling, his bald head glinting, then strode presidentially up the red carpet into the City Hall. There was a sea of people inside, the stage decked out in National Party colours. PW Botha stood before the forest of microphones, and silence fell.

Mahoney listened to the speech with rapt attention, waiting for the New South Africa. He waited, and waited: then he threw down his pen and groaned.

And across the world people groaned. For the President of South Africa, sweating under the spotlights, talking half-truths, hedging and fidgeting, did not, *could* not, because of his Afrikanerness, because of his Afrikaner constituency, cross the Rubicon . . . As a reformer PW Botha had feet of clay.

That night Mahoney wrote:

The world expected a great deal from PW Botha tonight: after all, he is the first Afrikaner leader to give us glimmers of hope, the first Afrikaner leader to announce that apartheid was a recipe for conflict, the first to talk of 'healthy power-sharing'. It was he who had the sense to decree that a middle-class of blacks was desirable, it was he who repealed the Mixed Marriages Act and the Immorality Act, it was he who created the Tri-Cameral Parliament, giving the Coloureds and Indians their own legislatures at the cost of splitting Afrikanerdom. This may sound small beer in Western ears but in South Africa it was dramatic reform indeed: in short it is old PW Botha who came close to admitting that his government's policies were a failure. And so, when South Africa was erupting in ungovernability and he announced he would make a landmark speech to the nation, it gave rise to great hope that a new South Africa would begin.

But instead the world finally lost patience with South Africa tonight. Our hopes are not to be satisfied as long as the old guard are in control. It seems clear he was bullied out of announcing significant reforms at the last moment. His body-language was very bad, he fidgeted, he even winked at his vast audience as if asking them to read between his lines. He announced no new reforms, saying only that the government was committed to 'negotiations to broaden democracy'. He did admit that Influx Control was 'an outdated concept', but said an African House of Parliament was 'impractical'. To sugar the bitter pill he announced that government will spend one billion rand to improve black townships – a mere clink in the begging bowl.

So now the trouble is really going to start. The escalation of international sanctions, the escalation of violence . . .

47

Mahoney had finished writing his third book, *Big Trouble*, which was a commentary on the politics of South Africa; it was to be published the following year. Now his publishers wanted to know what he intended writing next. 'We've invested a lot of money in you, Luke,' Bill Summers, his American editor said on the telephone, 'and you've got to keep it coming.' Mahoney had told him about his family journals which he was trying to keep up to date. Summers had been sceptical about the commerciality of diaries, but when Luke posted him a copy he was enthusiastic.

'It's fascinating stuff, Luke! They should sell well when they're properly edited. Keep them up and send it to us every month so we're ready to publish as soon as apartheid collapses. It is going to collapse, isn't it?'

'Yes, but that's still years away, the Afrikaner fights to the bitter end.'

Bill Summers said: 'Of course, what I really want from you is another love story, Luke. Preferably the sequel to *Alms for Oblivion*. The story of what happens when Pamela finally comes out of prison – the beautiful Indian martyr meeting Jack after twenty years. How do they feel? Are they still in love? *Yes* – but what has happened to Jack in twenty years? Is he married to somebody else? Has he got children? What do Pamela and Jack *do?* That would be a real tear-jerker. Couldn't you do it?'

But no, Mahoney could not do it. It would be too painful to try to imagine it, to try to live the story in his mind. It would be too . . . *unreal*. Too misty, too ghost-like, too heartbreaking. And too difficult – to summon back and relive all those emotions again, to *believe* so the poignancy came alive on the page. He did not *want* to go through that again, that pain.

And he doubted he could do it. How *did* he feel about Patti now? Oh, he admired her, and loved her, but was he still *in* love with her? The answer was no. Or: I don't know. So much water had passed under the bridge, so many other women had passed through his life that his heartbreak, his passion for Patti, often seemed a distant memory now, and it was too hard and painful to imagine how he would feel when and if he saw her again. Sometimes, now, it seemed that days passed without him thinking about her. Sometimes when he was alone, trying to work on his book, and had drunk too much, he got carried away and wrote her long passionate letters, but in the morning he tore them up. Once, in his cups, after hearing that *Alms for Oblivion* was to be published, he had written her a long letter, telling her how he admired her, and he had driven down in the middle of the night to post it so he could not change his mind. In the morning he regretted it; it was unfair to Patti, and he worried how much he had said. He had been relieved when she had not replied. Sometimes he would have a dream about her: suddenly, out of the darkness, she would be with him, and she was young and beautiful and full of life, sparkling, and he was joyously happy and wildly in love; but there would always be some dreadful danger lurking that threatened to tear her away from him, and he would wake up in a panic, horrified. When he realised it was a dream, he would desperately try to go back to sleep so as to be with her again, but he could not; and for days thereafter he would be under the spell of the dream, of her, and he would be filled with ineffable sadness, grief. No, he could not bring himself to write that book.

In the black township of Edendale, in Natal, the fighting between Inkatha and the United Democratic Front, the internal wing of the ANC, was very bad.

Out in the hills there were the desperate bands of homeless children totalling thousands, refugees from the fighting, sleeping in the forests, roaming in search of food, stealing from kraals and farmers, robbing travellers, marauding around the fringes of the fighting. They knew nothing about politics, they were the victims of it, they were on nobody's side. But in Edendale township you had to be on one side or the other, and God help you if you were challenged by the other.

Sam Mbene was an orphan. He was fourteen years old and he had a club foot. His parents had belonged to the other side: they had been attending an Inkatha meeting in a town councillor's cottage when a UDF gang hurled two petrol bombs through the windows. As the people burst out of the flaming house, the UDF gang slaughtered them with pangas and an AK–47. Now Sam lived with his widowed Aunt Matilda in her cottage. Sam's sixteen-year-old sister Princess was a trainee nurse in Edendale Hospital, about a mile away. She lived in the nurses' quarters, but on Wednesdays, when she was off-duty, she spent the night with Aunt Matilda too.

This Thursday morning Princess was late. There had been gunfire all night, people running up and down, the glow of distant houses on fire, shouts, battle cries. When Princess emerged with the sunrise, in her nurse's uniform, both ends of the road were blocked by youths, challenging the people going to work, demanding whether they were Inkatha or UDF supporters. Princess retreated back into the cottage. Sam was getting dressed for school.

'I will wait for you to walk with me,' Princess said.

Sam was nervous as they set out. He hobbled ahead on his crutch through the neighbour's back yard, onto the street beyond. He peered. There were no roadblocks. They set off into the early morning. When they came to the end of the block, a gang of youths burst out of the alley, with sticks and pangas. The leader grinned. 'Hullo, sister! Where you going, huh?'

Princess's heart was pounding, but she knew this gang was UDF because Inkatha gangs seldom spoke in English. She quavered in Zulu: 'To the hospital to work.'

'And who do you belong to, Big Sister, the UDF or Inkatha?'

Princess quavered: 'UDF.'

'Oh, to the UDF? And who is this cripple?'

'I am her brother, comrade,' Sam was trembling.

'Oh, you are her brother. And who do you belong to, Zulu-boy?'

'The UDF, of course,' Sam croaked.

'Oh!' the leader said. 'Also UDF. But tell me, brother, why your sister looks after Inkatha-dogs at the hospital?!'

Princess blurted: 'The hospital treats everybody, comrade.'

'Inkatha-dogs too!'

'Yes, also Inkatha-dogs, when they are wounded.'

The leader prodded her in the chest with his panga. 'You must not treat Inkatha! Anybody who treats Inkatha-dogs is a sell-out! You must let them die!'

Princess drew back. 'Yes, comrade.'

'Sell-outs must die! You will die if you treat Inkatha-dogs!' He raised his panga, and Princess shrank. 'Do you like to die?!'

'No, comrade!'

'Please!' Sam hobbled in front of his sister to protect her.

The leader said to his gang: 'Here is a UDF boy who likes to protect people who help Inkatha-dogs. I do not think he is UDF, I think he lies!'

'I am UDF, comrade!' Sam cried. 'And so is my sister!'

'I think the nurse who helps Inkatha must do some modelling to learn her lesson!' the leader cried and his gang shouted agreement.

'No!' Princess cried, and she turned to run, but two men grabbed her.

'*Modelling! Modelling . . . !*' the gang cried.

Princess burst into tears. 'No!' and she wrenched and struggled but they held her gleefully.

'*No!*' Sam cried and he tried to grab their arms. A youth swiped him across the head with a stick and he reeled and sprawled.

As she struggled and wept and cried out, the youths gleefully pranced around her, ripping off her uniform, buttons snapping, then her vest was torn off, and her bra wrenched apart. Princess struggled and cried out for her mother, trying to clasp her breasts, and gleeful fingers wrenched her knickers down. Princess writhed and crossed her legs but then her foot was grabbed and off came her knickers to shouts of applause. She cowered in the public road, mortified, weeping, one hand across her breasts, the other clutching her pubis, sobbing for mercy.

'*Stand up straight and model!*' the leader shouted.

'*Please comrade –* ' Princess wept.

'*Stand up straight!*' he shouted, and he swiped her across her buttocks with his stick. Then another youth hit her thighs and Princess lurched and she sprawled to the ground, weeping. They heaved her to her feet, and Princess began her modelling.

She walked down the early-morning street, the tears running down her face, one hand on her hip, the other arm swinging, and the UDF youths laughed and pranced about her, jeering and cheering and waving their weapons, shouting at her to swing her hips more, to smile, to toss her head, prodding to make her go faster, to shake her breasts, to flick her shoulders. The people going to work hurried past the spectacle, terrified that the same would happen to them.

For fifteen minutes the ordeal of nakedness in public went on midst the taunting: then the leader gave her a swipe across her buttocks and shouted: *'Go and tell your friends at the hospital what happens to people who treat Inkatha-dogs!'*

She was not allowed to recover her clothes. Nor would they let her go back to her aunt's house. They chased her down the main road towards the hospital, whooping and hollering and brandishing their weapons. Princess ran, stumbling, naked down the road, through the people going to work, the buses and taxis roaring past, everybody staring, and she wept and wept.

The self-governing homeland of KwaZulu, where Chief Buthelezi and his Inkatha party rule, is sprinkled down the length of Natal in isolated pockets. Just beyond the township of Edendale is a piece of KwaZulu. The afternoon following Princess's ordeal the Inkatha impi came over the hills.

Sam's school was on the fringe of Edendale. Most of the windows were smashed and the walls were pocked with bullets of many previous battles. Sam was in his crowded classroom when the commotion was heard in the streets, people running, the shouts, the wailing. Everybody scrambled to the window. The grassy hill was swarming with men running down it, armed with spears and pangas and axes and AK–47s. A chant rose up. The next instant there was a barrage of gunfire from the streets of Edendale and all hell broke loose.

'Out!' the teacher bellowed, *'everybody run home!'*

There was a rush for the door, children piling out onto the verandah, yelling. As Sam hobbled for the door he was immediately knocked aside by screaming children shoving back into the classroom, and simultaneously there was shattering gunfire from the playground. UDF men were running through the school grounds. Sam was sent reeling back into the classroom as Inkatha gunfire raked the windows.

'Flat!' the teacher bellowed. *'Lie flat!'*

Sam threw himself under a desk. Outside children were screaming, running in all directions for cover. A man burst into Sam's classroom with an AK–47, ran to the window and blasted at the hill.

The teacher shouted from under his table: *'Please do not fight amongst the children, comrade!'*

The gunman shouted: *'This school belongs to the UDF! The children belong to the UDF!'*

The teacher cried: *'Comrade, the children belong to God –'*

The man swung his gun on the teacher and let off a burst of gunfire. He roared at the terrified children: *'Anybody who does not belong to the UDF belongs to the cemetery! Who – ?'* He was cut off by a bullet through the head from outside.

The hillside was littered with bodies but most of the Inkatha impi had made it to the outlying cottages. Now the gun battle was from house to house, the occupants fleeing midst the wail of police sirens. In the school grounds Inkatha gunmen were shooting it out with UDF gunmen. The shattered window of Sam's classroom burst upwards and a man scrambled through. He saw the dead gunman and turned to the cowering children and roared: *'Why do you help the UDF in this school?!'* He snatched up the dead man's gun. *'Why are you not shooting the UDF?'* He shook the gun at them: *'Everybody must fight for Inkatha! Any person who does not join Inkatha will die!'*

On the main road two police vehicles had taken up position outside the hospital, which had a high-security fence. Terrified people were pouring through the gate, seeking refuge. A police officer was radioing for reinforcements from Pietermaritzburg, three miles away. A military vehicle was roaring down the road towards the hospital. The battle was raging only two hundred yards away. The military vehicle stopped and soldiers leapt out. The commander hurried to the police officer. 'What's the score?'

'Inkatha seems to be winning this one at the moment.'

'What're you guys going to do to stop it?'

'To stop it?' the policeman grinned. 'We want Inkatha to win, don't we?'

The army man said: 'For Christ's sake, Klasie, this is a police matter, *you've* got to tell *me* what you want my men to do!'

'Ja, I'm the policeman in charge right now, but this is a kaffir matter an' I'm telling you there're only eight policemen here right now and there's fok-all I can do right now about four hundred Inkatha kaffirs with AK–47s attacking four thousand UDF kaffirs with AK–47s until a hell of a lot of police reinforcements come.' He turned to his map of the township. 'We're here. Tell your men to go there, and there. Try and hold Inkatha across that line without killing too many of them, hey. Shoot the shit out of any UDF who resist you.'

'And both Inkatha and the UDF will shoot the shit out of us.'

'Ja,' Klasie agreed, 'that's a problem, hey, but that's the name of the game if you join the army. Or the police,' he added.

'But there aren't really four thousand UDF in this battle, are there?'

'Maybe not,' Klasie said reasonably, 'but there will be tonight when the bastards start coming home from work. And there'll be four thousand Inkatha when they start coming home from work . . .'

That battle for Edendale raged all night, as it had many times before. The police and army reinforcements arrived but there was little they could do without a pre-ordained curfew and a shoot-on-sight order, for the battle raged behind them and between them and to the side of them and in front of them, and the streets were full of screaming people fleeing in all directions. As Klasie had said, this was a black man's war and only the black man could stop it. But the black man did not want to stop it: this was part of the battle for the new South Africa.

It was after dark when Sam got back to Aunt Matilda's house. He had lost his crutch and he had crawled most of the way, creeping along ditches and hedges before scrambling up to limp flat out across a road or open ground. All the time the cacophony of the gunfire, the sirens, the clattering of the helicopters overhead, the stink of tear-gas, the flames leaping up from the houses, war cries of new impis descending from KwaZulu. Sam hobbled down the dirt road where Aunt Matilda lived, crouched behind a bush and peered.

Up the road a house was on fire and people were running down past him. At the other end another fire raged. Sam hobbled on. He was about a hundred yards from Aunt Matilda's house when the gang of UDF youths came pounding down the alley.

'Oh-hoh! Here is the cripple boy who is relative of Matilda!'

First they beat him, sticks and kicks and punches, then they dragged him down the road to see what the UDF did to Inkatha sell-outs. Aunt Matilda's house was in darkness. Inside Aunt Matilda lay in bed with her two children, curtains drawn, listening fearfully to the commotion. She did not hear the UDF boys creeping around the side of her house; Sam could not cry out to warn her because they had put a gag in his mouth. A UDF boy took up position under each window with a panga, while wire was wrapped around the handles of the front and back doors and made fast to the frame. Sam struggled and gargled in horror. Then the wicks of two petrol bombs were lit, and they were hurled through the windows.

All Aunt Matilda knew was the sudden crashing of window panes, the bottles smashing against the wall, the flaming petrol flying in a great whooshing explosion. And Matilda and the children were on fire, flaming petrol all over them; they screamed and scrambled out of the burning bed onto the flaming floor, beating at the flames with their hands. Aunt Matilda grabbed a wrist of each screaming child and dragged them to the door. And the living-room was on fire, great clouds of black smoke barrelling from leaping flames, and Aunt Matilda plunged wildly into them, gasping, choking, on fire, dragging the screaming children, and she grabbed the front door handle and wrenched, but the wire held it closed. And she screamed and wrenched and wrenched, then turned and plunged wildly towards the kitchen. But the kitchen was ablaze, flames leaping to the ceiling, and Aunt Matilda tried to make it to the children's bedroom. She lurched wildly through the flames, in agony, desperately trying to breathe, choking, coughing, her head reeling, and that bedroom too was on fire. Matilda dragged the children towards the window, and she collapsed. She tried to clamber to her hands and knees to crawl to the window, and she collapsed again. The children were writhing, faces contorted in choking screams, burning bodies jerking. Aunt Matilda's whole body was blistering; she tried one more time to clamber up. She got to her hands and knees in the leaping flames and she tried to reach the window, and she collapsed again. She collapsed onto her side, writhing, and she tried to curl herself into a ball, and she lost consciousness.

Outside the UDF boys pranced and toyi-toyed and they told Sam to rescue his Inkatha aunt. Sam hobbled desperately to the back door, ripping off his gag, and grabbed the handle crying: 'Aunt Matilda!' He wrenched at the wire as smoke poured through the cracks and the UDF boys toyi-toyed around him, shouting encouragement. But Sam could not undo the wire and he hobbled desperately around the side of the house and the gang toyi-toyed joyfully after him. Sam threw himself at the front door. Smoke was billowing around the frame. Sam wrenched at the handle but the wire held it.

Sam sobbed desperately: 'Please, comrades, do not kill my aunt!' He kicked at the door with his club foot, and he collapsed on his back, and the UDF boys screamed in mirth. He scrambled up and he tried to kick again, his withered toes smiting the hot wood, then he hobbled to the window and the boy guarding it raised his stick but Sam lunged past him, his fist on high, and he plunged it through the window pane. The hot glass shattered, and the guard hit Sam across the head. Sam lurched but his hand reached desperately through the broken glass and found the red-hot handle. He wrenched at it, and the stick swiped him again.

He sprawled unconscious in the dirt outside the inferno of Aunt Matilda's house, his knuckles and wrists slashed by the glass; the boys gave him a few more blows for good measure, then they gleefully ran off into the cacophonous night.

The neighbours on all sides had seen the whole thing, and thanked God it wasn't them.

48

And so Mahoney wrote up the family journals, using the lamp-post format that Lisa Rousseau had taught him.

VIOLENCE INTENSIFIES FOLLOWING RUBICON SPEECH

ANC ANNOUNCES 1986 IS 'YEAR OF PEOPLE'S ARMY' – 'CIVILIANS WILL BE CAUGHT IN THE CROSSFIRE'

AS VIOLENCE CONTINUES GOVERNMENT ANNOUNCES NEW REFORMS

Opening Parliament, President Botha said he proposed to create a National Council pending negotiations on power-sharing. This council will include black leaders from all walks of life, but will be an advisory body only. 'Those who oppose this evolutionary reform must know that the alternative is revolutionary chaos.' He also announced that Africans would now be given freehold rights to property in the black townships, and that there would be a uniform identity document for all races.

However, the Minister of Education, FW de Klerk, said the government stands by its policy of separate residential areas for different races, separate schools and separate institutions, saying this 'is not discriminatory, but the prerequisite for peaceful co-existence: each racial group must handle its own interests'.

US CONGRESS IMPOSES SANCTIONS ON SOUTH AFRICA – BUT PRESIDENT REAGAN VETOES

The United States Congress has shown its exasperation with South Africa by voting for comprehensive economic sanctions against the country. However, President Reagan used his powers to veto the legislation for six

*months, reiterating his policy of Constructive Engagement by which he hopes
to influence the South African government with carrot-and-stick tactics.*

GREAT INDABA STARTS IN KWAZULU/NATAL

*A great indaba has been convened in Durban by the (black) KwaZulu
Administration and the (white) Natal Provincial Council to draw up
proposals for a non-racial, democratic legislature to govern Natal. If
accepted by the government, this will be a breakthrough for a New South
Africa. The indaba, expected to last six months, is to be attended by representatives of chambers of commerce, trade unions, political, cultural, religious, educational and business organizations, black and white. The
government has refused to participate.*

S.A. COMMUNIST PARTY
INTENDS REVOLUTIONARY SEIZURE OF POWER

*A document leaked from the politburo meeting of the South African
Communist Party reveals that its strategy is the revolutionary seizure of
power. The National Executive Council of the ANC has thirty members:
nineteen of them are members of the S.A. Communist Party. ANC guerillas
are trained in East Germany, Libya and Russia, get their arms from the
Eastern Bloc and use the communication facilities of the Palestine
Liberation Organization. Libya's Colonel Gaddafi has disclosed that he is
cooperating with the ANC.*

*The South African Minister of Defence said: 'We don't negotiate with
terrorists, we fight 'em.'*

MASSIVE EXODUS TO JOIN MK

SANCTIONS INCREASED BY CANADA, EEC, JAPAN

AMERICA APPLIES SANCTIONS

*The Comprehensive Anti-Apartheid Act vetoed by President Reagan for
six months has now become law. The act also requires the US government
to pressurise South Africa to repeal the State of Emergency, to release
Nelson Mandela and all political prisoners, to permit free political expression, scrap apartheid, negotiate a new political system and end military
activities in neighbouring states.*

ANC DECLARES WAR ON INDUSTRY

On Radio Freedom, Chris Hani, the communist commissar of MK, urged black workers in South Africa to 'use revolutionary violence in factories, plant mines, deal with all managers who display hostility.'

BLACK-ON-BLACK VIOLENCE ESCALATES

The S.A. government's control of the media means that the general public is not fully aware of the extent of the violence.

While all black political groups have been getting stuck into each other, the worst violence has been between Inkatha and the UDF. As their respective supporters rage through the Natal countryside slaughtering each other, their leaders hurl abuse at each other on the radio. The president of the ANC, Oliver Tambo, has said that Chief Buthelezi 'tells people he is governing KwaZulu but our people scorn these ravings.' Buthelezi retorts that the ANC leaders 'strut up and down the corridors of the international community . . . loudly proclaim themselves to be the sole representatives of the people of South Africa. They tolerate no opposition. They murder them brutally by hacking them to pieces and burning them alive. That is democracy for the ANC. They are making hideous mistakes. If we reduce the country to ungovernability now, it will remain ungovernable after liberation.' Buthelezi has called on the government to release Nelson Mandela, adding that the continued banning of the ANC produced sympathy which allowed them to 'bask in the illusion of popularity'. He called for unity talks with them, but the ANC responded that he was deliberately dividing the people. 'The puppet Buthelezi is being groomed by the West and the racist South African regime. The Buthelezi snake is poisoning the people. It needs to be hit on the head.'

Meanwhile, as the hate-campaign of the airwaves goes on, the butchery continues on the ground.

Of course the tap-roots of the violence are buried in the bedrock of heartless apartheid, in the poverty it created, but the grass roots lie in the power struggle between the UDF and Inkatha for political control of Zululand and Natal. But the real prize is the new South Africa when it comes into being. Both Inkatha and the UDF are hostile to apartheid, but whereas the UDF has a policy of violence to overthrow the government, Buthelezi has decided to work for that same goal from within, from the legitimate power-base of KwaZulu. So whereas Inkatha worked with the Natal Indaba to negotiate a constitution which would become a model for the new South Africa, the UDF attacked the Indaba as an unholy alliance of Inkatha and big business plotting to suppress the worker and the ANC. Expressed

*another way, the violence is about whether the New South Africa is going
to be ANC-socialist or Inkatha-capitalist. Expressed another way, the
bloodbath is about whether the New South Africa will be Zulu-dominated
or Xhosa-dominated. Expressed yet another way, it is typical African
democracy at work: kill the opposition.*

*The differences in ideology between the UDF and Inkatha, between
socialism and capitalism, are barely understood by the semi-literate populace
traumatised by the bloodbath. Ideology has long since been trampled underfoot by a reckless unemployable youth who understand little, but imagine
they are participating in 'The Struggle' – as much against their feckless
parents who bowed down to the white man as against apartheid itself . . .*

49

Mahoney heard the story of Sam Mbene from his sister: it was Jill
Dawson who had stopped her car when she saw the lone cripple hobbling up the dark road and offered him a ride. 'Where are you going?' she
said. And Sam had replied: 'I am looking for a better land, Nkosikazi.'

She had taken him home to the mission's farm, dressed his cuts, and
then given him a job while he studied at the mission's illegal school.

'Looking for a better land.' It made Mahoney's eyes burn when he read
his sister's letter. He must use that in his journals. Are not many South
Africans looking for a better land? Patti Gandhi and Nelson Mandela
withering in prison for trying to make a better land; his sister Jill, working on her husband's mission station, trying to make a better land;
Justin Nkomo somewhere out there in the bush fighting for a better
land; Lisa Rousseau, teaching her students about a better land. And
what was he doing? Sitting on his arse in a better land, coining money
by writing about his bad old land, pontificating about how to make it
better but not putting his money where his mouth was. *God*, it made
him feel guilty. And, God, he wanted to go home . . .

And then had come the news that his father had died of a heart attack.
It was like a blow. He brooded about how the old man had devoted his
life to the blacks, fighting for them in parliament, trying to make a better
land for them – and all Luke Mahoney had done was make money out of
criticising them. And now even his old mother was helping make a
better land: she had gone to live with his sister on the mission station in
Zululand and the old girl was busy teaching needlework and stitching
heads. And, God, he wanted to go home . . . But he could not, because
those Afrikaner bastards might arrest him.

346

He received a long letter from Lisa Rousseau – and that made him want to go home – oh, to be in the thick of it. Her letter was in response to one he had written her, asking for her historian's advice on the family journals he was updating for publication. He also sent her all the new work he had added, for comment. She wrote:

> *I've made some important comments in the margins, but your grasp of current events is excellent, dear Luke. I have taken the liberty of checking certain passages with a friend of mine, Professor Katrina de la Rey of the University of South Africa – I taught her too! – and when I've got her response I'll fax them to you. Meanwhile, I thought you might like the following digest of what's happening in our unhappy land you so hanker for.*

VIGILANTES

> *A new phenomenon has appeared: black workers who've had a gutful of the UDF Comrades have banded together and set upon their persecutors. In June a pitched battle between 3000 vigilantes and 8000 comrades was fought at Crossroads Squatter Camp outside Cape Town: 60 people were killed and 70,000 left homeless. Shocking. In Soweto, Zulu hostel-dwellers went on the rampage for three days searching for UDF comrades, killing fourteen. In Natal pitched battles are fought daily between Inkatha and the UDF, while in the Eastern Cape – where there are almost no Zulus – there are bloody battles between the UDF and AZAPO, the followers of Steve Biko's Black Consciousness.*
>
> *In short, the government has lost control of large areas. The conservatives scream for a 'shoot-on-sight' curfew for blacks, while the AWB bellows that it is going to 'restore law and order'. Meanwhile the government demands that violence be abandoned by the blacks before negotiations on power-sharing can start. Some hope! I suspect this is an excuse on government's part. Meanwhile . . .*

SA ARMY RAIDS ANC FOREIGN BASES

> *In one day army commandos launched three simultaneous attacks on ANC bases in Botswana, Zambia and Zimbabwe. Defending the raids as necessary to eliminate Russian lines of supply, President Botha said: 'We have only delivered the first*

instalment. The ANC is not engaged in a so-called liberation strug-
gle, but is hell-bent on the destruction of South African society.'
True. But who can blame them?

'TOTAL STRATEGY' AGAINST 'TOTAL ONSLAUGHT'

*Luke, so far you haven't sufficiently emphasised the importance
of this. So here's a rundown.*

*The government says that South Africa is now facing a Total
Onslaught by the Marxist forces of darkness. The 'front-line states'
of Mozambique, Zimbabwe and Angola are all hostile Marxist
regimes who're providing military bases for the ANC and PAC,
requiring South Africa to have a 'Total Strategy': i.e. a ring of steel
defending the borders, cross-border raids to hit terrorist bases, and
destabilization of the hostile governments to discourage them from
succouring the ANC. This Total Strategy is controlled by the
'Securocrats' in the National Security Management System.*

*Here is how that system works: at the top is the State Security
Council (SSC) headed by President Botha, and it includes the
ministers of Defence, Law and Order, Foreign Affairs, plus numerous senior officials. Its purpose is to 'advise the government on security strategy and to coordinate the country's intelligence systems.'
The SSC is the topmost body which decides the Total Strategy.*

*Below the SSC come 12 regional Joint Management Councils,
(JMCs) centred on the main cities, each headed by a military or
police brigadier and composed of officials from all government
departments. Below these JMCs come 60 sub-JMCs, consisting of
city officials and local army and police commanders. Below these
come 400 mini-JMCs at the local authority level.*

*The function of all these 472 JMCs is to identify potential points
of unrest, to neutralise activists in the townships and to 'win hearts
and minds'. The good news is that they have spent large sums on
upgrading projects in black townships and establishing new sports,
cultural and church bodies. The bad news is that these JMCs rely
extensively on networks of spies. It must be borne in mind that
these JMCs function in addition to the Security Police and the
National Intelligence Service, whose business is spying. All this is in
addition to Military Intelligence and their spies! Phew!*

*President Botha has refused to tell Parliament the number of
persons thus employed, or the amount budgeted to pay them, and
whether they have infiltrated political parties, trade unions,*

community and student organizations. So, Big Brother is watching you. And Big Brother ain't answerable to Parliament! The Progressive Federal Party has denounced this Securocratic system as a 'creeping coup d'état' saying the Botha regime has become one of executive despotism, in which the security forces are answerable only to the president 'and the president only to himself'. And they're damn right, Luke.

So is the South African Parliament relevant anymore? Is Parliament accountable to the electorate anymore or are the president and his 'securocrats' running the bloody show like Hitler ran Germany, Stalin ran Russia? How Shaka ran Zululand? Is South Africa a 'Western-style democracy' anymore, as the government so loudly claims, or is it being ruled the 'African Way'? Is the Afrikaner white tribe any different from the black tribes they denounce, whose leaders rule by the sword and scorn the ballot-box? Make this point in your journals, Luke.

MK HIT MANY MORE 'SOFT' TARGETS

As you know, there's been a dramatic increase in the number of landmines on farm roads, bombs exploding in hotels, restaurants, supermarkets etc, and some gun battles between police and MK insurgents. Several major caches of Russian arms have been found. Police stations have been bombed and many policemen killed. In some areas black policemen and their families have had to be moved to tent-camps adjoining their police stations! Black township councillors have had their homes attacked, their families shot and hacked to death. The government's had to move Soweto's councillors to a guarded apartment block in Johannesburg, and this too was attacked with limpet mines. Government had to spend a fortune on arming councillors! Also there have been as many attacks on black anti-apartheid activists, mainly members of the UDF and AZAPO.

WHITE VIGILANTES ARE ON THE WARPATH

They are raising hell, especially around Jo'burg, where nearby black townships are perceived as a security threat. The AWB leader, Eugene Terreblanche, announced that because of 'the government's ineffectual handling of the unrest crisis' all his branches will form *vigilante groups to fight the 'onslaught of leftist Marxist forces'. Oh boy. Meanwhile a black consumer boycott of white shops and the death of two policemen have raised the fury to boiling point. Attacks by white vigilantes on blacks in certain townships are almost nightly occurrences. They wear balaclavas and indiscriminately attack blacks with tear-gas, sjamboks, batons and firearms, and they are sometimes accompanied by black men in uniform. Who are these blacks? Hired guns?*

AWB BREAKS UP GOVERNMENT MEETINGS

Infuriated by the government's 'reform' policy, denouncing poor old Botha as a traitor to the Afrikaner volk, wearing their khaki uniforms and swastika insignia, the AWB broke up a meeting in Brits where the Minister of Information was explaining government policies to the party faithful. A month later they broke up a similar meeting held by the Minister of Foreign Affairs in Pietersburg, ignominiously driving the minister from the hall midst fierce fist-fighting. Hereupon the AWB leader was carried shoulder-high to the podium where he delivered a fierce anti-government speech, reiterating his demands for a white Boer state consisting of the old Boer republics. Meanwhile . . .

CONSERVATIVE PARTY LAMBASTS
GOVERNMENT'S REFORM POLICY

The CP has only 18 seats in Parliament but, as you say, it speaks for a much greater segment of white South Africa. And their leader, Dr Treurnicht, being a theologian, has a lot of clout. He loudly declares that the CP will return South Africa to 'strict Verwoerdian apartheid', remove the rights given to non-whites in the Tri-cameral Parliament, re-enact the Separate Amenities Act and the Immorality Act and eject Indians from the Orange Free State and northern Natal. The Conservative Party will never negotiate with the ANC. To reject apartheid, as the government is 'methodically and recklessly' doing, is to 'reject the past, future, and the very existence of the Afrikaner people'. The CP also denounces the government for allowing black trade unions, 'whose purpose is to seize political power'. God help us from the CP!

Meanwhile, across our bloodied land there are boycotts of white-owned shops, rent boycotts protesting at township conditions, school boycotts – all demanding the lifting of the state of emergency, the withdrawal of troops from the townships, the rebuilding of schools (which the blacks burned down!), and the opening of municipal facilities to all races. On Radio Freedom the ANC urges the people to destroy 'the monstrous apartheid system' with 'our own version of economic sanctions, crippling the economy from within.'

And they're succeeding, Luke. The Associated Chambers of Commerce roundly blames the Group Areas Act for making boycotts successful because the legal differentiation between black and white trading areas makes the white targets clearly identifiable. True! In East London the boycott was so effective that the City Council has opened residential areas and municipal amenities to all races in defiance of apartheid! In Queenstown a seven-month boycott closed down 35 white-owned businesses and only ended when the government committed R16,000,000 to upgrading the adjoining black township. In Port Elizabeth the Chamber of Commerce loudly called on the government to release detainees, adding that the only people capable of calling off the boycott are in detention or in hiding. In Howick the boycott has glutted the real estate market with white houses for sale. Of course intimidation to enforce the boycotts is widespread. Scabs are beaten, made to consume their purchases on the spot, murdered with dreadful brutality. In townships outside Port Elizabeth black-owned liquor stores were ruthlessly destroyed to enable boycotters to prove that anybody found with liquor must have bought it in white-owned shops. Oh boy, are the chickens of apartheid coming home to roost!

BIG BUSINESS GIVES GOVERNMENT BIG STICK!

Businessmen are realists. They prospered under apartheid and pretty much kept their mouths shut. Now that business is bad because of apartheid the government is coming under heavy fire. In January the Chamber of Industries demanded that government scrap all discriminatory laws, negotiate power-sharing up to highest level, grant equal citizenship to all races, grant full participation in private enterprise to all races, grant equality of education. In March the Midland Chamber of Industries told the Minister of Law and Order that the banning of 'accepted black leaders' raised doubt over the government's sincerity about negotiations. In May the Association of Chambers of Commerce urged the government to repeal the Group Areas Act and the Black Land Act. In July the Cape Chamber of Industries advised its members not to dismiss workers detained under the emergency regulations, while the Sugar Growers Association 'denounced apartheid'. In August the South Africa Foundation, the diplomatic arm of the business community, told a British Parliament select committee that the SA government must release black political leaders and unban political organizations.

But does this government learn, Luke? Does it hell. In November the president convened an 'economic summit' of business leaders, but the eventual report made no reference to the businessman's demands. In December the Associated Chamber of Commerce issued a hard-hitting homily: 'We cannot afford to waste precious months, even days, on repetitious debate, on preparing serialised memoranda. Time is running out fast and it must not be wasted by temporising, procrastination, and the shuffling of papers.'

NECKLACING IS NOW COMMON

As political violence rages across this bloodied land, the 'necklace' has become a favourite form of political execution. There have been over 300 cases this dreadful year. Now gangs of UDF Comrades terrorise the townships by shaking matchboxes. The following is the shocking procedure (I'm quoting from the journal of the South African Institute of Race Relations which, as you doubtless know, is a very liberal organization).

First the victim is beaten up before being tried by a 'People's Court'. Predictably sentenced to death as a collaborator, he or she is then taken to the place of execution, where a large crowd has gathered. The following ritual is observed:

(1) The executioners bind the condemned person's wrists with barbed wire or chop off the hands at the wrist or elbow with an axe. (2) A used car tyre is hung around the condemned's shoulders, and filled with petrol or diesel oil. Diesel is preferred as it clings to the skin. (3) The fuel is lit with a match. If the victim has not had his hands chopped off he is often forced to light his own necklace. (4) The tyre bursts into flames about the condemned's head and releases thick clouds of smoke, reaching temperatures of 400 degrees

Celsius. Inhalation destroys the lung tissue. (5) The burning tyre melts as the condemned struggles with bound hands or stumped arms to throw it off. It burns deep into the flesh. Once this has happened the tyre cannot be removed. For the greater amusement of the crowd, the condemned's relatives are encouraged to help him or her. This is impossible due to the tyre's enormous heat, and the melted rubber cannot be pulled off the scorched tissue. It takes about twenty minutes for the condemned to die.

Winnie Mandela attracted international outrage when, addressing a crowd of supporters, she said: 'Together, hand in hand, with our boxes of matches and our necklaces, we shall liberate this country.' Foreign newspaper reports tell us that she has lost much support amongst British liberals. Oliver Tambo, at a London press conference, criticised the use of the necklace by 'radicals' but did not condemn it. An ANC spokesman in London told the Sunday Times: 'Collaborators have to be eliminated. Whatever the people decide to use is their decision. If they use necklacing, we support it.' Necklace killings have horrified the world, and the failure of Oliver Tambo to condemn it is widely noted. He drew harsh criticism in his fund-raising tours of Australia, New Zealand, America and Japan. In New York demonstrators carried out mock-necklacings of effigies, which the South African Foreign Minister described as 'a billion dollars' worth of free propaganda.'

Although the government is responding to all this trouble with its customary kragdadigheid, I think it is a sign of its insecurity that it is calling a new general election for whites in 1987 to seek a new mandate. Radio Freedom responded by announcing that the ANC's Armed Struggle is to be taken into the white civilian areas, saying 'the white minority is the cause of all our sorrows and suffering . . . the time has arrived for an eye for an eye, a tooth for a tooth, a life for a life.' MK has now promised 'sensational' attacks before the end of 1987. 'This time we will be ruthless.'

Well, dear Luke, that brings you up to date on my lamp-posts – I hope they're of some use. If you'd like to keep sending copies of your chapters for comment, I'd be delighted, and flattered.

I've received a most amusing letter from Sally Freeman, the black American lass I suggested visit you in Hong Kong. (Should I apologise?) Anyway, she gave a hilarious account of being caught in your boudoir by your Chinese lady-friend. It seems you lead a hectic love-life! You'll be interested to learn she is definitely coming to South Africa in the next few months 'to experience apartheid'. I hope she doesn't get into too much trouble. She describes you as a 'latent racist'. Luke, I know you're not a racist, only a realist, but I do think you must be careful not to create the wrong impression in your books, especially in your comments about the mess the blacks have made of self-government in Africa. They are valid comments, but remember that South Africa is so unpopular because apartheid is such a beastly system that the world is very sensitive about adverse views on blacks. Try to sugar the pill more. (Tell me to shut up! Once a teacher . . . You can't expect too much of us.)

In closing – though I hesitate to mention this – I visited Patti Gandhi when I was in Jo'burg last month. She is well. She is very excited about the political developments. She is convinced this government is about to fall and that she will soon be free. Indeed it will fall but, alas, not as soon as she thinks, though I did not have the heart to dampen her optimism. The point is, however, for the first time in a long time she mentioned you: she had recently read Alms for Oblivion (a friendly wardress had smuggled a copy to her), and she was deeply moved by it. She wept while she spoke about it. Said she knows it almost by heart now. She said she'd written several letters to you, but torn them up. She also said she'd received a letter from you year before last – said it looked as if you were drunk when you wrote it. I gather it was not a love-letter but more an outpouring of your admiration for her and your sense of guilt. Luke, I do urge you not to do that again. It really shook up her equilibrium. She said she resisted reading it for days. Remember that you can dull your memories with other women and another life; she has nothing but time to help her. Now Alms has reawoken all her memories and pain. And for your sake, Luke, you must put her behind you: it will be years before she is released and I fear it will be a sad anticlimax for both of you if and when it happens. And as for your sense of guilt, forget it. Not only is it irrational, it is destructive. I hope that is not the reason why you are still unmarried: I hope it is because you're having a helluva good time.

I eagerly await your next batch of lamp-posts, dear friend.

With great affection

Lisa

Mahoney held his head. Just seeing Patti's name brought a flush to his breast. And, oh God, yes, everything Lisa said was true: he shouldn't have posted that letter, he must not do it again. For her sake and his. Because, yes, Lisa was right that this whole Patti thing was the reason why he'd been unable to commit himself to anybody else. Oh, it was also true that he was having a helluva good time, but it was also his irrational sense of guilt. And that was wrong. Destructive. And it would indeed be years before Patti came out. And, if and when it happened, it *would* be a sad anticlimax . . .

50

Sally Freeman had not gotten around to divorcing her sumbitch of a husband, partly because her marriage to a South African might facilitate her entry into the mother-fuckin' country, and partly because she still loved the asshole.

Her uncle in the United States diplomatic service had arranged her visa, vouching for her. She carried two references, one from her bank manager, the other from a university professor, perjured, testifying to her apolitical academic interest in African art. She also had a wad of American Express traveller's cheques, an American Express card and a copy of her degree in Social Anthropology. Her uncle in the Pretoria office of the American Embassy sent a car to meet her at Jan Smuts Airport. But, as she complained loudly, for all the good all these credentials did her she might as well have stuck them up her sweet ass. 'What more does a darky damsel need to get into this fuckin' country? That Special Branch oaf at the airport treated me as if I had made the visa myself – read me the riot act about keeping my nose clean.'

'What did you say to that?' her uncle asked.

'Told him where to stick his advice – I'm a United States citizen. *No*, I simpered and flapped my eyelashes so much he almost charged me under the Immorality Act.'

Her uncle smiled. 'Well, you *better* keep your nose clean or they'll deport your sweet ass.'

'Can you arrange for me to visit Nelson Mandela on Robben Island?'

'Definitely not,' her uncle said. 'Even MPs can't visit him without the Minister of Justice's permission. Anyway, he's not there anymore, he's in Pollsmoor prison, near Cape Town. He's had treatment for tuberculosis.'

'Shit. Are they ever going to let the poor guy out?'

'President Botha offered to release him provided he renounces violence. Mandela told him to go to hell, told *him* to renounce violence.'

Sally grinned. 'That's my boy, Nelson! And Winnie Mandela, what's she doing?'

'Well, she's back in Soweto. She was banished to Brandfort, a village in the Orange Free State, where she lived for years, then her house was petrol-bombed, by some right-wing Afrikaners presumably, and she said to hell with her banning order and returned to this area. For some reason the government's decided not to deport her back – I guess they're scared of the international fuss. She's living on donations from Americans and royalties from her book, *Part of My Soul*. She's quite a gal. She's not allowed to say anything, but she defies the banning order all the time. She made a shocking speech recently in which she extolled necklacing as a form of political expression. As punishment for collaborators. She said "With our matches and our necklaces we shall liberate the country".'

'But she denies saying it,' Sally said. 'It's a frame-up.'

'Unfortunately it's not,' her uncle said. 'Associated Press was present and recorded the whole speech on video.'

'Well, she didn't *mean* it.'

'Then what did she mean? Sally,' the diplomat said, 'you're in for a surprise. This ain't America. Politics is a very violent business in Africa.'

'Shit, who bumped off President Kennedy? An American. Anyway, Winnie Mandela is a hero of mine, can you arrange for me to meet her?'

'I could,' her uncle said, 'but I won't. You're in this country as my guest and I'm a senior member of the United States diplomatic service; my guests cannot upset the host government, and you talking to Winnie would upset them. She's a banned person.'

'Jesus, Uncle Gerry, I thought America supported *democracy*.'

'America's policy,' the diplomat said, 'is one of constructive engagement – to influence the South African government by *talking* to them, by holding out rewards for reforms and penalties for bad behaviour. Hobnobbing with Winnie Mandela, no matter how democratic, would not do our friendly but firm policy any good.' He held up a finger. 'And furthermore this is a delicate time for America, Sally. The Cold War has been raging here for twenty-five years, and almost the entire continent has gone communist. Except here.' He pointed at the floor. 'South Africa is the only bastion against communism. Mozambique is communist, so is Angola, Zimbabwe virtually the same. And the Cape sea route is very important, because Suez is dominated by South Yemen, which is a communist puppet, and the Panama Canal is potentially unreliable since Jimmy Carter gave it away. And that's why,' he raised a finger again, 'America is involved in the war in Angola on the same side as South Africa, helping UNITA fight the Cubans. Do you understand what's happening up there in Angola?'

Sally shrugged. 'Nope.'

Her uncle said: 'Well you must, if you want to understand America's relationship with South Africa. When the Portuguese collapsed and pulled out of Angola, the communists seized power illegally, forcing the capitalists, UNITA, out into the cold – so UNITA started a civil war. Russia ordered Cuba to send troops to support the illegal communist government – so America sent arms and instructors to help UNITA, and so did the South African government – because they don't want another communist government on their northern border either. And to complicate matters the South Africans are fighting another *separate* war on that same border with SWAPO, the liberation movement which is trying to take over Namibia, which South Africa governs – and technically America supports SWAPO because it's a democratic movement. So the whole thing is a mess. Delicate. In short, we need South Africa and South Africa needs us. So our policy often has to be sometimes more carrot than stick. And before you pull a face, young lady, let me tell you that's diplomacy – and Britain, France, Germany et al agree with us. So, *please*, no trying to meet Winnie Mandela. In fact don't go near Soweto, or any other black township. It's chaos, a State of Emergency, nobody is safe – least of all a black like you.'

Sally snorted. *Not go to Soweto?* That's where she was going to *live*. To *suffer* . . . 'Well, where the hell else *can* I go? I thought Soweto was the only place I'd be allowed to stay, for Christ's sake.'

Her uncle shook his head and poured more wine. 'You stay right here in the embassy, young lady. But you can go out and do your sightseeing. Times have changed in South Africa. They now have "international hotels" in most cities where blacks and white can stay. Even right here in Pretoria. And – would you believe? – downtown Johannesburg has become *legally* colour-blind. Blacks can now have a drink or a meal anywhere there. I'll tell an embassy chauffeur to show you the sights. The mines, for example, I can arrange that, very interesting – '

'Oh *yeah* . . . '

'And there are a lot of museums. And go to the Kruger National Park, see all their fabulous game – '

'Oh *yeah*,' Sally said, 'like to spend a week there!'

'Well,' the diplomat said, 'I'm afraid it will have to be a day trip because blacks aren't allowed overnight.'

Sally stared at her uncle. 'Why the hell *not*? It's the *bush*, ain't that where us darkies supposed to *belong*?'

Her uncle grinned. 'Unfortunately President Botha's reforms have not yet extended to the rest camps in the Kruger Park. But on the other hand you can go to the Republic of Bophuthatswana, which used to be part of South Africa until a few years ago – ' he pointed – 'just a hundred miles over there, and it's completely multi-racial. They've got a magnificent tourist joint called Sun City, like a mini-Las Vegas, gambling, girlie shows, the works. And you can go just a hundred miles in the opposite direction to the Kingdom of Swaziland, where they ain't got any apartheid either; it's lovely there. And you can go to the Transkei.'

Damn right Sally was going to the goddamn Transkei, to find Justin's parents and discover her roots, but she wasn't interested in the Mickey Mouse joys of the Republic of Bophuta-whatchacallit or the Kingdom of Bongoland, she wanted to suffer in Soweto. 'How the fuck have *you* put up with this apartheid shit all these years, an honest Injun like you?'

Her uncle laughed. 'Times have changed. When the ambassador and I first came out here we were guinea-pigs, a test-case for the South African government – black diplomats of the almighty United States, in the land of apartheid, with all the diplomatic privileges. We had diplomatic immunity, theoretically we could go anywhere. And that's why Ronnie Reagan sent us – to be an embarrassment to the apartheid government. And we were. Not on the diplomatic cocktail party circuit, of course, but when we went around in Pretoria we set the cat amongst the apartheid pigeons. At first we were refused admission to all kinds of restaurants and hotels and theatres, and we made a genteel fuss and wrote angry diplomatic notes and received mumbled apologies. But finally the word got around.' He grinned. 'Like the Japanese Consul – the government had to declare him an honorary white man.' He shook his head. 'Ridiculous, made a diplomatic laughing-stock of the government. But – ' he held a finger out at his niece – 'don't you dare attempt the same thing.'

Sally had every intention of attempting the same thing.

Her first few days she walked around Pretoria, trying to get herself thrown out of coffee shops and restaurants and hotels, to no avail: there were blacks everywhere. And where the hell was the violence? She had expected battles in the streets, but there was hardly a goddamn cop to be seen. She read in the newspapers that there was mayhem in the townships but here in the city the only menace was traffic wardens. She drove around the leafy suburbs and the only disturbance she saw was a dog chasing a cat. She looked for whites-only signs to defy, but there were none. She had read in the newspapers about the AWB and the White Wolves, and expected to be shoved off sidewalks by louts with swastika insignia, but here she was sitting on an unmarked public bench in Strydom Square, the heart of Afrikanerdom, and nobody paid any attention. What a fuckin' anticlimax! That is what Sally was thinking as she walked back to her uncle's diplomatic car, which she had parked outrageously illegally in the hopes of getting an undiplomatic ticket. She was half a mile away when a young man called Barend Strydom entered the square where she had been sitting and started committing mass murder.

Barend Strydom was twenty-five years old, nice-looking, fair-haired, blue-eyed. He had been a policeman until he resigned in order to devote his attention to the Third Boer War of Liberation, and to leading the Wit Wolwe.

Wit Wolwe means White Wolves. They took their name from the Nazi organization that tried to mount a last-ditch defence of the Third Reich in the dying days of World War II, the fanatical young Germans who took to the forests to fight tooth and nail against the invading allies. The South African newspapers paid scant attention to the Wit Wolwe when they announced their hit-lists over the telephone and then gave a wolf howl. Their hit-lists included PW Botha, who they branded a traitor to the Afrikaner Volk for betraying the ideals of Verwoerdian apartheid with his talk of 'healthy power-sharing'. The Wit Wolwe got into the newspapers occasionally, but were regarded as just another small, fanatical, right-wing splinter-group. Until that sunny day in Pretoria when Barend Strydom sallied forth.

That morning Barend wrote a letter to his parents, explaining that he was firing the first shots of the Third Boer War. Then he dressed in his policeman's fatigues, and set out into Pretoria to kill kaffirs.

He made his way to the heart of it, to Strydom Square. It was lunchtime and the square was thronging with people, black and white. Barend sat down on the City Hall steps and surveyed the scene, a little smile on his face. For twenty minutes he sat there, making up his mind. Then he stood up, reached into his shirt for his pistol, ran down the steps, raised his pistol casually, and started to fire.

There was a bang and a black woman eating an ice-cream sprawled dead. Everybody turned to look, and Barend's gun cracked again. A black woman screamed and contorted and fell, and pandemonium broke out. People screaming and surging everywhere, running and bumping into each other. Barend's gun cracked twice again in rapid succession, and two more black people sprawled, splatting blood. Barend loped on, with a smile. He fired again and a black man sprawled, and he fired again and a fleeing black boy fell. He came to the bottom of the now-deserted square. Across the street was a row of shops, terrified people fleeing along it. Barend started across the road, reloading his pistol; there was nobody within range when he reached the shops and he loped along to the intersection.

As he turned the corner a black woman was coming around it, and Barend shot her and ran on. Again and again Barend fired at the people fleeing down the street, and more screaming people fell. Now the wail of police sirens was to be heard. Barend came to the bottom of the street and he turned into a shop to reload. The shopkeeper cowered, gabbling, and three black customers fled, screaming. Then, as Barend clipped the new magazine into the pistol, a black man came hurrying into the shop and gabbled in Afrikaans: *'Excuse me, baas, but that baas over there – '* he pointed to the street – *'wants to speak to the baas – '*

Barend looked in the direction indicated, and the black man jumped at him. In one bound he grabbed the gun and his fist hit Barend on the ear, and he wrenched the gun from him. He hurled it out into the street, leapt on Barend and crashed him to the floor.

They were still fighting when the wailing police car screeched to a halt outside.

51

Sally was outraged when she heard about the Strydom Square massacre – and she was thoroughly pissed off with herself. Doggone it, she'd been right *there* only minutes before! What a diplomatic incident that would have made if she'd been shot (but only wounded) – *American Diplomat's Niece Victim of Apartheid*. What a mouthful she could have given the press. And even if she hadn't been wounded she would have made a very impressive witness, she would have told the court and the press a thing or two about apartheid: *American Speaks Out on Witness Stand*. Goddamn it, she'd missed a *golden* opportunity! Maybe, if she'd been there, she would even have been the one to overwhelm the bastard with her karate: *American Arrests Apartheid-Slayer*. Well, she was through with pussy-footin' around white towns. She told her uncle she was going to the Republic of Transkei to rediscover her roots. Instead she went to live in Soweto, to *suffer*.

And Soweto was another goddamn disappointment.

Soweto was quiet. Where was the violence? Three days ago the newspapers were full of the mayhem; now the fuckin' joint was all business-as-usual. Sure, there were soldiers to be seen, and military vehicles driving around, but nobody seemed to be paying them any attention. Sure, there were burned-out buildings, mostly shops and schools, and there were remnants of barricades littering the road-sides, but where was the fuckin' *action*? The only action seemed to be people thronging to and from work – where were the *strikes*?

Another disappointment was the number of big, new, middle-class houses. Oh, there were plenty of tin shanties, and most of the vast township consisted of rows of depressing little cottages, but those middle-class houses obviously belonged to rich blacks. Sally didn't want rich blacks, she wanted poverty. Another disappointment was her accommodation: she had expected to live in one of those tin shanties and form deep bonds of suffering with the masses, but those shanty people wanted nothing to do with her. She had ended up becoming a lodger in the cottage of a taxi-owner called Texas Khumalo and his family, who were quite uninterested in politics, liked Soweto, had a telephone, a large television set and the latest microwave oven.

And going to see Winnie Mandela had been an even greater disappointment. In defiance of her uncle Sally had asked the way to her house, got lost and finally taken a taxi there to offer Mrs Mandela her services to the ANC cause. En route, the taxi-driver pointed out the big red-brick house that Winnie Mandela was building on the ridge called Beverly Hills, and Sally couldn't believe her eyes. She expected the Mother of the Nation to live in a humble cottage like the Khumalo family, for Christ's sake! But the driver dropped her outside just such a cottage a little further on, and Sally was mollified. But not for long.

She knocked on the door, expecting the Mother of the Nation herself, or one of her children, to open it, but instead she was confronted by half a dozen youths wearing football jerseys bearing the words *Mandela United*, who belligerently asked her what she wanted. When she replied in English that she wanted to see Mrs Mandela to offer her services to the ANC cause they had immediately identified her American accent and accused her of being a CIA spy. When she protested in Xhosa they accused her of being a police spy. They had pulled her inside and frisked her for murder weapons, paying particular attention to her bosom and thighs. When she had protested they had threatened to beat her up. It was her American Express card which saved her. This confirmed that she was an American spy whom they had better not treat too roughly because America was a powerful country. They shoved her back out the door and slammed it.

'Well, fuck me,' Sally shouted. 'Can't get thrown out of a bar in Pretoria but I do here!'

Nothing went right for Sally during her first three weeks in Soweto. She saw no violence. She wrote Winnie Mandela a letter, giving her the Khumalos' telephone number and hired a taxi-driver to deliver it, but Winnie Mandela, if she ever got the letter, did not respond. Sally tried to make contact with an ANC underground cell, but nobody came forward. She asked people how to contact Black Consciousness, but nobody knew what she was talking about. Or so they said. A sullen veil of suspicion seemed to settle on faces when she asked anybody anything to do with politics. She finally learned, from a newspaper editorial, that the mantle of Black Consciousness had been taken over by AZAPO, now a banned organization. When she asked how to contact AZAPO she was visited by a group of UDF youths who threatened her with death if she joined AZAPO or Inkatha. When she asked them how to join the UDF – 'take me to your leader, you guys' – they swiped her on the head with a stick and told her to go back to KwaZulu.

'Maybe I fuckin' will!' Sally shrieked, clutching her head, and they came back and gave her another whack.

And she was bored. 'Bored shitless.' She had hoped to do voluntary work for the ANC or any other black organization, but all she seemed to do was wander around looking for somebody to help her until she went back to the Khumalo cottage and sat in a lump and read the newspapers, waiting for Winnie Mandela to telephone. The tiny cottage depressed the hell out of her. Mrs Khumalo worked as a domestic servant in Johannesburg, and the two kids she shared a bedroom with were at school all day, she had the joint to herself but she was *lonely*, empty-handed – fuckin' *bored*. Maybe she *should* go to KwaZulu – that's where the action seemed to be. Inkatha and the UDF were knocking the living shit out of each other there.

When the Khumalo family came trickling home she was even more bored. She had nothing in common with them except her pigmentation – she had expected them to have the same vocabulary as American blacks. And yet they were so fuckin' *detribalised*: Texas Khumalo was a Shangaan, Mrs Khumalo was a Tswana, and the two kids were just plain Sowetan. Where were their proud tribal artefacts, the likes of which decorated her walls in Miami? And their food was *awful*. Sally was accustomed to fruit juice, cornflakes and two eggs for breakfast (sunny-side up), steak, salad and ice-cream for supper; here it was plain mielie-meal porridge for breakfast, mielie-meal porridge with a vegetable gruel for supper, with a piece of chicken as a big deal. And the sanitary conditions were *hideous*. Texas Khumalo, at great expense, had installed a hot-water shower in the privy, but the privy was a long-drop out back in the yard. *And no toilet paper* – newspaper was what you used! Sally bought toilet paper, left it in the privy and the next morning it was gone. She bought more and it also disappeared after only one crap. So now she took out what she needed in her pocket and left the rest of the roll under her bed. It was mean, but what's a gal gonna *do*? Is this how Alex Hailey had to discover his *Roots*? Martin Luther King had a dream, not a fuckin' nightmare. She had come here to suffer apartheid, not long-drops. And certainly not *boredom* . . .

The Mandela United Football Club, whose members had been so unpleasant to Sally, did not play football, though they wore club jerseys: they lived in the backyard of the Mandela home. The football club members were Winnie Mandela's bodyguards, her musclemen. If Winnie wanted to know who was up to what, her football team found out. If she wanted something done, they did it. If somebody crossed her, they uncrossed them. If anybody defected they 'disinfected' them – or, as certain uncharitable policemen put it, 'if anybody informs, the football team deforms them.'

Like Stompie Seipei. Stompie means 'shorty' in Afrikaans. He was fourteen years old. He was a hanger-on of Mandela United, a tough little bastard, good at throwing stones, building roadblocks and enforcing consumer boycotts, but too small to be a full-time heavy. He was allowed to eat at the Mandela house, and usually slept there. He was one of the Mother of the Nation's favourites, and he had a good future as a member of her extended family when the Armed Struggle eventually succeeded. It is not known, therefore, why Stompie took it into his head to disappear from the house and move into the manse of the nearby Methodist Church, where a number of other juveniles took refuge from the slings and arrows of Soweto's tumultuous life. But it is known that he was regarded as a defector and that Winnie Mandela issued instructions to her Football Club to kidnap him and bring him back for interrogation, on the excuse that he was being seduced into homosexual practices on the church premises.

It was late at night when the Mandela United Football Club broke into the manse, clamped a hand over Stompie's mouth, carried him to a car and drove him back to the Mandela house. His interrogation began in the kitchen, under bright electric lights, surrounded by the latest culinary equipment.

Dr Asvat was a black physician who lived in Soweto. He was a member of the ANC and his patients included Winnie Mandela's entourage. At two o'clock that morning members of the Mandela United Football Club woke him and told him to come urgently to the house. When he arrived he found Stompie unconscious, his face grossly swollen, his body covered with contusions, blood oozing from his mouth. Dr Asvat advised that he be taken to hospital immediately as he showed all the symptoms of brain damage. Dr Asvat left immediately.

The next day masked black gunmen walked into Dr Asvat's surgery and shot him dead as he sat at his desk. The following day Stompie's rigid body was found on vacant ground several miles from the Mandela house. His throat had been cut from ear to ear.

Stompie's murder was thoroughly investigated by the police. They were delighted to find the trail led to the Mandela United Football Club. Several club members were arrested. Winnie Mandela was questioned. She admitted she had told her men to persuade Stompie to come back to the house because she feared he was getting involved in homosexuality at the church, but she claimed she was far away in Brandfort on the days they interrogated him: she knew nothing about that. The police charged her with complicity in the murder and made sure the press gave the scandal good coverage.

Sitting, bored shitless, a few miles away, Sally read about the scandal and perked up – here was something to get her teeth into! *Police Frame Winnie Mandela*. What was needed was a campaign, a massive wave of protest about police persecution of the Mother of the Nation! Of course she was innocent! Winnie Mandela wouldn't do *that*. Nor would those guys in football jerseys who challenged her at the gate – okay, they were jerks, but they *meant* well, protecting Winnie against just this sort of persecution! A worldwide campaign was needed, an international outcry that would intimidate the apartheid regime into dropping these *spurious* charges – outcry in the UN, the whole nine yards. And she, Sally Freeman Nkomo, would spearhead it!

Sally spent the next two days composing a long, sympathetic letter to Winnie Mandela, setting out her plan in great detail. She paid a taxi-driver to deliver it. The taxi-driver was an AZAPO supporter who drove round the corner, read the letter with difficulty, and chucked it out the window. Sally spent five restless days in the Khumalo cottage waiting for Winnie Mandela to telephone. When she could stand the confinement no longer, she took a bus into Johannesburg and bought an expensive answering machine in case the Mother of the Nation telephoned when she was out. On the tenth day she screwed up the courage to telephone her and was brusquely told that the Mother of the Nation was out of town.

Oh, fuckin' shitbombs . . .

She had come to Soweto to suffer and all she was suffering was fuckin' frustration and boredom.

Then, suddenly, the violence broke out again. And, sweet suffering Jesus, did she suffer.

Suddenly, overnight, the word went out that the UDF were on the warpath, that tomorrow they were enforcing another strike, another school boycott, another boycott of shops in Johannesburg. That night Sally heard the rumble of military vehicles passing the Khumalos' cottage; in the small hours of the morning she heard shouts and running feet, distant gunfire. When she heard Texas Khumalo getting up at four a.m. to start work she dressed hurriedly and begged to accompany him, to see the fun.

But it was not funny. People were streaming through the pre-dawn to get to the bus-ranks and railway stations, and out of darkness came the stones raining down, making them run, stones clattering on the minibus, smashing the windscreen. When Sally and Texas reached the taxi-rank the vehicle was battered, and the place was half empty because many of the workers had turned back. Many of them were bloody.

Sally was enthralled by the action, the men in uniform, the bloody, frightened, angry people, the rumbling buses and taxis, the distant sounds of gunfire. She insisted on accompanying Texas on his journey, paid him a fare and grabbed the front seat beside him. *Yeah, go for it*, she urged the invisible UDF rioters out there in the darkness who were throwing stones and setting up roadblocks. *Boo*, she silently hissed at the policemen and soldiers guarding the bus-station.

Texas Khumalo's minibus ground out into the pre-dawn streets, heading for the distant skyline of Johannesburg. They roared down the roads of Soweto, past the rivers of people heading for the train stations, past the military and police vehicles standing by to protect them. Then they rounded a corner, and in the headlights they saw youths dragging car tyres and rocks across the road. Texas swore and slammed his hand on the horn and trod on the accelerator and charged them. He roared his minibus flat-out at them midst a hail of stones, swerved around a boulder and hit a tyre. The passengers cried out as the minibus leapt into the air, then crashed down on its wheels again.

'*Bastards!*' Texas shouted.

He roared on towards the skyline of Johannesburg. He crested the last hill in the dawn, and there were the reassuring sky-scrapers rising up. He drove over the system of flyovers and underpasses, down into West Street and swung into the bus rank. Hundreds of minibuses were disgorging passengers. He swung into the rank for passengers bound onwards to the Eastern Rand, for Germiston and Benoni and Boksburg. He said to Sally: 'Go home!' He pointed at another rank. 'Over there!'

Oh what fun! Sally thought – the real South Africa at last!

But Sally found out that it was not fun.

The riots, the running battles, the cops and soldiers everywhere, the stink of tear-gas and cordite, the baton charges, the wail of sirens and the roar of guns, the barricades thrown across the rutted streets, the burning houses, the gangs of youths, the impis from the Zulu hostels, the boycotts – it was terrifying.

Every day Texas and Mrs Khumalo braved the embattled streets to go to work, but Sally, far from having any fun, spent all her time locked in the cottage with the children, terrified of the roving gangs that beat on doors demanding to know which party you belonged to. She had come to suffer but not to *die*, for Christ's sake. She'd come to help these people tackle the apartheid state, but they seemed to be doing just fine out there without her. The only time Sally left the cottage was to run to the nearest shops to buy food. The shops were sold out of almost everything – *including* toilet paper – because the gangs would not allow the suppliers' trucks to enter Soweto. Sally was heartily sick of mielie-meal, she'd have given her left tit for a steak, but no way was she going to go into Johannesburg just for a feed. But it was the problem of toilet paper that made her take her life in her hands.

She had a hair-raising bus ride into town through hailstorms of stones, but in Johannesburg it was quiet. There were plenty of blacks on the streets, but almost none in the shops. Sally went into a super-market. She bought only one toilet roll because that was all she could conceal from the gangs in her handbag. She added a bottle of shampoo and a bar of soap. She paid, then hurried out to find a restaurant. She found a Wimpy joint and got stuck into a row of hamburgers, french fries and salad. 'Keep 'em comin', honey,' she said to the black waitress.

Christ, it was great to be in civilization . . .

She dreaded going back to Soweto. It was hard to believe, sitting here peacefully with a full gut, that just a few miles away the shit was hittin' the fan. South Africa was a sick society – apartheid kept the black troubles out of white sight. She spent the day wandering the central business district, window-shopping, revelling in being normal. It was with great reluctance that she eventually made her way back to the bus-ranks. It was after five o'clock and the station was crowded with blacks queuing to get home. It was dusk when they entered the outskirts of Soweto, turned down the side roads and encountered the roadblock.

The barricade of old motor tyres was manned by a score of youths with sticks and spears and axes. Two other taxis were stopped ahead of

Sally's vehicle. The youths were pulling the passengers out and searching their baggage for goods purchased in the city. Sally stared, horrified. She opened her bag and grabbed the toilet roll and threw it under the seat in front of her, then a youth burst up onto her minibus. 'Everybody out!' He strode down the aisle, grabbing people by the collars and wrenching them. *'Out! Out! Show us what you bought today!'* He grabbed Sally. She lurched to her feet, her heart pounding. In terror she threw her bag under the seat. But the comrade saw her do it.

'Oh ho!' he shrieked. He snatched it up and held it aloft like a trophy, then grabbed Sally by the scruff of her neck again and wrenched her to the exit. She reeled out onto the road, terrified, into a ring of gleeful youths who were searching passengers' baggage. Her bag was ripped open and a shout went up as the shampoo was pulled out. Then the soap. Then everybody was shouting at her. And the beating began.

A stick swiped her arm and she cried out and staggered, shocked, then another, and they were onto her from all sides. Sticks swiping and thudding, beating her shoulders and back and arms and legs. Sally reeled, her arms curled over her head, crying out. For a full minute they beat her from all sides, having great sport, then they made her eat her purchases, and the real fun began.

The shampoo was the first. The youth thrust the plastic bottle at her. *'Puza!'* Sally cowered, aghast, not believing this was happening to her, and the youth seized her hand and clamped her fingers around the bottle, then he raised his stick and threatened her. Sally cowered, tears streaming, and cried *'Please, I can't –'* and the youth swiped her on her shoulder. She reeled, and he hit her again, then he grabbed her by the hair and wrenched back her head and he rammed the shampoo bottle into her crying mouth.

He rammed it in deep and he squeezed the bottle and the green liquid jetted into Sally's gullet. She struggled and screamed as the soap gurgled in her throat, and the youth squeezed the bottle harder. There was nothing Sally could do but swallow. And she gagged and frothed and writhed, suffocating, liquid soap spewing out of her mouth and nostrils. The only desperate way to breathe was to swallow again. She gagged and tried to scream again, and she collapsed. She sprawled on her back, and the youth crashed on top of her, still clutching her hair and jamming the bottle into her mouth. She desperately tried to twist to vomit up the frightful stuff, but he wrenched her head back and rammed the bottle in deeper and squeezed harder. And there was nothing she could do but swallow to stop choking, and she choked again and swallowed again. Sally swallowed and choked and swallowed and choked – until the bottle was empty.

The youth got off her, and Sally twisted onto her side and retched, and green shampoo frothed out, and the youth kicked her. He kicked her in the buttocks and she retched again and more froth erupted, and she began to crawl. She crawled off the roadside, retching and gasping as the youths kicked her and beat her and jabbed her with their sticks; then she reached the ditch, and she collapsed onto her stomach. She hung her head and retched and vomited and retched, and all the time they beat her.

She had yet to eat her bar of soap.

PART VIII

52

Walter Kosagu was a Zulu, but he was no warrior. Indeed, he was a washout, as Walter himself admitted at the few left-wing social events to which he was invited. He hadn't personally managed to split open a head with a knobkerrie since he was twelve – and then only by good luck. In fact, the last split head he'd seen was his own, suffered in a stick-fight at Fort Hare University. Walter giggled rotundly as his white audience rocked with laughter. Nor, he insisted, was he a very good lawyer, because a good lawyer needs *brains* . . .

The truth, however, was that Walter was a very good trade union lawyer, and he was an astute politician. He was, his police dossier said, a cunning little bastard. He was an official of the banned ANC and the banned surrogate UDF, though not a shred of evidence could be found. The police could easily have planted some evidence on him, of course, or sweated a confession out of him, or detained him without trial indefinitely.

It was easier to send in the Platplaas boys.

Platplaas is a farm thirty miles outside Pretoria. It has a dwelling, a barn, outbuildings, workers' quarters; but no agriculture was carried on. Platplaas was a police base, though there wasn't even a gate that locked. Officially, Platplaas was a base of the Counter-insurgency Unit, which tracked down terrorists who had infiltrated South Africa. Unofficially it was a base for the police murder-squads. The squad members were either selected policemen or 'askaris', terrorists who had been captured and persuaded to join the unit, to use their inside knowledge to track down their former comrades. The pay was good and the alternative was a bullet behind the ear.

Captain Erik Badenhorst was the commanding officer at Platplaas when the instructions arrived from Police Headquarters for the permanent removal from society of Walter Kosagu. They came from General Krombrink, who had years ago arrested Luke Mahoney and Patti Gandhi. The instructions were, as always, verbal, so that no written evidence existed. Erik Badenhorst was briefed by General Krombrink, but the details were left to him to work out. Badenhorst was a bold, imaginative policeman who had no qualms about his job. He believed he was fighting against the forces of darkness which were bent on plunging South Africa into a godless communist bloodbath. He was only fighting fire with fire. He considered himself a James Bond-type of good-guy.

Erik Badenhorst worked out a plan and carefully chose his men: Daniel Sipholo as squad-leader, Simon, Moses and Pete. All were fit, and non-drinkers. Erik briefed them. The next day they left for Natal by car, Erik following separately.

The four hitmen first drove to the football stadium, where Walter habitually parked his car when he went to work. They identified Walter's car and familiarised themselves with the surroundings. Then they walked to Walter's office building, memorising the route. Then they retired to a nearby fish and chip shop.

The plan was far from water-tight. The murder was to take place in a public car park, and they did not know what time Walter would show up. But nobody was perturbed. If they were pursued and arrested they would be released, or allowed to 'escape', as soon as Captain Erik Badenhorst made a telephone call. They would take it in shifts in the fish shop, from where Walter's building could be seen, while the other two loitered at the car park, playing dominoes.

It was dark when Walter emerged, carrying a briefcase. Daniel and Simon left the chip shop separately and followed him. Walter turned down the dimly lit road towards the football field.

Pete and Moses sat on the kerb under the lamppost nearest to Walter's car, playing dominoes. Walter came busily through the patches of lamplight, Daniel twenty yards behind him, Simon on the opposite side of the road. Pete got up, and said to Walter in Zulu: 'Umlungu, we have been guarding your car from the tsotsis; will you not give us fifty cents for bread?'

Walter grinned chubbily, his car keys in his hand. 'I think you have been playing dominoes, madodas.'

Pete walked towards him. 'But we are hungry, umlungu – we have been keeping the tsotsis away with our dominoes.'

Walter delved his hand into his pocket for some coins; and Daniel came bounding up from behind him with a knife, and plunged it into Walter's back. Simultaneously Pete whipped his knife out and sank it into Walter's ribs. Moses came running with another knife, and from across the street came Simon. Walter reeled backwards, shocked, gasping, terrified, blood pouring from him.

Daniel had intended to strike Walter's heart from the back, Pete from the front. Simultaneous frontal and rear assault on an unarmed victim can hardly go wrong. But Daniel's knife had skidded on Walter's shoulder-blade, out of his expert hand, and Pete's knife missed the heart, twisted between the ribs and he could not pull it out.

Walter reeled, one knife in his back, another in his front, and crashed against the stadium fence, desperately grabbing at the knife in his ribs. He wrenched it out, eyes wide, spouting blood, and brandished it on high, mouth agape. Moses lunged at him, and Walter swiped wildly. The knife flashed and Moses reeled backwards, head thrown back, blood gushing. Simon lunged with his knife like a bayonet. It sank into Walter's ample guts, but simultaneously Walter's knife slashed wildly down into Simon's shoulder, and Simon sprawled, clutching his neck.

Staggering, Walter pulled Simon's knife out of his guts, and crouched, a knife in each hand now. Daniel and Pete were astonished. Daniel's knife was still in Walter's back. Pete produced another knife from his pocket, then he pranced in front of Walter, flicking the knife, circling, to make him turn his back on Daniel, and Walter gave a rasping roar and he charged.

He lunged, both knives on high, and Pete leapt aside. Daniel sprang and struck Walter across the neck with the edge of his hand with all his might and wrenched the knife out of his back, and Walter sprawled. He twisted wildly and tried to scramble up, but Daniel kicked him in the head and Pete stabbed him again. Walter cried out and began to scramble up, and Daniel bounded to kick him down again but Walter's knife slashed out and Daniel had to dodge. Walter scrambled to his feet, lurching, wild-eyed, covered in blood, and he staggered backwards against the fence. He leant there, rasping, blood flooding, knives in both fists.

Daniel and Pete crouched, panting, staring at the fierce little lawyer; then Daniel rasped 'Now!' and they both charged. Walter lashed out blindly, frantically flailing his knives on both sides, but Daniel's knife sank into his back again. Walter sprawled on his face, and Daniel jumped astride his back, his knife on high, and plunged it down – again and again. They stabbed and stabbed him a total of forty-three times before Walter stopped struggling.

For trained killers they had made a terrible botch of it. As Daniel was to testify years later, Walter Kosagu, the washout Zulu warrior, had fought like a lion.

The murder of Walter Kosagu was hardly reported by the press, who saw it as just another robbery. But Mrs Kosagu had a very different view and within days all the UDF's underground knew about it.

Professor Lisa Rousseau was an office-bearer of the Stellenbosch branch of the UDF, and she was convinced it was the work of a government hit-squad. She wrote to Mahoney:

> . . . You probably don't know about the murder of Dr Rick Turner about ten years ago. He was a popular academic at the University of Natal, and a prominent member of the ANC underground. One night he answered a knock on his door, and he was shot at point-blank range by masked gunmen. He died in his daughter's arms. The motive was not robbery because nothing was taken. Who but the government would want to kill Rick Turner? And Dulcie September, the ANC's representative in Paris, was gunned down one fine morning as she unlocked her office door. Ever heard of Albie Sachs? He was a senior ANC officer in Mozambique: he got his arm blown off by a bomb rigged to his car door. Ruth First, the wife of Joe Slovo, was blown up by a letter bomb. You must refer to these dark goings-on in your journals, Luke. There have been numerous other cases of activists meeting violent deaths: Matthew Goniwe, a black school-teacher from the Eastern Cape, was gunned down in his car in the bush, along with his companions, their bodies thereafter burned. Matthew Goniwe had been giving the government lots of trouble. And, of course, suspects are always having unfortunate fatal accidents while in police custody. Duncan Buchanan, the Anglican Bishop of Johannesburg, recently found a monkey's foetus hanging in a jar from a tree in his garden. His bishopric was until recently occupied by Archbishop Desmond Tutu, and Duncan is convinced that the foetus was placed there by the police as a sick warning. The Early Learning Centre in Cape Town, part of a UDF community programme, was recently bombed. There are many other examples. The common denominator of all these local cases is that the victims are 'middle class', against whom no specific offences can be proved. One can only conclude that a Dirty Tricks department exists, at work against the 'Total Onslaught'. You must deal with this in your journals. I will do some research and try to send you a dossier.
>
> Meanwhile, who should show up on my doorstep in Stellenbosch, rather the worse for wear, but our mutual friend Sally Freeman Nkomo! The poor girl has some hilariously hair-raising tales to tell of her experiences in Soweto which she fled after being force-fed a bottle of shampoo and a bar of soap, an experience that 'did her bowels no end of good'. Having had enough of 'that shit', she valiantly journeyed down to the Transkei to trace Justin's family, to discover her roots. In Umtata she bought herself a nice

new red blanket, a pipe, umpteen brass bangles, a head scarf and a jar of red ochre, daubed herself suitably, then hired a taxi, at enormous expense, to find Justin's kraal. This journey took two days, the taxi-driver trudging with her from kraal to kraal. When she finally found the right one, she waltzed in wearing her red blanket, lugging her suitcases, all smiles, full of dutiful respect, and announced she was Justin's lawfully wedded wife under United States law, only to be greeted by Justin's astounded family as a nutcase. Evidently that no-good husband of hers hadn't told them about his marriage.

Facilities for nutcases being rather poor in the Transkei boondocks, Justin's father (having politely offered her a hut for the night, for the Xhosa are hospitable folk) summoned the local witch doctor to sort her out with muti, whereupon poor Sally got the message and fled, lugging her suitcases over the uncharted hills. It took her almost a week to hitch-fuckin'-hike back to Umtata, whence she caught a series of 'disgustin'' buses down to Cape Town, and fetched up here.

She really is a gutsy, amusing girl and she's kept me in hysterics about her adventures, of which she sees the funny side only with difficulty. I don't know how long she will be with me. Of course, because of the Group Areas Act, she can only safely sleep in my servants' quarters, masquerading as my maid, a role she has adopted with gusto. She's bought herself a maid's uniform and, when I have guests, she takes great delight in serving tea and drinks, addressing everybody as 'baas' and 'madam' and making wise-cracks. During the day she disappears into Cape Town and the surrounding townships of Crossroads and Kayelitsha and Mitchell's Plain, doing God knows what. Each night she comes home with another graphic injustice to report. She is desperate to contact her husband in MK. I am unable to help. She roundly condemns the man as a 'sumbitch' but it is clear to me that the poor girl's still in love with him . . .

53

Mbokodo, as Justin Nkomo had discovered in London, was the ANC's police force. It was their function to maintain discipline amongst ANC cadres worldwide, to run the ANC's prisons, to carry out punishments and, above all, to search out spies, particularly in MK, the Spear of the

Nation. The ANC executive had given the administration of Mbokodo to their Communist Party allies, and every member of Mbokodo was a communist. Mbokodo saw a potential spy in every recruit who fled South Africa to join the ANC. Now Dr Justin Nkomo, who was a captain in MK, stood to attention before Comrade Dumiso in the Mbokodo office in Angola, trying to control his fear.

'I only said that the troops are dissatisfied because they are not sent to fight the Boers, comrade. They have risked their lives to get here, they have been trained as soldiers and now they want to fight the real enemy, not UNITA, comrade.'

Dumiso was a self-important, hard little man. 'So you don't think UNITA is the enemy?' Dick-my-darling, his side-kick, snickered. So did Ben Bazooka.

Justin swallowed. 'The men say that UNITA is an Angolan government problem, sir, not the ANC's war against the Boers.'

'The Boers are supporting UNITA! And so is America!'

Justin swallowed again. 'Yes, but the men have not seen a single Boer or American, only UNITA soldiers, and they want to fight Boers.'

Dumiso roared: 'The men are fighting on the side of Cuba and Russia! Didn't Comrade Chris Hani fight alongside you in your last battle?! If he can fight for the Revolution so can you! You insult him!'

Justin said resolutely: 'No, comrade, I only said – he asked me first – I only said that the men wanted to fight the Boers.'

Dumiso screamed: '*You told him that the men are bored!*'

Justin nodded. 'Yes, comrade. They have only recently been ordered to fight against UNITA, and they do not understand why they are not fighting on the South African border.' He added: 'And Comrade Hani will verify that – '

'Comrade Hani has gone back to Lusaka! Now you're speaking to me! And I see you are a troublemaker!'

Justin said: 'No, sir, I am a soldier who wants to do his duty.'

Dumiso glared. 'And what else did you complain about?'

'Comrade Hani was asking me about the men's morale. I told him they complained that the food was bad.' He added hastily: 'They want more. And more meat.'

Comrade Dumiso nodded slowly. 'More meat. Anything else?'

Justin swallowed. 'They say the rations are old military supplies from Russia, left over from World War II.'

Dumiso leered. 'And what do you think, Comrade Captain?'

'Of course tinned food could not last that long.'

'But do you like the food?'

Justin would dearly have loved to lie, to save his skin, but he could not betray his men. 'The food is not good, Comrade.' He added: 'Napoleon said an army marches on its stomach.'

'*Napoleon was a capitalist!*'

Justin closed his eyes. 'Yes, comrade.'

Dumiso glared at him furiously, then whispered: 'And that is all you told Comrade Chris Hani?'

Justin wished to God he dared lie. But Chris Hani had obviously reported their entire conversation. He said: 'He asked me how the men honestly felt about the ANC leadership.'

Dumiso's eyes shone. 'And what did you tell him "*honestly*"?'

Justin said resolutely: 'I told him that the men feel the leadership of the ANC should be elected at a new congress. They should not be appointed. The last congress was sixteen years ago, and the men think it is time for a democratic election.'

'And why do they want new leaders of the ANC?'

Justin trusted Chris Hani: he did not believe the man had authorised this. He said: 'They feel the leadership is too autocratic. They want democracy.'

Dumiso leaned towards him. '*Democratic? About better food? About more meat? About not fighting UNITA?*'

There was no point lying: Chris Hani had obviously told Mbokodo everything – doubtless in good faith, for Chris Hani was a good man who wouldn't intend this shit to result. 'No, I told Comrade Hani, man to man, that the men want democracy, that is why they fled to join the ANC. And they want to fight against the Boers. But instead they have waited in the camps for three, four, six years, doing nothing. And it is bad for soldiers to do nothing, comrade. Soldiers want to fight, or they get restless. In all the years they have been here they have not fought one battle against the Boers – only against UNITA, who are not their problem. That is what the men are saying, comrade, and Comrade Chris Hani told me he was sympathetic to our problems. Please ask him yourself – Comrade Hani is a man of honour.'

Dumiso said quietly: 'And what else did you tell Comrade Hani about?' He waved his hand airily. '*Money?*'

Justin sighed tensely. 'I said that the men were worried that the leadership might be wasting the money that the world gives the ANC.'

Dumiso roared: '*You said the leadership was corrupt!*'

Justin cursed himself for talking to Chris Hani. He was a good man but Mbokodo were thugs. 'I said the men were *worried* that the leadership *may* be corrupt.' He added: 'We were talking frankly, as fellow officers.'

'Oh, the *men* are worried. Not you? We'll see. But first tell me what else you told Comrade Hani about Mbokodo?'

Justin's frightened heart sank. He said grimly: 'I told Comrade Hani that the men are very angry about the detention camps, yes. Because the camps are unjust.'

'Oh, unjust? Should spies be allowed to operate?'

'No, but it is unjust that there is no trial. Soldiers are thrown into detention on suspicion. Some of our comrades have been in detention camps for many years, without a trial. And the punishments are cruel.'

'Should spies have a luxury hotel?'

'No, comrade. But the men live in fear of being arrested on mere suspicion when they are honest ANC soldiers who only want to fight the Boers, but instead we are kept here in Angola for years, a thousand miles away from the South African border!'

Dumiso shouted: *'You are a spy, trying to cause discontent!'* He snatched up a file and shook it at him: 'You worked at *Drum* magazine in Johannesburg with a man called Luke Mahoney!'

'Yes, comrade, I wrote that in my biography. He got me the job.'

'He is your friend! And he was a spy! He spied for the police on his own girlfriend! And she was sent to jail for life!'

Justin said: 'No, comrade, I believe Miss Gandhi told the court that Mr Mahoney knew nothing about the explosives, so he could not have told the police about them.'

'Then how did the police catch her?! And your friend Mahoney tried to infiltrate the ANC in Botswana! Then he let his girlfriend return to South Africa to be arrested!'

Justin did not believe it. He said: 'I did not know that, Comrade.'

Dumiso hissed: 'And then he became a journalist and wrote lies about our comrades in Africa! Lies about all the black governments!' Dumiso slammed his hand on his desk. 'Lies for the Boers! And you call him your friend!'

Justin swallowed. 'I did not know that. Such a man is not my friend.'

Dumiso leant forward: 'Have you written letters to him?'

Justin closed his eyes. How could Mbokodo know whether he had written or not? But it was safer to tell the truth. 'I have not written to him since I left South Africa to join the ANC. Before, yes.'

'What did you write?'

Justin said: 'Just local news. Because we were both interested in that.'

'You were supplying him information for his lies!'

Justin sighed. 'I only told him what the government was doing to our people. He was not even a journalist anymore when last I wrote to him, he was working in Hong Kong, as a lawyer.'

'Yes!' Dumiso hissed. 'Working for the fascist colonial government!

Persecuting our comrades, the poor Chinese people who want to liberate themselves from the capitalists!'

Justin took a tense breath. 'He only told me in his last letter – several years ago – that he was a government lawyer and he was to be transferred temporarily to the British Solomon Islands as the chief magistrate, then he would get a promotion when he returned.'

Dumiso shouted: 'He has written two books about Africa! Spreading his lies! Saying the ANC is no good!'

Justin said: 'I know nothing about that. He only told me in his letter that he was writing a book. He said it was a love story.'

'About his girlfriend in the ANC! And it says the ANC is no good! And he has written a second book – he says there will never be peace unless the Boers are given their own white republic because they will never accept the ANC!'

'When I knew him he did not support the Boers.'

'He was a Boer spy when you knew him. Spying on the ANC through his girlfriend! And in his book he says the Zulus must also have their own republic because they will never accept the ANC!'

Justin took a deep breath. 'I know nothing about that.'

Dumiso shouted: 'I will pump the truth out of you! *Pompa!*'

Justin blurted: 'I have told you everything, Comrade – '

'*Pompa!*' Dumiso's fist smashed into Justin's guts.

Justin staggered backwards against the wall, doubled up. '*Pompa!*' Dumiso shrieked, and he swung his fist again, low, into Justin's crotch. Agony exploded into his legs and stomach. Justin crashed back against the wall, gasping, head down, hands clasping his crotch. Dick-my-darling wrenched his hands away – and Justin knew he could not take another blow like that. He raised his head, his eyes screwed tight in agony, and he clamped his lips shut and inflated his cheeks for the dreaded pompa.

Dumiso savagely slapped his hands simultaneously on the bulging cheeks, and Justin's eardrums exploded in red-black agony and he collapsed as if pole-axed, stunned with the new pain on top of the agony of his testicles. Dumiso, Dick-my-darling and Ben Bazooka then proceeded to kick him.

When Justin regained consciousness the pain was excruciating. Then he became aware of the suffocating heat, the stink of shit, the hot metal beneath him. *Was he in Hell?* He desperately began to scramble up, to try to get air, air, *air* – but he collapsed again in agony. Agony in his loins, in his head. He lay there rasping, his broken face scrunched against the hot metal, but his desperation for air drove him up again, to his knees, then he clawed his way up the wall. *And the wall was metal.* In total blackness, Justin desperately clambered up, eyes screwed up in agony, trying to get up above the stench and the roasting heat below, and his fingers found some holes. He saw daylight through a short row of round apertures, and he rammed his broken mouth against them and sucked. He sucked and sucked, desperately trying to fill his gasping lungs.

He was in an iron shipping container. On the opposite wall was another short row of ventilation holes. The container sat in the middle of Quatro Detention Camp in the tropics of Angola. The sun beat down on it. He was alone. The stench of shit was from previous occupants. His clothes, his hands, his face was smeared with the stuff. He clawed at himself desperately as he gasped at the holes, his nostrils pressed against the hot iron trying to blow the cloying stench away through his smashed mouth. He sucked and blew and sucked and blew, trying to get air into his lungs while his hands clawed at the shit on his face and chest. After a long time he got just enough air, and he was able to think.

He peered about through swollen eyes, rasping fetid air. Blackness, but for pin-points of light from the ventilation holes. He saw a row of redbrick buildings, the heat shimmering off the tin roofs. Bars on the windows. A big steel water bowser. There was silence. He limped across the container, pressed his swollen face against the hot iron, and peered. He saw a tree in a big open space. A parade ground. To the side, a row of buildings that looked like offices. Beyond, and all around, was the dark green subtropical scrub of Angola under a mercilessly blue sky.

The stinking heat was unbearable. Justin filled his lungs with the fetid air and beat his hands on the hot iron and bellowed: *'Let me out!'* His cry was deadened in the stifling container. And he filled his lungs again and bellowed again. And again. And again. Then he could bear the stink no more and he just wept against the ventilation holes, sobbing: *'Please let me out!'*

But they did not let him out. In the middle of the stinking, stifling afternoon he heard distant shouts and he peered. He saw a group of men emerge from the bush, up the steep track. They were pushing a big water bowser. Six men were heaving on it, staggering, trying to run as half a dozen guards beat them with sticks, shouting, punching, kicking. The big bowser came creaking slowly up the slope, the men desperately shoving as the guards lashed them. They came lurching across the parade ground, and now Justin could see that the prisoners were thin, weak. He could see blood. One of the guards was Dick-my-darling, another was Ben Bazooka. The bowser came to a halt near the tree, and the prisoners slumped against it, panting, exhausted.

Dick-my-darling shouted: '*Stand up!*' He swiped the nearest prisoner across the face with his stick. The man reeled and the other prisoners staggered up, chests heaving, arms hanging. Dick-my-darling shouted: '*Everybody who was lazy must apologise to the tree five times! Pig first!*' He swiped the nearest man across the shoulders.

The prisoner called Pig reeled up to the tree. 'I am sorry, Tree,' he rasped, and he banged his forehead against the trunk once.

'*Harder!*' Dick-my-darling shouted, and he swiped Pig. 'Tree likes to feel you are sorry!'

'I am sorry, Tree!' Pig banged his forehead again.

'*Harder!*'

'*I am sorry, Tree!*' Pig sobbed.

Justin stared. One after the other the prisoners were made to beat their heads against the tree. The prisoners clutched their heads, dizzy, gasping. The guards were having a good time. Then Dick-my-darling opened the spigot on the bowser and the water gushed out onto the ground.

'*Now Tree is happy! Now Pig propose love to her!*'

Pig knew what he had to do. His forehead was bloody. He lurched to the tree and spread his arms wide and croaked: 'Oh, Tree, you are so beautiful. I love you.'

The guards were laughing. The other prisoners watched dazedly. '*Louder!*' Dick-my-darling shouted, and he swiped Pig across the back.

'Oh beautiful Tree,' Pig rasped, 'I want to make love to you.'

'*Louder!*' Swipe.

'Please, beautiful Tree, let us get married.'

'*Louder!*' Swipe.

'I love you, Tree, please let me fuck you . . .'

Dick-my-darling shouted: 'Tree says yes!' And the other guards shouted: '*Yes! Yes!*' And Pig proceeded to fuck the tree.

Justin stared through the ventilation holes, shocked, disgusted. For there was the prisoner called Pig, a soldier in the ANC army, his arms wrapped around the tree trunk, kissing it, simulating the motions of ardent sexual intercourse, his pelvis grinding against the bark, his buttocks going back and forth as the guards laughed uproariously and Dick-my-darling whacked his arse to make him do it harder. And Pig clasped the tree tighter and ground his hips harder, his face contorted in pain and mortification. On and on the spectacle went; then at last it was time for the best bit when Dick-my-darling shouted *'Now!'*, and Pig simulated orgasm. He threw back his head as he knew he had to and he cried out *'Ooooh!'* And his buttocks jerked back and forth frantically and his hips pounded against the bark.

Justin staggered across to the other side of the container, and retched. Outside the guards were ordering the prisoners to push the bowser back to the river, on the double, to fill it again.

It was dark when they took Justin out. As he staggered out of the stinking container, gulping in God's sweet hot air, Dick-my-darling said: 'What do you prefer, sir, coffee or guava juice?'

Justin wanted to weep with gratitude. He had had nothing to drink for ten hours. He sobbed gratefully: 'Guava juice, please.'

'Good.' Dick-my-darling examined the two stout sticks in his hand and selected the one cut from the guava tree, then lashed Justin across the face so he reeled, shocked, then Dick-my-darling was lashing him, shouting: *'Run, Cowdung! To the office!'*

Justin tried to run but stumbled, and Dick-my-darling kicked him in the ribs, and Justin clambered up again. He staggered across the parade ground, Dick-my-darling lashing him, up the steps and collapsed into the doorway of Dumiso's office.

'Get up!' Dick-my-darling roared.

Justin got to his feet, rasping. Dumiso said from behind his desk: 'Cowdung does not know how to use the toilet, he has shit all over, he must be taught. But first he must tell us some facts. Cowdung must write his biography.'

Justin whispered: 'But I have already written my biography, comrade: I wrote it five years ago in Mozambique when I first reached the ANC – '

Dick-my-darling's stick swiped him across the shoulders. Dumiso shouted: 'You will write it again, Cowdung! And if you make one mistake we will hang you!'

Justin was kept in the iron container under the broiling sun for one week. Each day he wrote his biography again, each day he was beaten as Dumiso interrogated him, comparing his new biography with his previous ones, looking for discrepancies. There were none, but when he supplied more detail under interrogation, such as the colour of Luke Mahoney's eyes, or that one of the boys he played cricket with was the police commander's son, he was thrashed for omitting the detail earlier. On the eighth day he was put in a communal cell.

In the corner was a plastic bucket for excrement. It overflowed.

There was a small, high, barred window. Each man had a blanket but there was no bedding. The roof was corrugated iron and the heat beat down from it. It was hotter inside than out in the sun.

'How long have you been here?' Justin asked.

'Two years,' Pig said.

'What did you do?'

'I was caught smoking dagga.'

'How long is your sentence?'

'I have not been tried.'

Dogshit said across the gloom: 'I have been here two and a half years and I did not do anything. I have not been tried either. They only interrogate.'

'About what?'

'About being a spy. They make us write our biographies. I have written mine seventeen times. Then they beat you to try to make you admit. How did they beat you?'

'With sticks,' Justin said. 'And fists. And pompa.'

'The pompa is very bad,' Cunt said. 'My ears still ache from pompa. But the gas mask is worse. I was almost dead from the gas mask.'

'What is the gas mask?'

'They hold a pawpaw skin over your face like a gas mask so you cannot breathe.'

'I also thought I was dead,' Asshole said.

'I wish I were dead,' Justin said.

'You will wish that many times, comrade,' Dogshit said.

'My head is splitting open. Is there a camp doctor?'

'There is only a medical orderly, his name is Six-gun, but he is one of them. He and Ben Bazooka and Dick-my-darling are the worst. Six-gun's favourite is the red ants.'

'Oh, the red ants . . . ' Cunt said.

'What is that?'

'They cut open an ant-hill and make you sit on it naked. The ants bite all over your body and it is agony, you cannot run because they tie your feet and hands together. That pain is very bad. And the other terrible one is "napalm".'

'What is that?'

Prick said from across the stifling gloom: 'The bush they call napalm. It's leaves are poisonous, if you touch them it is like touching fire. They make you crawl through it naked.'

Justin breathed into his shirt. He shook his head. 'Why do they do this to us? We are their soldiers.'

Pig said into his hands: 'To humiliate us. They do not know what else to do because they are too stupid to prove whether we are spies or not. They only know how to make us keep writing our biographies and beating us to try to make us contradict ourselves.'

Asshole said: 'Quatro is a "rehabilitation centre"; they can do as they like. Joe Slovo was here, and he saw these cells, and we were hopeful he would do something to reduce our pain, but he did nothing. And Oliver Tambo was here, but he did nothing.'

Justin raised his head and stared across the fetid gloom at Asshole: *'Oliver Tambo was here in Quatro?'*

'He was here,' Pig said. 'And Chris Hani, and they did nothing to ease our suffering.'

Once a day the latrine bucket was emptied. Once a day food was delivered. Once a day they were called out for ritualised beatings and sent out for hard labour. Once a week or so they got called out for interrogation, for more guava juice or coffee, for more pompa, gas mask, red ants, napalm, more re-writing of their biographies. Once a month they washed their clothes. A barrel of water was pushed from cell to cell: by the time it reached the last cell it was soupy with dirt and almost empty.

'Why? Justin whispered. 'There is plenty of water, every day we have to fetch it with great pain.'

'There is also plenty of food,' Asshole said.

There was plenty, but the prisoners had only enough to keep a man alive. The guards had good food. Every day the prisoners had to throw the leftovers to the pigs. Out in the forest fruit grew in abundance, guavas and pawpaw and wild apples, but when the prisoners were sent to fetch firewood they were not allowed to eat any. On his second firewood detail Justin was caught eating a guava. First he was thrashed. Then, when they returned to camp, dragging their loads of wood, he was given to the red ants.

All the guards turned out for the spectacle. On the edge of the camp there were many anthills, cones of earth several feet high. Justin was ordered to take his clothes off. The anthill was slashed open, and angry ants came boiling out with a hissing noise. They were the length of a fingernail. Justin's hands and ankles were tied, so he could take short steps but not run. Dick-my-darling shoved him, and Justin sprawled. And his howl of agony rose up to the sky.

In a moment he was covered in angry ants, swarming between his legs and up his chest and arms and face, biting, and he howled and scrambled up and tried to beat at them with his bound hands, and he sprawled again. He scrambled to his feet and tried to jump-hop out of the nest, and Dick-my-darling swiped him across the head and knocked him down again. He writhed, trying to beat the ants off his face, and he cried out in agony. Clambering to his hands and knees, he tried to crawl and crashed onto his side. And he writhed and tried to beat off the ants, and clambered up again and tried to hop, and Dick-my-darling swiped him and he crashed again. For ten minutes the spectacle went on, midst the laughter and swipes, then the best part of the show began.

Justin was allowed to make it out of the swarming nest, his stinging flesh crawling with ants, and instinctively he tried to run, and he sprawled again. And he frantically scrambled up and he began to hop. He went hop-jumping away, trying to claw the ants off, crying out, frantically twisting and writhing, and the guards and Dumiso followed, jeering encouragement. Justin threw himself onto the ground and writhed on his back like a dog, thrashing his bound legs, and he twisted onto his stomach and writhed, then he lurched up to his feet again and began to hop-jump again.

And all the time the laughter and the jeering and the glee.

54

'*Mkatashinga*' means a yoke or burden that has become unbearable. A mutiny is a revolt by soldiers against their officers. The ANC soldiers who revolted in Angola deny it was a mutiny: they say they only wanted to reform the army. They say it was a case of *mkatashinga*.

Mkatashinga was the word on everybody's lips when Justin returned to his base in Kangandala after months of hell in Quatro. There was great excitement because an ANC delegation led by the ANC President, Oliver Tambo, was coming to hear about the *mkatashinga*. The soldiers had sent him a message setting out their demands: the dissolution of Mbokodo and the closure of all detention camps; an end to MK being used to fight UNITA; the immediate commencement of a military campaign against South Africa; the holding of democratic elections to elect a new ANC leadership.

But then Oliver Tambo refused to entertain these demands, refused to address his troops. The angry word spread that he was not coming after all, it spread to the eastern front where MK were fighting UNITA, and the mutiny began. From all over the area the decision was taken to proceed to the capital of Luanda en masse to confront the leadership. Then Oliver Tambo sent word that the eastern front against UNITA would be closed and all soldiers must proceed to Luanda for a conference. And excitement was high again as the convoys of vehicles began to converge on Luanda.

In the days when the Portuguese governed Angola, Luanda was a good-looking, Mediterranean-style port spread-eagled elegantly around a big bay. Now it was grubby, run down. On the outskirts was a big fenced camp called Viana, loaned by the communist regime to the ANC as a transit base for new arrivals to the Armed Struggle. The ANC had evacuated all the recruits from Viana in order to accommodate the mutineers on their arrival. It was here that the ANC laid its trap for them. Here a heavily armed roadblock barred the way into the city.

Justin was in the leading vehicle of the first convoy to reach the roadblock. The driver pulled up and an officer approached the cab. 'All troops are to be put in Viana!' he ordered. 'That is where the meeting will take place!'

The driver turned into the gates of Viana, and all the vehicles behind followed. The troops on the back were in high spirits. They disembarked cheerfully. The boisterous soldiers fired gun salutes into the air. Soon there were several hundred soldiers in the camp. There was a carnival atmosphere as they obeyed orders to fall in on the parade ground. Then the camp commandant made his appearance, and a murmur went through the ranks: many recognised him as an Mbokodo officer at Quatro detention camp.

He shouted: 'All troops must hand in their weapons now! This is the order of President Oliver Tambo! This is because it is dangerous for the people of Luanda to have armed men so close to the city.'

Then the shouting began. No way were the men going to surrender their arms. Justin shouted to the commandant: 'We refuse! Once we surrender our arms Mbokodo will crush us!'

'I am the camp commandant and this is my order to you! It comes from President Tambo himself!'

'Tell President Tambo to come here himself to order us!'

Someone shouted: 'Let Mbokodo surrender their arms to us!' and the men surged forward in a ragged unity. The commander and his guards retreated in alarm, but in a moment they were surrounded by soldiers. Their weapons were seized midst roars of approval, and they were frisked none too gently for handguns. The hated Mbokodo stood there defenceless, the soldiers were in joyful command of Viana, waiting for Oliver Tambo and his executive to arrive for the big meeting.

But they did not arrive. The ANC roadblock dissolved and retreated into Luanda to report. And rolling in from the bush came more vehicles full of jubilant soldiers, streaming to the great conference that would put their army right. The numbers in the camp swelled to five hundred, then to seven, and more vehicles came streaming down the highway to join the soldiers. That afternoon the ANC leadership laid ambushes to intercept mutineers. There were a number of running firefights but the mutineers got through and their numbers at Viana rose to nine hundred.

At sunset a great meeting began. It was a noisy, ragtag, but democratic meeting, with many speeches, much cheering and much laughter. A semblance of order was maintained by Justin, who took it upon himself to act as chairman. It was resolved to elect a committee to present their demands to the ANC leadership and negotiate the reform of the army. Justin was one of the Committee of Ten who finalised their demands.

He shouted through a loudhailer to the assembly: 'Comrades, according to my notes, the following are our demands to our president Oliver Tambo and the National Executive Council of the ANC; I will read them out to you, and if you agree answer yes at the end of each one.' He consulted his notes then read: 'We, the loyal soldiers of MK, demand of the ANC leadership the following. *One*: That Mbokodo be disbanded to stop them killing us with their tortures and suspicions and starvation, because we are not spies of the apartheid regime.'

'*Yes!*' roared the mob of soldiers joyfully, and many of them began to toyi-toyi, weapons thrust aloft.

Justin called for order, then said into the loudhailer: '*Two*: that the tyrants of Mbokodo be brought to justice before a people's court!'

'*Yes!*' roared the soldiers.

'*Three*,' Justin shouted: 'that the ANC leadership immediately convene a congress of all the people in exile in order to hold democratic elections for new leaders because democratic elections have not been held for fifteen years . . .'

'*Yes!*'

'. . . and *because*,' Justin shouted, 'we want leaders who are answerable to the people! We no longer accept the leaders' argument that democratic elections are impractical and that we must blindly accept their rule because it is "tried and tested"!'

'*Yes!*' the mob roared, then a man shouted: 'And they are corrupt!'

Justin shouted: 'We cannot prove that because we do not know how much money they have received and how they spent it –'

The man shouted: 'They live in nice houses with good food and have nice cars but we have very poor food! And they give all the good jobs and promotions and scholarships to the Xhosa!' There was a rumble of agreement from parts of the mob.

Justin shouted: 'We can say that we *worry* that they *may* be corrupt because we have no democracy to enable us to check on them –'

'*Yes!*'

'Very well.' Justin made a note, then shouted: '*Four*: we demand not to fight against UNITA anymore because that is an Angolan problem, not ours – '

'*Yes!*' the mob roared.

'And *five*,' Justin shouted. He thrust his fist aloft and punched with each word: '*we demand to be sent to South Africa to fight the Boers, because that is why we joined MK! But instead we are waiting in our camps for years suffering under Mbokodo, or suffering casualties from UNITA!*'

'*Yes!*' the mob cried ecstatically, and a man shouted: '*Write Mkatashinga!*' and the cry went up, '*Mkatashinga!*'

Later that night Chris Hani, who was both the political commissar of MK and a member of the National Executive Council, arrived in a jeep with his bodyguards to confront the mutineers; the demands were presented and he was harangued by the mob of soldiers. Chris Hani was astonished at the level of anger, appalled that the 'tried and tested' ANC leadership was under such attack. It was in bewilderment and anger that he cried: '*You are stabbing us in the back!*'

He retreated into Luanda to report to the leadership.

That night many soldiers slept in the bush outside the camp for fear of reprisal. At dawn the Angolan army struck at the request of the ANC leadership. They encircled the camp; then a strike force burst through the gate in armoured personnel carriers, guns blazing. And pandemonium ensued, soldiers scrambling in all directions, firing back, the clatter of AK-47s and pistols. Then the Angolan troops outside the fence found themselves under fire from the soldiers who had slept in the bush. But it was short-lived: suddenly there was the thud of a bazooka and an Angolan personnel carrier was shattered, its entire crew blasted to bits, and everybody stopped fighting. A clamour rose up from the soldiers trying to explain to the Angolans why they were in mutiny; and several recognised Angolan officers as men they had trained with in Russia and Cuba, and they appealed to them.

The Committee of Ten negotiated the truce that followed. The Angolan colonel, on behalf of the ANC, demanded an unconditional surrender, but the Committee were having none of that. At first they refused to surrender their arms at all until their grievances were met: but the hard fact was that the camp was surrounded and virtually indefensible against bombardment, and supplies and ammunition would not last long. Finally the Committee agreed to surrender their arms on the strict condition there would be no victimization of any 'mutineer' –

'Remember this is a case of *mkatashinga*' – and that their grievances be addressed immediately by the ANC leadership. 'Especially the matter of abolishing Mbokodo . . .'

The Angolan colonel sent messengers into Luanda to the ANC leadership, setting out these terms. An answer promptly came back.

'It is agreed,' the colonel solemnly announced.

The men were far from happy as they loaded their weapons onto the vehicles. There were plenty who muttered that this was madness because the ANC leaders were not to be trusted. But most were convinced that this was the only solution: they were not mutineers, they were loyal soldiers who wished only for the *mkatashinga* to cease. They had come to Viana on the ANC's instructions for a conference; they had formulated their just demands in a democratic manner; they had tried to persuade Chris Hani of the reasonableness of those demands; this morning they had opened fire on the Angolan troops – *not* fellow ANC comrades – only in self defence. And now they had surrendered on conditions which had been promptly accepted by the leadership. Surely there was nothing to worry about. The whole of Luanda knew what had happened, so surely the ANC leadership would not dare break their bargain.

That was the mood in Viana camp, a mixture of optimism and anxiety, as the mutineers watched the vehicles drive out of the camp with their weapons. The Angolan troops surrounding the camp remained.

A few minutes later a convoy of vehicles came racing up the road and swung into the camp. They were loaded with armed Mbokodo.

Chris Hani, the Political Commissar was amongst them. So was Joe Modise, commander-in-chief of MK. But there was no conference, no meeting to address the demands. Instead there was a parade of unarmed mutineers, at gunpoint.

Joe Modise read out a list of names. The Committee of Ten and several others were arrested and taken to the State Security Prison, called Nova Instalacao, a courtesy of the Angolan president to the president of the ANC, Oliver Tambo.

55

Two months later another mutiny broke out in Pango military camp. The mutineers' anger was inflamed by the ANC leadership having done nothing to meet their demands, and Mbokodo was even worse now. Several Mbokodo men were shot dead before the mutiny was crushed.

The mutineers were arraigned before a tribunal presided over by an Mbokodo officer. Seventeen were sentenced to death, without legal representation, or appeal. They dug their own graves and were shot by firing squad. The other mutineers were tied naked to trees for three weeks before being transferred to Quatro.

Justin Nkomo heard about the Pango mutiny when he was in Nova Instalacao. It gave him the reckless courage to attempt escape, despite his broken physical condition.

Justin had been in bad shape from his treatment in Quatro when he had been thrown into Nova Instalacao, his body undernourished, his ears still aching from the pompa, his feet traumatised by sole-beating, his ribs painful. It was only his anger and guilt that enabled him to survive the three months of hell at Nova Instalacao. He felt guilt because, as a member of the Committee of Ten, he was responsible for the surrender at Viana, for persuading the men to trust the ANC leadership, responsible for the agony they must now be suffering. His guilt was not assuaged by the certainty that they would have stood no chance if they had refused to surrender, that if they had tried to shoot their way out of Viana the entire Angolan army would have been launched against them. But his guilt and anger at the treachery made him furiously determined to survive to bring the bastards to account, to reform the army and make it do its job of fighting the Boers.

His fury enabled him to endure the horrors of Nova Instalacao; the stinking dark, with no blankets or mattresses, the overflowing lavatories, the appalling food, the dirty water, the raging thirst, the daily brutal beatings and electric-shock tortures. Then came the day that the Angolan guard told him that the Pango mutineers had been executed, that the Viana mutineers would be next. Justin knew that if he was to escape it had to be immediately.

And that very day, something happened to make escape possible: the mutineer who shared his cell died. He had been dying for several days. In the small hours of the morning Justin heard his death rattle. He felt the man's pulse, then put his ear to his chest: there was no heartbeat. Justin crouched beside the corpse, desperately thinking. This was the second mutineer to have died in this cell and he knew what happened. There was no formality: the guard would check the body, within half an hour a burial squad would drag it outside, throw it onto a truck, take it into the bush and bury it in a shallow grave.

Justin went to the door and shouted through the grille: 'Guard! Justin Nkomo is dead! Guard!'

The Angolan guard entered the dark cell and prodded the body. Justin lay in the far corner, watching. The guard left. Justin dragged the body to the corner where he had been lying. He arranged it in an attitude of sleep. Then he lay down where the corpse had been. And prayed.

Ten minutes later the guard returned with an assistant. Justin lay completely still, eyes closed, holding his breath, his heart pounding. The guards dragged him out of the dark cell, into the corridor. They lugged him out of the building, into the yard.

A truck was waiting, engine running. The guards swung him, and he landed on the back of the vehicle, on top of two shovels.

Justin lay sprawled on his back, taking desperately shallow breaths. He heard one of the guards slam the cab door, say something to the driver. The vehicle began to grind out of the prison compound. And Justin felt faint with relief.

It was not until he felt the open road under the wheels that he dared open his eyes and take a deep breath. Roadside treetops were flashing past. He dared not raise his head to check but he guessed they were driving away from Luanda. He lay on top of the shovels, vibrating, trying to think about what to do now. He had had no time to work out his plan. He had no idea how far they were taking him, how much time he had. He had no idea what he was going to do after he jumped, except run like hell. He tried to think whether he should try to take the guards by surprise, hit them with a shovel, steal their vehicle, steal their weapons – but he was too weak to fight two men.

The vehicle was doing about thirty miles an hour when Justin rolled over onto his hands and knees. The rear window of the cab was four feet from him, he could see the guard and the driver. Bush was flashing by on either side. He estimated he was about three miles from Nova Instalacao when he jumped. In one desperate scramble he got to his feet and leapt.

He hit the flashing road with a bone-jarring thud, and he rolled to take the shocking impact. Justin rolled across the road to the verge, then he scrambled desperately to his feet and went lurching wild-eyed into the bush.

The vehicle's tail-lights disappeared.

PART IX

56

Mahoney had promised his publisher he would do a publicity tour of America for his new book, *Big Trouble*, during his forthcoming annual leave. He decided he had better catch up on his journal before he left: it was the current events in South Africa which he was likely to be asked about on his tour. He was heartily sick of writing and it was with great reluctance that he spread out his newspaper clippings and began to make notes. Two days later he began to type.

MK ANNOUNCES WHITE CIVILIANS WILL BE TARGETED

As black-on-black violence escalates, Radio Freedom announces that MK will 'intensify their confrontations with the South African army and disperse their forces,' vowing to 'undermine South Africa's economic base . . . striking powerful blows at the enemy's military, economic and administrative structures.'

Which is bullshit, of course: MK has never yet fought a battle against the South African army and they don't intend to because they know they'll get the shit kicked out of them. In fact, some experts say that the only reason MK exists is as a dumping ground for refugees, an excuse to ask donor nations for more money, and for eventual use against Inkatha when apartheid collapses.

Much closer to the truth is their announcement that white civilians will now become specific targets of the ANC's violence. As attacks on policemen become common occurrences, soft targets are being hit more frequently. A bomb exploded recently in the Johannesburg offices of the life insurance giant Sanlam, two limpet mines exploded in OK Bazaars, three bombs have exploded in Newcastle, an 'extremely heavy' car-bomb exploded outside the Johannesburg magistrate's court, three land mines exploded in the Transvaal, a limpet mine exploded in a Johannesburg hotel, another in Cape Town's airport . . . Bombs scare the shit out of anybody, but such attacks hardly constitute an 'intensification of confrontation with the South African army' by MK, which is a thousand miles from the border.

Meanwhile, as the ANC radio urges whites not to vote in the forthcoming elections, and to join blacks 'in a massive democratic coalition to oppose the racists', the government warns that terrorists are massing in neighbouring states to disrupt the elections, making it necessary for the army to make cross-border raids.

SENIOR POLITICIANS DEFECT FROM GOVERNMENT

Protesting that the government's reforms have come to a standstill, a number of prominent Nationalist MPs have resigned from the party to stand as independents in the coming elections, while 301 academics from the prestigious University of Stellenbosch have called on the government to abolish apartheid.

AWB URGES RIGHT WING TO UNITE

As election temperature rises in this bloodstained, over-heated land, the leader of the AWB, Eugene Terreblanche, is begging the numerous Afrikaans splinter groups to unite behind the Conservative Party to fight the common enemy, namely the government and the ANC. Calling President PW Botha a 'deaf dog', and vowing that the AWB would 'take power by force' if the government continues with its 'reforms', he promises to 'blast black nationalists off the face of the earth'.

The government retorts that the AWB is a neo-Nazi organization which rejects freedom of speech and freedom of the press.

Jesus – the pot calling the cook-boy black.

But what is the government's platform in this election? It's hard to say – they are long on abstract nouns but short on specifics. Their manifesto promises a 'Five-Year Plan' of reform in which they will give 'full participation to all', 'freedom, prosperity and security for all', and 'continue to broaden the democratic base'. But they don't say how.

I don't think they know how. The only acceptable way is by a Great Indaba of all races, but that would be unacceptable to the world without the ANC, UDF, PAC and AZAPO participating – they are all banned, and the government intends to keep them that way. The government is ramming home the ANC as the enemy of reform because they are manipulated by the Communist Party and Russia, and promises to fight 'the revolutionary onslaught'. When President Botha was asked whether there would ever be a black government of South Africa he answered: 'Never! There will only be power-sharing, in which no racial group will dominate the other.'

Well, fuck me, what does that mean? Does it mean a massive jigsaw of dozens of little states, something like counties, each statelet predominantly one race, each ruling itself at the statelet level but sending representatives to a federal South African parliament? No, the government cannot mean this because such a system would result in more black statelets than white statelets, so the black statelets would dominate the white, which is exactly what the government is promising won't happen if you vote for them. So does the government intend to 'broaden the democratic base' by adding to the Tri-Cameral Parliament a Fourth House for 'urbanised blacks' who will have control over their 'Own Affairs'? Or what?

That, at best, is what their election bullshit is saying. Which means they wish to perpetuate apartheid in some more acceptable form, but they cannot agree amongst themselves how far they are prepared to go. And they are frightened of splitting their ranks further. After forty years, they are so accustomed to power that even the reformers amongst them only want to reform apartheid, not abolish it.

However, the other side of Afrikanerdom, the Conservative Party, knows exactly what they mean: to perpetuate apartheid and a white South Africa. They say the only solution is to partition it into white and black states – the white one to comprise 87% of the land – and to translocate 70% of the present black population back to their homelands, 'using modern techniques'. They promise to 'clean up the revolution in black townships within two months'.

The Progressive Federal Party's manifesto calls for the scrapping of all discrimination, the sharing of political rights 'without the domination of one group over others' in a federal constitution, a bill of rights, all of which requires urgent negotiations between all acknowledged leaders – including the ANC. 'Whilst law and order has to be maintained, the state of emergency, with its police powers, its abrogation of the rule of law, its assault on civil liberties, its muzzling of the press, its bannings, its jail without trial, is proof that the government is incapable of governing by democratic means.'

Which is dead right, of course. But notice that the PFP is also talking about 'power-sharing without domination of one group over others' – the same as the government. The fear of domination stretches across the political spectrum. In Africa, domination by one tribe over others is the norm, and it has led to bloody disaster all over. The same disaster must not happen in the new South Africa. And so the PFP is absolutely right in calling for a federal constitution, as in America: a federation of states, which would have to be divided along geographical tribal lines. But where does this leave the white tribes? In what geographical area do they predominate?

Nowhere. Only in the cities. And each white city is accompanied by an adjoining black 'township' which is bigger in population. So? Unless you *carve up South Africa into umpteen city-states (like Hong Kong and Singapore and Andorra – which might not be a bad idea), where the hell is the white state going to be?*

More important – much more important – where is the Afrikaner white tribe going to have their state?

'Nowhere,' you say?

'Fuck the white Afrikaner tribe,' you say?

Did I hear you correctly? Well, you're very, very wrong, my friend. You know not what you say. Because I'm telling you that there will never be peace – as with the IRA. There will never be a solution to South Africa's problems, unless the Afrikaner white tribe has its own state in which they can govern themselves.

Like the Jews got their Israel. Carved out of hostile Palestine. That works. So why wouldn't an Afrikaner state work?

Of course the right-wing Afrikaner movement, as politically embodied by the Conservative Party, is demanding the whole of 'white' South Africa, while the AWB is only demanding the old Boer republics of the Transvaal, the Orange Free State, and northern Natal. But, in the end, they will settle – they will have to settle – for a fraction of that. But where?

Two days before Mahoney left on his annual leave the election results came out. He sat in front of his radio, notebook in hand, writing down the results, shaking his head.

'They'll never fucking change.'

At midnight, when the final results came through, he sat down at his word processor.

THE DEVIL'S HOUR OF GLORY

Okay, so the government won the elections again. Nothing surprising in that, as they have won the last ten. But what is very significant is the number of seats the Conservative Party won. There was a massive swing of voters away from the government, in favour of the Conservatives, making them now the official opposition.

This dramatically illustrates the split in Afrikanerdom caused by President Botha's 'reform' policy. It is the first time since 1948 that the official opposition accuses the government of being too liberal. That was the year the Nationalist Party, the official opposition whose policy was apartheid, defeated the ruling United Party under General Smuts. Today we have the same situation.

It is a terrifying thought that history may be repeating itself. Chief Buthelezi says he is appalled by the massive swing towards the Conservative Party and calls it 'the devil's hour of glory'. He warns that moderate, peace-loving blacks are angry that so many whites clearly reject reform, saying he leads a 'very angry people that could go on a violent rampage . . .'

57

Lecture tours pay quite well for authors, but the real pay-off is the publicity for their books. However, most of the people in the New York University auditorium tonight looked like students – and unlikely to buy many books, Mahoney thought regretfully as his publisher introduced him to yet another audience. But another spin-off was getting laid. Writers aren't pop-stars, but some women feel it would be interesting to go to bed with one whose work they like. Or even if they don't like it. 'You do it better than you write,' a Boston housewife had said last week after a literary luncheon. Another, in Toronto, had said, as she dressed, 'Actually I've never read anything of yours but I'll get you out of the library.' (There's no money in libraries, either.) A beautiful geography teacher in Detroit had said: 'Never heard of you till tonight and I don't like South Africans but I love your voice, everything you say sounds so intelligent, bwana.'

'They only say bwana north of the Zambezi, baby.'

'That's where South Africa is, ain't it?' the geography teacher said.

It was when they brought their books to be autographed that they gave the how-about-it signal, if that's what they had in mind. And right now, sitting in the front row was one of the most beautiful women Mahoney had seen, with two copies of his book on her lap, looking at him very speculatively as the publisher wound up the introduction of him as 'one of the best political commentators on Africa'. To the sound of polite applause, Mahoney went to the rostrum.

'Ladies and gentlemen, first I must apologize for my footwear. I don't usually show up at lectures in my running shoes – I'm not that big an optimist . . . (laughter) But when I arrived in America last month, I took myself to a health farm. Now, I was perfectly healthy when I went *into* this health farm . . . (laughter) but I came out a shuddering wreck. Apart from the shock to my liver, which went into spasm (loud laughter), all that heavy-duty aerobics they made me do has resulted in my having to undergo major therapy when I get back to Hong Kong; meanwhile I

399

must even wear these cushioned all-American athletic shoes to bed – in case I want to go to the john in the night . . . (screams of laughter)

'However, I'm here to tell you about my latest book – and, thereby, my publisher desperately hopes, help sell them. And let me say at the outset – and please get this straight – I come here to *bury* Caesar, not to praise him. My book seeks to condemn the Caesar of apartheid, not to point out what little merit there was in it. My book does *not* seek to excuse apartheid, but to *explain* how and why it came about, and to explain *why* the process of reform initiated by President Botha is going so slowly. And to explain *why*, therefore, the world must be patient. Because, ladies and gentlemen, with South Africa, you are not dealing with the standards that govern *your* daily lives in America. You are dealing with, and *up* against, two very special mind-sets: the *African* mind, which is authoritarian rather than democratic, and the *Boer* mind, the mind of the voortrekker who opened up darkest South Africa, just as your pioneers opened up America – and killed most of the Indians in the process.'

The hall was suddenly silent.

'Please, let it be clearly understood that we agree – wholeheartedly – that apartheid is wrong. *Immoral. Cruel.* A proven failure that should be abolished. The real question is, what system should replace it?

'What system? Democracy, of course. Ah, but we must be careful here because democracy has also been a failure throughout the rest of Africa. One-man-one-vote has meant one-man-one-vote-*once*, followed by a one-party dictatorship. We don't want the same to happen in South Africa – nobody wants to see white oppression replaced by black oppression. So the *real* question here is: what kind of constitution does the new democratic South Africa need, to avoid the undemocratic fate of the rest of Africa?

'The first problem is the African mind. They have no tradition of democracy in the sense of having a *loyal* official opposition, of tolerating the other man's point of view; they are largely unsophisticated tribesmen who vote for their tribesmen, not for a policy. This means that they are intolerant of rival tribes and try to impose their political will on them, and if necessary *crush* them. I am not being racist when I tell you this, I am being an historian. This is the story of Africa, and the new South Africa must avoid this fate. So, obviously, the new constitution must ensure that the rights of a loyal opposition are *entrenched*.

'The second massive problem is the Boer mind – their resistance to reform, their fear that what's happened in the rest of Africa will be repeated in their country. About half of the Afrikaner volk are like this

– they are *white* tribesmen who vote for *their* tribe's survival. And, like the black man, they will wage *war* to get their way.

'Ladies and gentlemen, this Boer mentality is the greatest obstacle to the new South Africa. They are collectively known as the right wing, their parliamentary representatives are the Conservative Party, and their military wing is called the AWB – though there are dozens of other splinter military groupings. The AWB are the guys you've seen on television in khaki uniforms, with swastika-like insignia, who break up government political meetings because they regard President Botha and his ilk as traitors to the Afrikaner – *and to God,* who, they truly believe, is on their side. They demand an Afrikaner homeland, consisting of the old Boer republics – the richest part, where all the gold mines are, which caused the Boer War. I do not believe they will succeed in securing this piece of real estate for themselves – about the size of France – but I do believe that they will create chaos and civil war while they try.

'I further believe that it is advisable for the new South Africa to offer to grant them a *smaller* piece of the country as a homeland, where they can govern themselves – without apartheid – to avoid this civil war. That proposition – and *these* people – are the major topics of my book . . .'

A hard core tried to give him a rough passage during question time, but he handled it. They seemed to have forgotten he was vehemently opposed to apartheid; because he had said that Westminster-style democracy had failed in Africa, that one-man-one-vote meant one-man-one-vote-once, he was a racist. They particularly resented his suggestion that President Botha was not such a bad guy and, like Mr Gorbachev, had his problems – 'Gorbachev is the first reformist Russian we've seen,' he said, 'so don't shoot Mr Gorbachev. Mr Botha is the first reformist Afrikaner we've seen, so don't shoot Mr Botha either – realise the problems he's got with the right wing.' But they seemed to think that the whole of South Africa – corporealised by Luke Mahoney – *was* right-wing. Nevertheless, when they were invited to have their books signed, Mahoney was surprised how long the queue was.

And the beautiful woman was in the line, at the very back. Mahoney had declined two invitations to cocktail parties before her turn came. She was tall and svelte, with flaxen blonde hair pulled back in a bun, her lovely eyes were very blue and she had a wide sensuous mouth. She was in her mid-thirties. As she presented her books she said: 'This one is for my father. Would you write *"Vir oubaas, hou vas"*. That'll amuse him.'

Mahoney was taken aback. 'You're South African? With *that* accent? I thought you were English.'

'My international camouflage. And Americans love it; they think everything you say is intelligent.'

'Isn't it?'

'Damn right.'

He grinned and started inscribing the book. 'And, what are you doing in darkest America, Miss . . . ?'

'Katrina. I'm researching their Native American policy at Princeton. I'm making a study of colonial history as regards the native peoples.'

His pen was poised for his autograph. 'Is this for a book?'

'For a doctorate. I teach political science at the University of South Africa.'

'I *see*. So you're on your way to becoming a professor?'

'Actually, I am a professor. I did my first doctorate years ago. This is another one.'

He smiled. 'For fun, huh?' He signed his name. 'Look, have you got time for a drink? And maybe some dinner?'

She grinned: 'I thought you'd never ask. If you hadn't, I would have. Because, Mr Mahoney, I've been involved in checking aspects of your family's historical journals. Our mutual friend Lisa Rousseau sent them to me for comment.'

'Good God. Professor de la Rey?'

'Yep.'

They sat in the stall of a Brew 'n' Burger. He had wanted to take her somewhere more upmarket but it was the nearest place. They had ordered a carafe of wine and a plate of spare ribs – it was too early for dinner yet.

He said: 'When Lisa told me she'd sent some chapters of the journals to you, she mentioned that you're one of *the* De la Reys, of Boer War fame?'

Katrina smiled. 'Right. My great-uncle was General de la Rey, the bitter-ender who didn't want to surrender to the British in 1902 – there's a monument to him in Delareyville.'

'And he was killed in the 1914 Rebellion.'

'Correct. And my father is General de la Rey too, in the South African army. He's spent the last ten years fighting in the border war, in Angola.' She added: 'About to retire, now that the battles are all but over.'

'Is the Angola war all but over?'

'Oh, I think so, the writing's on the wall – thanks to Mr Gorbachev and his new-look Soviet Union. *Glasnost* and *perestroika* and all that jazz. Angola is the USSR's Vietnam, financing fifty thousand Cuban troops to fight UNITA, South Africa and the United States – which is a war they can't win. And Angola is South Africa's Vietnam too – all our young men sucked out of the economy and drafted into the army just to fight yet another African communist regime and SWAPO over Namibia – crazy money. But now Gorbachev's pulling the Soviet Union's horns in and counting the roubles, so the Cubans will have to go home soon, Fidel Castro will fail in his ambition to be the conquistador of South Africa, and so the communist threat is removed. So South Africa can draw a deep grateful breath and withdraw too.'

'But what about SWAPO, and Namibia?'

Katrina waved a hand. 'I'm sure South Africa will sacrifice Namibia to SWAPO as part of the deal. Namibia has been nothing but a headache for years, in the United Nations, and now that Mr Gorbachev has decided that he can no longer afford to support overseas wars, the danger of Namibia being a launch-pad for communist strikes against South Africa has passed. So, she can afford to wash her hands of Namibia very soon.' She added, with a professorial smile: 'You forecast something like that in your journals, but not strongly enough. I've added some notes in the margins for you.'

'Thank you very much.'

'Not at all, I'm fascinated. And I'm pleased to help any friend of Lisa's. She taught me history, years ago at Stellenbosch. And she's the one who gave me *Alms for Oblivion*, when it was still banned. Tell me – I'm sorry, everybody must ask you this, but I'm dying to know – is *Alms* an absolutely true love story? I mean, the passion? The heartbreak.'

'Yes.'

She nodded. 'Yes, nobody could write like that if they hadn't felt it. I wept like a girl. I think that book did more to show up the cruelty of apartheid than all our other literature – that's why the government banned it for so long. And tell me – I hope this isn't too personal – but you've never married, Lisa says? Is that because – tell me to go to hell if you like – but is that because of her? Patti Gandhi, I mean, though you call her Pamela in your book.'

Mahoney shifted. People often asked the question. He usually dodged it, unless it was a pressman asking, in which case he gave the answer that sold books: yes. Which was also the truth. But he very much wanted to make love to this gorgeous woman and talking about Patti wasn't the way. He said, almost truthfully: 'It's a long time ago now. I'm used to being single, and I work hard at two jobs – law and writing.'

'And,' she smiled, 'the Far East is a bachelor's paradise?'

He smiled. 'Used to be, until AIDS came along.'

'Ah yes, AIDS. It's dealt a numbing blow to the one-night stand.'

Mahoney laughed. She had said it almost ruefully. He grinned: 'And, are you married?'

'Once. It didn't work out. No children, thank God. Boring story. Please, let's talk about you, that's what I came from Princeton to hear at enormous expense.' She glanced at her wristwatch. 'So tell me – why are you still a lawyer; why aren't you writing full-time?'

Mahoney sighed. 'It's years since I wrote *Alms for Oblivion*. Since then I've only written *Not Enough Tears*, which didn't enjoy the same success, and now this one – ' he tapped *Big Trouble* – 'which is a documentary account. So? Maybe I'm not a novelist – I'm really a newspaperman, and writing documentaries is all I'm good for. In that case, I should do it in my spare time.'

She had listened judiciously. Then: '*Bullshit!* Anybody who can write *Alms* and *Tears* is a novelist; *Tears* was *bloody* good. This – ' she smacked *Big Trouble* – 'is a lucid but emotional account. But you're really a story-teller.' She looked at him earnestly. 'Come on. What have you got next for your fans?'

'Those family journals. Update them and get them published.'

'Okay, good, but what then? You can't have a talent like that and not use it, Mr Mahoney.' She raised her eyebrows. 'Okay, so tell me about yourself as a lawyer. Do you like it so much that you're prepared to treat your real talent as a hobby? What kind of law do you do?'

'Crime.'

'And, are you good at it?'

Mahoney smiled. 'Expert. Meaning that I've practised criminal law, in the courtroom, ever since I quit journalism. And I know it backwards. It seems that any case that lands on my desk, I know exactly what to do.'

'"Been there, done that"?' She nodded. 'Same with me. I've been doing political science so long it seems I've read, argued, taught and done it all. Any new idea that's thrown at me, I have at my command the wisdom of the ages to answer it. Right?'

'Right.'

'Are you bored?'

'Yes.'

'Right. So tell me what's so compelling about your lawyer's job that you don't chuck it and become a full-time writer? What's your actual position? Are you the boss?'

'No, I'm the Deputy Director of Public Prosecutions.'

'I read somewhere that you were a judge.'

'I've been a District Judge. In faraway places with strange-sounding names, like the British Solomon Islands. But not a Supreme Court judge.' He added: 'I started later than most.'

'Do you want to be one?'

'No.' He shook his head. 'I'd rather be fighting the case than sitting there patiently listening to it.' He added: 'But I'll have to do it soon, I suppose.'

'Why?'

'Because it's the next logical step if I'm going to stay in the service. The Director of Public Prosecutions is younger than me and has more years of service and doesn't want to move.'

She sat back. 'Would you consider coming back to South Africa?' She added: 'Where you belong?'

Mahoney smiled wanly. The question he so often asked himself. 'I would really *love* to be back in South Africa. To be experiencing history in the making. To participate daily in the developments. Yes, I feel I belong there. And, believe me, I'm bored with Hong Kong. It's beautiful, exotic, all that, but I've had years of it, and I'm bored with the politics. Communism may be on its way out in Europe, thanks to Mr Gorbachev, but those Chinese communists will hang on for a very long time yet. And I'm bored with the colonial life – with the dinner parties, and all that colonial bullshit. And I'm *bored* out of my *mind* by living in an apartment.' He looked at her. 'I'm used to wide-open spaces, to wildlife, but in Hong Kong – like in Manhattan here – you *have* to live in an apartment. Would you like that?'

Katrina shook her head. 'I couldn't bear it.'

'No. But, you get used to it. And our government apartments are very nice. But no garden. Know what I really miss? Not having chickens in my backyard.'

Katrina grinned. 'I know, I'm a farm girl.'

'Yes, you look like a healthy, *beautiful* country girl. Roses in her cheeks. Milking cows and eating her wheaties.'

She grinned. 'Yes, all that. Collecting the eggs, dipping the cattle, growing her own vegetables, going to market. My family have been farming the Western Transvaal since the Great Trek.' She waved a hand. 'But please carry on. About why you won't come back to South Africa, despite being so *bored*.'

Mahoney held up three fingers. 'One: twenty years ago there was, and probably still is, a warrant out for my arrest as an accomplice to Patti Gandhi. Even though Patti exonerated me at her trial, I don't relish the prospect of proving my innocence. I couldn't even go back for my parents' funerals. Two: I'm simply not willing to live under apartheid again. Okay, apartheid is crumbling before our eyes, but it could last for years yet, like communism in China. And three: If I go back to South Africa, what do I do? Start a law practice?' He shook his head. 'I couldn't bear it, starting all over again.'

'You could write books.'

Mahoney smiled. 'Thank you for your confidence. But the truth is I'm a journalist by talent, *not* a novelist. So what do I do if I return to South Africa – assuming I'm not thrown in jail? Write another book – called *Huge Trouble*? Or *I Told You So*?' He shook his head.

Katrina de la Rey sat back. 'So,' she said, 'you'll go back to Hong Kong, become a judge against your will and publish your journals, huh? And, when do you think you'll finish those?'

'When the new South Africa comes into being. That's the natural ending of the long story.'

'And when do you think that will be?'

Mahoney spread his hands. 'You're the political scientist. But my feeling is that President Botha is running out of elastic, despite his recent re-election victory. I think he may be replaced as president. Depends who replaces him.'

She nodded. 'The buzz is that there's a lot of dissatisfaction in the party. A power struggle is on.' She shrugged. 'But, what do you think the new South Africa is going to be like? A ruin, like the rest of Africa?'

Mahoney sighed. 'I have little hope. PW Botha is only talking about power-*sharing* with the blacks – whatever that means. It sounds like wishful thinking to me – when this government finally collapses there's going to be black majority rule. That means the ANC. How good or bad are they going to be? They've been in exile twenty-five years: what experience have they got? They've been living in an unreal world of hand-outs. We know they're autocratic because they haven't had an election for their executive council since 1969. And we know that their executive council is dominated by communists.'

Katrina nodded. He continued: 'It depends partly on the new constitution, of course – is it going to be a federal one, like America, with each state largely running its own affairs; is it going to be *con*federal, something like the EEC; or is it going to be unitary, like England, with a Westminster-style winner-takes-all constitution – which is what the ANC will want so that they have all the power.' He shook his head. 'If the constitution is a unitary one, I have no hope at all. If it's a federal one, maybe. There are some things going in our favour: communism is on the way out, so maybe there won't be wholesale nationalization of the economy. And the ANC could never defeat the South African army, even with the USSR's help – so it's not going to be a Rhodesia situation, where the white man went to the negotiation table defeated. Maybe we'll get a workable federal constitution which will limit the black man's power, and maybe the economy will remain in responsible hands.'

She said: 'Communism is a proven failure but communists dominate the ANC and a leopard doesn't change its spots. A black government will nationalise. The masses will demand it. Their expectations have been raised. Oh sure, I think we'll end up with a lovely constitution, on paper, protecting property-rights, et cetera. But that can be torn up as quickly as all the pretty Westminster constitutions in the rest of Africa. Just declare a state of emergency, martial law, and ban all political activity – or just ban certain political parties, as we've done.' She smiled wryly. 'And you don't have to be a clairvoyant to foresee that the new black government is going to have plenty of emergencies. Because the ANC are mostly Xhosa, and I don't believe the Zulus are going to sit still to be ruled by the Xhosa. Result? Trouble. Result? Martial Law. Result? Dictatorship. Result? Economy in ruins.'

Mahoney poured more wine. 'So you have no hope? But surely you don't think South Africa should stick to apartheid?'

'*Apartheid*? *God*, no! Apartheid is also a proven failure. And unjust. Et cetera, et cetera. I've known that from the time I reached the age of reason.' She rummaged for a cigarette. She lit it with her cheap plastic lighter and inhaled deeply. 'Damn cigarettes – I'm giving them up, this is my first today. But, yes, I do have hope. And there is a solution.'

Mahoney was eating her up with his eyes. She had a breathtaking cleavage which he had difficulty not staring at. 'And that is?'

She tapped his book. 'The solution you put forward. The Israeli model.' She looked at him professorially. 'The Jews were granted their homeland after World War II. It was carved out of Palestinian territory but historically that land belonged to the Jews. The whole Arab world was hostile – but Israel succeeded. Because the Jews were tough, and because the rest of the world supported the principle. As you said tonight, that's the solution for the Afrikaners in South Africa. For the "white tribe" of Africa. The Boers have been in southern Africa as long as the Zulus and Xhosa, so they have as much moral right to a home-land as they do.'

Mahoney had expected that as a political scientist she would reject his argument. *So she really was a Boer.*

'But is it *practical*?' he said.

'It'll be *difficult*. But it's as practical as carving Israel out of Palestine. As separating Austria from Germany. Or Lithuania from Russia. The

Lithuanians want to be Lithuanians, not Russians. The Pakistanis don't want to be Indians.'

'Okay, but where is this Afrikaner state going to be? The old Boer republics of the Transvaal and the Orange Free State?'

'No, that *would* be impractical, like trying to give Manhattan back to the Red Indians.' She looked at him earnestly. 'Don't get me wrong, I don't support those die-hards in the Conservative Party who demand that white South Africa remain white. Nor those neo-Nazis in the AWB – but I do belong to the Afrikaner Volkswag.'

'The Afrikaner People's Sentinel?'

'Right. We want to preserve our Afrikaner heritage. Our language, our culture, our religion. And to do that we want our own homeland. Like the Jews.' She spread her palms reasonably. '*Where* must be negotiated, of course. And if necessary we must be prepared to buy the land. The most practical area is the northern Cape, plus part of the south-western Transvaal. Along the Orange River, to the Atlantic. To Saldanha Bay, which would be our port. That could give us a chunk of land about the size of England. Not a lot to ask, considering South Africa is almost as big as Spain, Portugal, France and England combined.'

Mahoney said: 'But that land is mostly desert. Karoo.'

'So was Israel. But we'll make it bloom with irrigation from the Orange River. Like the Israelis did. Boers are good farmers.'

Mahoney nodded. 'Oh, you people could make it work. I just don't think you'll be allowed to do it. How many blacks live in that area now?'

'Half a million. But they're mostly *brown*. Coloureds. Only a hundred thousand are blacks.'

'And how many whites?'

'About a quarter of a million.'

'And how many Afrikaners will emigrate to the state?'

She sat back. 'In the first instance, who knows? Israel started with only a handful of Jews. Then they came flooding in. The same will happen with the Boers, once the problems of the new South Africa become a reality.'

'But the Afrikaner will still be in the minority. What about the half million Coloureds?'

'Wrong. We'll be in the *majority*. Because the Coloureds are Afrikaners too! They are descended from us, they speak our language, share our culture. As far as I'm concerned, they stay. And no apartheid. However, those that want to leave, we'll buy out their properties at fair prices.'

This was news to Mahoney – if the Coloureds were regarded as

Afrikaners, it put a whole different complexion on the practicality of a volkstaat. 'Is this the official position of the Afrikaner Volkswag?'

She smiled. 'The reason I've joined Volkswag is to ensure that that *becomes* the official position. I'm a professional political scientist – *and* educator – and I consider I've got a lot to contribute to my people. Not many people take us seriously yet – it's part of my job to ensure they do. The idea of a Jewish state wasn't taken seriously for a long time either: the Balfour Declaration which declared the principle of a Jewish state was in 1917, but Israel didn't get going until 1948. That's why this book of yours is important to us: you support the idea of a volkstaat as part of the solution to South Africa's problems, even if you doubt it's practical. We say it *is* practical. For a volkstaat to be practical there must be no apartheid, and there must be one-man-one-vote – otherwise the world just wouldn't tolerate it. It follows that *all* people in our volkstaat will be regarded as Afrikaners, be they white, brown or black, like all people in England are regarded as English, be they white, Asian or black: they are bound together by the predominant English language and the broad English values.'

She paused and stubbed out her half-smoked cigarette. She continued: 'You can take it from me that that is how it's going to be in our volkstaat. However, I must admit that as of this moment that is not yet the Volkswag's official position – it's a conservative organization and they're still wrestling with that one. Volkswag was founded by Hendrik Verwoerd's daughter, after all. But apartheid is crumbling before their eyes, and the conservatives will change. And it's my job – ' she tapped her breast – 'and that of people like me, to make sure they change.'

Mahoney sat back. Impressed. 'Wish I'd known this before the book went to press. However, is your volkstaat idea *economically* practical? Viable?'

'*Yes.*' She smiled. 'At the risk of sounding professorial, that's another mistake you make in your book which I hope you'll put right before the paperback is released. I will post you a very impressive analysis of the economic picture. It's a popular misconception that our volkstaat would be economically unviable. The area we've earmarked is viable right *now*, as a successful farming area with some industry and some mining, so why should it not continue to be when it's intensively developed? And what everybody seems to misunderstand is that we'll be economically integrated with the rest of the South African federation – just as the state of Colorado is economically integrated with the rest of America. We'll use the same currency, share their railway system, their electricity, their roads, their communication systems. We'll have to pay federal taxes for it, just like in America. There'll be a common market, so there'll be no customs barriers for our exports – or imports. We'll have our own civil service, of course, which we'll have to pay for, but it will be a *lean*, well-run civil service. For example, the army will be a people's militia and largely unpaid. The police will also be lean.' She nodded. 'We won't be the richest state, but we'll be economically viable, all right. Especially when immigrants start arriving with their capital and know-how.'

'But what about your poor immigrants? Can your volkstaat carry them?'

'The poor-whites?' She nodded. 'Okay, that will be a problem, if they arrive in large numbers. As they might. *As* they did in Israel. And in America in the last century.' She spread her palms. 'With the destitute, if they can't find jobs, we'll have to have some kind of kibbutz scheme, like Israel's. And teach them a trade. Or give them a state small-holding to farm. As for the no-hopers? Every society has its share of those.'

Mahoney was impressed. 'I'd be grateful if you sent me that analysis. I'll put it into the paperback edition.'

'Oh, rely on it. Your book's important to us. That's why I'm here.'

He smiled. 'I was hoping it was because of my big blue eyes.'

She grinned. 'Those too. Lisa Rousseau told me you were *very* attractive.'

Mahoney's hopes rose. 'As are you. Very, *very* attractive.'

The beautiful mouth twitched as she inclined her head elegantly. 'Thank you.'

'One of the most attractive women I've ever met.'

The mouth smiled widely. She sat back. 'Now, where were we with our volkstaat?'

It was time to stop blandishments. Mahoney said: 'But do you intend to live in the volkstaat?'

She looked surprised at the question. 'Oh, yes.'

'*All* your life?'

She shrugged. 'As long as I can usefully serve.' She sat forward earnestly. 'Luke, you think I'm a good-looking Afrikaner academic who talks a good game but won't be able to play? Who would be bored out of her mind in the Karoo?' She frowned. 'Maybe at times I will be bored, socially. But look at the rewards. The excitement of creating a whole new *state*.' She waved her lovely hand. 'I can think of no under-taking so professionally challenging for a political scientist. Imagine!' She spread her hands. 'We're going to build a whole new piece of history. From the bottom up, like Israel! Imagine the sense of *achieve-ment*, in being one of the founding fathers. The work required, the brains, the worry – planning the culmination of three hundred years of South Africa's history! And in building the future of Africa, because the Afrikaner is going to be the dynamo which drives Africa upwards out of its chaos.' She frowned at him. 'I'm very, *very* privileged to be a founding father of that. I wouldn't miss it for *worlds*.'

Mahoney was smiling at her, enraptured by her beauty, her enthusiasm.

She continued: 'You're thinking: how can a sophisticated academic like me go and bury herself in the backwoods of an Afrikaner volkstaat?' She raised a finger. 'But there are a lot of Afrikaner academics who are keen to make the commitment. So I won't be lonely. And put this in your book: we intend to build a *modern* Afrikaner state. Get that – *modern*. People imagine we want to recreate a hill-billy, voortrekker state. Nothing could be further from the truth! The modern Afrikaner – ' she tapped her beautiful breast – 'intends his volkstaat to be state-of-the-art: modern agriculture, modern factories, making modern products, using modern marketing techniques. If we make a transistor radio, or a car-part, or a shirt, we must make it as well as Taiwan and Japan. Health – our Afrikaner doctors are as good as anywhere in the world. Education?' She shook her head at him. 'Education is the most important thing of all! We must educate our youth to be as good as the rest of the big wide world, so that our *future* is secured. Our schools, our university, must be first class. And that's where I come in.'

Mahoney was entranced by her beauty and her vision. 'Minister of Education?'

She smiled. 'I would *love* to be Minister of Education. What a job, educating a whole new nation. *But*,' she shrugged, 'there will be candidates just as qualified as me. I'll be quite happy to do whatever comes up.'

'A member of parliament?'

'Oh yes, I'd definitely want to be a member of the Raad.'

Mahoney was impressed. Yes, he would vote for her if he was a volkstaater. She would kick ass, as the Americans say. And she made a volkstaat seem a certainty. 'And your family? Are they involved in this?'

She smiled. 'With the name De la Rey? They're involved in *politics*, but not in my volkstaat. My father was staunchly Conservative Party. Now he's finally come to realise that apartheid was a mistake that cannot be defended, but he's a leading light in the Boerestaat Party, which demands the old Boer republics back. He thinks my volkstaat is far too small a demand. He dismisses it.' She added: 'He's also one of the kindest men I know. He finally disapproved of apartheid because it took away the black man's dignity. And he's all in favour of the black man having his independence and governing himself any way he wishes. He just doesn't want a black man governing *him*. But he'll finally see that my volkstaat is the only way.'

'And your mother?'

Katrina smiled. 'My mother is a very switched-on lady. But when it comes to politics she thinks the world is flat.' She made a fist and lowered her voice. '"The good Lord made us different for good reason".'

'Have you any brothers and sisters?'

'Three brothers. One's a dominee in the Dutch Reformed Church. The eldest is in the army. The other's in the police.'

'And do they support the Volkswag? Or your father's idea.'

'My father's. But my youngest brother, he's a captain in the police, he doesn't think it's practical.'

Nor did Mahoney. 'And, if the new South Africa does not agree to this Afrikaner state, what will you do? Are you prepared to fight?'

She sighed. 'I think there will be a civil war, or at least a rebellion, if the Afrikaners don't get their volkstaat. And once it starts it would become very hard to stay above it. Civil wars are like that.' She sighed again. 'However, when the new South Africa is launched there's going to be so much tribal fighting anyway, we may not have to fight – we'll just secede. Just retreat into our laager, if you like, and let them get on with fighting each other. We may have to *defend* our secession by fighting.'

'And you would fight in that situation?'

'Yes. If the secession were morally justified.'

He sighed. 'So you think there will be a rebellion at least?'

'There will be enough who are *prepared* to fight. For a start, there's the AWB. Take them seriously. And possibly half the police force and half the army support them emotionally. It wouldn't take much to make them defect – maybe just one successful rebel battle. Then there's the Citizen Force – all those guys who've been trained for years to fight the ANC. It wouldn't take much to mobilise them, particularly if their farms were threatened. And land is going to be a hell of an issue in the new South Africa – the ANC is going to redistribute land and that means dispossessing a lot of white farmers.' She shook her head. 'Oh, there'd be enough to put up a hell of a fight.'

Mahoney rubbed his chin. 'But are they organised enough to take on a real army? Have they got a battle plan?'

'All the battle plans they need are in the military manuals in use right now against the ANC. All those Citizen Force officers know exactly what to do. All they need is an overall commander to press the right buttons.'

'And is there an overall commander?'

She smiled, 'How about my father – a retired general?' She shook her head. 'There must be many conservative officers who've put their heads together.'

'But it would be treason, and most people balk at that.'

'*Enough* men would follow them. Remember, most Boers will feel that handing over to blacks – let alone to the ANC – would itself be treason. To them it would be justified rebellion. *Die Derde Vryheid Oorlog*, the Third War of Liberation. Sufficient would follow.'

Mahoney sat back. 'The Third Boer War,' he said. 'History repeating itself. I hope it's not Slagters Nek repeating itself.'

Katrina snorted. 'I hope so too.'

God, it made him want to go home. 'And when do you go home?'

'In six weeks. Then, next year I go to Australia for a couple of months to look at their Aboriginal policies. For my thesis.'

'Australia? Any chance of you coming to Hong Kong?'

She shook her head. 'No. I've been to Hong Kong twice. It's beautiful but it's out of my way.' She glanced at her wristwatch.

Mahoney ached to take her hand. He said: 'Come to Hong Kong, I'll show you around.' He added: 'Would you like to dance while we talk about it?'

She was taken aback. 'But there's no music.'

'There must be a night-club nearby. Or I could *croon*. Right here.'

She had a twinkle in her eye. Then: 'I don't think so, Mr Mahoney, dancing ain't my forte. And it's time I thought about driving back to Princeton.'

Mahoney hunched forward. '*Please* don't think about driving back to Princeton. We're only just getting to know each other.'

She smiled. 'And dancing would promote such knowledge?'

'Oh, indeed.'

'I've always thought dancing a rather mindless process.'

He said: 'It's part of the courtship ritual. I'm aching to feel you in my arms. And whisper how beautiful you are.'

She smiled. 'Ah. You refer, therefore, to *carnal* knowledge? You're inviting me to a one-night stand?'

Mahoney grinned. 'Perish the thought! Beyond my wildest *dreams*. I simply can't bear you driving into the night out of my life.'

'But tomorrow *you're* flying away.'

He said conspiratorially: 'Here's an irresistible proposition: I could stay another day, and take you to dinner tomorrow night as well.'

She grinned. 'Ah. So you're inviting me to a *two*-night stand?'

Mahoney threw back his head and laughed. 'Would that I had the courage! I just want to . . . *be* with you.' He added ardently: '*Know* you.'

She lit another cigarette, looking at him steadily. 'Why?'

'Because you're the most alluring woman I've met!'

She smiled thoughtfully. Then stubbed out her new cigarette. 'Damn tobacco. I won't ask you what happened to the others. No, Luke. Attractive thought though it is. We're just ships that pass in the night.'

Mahoney took her hand in his. It was warm and deliciously smooth. He said: 'Just dinner tomorrow night in Princeton, where all the beautiful people hang out!'

She smiled widely, then put her fingertip on his lips. 'No, Luke. Too dangerous.'

He kissed her finger. '*Me?*'

She grinned. 'Maybe me? Because I would probably go to bed with you. And there's no future in that.' She tried to extricate her hand.

Go to bed with him? Mahoney held onto her hand ardently. '*Please* – another bottle of wine at least.'

She stood up. 'In Pretoria. You know where to find me.' She gently but firmly extricated her lovely hand. She smiled down at him: 'But you can walk me to my car, you handsome, talented man.'

Handsome and talented? As she preceded him out of the door he thought: *What a gorgeous woman. What lovely legs. And a goddamn Boer . . .*

PART X

EMBATTLED PRESIDENT BOTHA
ADVERTISES FOR BLACK SOULMATES

ZULUS CALL FOR
BLACK UNITY AGAINST GOVERNMENT

AFRIKANER DELEGATION
VISITS ANC IN LUSAKA

AMERICAN GOVERNMENT CRITICISES
COMMUNIST INFLUENCE IN ANC

AUSTRALIA, NEW ZEALAND, JAPAN,
BRITAIN CRITICISE ANC

AFRIKANER RIGHT WING ON WARPATH

58

When they had said their goodbyes in the car park she had offered her hand, and he had kissed it. Then, with her silent consent, he had taken her in his arms and kissed her mouth. It was an ardent kiss, their lips crushed together, and for a wonderful moment he felt her soft loins against him, and the most desperately urgent thing in the world was to possess her. Then she had broken the embrace and turned for the car door, her eyes smouldering. 'Wow . . . ' He had tried to take her in his arms again, but she had slid resolutely into the seat: 'See why dinner would have been unwise?'

'Please reconsider,' he had said.

She had laughed. 'What a lovely word for sexual intercourse!' She twisted the ignition. 'I'll send you that economic literature,' she had grinned, and driven off.

He had watched her car lights disappear with much more than intense regret and sexual frustration: it was actual sadness. *What a beautiful, exciting woman* . . . And he would never see her again.

Two months later the literature she had promised arrived in Hong Kong; but there was only a compliment slip from the Afrikaner Volkswag, on which she had written: '*Meanwhile, the violence continues* . . . ' He had written a long letter thanking her. She had not replied.

The success of Mahoney's publicity tour was reflected in the sales. 'Luke,' his publisher said on the telephone, '*Big Trouble* is going well for non-fiction, and the spin-off is that sales of *Alms* and *Tears* are picking up again. Now, it really is important that we keep your name in front of the public. So, when can I expect to publish those family journals?'

Mahoney was standing at his study window, looking down on the magnificent harbour. 'Not until the new South Africa comes about. And that might not be for years.'

'Sounds like it could be any moment, with all the violence. Well, keep the chapters coming so we can edit them and be ready to burst into print the moment the new South Africa breaks. Concentrate on the violent nature of Africa, the failure of democracy as a consequence, the struggle of the Afrikaner for freedom and security. D'you still think there's going to be a civil war if the Afrikaner doesn't get his volkstaat?'

'I think there'll be a *rebellion*, at least. How long, how successful, is a guess. But once it starts, anything can happen.'

'*Excellent*,' his publisher said. 'Meanwhile, have you started writing anything else?'

'No, Bill. I'm in court most days. And next month I've got to go to goddamn Borneo on relief again.'

'I wish you'd give up that job of yours. What we really want is the sequel to *Alms*. Couldn't you do that? About when Pamela comes out of prison after twenty years?'

Mahoney sighed, and shook his head. 'I don't think so. I can't realistically *feel* how they would feel.'

'Use your imagination, that's what writing's all about! Suppose Jack is happily married, but when he sees Pamela again he still loves her? There's drama for you. Sit down with a case of beer and start imagining. I haven't invested all this money in you for nothing.'

About once a week Mahoney reviewed his newspapers, wrote up his journal and posted his work off to Lisa Rousseau for comment. He considered himself fortunate to have a tame university professor advising, but it was really Professor de la Rey he hoped Lisa would put on the job: he'd love to open a correspondence with *her*. But Lisa didn't do that, despite his hints. *Damn*. He wrote:

PRESIDENT BOTHA ADVERTISES FOR BLACK SOULMATES

As Inkatha and the UDF continue to butcher each other in Natal, President Botha has placed a swashbuckling lonely hearts advertisement in leading newspapers calling for 'all wise black leaders who reject violence' to join him in 'an honest meeting of men of goodwill to solve our problems'. In parliament, however, he said that he would crack down on organizations which send delegates to talk to the ANC, and he warned businessmen to stick to business. He has had no takers. 'Wise black leaders' realise that to talk to government would be a kiss of death when the ANC comes back.

Meanwhile, to prove how serious he is about reform, the president announced that, although he will never *repeal the Group Areas Act, which segregates residential areas, he is going to allow for 'grey' areas where people of different races who wish to do so may live as neighbours. However, he warned, wagging his finger, the remainder of the Group Areas Act 'will be strictly enforced'.*

CONSERVATIVE PARTY LAMBASTS GOVERNMENT REFORMS

Proposing a vote of no confidence in the government because of its reforms, its failure to restore law and order, and for 'stubbornly clinging to notions of power-sharing', the leader of the Conservative Party, Dr Treurnicht, vehemently declared that apartheid has not failed – it is the government who has failed the divine ideal of apartheid. 'My Bible tells me that God was responsible for the division of peoples!' he declared to roars of applause.

ZULUS CALL FOR BLACK UNITY

As bloody mayhem escalates, Chief Buthelezi continues to call for the unbanning of the ANC. He refuses to participate in the proposed National Council, intended to be an advisory chamber pending negotiations for a new constitution, unless Nelson Mandela, his arch rival, is released from prison. He rejects the president's lonely hearts advertisement – 'unless the reality of a black majority rule is recognised'. Calling for black political parties to unite, he says, 'Let us not tear each other apart like a pack of dogs fighting over who will take over PW Botha's seat.' Buthelezi says he has tried time and again to seek reconciliation with the ANC. A high-level talk between the two sides in New York was to have been followed by a meeting in London; but when the Inkatha delegation arrived no meeting took place. Buthelezi says that Inkatha supports the ideals of the ANC as founded in 1912, but rejects their socialism, their Armed Struggle and their policy of rendering South Africa ungovernable.

The ANC retorted on Radio Freedom that they would not talk to Buthelezi because his hands are 'just as bloody as the government's', adding that he is 'part of the apartheid regime'.

NECKLACING INCREASES

The head of the security police testified in the Supreme Court that 400 people have now been murdered by the notorious 'necklace', another 200 burned alive. 'These killings are part of the ANC campaign of terror to make the country ungovernable.' The mining industry says violence has increased dramatically. Fifty-two miners have been murdered in three months. Meanwhile, COSATU House, headquarters of the largest federation of black trade unions, has been rendered useless by two large explosions.

I wonder who did that . . . ?

STRONG AFRIKANER DELEGATION VISITS ANC

Sixty-two Afrikaner academics, clergymen, businessmen, politicians and journalists have visited the ANC in Dakar – in defiance of finger-wagging President Botha. After the talks a joint communiqué called for a negotiated settlement, the release of political prisoners and the unbanning of the ANC. Everyone was deeply concerned about the violence. The ANC, however, drew a distinction between that and their Armed Struggle. Further, the ANC said: 'We do not approve of necklacing, nor do we encourage it, but we are not prepared to condemn publicly those who carry it out.'

(Well, what the fuck is that if it's not encouragement?)

Upon their return to South Africa the delegation was awaited by a howling mob of 400 AWB members. A violent fight ensued between them and students applauding the delegation. In Parliament President Botha wrathfully denounced the delegation, saying: 'The ANC is laughing up their sleeves at the naiveté of "useful idiots" who, as Lenin puts it, can be used to further the first phase of the revolution.' Shortly afterwards a bomb exploded in central Johannesburg, outside the army's headquarters, leaving sixty-eight people seriously injured, many of them black. The Minister of Defence said: 'Those who talk to terrorists owe South Africa an answer'.

Gutter politics.

US GOVERNMENT CRITICISES
COMMUNIST INFLUENCE IN ANC

President Reagan has refused to meet the ANC leader, Oliver Tambo – causing bitterness because Reagan met Chief Buthelezi last year. But Tambo did manage to meet George Schultz, US Secretary of State, who warned him that violence would lead to catastrophe, and asked the ANC to outline its vision for the future 'more specifically', expressing American opposition to 'the replacement of apartheid by another unrepresentative government'.

Schultz also expressed US concern about Soviet influence in the ANC. A recent publication by the US government says that half of the ANC's thirty-member executive council are communists, who also dominate the ANC's military wing, MK, and the Congress of Trade Unions. It says a vast network of communist cells exists in South Africa, adding that the ANC is beholden to the Soviet Union for its arms and military training.

But if the US thinks this is bad news it should look at AZAPO, the successors to Black Consciousness. AZAPO denounced the SACP because of its alliance with the ANC which is 'multi-class', therefore unable to construct 'a socialist dictatorship of the proletariat'. Meanwhile the PAC, with their slogan 'One Settler One Bullet' and their demand that all the land be returned to blacks, is committed to the 'total destruction of capitalism', and rejects parliamentary democracy as inimical to socialism.

Meanwhile black children are pledging the allegiance of their schools to either AZAPO or ANC, knocking the shit out of each other . . .

AUSTRALIA, NEW ZEALAND, JAPAN, BRITAIN CRITICISE ANC

In a diplomatic tour to ask for tougher sanctions against South Africa, Oliver Tambo has had a less than warm reception, due to the mind-boggling violence and the horrific necklace, which the ANC refuses to condemn. Further, the world is exasperated with the mess Africa has made of itself under the combined influence of communism and the African Way.

In Australia, Tambo was given a repeated roasting by the media on the ANC's view of necklacing, and prime minister Bob Hawke bluntly told him that though he understood black frustration he did not condone violence. Mr Tambo then visited New Zealand, which refused to support tougher economic sanctions. Next came Japan, which also rejected comprehensive sanctions and told him they were opposed to the ANC's Armed Struggle. And British prime minister Margaret Thatcher said that the ANC is a 'typical terrorist organization which people should fight, not embrace'.

Meanwhile Chief Buthelezi continues to denounce everybody and oppose sanctions loudly. He says that African workers who barely understand disinvestment are facing the brunt of ANC strategy. 'The people who travel the world campaigning for sanctions still have their jobs while the victims of sanctions are losing theirs in droves.' He tells the West that apartheid is best attacked by diplomatic offensives, not sanctions. Recently Inkatha transported 400 supporters to Ladysmith to break a shopping boycott organised by COSATU. Buthelezi said he was not challenging the legitimacy of the boycott, but the method, which was a typical example of thugs using terror tactics to intimidate the public.

Jesus. Spare a thought for old President Botha. One of his difficulties, of course, is his own inability to grasp the nettle because he is a dyed-in-the-wool Afrikaner. But the main stumbling block is the fact that most Africans are notoriously undemocratic by culture. Another problem is Africa's appalling economic track record. Due to incompetence and dishonesty Africa has bankrupted itself. All of which leads PW Botha back to his own Afrikaner volk's resistance to reform. To succeed, PW must persuade his own people to follow him. Not only do they honestly believe that apartheid is God's will, they are aghast at the prospect of being ruled by people they consider undemocratic, incompetent, communist and savage. And the Afrikaner is a fighter: fighting for his life against the Xhosa, against Dingaan's Zulus, against Mzilikazi, against the British in two wars of liberation, against the modern-day Swart Gevaar (black peril) is not only his tradition, he believes it is his God-given destiny. God, he believes, has cast him in a heroic role in Godless Africa, and the current Total Onslaught is but another battle to be overcome with fortitude.

And now, as if the Hitlerian AWB were not enough of a headache, along comes the BBB, the Blanke Bevrydings Beweging or White Liberation Movement. They are led by Professor Johan Schabort of the Rand Afrikaans University, who says his movement stands for 'the white man first under all circumstances', and 'the removal of all non-whites from white South Africa'. The BBB works in close contact with the National Alliance and White Power Movement of the United States, the National Front of France, the National Front of Britain, the Voorpost of Belgium, right-wing organizations in Australia, West Germany and Scandinavian countries, and 'sister organizations' in South Africa.

Mahoney stopped typing. He pressed the button, and his machine began to print out. Ready for Lisa Rousseau to evaluate.

He walked to the window with his glass of whisky. Katrina de la Rey had said that PW Botha was on his way out. If a real reformer took over and real negotiations began with the ANC then surely 'political prisoners' would be released. It was quite possible, therefore, that soon Patti Gandhi may be coming out . . .

And for a moment he glimpsed the delicious fleeting feeling of Katrina's body when he kissed her. *But how would he feel about Patti?* He had to force himself to concentrate. Overjoyed, of course, that she would be free again. He would weep with joy for her. His eyes burned, just imagining it. And he would feel guilt. Irrational, but guilt nonetheless, that he had lived the last twenty years *free*, while she had suffered the *dreadful* ordeal of incarceration.

But how would he feel about *her*?

He closed his eyes, and tried to feel, tried to imagine it, as his publisher had urged.

But all he could feel was . . . unreality. He could not imagine it. All he could feel was . . . responsibility. Responsibility for trying to make her happy? To be *kind* to her. To do everything he could for her. But if she wanted to come back to him, to rush into his arms?

He stood at the window, overlooking Hong Kong harbour, and tried to imagine her in his arms again. Her beauty of long ago. And, yes, he could imagine it. Almost see it. The feel of her silken nakedness. Her loins, her belly, her breasts. Her face. Her long black hair. Yes, but it was blurred. *Theoretical.* In theory, yes, he could imagine passion for Patti Gandhi. But as he stood here, half drunk, looking down at the lights of Wan Chai, it was unreal. Not dead, just past. Over.

He only wanted to do everything in his power to make her happy.

59

Richard Barker was a short man, about forty years old, with a tanned, weathered face. His visiting card advised that he was a geologist employed by a South African mining group.

'How did you find me?' Mahoney asked. They were seated in his chambers.

'I'm on holiday here. It says on the dust-jacket of your book that you're a lawyer in Hong Kong.' Barker opened his briefcase and took out a copy of *Big Trouble*. 'You understand the South African political situation. The tale I'm about to tell you now, in the strictest confidence at this stage, is very relevant to your book. And if anything untoward happens to me, I hope you will publish the tale. And not just in a newspaper article, which is here today and gone tomorrow, but in a book.'

'"Untoward"?'

Barker said: 'If I am murdered. By agents of the South African government. Or detained without trial.'

'Jesus.' Mahoney sat forward. 'Okay.' He picked up a pen.

Barker sighed. 'I don't know how much you know about Renamo? Your book hardly deals with it.'

'Not much. Nobody does, it seems. So start at the beginning.'

'Okay. When the Portuguese collapsed in Mozambique in 1975 and the Frelimo communists took over, the Renamo resistance movement started a guerrilla war against the new government. Renamo was sponsored by the Rhodesian government, in the hopes that the communists would be overthrown. When Rhodesia collapsed in 1980 the South African government took over sponsoring Renamo. In fact Renamo headquarters were actually *inside* South Africa and South African military officers directed operations. Renamo wrought havoc in Mozambique. When President Botha decided Mozambique had been softened up enough, he invited the Mozambique president to a peace conference at Nkomati, on the border. The deal he offered was, "We won't support Renamo anymore if you don't allow the ANC to have military bases in Mozambique any more." Mozambique had little choice, so the much-heralded Nkomati Accord came about. It was a big blow to the ANC. But the rumours were that South Africa was still secretly supplying Renamo, in breach of the Nkomati Accord – and Renamo continued to wreak havoc. Mindless anarchy. But, of course, South Africa piously denied supporting them. And then, a few months ago, I went on a geological expedition into Mozambique.'

'Did you enter legally?'

'Oh yes. Via Swaziland. I go all over southern Africa. Anyway, I got to my work-site, about fifty miles from the South African border, and set up a camp. I saw nobody. Then, at dusk on the second day, I heard a vehicle. I climbed to a higher spot, with my binoculars. About a mile away, I saw two vehicles coming to a big clearing. Some blacks got out and started to prepare fires, demarcating an area about a couple of hundred yards square. I was sure that I had witnessed preparations for an arms-drop for Renamo, so I resolved to stay where I was. At about midnight my patience was rewarded when the fires were lit. Half an hour later I heard an aircraft approaching.'

'From which direction?'

'From the west, from the South African border. I could not see the plane because it was showing no lights. Then I saw parachutes against the stars. Five or six came floating down towards the fires. They were carrying crates. They hit the earth and men ran for them. Then the plane disappeared off to the west.'

Mahoney was making notes. 'Then?'

'I wanted to know what was in those crates, so I started down the hill towards the fires.'

'That was courageous.'

'Well, I eventually got within about a hundred and fifty yards of the nearest crate. A gang of blacks were smashing it open and emptying the contents – AK-47 automatic rifles.'

'But that's a Russian weapon. Are you saying that was a Russian plane?'

'No. The South Africans capture the weapons in Angola and give them to Renamo. Anyway, I wanted to see what other weapons were in other crates. So I crept around the perimeter of the illuminated area. More rifles. In the third crate I saw mortar launchers and shells. I had enough evidence and I should have crept away, but I wanted to see more, and that was my undoing. Suddenly there was a shout and a man pointing in my direction – and all hell broke loose.'

'Jesus. And?'

'And I ran like hell. Midst a fusillade of gunfire. Fortunately I had a hundred yards' start on them. Bullets flying everywhere – I was terrified. Those Renamo bastards think nothing of lopping off your nose and ears while they interrogate you. I ran. Dodging trees. Bullets flying everywhere. And then I tripped and sprained my ankle. I tried to run again, but my ankle was buggered, in agony. I desperately tried to hide. To cut a long story short, they found me. And, I thought my last day had come.'

'What did they do?'

He snorted. 'They knocked the living daylights out of me. They dragged me back to their commander. But they only spoke native dialect and some Portuguese – no English. Oh God . . . They came at me with knives, threatened me with burning logs, the works. But they could see we couldn't communicate, so they decided to take me back to their base where somebody spoke English. But first I showed them my camp to try to convince them I was a geologist. They seized everything, threw me in the back of my Land-Rover, chained me up with my towing chain and padlock, and set off. You can imagine, I thought I was going to my untimely and highly unpleasant death.'

Mahoney was making notes. 'Yes. And?'

'I only knew we were heading north, roughly parallel to the South African border. We ground along bush tracks for hours. Then, at dawn we reached a communal farm, set up by Frelimo, part of their agricultural collectivization – the peasants are moved from their kraals into new villages where they have an administration of sorts – '

Mahoney added: 'Which was a predictable communist failure.'

He waved a hand. 'You don't have to convince me – I'm an ANC supporter, but not a communist.' He took a deep breath. 'We roared into the village, all guns blazing.' He closed his eyes. 'And, I've never imagined anything so horrific.'

'Jesus.' Mahoney waited.

Barker sighed, then continued: 'There were maybe a hundred huts, in rows. The village was just coming to life, cooking fires starting. And, oh God, the carnage. We roared into the middle, guns blazing, just mowing down everybody, women, children, just mowing down screaming people. Then the bastards went running between the huts, firing into doorways. I saw children gunned down, old ladies, young girls, old men. Just killing for the malicious joy of it.'

'God.'

'I remember I was screaming. Screaming *Stop, stop, for Christ's sake!* But I couldn't even hear myself above the gunfire, it was like a nightmare. I saw one bastard corner a mother and three screaming children and dance gleefully as they cowered, begging for mercy. He shot the youngest first, in the guts, to make the mother go mad, then the next, then the next, before blowing the woman's chest apart.' He held his head.

'Go on.'

'They started setting fire to the huts. The thatch went up like an inferno. They set fire to the school, burnt the books, they smashed up the administration hut and hurled all the files on a bonfire. They even burnt the clinic.' He looked at Mahoney in wonder. 'The health clinic – the one thing in the whole Mozambique fuck-up which brings some relief, even if it is so primitive that it's only first aid? Why did they do that?'

Mahoney shook his head. Barker went on: 'Absolutely incomprehensible anarchy. All the medicines being gleefully thrown on the bonfire!' He sighed. 'And then I escaped.'

Mahoney looked up. 'How?'

'I had a spare set of keys for both the ignition and the padlock. They were in the toolbox. I managed to fish them out, got the padlock undone, then scrambled over into the front seat. I had nothing to lose – shot now or shot later. I gunned the engine and just roared out the village. Trying to keep my head low in the gunfire.'

'And you weren't hit?'

'The Land-Rover was shot up to hell. But by a miracle I was missed. I was covered in flying glass. I just kept my foot flat. I suppose the dust I was throwing up gave me some cover.'

'And they didn't give chase?'

'I don't know. I couldn't see through the shattered windows. But their lorries were old and probably couldn't catch up.'

'Did you know where you were?'

'I reckoned I was about a hundred miles from the Swazi border-post I'd entered by. And, *God*, did I drive? And pray. About three hours later

I reached the Swaziland border. God, was I relieved. I was asked about the bullet holes. I said I'd been ambushed by robbers. I wasn't going to tell the truth yet, I was going to do some further investigation, then discredit the South African government for breaching the Nkomati Accord. And that's why I didn't take my Land-Rover back into South Africa – to avoid awkward questions. I left it in Swaziland to be repaired and caught a plane back to Johannesburg. I had to wait the whole day for the flight. I bought a notebook and made notes while my memory was fresh. At nine o'clock I got into Jo'burg. I phoned my girl-friend from the airport. Just before ten my taxi got me back to my house. I have a high wall. And a bloody great Alsatian dog who runs around the garden barking for a living.' He took a deep, tense breath. 'I let myself through the big iron front gate. And, the first thing I see is Fred, my Alsatian, dead on the lawn. And then I was jumped by three big bastards.'

'Black?'

'Yes. They wore balaclavas, but they were black all right. But that doesn't mean they weren't a fucking government hit squad.'

'Hit squads?'

'Oh yes sir. That's what I'm here to place on record with you.' He sighed, then continued: 'They grabbed me, snatched my bag containing my notes. They repeatedly demanded where my Land-Rover was – said they were stealing it. I said it was in a garage. They dragged me inside and tied me up. They proceeded to "burgle" my house. Ransack it, to make it look like a burglary. Said they were looking for money and jewellery. Finally they just took a portable radio and fled. Fifteen minutes later my girlfriend arrived and untied me.'

'So you think they were security police?'

'I *know* they were. All of which is further proof that that plane was a South African one. Look, those Renamo bastards had the registration number of my Land-Rover. So after I escape they report my number by radio to the South African army. The security forces trace me and send some heavies to seize any evidence I've come back with – including my shot-up Land-Rover. All they can get is my bag with my notes. They make it look like a burglary and run.'

Mahoney sighed. 'Okay.'

'The next point is my dog. Rigor mortis had already set in. That means that he had been dead several hours. So those bastards had been waiting for me for hours. If they were ordinary burglars they would have broken in and left long ago. But they waited for me to come home. Why?' He held up four fingers. 'One: they badly wanted that Land-Rover – to destroy my evidence of the bullet-damage. Two: they had already *been* inside my house – by picking the lock – and gone through my files, looking for evidence that I was spying on Renamo. I know because when they were ransacking my house they did not touch my filing cabinet – I could see it. But the next day I realised all my files were in the wrong order. Somebody had been through them *before* they jumped on me.'

'Was anything missing?'

'No. But at least one document had obviously been photographed.'

'How did you know?'

'The pages were back to front.' He held up his third finger. 'If you're still in any doubt: the next day the garage in Swaziland phoned to say my Land-Rover had been stolen during the night.'

Mahoney sat back. 'Okay, your theory is sounding impressive.'

'I haven't finished yet.' He held up a fourth finger. 'I had planned this trip to Hong Kong some time ago. But I was scared of staying in South Africa a day longer. So I advanced my bookings and left the next night –'

'Pause there. Did you report your burglary to the police?'

He snorted. 'Yes – in order to make myself appear an innocent victim. I just told them what had happened since I entered my front gate – nothing else. I *didn't* mention the Land-Rover. They took photos, made sympathetic noises and left.'

'You think they knew?'

'No. These were two dumb constables.' He snorted. 'But when I arrived in Singapore I noticed a furtive Chinese gentleman who was around wherever I was, trying to look unobtrusive. The next day I left Singapore for Hong Kong. Arrived yesterday. And last night I saw the same guy, in my hotel foyer.'

'*Sure* it was the same man?'

'Absolutely. This time he was with a white man.'

'And did they follow you anywhere?'

'I was on my way to bed when I saw him. This morning the Chinese was in the foyer again. And so I called you.'

'Did he follow you when you left the hotel?'

'I had the receptionist call for a taxi. As I drove off I looked back but there were so many people I couldn't be sure.'

Mahoney sat back. 'Okay,' he said, 'it sounds suspicious. But Hong Kong is a tourist place, I've seen people in Singapore whom I've seen again on my plane to Hong Kong. And there's the improbability that the South African government has hitmen all over the world.'

'Why? This is the era of Total Strategy.'

'Okay. Now, what exactly do you want me to do?'

'I would be most grateful if you could record an affidavit from me, in the proper legal form, and keep it in a safe place. Meanwhile I'm returning to South Africa to do further investigation and I'll send you any more evidence I uncover. Then, I want you to release the affidavit when I tell you to go ahead.'

'Release it to whom?'

'To the international press. To prove to the world that South Africa is still up to its dirty tricks supporting Renamo. *Or,*' he added, 'if you hear that I have died. I will instruct my girlfriend to advise you if that happens. And,' he added, 'I hope you will be able to place it in a book. Is that possible?'

'Oh,' Mahoney said, 'I'm very grateful to be able to use it. And, yes, I know the newspapers would go for it. But I cannot act as your *lawyer* because I work for the Hong Kong government. If you want somebody to act as a *trustee* of this story, and release it on certain conditions, you should appoint an attorney in South Africa.'

'But I want *you* to put it in a book.'

'Once it's in the newspapers, anybody can put it in their book. As it happens I *am* writing a book, in which I can use this. And, yes, I can type up an affidavit and you can swear it right now. But,' Mahoney sat up, 'if you think your life is in danger, we should tell the Hong Kong police. There's insufficient evidence to arrest anybody, but they can check this Chinese man out.'

'*No,*' Barker said. 'I don't want the South Africans to know I'm wise to them. That'll screw up my investigations.'

Mahoney doubted this Chinese was a South African agent. But he said: 'It's better than being dead. And aren't you being foolhardy continuing your investigations in South Africa?' He tapped his notes. 'You've got enough evidence here to publish the story.'

'But not to *prove* it beyond doubt! They'll just deny it. I want to blow this case wide open – it's my duty.'

His duty. Yes, and what have I done? 'How will you investigate further?'

Barker sat back earnestly. 'One: return to Mozambique. At least one parachute got snarled up in trees – fragments of it must still be there and may lead us to its origin. The crates – can chips of that wood be traced, forensically, back to the South African army? And I've got a contact in civil aviation who's got a contact in the air force – maybe that plane's flight is recorded. And so on.' He ended grimly: 'I'm leaving no stone unturned.'

'And what about this guy you think's following you?' Mahoney sighed. 'Look, you'd better move out of that hotel.'

'I've already decided that. I've already paid. I've booked a room at the Peninsula. I've just got to get my bag.'

Mahoney shook his head. 'He mustn't see you move your bag, or he'll follow you.' He looked at his watch. 'Look, I'm leaving for Borneo tomorrow, or you could have stayed with me. Give me your hotel key – I'll get your bag to the Peninsula Hotel.'

It was mid afternoon when he got to the Capitol Hotel in Kowloon to collect Richard Barker's bag. He told his taxi to wait.

It was a small, cheap hotel. There were a few Chinese and Japanese around. There was no elevator. Mahoney started up the stairs. He found room 204. He looked back at the stairway. Nobody. He put the key in the lock and walked in.

The beds had been made, everything neat. Mahoney opened the wardrobe. There hung one jacket and a few shirts. In the drawers was underwear. At the bottom was one hold-all. He stuffed everything into it. He opened the bathroom door to collect Barker's toiletries. And the plastic shower curtain swept back and there stood a white man.

Mahoney stepped backwards, shocked; confusion crossed the man's face, then he bounded, his hand on high. Mahoney tried to swing a desperate fist, the man's hand swiped down. Mahoney crashed into the corner, and everything went black.

He came to on the floor. He had a humdinger of a headache. He clambered to his feet. He looked into the mirror: but there was no blood. He turned unsteadily for the bedroom: Barker's bag was still there. The door was closed. He locked it. He held his head, sat down on the bed and tried to think.

A white man.

Would he recognise him again, from those few shocked seconds? No. Blue eyes, about forty – but that was it. But for sure this had to be reported to the police. Jesus, this was a hit-job he had stumbled into. That meant a professional. That meant he was not going to be found in teeming Hong Kong very easily. And that meant calling in the police was probably wasted effort. And the opposite of what Barker wanted – it would alert the South African 'authorities'. And, by God, he wanted Barker to be onto them. *But the man's life was in danger.*

Well, Barker had to get out of town. Mahoney picked up the toiletries, stuffed them into the bag, and left the hotel via the emergency stairs. He emerged into the sanitary lane and walked briskly to his taxi.

* * *

It was six o'clock when Mahoney got back to his apartment. He had told Barker, and informed the police. The police had found no clues in the room: they had persuaded Barker to leave Hong Kong and had taken him to the airport.

He poured a large whisky. Then looked at himself in the mirror, trying to think. About what Barker had told him, what it meant: what Lisa Rousseau had said about the murder of Walter Kosagu – 'a Dirty Tricks department' exists. But all he could think was that he wanted to go back to South Africa. Even if there was no hope, he wanted to *be* there, to see, to smell, to worry, to argue, to *participate*. Like Barker was doing. Like Katrina de la Rey was doing. Like Lisa. Like Patti. Like even that dizzy Sally was doing. Once a South African, always a South African. And once a writer always a writer.

And instead where was he going to go? Fucking Borneo again.

He looked at his reflection. It was definitely a forty-something face. Mature? Approaching his prime? Bullshit. His prime had passed, sitting on his arse doing Regina versus Chan Fat which any beat-up lawyer could do, when he could have been writing full-time like Bill Summers said, like Katrina de la Rey said. Without difficulty he tore his eyes off that well-fed, well-paid, beat-up colonial servant in the mirror and stomped through to his study. He pulled the journals off the shelf, thumped them on the desk. His notebooks. His typescript.

He looked at the daunting array of writing, and half-written material. The pile of unwritable material. He sat down and held his head.

Think. Try to think of the big picture. What are the main threads of the big story? *That's* your job. As the historian you want to be. That Lisa Rousseau wanted you to be. As the journalist you used to be. As you really deep-down want to be, the guy with the fag hanging out of his mouth, the opinion-maker, the air ticket somewhere in his pocket, *happy* to be a hack.

He switched on the word processor, and stared at it grimly.

60

Borneo was worse than anticipated. He had been bored in Hong Kong, but in Borneo he was 'stultified,' he wrote to Lisa when he posted his latest batch of journals to her, 'and no women . . . ' Until the Pig Case.

When the blonde with the spectacles and the floppy Panama hat came into the courtroom, she seemed to bring the sunshine in with her. She sat in the front of the gallery under the slowly turning fan, which moved wisps of hair about her beautiful shadowed face. She opened a notebook and prepared to take down his judgment.

Mahoney tore his eyes off her and began: 'The defendant, Mobongo, is a forty-year-old tribesman, and he is charged with murder, in that upon or about the eighteenth of September 1988 he did wrongfully, unlawfully and maliciously kill Shilling.'

He paused to allow the interpreter to translate. The woman certainly brightened up the old courtroom. He continued: 'The facts are hardly in dispute. Argument by both counsel has largely been confined to the question of extenuating circumstances which, if they exist, enable me to pass a sentence other than death.

'The evidence is that the defendant has been married by tribal custom for three years to a woman of about twenty years, called Mary. She has not yet conceived a child, a matter for some concern in tribal eyes. It is also the local custom that each time a married woman has sexual intercourse she makes a knot in her ceremonial grass skirt – the number of knots a woman displays being a sort of badge.

'Now, on the second of September, the defendant left to go on a hunting expedition. When he returned twelve days later he counted the knots on Mary's skirt and found three more than he remembered. He challenged Mary, who eventually, shamefacedly, confessed that she had had sexual intercourse with three men during his absence: with Sunku of Chief Ganga's village, with Joshua of Chief Wumpa's village, and with Shilling of Chief Wozom's village.

'The defendant was greatly angered by these adulteries. However, I am unable to agree with Mr Williams, counsel for the defendant, that he was "blinded by hurt" and "maddened with the disgrace of it" to the point that he did not know right from wrong. What is clear to me from the evidence is that the defendant, angered, methodically set about setting the record straight amongst his aboriginal peers. Daubing himself in war paint, taking up his spear, he set off to Sunku's village to claim compensation before Chief Ganga.

'He arrived the next day. He raised his hue and cry, brandishing his spear, and demanded compensation. The chief summoned his people, Sunku confessed his guilt and, as tradition required, offered compensation in the form of one pig. This was accepted by the defendant. Satisfied, he set off for the second village, with his pig.'

Mahoney glanced at the blonde woman. She crossed her legs and he caught a glimpse of lovely knees. He went on: 'The defendant arrived at the second village the next day. He raised the hue and cry, Joshua was summoned and he also confessed guilt. And he offered, as tradition required, one pig. This, again, the defendant accepted. And he set off for the third village.

He glanced at the woman, then said: 'I pause here to point out that this was the third day of his travels.

'The defendant arrived on the fourth day. With his two pigs. He laid his complaint to the chief and Shilling also admitted intercourse. Shilling then proffered a pig as compensation, whereupon the defendant brandished his spear and thrust it through Shilling's heart, killing him instantly in front of hundreds of witnesses.' Mahoney sighed. 'None of these facts is disputed. The accused's reason, given to this court, for so murdering him is that he was offered an *inferior* pig.'

He paused, then ended matter-of-factly: 'I have no hesitation in convicting the defendant of murder. However, Mr Williams has argued strenuously that this insult of the inferior pig, together with the defendant's other hurt, constitute extenuating circumstances which empower me to pass a sentence other than death. I will consider Mr William's arguments overnight. Court will adjourn until ten o'clock tomorrow morning.'

The registrar called: 'Silence in Court', and everybody stood. Mahoney rose and walked out, into his chambers.

And, oh God, he hated this job. He tossed his wig onto the desk and shucked off his red robes. The registrar came in and started hanging them up. Mahoney combed his matted hair. He tried to sound casual: 'That woman in court today – is she a member of the press?'

'Don't think so, sir, she'd have sat at the press table.' He added, with a small smile: 'Shall I ask?'

'No.' That was another thing about this job – judges are supposed to be so fucking respectable.

Mahoney returned to his suite in the old Victorian hotel. He had a shower, draped a towel around his waist and ripped open a can of beer. It went down like a mountain brook. He opened another can, then turned to his desk. The registrar had brought his notebooks from the courthouse. But he couldn't bear to comb the evidence yet, looking for any detail in the defendant's favour.

And he could not bear to confront the other books on his desk either: the pile of family journals. But he took a grim breath and made himself sit down and confront them.

He pulled his portable word processor towards him grimly.

The magistrate's cocktail party that night was the usual colonial affair, in the Residency's big tropical garden, the town's dignitaries standing about being frightfully polite and hot. A native police band played chamber music and waiters circulated with trays of drinks and hors d'oeuvres. The Honourable Mr Acting Justice Mahoney was the guest of honour and had to be introduced to everybody. He thoroughly disliked cocktail parties: but there, amongst the guests scattered across the lawn, he spotted the beautiful blonde and he immediately cheered up. She was even more beautiful without her Panama hat. When he was finally introduced to her by the magistrate he stared.

'Good God! Katrina de la Rey. Now I remember!'

'Oh, you know each other?' the magistrate said jovially.

Katrina smiled. 'Last tore my eyes off him in the Brew 'n' Burger in New York.'

'What on earth are you doing *here*?' Mahoney demanded happily.

She smiled. 'That thesis, remember? Just been down in Australia, studying their Aboriginal policy. Now I'm having a look at the Borneans, on my way home. I'm staying with the American consul, I'm a friend of their daughter.'

'But you didn't wear glasses in New York.'

'I had contact lenses, but got fed up with losing them. Needed glasses every morning to find my lenses!'

The magistrate began to move him on to the next introduction, and Mahoney held out a finger at her. 'You can't claim you've got to drive back to Princeton tonight.'

Fifteen minutes later he managed to make his way back to her. He said: 'I know what I recognised about you, despite the hat and the spectacles – it's your beauty.'

She grinned. 'What the hell does a woman of maturity say to blandishments like that?'

'You can say you'll have dinner with me tonight.'

She grinned. 'I thought you had a judgment to consider.'

'I've already considered it.' The magistrate's wife was heading purposefully towards him to lug him away to another group. 'Okay?'

She grinned, 'Okay, Judge.'

'And don't call me judge!'

'There you are, Judge!' the magistrate's wife gushed, as if he had been hiding. 'You must come and meet our late arrivals.' As she led him away she said: 'And after the party you will stay and have a bite to eat, won't you?'

'Thank you, but I really can't,' Mahoney said. 'I've got a judgment to consider.'

* * *

Peter Chan, his registrar, had to fetch Katrina de la Rey from the American consul's residence and bring her to dine in his hotel suite because Mahoney could not be seen doing it himself after declining the magistrate's bite to eat. 'I feel like a paramour being smuggled into the palace,' she said.

'Perish the thought!' He passed her her glass of wine. 'This really is a great unexpected pleasure.'

She smiled. 'Not as unexpected as you think . . . Lisa phoned me in Australia to tell me you were in Borneo.'

Mahoney was taken aback. '*Lisa* did . . . ?' *Well, good old Lisa!*

'But, I hasten to add, I was coming here anyway . . . But, I do admit that her information made me tiptoe into your courtroom to observe her protégé at work.'

Lisa's protégé? He grinned. 'Well, so I'm indebted to Lisa – again . . . ' He went on: 'I would have preferred to go to the yacht club for dinner – it's pretty there. But, alas, goddamn judges should not be seen being attentive to beautiful ladies in public places.'

She grinned widely. 'And you're feeling very attentive? With half a dozen of the magistrate's whiskies inside you?'

'I assure you, even without the whiskies . . . '

She sat down in an armchair. 'You don't like being a judge, do you? All the protocol.'

Mahoney wasn't sure whether this was a change of a promising subject. 'No. I feel a fraud. I'm only a judge because I didn't blot my copybook over the last umpteen years. And I'm only an acting-judge, anyway.' He shook his head. 'I'm not cut out to be a judge, Katrina, I'd much rather be down there in the well of the court, having a good scrap, instead of sitting up there listening patiently.' He added: 'And judges are supposed to be so damn respectable.'

'And you're not? Beneath that wig and scarlet robes there's a hard-drinking scribe who really wants to be one of the boys?'

'Now you're talking.' He wanted to take her in his arms. 'Come and look at the view from the balcony.' She got up. The moonlight shone on the garden below, the sea silvery between the palm leaves. 'Pretty, isn't it?'

'Yes.' Then: 'Have you done many capital cases?'

'Hundreds, over the years. Tell me about Australia.'

'God. And were they all sentenced to death?'

Mahoney sighed inwardly. 'Many of them.'

'And did it worry you?' She looked at him earnestly.

He said. 'I was only the prosecutor. You learn to be objective. Or you'd become a shuddering wreck. Each case is just another set of facts. And the ultimate decision is the judge's.'

'But now you *are* the judge. So, how many death sentences have you had to pass?'

'None until – ' He corrected himself. 'None.'

She looked at him with wide blue eyes. He put his hands on her hips, leant forward and gently kissed her lips to shut her up about death sentences. She stood still, arms at her side, eyes open. 'Until tomorrow?'

Mahoney whispered against her cheek: 'I didn't say that. I'm going to sleep on it.'

She tilted back her head. 'The Realist School of Jurisprudence, huh? The judge's verdict depends on the state of his liver. How he slept. What he had for breakfast?'

Mahoney grinned. 'How do you know about the Realist School of Jurisprudence?'

She appealed: 'Oh, please don't sentence him to death!'

Mahoney held her hips. 'I'm afraid we can't discuss it, Katrina.'

She looked him. 'It wouldn't be proper? But surely judges can discuss things like that with their wives, for example?'

'They shouldn't. It would mean that the defendant was tried twice: once in the court, and again at the dinner table.'

'Or in bed?'

Mahoney smiled. 'Indeed.' And he pulled her against him and kissed her mouth again.

She let herself be kissed but did not yield. She said against his cheek: '*Oh, please don't hang him, Luke!*' Then: 'Oh, this is obscene!' Her eyes bright with tears.

He took his hands off her hips. He picked up his glass and drained it, looking her in the eye. 'What is?'

She declared: 'Us. Here we are, making love, while a man sits in a cell with his life in our hands.'

Making love? The most delicious statement he'd ever heard. He smiled. '*Our* hands?'

'*Yes*. Isn't that what the Realist School of Jurisprudence is about? How well the judge slept, and *who* he slept with! Was it good, was it disappointing? So I'm in on this too, Luke!'

Mahoney threw back his head and laughed. He wanted to hug her tight. He turned back into the sitting room, to the liquor cabinet. 'Let's talk about you, Katrina.'

She followed him earnestly. 'Like hell! If I'm going to sleep with you. And be part of that mystical process of deciding on a man's life called "sleeping on it".' She pointed out into the night. 'That's a primitive man! He should be judged by *his* standards, not by *ours*. His standards are the quality of a pig!'

Mahoney poured more whisky into his glass. 'Tell me about Australia. About your thesis.'

She demanded quietly: 'Are we going to make love? That's what all that kissy-face out there on the verandah was about, wasn't it? You want to make love, right?'

Mahoney wanted to burst into laughter and holler, Yes please! 'Right.' He grinned.

'*Right*,' she said. 'So I *am* involved.' She took his whisky glass and put it down. Then she plunged her mouth onto his.

And, oh, the blissful taste of her, and the wonderful feeling of her body thrust against him, her lovely breasts and loins and the warmth of her, the feel of her back and hips under his sliding hands. And to possess her was the most desperately important thing in the world; but she broke the kiss and leant back in his arms. 'On one condition.' She held up a finger. 'That you eat your dinner first.'

He wanted to laugh. 'And if I'm not hungry?'

'Nor am *I*. But you're not going to sleep on that decision on an empty stomach after all that booze. And – ' she picked up his whisky glass and tipped it into the ice bucket – 'wine only. And then . . . ' She leant forward and murmured into his mouth: 'Then I'm going to make sure you sleep so well you'll wake up feeling *wonderful* for that poor man . . . '

61

And he did wake up feeling wonderful. Absolutely shagged out, but absolutely wonderful.

The night was like a dream. He had lived long enough to know about love – and this felt very like it. Like honey, was his waking thought. Honey for the colour of her hair, honey for her skin, honey for her glorious body, honey for the taste of her. And all the hangovers in the world did not matter.

But he had not finished formulating his judgment.

He swung out of bed, went into the bathroom and slammed on the cold shower. He let it beat down on his head, trying to knock out the stunned feeling. He brushed his teeth vigorously, combed his wet hair and pulled on a tracksuit. He went back to the bedroom.

Katrina was in her long red cocktail dress, frantically pulling a brush through her tousled hair. 'Oh my God, this is dreadful, I slept right through.' She held a finger out at him, her brush arrested in mid-stroke. 'This is truly obscene!'

His mind wrestled briefly with that long red cocktail dress leaving his hotel. 'What time does the consul get up?'

'To hell with *my* reputation – it's *yours*! You – ' she jabbed a finger – 'haven't slept on your judgment!' She turned to the bed and tried to straighten it. 'Oh God, this is obscene!'

'Let me worry about my judgment. And I did sleep on it.'

'Like hell – you mostly slept on me!'

He grinned. 'Stop fussing with that bed and I'll drive you home.'

'You can't be seen driving me home at this hour! I'll walk!'

'In your cocktail dress?'

'I could be returning from a party at anybody's house. You – ' she jabbed a finger ' – are going to sit down with a pot of black coffee – ' Then she noticed the tracksuit he was wearing. 'Hey, why don't you lend me that? Then it'll look like I'm out for an early morning jog. Come on.'

'It'll be a bit big.'

'I'm a big girl, didn't you notice?' She unzipped, wriggled and the dress fell to her feet, and her lovely breasts bulged in her lacy red bra, her brief red panties clung. The beauty of her long legs made his heart turn over. She pulled the tracksuit trousers up to her waist, then rolled the top over. 'Now your sneakers. Three pairs of socks, please.' She feverishly pulled on the socks, rammed her feet into the running shoes. 'Flipperty-flop. Okay! Now *please* sit down and work!'

'Will you have dinner with me tonight? And lunch?'

'God, how can you even *think* about that now?' She kissed her finger and put it on his lips. 'Please work! Bye.' She started for the door, then pleaded: 'And *please* remember what I said! Okay, I won't say it again.' She hurried out the door.

Mahoney turned out onto the verandah. The sun was just coming up, golden green on the bananas and palms, and the world was young and soft and beautiful. Katrina emerged from the hotel onto the quiet street. She began jogging, towards the fragrant suburbs. Her feet flopping.

Mahoney watched her go, grinning. He thought: *What a lovely woman. What lovely legs.*

The courtroom was full when Mahoney entered at ten o clock.

Katrina was sitting in the front row of the public benches, in a very sober dress, looking very solemn. Mahoney sat down and everybody followed suit. He cleared his throat and said: 'Yesterday, the defendant was convicted of murder. The only matter for me to give a judgment on today is whether extenuating circumstances exist.' He paused to allow the interpreter to translate. He continued: 'Extenuating circumstances are facts surrounding the case which reduce *morally* – albeit not *legally* – the degree of the accused's guilt.' He paused. 'Mr Williams has argued strenuously that in the defendant's primitive community Mary's adultery so humiliated that it required him to make a dramatic response, to show his manhood, daub himself in war paint and to be very aggressive. He argued that this compelled the defendant to kill the deceased very dramatically when that man *further* insulted him – or appeared to do so – by offering him an inferior pig. Furthermore, argues Mr Williams, the defendant was in emotional turmoil, of jealousy. All this, Mr Williams argues, diminishes his moral, albeit not his *legal*, guilt in the eyes of a reasonable man, viewed both objectively and subjectively.'

Mahoney glanced across the courtroom at Katrina. She was staring at him. He went on: 'Against this argument I must, however, weigh some sobering facts. First, the matter of compensation. And this strikes at the root of Mr Williams' arguments – it is clear that just one, decent, presentable pig was enough to soothe the defendant sufficiently for him to control himself.' He glanced at Katrina, then repeated: '*One* pig. I do not consider that a reasonable man would consider a man who is so easily consoled as being in great emotional pain. Had the deceased but offered one *decent* pig, the defendant's humiliation, his loss of face, his pain, would have been assuaged.' He held up a finger. 'One respectable pig. Furthermore, a society which considers adultery so simply compensated is not a highly censorious one.' He paused for translation. Avoiding Katrina's eye. 'This brings me to Mr Williams' catch-all argument: namely that the defendant, labouring under an accumulation of his humiliation and personal pain, acted in hot blood in stabbing the deceased.' He sighed. 'But, unfortunately, the facts preclude such a finding.'

He saw Katrina put her hands to her face. She was staring at him through parted fingers. He continued grimly: 'Had the deceased been stabbed at the very first village, hot blood *might* have been a compelling argument in his favour. But the deceased was stabbed when the defendant had had plenty of time for his anger to cool. It had taken him a day to get to the first village – time in itself to cool off. There he conducted himself reasonably by local custom. It took him *another* day to reach the second village – more time to cool off. Where he again behaved properly, then he proceeded to the third village, which gave him yet another day to cool off. There, offered an *inferior* pig, he slew the deceased without any ado.' Mahoney spread his hands. 'Doubtless he was angered, but it was *not* his pain over Mary that angered him, but the inferiority of that pig.'

There was a stifled sob. Mahoney glanced up and saw Katrina's head down, in her hands. He sighed and continued: 'Accordingly it is clear that, in law, no extenuating circumstances should be found in this case.'

The interpreter translated. The defendant looked grimly passive. The two counsel got up, gave a little bow and sat again. Mahoney consulted his note, then took a breath to continue, when there was an anguished cry: *'Wait a minute!'*

Mahoney looked up, astonished. Everybody turned.

Katrina was bursting from the public benches into the well of the court, her eyes alight. She stopped beside Mr Williams at the bar. She blurted: 'I have something to say, please, My Lord!'

Mahoney stared at her, astonished. The orderly was striding towards her. 'Professor de la Rey – ' Mahoney began – 'this is the Supreme Court of Borneo – '

Katrina cried: *'And that's why I'm speaking up, My Lord, this man is Bornean and – '* The orderly grabbed her arm.

'Let her go, Mr Orderly!' Mahoney snapped. The orderly released her. Mahoney said tersely: 'Professor de la Rey, this constitutes contempt of court – '

'I'm not being contemptuous, My Lord – on the contrary I'm over-awed! *But this poor man – '* she jabbed a finger at the defendant – *'is too unsophisticated to say anything for himself – '*

Mahoney snapped: 'Court will adjourn for fifteen minutes!' He got up and turned for the door. As he swept through, he snapped to the registrar: 'Tell counsel I want to see them in my chambers!'

He slung off his wig and slumped down at his desk.

A minute later the two counsel were ushered in. Mahoney said, 'Sit down, gentlemen.' He sighed. 'Well, you will have gathered that I know Professor de la Rey socially. You probably saw me speaking to her at the magistrate's cocktail party. Nobody could fail to notice a lady as appealing as Professor de la Rey?'

Both counsel grinned, and nodded.

'Last night we had dinner together. During the course of the evening Professor de la Rey sought to discuss this case. Indeed, given the opportunity, she would have done her best to dissuade me from the judgment I have given so far.' He paused. 'Gentlemen, you have my assurance that not only did I refuse to discuss the case with her, but her would-be intervention affected me not a jot.'

Both counsel nodded.

'However,' Mahoney said, 'I have not yet finished my judgment – Professor de la Rey has jumped the gun. And the rest of my judgment is going to be that although, in strict law, no extenuating circumstances exist for the reasons I've given, I refuse to sentence him to death because one cannot apply strict English law to a man to whom human life is as cheap as the quality of a pig. I'm going to give him fifteen years – whereas if he was a white man I would undoubtedly have hanged him. If that's bad law, I don't give a damn. And that, gentlemen, was my decision before dining with Professor de la Rey last night. Okay?' He sighed. 'Now, turning to the question of what to do with her: to put her in the cells for contempt would be an unpleasant incident. That leaves me no alternative but to have her brought in here, reprimand her, and get her to shut up, so we get this business of sentencing over. Now, I would like you gentlemen to be present.' He called out: 'Mr Chan . . . '

A minute later Katrina was escorted in. The men stood up. Mahoney had to force the image of her nakedness from his mind. 'Sit down, Professor.'

'I'd rather stand, thank you, Your Honour – I mean My Lord.'

'Very well.' Mahoney sat. He said: 'Professor, I admire your courage in speaking up in court today. And I accept that you did so with the best of intentions. *But*, I must severely reprimand you.'

She stared at him defiantly. Her nervousness seemed to have gone. Mahoney continued: 'Now, the purpose of this meeting is not to hear what you want to say but to extract a promise that when court reconvenes you will keep quiet. Otherwise I will have you put in the cells.'

A wisp of a smile crossed her lovely lips and her eyebrows rose a fraction in challenge. Mahoney glared at her, then ended: 'And I wish to impress upon you that your well-intentioned intervention is totally irrelevant.'

She demanded: 'How do you know when you haven't listened to me?'

Mahoney sighed. 'Do you promise?'

Katrina's eyes widened. 'I apologise for disturbing the court! But I don't care if you lock me up, I'm going to say what I have to on behalf of that poor man you're about to sentence to death, Luke!' Both counsel suppressed smiles at her use of Mahoney's Christian name. She banged her breast. 'I'm a political scientist and I'm telling you that the big mistake you made today is in applying the Reasonable Man test to a primitive tribesman whose values are entirely different!'

'Professor de la Rey, I did not apply any so-called Reasonable Man test: I said, if I remember rightly, that the question of extenuating circumstances must be viewed through the eyes of a reasonable man, like the question of "reasonable doubt". Now this meeting is over.'

'I haven't finished yet! Here!' She thrust out her wrists dramatically. '*Manacle* me and throw me in the cells but I'm going to finish while you do so!' She glared, wrists outstretched. 'What about the Realist School of Jurisprudence?! Apply that to your reasonable man, My Lord, and see what you come up with! The Realist School of Jurisprudence says that justice all depends on the state of the judge's liver – whether he had a fight with his wife, et cetera – right? Well, this morning you had to assume the *role* of the reasonable man yourself! But were you fit for that job? What was the state of *your* liver this morning, Your Honour, after a heavy night's boozing and – ' she appeared to change it in her mouth – '*gallivanting*?'

Williams coughed to smother a guffaw – Davidson wiped his hand across his mouth. There was a moment's silence. Mahoney glared at her, then turned to counsel: 'If you gentlemen would excuse us?'

Williams and Davidson got hastily to their feet. They filed out straight-faced. Mahoney turned to Katrina. She said, wide-eyed: 'Oh God, I'm sorry, Luke.'

Mahoney sat down slowly. 'I don't believe this. You're making yourself very unpopular, Katrina de la Rey. You have one more minute.' He glanced at his watch.

She snorted. '*One* minute, huh?!' Her contrition was gone. 'Luke,' she held a finger out at him, 'you were a *wreck* this morning when you woke up. Hungover as hell! Hadn't eaten your dinner. Hadn't slept enough because you were banging me all night! And I *bet* you didn't have any breakfast! Did you?'

He was about to lie, to shut her up, but he murmured: 'Two Alka-Seltzer.'

She smote her forehead. '*God*! Do you honestly consider that you were in a fit state to assume the role of a reasonable man in judging a matter of life and death?'

Mahoney closed his eyes. 'Katrina, I've been dealing with matters of life and death all my life.'

'Hungover and all?'

He was about to assure her that, yes, like many lawyers, he had been dealing with hangovers all his life too. 'Anything else?'

'Yes! That Reasonable Man test is bullshit, Luke! You should be applying the standards and values of the defendant!'

Mahoney murmured: 'The Reasonable Tribesman's test?'

'Exactly!'

Mahoney nodded wearily. 'I see, I shouldn't view the facts through the eyes of a reasonable man – which is all I did – I should put myself into the skin of a primitive tribesman? And if Adolf Hitler were on trial today I should apply the Reasonable Nazi test? And if he was a soccer hooligan, I should apply the Reasonable Hooligan test?' He sighed. 'Anything else? Your minute's up, Katrina.'

Katrina snorted. She slumped her shoulders.

'No,' she said. 'That's it.' She added sullenly: 'Have I made *any* impression, Luke?'

Mahoney reached for his wig. 'Yes. You impress me as a very brave woman.' He came around the desk, and put a hand on her shoulder. 'I'm going back into court. Now, do you promise to keep quiet?'

She averted her eyes. 'I won't come in, I couldn't bear to hear the sentence. I'll go home and pack.'

He was astonished. '*Pack?* For what?'

She said wearily: 'Home. My plane to Singapore is tomorrow.'

He frowned at her. '*Tomorrow*. You didn't tell me *that*. You told me next week.'

'I'm due back at my desk on Thursday.'

Mahoney said: 'You're *not* leaving for South Africa tomorrow, Katrina. Your job can wait another week.' He added with finality: 'We'll talk about it over lunch.'

She sighed. 'How the hell can we be talking about a nice lunch at a time like this? I couldn't eat a damn thing.'

'You can't spend the *night* with me, kick up a fuss in *court*, and refuse *lunch*, for Christ's sake!'

She snorted softly. 'Is it proper for judges to be lunching with ladies who're in contempt . . . ?'

62

He took her to lunch at the yacht club, to get her away from the judicial associations of his hotel suite. But it didn't work. 'Oh *Gawd*,' she moaned, 'I made such an ass of myself. Why didn't you *tell* me you weren't going to hang him?'

Mahoney smiled. 'I told you I couldn't discuss it. Now forget it, Kat.'

She put her hand on his. 'Oh, forgive me for blurting out, Luke. But I'd never have forgiven myself if I hadn't spoken up and you had hanged him – as your judgment gave every indication of doing.' Then she smirked wanly. 'And, I've never been to bed with a judge before. Even an acting one.'

'Yes,' Mahoney smiled, 'I can tell.' Then he sat forward and said: 'This is a very important matter I'm going to put to you, Katrina, so hear me out. After that we can discuss it.' She looked surprised. 'Kat, you can't leave tomorrow. Your work can wait. It's much, much more important that we have more time together. It's vital. To learn more about each other. Because I want you. I know enough about life to know that I can't know yet, but it feels like I'm well on the way to being in love with you, Katrina de la Rey.'

She looked at him steadily. 'After one night?'

'One *glorious* night. And twelve months of remembering our meeting in New York. And one murder trial.' He gave her a solemn smile. 'And I want you to know how much I admire your courage for speaking up like that. Courtrooms are very daunting places. I could see you trembling. But you nonetheless had the sheer bravery to throw yourself into the fray for what you believed was right.' He smiled at her. 'You are a very principled person, Katrina.'

She averted her eyes. 'Principled, My Lord?. I went to bed with you last night with the express purpose of persuading you, with sexual blandishments, to change your mind. To *seduce* you into not passing the death sentence.'

He frowned at her. 'That's the reason you made love?'

'Fucked you. Yes.'

He wondered whether he had heard that right. 'The *only* reason?'

She said firmly: 'Yes. Because there's no future in it, Luke.'

He said: 'I don't believe you.'

She sighed. Then: 'No, I don't either, though I'm trying hard. I also did it because I wanted to. I wanted to that first night in New York. There was no future in it last night either, but when you came on heavy I thought what the hell, kill two birds with one stone, get laid and get that poor man off the hook.'

Mahoney laughed. She smiled wryly. 'But,' she said, 'you refused even to discuss it, despite my spectacular performance. And for that I have grudging respect.'

Mahoney put his hand on hers. 'But maybe there *is* a future in it, if you stay another week.'

She fiddled with her glass. 'What will we find out in a week? We won't be over the honeymoon, we'll still have stars in our eyes.'

'Have you – got stars in your eyes?'

'You can't see them? Good. I'm trying hard not to have.'

He squeezed her hand. 'Okay, make it two weeks.'

She looked at him. 'I'm quite sure I'll still have stars in my eyes. And after that, what then?'

He said: 'We decide whether we want to stay together.'

She sighed and shook her head. She said sadly: 'After two weeks I've got to give up my university post, sell my house, my car, my furniture? One only makes a big decision like that after a much longer time, Luke.' She shook her head again. 'And, what about my *politics*. I would have to be the one to change, not you. I would be the one to have to leave all the things I hold dear. And one can't make momentous decisions like that after fourteen nights, no matter how wonderful.' She looked at him. 'So it would be an exercise in futility.'

And, oh God, he wanted to go back to Africa. It wouldn't be futile if he was going back to Africa. 'And happiness.'

'Not if we can't do anything about it. That will bring unhappiness.'

'If you stay for two weeks, I'll go to see you in South Africa.'

'I thought you dared not go back to South Africa because they may arrest you over those explosives found in your car.'

'That was over twenty years ago. And anyway, Patti Gandhi cleared my name. I'll take the chance.'

She sighed. 'When? And for how long? Six weeks?' She put her other hand on his. 'Luke, it's not going to work. We don't live in the same country. It's simply not practical. And I don't *want* it to work, I don't *want* to fall madly in love with you and break my heart.' She shook her head. 'I don't want to leave my country, my people, my culture.' She looked at him earnestly. 'If I spent another week with you it would break my heart to leave. I want my heart intact.' She smiled at him sadly. 'We're two ships which collided in the night, Luke. We must now sail on, grateful the incident was without serious structural damage.'

'You can take it from me that ships that collide in the night have to undergo an Inquiry. That takes two weeks at least.'

She smiled. 'This is a case of hit-and-run.'

He held up two fingers. 'Just a fortnight.'

'Hit-and-run.'

He held up one finger. 'Okay, one week.'

'Hit-and-run. Defendant in default.'

'Okay, then I'm giving hot pursuit.' He snapped his fingers for the waiter. 'The bill, please. '

'Aren't we having lunch here?'

'In the privacy of my hotel. Where I can begin my hot pursuit. Nobody collides with me and gets away with it!'

63

It was a wonderful week. And tremendous fun, getting away with it so nobody knew that the American consul's guest – that good-looking blonde who was seen jogging every sunrise – was having a wild fling with the visiting judge. It was the talk of the town, from the consul's maid who reported in the market that the blonde missie slept till noon, to the hotel waiter who confirmed that she had lunch and dinner in the visiting judge's suite every day, to the chambermaid who confirmed that two people had definitely slept in the judge's bed – 'You can always tell' – to the police officers who reported that the judge looked shagged out, to Williams and Davidson who said he had a hard time keeping the smile off his face, to the Garuda Airways clerk who confirmed that Miss de la Rey had postponed her departure. The only place where the affair wasn't published was the *Borneo Weekly Mail*, which confined its attention to Mahoney's light sentences.

Not until Saturday did they discuss what was going to happen. When she arrived back at the suite for lunch, Mahoney took her in his arms. He said: 'It can't end tomorrow, Kat.'

She looked at him. 'But it must.'

'Stay another week.'

She smiled sadly. 'No, darling Luke. It's been wonderful. But now I must go home. We've held our Inquiry.'

'And what did it reveal?'

She turned out of his arms. She walked out onto the verandah and looked down at the garden.

'That it was unwise of me to stay. That now I must pay the price. If I had gone home last Sunday it would just have been an . . . accident, a one-night stand. Now it's an international disaster.'

'There doesn't have to be a price, only a prize: happiness. You must stay.'

'And *really* break my heart? At the moment it's only cracked.'

He put his hands on her shoulders. And, oh, the feel and scent of her. He heard himself say: 'Stay forever. We'll get married.'

The words hung in the air. Awesome and simple. And wonderful. Get married, it was as wonderful and simple as that. She stared out over the garden, quite still.

'After one week you ask me to marry you?'

'Yes!' It felt wonderful. He had never felt more certain of anything in his life.

She closed her eyes and smiled. 'And I'm almost sufficiently crazy to accept. But, a small corner of my mind remains unaddled.' She turned and faced him. Her eyes were moist. 'Thank you, darling Luke. But it wouldn't work.'

'But you love me.'

She closed her eyes for a moment. 'I'm *in* love with you, maybe. In *lust* with you, certainly. Crazy about you, definitely. But it's impossible that I *love* you yet. Or you me. And I don't want to love you, Luke. I don't want to leave my country, my people.'

Suddenly Mahoney knew loud and clear what he had to do. He finally made the decision he had been trying to make for years, the decision that had been coming to a head all week. *And no way was he going to let this woman out of his life*. He said: 'Marry me, and I'll leave the service and we'll live in South Africa.'

She was taken aback. She said: 'I won't accept responsibility for your abandoning your career, your whole way of life – '

He wanted to laugh it: 'You don't understand, Kat – I've had enough. Life's been good, I even find law quite interesting in a perverse sort of way – but I've *done* that now. There's nothing for me in the service except another twenty years of the same. I can do this job with one hand tied behind my back. And if I go to one more colonial cocktail party I'll go right up the fucking wall. Or if I have to listen to one more counsel fucking up a perfectly good case.' He shook his head. 'I want to make the most of the rest of my life – '

'How?' she asked quietly.

He said: 'Writing, Kat. That's what I've always wanted to do, that's what I used to do pretty damn well. I only quit journalism because I was fired.'

'You'd go back to being a journalist after being a judge?'

'No, Kat – a *writer*. A thinker. A contributor – an historian. Perhaps a novelist.'

She said soberly: 'You yourself said there's no hope for South Africa. And I tend to agree with you – '

'We're not going to discuss that again, Kat – in fact I *do* think there's some hope. Mr Gorbachev is winding down communism's global ambitions, when they pull out of Africa the communist tyrants are going to collapse and there's going to be a whole new ball-game.' He took her in his arms urgently. 'Let *me* worry about what I'm going to do in South Africa.'

She shook her head against his cheek. 'You're English and I'm an Afrikaner, and that's how I intend to continue – '

'I'm a South African.'

'An *English* South African. And they're the second-worst kind!' She half-giggled against his shoulder. She squeezed him and continued

447

resolutely: 'We have irreconcilable differences. What are you going to do in my volkstaat?'

'Let's worry about your volkstaat when it happens.'

'You don't believe it'll happen, huh?'

He started to say No but changed it in his mouth: 'I don't believe it's a problem between us – '

'Because you don't believe it'll ever come to pass?' She turned out of his arms and walked to the balcony rail. 'Luke, do you think the Afrikaners are any less determined than the Israelis?' She shook her head. 'It's what the Great Trek was all about. It's the culmination of the Kaffir Wars, the Battle of Blood River, the Boer War, the 1914 Rebellion. *That's* our irreconcilable difference. Because I believe it will happen. And I want to do my utmost to make it happen.' She shook her head at him. 'You wouldn't want to live there, Luke. And I wouldn't want you to try. You wouldn't be happy. And that would make me unhappy.' She took a deep, sad breath, then came back and kissed him. 'No, darling Luke. It's been wonderful. I'm going to keep it wonderful. As a memory to be cherished.'

He started to speak but she put her finger on his lips.

'Please don't let's talk about it anymore? Please let's be happy? Shall we have a drink?' She made her lovely eyes sparkle. 'Do you want to make love?'

Then she dropped her face into her hands and sobbed.

That Sunday morning was very sad. She made no pretence of jogging back to the Consul's residence. They were awake at sunrise. They lay in each other's arms in the awfulness of parting. They had hardly slept.

Finally she whispered: 'I'd better get ready.'

He tightened his arm around her.

'Please let me get up.'

He let go of her. She got off the bed. She walked to the window.

'It's a beautiful day.'

'It's a terrible day.'

She smiled sadly at the morning. And her naked beauty in the sunrise made his heart turn over. Her golden, curvaceous body, her long strong legs, her long blonde hair glinting down her golden back, the line of her shoulders, her neck, her perfect breasts.

'I love you,' he said.

'I know the feeling,' she said.

*   *   *

At nine o'clock he drove her to the little airport. The first passengers were already crossing the tarmac to the aircraft. After she had checked in she said: 'Please don't wait.'

'Of course I'm going to wait.'

'Please, I couldn't bear it. Go now.'

'I'm waiting.'

Her eyes were moist. 'Goodbye, darling Luke.'

'I love you.'

She smiled. 'It's been lovely.'

'I love you and I love you and I love you.'

Her eyes brimmed. 'Goodbye.'

'And you love me!'

She shook her head.

'Not yet.' She kissed him hard, then turned to go.

He held her. 'Will you write?'

She kissed him again, hard. 'No,' she whispered into his mouth. 'Please go now.'

She turned abruptly for the door. She held out her boarding pass and walked through.

Mahoney watched her cross the tarmac. She walked briskly, carrying her briefcase, her long hair adrift in the small breeze, shiny in the sun.

She did not look back. She mounted the stairs, and she was gone.

He stayed until the aircraft had disappeared into the sky. And even then he stayed, sitting behind the wheel of his car, staring through the windscreen. His eyes were burning. And he knew what he had to do.

PART XI

VIOLENCE, VIOLENCE, BOYCOTTS, BOYCOTTS

ANGOLAN WAR ENDS –
CUBAN AND SA TROOPS WITHDRAW

POWER-STRUGGLE AFTER
PRESIDENT BOTHA SUFFERS STROKE

FW DE KLERK BECOMES PRESIDENT OF
SOUTH AFRICA – PROMISES 'GREAT INDABA'

64

She did not write. He telephoned her a dozen times in the next month but he only got her answering machine: he left impassioned messages, but she did not respond.

He hated Borneo. It had been a wonderful place when she was here, but now it was dead, empty. And he was powerless to do anything about it: he was nailed down here for another two months. Had he been in Hong Kong he would have wangled some unpaid leave and flown to South Africa to talk some sense into her.

'To *fuck* some sense into her?' Max said on the telephone.

'Max, this is serious.'

'How serious?'

'*That* serious.'

Max paused. 'You don't mean *that* serious? Not . . . *marriage*?'

'Yes,' Mahoney sighed.

Silence again. Then: 'Please tell me you mean "if needs be". Please reassure me, your old buddy and long-suffering boss, that you only mean "*if absolutely necessary*". Please don't tell me that after one week of carnal passion, following a veritable lifetime of carnal passions, you've lost your marbles? Didn't you say she was a Boer?'

'I said that she is an Afrikaner. There's a difference. She's a *patriot.*'

'*Who wants to perpetuate apartheid?*'

'I expressly said that she does not, nor has she ever approved of apartheid.'

'But her buddies do?'

Mahoney sighed. 'Max, I am hereby formally putting you on notice that when I return to Hong Kong I am applying for – and expect to *get* – two months' unpaid compassionate leave, so I can go to South Africa and bully this woman.'

'Sounds as if she may bully you. Well, I promise you nothing, me ole mate. Because the Chief Justice tells me that when you come back he needs a judge in Tuvalu for three months and he fancies you for the job, you're his boy – '

'No!' Mahoney cried. 'No, no, a thousand times no!'

'Listen, he told me he wants to *confirm you* as a full-blown judge now after the stout job you've done in wildest Borneo. That's a nice little salary-hike. Fortunately, he doesn't know you've lost your marbles over this Boer woman, or he'd think again.'

'Max,' Mahoney said, 'get this straight, I do not wish to be a judge. Anywhere.'

'So you wish to play second-fiddle to me for the rest of your professional life. *Deputy* Director? Fine, that suits me, you're a good deputy. But the salary's not as good as a judge's, is it? Okay,' Max sighed, 'so you want some unpaid leave when you get back. I can't guarantee anything, but I won't tell the Chief Justice that you say he can stick Tuvalu up his arse, in the hopes you return to your senses.' He added: 'Luke? Is this really love?' Mahoney snorted. 'Can't you persuade this woman to come out here? Nice life.'

'*That*,' Mahoney said, 'is the purpose of my application for unpaid leave.'

'Okay.' Max brightened. 'Now you're talking more sense. Surely to Christ you're not seriously thinking of resigning and going out there to live? It sounds like chaos, on the news. A bloodbath . . .'

Every day Mahoney got the news on the BBC, once a week or so his South African newspapers came trickling through the mail via Hong Kong, but he could not sit down at his word processor because of *her*. All this news was about *her*. And *she* did not answer his letters.

'It's all good news,' Mahoney shouted on the telephone to his New York publisher, 'because apartheid is almost finished. But it'll take a couple of years yet – '

'No rush?' Bill Summers complained. 'I haven't had anything from you for two months and things are moving fast. Remember we want to be the first book published. I wish you'd stop playing at lawyers and fax us an update. For example, how important is it that the war has ended in Angola?'

'It's highly important. The fifty thousand Cubans fighting for the Angolan government were paid for by the Soviet Union, and after the war the Cubans were going to invade South Africa. But it's turned into the USSR's Vietnam so Gorbachev's said the Cubans have to withdraw. Sighs of relief. So peace has been negotiated. Furthermore the peace treaty says that Angola cannot allow the ANC to have any bases there, which is another blow to them: not only have they lost their paymaster, but they've had to move. They're even less of a threat now.'

'So the reform process is likely to be speeded up, surely? Luke, you've got to send us this stuff. What is the significance of the row over the presidency after PW Botha had his stroke?'

'The reformers in his party wanted to get rid of President Botha because he was too slow. But he didn't want to relinquish control. For health reasons he had to resign as leader of the party but he wanted somehow to hang onto being president. There was a showdown in the cabinet. He threatened to fire them all. Finally he resigned and this new guy FW de Klerk became president.'

'And that's good news?'

'Look, Botha was called the "Big Crocodile" because he was so auto-cratic. Although he's earned his place in history for taking the first steps in reform – the Tri-Cameral Parliament, for example – he was too dyed-in-the-wool to abolish apartheid – he just wanted to give it a human face. Like Gorbachev wants to reform communism, not abolish it. But, as Machiavelli said, the lot of the reformer is that he is the first victim of his reforms. And the same is likely to happen to Gorbachev, by the way.'

'Brilliant!' Bill Summers cried from twelve thousand miles away. 'Write it just like that! Throwing in all that Machiavelli shit. And Gorbachev. So, what do you make of this new guy, De Klerk, is it?'

'We don't know much about him, Bill. I remember him saying a couple of years back that his party would never repeal the Group Areas Act, residential segregation. So maybe we can't expect too much of him. However, yes, I'm cautiously optimistic about him, he may grasp the nettle which Botha couldn't. He's in his early fifties, he's a lawyer, and in his first parliamentary speech as the new leader he promised the nation "a totally changed South Africa, free of racism and domination of any kind". He also said the time has come for the "Great Indaba".'

'Does that mean he's going to unban the ANC?'

Mahoney sighed. 'I don't know. The ANC has been the enemy too long. But he'll have to release Nelson Mandela for the Great Indaba – it will lack credibility if Mandela isn't present. So, he may unban the ANC.'

'Christ,' Bill Summers said, 'that would be something – the world's most famous prisoner coming out.' He added: 'And if Mandela is released surely others will be too – like your Pamela? Sorry, I mean Patti Gandhi, I always think of her as Pamela Patel.'

Mahoney closed his eyes. 'I hope so. But I'm not counting on it.'

Bill Summers snorted. 'I wish to hell you'd write *that* book, the sequel to *Alms* – we'd get great publicity from Mandela's release.'

Mahoney said, to shut him up: 'I'll think about it.'

'Please. Meanwhile, what'll the right wing do about the Great Indaba, and Mandela being released? Up in arms? A civil war,' he added optimistically. 'Luke,' he sighed, 'you want these journals published, don't you? They're very timely, with South Africa coming to a head. But you've dried up on me. *Please* get your ass to an anchor.'

Mahoney got his ass to an anchor. He spread out his newspaper cuttings. His notes. He sighed. He paced.

NEW ELECTIONEERING HOTS UP

As violence rages, President de Klerk has called a new election to refresh his mandate.

As the Conservative Party howls for a return to Verwoerdian apartheid, FW de Klerk promises to negotiate a new non-racist constitution with black leaders. He promises one-man-one-vote, participation of all races in government, protection for minority and group rights, guarantees for all to pursue their own culture, checks and balances to ensure that no group dominates the others. He promises to submit this new constitution to the electorate for approval.

Sounds good, but haven't we heard this before?

The snag lies in the guarantees on group rights. Bluntly, this means the preservation of whites-only residential areas and whites-only schools, while the whites will have a veto over uncongenial legislation. Will the blacks accept that?

And with which black leaders will the government negotiate? Will it unban the ANC, PAC, AZAPO, et al for this purpose? Will the right-wing Afrikaners accept that?

There is no promise to repeal the Group Areas Act – only to allow for more 'grey' areas. Nor is there a promise to repeal the Separate Amenities Act – only to upgrade amenities and to desegregate 'where practical'.

But does this manifesto conceal a greater secret agenda? With the Conservative Party baying for their blood, does the government dare to tell the electorate what they really propose to do?

I suspect they are stealing a march. With the Cubans withdrawing from Angola, the albatross of Namibia and the Angolan War off the government's back, with the USSR in shambolic retreat, De Klerk will be able to negotiate from strength with an enfeebled ANC. Why risk that opportunity by frightening the voters?

President de Klerk has won his mandate to reform South Africa. The ruling National Party has now been in power for a remarkable forty-one years. What is truly remarkable, however, is how much that party has changed in those years: the Conservative Party has hijacked the old National Party programme of apartheid, the National Party has hijacked the Democratic Party's programme of reform, leaving the Democrats looking around for somewhere to sit. And equally remarkable is the way the electorate has acquiesced in this game of musical chairs.

The majority of the electorate has gone along with whatever the National Party have proposed as they shifted from hard right in 1948 to left in 1989. What does this prove? That they realise at last that apartheid is a failure? Yes, partly. But would they have voted for the Democratic Party if the Nationalists had not hijacked their policy? Definitely not. Why not? Because South African voters are sheep? Partly, but it goes much deeper than that: it goes into the South African soul – their fear of the Black Peril. But if the Nationalist leaders say it's okay to venture out of the laager, then it's okay. If anybody else says so, forget it. It has to be the Afrikaner who leads this country belatedly into the twentieth century.

That is why Botha was so important in history. It was the Big Crocodile himself who said to his volk 'Adapt or Die'. So the volk braced itself to adapt.

De Klerk claims to have a mandate for all kinds of wonders. All beaches have already been declared open to all races. Wow. He has announced that the Separate Amenities Act will be totally repealed early next year, in 1990. This is a big deal. It is a direct breach of his electoral promise that the act would only be 'amended where practical'. The Conservative Party is outraged. They have taken to the streets, vowing to enforce God's law. And so we have grotesque scenes at public places like Boksburg Lake . . .

Boksburg is one of the numerous satellite cities on the gold reef surrounding Johannesburg. It is a mining and industrial town with unlovely suburbs of drab, lower-middle-class houses of depressing post-war architecture. One of the few pretty places is Boksburg Lake, in the centre of town. It is man-made, surrounded by lawns, and trees, where white people go to have barbecues on a Sunday, paddle and maybe row a boat.

Unlovely Boksburg is typical of many industrial towns in South Africa; it is predominantly Afrikaans-speaking and the city council is very much Conservative Party oriented. Apartheid is strictly enforced, and the numerous non-whites in the surrounding townships know better than to argue about it. But now that this new President de Klerk had announced that the Separate Amenities Act would be repealed, the Conservative Party was up in arms, and the non-whites were getting uppity. A nationwide conference of four hundred officials from Conservative-controlled town councils met and noisily agreed to reinforce apartheid strictly in their municipalities, in defiance of the president.

This sunny Sunday, a convoy of half a dozen cars carrying non-white families arrived at Boksburg Lake to have a picnic. They were mostly Indians and Coloureds. One was a Mr Patel, a shopkeeper; one of the Coloureds was a Mr Solomon Botha, a school-teacher, distant relative of the many Afrikaner Bothas that inhabit South Africa whose forebear had been born on the wrong side of the blanket. Mr Botha had brought his black cookboy, Edward, along to make the barbecue, and Mr Patel had brought along his black maid, Elizabeth, to help Edward. Another Coloured couple, the Bezuidenhouts, also shopkeepers, were also Afrikaner-descended. The only real black members of the party were Mr Simon Tandiwe, a plumber, and his wife, Pakitcheni – so named because she had been born in the kitchen – and their robust son, Samson. They were all solid citizens and members of a UDF street-committee; encouraged by President de Klerk's announcement they had resolved to picnic together at Boksburg Lake in defiance of the City Fathers.

The AWB were waiting for them, in force, wearing their khaki uniforms, with the swastika-like emblems on their sleeves, pistols in their holsters, truncheons and sjamboks in their hands. The Separate Amenities Act was still the law until formally repealed, and so were the municipal by-laws made thereunder, and they were going to teach these cheeky bladdy kaffirs – and President Frikkie de Klerk – who was boss in Boksburg, hey. The AWB were waiting around the gate to the Boksburg Lake, lining the entrance road, patrolling the barbecue stands, slapping their sjamboks at weeds and butterflies in anticipation.

At eleven o'clock the convoy of non-whites arrived. The AWB stalwarts allowed them to pass through the gate unchallenged, then followed them along the lakeshore to their picnic spot. They allowed them to unload their baskets, to proceed to their selected barbecue stand; allowed them to start preparing their fires and start unpacking, so that they were definitely contravening the Separate Amenities Act. Then the AWB moved in.

A hundred beefy khaki-clad stalwarts encircled the families, and the AWB leader strode up to Mr Botha and said: 'Get out, in the name of the law, hey! This lake is for whites only!'

'But – ' Mr Botha began, and the AWB leader, whose name was also Botha, slashed him with his sjambok, and the grotesque spectacle began.

The spectacle of a hundred AWB men chasing a score of non-white men, women and children, thrashing them with their sjamboks, kicking over their picnic baskets, their camp chairs, hurling their food and drink into Boksburg Lake, thrashing screaming women and children as they fled back to their cars. Mr Patel and Mr Solomon Botha and Mr Bezuidenhout and Mr Tandiwe tried to stand their ground and to defend their fleeing families, but they were thrashed and punched and kicked. Samson kicked an AWB man in the balls and had ten men kick his ribs in before he was dragged into his father's car. The convoy of cars containing the screaming, weeping, bruised and bloody women and children was chased as it fled, the AWB men beating the vehicles with their sjamboks. Then, as the last car roared through the gates, a cheer went up, and the AWB leader shouted: '*And tell your friend President de Klerk the same will happen to him . . .* '

And then the Berlin Wall came crashing down.

It was astonishing melodrama; it brought tears to the eyes and a laugh to the heart. There on the television screens was the spectacle of the Berlin Wall being demolished by thousands of jubilant Germans of both east and west, cranes taking great bites out of it; slabs of mortar tumbling down; dust rising up; Germans joyfully getting stuck into the hated wall with picks and sledge-hammers. There was not a sign of the killer East German guards who had manned the watch-towers. The Checkpoint Charlie gates were wide open, people flooding through tumultuously.

It was the night before Mahoney left Borneo. He stared at the television, a smile all over his face. It was wonderful, this physical destruction of the symbol of oppression, this dancing on the grave of communism, this taunting jubilation – it was a wonderful malicious outburst of the triumph of freedom at last, of People Power. It was wonderful to imagine the scenes beyond that crumbling wall, the Stasi security police scurrying, frightened, disowning their uniforms. And over there in the suburbs the tyrant Honecker frantically packing his bags to flee to Moscow . . .

Mahoney went to the liquor cabinet and poured himself a stiff whisky. Then he walked to his word processor, and rubbed his hands with relish. He flexed his fingers and began to type: 'And next will be the apartheid wall.'

65

When you're lying in the arms of a beautiful woman, it's easy to say: Love was never like this. When you're dining by candlelight, looking into her lovely eyes, at her sensuous mouth, her shiny hair, talking about everything under the sun, being immensely intellectual, so reasonable, granting points of view, understanding each other, then it's easy to say: Conversation was never like this. When you're swimming naked together in the sultry sea, her lovely body silvery in the moon-light, it's easy to feel that lust was never like this. When you're watching this woman walk away from you across the tarmac with tears in her eyes, it's easy to convince yourself she's really madly in love, even though she's just told you she isn't yet. When you're back in congested Hong Kong and tonight you've got to put on your dinner jacket again and go to yet another goddamn colonial party and tomorrow you're going into court again for yet another goddamn case and it's going to be like this for the next twenty years it's easy to say: What the hell am I doing this for? When you're writing the family journals and Africa is so vivid and romantic, it's easy to feel that back there is where you really belong.

But then you watch the news on television and there's the smoke barrelling up from the townships, the running battles, the bodies, the Caspirs, the riot police, Inkatha and the UDF knocking the living shit out of each other, UDF knocking the living shit out of AZAPO and the PAC, and you think, Oh God, will Africa never change? And you wonder what the hell you're doing, thinking about going back to Africa. And you read about the economy in crisis, the workers on strike again, and you look at your bank balance and you think: Where the hell can a beat-up lawyer like me earn money like this? And that view down there is beautiful, and this A-Grade apartment is spacious and gracious, and the trial starting tomorrow may be a pain in the arse but nobody promised you a barrel of laughs if you became a lawyer. You don't have to accept these fucking dinner parties. And she's just returned the air ticket you sent her and she doesn't write and so she *doesn't* love you, you're fooling yourself, the woman is *serious* when she says we're just two ships that passed in the night, a holiday fling, a one-week stand. And there really *is* no future in it: what have you got in common with a bunch of Boers trying to live in a volkstaat? They're talking bullshit anyway, they won't get their volkstaat but they'll cause a bloodbath while they try. Goddamn Boers, still fighting the Kaffir Wars. So what are you doing, imagining you're in love with one of them? Just give it another month or two and your imagination will go away.

But his imagination did not go away, it did *not* feel like he was imagining it. And he did not know what the hell to do.

Then a letter from Lisa Rousseau arrived.

Ironically, it was not her reference to Katrina which made him put in another application for unpaid leave, nor was it her conviction that a new era was about to dawn in South Africa – what made up Mahoney's mind were the last two paragraphs:

> *I have it on good authority that, as a gesture of goodwill, a number of political prisoners will soon be released, the most important being Nelson Mandela (what a splash that will make!). But this may include your famous friend Patti Gandhi. I visited her in prison last week; she is very excited, and convinced she'll be free soon. She is as beautiful as ever – Asian women have a way of improving with age. I am telling you this, dear Luke, because again she wanted to talk about you. I told her what little I know from our few letters. She is very impressed by* Big Trouble *and is very proud of* Alms for Oblivion. *'My book' she calls it. She said it had 'sustained her for years'. She asked me to send you her love.*
>
> *I am quite sure, from her demeanour, that she thinks she's still in love with you, Luke. The purpose of this letter is to advise you, as my dear long-standing friend (note that I did not say 'old'), that you may face a certain emotional confusion when and if Patti is released, because I gather from Katrina (though she refuses to discuss it) that you got rather fond of each other in Borneo. I feel dreadfully sorry for Patti, and I know you do too. Nuff said.'*

Mahoney stared across his chambers.

Patti Gandhi being released.

And, *oh*, the thought of it brought tears to his eyes. Of joy, for her sake. He could hardly bear to imagine her feelings on walking out of those prison gates, the feelings of the open sky, the open land. What he wanted was for her to be happy. Gloriously happy for the rest of her life.

It was the first time she had sent a message to him in twenty years.

'Certain emotional confusion,' Lisa had said.

Mahoney closed his eyes. Yes, confusion. Oh yes, he wanted to see her, and hold her tight. Rejoice with her, welcome her back into the world. And yes, he could imagine the feel of her in his arms, her lips, her body which had given him such bliss . . . But the hard, emotionally confusing fact was that though he wept for joy for her he could not take her back. Too much had happened. Too much water had passed under the bridge. The hard fact was that it was Katrina's body he wanted in his arms – he thought he was in love with Katrina now.

And the only fair thing to do was to go to South Africa to verify this fact.

As he was paying for it himself – and not the Hong Kong government – he flew economy class and not first, and that was enough to remind him that working in Hong Kong wasn't so bad: he'd forgotten the difference. The Chinese man sitting next to him had a basket of live crabs which didn't smell too good, and from Bombay he found himself next to a black man who smelt no better. At Nairobi he upgraded himself to first class to get some sleep. But he could not, and as he looked down at the mauve-brown vastness of Africa, knowing that the roads were broken up and the forests destroyed and the wildlife shot out and nothing worked anymore, Hong Kong and his apartment did not look so bad at all. And when the plane came in over Johannesburg, spread over the vast brown veld with no reason for being there except those huge yellow mine dumps, no mountains, no sea, no rivers, the seething black townships sprawled all around, it was hard to remember the good times even with a row of beers inside him.

You can't go backwards in life, he told himself; there was never any hope and there isn't any now – if a new South Africa dawns the AWB will create a bloodbath while they lose their Third War of Liberation and the blacks will fuck up what's left. So what the hell had he been dreaming about when he burnt the midnight oil writing all that romantic bullshit about going 'home'? So, okay, he told himself, it's a good thing you came back to check it out, so the experiment is a success. All you've got to do now is see how you truly feel about Katrina after four months apart and then get your ass back to Hong Kong, with or without her. And be very prepared for the fact that it'll probably be without. Maybe, though it feels like the real thing, you'll realise when you see her it was just a wonderful holiday fling, to be kept only as a memory – and if that's the case the experiment is also a success.

In which case where does that leave Patti?

He stared out of the window, then sighed.

The same as last week, he said. You've made your decision about Patti. You love her as a person but the old feelings are all over. Irretrievable. Maybe this journey started out as an exercise to confirm that, and looking out of this window right now it is confirmed, so that experiment is a success also.

So that only left the experiment of Katrina de la Rey.

So enjoy the experiment! He tossed back his whisky and fastened his seatbelt for landing. And, oh yes, he was very excited about seeing Katrina.

It certainly did not feel as if he was coming home when he stepped out onto the tarmac. Hearing those Afrikaans accents again took him right back to Colonel Krombrink. (*Thank God Katrina didn't sound like that!*) And at the immigration desk the officer looked up his name on a computer screen, pressed a button and told him to stand aside. The unsmiling security policeman who appeared said: 'What's the purpose of your visit, hey, sir?'

Jesus Christ. 'To exercise my legal right of entry to the land of my birth!'

'And what's your job, hey?'

Jesus. He was angrily pleased to say: 'Director of Public Prosecutions, Hong Kong.' He left out the 'Deputy'.

The policeman appeared unimpressed. 'Where are you staying?'

'Where I like! By the way, *is* this the *new* South Africa we read about overseas?'

The policeman said: 'You're in the computer, Mr Mahoney, hey.'

'In the computer indeed? For what offence?'

'That's our business.'

'Then why the hell are you telling me?!'

'To let you know, hey.'

Mahoney seethed. 'Can I proceed now, or do I call a lawyer?'

The man thrust his passport back at him and turned away.

Mahoney was angry. He emerged into the huge marbled Arrivals hall. He found the Hertz desk and filled in a car-hire form. He gave the girl his credit card. Then the telephone rang. The girl answered, then said: 'Mr Mahoney?' She passed him the telephone.

'Hullo?' Mahoney said, mystified.

A heavy Afrikaans accent intoned: 'Welcome back to South Africa, Mr Mahoney!'

'Who is this?'

There was a chuckle. 'This, Mr Mahoney, is your old friend, Colonel Krombrink. General Krombrink now. How are you, hey?'

Mahoney was astonished. He looked around, almost expecting the bastard to be visible. 'Where are you, *General* Krombrink? Hiding in the Oude Meester brandy advertisement?'

Another chuckle. 'No, man, I'm calling you from Head Office, hey, one of my men jus' alerted me to your arrival and said you were at the Hertz desk. Thought I'd phone to say hullo.'

'Well, hullo there,' Mahoney snapped, 'and goodbye!' As he began to put the telephone down Krombrink said: 'Mr Mahoney, we're so pleased to see you've done so well. A top lawyer, hey. And all those books. I particularly enjoyed the scene about me in *Alms for Oblivion*, but why didn't you use my real name?'

'Go to hell!'

'Agh, Mr Mahoney, wouldn't you like to drop around to my office for a nice cup of tea?'

Mahoney closed his eyes. God, this frightened him. 'No, thank you. Now if you'll excuse me – '

'Where are you staying, Mr Mahoney? With your friend Professor Katrina de la Rey?'

Jesus. They even knew that? How? '*Is* this the new South Africa?'

'Agh, yes, this is the new South Africa, Mr Mahoney. The ANC is irrelevant, hey, now that Russia and the Cubans gone home because there's no more money in Mr Gorbachev's piggy bank and poor old MK has to move its pop-gun army, hey. They got egg all over their faces, now the Berlin Wall's come down and communism is such a disaster. Well, we all knew it except certain people like your old friend Miss South Africa Gandhi, who paid for her stupidity by a lifetime in jail, hey. Others, like you, were lucky, but hopefully they've also learnt their lesson.'

'General Krombrink,' Mahoney said slowly, 'I intend this to be a pleasant visit, and I will not tolerate any harassment. The Hong Kong government is expecting me back in eight weeks, unscathed. Unscathed and untroubled. I imagine that important people like President de Klerk would prefer that visitors like me speak glowingly of the new South Africa – and now, General Krombrink, goodbye.' He banged down the telephone.

He was shaking. He signed the credit card slip, picked up the keys and walked out of the building.

And, Jesus, he knew he could never come back to live in this country. Oh Jesus, he hoped the new South Africa gave the likes of Krombrink their comeuppance. But he was determined that Krombrink was not going to spoil his experiment. He was about to see the most beautiful Afrikaner in the world.

He drove out of the car park into the new South Africa.

* * *

It was all new to him.

Twenty years ago there had been none of these six-lane highways and flyovers sweeping around and between the city and mine dumps, none of this huge, neat industrial area, nothing like this massive volume of traffic screaming in all directions, nothing like as many skyscrapers over there in down-town Johannesburg. He considered himself an expert on African affairs, he knew what a dynamo Johannesburg was, but he was not prepared for this. It was not only impressive, it was exciting. This was an African country that really *worked*.

It was a beautiful African day, the sky so blue, the highveld out there turning to mauve, the vastness of Africa stretching on and on. He found his way onto the M1, the start of the Great North Road, and he saw the magnificent homes of the leafy northern suburbs, and it was hard to believe all this would go the way of the rest of Africa. Then on the horizon was the silhouette of the Voortrekker Monument towering hundreds of feet up against the sky, representing three million Afrikaners who had nowhere else to go. *There would always be those three million Afrikaners* – not the handful of Englishmen that were in Kenya, Tanganyika, Zambia and Zimbabwe, not the handful of Portuguese in Angola and Mozambique – three *million* white Africans who had been here over three hundred years – so *surely* to God this country did not have to go the way of the rest of Africa?

It was a strange mixture of feelings. He did not like that massive monument over there, the nationalism and the injustice of apartheid it represented, and he hated being threatened by Krombrink as he stepped off the aircraft, he disliked the Afrikaans accent, the language of the oppressor; but somehow that monument was also reassuring, it also represented the future of this country, and somehow it made him feel that he had come home. Then he came over the last hills approaching Pretoria, and there on the skyline was the massive modern University of South Africa, and somewhere in that huge building was Professor Katrina de la Rey, and he was grinning with anticipation.

He entered the big marbled foyer. He was impatient as he waited for the elevator. He rode up to the ninth floor. He was happily nervous. He walked down the long corridor, looking for her room. And there was her name above the door.

He ran a shaky hand through his hair, and knocked.

'*Kom binne.*'

He opened the door.

She was poring over papers on her desk, her blonde hair in a bun, her spectacles on the tip of her nose. And she was even more beautiful than he remembered and any doubts about how he felt went out the window.

'*Ja?*' she said, without looking up.

'Hullo, Kate,' he grinned. He closed the door behind him.

She looked up, and stared over the top of her spectacles.

'Good God,' she whispered.

She took off her spectacles. She stood up slowly, staring. 'Why didn't you tell me you were coming?'

He grinned. 'Because you'd have told me there's no future in it.'

She was still bemused. She nodded. 'Yes,' she whispered. 'Yes, I would have.'

Then she stepped uncertainly around the desk, and he took her in his arms, clutched her tight and kissed her. And, oh, the bliss of her against him again. He kissed her and kissed her, then she broke the embrace, and took a deep breath.

'We'd better lock the door.'

He said ardently: 'Let's go to your place.'

She moved out of his arms and turned the key. She ran a hand over her hair, then leant back against the wall. She looked at him, then said softly: 'There's still no future in it.'

He was trembling with desire. He repeated: 'Let's go to your house.'

'I'm supposed to be working.'

'To hell with work!'

She closed her eyes. 'Oh Christ . . . ' she whispered. Then she stepped towards him and slid her arms around his neck and clutched him tight.

He kissed her hard, and, oh, the bliss of her wide mouth again, the sweet taste and scent of her, the feel of her thighs and belly against him, and his hand slid to her breast, and she broke the kiss and grinned into his mouth: 'Not here.'

'Yes, *right* here.'

'*No*, take my house keys and wait for me at home . . . '

66

He felt on top of the world as he drove back to Johannesburg. Madly in love again, and so glad he'd come back. This time that voortrekker monument did not dampen his spirits: all he cared about was that the most beautiful woman in the world was coming to make love to him in two hours. And he was going to sweep her off her feet and they'd live happily ever after . . .

It was a pretty Victorian house in the trendy suburb of Melville. Jacaranda trees lined the streets and the gardens were luxuriant. Mahoney swung into her gate, went down a short drive and parked. Two big trees dominated the back lawn.

He mounted the red-cement stoep and let himself in the back door. He entered a big kitchen, and put down his bag.

An archway led to a dining room, and beyond that another arch led to a big living room, its windows opening onto a front porch and the pretty street beyond. All the floors were old polished pine and the ceilings were pressed with ornate patterns. A door off the living room led to a reception hall, with three bedrooms leading off it.

The front room had been converted into a study: a large desk dominated the centre and the walls were lined with books. Mahoney walked in.

Half a wall was taken up with photographs. They were dominated by a life-size picture of a glorious woman clad only in a G-string, her back to the camera. She was posed, one leg stretched like a ballet dancer's, one hand on her rounded hip, the other holding a weight aloft triumphantly. Her magnificent body was tensed, oiled, showing perfectly sculpted lines. Printed below her feet were the words *'Come to life at The Gym'*. She was a magnificent figure of a woman – then he realised it was Katrina he was looking at. He grinned – and, oh, he was glad he had come.

The other photographs were also of her: Katrina astride a huge motorcycle, dressed in red leather, her helmet under her arm – Christ, she didn't ride one of those dangerous machines, did she? – Katrina in the seat of a microlight – Jesus! – Katrina on horseback, jumping a farm fence, blonde hair flying; Katrina on a windsurfer . . .

She hadn't told him anything about these pursuits. He turned to the bookshelves. History, social anthropology, political science, in English and Afrikaans. Several shelves of novels, mostly in English. He was gratified to see his own books amongst them. A number of books on farming. A set of *Encyclopaedia Britannica*. The Time-Life series of famous artists. A number of books of photographic prints. He picked one off the shelf.

It was a study of the female form. Scores of evocative pictures of beautiful naked women. Some of the photographs were bordering on pornographic. He picked up another one. It was similar stuff: beautiful photography. There was a large compendium called *The Complete Book of Erotic Art*. Mahoney raised his eyebrows. He opened it. It was very erotic stuff indeed, a pictorial history of pornography down the ages. *Interesting*.

He turned out of her study and glanced in the second room. Obviously a guest room – he had no intention of sleeping *there* tonight. He moved on to the last bedroom.

It was feminine but untidy. There was a large double bed which had been hastily made, the pillows left unpuffed. A very sexy pair of high-heeled shoes and a frilly suspender belt lay abandoned on the rug. Hairbrushes and jars of cosmetics were scattered across the dressing table. Another door led to a bathroom. On the walls a number of framed prints of Impressionists. He walked into the bathroom, and was surprised. It was almost as large as the bedroom and it was festooned with indoor plants. Big windows looked onto the back garden. There was a shower booth, a toilet, a bidet and an old-fashioned claw-and-ball bathtub. But most of the room was taken up by a large whirlpool bath, decorated with small blue tiles and ornate borders. It was full. The water was warm.

Well . . . He was dying to get her into *that*.

He returned to the back door and fetched his bag. He slung it on her bed and unzipped it. He began to undress. He pulled out a bottle of whisky and went to the kitchen to find a glass. He poured himself a good shot.

He walked back into the bathroom with it. A pair of black stockings was hung out to dry, a lacy pair of very scanty panties beside them. He smiled. She had never worn stockings in Borneo, it had been so hot. And he *ached* to see her in these. Particularly with those high-heeled shoes.

He looked for soap and shampoo, then got under the shower. And, oh yes, it was good to be here in her pretty house, waiting for her to come home. He let the hot water teem down on him, beating out the jet lag, and sang as steam billowed up.

Later, scrubbed up and beautiful for the beautiful Katrina, he poured himself another whisky, then wandered back to her study. On her desk was a pile of photocopied literature. 'Economic Analysis of Israel's Kibbutz System' by Professor Horowitz of the University of Tel Aviv.

Then he heard the back door click open.

Katrina came in, carrying a shopping bag, beaming. '*Hi!*'

He strode towards her, a smile all over his face. He laughed, flung his arms around her and kissed her joyfully. Then he scooped her up in his arms and carried her through to the bedroom.

Afterwards she lay sprawled on her back, her hair awry. She gave a small sigh.

'What?' Mahoney said.

She smiled gently. 'Nothing. I'm happy, that's all.' She turned her head to him. 'Despite myself.'

'Why despite? Don't you want to be happy?'

She stroked his eyebrow with her fingertip. She said: 'Why did you come? I told you there was no future in it.'

Mahoney waved a hand. 'Oh, just for the fuck. Thought what the hell.'

'Be serious.' She smiled.

He got up onto his elbow. He said down to her: 'Because I don't believe there's no future in it. I came because you wouldn't come to me. Because I'm madly in love with you. And because the aberration refused to go away.'

She smiled. 'You can't be in love after only a week. You didn't give yourself a chance to aberrate.' She added, more seriously: 'I don't want to get married, Luke. To anybody. The life I want isn't normal.'

He lay back again, and looked at the ceiling.

'You mean this Afrikaner homeland? The Volkswag.' This was okay by him, because it would come to nothing.

She sighed deeply. 'That's part of it. But the real reason is . . . ' she hesitated, then continued resolutely, ' . . . is that I don't want to be married, Luke. Certainly not at this stage of my life. I've already made one man desperately unhappy – and a few lovers before that – and I don't want the responsibility of another one. Not even the *risk* of doing that. I want – I need to be free to do my own thing. And part of that is the Volkswag, yes.' She turned her head to him. 'And you certainly don't fit into that. But the real reason is for *me*. For my soul.'

'And what does that beautiful soul want? Apart from your volkstaat? And to be free.'

She smiled. 'Not Hong Kong. No matter how beautiful and exotic. And no matter how much I could love you.'

'"Could"?' That was good enough for him, for now. He had lived long enough to know he wasn't in love with her yet, either. Only in lust? Only besotted? He said: 'The question is, what else does your *soul* want?'

She took a deep breath. 'Marriage is very confining. And my marriage was very conventional, to a dominee. Your work, your ambitions, your recreation, your domestic patterns – they all come under this new regime called marriage. The basic rule of which is Love, Honour and Obey. All of which I tried to do. I tried my best and I failed the tests of wifehood. And I don't intend to make the same mistake again in a hurry.'

That was bullshit. But he let it go. 'Tell me how you failed?'

She sighed. And sat up, and swept her fingers through her hair. 'Not yet. Too involved.' She turned to him solemnly. 'But there's one detail I must tell you. And I should have told you this in Borneo.' She paused. 'I'm bi-sexual, Luke.'

Mahoney stared up at her. 'You're one of the most sensual hetero-sexuals I've met.'

'I didn't say lesbian.'

He looked at her. 'You mean you're not a practising bi-sexual?'

'I try not to be.'

'And is that difficult?'

'Sometimes. But usually not.'

'And this caused of the break-up of your marriage?'

'I never broke my marriage vows. But I told him.'

'And he couldn't take it?'

'Oh, he could take it. He prayed. It was I who couldn't take it. And left.'

'For a woman?'

'No. Just to be me.'

And he wanted to laugh. None of this mattered because he only half believed this melodrama. 'But now that you are free to be yourself, why the tension? You're a mature adult. An intellectual.'

She smiled bleakly. 'The Jesuits say give us a child up to age seven and we've got him for life. Same with the Dutch Reformed Church. But the Catholics are fortunate to have the facility of confession.' She got off the bed. She went to the dressing table mirror and began to brush her long blonde hair vigorously.

Mahoney looked at her glorious nakedness. And the image of her making love to a woman was both erotic and gave him a stab of anguish. 'So it's a sin? I didn't realise you were religious.'

'I fail at that as well. That's another reason why I had to leave my husband, I failed him in my piety.'

He couldn't help grinning. He tried to be serious. 'I don't know whether it's a sin, I'm not a theologian. But it seems to me it's no worse than heterosexual promiscuity.' He regretted that last word.

'I'm not promiscuous. At least that much I've succeeded in.'

He felt that stab of jealousy again. 'You used to be?' And he did not care as long as she was his now.

She smiled at the mirror. She tossed down the brush and walked into the bathroom.

Mahoney got off the bed and followed her. She was stuffing her hair into a shower cap. He said: 'Before or after marriage?'

'Both.' Then she raised her eyebrows in a parody of sauciness. 'But I'm a reformed character now.' She turned on the taps.

He sat down on a white cane chair. 'Both men and women?'

'Yep.' She turned her face up to the jets and reached for the soap. 'But mostly men, you'll be pleased to hear?'

He would rather she'd said mostly women. She washed the suds off her face, then began to soap herself vigorously. 'You don't want to know how many?'

No he didn't. What mattered was from here on in. And he did want to know. 'Okay, how many?'

She began to soap her beautiful loins. She looked at him through the steam. 'In my thirty-seven years – exactly forty people, counting you. Excluding four years of marriage and the years until I was sixteen.' She soaped. 'If you care to work that out, it makes seventeen years of sexual activity, making an average of two point three five sexual partners per annum.' She turned her belly to the jet, washing the soap off her pubic triangle. 'Not *too* bad, huh? Compared to who – you? How many have you had?'

'I've no idea.'

'How many hundreds? Three. Five? A thousand?' She began to soap her shins. 'Forget it, none of my business.'

He said, looking at the lovely line of her: 'And your history is none of my business, I don't want to know.'

She soaped a foot, dangled it under the jets, then slammed off the shower. 'But I want you to know. Because you've come ten thousand miles.' She stepped out of the booth, glistening, and grabbed a towel. 'It is your business, Luke.' She ripped her plastic cap off.

'You've just brushed your hair, and now the edges are wet.'

'Trying to brush out my pathetic Dutch Reformed Church conscience.' She thrust the towel to her face and dried it. She demanded into the towel: 'Don't you want to know how many of those forty sexual partners were female, Luke?'

Yes he did. And he did not care.

'No. But, okay, how many?'

She plunged the towel down over her loins. 'Isn't that unnatural, not to want to know how many *unnatural* affairs your woman has had? Well: eleven. But that includes four one-night stands and four that I terminated after about a week. Sent her on her bicycle. That leaves only three serious ones to worry about.' She tossed down the towel, walked into her bedroom and sat down at the dressing table. She dipped her fingers into a jar and began to smear cream on her face.

'I'm not worried.' He sat down on the bed.

She looked at him in the mirror, hands poised, her face daubed in cream. 'Why not?'

He grinned at the mirror. 'I'll take my chances.'

She frowned at him. 'If you're serious about me, why don't you find it worrying?' She placed a hand on her breasts. 'Because you have complete confidence in my sense of sin? In my reformed character?' Mahoney wanted to laugh. And he loved her. Before he could reply she said to the mirror: 'Because you find it erotic?'

'Because I find *you* erotic. And enchanting.'

'I know that. That's why you flew ten thousand miles. As I find you enchanting, and very erotic. The question is: do you find it erotic that I fancy ladies sometimes?' She looked at him in the mirror. 'You do, don't you? Because you imagine yourself in bed with us? My bi-sexuality is an erotic bonus?' She began to massage the cream into her face vigorously, eyes closed. 'Well, that won't happen, Luke. I've tried it and I hated myself even more.'

'You've got a strong sense of morality, haven't you?'

'I notice you don't deny what I've just said.'

'My optimism hasn't yet got that far,' he said, truthfully. 'Why're you telling me all this, Kat? And flagellating yourself in the process.'

She turned on the stool and faced him. 'Because, darling, I want to be entirely honest with you. I want you to know the dark side of me. If I'd told you this in Borneo you wouldn't be here now. I feel responsible for getting you here under false pretences.'

'You've got a strong sense of responsibility, too.' He got up and cupped her face in his hands. 'I would have come anyway.' He kissed her forehead. 'The "dark side of you", huh?'

'God, don't you consider it dark? Wouldn't you be uptight if it were you? And there's another thing you've got to know – '

'More darkness?'

'Please be serious.'

'I'm trying, I'm just so happy I came. Are you?'

'I don't know yet.' She closed her eyes. 'Yes, of course I'm happy, I just want to know what you're doing. Let me finish.'

He sat on the corner of the bed. 'Ready for the worst.'

She said: 'I know you think it's a lot of bullshit but I assure you I'm deadly serious, so I want you to come to the Volkswag offices and see our work. And then come to the northern Cape to see what we're doing in Orania. The land we're developing.'

'So you're trying to put me off?'

She continued: 'And I want you to meet people who *aren't* Volkswag but who are our natural allies – the AWB. Whether we like them or not, we're going to be on the same side. And see how you like me being associated with *them*.' She looked at him. 'I think that'll *really* put you off me.'

Mahoney kept a straight face. None of this mattered because it would not come to pass. He nodded reasonably. Katrina continued: 'And I want you to meet some *real* military men, the Citizen Force commandos in my neck of the woods. Representative of many across the country. They're highly willing to take up arms to defend their rights. I want to convince you that the Afrikaner means business. In short, he is prepared to commit treason. And we'll see how you like me being associated with that.' She shook her head. 'I think you'll want to wash your hands of me.'

He resisted a smile. She studied him solemnly. 'And I want you to meet my family, Luke. See how you like a real, *conservative* Afrikaner family. Our thinking. Our politics. Our religious conservatism. Meet my brothers and relatives, see if you want to be associated with them for the rest of your life.' She suppressed a smile. 'I think they'll drive you right up the wall.'

'Sounds like a fun weekend. When are we going to have all these laughs?'

'Ten days, buddy, not a weekend. Christmas time.' Then she dropped her head and giggled.

Jesus, ten days. But he was pleased she seemed to be cheering up. She put on a straight face. 'Is that a deal?'

'Of course, I ain't chicken. But on one condition. That you spend the equivalent amount of time with me in Hong Kong.'

She smiled. 'No deal. I refuse to waste your money.'

Mahoney sat forward. 'Listen, Katrina, when the new South Africa begins, the shit's *really* going to hit the fan. There's going to be even more blood than we've seen in a hundred and seventy years when the blacks really start getting stuck into each other for political power.'

She sat forward too. And took both his hands in hers. 'Luke, of course the shit's going to hit the fan. Of course there's going to be blood like we've never seen before. And that's exactly when – and why – the Afrikaner needs his volkstaat.'

He sighed and said apologetically: 'Kate, the Afrikaner isn't going to get his volkstaat – you're striving for the impossible, darling, the Great Trek is over.' He immediately regretted saying it.

She looked at him soberly. Then nodded. 'I know that's how you think, despite what you say in your book. And that's why there's no future for us, darling. Luke? The Great Trek is *living* history, believe me. Like the State of Israel is living history. And I intend to be part of it.' She looked at him soberly. 'The state of Israel exists today only because a handful of Jews worked hard, and lobbied and agitated and made a nuisance of themselves. People thought it was a fool's errand – demanding a Jewish state on a continent of hostile Arabs. And the Jews were powerless – they had no army, no infrastructure, no money, they were a decimated people. But a handful of Jewish leaders kept struggling for it, and finally the British threw up their hands in despair and granted them a chunk of Palestine the size of the Kruger National Park. And look where Israel is today.'

He wished he hadn't opened the subject on this happy day, but he had to finish. 'Yes, Kate, but there are differences between the plight of the Jews at the end of World War II and the plight of the Afrikaner at the end of apartheid. The Jews evoked sympathy, the Afrikaners do not. And it was the *British* who gave the Jews Israel, not the Arabs. If the Arabs had had any say in the matter Israel wouldn't exist today. And if the blacks in South Africa have any say, there won't be a volkstaat either.'

She smiled. And stood up. Her glorious nakedness above him. She said: 'I'm familiar with all the arguments. And the points you make are weighty ones. And I have an answer for each one. But, please, not now.' She put her finger on his lips. 'Tonight is meant for *fun*. You've come ten thousand miles to see little ole me!' She squeezed his hands with a bright smile.

'That's *right*.' And, oh, her breasts were beautiful. She grinned down at him. 'So I'm going to make us a delicious dinner.' She turned to her wardrobe, flung open the doors. 'So what shall I wear to this party?'

'A G-string. And nothing else. Like in that photo of you in your study.'

She grinned over her shoulder. 'How did you know it was me? My back's to the camera.'

'Who else has got such a perfect body? Do you go to The Gym a lot?'

'You must come with me. That's just an old publicity photograph which was never used, but I stuck it up there to remind myself to go as often as I can.'

He said: 'And the motorbike and the microlight?'

She reverted to her wardrobe. 'They're on my parents' farm. I hardly ever use them now.'

'Thank God. Never use them again. Sell 'em.'

She turned back to him. Her eyes were suddenly moist. She said: 'Oh, I feel so much better now I've made a clean breast. I was dreading you coming back here, not knowing.'

'What made you so sure I'd come? Apart from those magnificently clean breasts.'

She made her eyes sparkle and sauntered to him, swinging her hips, and kissed him hard.

'*Omdat*,' she said into his mouth, '*jy is 'n ware man*. Because you are a *real man*.'

67

When he woke up the sun was high, shining green-gold on the trees in the garden. He had no jet lag – he had slept it off in the dreamless sleep of the sexually exhausted man. It was the song of birds that woke him. Outside the window a weaverbird was busily building a nest for a female who sat on a nearby branch watching critically. 'I know how it feels, weaverbird.'

He swung out of bed, feeling good. He had a shower, looked at himself in the mirror. 'Isn't it nice we're not going into court today, weaverbird?' He dressed, then went to the kitchen. There was a note: *Welcome to sunny South Africa! Help yourself to breakfast.*

The first person he telephoned over his cup of coffee was his sister.

'Hullo, darling!' she cried. Jill was overjoyed. 'But aren't you taking a chance – this isn't the new South Africa yet . . . ?' And she was delighted to hear there was a woman involved. 'Who *is* this lucky girl?' Jill laughed. 'Are you bringing her down to meet her future sister-in-law?'

'She's busy marking end-of-year exam papers. She's a professor at UNISA. And she's an Afrikaner. And she's beautiful.'

There was a surprised pause. Then: 'Of course she's *beautiful*, you wouldn't go for a *plain* one! But she's not a *ware* Afrikaner, is she?'

'Dyed in the wool. Thinks the world's flat.'

'Luke, don't tell me she belongs to the Conservative Party!'

'She thinks the Conservatives are dangerous left-wingers.'

'You're joking, of course!'

'But she belongs to the Afrikaner Volkswag.'

'Oh *Gawd* . . . ' Another pause. 'I hope you know what you're doing, my brother. And what about Patti Gandhi?'

Mahoney sighed. 'That's over, Jill. After twenty-odd years. I feel very sorry for her, she's a very brave woman, but it's over.'

There was a sigh. 'Well, yes, but how terribly sad. She may be out of prison soon. And that wonderful book, *Alms*.' She added, more

475

brightly: 'I'm basking in reflected glory. What a wonderful movie it would make . . . But, the Afrikaner *Volkswag*? Oh, *Gawd*!'

They talked for an hour. 'Mother was hale and hearty to the end, Luke. You know how Britishly *precious* she was about maintaining her "standards"? There was old Mum, one morning stomping around in her no-nonsense tweeds giving the Zulu girls hell in their domestic science classes, the next morning she was dead. The Zulus were very fond of her and gave her a lovely funeral . . . ' It made Mahoney's eyes burn. Good old Mum – who would have thought it? God, he wished he'd been closer to her. And, God, it made him want to stay here. But it was mostly a laughy conversation he had with his dear sister.

Jill giggled: 'And remember a certain Sally Freeman *Nkomo*? The black American lass you so charmed in Hong Kong? Well, you'll never believe it, but she showed up here with a letter of introduction from your old heart-throb Lisa Rousseau. Hell-bent on becoming a *Zulu*!'

'A *Zulu*, now! And?'

'Oh, she's a dear girl . . . I really take my hat off to her – she's sure getting the most out of her "African experience". And *what* a sense of humour. . . '

Dear, funny, pretty Sally Freeman of the US of A, 'thoroughly pissed off with the Xhosa,' showing up in her Avis rented car at the mission with a Zulu phrase book and all the tribal garb purchased at expensive tourist shops in Durban, 'all tarted up like a Zulu umfazi,' demanding advice about finding her roots. Wanting 'to shack up with a nice Zulu family,' wanting to learn Zulu dancing, Zulu songs, Zulu folklore, Zulu cuisine, 'Zulu every-fuckin'-thing'. ('I *beg* your pardon?!' the Reverend Leonard Dawson said.) (Jill had been in hysterics.) Including a nice Zulu warrior to show a gal a good time. (The Reverend blanched.) Jill had telephoned friendly Zulu officials in Ulundi: it was arranged. But Sally first spent a week at the mission 'gettin' some Zulu know-how' and 'hands-on experience', before setting forth, all smiles, in her rented car. 'She gave the expression "sallying forth" a whole new dimension',' Jill laughed.

'And?'

And Sally came back a month later, wild and woolly, her feet blistered from 'workin' fuckin' barefoot all day', her back aching from 'hoeing fuckin' fields', her hands callused from 'choppin' fuckin' firewood'. And if she saw another cow's udder she'd fuckin' scream. 'And/or another pot of sadza. And/or had another crap behind a fuckin' bush.' And as for a gal gettin' a good time, forget it – 'biff-bam, thank you m'am'. The only Zulu warriors she had seen had been impertinent UDF youths armed with AK–47s who stole all her traveller's cheques. That had been the last fuckin' straw: after half-a-dozen baths and two nights in a nice clean bed at Jill's mission, she had washed her blistered hands of the fuckin' Zulus and driven ruefully back to Lisa Rousseau.

Mahoney's eyes were wet with laughter – but he also took his hat off to Sally. And, oh, it was lovely talking to his sister. He promised to go down to Natal to see her before Christmas.

Afterwards he telephoned Richard Barker and left a message on his answering machine. Then he telephoned Shortarse Longbottom at the *Star*. 'Good God!' Shortarse said. He arranged to meet him for lunch.

Then he telephoned Hugo Wessels at *Vryburgher*, the liberal Afrikaaner journal. 'I don't believe it . . . !' Huge Vessel said.

They met in the Press Bar of the Elizabeth Hotel, opposite the *Star*. It didn't seem to have changed in twenty years, but Shortarse had. He was still gangly, but his straggly beard was grey and his hair thin.

He hunched morosely over his pub lunch and said: 'The Volkswag will not get their volkstaat. I think it's a legitimate enough demand, but the new South Africa, *when* it comes, will not permit it because it smacks of apartheid.'

'The Jews got Israel,' Huge pointed out. 'I'm all for granting the Boers a separate homeland – get rid of the bastards.'

Shortarse said: 'But the Jews were a highly victimised minority and had everybody's sympathy. Even this present Afrikaner government isn't sympathetic to the Boers' demand. Nobody will be pressurising the new black government to be generous with die-hard old Afrikaners.'

Mahoney said: 'But the Volkswag doesn't intend to perpetuate apartheid. They acknowledge that as a failed ideal.'

'And what about the hundreds of thousands of Coloureds who live in the northern Cape where this Orania is going to be?'

'I have it from the horse's mouth that there'll be no forced removals, no apartheid.'

Shortarse shook his head. 'Who's going to trust half a million die-hard old Boers who think apartheid is God's will?'

'But surely the Afrikaner Volkswag – which is a very Christian institution, is it not? – surely they wouldn't be so *duplicitous* as to break trust on that? They know the world would come down on them like a ton of bricks?'

Huge grinned at Mahoney. 'I'm all for this Afrikaner homeland, who needs trouble-makers? It's a bargain.'

Shortarse snorted. 'Who would trust all those Nazis living in South America not to breach trust if they were given their own state?'

'But Volkswag isn't neo-Nazi,' Mahoney said. 'Is it?'

'No, but who's going to do their fighting for them? The AWB.'

Mahoney sighed worriedly. Jesus, Katrina had warned him loud and clear last night about this. Now he was getting it from two wise men. 'And could this Afrikaner homeland be economically viable?'

'Absolutely,' Huge said.

'No way,' Shortarse said.

'*Absolutely!*' Huge said. 'Is the state of Israel economically viable? Yes, because they work hard. And they've got a *mission* – a religious mission to survive, surrounded by all those hostile Arabs. And the Afrikaners also have a sacred mission to survive against the black hordes. That's what the Great Trek was all about. And they've got guts.' He nodded at Mahoney. 'They'll pump water out of the Orange River and turn that Karoo into a garden.'

'And where'll they get their revenue?' Shortarse demanded.

'They'll sell their produce to the rest of South Africa, which will be in deep shit because the ANC will have redistributed the land and agriculture will have gone to hell. Orania will probably become the breadbasket of southern Africa.'

Shortarse shook his head mournfully. Mahoney said: 'But if the Boers declared independence unilaterally, they couldn't win if they had to fight for it.'

'No way,' Shortarse said.

'*Maybe,*' Huge said, 'and maybe not. But they sure could make a hell of a lot of trouble. And possibly drive the enemy back to the negotiation table. The Afrikaner is a fighter. Look at the Boer War. The guerrilla is a hard enemy to beat. Look at the IRA – they're only a handful of hotheads but they've been tying down thousands of British troops for decades. And that is how the Afrikaner will fight – ambush, hit and run, sabotage, et cetera.' He nodded. 'And remember that they will have *many* sympathisers in the army and police. And in the civil service – they could paralyse the new government. For example, they could ground all the air force planes for days – and the airways – simply by tinkering with the computers. Easy.' He shrugged. 'Same with the railways, all the state institutions. The Afrikaners could create chaos.'

Shortarse shook his head. Mahoney said: 'But do you think they've got a strategy for all this? Plans. Military blueprints?'

Huge snorted. 'The AWB has been talking about the civil war for fifteen years. All their sympathisers in the army and air force and police force? Do you imagine they haven't thought it all out?' He added: 'I honestly wouldn't be surprised if they've even got a few nuclear weapons.'

'Jesus,' Mahoney said. 'Really?'

'Why not? The army has nuclear weapons, we make the enriched uranium at Pelindaba. What is so improbable about some senior officers letting a few get to the Boers?' He raised his eyebrows. 'They could do a Nagasaki. Deliver an ultimatum that, say, Port Elizabeth must be evacuated by noon on Tuesday because a nuclear device will be detonated unless Orania's independence is recognised.'

'Jesus.'

Shortarse shook his head. 'Never happen.'

'No? And anyway,' Huge said to Mahoney, 'the right wing in the citizen force *and* army and police hardly need to invent elaborate military plans – they've already *got* them, for the Total Strategy against the Total Onslaught.' He added: 'And I'm not so sure they couldn't win.'

Mahoney turned to Shortarse. 'Well?'

Shortarse shook his morose head. '*Oh*, they certainly have arms caches and plans. There will be a lot of posturing, yes, and a number of *incidents* – even dramatic ones. Maybe lasting weeks. But, they will be put down quickly.' He waved a skinny hand. 'Oh, there'll be a few pockets of bitter-enders who'll take to the bush and fight on for a while. But it will fizzle out.'

Huge sighed. 'I wish I had your optimism.'

Mahoney said: 'And if it doesn't fizzle out?'

Huge said: 'An IRA situation. Sabotage.'

Shortarse said: 'It will fizzle. Public executions will make sure of that.' He nodded over his shoulder at the City Hall. 'In the square. The gallows permanently rigged. Black mobs toyi-toying. For all Afrikanerdom to see.'

It was three o'clock when Mahoney drove into Pretoria, got lost around Church Square under the statue of Paul Kruger telling the day there would be no nonsense, before finding his way to the doors of Lawyers for Human Rights.

In the reception area, there were rows of blacks sitting on benches. He said to the black receptionist: 'Please tell Advocate Woodcock that the ex-Acting Mr Justice Mahoney would like to kick the paint off his door.'

A minute later Splinter Woodcock came striding down the corridor. 'Well, Jesus Christ . . . !'

They sat in his office. Splinter said: 'Certainly I take the Boers seriously. They're our problem people, who made the Great Trek, who fought all the wars, who mounted the rebellion against their own

479

government in 1914 because South Africa was fighting against the Kaiser in World War I. They're the guys who formed the Ossewa Brandwag against the Smuts government during World War II, they're the bastards who've defended apartheid for forty bloody years.' He raised his eyebrows. 'So when they talk about civil war to get their beloved Boer republic, I certainly take them seriously. Anybody with a sense of history should.'

'But can they succeed?'

'No. What they're demanding, the old Boer republics of the Transvaal and Orange Free State, is not only unreasonable, it's patently impossible for them to seize and defend.'

'But the Volkswag is only asking for a chunk of the northern Cape. Do you think that's unreasonable?'

Splinter sighed. 'Look, the Volkswag is respectable – they're not threatening war, they want to negotiate. But they're going to be tarred with the same brush as the AWB, who would use the Volkswag's territory as a military base, and that's one of the reasons they *won't* be granted it. And so they'll *all* end up going to war, the respectable and the disreputable.'

'And when will this happen? If ever.'

'When the Afrikaner can claim – ' he put his hand on his heart – 'that his God-given right to self-determination has been taken away. That means, when the long-awaited Great Indaba starts and the Afrikaner's demand for his republic is rejected. That's when the Afrikaner's "right to self-determination" will have gone, and that's when the trouble will start.'

'Next year?'

Splinter raised his palms. 'Communism is on its last legs now. That means the ANC is enormously weakened. When parliament resumes after the Christmas recess, the president will make an important announcement about the start of negotiations.'

Mahoney rubbed his chin. 'Do you think he'll unban the ANC?'

'No negotiations would be meaningful in the eyes of Africans if Nelson Mandela wasn't sitting there. And if he's going to release Mandela he must unban the whole ANC.'

It was almost impossible to imagine, after all these years. 'And do you think De Klerk is sincere about abolishing apartheid? Or does he only want to reform it sufficiently to get the world off his back?'

Splinter sighed again. 'Does a leopard change its spots?' He shook his head. 'He knows apartheid is a failure. But he's a very astute politician, and I don't believe he intends the Afrikaner to commit political suicide. He intends to somehow come out on top. He's got plenty of tricks up his sleeve, I'm sure. And I'm sure the security police have got plenty more dirty tricks in store for us.'

'Dirty tricks?'

Splinter snorted. 'Oh boy. Like the murder of Anton Lubowski on the eve of Namibia's independence?' He reached for a file. 'There're many examples. And they can't all be attributed to right-wing thugs. There's a government hit squad lurking somewhere. That may not surprise you – many governments in this sad world have dirty-tricks squads, even Great Mother Britain.' He shrugged. 'But my guess is that De Klerk is capable of running rings around the ANC when the Indaba starts.' He added: '"Capable", note. I'm not necessarily saying he'll be dishonest. But I'm quite sure he'll have kept his powder dry.'

'I don't doubt that: gunpowder has always been the Afrikaners' political stock-in-trade.' Mahoney nodded at the file. 'And what're you guys doing? Collecting evidence? Like Amnesty International?'

Splinter said: 'We investigate cases of abuse of human rights. We have regional offices all over, who monitor anything that looks suspicious. We make representations to the police, ask questions, and if we collect enough evidence we brief a local lawyer to put matters right. These offices here are our headquarters. We give legal advice, kick up a fuss with the authorities, with the press, et cetera. We also monitor all the cases awaiting execution on Death Row. We review the evidence, make sure all the condemned man's rights have been exhausted. It's amazing, but we've found mistakes and saved a lot from the gallows at the last moment.'

'Jesus.'

'And from here we also run an education programme teaching the blacks what human rights is all about, so they don't take abuses lying down. In other words, we're trying to develop a human rights *culture*, which won't be abused as it has been for forty years under apartheid.'

'And in the rest of Africa.'

'Indeed. Africa has a terrible track record on human rights. We hope to work ourselves out of a job in the new South Africa.'

Mahoney was amazed by this optimism. 'It's the African *way*, Splinter. Do you imagine the Zulus are ever going to accept domination by the Xhosas? Or vice versa?'

'You must have heard of the Third Force?'

'Oh,' Mahoney said, 'you can't convince me that all this violence is being done by the government's shadowy Third Force. This violence is a struggle between the Zulus and the UDF-ANC alliance over who'll dominate in the new South Africa. A so-called Third Force may be *exploiting* it, rogue policemen may be encouraging it, but the *cause* of the violence is traditional African politics – crush the opposition. And that will continue after a black government takes power, Splinter. You'll have your job for a long time.'

Splinter said: 'Certain rogue policemen? Plus certain rogue army officers? Plus the government's dirty-tricks department, which must exist? Plus the government's traditional policy of divide-and-rule? When can all that be said to become a Third Force? And when does "exploitation of violence" become "organization"?'

'If the government is organizing this Third Force, that must mean De Klerk himself. If so, why isn't this violence more efficient? Even more devastating?'

'Perhaps it suits government to draw out the conflict to show the world the blacks' inability to be democratic. Perhaps if it was more efficient it would arouse suspicion? I don't know, I haven't got enough evidence, but that a Third Force is operating is clear. And, yes, President de Klerk *must* know about it, although he publicly denies it. He doubtless keeps himself aloof from it – doesn't *want* to know the details. All politicians need a psychological cut-off point they can shield behind – but, yes, I believe he knows.'

'And approves?'

'He may disapprove. But he's powerless to stop it. He calls in the Ministers of Defence and Police and says: "What's this I hear about a Third Force?" They say: "President, there is no such thing, it's just rumour, sponsored by the ANC." "Well," he says, "investigate it, I want a full report." A week later they come back and say "Mr President, here's our report, but there is no Third Force." So? His conscience is clear. He knows, yet he doesn't know.'

Mahoney sighed. Thank God it wasn't his problem. But Katrina was his problem. 'And, what can you guys do about it?'

Splinter grinned. 'Why, want a job?'

'I've already got a job. I'm on holiday.'

'And while your girl's at work all day, what're you doing?'

'Drinking beer. And I've got a book to write.'

Splinter sat back and said: 'We pay peanuts. You don't become a human rights lawyer for the money. But I could put you on the pay-roll as a temporary legal advisor.'

Mahoney smiled. 'No thanks. I don't know any human rights law.'

'You don't have to. There's no Bill of Human Rights in South Africa. Cynics may say there's no acquaintance whatsoever between South Africa and human rights. Tell me – how much of your wealth have you put back into the world?' He got up. 'Come with me.'

Splinter opened the door and pointed down the corridor. Two dozen black faces turned to look at them.

'Look at those people, Luke. They're poor. They're uneducated. They're in trouble and they're scared. All are here because they feel they have suffered some injustice at the hands of the authorities. Or their family has. Or their son is about to be hanged next week. Now, our clerks will interview each one, then bring them to one of our legal advisors – for free advice, and action. Digging into the case, going through court records with a fine-tooth comb, then rushing to court, ringing the Minister of Justice in the middle of the night for a stay of execution. And we have to do it *properly* – because our reputations are on the line. If we cry wolf, or make a dumb mistake, we lose credibility.' He looked at Mahoney. 'And we do this for a pittance. Why?' He tapped his chest. 'Because we feel it's our *duty*, as lawyers. Because, if you like, we're *compassionate*.' He hollered: 'Steven!'

A head appeared round a doorway. Splinter beckoned and turned back to his desk. A lanky black man entered.

'Steven is our senior clerk. He's our Death Row specialist – he monitors who's due for the high jump, he's got contacts amongst the black prison staff, which is vital because we have no right to get into Death Row – only the condemned man's own lawyer has that privilege. And most of those lawyers are fresh out of law school, with zero experience, assigned to the case *pro deo*. Directly and indirectly, Steven has saved many men from the gallows, days before their execution, a couple of whom are walking around free today, the rest serving life sentences instead. Tell Mr Mahoney how you do it, Steve.'

Steven gave a brilliant, modest smile and shuffled.

'Well, sir – you see in this country there is no automatic right of appeal against the death sentence – '

'God,' Mahoney said.

'Well,' Steven said, 'the accused sentenced to death must apply to the trial judge for "leave to appeal". But if he refuses, the accused can still write to the Chief Justice for leave to appeal, from Death Row. The next stage is that the condemned man can write to the president asking him for the prerogative of mercy. But these prisoners are usually uneducated. And they are without hope. They believe all is over after the trial. So many do not write to the president. Or they cannot write. Or they write stupid letters. And the president – '

'Or one of his staff,' Splinter murmured.

' – just reads the letter, reads what the judge said, and then confirms the sentence.'

Splinter said: 'What time has the *president* got to read hundreds, maybe *thousands* of pages of trial evidence and judgments? So, he relies on staffers to tell him what to do. And *that's* where Lawyers for Human Rights come in. And we have saved a lot of men from the gallows.' He pointed at Steven: 'And it's all largely thanks to this man. Who's got the contacts, the sympathy, the energy, the black skin, to get into Death Row on the pretext of visiting one prisoner legitimately, and comes out with information about others who need help desperately. Who're facing the hangman next week and who haven't even written to the Chief Justice for leave to appeal, let alone to the president.' He took a weary breath. 'And that's when we go to work.' He turned to Steven. 'Okay, thank you, Steve.'

The man smiled and turned to the door. 'And, Steve?' Splinter said. 'Mr Mahoney may be coming to help us out temporarily. Show him the ropes, will you?'

68

It was after five o'clock when Mahoney found Richard Barker's modest suburban house in Westdene.

'I should have warned you not to leave messages on my answer-phone,' Barker said. 'I'm sure my line is tapped. By Military Intelligence. And that means you're known to them now. Not the healthiest thing you could have done.'

'Okay. But what's happened since we spoke in Hong Kong?'

'Ah, the plot thickens.' He smiled. 'I returned to Mozambique. I did find chunks of the crates that were parachuted down. And nails. And I recovered a piece of parachute caught in the trees. I took them to a scientist friend at the university for analysis.'

'And?'

'The crates were made of South African pine – the type used by the Defence Force. The nails were the same as those manufactured by suppliers to the Defence Force. And the parachute material the same – in thickness, substance and colour of the fibre.'

'Could your friend in Civil Aviation trace a record of that flight?'

'No record in Civil Aviation of any aircraft filing a flight plan in that area that night. So the fact that there's *no* record is further proof, isn't it? But there's more: my Land-Rover has never been found in Swaziland. My insurers investigated thoroughly before paying me out. Nothing. Vanished.' He raised his eyebrows happily. 'And, I've received threatening phone calls since I returned.'

'Oh? What was said?'

Barker smiled grimly. 'Nothing. Just a wolf-howl.' He uttered a soft, long, ululating imitation.

'Jesus.'

'That's the signature tune of the White Wolves, the Nazi bastards. Like Barend Strydom, who shot all those blacks in Pretoria. They howl down the telephone at people they intend to hit.'

Mahoney frowned. 'But if Military Intelligence were after you because you'd seen the arms-drop to Renamo, they wouldn't warn you by howling down the phone. They'd just rub you out.'

'Unless,' Barker said, 'they're trying to make it appear that it's these White Wolves who're guilty of rubbing me out.'

'Okay, but why haven't they rubbed you out already?'

Barker shook his head. 'Look – assuming that there *is* a branch of Military Intelligence, or Special Forces, whose job it is to carry out special assignments like assassinations of trouble-makers like me, there must be a chain of command – local commanders, then district commanders, up to the top man who gives the final orders. That's obvious – you don't want your hitmen going off half-cocked and giving the game away – everything must be *deniable*. No clues. So maybe they're still working out my case.'

'If you believe that, you should make yourself scarce, surely.'

'Don't *you* believe it?'

Mahoney sighed. 'Yes, I think I do. Speaking as a criminal lawyer, there's insufficient evidence to prove who did anything. That arms-drop *may* have been done by ordinary arms smugglers. But, what are you going to do about it? Leave?'

'Like hell! And go where? This is *my* mortgaged house! This is where *my* friends are. Where my work is! And,' he jabbed a finger, 'I'm going to get to the bottom of this!'

Mahoney thought for a moment. 'Surely for the sake of your skin, you should publish your story. Then they dare not hit you? Because the finger of guilt would point to them.'

Barker nodded emphatically. '*Right*. But first I've got to get some more evidence.' He smiled. 'I'm getting evidence from my junior geologists that the army is training a corps of Zulus in the Caprivi Strip at a place called Hippo Camp. And these Zulus have been infiltrated back into Natal to fight the UDF.'

Hell, *this* was important. 'What's your evidence?'

Barker said: 'My geologist only has it second-hand from natives in that area. He's working on finding better witnesses.'

'How does the informant know they're Zulus?'

'Heard them speaking.'

'How does he know they've gone back to Natal?'

'That's what they said. Going back to fight the UDF, they said.'

'Where is this informant now?'

'He's a Bushman, whom my geologist hired as a guide. I've told him to try to find him, get the full story and write it all down.' He held up two fingers. 'Now the second piece of evidence I'm collecting is that the South African Defence Force is not only supplying arms to Renamo, they're actually taking ivory in payment!'

Mahoney looked at him. 'Ivory?'

'*Ivory*,' Barker nodded. 'And I've got another geologist working the coastal area bordering Mozambique. He's heard stories of Mozambicans exchanging ivory for arms. The arms arrive in great big trucks. The Mozambicans arrive carrying ivory.' He nodded in satisfaction. 'No, I haven't got sworn affidavits yet, Mr Lawyer, but I've told my men to work on it.'

Mahoney sat back in his chair. God, this was important stuff. 'And what do you want me to do?'

'You tell me. Will it be strong enough to publish?'

'Yes. What you'll publish is what you saw, plus the hearsay. But it doesn't prove the government's doing it, not in a court.'

'I'm not talking about a court of law, I'm talking about the Government Department of Dirty Tricks! I'm talking about the court of international opinion.' He took a determined breath. 'So, I'll wait for my geologists to get those statements. Then will you write it all up for me . . . ?'

It was seven o'clock when he got back to Katrina's house. It was in darkness. He poured a generous whisky and stood, thinking about Barker's story.

It was important, exciting stuff. If it was true that the South Africans were continuing to supply Renamo in breach of the Nkomati Accord, the government would have egg all over its face. There would be an international uproar. Increased sanctions. And if the government *was* training Zulus to fight the UDF? Jesus. What do you say about a government that trains its citizens to kill other citizens? It was mind-blowing criminal behaviour. Mass murder. And, *God,* he was excited that he was in on the story! Once a journalist always a journalist! And once a South African always a South African. You cannot leave the bloody place alone.

The telephone rang. He walked into the hall and picked it up. 'Hullo?'

There was silence for a moment; then came a long, spine-chilling wolf-howl: '*Wo-wo-wo-wo-wo-oooh . . .* '

Mahoney felt gooseflesh. '*Who the fuck are you?!*' he shouted.

'*Wo-wo-wo-wo-oooh . . .* '

Mahoney took a furious breath. '*Tell me who you are, you bastard, and we can meet and talk about it –* '

The howl came again.

'*Go to hell, you stupid bastard!*'

He slammed down the telephone and leant against the wall. His whisky glass was trembling in his hand.

Jesus, that had frightened him. Jolted primitive fear right through him. *What the hell was he going to do?* Report to the police? That's what he would have done in Hong Kong. Yes, and what would the police do? What *could* they do? They couldn't trace that call. And the police would want to know why. And that would draw attention to Richard Barker, to whom he was bound in secrecy.

Mahoney drained his glass. Then shoved himself off the wall and walked into the kitchen to recharge it. And the telephone rang again. He returned to the hall. '*Hullo?*'

There was a moment's silence, then a female voice sobbed: 'Mr Mahoney? You don't know me but I'm Janet Forsythe; I'm Richard Barker's girlfriend. Please come – something terrible has happened.'

Richard Barker had walked to the nearby mini-market to buy milk and cigarettes when Mahoney left. He was returning in the dusk, approaching his front gate, when the car came cruising slowly down the street from behind.

There were two men in the front seats, one in the back. As they drew close the man in the back raised a shotgun through the window and took aim. As they drew level, he fired. Richard Barker was blown off his feet by the shocking blast. He was thrown across the sidewalk and crashed against his garden wall in a mass of flesh and blood, as the car sped away down the avenue.

By the time Janet Forsythe came bursting out of the gate it was two blocks away. Richard Barker lay in a flood of blood, his chest blown to pulp. She screamed, fell to her knees beside him and lifted his head, aghast. With his dying breath he was trying to say something.

'What?!' Janet cried.

Barker whispered four words, and slumped dead in her arms.

The police had not yet arrived when Mahoney pulled up at Barker's house. Neighbours were milling. Richard's body lay where it had fallen, blood running into the gutter, splattered on the wall.

Mahoney found Janet in the living room, being comforted by a dozen neighbours. When he told her who he was, her face crumpled and she struggled to her feet. She led him to one side.

She sobbed: 'He only said four words before he died: "Tell Luke grey Cortina."'

69

Colonel Floris Klaasens, officer in charge of the Murder and Robbery Squad, was an avuncular hulk in his mid-fifties with kindly blue eyes.

He said in a heavy Afrikaans accent: 'Please call me Floris, my mother was a florist and she hoped I'd be one too, but *Got*, man, here I am, jus' an honest dumb cop, hey. Mr Mahoney,' Floris said, hunching forward, 'it's a great pleasure to have one of the legal fraternity on our side, hey. Now tell me, you were there last night comforting poor Janet when the police arrived, but you didn't tell them what you just told me, about the arms-drop to Renamo in Mozambique. Why is that?'

Mahoney held old Floris's eye. 'I don't trust your police, Floris.'

Floris frowned. 'Oh? Why not?'

'Because this is a police state.'

Floris sat back. 'Agh, come on, Mr Mahoney, this is the new South Africa, hey, old PW Botha is gone.'

'Floris, we've been hearing about this new South Africa for years. So why was the government still supplying arms to Renamo less than a year ago? Mr Barker saw them doing it. And that is why he was murdered last night. So, who murdered him? Obviously somebody acting on the orders of the government. That means either the army, or the security police. That's why I don't trust the police.'

Floris said reasonably: 'But it might be just a few rogue officers in the army – or the security police – who supplied Renamo.'

'Maybe so, but a clique of rogue securocrats is just as dangerous. Indeed *more* dangerous because they're a *secret* clique.'

'Or,' Floris said, 'maybe it was one of those crazy Wit Wolwe who murdered him. You received a wolf-howl just after he was shot.'

'I can't imagine a bunch of White Wolves managing to arrange a parachute-drop of arms to Renamo.'

'So you think it was just a coincidence that you received a wolf-howl moments after Barker was gunned down?'

'Not at all, I think it was intended as a red herring, to make Barker's murder look like the work of a bunch of crazies. Nor do I think it's a coincidence that as I stepped off the plane in Jo'burg I received a phone call from General Krombrink. Nor do I think it's a coincidence that Mr Barker was murdered the day I met him in Johannesburg – I think he was murdered because they suspected he had told me about the arms-drop and they suspected he was giving me further information about it. Put those three together and they don't look like coincidences to me.'

'So you think it's General Krombrink and his merry men who made the Renamo arms-drop, chased Mr Barker in Hong Kong, shot him last night, and gave the wolf-howl to you?'

Mahoney said dryly: 'I think it's a worthwhile line of investigation. I think they gave me that wolf-howl to intimidate me from sticking my nose into Barker's story.'

'I see. And, are you intimidated?'

'Damn right. But I've already stuck my nose in.' He paused. 'I've already filed his story with my old newspaper. I sat up most of the night writing it. It'll be published today.'

Floris stared at him. '*Got*, man, now the bastards have been alerted, they'll run for cover! We'll never find them!'

Mahoney snorted. 'And the other reason I published in such a hurry, Colonel Klaasens, was to get the bastards off my back. Barker was murdered to stop him spilling the beans. But once I've published his story, there's no point in murdering me, is there? I've done the damage, murdering me now would be an unnecessary risk.' He raised a finger. 'And the other reason was to protect Janet – they must suspect that she knew the story.'

Floris shook his head wearily. '*Got*, man, Mr Mahoney, you make life difficult for me, hey? Now they've gone really underground. An',' he held up a finger, 'you better watch your back. Don't count on these bastards not shooting you out of revenge, hey. If they're the Wit Wolwe they wouldn't think twice.'

Mahoney said grimly: 'They're not White Wolves, Colonel. They're security police. Or Defence Force.'

Colonel Klaasens sighed. 'And therefore you don't trust the police, hey? Tell me, Mr Mahoney, do you trust me?'

Mahoney smiled. 'I don't know, Colonel, I don't know. Because you're a member of the security establishment. Which means they can give you orders to shut up. To stop a line of investigation. But they can't do that to me. Unless they shoot me.' He smiled thinly. 'And that's why I sat up all night and filed my story.'

The colonel smiled. 'I like your style, Mr Mahoney. And I'm not going to try to convince you that old Floris Klaasens is an honest cop. Now, have you told me everything?'

'Yes,' Mahoney lied. He wasn't going to tell the South African police about the training of Inkatha cadres in the Caprivi Strip, nor about rumours of ivory trade for guns on the northern Natal coast.

'Can I please have a copy of your story?'

Mahoney put his hand into his jacket pocket. 'I knew you'd ask.'

'Thank you. And may I ask you, *please*, to contact me immediately if you find out anything else?'

'Certainly.' Mahoney stood up.

So did old Floris. He extended his hand. 'I hope you come to trust me, Mr Mahoney. And murder is murder, whoever did it, hey, and murder is my business. I've been at it almost all my life. Mr Mahoney, would you like some police protection?'

For an instant Mahoney thought the man may be issuing a veiled threat. Then the sincerity of the eyes dispelled that. 'Thank you, but no. I think I'm safe as soon as the story is published.' He grinned. 'I couldn't bear having a policeman around all the time, and Professor de la Rey and I are going away soon for the Christmas holidays.'

'Oh, good. But I think I'll sleep easier if I have a chap watching your house tonight.'

'Okay, thank you. But the best way to protect me is to pick up that telephone and tell General Krombrink to get off my back.'

The gangland-style murder of Richard Barker had been on the front page of every newspaper that morning. On the way back from work, Katrina had heard on the radio the further detail that Luke Mahoney had broken the story as to why he had been murdered – the arms-drop to Renamo in breach of the Nkomati Accord. She was astonished. And she was flabbergasted to arrive to find a policeman in her back yard.

'For God's sake, what's happening?' she demanded.

The constable touched his cap. 'I'm here to protect you, madam.'

'Against what?! Is Mr Mahoney all right?'

'Ja, he's been drinking but I think he's still o'right, hey.'

Katrina clattered up the steps and burst into the house. 'Luke?!'

She saw him coming from the hall. She ran into his arms.

'Oh, thank God,' she cried. 'I hope you haven't got any more surprises for me . . .'

But there was another surprise.

Late that night, as they lay in the whirlpool bath together the telephone rang. Mahoney heaved himself up, walked to the hall and picked up the receiver. 'Hullo?'

'I've got another hell of a story for you,' Splinter Woodcock said. 'Does the name Walter Kosagu mean anything to you? He was a leading ANC activist, a black lawyer who was stabbed to death in Durban a few years ago, supposedly by robbers.'

Mahoney listened intently, water dripping onto the floor. Then he said: 'I'm on my way!'

He hurried back to the bathroom and grabbed a towel. 'Where are you going?' Katrina demanded.

'To Lawyers for Human Rights. To pick up the affidavit of a condemned man who's due to be hanged tomorrow. The shit,' he promised her happily, 'is *really* going to hit the fan.'

70

You soon come to believe that you're totally above the law when you're a government-paid killer. When you are assured that, if you are caught, wheels within wheels will ensure your speedy release; when you're constantly told that you're a member of an elite, it's easy to come to believe that you'll be let off the hook for your own crimes. And murder becomes an easy job after a while: you are in a tough business and the tough cannot be squeamish. It is usually quick, almost perfunctory, in and out. After a while, you convince yourself that as you can get away with murder you can surely get away with illicit diamond buying.

It was an illicit investment in diamonds that led to the downfall of Daniel Sipholo, the policeman from Platplaas who led the hit squad that murdered Walter Kosagu.

The big diamond that caused the trouble had been stolen the hard way. The mines' security to prevent thefts was so elaborate, including X-rays to detect swallowed diamonds and body searches for diamonds stuffed up the anus, the black miner who found the stone deliberately drove his pick through his own foot, stuffed the diamond into the awful wound, then screamed for help. He was rushed to the surface, past the security apparatus. In the ambulance he dug the diamond out of the wound, and buried it in his anus. He was rushed into the hospital, and immediately anaesthetised.

When he came round the diamond was gone. His bowels had expelled it under anaesthesia, causing the black nurse considerable annoyance: but when she removed the soiled linen she spotted the stone. She hastily thrust it up her own anus. A week later she offloaded the diamond to a taxi driver. Three weeks later it was one of eleven stones bought by a white farmer, Hendrik van Rensburg, in the Transvaal. Mr van Rensburg was an illicit diamond buyer from way back. Daniel knew of him by repute. A meeting was arranged by telephone. It took place on a deserted farm road.

Mr van Rensburg did not like dealing with kaffirs, even good ones who showed due respect, and he virulently detested ones like Daniel. In Mr van Rensburg's view there was only one *really* good kaffir, and that was a dead one. But a cheeky bladdy kaffir's money was the same colour as a white man's. And if you could cheat a cheeky bladdy kaffir, so much the better. Daniel did not know much about diamonds: he could only tell a very good stone from an obviously flawed one. Daniel did not like Boers either. He was employed by Afrikaners, was well paid by them, and with those he worked with he had esprit de corps. But the Boers at large, like Van Rensburg, he detested. It was with satisfaction that he dismissed his small diamonds with a disparaging click of his tongue. 'All rubbish. But maybe I pay one thousand rand for the big one.'

To make matters more maddening, Hennie knew that the kaffir was right: the small stones *were* third-grade. But the big one was also flawed and Daniel did not know it. He took pleasure in angering the Boer; he thought the diamond was a bargain at three thousand rand. He had a pocketful of easy money to invest. Easy come, easy go. Daniel let the Boer posture and beat him up to two thousand, counted out the money with a contemptuous flourish, then theatrically offered him his black hand. To his surprise Hennie accepted it, with a carnivorous smile. For Hennie rejoiced that he had flogged this cheeky bladdy kaffir a flawed diamond, worth only one thousand on the black market, for two.

When, four days later, Daniel discovered that he had been cheated, he drove out to Hennie's farm to demand the money back. He had to ask directions, and it was ten o'clock at night when he arrived. He parked outside the fence surrounding the homestead. He climbed over the gate, checked his gun, pulled on woollen gloves, and walked towards the house. He could make out the glow of a television screen behind curtained windows. He walked to the back door and knocked loudly.

As they were arguing inside the kitchen, Daniel pulled out his gun on Van Rensburg, and in the ensuing fight shot him dead. It was a piece of drama that would have daunted most women, but not Mrs Maria van Rensburg: she tried to reach the gun rack, and Daniel shot her too.

It was intended only as a warning shot but Daniel thought he had killed her. He failed to recover his money, but he did take an emerald brooch from her body before disappearing into the night.

But Maria van Rensburg was not dead. Within ten minutes she was crawling to the telephone.

The police found the peasants from whom Daniel had asked directions, and one happened to remember the number of Daniel's car. The tyre marks outside Hennie's gate matched exactly the tyres on Daniel's car when it was traced back to Platplaas. Wool fibres found on Mr van Rensburg's face matched the gloves found in Daniel's room, in thickness, substance and colour. Daniel had got rid of the gun, but in his possession was Mrs van Rensburg's brooch. At the identification parade, she unhesitatingly identified him as the killer.

Daniel was surprised that matters had got as far as a formal charge: he had expected Captain Erik Badenhorst to have given a few nods and winks resulting in his speedy release. However, Daniel figured that the wheels within wheels took time: after all, 'unofficial and deniable' was the name of his corps' game. During the next six weeks he telephoned Platplaas frequently from the prison, but Captain Badenhorst was never in and never returned his calls. Even so, he wasn't unduly concerned when the indictment of murder was served upon him. He was still unconcerned when the young advocate assigned to defend him *pro deo* came to see him.

The advocate was astonished at Daniel's attitude. The evidence was stacked against him: the car number, the tyres, the woollen fibres, the brooch, the eye-witness account of Mrs van Rensburg. Nobody could have got Daniel off the gallows, unless maybe he came up with a convincing story of self-defence: but Daniel insisted that it was all a case of mistaken identity. 'I am innocent,' he said. 'Ask Captain Badenhorst, and if he is out, ask General Krombrink.'

'And what will they tell the court? That you were with them on the night Mr van Rensburg was murdered?'

'I've told you, I was at home in bed. Just ask Captain Badenhorst, and everything will be all right. Just say: "Remember Walter".'

'"*Walter*"? Walter who?'

'Just Walter,' Daniel said. 'He'll understand.'

Platplaas is not in the telephone book. When the lawyer was eventually put through by the central police exchange Captain Badenhorst said apologetically: 'Sir, I don't know anything. Except that Daniel was on my squad, yes. But I don't know where he was that night.'

'He said I must mention Walter to you.'

There was a moment's silence. Then: 'I don't know what he's talking about.'

'But you know who Walter is?'

'I've no idea, man.'

The lawyer said crisply: 'Very well, I'll try General Krombrink. He's your over-all superior officer I believe?'

But General Krombrink was not helpful at all:

'I don't know anything about this bloke Daniel. I'm told he was a member of Platplaas under Captain Badenhorst but I can't even remember hearing his name until this murder case came up, hey. Now he's sending mysterious messages about somebody called Walter. Please tell your client to stop bothering us.'

When the lawyer returned to the prison to report this, Daniel was still not unduly perturbed. Evidently his release would be achieved *after* the trial. 'For Christ's sake, Daniel,' the lawyer groaned, 'give me something to defend you with! If you don't I promise you're going to hang.'

'I will not hang.'

At the other end of the prison, on Death Row, another man was quite certain he would not hang. He was Barend Strydom, the man who had shot all those blacks in Pretoria. He had written his letter to the president a long time ago, asking him to exercise his prerogative of mercy. The president had not yet replied. Barend knew the Afrikaner right wing would be up in arms if he was hanged, he knew the president was scared to hang him for fear of a right-wing backlash.

Every man is presumed innocent until proven guilty, and it is the defence lawyer's duty to test the prosecutor's case to the utmost with cross-examination. Daniel's lawyer did the best with what slender ammunition he had: the natives who noted Daniel's car number were mistaken; there are millions of tyres that would have left identical marks, millions of woollen gloves made from the same material as Daniel's; Mrs van Rensburg was in terrible shock so her identification across a half-lit room was unreliable; Daniel's story, that he bought her brooch from a peddler, was feasible. Daniel declined to go into the witness box but instead made an unsworn statement from the dock saying he was in his quarters that night. It was an unnerving experience when he was sentenced to hang by the neck until he was dead, but he was still not really worried. Indeed, he wanted to get the judicial process behind him so that the wheels within wheels could get him out.

But being transferred to Death Row was a sobering experience. It was in the maximum security section, gun turrets dominating the courtyard. A series of iron doors clanged behind him. And just down the corridor, above the chapel where the condemned said their last prayers, was the gallows chamber, and the last-night holding cell, called The Pot.

Daniel was told that he had the right to petition for leave to appeal, and to petition the president for mercy. Daniel was not interested in an appeal but he was desperately tempted to write to the president threatening to tell the world about police hit squads. But he was scared to interfere with those wheels within wheels. Every day he expected to be told that he had been reprieved. He sent more messages via prison authorities to Captain Badenhorst. But he received no response. His anxiety mounted; and when the first executions since his arrival took place, and the condemned men were taken to The Pot and the all-night singing started from the vast prison to give them courage, Daniel became frantic. And at dawn when the singing reached its crescendo and the footsteps of the hangman passed his cell and he heard the bang of the trapdoor, Daniel vomited.

That day notice of execution was served upon him. The document advised him that the death sentence would be carried out seven days hence. And Daniel beat against his door, screaming that he'd tell his lawyer everything he knew about the police unless General Krombrink came at once. This threat got through, relayed by the superintendent. The next day a verbal message came from General Krombrink that he would come the following day. Daniel heaved a massive sigh of relief.

But the General did not appear the following day. Daniel sent another message. A reply came back that he must be patient. When he did not appear the following day, Daniel sent a desperate instruction to his sister to visit the General. She did so, and the General told her he would visit Daniel the following day. That was the day before his execution.

Something else happened that fateful Wednesday morning: Luke Mahoney's story about the arms-drop to Renamo and the murder of Richard Barker was published internationally. The common motif of the headlines was: SOUTH AFRICAN HIT SQUADS EXPOSED? The news went through Pretoria Central Prison like wildfire. Daniel kicked the door of his cell and screamed: '*Tell General Krombrink to come or I will tell everything to the newspaper . . . !*'

That message also got through, promptly. But it was not General Krombrink who arrived. It was a black sergeant. Daniel cried: '*Where's General Krombrink?*' The black sergeant whispered: 'He cannot come.

And nobody will believe you, they will say you are a desperate man trying to save his neck. He says you must take the pain and keep your mouth shut.'

'"*Take the pain*"?' Daniel bellowed.

'And Captain Badenhorst has left the police.'

'*Left the police?*' Daniel smashed his hand on the table. '*I'm going to tell the newspapers about the murder of Walter Kosagu! Tell them everything about Platplaas! Call my lawyer! Call the newspapers!*'

But Daniel's lawyer was not at home. It was Steven of Lawyers for Human Rights who came.

Darkness had fallen and the singing for the condemned man had already started when Steven arrived. He listened to the sweating, frantic Daniel, then he hurried to telephone Splinter Woodcock. Splinter telephoned Katrina's number, got Mahoney out of the whirlpool bath and told him to get his ass over to Pretoria because he had a helluva story. Then he telephoned the Minister of Justice.

'Sir, this is a matter of grave national concern; tomorrow this story will be trumpeted around the world whether or not you grant the stay of execution I am about to seek. If you refuse, the president will forever be accused of hanging a man to cover up evidence of the state's hit squads. If you grant the stay of execution, your government can only be praised for grasping the nettle and investigating these shocking allegations.'

71

It was major news across the world: CONDEMNED MAN'S REVELATIONS WIN STAY OF EXECUTION. President Reagan demanded a full investigation, the British government demanded that Daniel not be made the scapegoat. There were howls for a judicial inquiry. But President de Klerk said a judicial inquiry could take years and he ordered the Attorney General to investigate, to 'cut this matter to the bone'. Senior policemen implicated by Daniel were running for cover. General Krombrink roared: 'It's all lies,' before slamming down the phone on Mahoney. And Erik Badenhorst, the man most directly implicated by Daniel, was a very worried man, and he was talking to nobody.

Mahoney was delighted by the police discomfort. Every writer loves a scoop, but to him it meant more – sweet revenge on Krombrink for what he had done to him and Patti Gandhi. But it was alarming proof of forces entrenched deep in the system that could sabotage reform and might even drag South Africa into a civil war. God, he wanted Katrina out of this. And he was disgusted that there was going to be no judicial inquiry to get the rest of the story.

'This is just the tip of the iceberg,' Katrina said. 'Thank God that De Klerk has just taken over the presidency and can honestly say he knew nothing about it.'

'Do you believe him?'

'Oh . . . Didn't we *all* know that South Africa must have a Dirty Tricks Department? Like America, Britain, France – even the goody-two-shoes Swiss. Even as we speak other countries' agents are up to dirty tricks. But it's a matter of *degree*, isn't it? Sure I'd have said that South Africa had some kind of Dirty Tricks Bureau – but the *sordid* stuff Daniel's told you about stabbing Walter Kosagu to death because he opposed apartheid? And they must have shot Richard Barker. And Dr Rick Turner. And Anton Lubowski. Who made *our* decisions to commit those murders – and why? Did *my* government really murder all those people just because they opposed them? If so, it's appalling. That puts us in the same brutal league as the KGB and the Gestapo. In the same league as all these African dictators.' She looked at him grimly. 'Would you believe that of the British?'

Mahoney murmured: 'History proves that the British perfected Dirty Tricks three hundred years ago.'

Katrina snorted. 'True, but I simply do not believe it of *my* government. Those hit squads are the work of a rogue clique of securocrats, Luke. Remember that the Afrikaner, even though he's rough and ready, expects his leaders to be straight – legalistic, God-fearing. I think the decisions to murder those people were made by the likes of General Krombrink, by certain policemen grown too big for their boots. People who've grown to believe they're a law unto themselves during the Total Strategy era. So, no, I don't think FW de Klerk knew.'

Mahoney demanded: 'So why the hell doesn't he fire the Minister of Police now he *does* know?'

'To let him draw the flak, perhaps? Let *him* stand up in Parliament and face the music. It's better than De Klerk wringing his hands and saying he doesn't know the answers.'

'He should fire him with a crack of thunder and let him answer the questions before a judicial commission of inquiry!'

'He will fire him, after he's served his purpose.'

'As a scapegoat? We don't want scapegoats – we want *all* the fucking goats!' He shook his head. 'De Klerk doesn't want to upset the security establishment, that's why he doesn't fire the minister!' He snorted in disgust. 'He says he's going to wrest power from the securocrats and restore it to Parliament, so now is the golden opportunity. Fire the bastard!'

Katrina said quietly: 'And risk a rebellion amongst the security forces? That's a very real risk, Luke – the securocrats have been calling the tune for so long they think they *are* the government. And they think they can wipe out the ANC if De Klerk would only let them get on with the job. It wouldn't take much to bring about a rebellion by a big chunk of the security forces. A coup d'état? Where would the reform process be then?'

Mahoney snorted. He took a swallow of beer. 'You'd get your Afrikaner homeland then.'

'For Christ's sake,' she groaned, 'we want a negotiated homeland. We do not want to seize our land with a gun. We don't want any more bloodshed – this country is soaked in blood. We don't want trouble – we want *peace*. And the only chance of peaceful negotiation is by De Klerk organizing it! So the last thing we want is a rebellion. And starting a witch-hunt now by appointing a judicial commission inquiry could cause a rebellion!'

Mahoney shook his head. 'He'll have to do it,' he warned.

But the president did not do it. To hold a judicial inquiry, he said, would take years of bitterness and be destructive to the climate for negotiations: a quiet investigation by the Attorney General was better. And the outcry redoubled.

More alarming news followed. The next week the police arrested five white men who called themselves the Order of Death, and charged them with murdering blacks at random to prepare themselves for wholesale killing to come: their hitlists included President de Klerk and the Foreign Minister. Then the news broke of a right-wing organization of professional people from every branch of society, government, the security forces and the civil service, who were dedicated to derailing the president's reform process, and their information network reached right into the cabinet. And then it was announced that on 12th December Daniel Sipholo would appear in court in Durban at a preparatory examination into the murder of Walter Kosagu.

Mahoney was delighted. This was high drama. The only evidence against Daniel was his own confession, which had temporarily saved him from the gallows. If he now pleaded guilty to Walter Kosagu's murder he would be committed for trial in the Supreme Court; he would condemn himself to the gallows yet again but at the same time drop the police right in the shit. If he pleaded not guilty it would be an admission that his story was lies, and he would re-condemn himself to the gallows for Hennie van Rensburg's murder. So he had nothing to lose by telling the truth. The police desperately wanted him to plead not guilty.

Mahoney telephoned Splinter Woodcock. 'What have you advised him?' he demanded.

'What any lawyer would advise in a capital case: to reserve his defence until his trial in the Supreme Court.'

Oh, Mahoney wanted that Supreme Court trial to take place. He wanted the whole sordid story laid bare. He badly wanted Daniel to plead guilty. He badly wanted to see General Krombrink on trial for his life.

Luke and Katrina were to spend Christmas with Katrina's family, and now that Katrina's university vacation had begun, they set off. Luke planned to make the most of the long journey: they would be able to go to Durban to observe the proceedings, and also visit his sister in KwaZulu, but first Mahoney wanted to see some historical sites for his journals.

It was the route of the Great Trek and its battle-sites Mahoney wanted to see. They left Johannesburg in the early morning with a cold-box of booze, heading south, and crossed the Vaal River into the Orange Free State. In the late afternoon they saw the mountain Thaba Nchu rising up: this was where the voortrekkers had gathered in their multitude of wagons after crossing the Orange River, to decide where to go.

Luke and Katrina spent the night at the Thaba Nchu Sun casino. One side of the historic mountain was largely owned by the casino consortium and the surrounding grasslands were green and clean. Now gaming salons glittered where a hundred and sixty years ago the wagons had outspanned, and down the passage the cinema was showing American pornographic films. Mahoney and Katrina stood on their balcony, drinking wine, watching the sun go down. 'This is where South Africa's troubles began.'

'My people have caused trouble? It was you British who were the trouble, buster!'

He took her in his arms. 'You ain't seen nothin' yet.'

The next morning they drove round to the other side of the mountain. The earth was cropped bare, plastic bags littered the veld, the slum town of Thaba Nchu sprawled. It was part of the patchwork independent Republic of Bophuthatswana, home of the tribe which had helped the voortrekkers after the Battle of Vegkop against Mzilikazi. Now they found miles of mud huts with rusted tin roofs, rutted roads, scrawny cattle, the shells of cars, plastic bags flapping, people teeming. Mahoney followed the pitted street of joyless native stores.

He was looking for the church that Reverend Archbell had built. They found it at the top of the decrepit main road, at the foot of the mountain. Made of carved stone, it stood in an unkempt garden. Behind it were a number of huts under bleak blue-gum trees. Mahoney looked at the run-down church; then he looked back down the dusty, dirty main road. Christ.

'This building is a national monument,' he said. 'Around this historic site the voortrekkers gathered to discuss their future. Here the first cornerstones of South Africa were laid. *Here* all the fears and beliefs of the Afrikaners were given the first articulation. Here they sealed their fate, the fate of our nation. And what has this historic site become?' He waved a hand down the road. 'Part of an African slum.' He shook his head. 'And I'm afraid that the rest of South Africa is going to become like this, Kat.'

'And that's why we have to have our own state,' she said quietly.

Mahoney wanted to say, Oh Christ, woman, stop your daydreams and come to live with me in Hong Kong.

They crossed the invisible state line back into South Africa and immediately the fields were laden with summer crops and the cattle sleek.

In the afternoon they arrived at the battlefield of Vegkop. Here Potgieter's laager of fifty-four wagons had stood beneath the flat-topped, rocky hill. The site was marked by a monument – a great pile of boulders, from which rose a bronze statue of a triumphant voortrekker brandishing a rifle in one hand, a bunch of broken assegais in the other. The surrounding lawns were green, and well mown. As he looked at the hill Mahoney imagined the lookout raising the alarm, the feverish activity as men, women and children hurried to their battle stations; the anguish of leaving their cattle outside; their mounting dread as the veld began to turn black as ink as five thousand warriors appeared; their battle hiss rising up, the sun glinting on their assegais, the head-dresses dancing. He imagined the commando riding out to parley, the warriors charging, the commando galloping back to the laager.

'This is where Ernest Mahoney met his beloved Sarie for the first time. If he hadn't, I wouldn't be alive today.'

Katrina smiled. 'Thank God he did.'

In the late afternoon they crossed the Drakensberg at the pass where, a hundred and sixty years ago, Piet Retief, the newly elected Governor of the United Laagers, had descended into Zulu country to parley with Dingaan. They drove down through the rolling green hills of Natal, to Durban.

The next morning they went to the Magistrates' Court to attend the preparatory examination of Daniel Sipholo.

The press corps was there in force. Everybody wanted Daniel to plead guilty and drop the government in it. The august courtroom was packed with local journalists and foreign correspondents. Mahoney and Katrina sat in the front row, with Splinter Woodcock. At five minutes to ten the public prosecutor appeared, in his gown, and sat down at the Bar. A number of senior policemen huddled around him for last-minute consultation. At two minutes to ten Daniel emerged from the holding cells below the court, into the dock. He was a medium-sized, lean man with a sullen expression. And he gladdened Mahoney's heart. Here was an angry accused, already under sentence of death, who had nothing to lose by telling the truth and dropping his erstwhile employers, particularly General Krombrink, right in the big bad shit. Then the orderly cried: 'Silence in Court,' and the magistrate walked in.

The evidence was simple. The evidence of the police patrol who found Walter Kosagu's mutilated body outside the football stadium. The evidence of the pathologist that Walter Kosagu died of multiple stab-wounds. The evidence of Steven that he had spoken to the accused on the eve of his execution, as a result of which he had summoned his superior, Advocate Woodcock of Lawyers for Human Rights, to Death Row. The evidence of Advocate Woodcock that he had recorded an affidavit from the accused, as a result of which he had secured a stay of execution from the Minister of Justice. The evidence of a police officer that he had subsequently formally charged the accused with the murder of Walter Kosagu; the accused's replies to the charge, voluntarily given, confessing to the murder, were handed into the court.

That was it: the prosecutor closed his case, and the charge of murder was formally put to Daniel. And everybody waited with bated breath for Daniel to respond.

'I plead guilty. I committed this murder with three police accomplices on the orders of Captain Erik Badenhorst and General Krombrink of the South African Police. I will give full details at my trial in the Supreme Court.'

501

72

It was a good start to their holiday, at the end of that fateful year of 1989, the year FW de Klerk came to power in South Africa. Oh, in his sound and sober senses, Mahoney wanted Katrina out of this, but right now he was in the thick of it, and it was *his* country and, *God*, it was exciting, and he loved it. With Daniel's plea of guilty yesterday General Krombrink was going to get his comeuppance at last, and now it was the Christmas season and he had almost one whole glorious month's holiday with his beautiful woman.

That afternoon they drove up the Natal coast to visit Mahoney's sister, Jill. Katrina was nervous. 'Supposing she doesn't like me?' 'How could anybody not *adore* you?' 'But maybe she'll think I'm a typical Boer?' 'She'll think you're as wonderful a Boer as I do.' They drove up the undulating, sultry eastern coast, with vast rolling fields of sugar cane on one side of the highway, the long beaches of the Indian Ocean on the other. At sunset they left the lush coastland behind and turned up into the bushy hills, and followed the signs to Shaka's Place.

Shaka's Place was a hotel, consisting of two dozen large reed huts in the traditional Zulu shape of beehives. The complex was surrounded by the high traditional fence of rough-hewn poles. Clean-swept earth, flower beds and lawns separated each hut. In the centre of the complex was a large thatched dining hut with tables made of local wood, a thatched bar which served every kind of booze including Zulu maize-beer in calabash gourds, and a big kitchen hut which cooked only traditional Zulu dishes in big black iron pots over open fires. All the staff, except the white manager, were dressed in traditional Zulu garb. Mahoney was enchanted: nothing like this had existed in South Africa when he lived here. 'How did you know about this place?'

'*Aha* . . . ' she smiled.

'Okay, I don't want to know.'

They dined by candlelight on Zulu stew and maize porridge, drinking excellent Cape wines, surrounded by jolly American and German tourists, served by pretty, bare-foot Zulu girls in short beaded loin-cloths that just covered their buttocks.

'Now you understand,' Katrina said with a grin, 'why it's alleged that the average Afrikaner has about ten per cent black blood in his veins.'

'Is that true, d'you think?'

'Oh yes. We're a very mongrel race, the so-called White Tribe of Africa. Dutch, French, German, Hottentot, Xhosa, Zulu – even some British ones, alas. And all those Malay slave-girls of yore . . . '

'How much have you got?'

'Can't you tell, baas?'

It was improbable, with that fresh-faced Dutch beauty. 'Do you think I've got any?'

She put on a Cape Coloured accent: *'Agh sis no, Master, so it's time you got out in the sun, hey.'*

After dinner there was an exhibition of Zulu dancing in the Great Place, the giant beehive hut in the centre of the compound. The tourists lined the walls on benches with their cameras and videos, and in came a troupe of gleaming Zulu warriors in traditional battle-dress, with oxhide shields and gleaming spears, skirts and leggings of animal tails. They stamped their feet on the raw earth so it shook, and in magnificent unison they danced and gave their war-cries and made terrifying charges that startled everybody and drew roars of applause afterwards. Then on came the bare-breasted Zulu girls who did the traditional love-dance of the maidens lying in wait for their warriors, leaping up in unison as their paramours came home from Shaka's wars, going into a savage dance to seduce them, their feet stamping and their legs kicking to the sky, their breasts bouncing, their wide smiles flashing, their sensuous shouts.

Afterwards, lying in Katrina's arms in their Zulu hut between crisp sheets on a soft mattress, Mahoney said: 'It stirred my blood. I saw those warriors at the Battle of Blood River. At Isandhlwana and Ulundi. God, what a magnificent tradition the Zulus have. What a tragedy if that is lost, if they become a nation of urbanised blacks in white man's clothes.'

Katrina said in the dark: 'Zululand will remain Zululand in the new South Africa. They will never accept the ANC as their overlords. The Zulus must have their own volkstaat, like the Afrikaner must have his. Chief Buthelezi will see to that.'

The next day they crossed the invisible border into KwaZulu, and immediately the lushness gave way to hard hills and scrub and over-grazed land, and the woven beehive huts were replaced with run-down mud kraals with rusted iron roofs, plastic bags littered the roadside, and the Zulus were not wearing their romantic tribal dress, they wore white man's tatters.

'This is what apartheid has done to a proud people,' Katrina said.

Thus they came to Dingaan's Kraal, where a hundred and sixty years ago Piet Retief had been murdered when he went to parley with the Zulus for land for his voortrekkers.

Mahoney was both disappointed and enthralled. Disappointed because the Place of the Elephant was dusty and run down, enthralled because he could imagine how it looked all those years ago. The perimeter of the kraal city was still visible, and he could make out the remnants of a few huts.

'Here,' pointed the bespectacled KwaZulu guide who had sold them their entrance tickets, 'is where the Great Place stood, Dingaan's own hut.'

Beyond was Execution Hill, where the daily killings were carried out, where vultures always flew, where Piet Retief and his party were clubbed to death. They climbed up it. There was a tall stone monument there, erected by the South African government, with a weathered bronze plaque commemorating the names of the murdered voortrekkers. On another hill the huts of the mission station had stood, where the Reverend Owen had prayed as he watched the fearful executions and afterwards confided to his diaries that it was 'a trying moment'. There was the communal grave beside the monument, where the bones of the murdered voortrekkers were interred.

Katrina said: 'This is where Piet Retief's satchel was found after the Battle of Blood River, bearing the parchment on which Dingaan had made his mark, granting the land south of the Tugela River to the voortrekkers as their first volkstaat.'

Yes, the place was drenched in history which stirred Mahoney's blood and made him want to come back to South Africa. But he wished she'd stop thinking about her volkstaat.

That morning they drove on to Ulundi, the new capital city of the self-governing homeland of KwaZulu. This was the stronghold where Chief Buthelezi lived, and the Zulu monarch, King Goodwill Zwelithini, both direct descendants of Shaka, Dingaan, Cetshwayo. And this was the site of the Battle of Ulundi, where the British Empire had finally broken the might of the Zulu nation. The monument to the battle was well kept by the KwaZulu government: the cemetery, in the big square which the British had formed on the hilltop as the Zulus charged, wave upon wave, to 'wash' their spears, was well tended. A mile away, on the hills, the new Ulundi rose up.

They drove through it. It was modern and raw. The big buildings stood bleakly on bulldozed earth amongst newly tarred roads alongside which no lawns or trees yet grew. There were the new KwaZulu Legislature, the new civil service blocks, the residence of Chief Buthelezi, the palace of King Goodwill, the acres of new houses for KwaZulu government ministers, the new shopping malls, bus stations. Beyond were the hillsides of suburbs with rows of little concrete cottages, not unlike Soweto. It was all the creation of apartheid, all paid for by the South African government and the taxpayer. They drove slowly through the new little purpose-built city.

Katrina stopped the car and said: 'Impressive, isn't it?'

It was. 'But also an impressive waste of money. And precious time.'

'Okay. But is it entirely wasted? Look, I don't defend the sin of apartheid. Because all this,' she waved a hand, 'was built for the wrong moral reasons – to get rid of the Zulus and deny them their rightful place in South Africa as citizens so that the whites could lay claim to the rest of the land. But, as you say in *Big Trouble*, gradualism is necessary to teach the blacks the art of democracy, to avoid the fate of the rest of Africa. This land historically belongs to the Zulus, and when the new South Africa comes, the Zulus will want to keep this part of the country Zulu, with their own self-government, they won't accept the Xhosa – they will want to be an autonomous state in the Federation of South Africa. And most of the whites in Natal will support them. And this,' she waved her hand again, 'has given them a physical base and infra-structure – and practical experience of self-government – from which to start pressing those claims. So, although apartheid was a failure, and unjust for all the familiar reasons, some good may come out of it. Maybe it wasn't a complete waste of money – and it gave them some learning time.'

That was also true. Maybe, if the Afrikaner had given the Zulus the whole of Natal and not just a patchwork part of it, as it gave the Xhosa the whole of the Transkei, the system might have worked.

They turned south again and headed through the rolling hills towards the midlands. It was mid-afternoon when they approached the American Zulu Mission, overlooking the Tugela River. As they approached the cluster of thatched buildings on the hilltop the door of a house burst open and Jill came running down the garden path, a laugh all over her face. Mahoney stopped the car and scrambled out, grinning, and ran into his sister's arms.

'Darling, she's *gorgeous*,' Jill whispered in an aside over dinner – 'and such a conversationalist . . .'

Mahoney wished he could say the same for his brother-in-law. The Reverend Leonard Dawson was as American as apple-pie and expressed his opinions as if he were the only person to have thought of them, and used American clichés as innocently as if he had coined them himself. The American Way would solve all the problems of the world – 'Uncle Sam wouldn't hand you guys a lemon' and 'We won't leave you guys behind the eight-ball', and communism was a 'basket case'. What was good for General Motors was good for America and what was good for America was good for South Africa. 'We're all God's happy family' and American family values of motherhood and Father's Day was what black Africa needed to 'stop tribalism at first base' and allow 'the commandments to hit a home-run'. It followed that polygamy and tribal customs were a 'no-no' and one of apartheid's many 'boo-boos' was permitting it. Democracy would flourish once apartheid was 'garbage-canned', and politicians would 'keep their hands out of the cookie-jar' once they 'tuned in to Jesus'. As for Katrina's volkstaat, it was a 'non-starter'.

'I don't agree,' Katrina said, putting on an American accent, 'but I'll sure defend to the death your right to say it.'

'Hey – that's a saying we've got in America!'

'Oh darling,' Jill whispered to Mahoney, 'I do so hope you marry her. And don't be put off by her volkstaat notions – it'll never happen. Bring her to live in Natal, so you're near me. It's so *British* here. The Last Outpost of the Empire, we call it . . . '

They spent two days at the mission. Mahoney and Katrina accompanied Jill as she did her work, he sat in classrooms listening to her teach, followed her through the craft workshops, the carpentry shop, the clinic, trudged through the landscaped fields listening to her lectures on crop rotation, fertilization, irrigation. The mission was an oasis in the exsanguinated scrub of KwaZulu. He was vastly impressed, and very proud of his sister. He even sat in church and listened to his brother-in-law preach, and he was equally impressed. The man spoke fluent Zulu, albeit with an American accent, and he used just the right degree of showmanship to carry his congregation with him – the Zulus loved it, even though Mahoney doubted they believed the meek would inherit the earth. Their singing was superb, the choir brought a burn to his eyes. Mahoney changed his opinion of his sister's husband: the man was doing a bloody good job, he was proud of him too. And, God, the whole thing made him feel guilty: what was *he* doing for this country?

On the second evening Mahoney took them out to dinner at the St George Hotel across the Tugela River, outside KwaZulu. Yes, as Jill had said, it was so British here. The grand old thatched hotel nestled in rolling green pastures that could for all the world be England except for the sultry temperature. The sprawling gardens with the big pond, the swans, the lawns, could be a tranquil English country garden. It was hard to believe that just out there beyond the Tugela River the earth was stripped by over-grazing, that there was mayhem as Inkatha Zulus fought UDF Zulus.

The hotel was jolly with landed gentry speaking in well-bred English accents, and he thought of the vast scrubland of the Karoo they were heading for tomorrow, where Katrina wanted to build her volkstaat, hot, hard, dusty, gritty, where all you heard was Afrikaans, all you saw was sheep and bushes and distant kopjes, stretching all the way to the horizon: and he thought, If I'm going to live in South Africa this is where I want to be – amongst my own. *And Katrina was going to live here with him.* Yes, of course he could forget about her Afrikaner volkstaat. But marry her first, that was the trick. Now he knew with absolute certainty that that was what he wanted to do.

73

The next day was 16th December, the Day of the Covenant, the anniversary of the Battle of Blood River when the Boers had defeated Dingaan. There was to be a big memorial service at the battlesite, and Mahoney wanted to see it. They took leave of his sister and brother-in-law, and found their way down winding tracks to join hundreds of vehicles carrying thousands of Afrikaners through the rolling hills, down to the historic site on the river, where the laager of life-size bronze wagons commemorated the battle.

It began with a massive religious service. Then speakers railed against the government for breaking faith with the Lord and with the Afrikaner volk. Finally the man everybody had been waiting for got to his feet: Eugene Terreblanche, the leader of the AWB, dressed in khaki, with his veld hat and beard.

Mahoney sat on the grass with Katrina inside the great laager and listened to the deep ringing tones rising up to the Zulu sky. It made Mahoney's blood stir. The man was a superb orator. It took a minute before Mahoney realised the man had opened his speech by quoting poetry; then it was hard to tell where poetry ended and political oratory began. The speech flowed brilliantly into historical detail which also seemed to rhyme. The effect was hypnotic. Mahoney sat, hearing the thunder of the guns, almost smelling the gunpowder, the sweat of the glistening hordes charging down the hillsides, wave upon wave trying to breach these ramparts of wagons, assegais flying: he could almost see his great great grandfather frantically firing and reloading, the barrel red-hot, the bang as he fired into the mass of black charging flesh. Yes, Mahoney felt his blood stir. Then Terreblanche rolled on to the Boer War, to the legions of Great Britain arrayed against the fledgling voortrekker republics, against the lonely women and children in the far-flung homesteads keeping the homefires burning while their valiant men were off at the war, he could hear the cries as the British kicked down the doors and dragged them out, he could see the cornfields going up in flames, hear the crackle of the homestead being put to the torch, hear the weeping of the women and children as they were herded off to the faraway concentration camps. As Terreblanche's hypnotic voice rumbled on he saw the horror of those camps, the bleak rows of tents under the winter sky, the malnourished children dying in their mother's arms of dysentery and cholera, he saw the burial carts, the little graves, he heard the cries of grief.

And he saw the poverty when the dreadful war was over, the scorched earth, the bones of slaughtered livestock littering the veld. He felt the despair as the Afrikaner trekked off the land to the towns to compete for lowly manual labour against blacks. He felt their humiliation as poor whites in their own land. And he felt their anger at being asked to fight for the British victor in two world wars. He felt the fury of the 1914 Rebels and the wrath of the Ossewa Brandwag. And then, as Terreblanche's voice rose, he felt the joy of the 1948 elections as the Afrikaners were swept to political power, getting their country back, empowered at last to govern their country according to God's will. And a golden age of peace and prosperity had ensued, for God had chosen the Afrikaner to be His fortress in godless Africa. And now President de Klerk was flying in the face of the Holy Bible, tearing down the pillars of Christianity itself!

'*Apartheid has not failed! It is the government that failed God . . . !*'

So the time had come for the true servants of God, the true Afrikaners, to re-affirm the holy covenant and gird themselves for the war that was coming, the war against the godless ANC and the South African Communist Party – war that would ultimately be won by the righteous, for God would as surely stand by His chosen people as He stood by them at the Battle of Blood River, and the Christian law of apartheid would be restored to this holy land.

It was a brilliant speech. Mahoney glanced at Katrina. She was watching the man with steady, calculating eyes. And, oh God, he wanted to get her out of all this. Out, out, out. Then Terreblanche asked everybody to stand and take the vow that the voortrekkers had taken this day a hundred and fifty-one years ago.

Mahoney had no objection to standing, but no intention of taking the vow. Katrina understood. They got to their feet, with the thousands. Terreblanche, his baritone ringing, asked everybody to take the hand of those on either side of them. Mahoney glanced at Katrina, and gave a small shake of his head. They stood, their arms at their sides, while all about them thousands joined hands. And Terreblanche began to administer the oath.

'Almighty God . . .'

Mahoney kept his eyes open. Then he felt a hand take his. It belonged to an elderly lady on his left, and she gave him a smile. He glanced at Katrina; an old man beside her had taken her hand too. She looked at Mahoney, her eyes moist. Then, as the resonant vow rolled over them, she slipped her hand into his. And she closed her eyes and lowered her head.

Mahoney watched her out of the corner of his eye, his heart sinking. She held his hand tight, and her lips moved silently.

The next day they drove up the rolling hills into the Drakensberg mountains, roughly following the route the voortrekkers had taken. They reached the crest at Kerkendal, where Piet Retief had ordered his people to wait whilst he rode down to parley with Dingaan: this was the place where Ernest Mahoney had found his Sarie again, the girl who had been his loader at the Battle of Vegkop, learned she was pregnant and started the line of descendants which ended in Luke. They followed the track to the cluster of huge boulders which the voortrekkers had used as a church to give thanks to the Lord when they received Retief's news that Dingaan had granted them their promised land, before butchering them at Blaukrans and Weenen – meaning 'weeping', the 'place of tears'. They walked to the outcrop where stood the statue of the barefoot trekker woman, her back to the promised land below, who had said she would rather walk thus over the Drakensberg than submit to British rule again. It was Mahoney's great great grandmother, Sarie, who had said those words.

They sat on the grass and drank a bottle of beer.

'No, I did not repeat the vow,' Katrina said in answer to his question. 'It was the solemnity of the moment that moved me – I was saying my own prayer for the new South Africa. I do not believe apartheid is God's will, Luke. But God did make the races different and the hard fact is that it's not easy to mix them politically. And it's every nation's right to govern themselves. The Afrikaner nation does not have the right to the old Boer republics, as Terreblanche was demanding. But he does have the right to his own part of it. That's what I was praying for.'

He was immensely relieved to hear that. 'And do you believe you're a chosen race?'

She smiled. 'Ja, learned it at my mother's knee.' Then she said seriously: 'I think God has given a special role to the Afrikaner, yes. As He had a special role for the Jews. Apartheid was a dreadful mistake, but the *purpose* of the Afrikaner remains: to be a permanent bastion of

Christianity and Western civilization on the dark continent of Africa. To be an example to the rest. The English did not have such a role, nor the French, nor the Portuguese: they packed up and went home. It's God's intention that the Afrikaner stays in order to fulfil His purpose. And that can only be done properly if he has his own homeland which is properly run. In that sense I think we're a chosen people, yes.'

It was only mid-afternoon but the Drakensberg cast long shadows down over the old promised land. And Mahoney remembered what the witch doctor told him, and Ernest's entry in the family journals, the warning of the old trekker who had said: 'Woe unto the land whose borders lie in shadow.'

The next day they crossed into the vast Orange Free State again, through great wheat fields and verdant pastures with the distant flat-topped kopjes that the voortrekkers had navigated by. In the late afternoon they crossed into the northern Cape. And the green highveld gave way to the hard, gritty Karoo, the scrub stretching to the mauve horizon.

God, this hard country was where she intended to live.

They came to the bleak village of Hopetown. Katrina stopped the car. 'Now then . . . ' She reached into the backseat for a large map.

It showed the northern Cape Province, stretching to the Atlantic Ocean. She said: 'This covers the heartland of our volkstaat. It's about ten per cent of South Africa's surface, about ten times the size of Israel. We don't expect to get it all, we'll be delighted with half. Happy with a third. Okay?'

'Okay,' Mahoney said solemnly.

'Now, there are three massive irrigation projects in or around this proposed heartland. Millions of hectares of this desert could become irrigated. Indeed it could become the breadbasket – or a major part of the breadbasket – of the new South Africa. Because the blacks will redistribute land and agriculture is going to suffer.'

Mahoney nodded. Oh, he agreed. And he agreed the Afrikaner should have his homeland. He just didn't believe they would get it.

'Now grasp *this*, Mr Mahoney. This Orange River Project I'm about to show you is one of the most comprehensive in the world. It includes two existing dams, largest of their kind in the southern hemisphere, and one of the longest water tunnels in the world. The nucleus of the project is the Hendrik Verwoerd Dam. The water flows from there through the Le Roux Dam, through the tunnel – ' she pointed at the map – 'to the Great Fish and Sundays River valley. Both the dams generate electricity. And the scheme includes more dams yet to be built downriver, the Torquay

Dam here – ' she pointed – 'the Boegoeberg Dam here, the Augrabies Dam over here. Then there are the Olifants River Scheme and the Doring River Development Project, here. Add it all up and you've got a highly viable economic area *much* better than Israel. *Much* more potential than Israel. And we probably also have mineral wealth which has yet to be checked out. Israel ain't got any of that.'

Mahoney wanted to kiss her earnest, beautiful blue eyes. And it was a hell of a lot more impressive than he had realised.

'Transport? Show me the rail-line and so forth?'

She pointed at the map again. 'In Upington there is an airport capable of handling international jets. There are good roads over the whole area. The Sishen to Saldanha railway line – ' she traced her finger – 'connects us to the sea, and we're researching the feasibility of another railway along the Orange River. Saldanha Bay is a natural deep-water port. *And* it's quite possible to make the Orange River navigable, for barges.'

'And how many people can this area support?'

'The beauty of this area is that it is so underpopulated because it is still desert. The whole area could easily support five million Afrikaners – little Israel supports six. At the moment there are only about two hundred and twenty thousand whites, all Afrikaners. And about five hundred thousand Coloureds, but they're Afrikaners too, they'll fit in fine.'

'You told me in New York that assimilation of the resident Coloureds is not yet official Volkswag policy. Has that changed?'

'No, but it will be, believe me. We have no intention of repeating apartheid's mistakes. Sure, there will be natural class differences socially, and some prejudice, particularly at first, but people like me will ensure that prejudice is eliminated.' She added: 'The same applies to the vote. Yes, at the moment our policy seems to be that only white Afrikaners will have the vote. But that won't stick, the world wouldn't permit it. That point will be bargained away at the Great Indaba. And any Afrikaner who imagines otherwise has got his head in the clouds.'

Mahoney had difficulty imagining the AWB and the Conservative Party accepting that. But her earnest enthusiasm and confidence was almost infectious. 'But how many Afrikaners are going to move? Sell up, pack up, leave their jobs and farms to come here?'

She said: 'At present there are about seven hundred thousand Afrikaners here, whites and brown. How many Jews lived in Palestine at the end of World War II? Only fifty-five thousand. How many Jewish immigrants were estimated would arrive at the end of World War II? "These wailing Jews", as Churchill described them. Nobody had any idea. In fact there were so many the immigrant ships had to be turned back by gunboats.' She nodded. 'We'll encourage the Afrikaner to have large families again. And they *will* because they'll need the help of the children, because it's our policy that we do all our manual labour ourselves, and not rely on black labour any more. Remember that the first priority of the new black government will be to redistribute land. And their first step will be to withdraw Land Bank loans from farmers who can't repay their debts. Foreclose on their mortgages. About forty-five thousand Afrikaner farmers would have their farms repossessed under such a tactic. Representing several hundred thousand mouths. Where're those people going to go? Unless they take up arms.' She nodded at the desert. 'Right here. Because we'll have a land-settlement scheme to encourage people to pioneer. And the new government will doubtless also make a compulsory purchase of many other white farms as a quick-fix to black land hunger. Where will those farmers go with their money? Many will come here to start again. And the new government won't have enough money so they'll pay the farmers out in government bonds, payable in, say, twenty years, with a small rate of interest. What are *those* farmers going to do? Can they retire? No. But they can come here and sell their bonds to the Volkstaat Bank which will enable them to start again.' She looked at him earnestly. 'Oh, we're confident we'll get plenty of immigrants.'

Mahoney smiled. Her conviction infectious. 'Okay.'

'Okay what?'

'Okay, sounds impressive.'

She punched him on the knee. 'Don't make fun of me, Mahoney!' She held up her finger. 'Remember the Israelis, buster!' She put the car into gear.

The harsh Karoo gave way to big circular fields of lucerne and wheat irrigated with huge overhead mobile sprinklers, hooped contraptions spewing water. Cattle and sheep grazed in paddocks, and over there the Orange River flowed between green banks. In the distance was a row of ten massive wheat silos, the mauve koppies rising up beyond.

'See what the Orange River can do?' Katrina said. 'Properly harnessed, it can turn the Karoo into a Garden of Eden.'

Yes, it was impressive. But Mahoney's idea of a Garden of Eden was tropical palms, bananas, waterfalls, blue lagoons and tumbling streams. 'Are farmers allowed to irrigate as much as they like?'

'Yes, but the further they pump the more expensive it gets.'

'And how much does one of those overhead sprinklers cost?'

'Depends on how many sections of pipe. Between seventy and a hundred thousand rand. Fifteen to twenty thousand pounds. Not bad. Look what a new car costs these days. And you can move your sprinkler system on to your next field. Reliable rain.'

Mahoney sighed. 'Okay.'

'What does that sigh mean, Smart-ass?'

'Talking about ass, I haven't had any since breakfast, how far is this hotel?'

Just then they came over a rise and in the distance was a cluster of rooftops, a church steeple rising up. She stopped the car.

'There it is,' she said proudly. 'Orania. Owned by Volkswag, lock, stock and barrel.'

Mahoney thought: *Rock*, stock and gun-barrel? But he didn't dare say it.

The village was originally built by the government to house its white workers building the PK le Roux dam, further upriver. There were about fifty pre-fabricated houses, on suburban-size stands. The streets were wide, made of concrete, tree-lined. The gardens were neat. A large sign read in Afrikaans: '*Welcome to Orania, the kernel of the Boerestaat.*' There was a miscellany of buildings, originally the administration offices of the dam workings; now they housed the Afsaal Cafe, and some cottage industries.

Katrina drove slowly down the concrete streets.

'We set up a company and bought the entire village from the government – it had been empty since the dam was finished. We restored it without using black labour. Now we have over three hundred permanent residents – and more are buying all the time. We're buying more land as it becomes available. We already have over three thousand hectares around here, including sixty-hectare small-holdings for farming. We do all our own donkey-work. We must think in terms of small, scientific farming methods and forget about huge farms worked by abundant cheap black labour – that was the Afrikaners' undoing. It gave him a feudal mentality. And his desire for huge farms made him trek further and further into troubled waters. We must become a small, modern state.' She added: 'The Volkswag leadership went to Israel recently and aroused a lot of enthusiasm. And an Israeli expert came out here and he was very impressed.'

The Israeli was impressed? 'Uh-huh?'

Katrina stopped the car. She said solemnly: 'For God's sake, this is just the beginning, Luke – the seedling which will grow – it is purely a demonstration model. God, we've only been going a short while and we already have our own doctor, a dentist, and seven qualified nurses amongst our permanent residents. We're building our own hospital. We have a retired magistrate, who's our legal advisor and ombudsman. We've got an elected town council. And a fully fledged school!' She waved a hand at the big building before them, standing in neat gardens. 'We've got almost a hundred pupils enrolled already. And a well-trained teaching staff! Christ, Rome wasn't built in a day!'

Mahoney put his hand on her knee. 'I'm sorry, I didn't mean to be flippant. I am also impressed.'

'Uh-*huh*?' she echoed him. 'I never promised you a rose garden, buster.' She shoved the gear lever and drove off towards the river.

Mahoney held her knee. 'I've said I'm sorry, Kat.'

'Nothing to be sorry about – the purpose of the trip is to get your reactions to my life's work, and we're getting them. Anyway, this,' she waved her hand to the left, 'is our so-called sports club.'

Mahoney squeezed her knee hard. 'Katrina, please stop the car.'

She jerked on the brakes. She looked at him grimly. 'Uh-*huh*?'

Mahoney spread his hands. 'Darling, you're understandably sensitive about this volkstaat issue. And justifiably hurt, because there is indeed impressive evidence here of will and progress. So let's talk about it. Like lovers, with serious decisions in mind.' He waved a finger over his shoulder earnestly. 'Yes, that's an impressive school. But the question arises as to where these kids are going to find work when they finish.'

'They'll have the whole volkstaat to choose from.'

'And if they can't find work they want?'

She looked at him grimly. 'You haven't grasped that the volkstaat is going to be part of an economic common market with South Africa. So if our kids can't find work here they'll look for it in the rest of South Africa.'

'Will South Africa – or Azania as it will probably be called – will it permit them to work?'

'Yes. It will be part of our common market treaty.'

'That means that workers from Azania can also come to work here?'

'Correct.'

'Okay. And if they stay long enough they will be eligible to become citizens? So many may come that they outnumber the Afrikaners. Then you'll be back to square one.'

She said: 'That's a possibility, yes. Though a very unlikely one. You're looking for difficulties where there are none.'

'Paul Kruger faced that very problem. Foreigners precipitated the Boer War. History may repeat itself.'

'True. But there's unlikely to be so much work that we'll be swamped by hordes of "foreigners" as Paul Kruger was because of the gold mines. And most people who go to work in neighbouring countries prefer to keep their own citizenship – Spaniards working in France tend to remain Spaniards. Certainly most Xhosa and Zulu would prefer to remain what they are. So I doubt the problem will precipitate the Fourth Boer War.'

He smiled. 'The Fourth? What happened to the Third?'

'The third, my darling, is the one we want to avoid. It's the one that will break out if the Afrikaner is refused his volkstaat.' She turned to the sports club. 'There's a full-scale swimming pool behind that wall which we've resuscitated. We've got to tidy this up yet.' She made a wry joke: 'When we come for our honeymoon it'll all be beautiful.' She shoved the gear lever and drove on.

Mahoney grinned. 'You don't put me off that easy, mevrou.'

She slammed on the brakes again. 'No?' Then the corners of her mouth twitched. 'You still don't believe me, do you? Luke, this piece of God's earth is mine, my volk's, and it's my life's work. I think it's all terribly exciting and worthwhile. History in the making. This, Luke,' she jabbed her finger at the real estate, 'is going to take up most of my life. Got that?'

'Got it,' Mahoney smiled.

She drove on, towards a large hall, just beyond the houses.

'Our club house,' she said, 'and civic centre.'

It stood on a hillock, surrounded by hard, harsh Karoo grit and bush. A wind swirled dust around it. The building was locked. They peered through a window. The cavernous hall was empty but for some bales of hay left over from a barn dance.

She said: 'When it's cleaned up it's going to be fine.'

God, it was depressing. 'Sure.' He hoped he sounded sincere. She shot him a glance, but gave him the benefit of the doubt.

She drove out of the village, climbing a scrub-covered hill. They passed two big, single-storey buildings, standing bleak in the windy sun. 'Our town council. That other building is our hotel. They've done it up very nicely inside.'

'Are we staying there tonight?'

'Nope, I'm taking you somewhere *really* exciting.'

They passed a tall billboard which read: ' 'n Boer is trots daarop'. A Boer is proud to be so. They crested the hill. On the right was a small supermarket, on the left a number of big sheds with cars and trucks parked around. Katrina said: 'Garage, panel beaters, blacksmith, electrician. They take in work from farmers for miles around.' Beyond stretched acres of small white houses. Katrina braked to a stop again.

'And those are the houses that the government built for the Coloureds and blacks who were working on the dam. They're ours now, all for sale. Much cheaper than the big houses back there. How many would you like?'

Mahoney smiled. The houses stood in small, treeless, unfenced yards, row after row of pre-fabricated cottages, the bleak Karoo extending beyond them. 'How much are they?'

'About five thousand rand a throw.'

'One thousand pounds each? Freehold?'

'All the way to the centre of the earth.'

'Make it a dozen.'

She smiled. They drove on slowly through the township on broad gravel roads, the dust swirling. Many houses had broken windows. Here and there were signs of occupation, a battered car, washing on a line. Katrina said: 'Poor, unemployed Afrikaners with no place to go.'

'Have they bought?'

'Most are renting from our town council. They're on the road, looking for a job. The rent is minimal. This is a haven for them, for a while. But we're not a kibbutz. We help them to find work in the area, their kids go to our school, we won't see them go hungry, but the idea is they've got to put their shoulder to the wheel, we're not a benevolent society. Afrikaners must sink or swim.'

They turned into the next road of empty little houses. A child was playing on a tricycle. A fat woman was hanging out washing. Otherwise, nothing moved but the swirling dust. But there, on the next corner, was a splash of green, a purple bougainvillaea climbing. Katrina stopped.

'And now, at *enormous* expense, we bring you *my* house.'

74

The cottage was freshly painted. It was surrounded by a little lawn and flower beds. The bougainvillaea grew up the front wall. There were two orange saplings. Mahoney was taken aback. She had never told him she owned a cottage here.

'Well?' she smiled.

'It's pretty.' It was, quite.

She grinned. 'It's not. But it shows people what can be done. If this whole street had gardens like this it would be quite cute.' She switched off the engine. 'Come.'

They walked into a small living-room. There was an old lounge suite, re-upholstered in corduroy. Woollen rugs were scattered on the cement floor. A doorway led off into the main bedroom. It had a double bed made of pine.

'Made that bed myself. It's just planks nailed to four legs, topped by beaver-board. Cost almost nothing. Try it.'

Grinning, Mahoney lay down on the foam mattress. The bed was solid, and very comfortable. 'Very good, Kat.'

'And I made that built-in wardrobe myself.'

He examined it. Two doors fitted snugly. Shelves lined one side: a length of plumbers' piping served as a hanging rail. 'I didn't know you were good with your hands.'

'I'm not. But it's dead easy if you use your head. Measure up the space, get the shop to cut the wood to size. Then knock it together. The point is, it cost almost nothing. I did it to demonstrate what can be done very cheaply.'

She led him back to the living room and opened the next door. It was the second bedroom. There were two single beds.

'Made them myself too. And the built-in wardrobe.'

Mahoney said sincerely: 'Kat, I'm really very impressed.'

She opened a third door. 'My study.'

A small desk had two ornate lamps on it. Pine shelves lined the walls. 'You made this desk yourself too?'

'Obvious, is it? I thought it was a rather professional job.'

'It's excellent, Kat.' He turned to her, and took her in his arms. 'You're bloody clever.' He kissed her. 'But about that double bed in there? I'd like you to demonstrate it can take the weight of two people.'

'Piece of cake, but later.' She led him back into the living room and opened the fourth door.

The kitchen. And Mahoney really was impressed.

It was rather crowded by kitchen paraphernalia, but it was cosy. Shelves lined the walls, laden with cooking utensils. In the centre was a table she had knocked together herself. A refrigerator, a small electric oven. Against the other wall stood a black wood-burning stove, its metal chimney leading up through the roof. Firewood was stacked neatly. From the walls hung a miscellany of old copper utensils and bunches of corn.

'It's absolutely charming.'

'The kitchen is the heart of any home – particularly the simple man's home. So I went to some trouble here. The fridge is essential, of course, but the electric stove is expensive for the poor to operate. Whereas as this – ' she indicated the big black stove – 'is not only typical of Africa, it's full of charm, heats the whole house beautifully – except it's inconvenient. I love it, but many women wouldn't like to cook on it. So, I've shown both options. And – ' she opened the back door – '*voilà!*'

A burst of greenery took Mahoney aback.

The backyard was only about fifteen paces long by ten paces wide. Overhead was trellis, festooned with vines. Beyond were fruit trees, perhaps ten saplings, in bloom. Beyond them, a small vegetable patch, with a poultry run.

Mahoney walked outside. The overhead vines were young, but budding grapes. The fruit saplings were as high as a man. He walked to the vegetable patch. There were two rows of cabbages, one of cauliflower, one of tomatoes.

'Did you import the soil?'

'No, just got rid of some stones. It's perfectly good soil if it gets water. And a bit of chicken and duck shit helps.'

Mahoney turned to the poultry run. It was new, the netting wire shiny. In the middle was a little cemented pond. Two ducks and a drake were quacking in consternation at the visitation. There were three hens and a rooster. Katrina said: 'There's enough livestock in there to keep a family. Each hen will hatch out about thirty chicks a year. Each duck will produce about a dozen ducklings. And here is the rabbit hutch.'

It was on ground level. In the corner was a breeding room. Two rabbits, a buck and a doe looked at them amiably, noses twitching.

'Rabbits breed like hell. These are Angoras, their pelts are worth a bit too. These two dear rabbits will breed about sixty offspring this year. That's a lot of meat. For the deep-freeze or for sale.'

Mahoney was grinning. 'And the purpose is to show poor-whites they can feed themselves?'

'And even make a bit of money. And rabbits and poultry are fun.'

'Who looks after them while you're away?'

'I pay the town council a modest fee. And, finally,' she took his hand, 'look at *this*.'

Adjoining the back door was a small toilet and shower. She switched on a tap. 'Feel that.' Mahoney did so. It was hot. 'Now look there.' She pointed upwards. On the toilet roof was a solar panel. 'I built that myself too. Free hot water for life.'

'*You* built it?'

'Easiest thing in the world – got it out of the Reader's Digest DIY manual . . . '

* * *

She cooked on the woodburning stove, thoroughly enjoying herself. Mahoney sat at the table, peeling vegetables – the flames flickering, the pots simmering, the sun going down over the Karoo in a riotous glow of yellow, orange and red.

'And the lovely silence of the Karoo,' she said. She was getting along with the wine, having a lovely time in her doll's house.

He grinned at her. 'I love you,' he said.

'Stop changing the subject to lusts of the flesh.' She waved a hand. 'Don't you think I've done a splendid job? I could live in it quite happily. Couldn't you?'

'Absolutely.'

She grinned. 'Liar, now I can't believe anything you say. I've got a confession to make. I've bought the cottage next door, as well.'

'You've *what*?'

She burst out laughing. 'Your *face*!'

Later, as they lay in each other's arms in the double bed, she said to the darkness: 'Don't worry, I don't intend living in this little cottage. I'm just setting a good example. And showing the flag. And it's going to work, because it's morally right. And politically sensible. The Afrikaner's going to make an unhappy bed-fellow if he's forced into bed with another people. All over the world nationalism is re-asserting itself – Estonia, Latvia, Lithuania, they all want to be independent of Russia, so do the Eastern Bloc countries. The Tyroleans want to be independent of Austria, the Kurds want to be independent of Iraq, Basques want to be independent of Spain. All over Africa artificial boundaries were drawn by the colonial powers, lumping different tribes together and we've had nothing but trouble ever since – bloodshed, civil war, dictatorships trying to enforce unity on people who are traditional enemies. It would be absolute *madness* to repeat the same mistake when the new South Africa comes into being. Do you believe the Zulus are going to accept domination from the Xhosa – never. Madness to try it. The same applies to the Afrikaner. Those Afrikaners who don't care about their Afrikanerdom will do what they like, but those who *do* care must have their own homeland. That's a legitimate aspiration for any people. And this area is ideal.' She sighed happily in the dark. 'The example I am setting will slowly result in poor Afrikaners settling here, taking pride in their cottages, fixing them up, increasing their value.'

He did not want to dampen her enthusiasm but he had to say it: 'But how will they make a living, Kat?'

'The same way the penniless Jewish immigrants made a living! They arrived by the boatload without a penny. With human *initiative*, that's how they made their living! With cottage industries and small-time farming and starting workshops. And we'll have assistance schemes to get them started, loans to buy tools and so forth. What's the inscription on the Statue of Liberty in New York harbour? "Bring me your poor, your dispossessed, your oppressed, and I will make them free"? Okay?' She squeezed his arm. 'Be honest, please. And you can sigh audibly.'

Mahoney sighed audibly. He weighed his words.

'Yes, you have a moral right to your volkstaat, I said that in my book. And maybe it could be economically viable – provided you have the cooperation of the rest of the world. Favourable trade treaties, et cetera. And provided you get some industry going. But, my darling, I don't believe that you're going to get the land granted to you.'

She said firmly: 'I believe it will be. When our case is properly presented. Skilfully. And that's part of my job.'

Mahoney was taken aback. 'You're going to be a negotiator at the Great Indaba?'

'Part of the Volkswag team, yes.'

'You never told me that.'

'There's a lot I haven't told you. Like my rabbits and ducks.'

'But you're actually going to be at the negotiation table?'

'Yes.'

Mahoney took a deep breath.

'Okay. But if it is refused? What are you going to do? Fight?'

She said carefully to the ceiling: 'It will depend on the circumstances at the time. But I think the new South Africa is going to be such a mess, everybody fighting and the ANC trying to nationalise the economy, et cetera, that it will become entirely justified for the Afrikaner to secede, make a unilateral declaration of independence.'

'And in those circumstances – would you take up arms?'

She said quietly: 'Yep.'

He persisted: 'Well, obviously, in a chaotic situation you have the right to secede. But the real question is: if you're refused a volkstaat at the Great Indaba are you willing to take up arms and fight for it?'

She weighed her words. 'I, personally, don't want to fight for it. Few things are more awful than a civil war. But I can tell you with absolute certainty that thousands of Afrikaners *will* rise up and fight for it. And they are prepared. And when they rise up, yes, I will feel compelled to join them.'

Mahoney suppressed a sigh. Oh Jesus. Was his personal history repeating itself? First Patti Gandhi, fighter, now Katrina de la Rey. 'Do you know their battle plan? What exactly they plan to do, militarily? Where? When?'

She started to speak, then hesitated. 'No.'

He did not believe her. 'I think you do.'

She sighed. 'Volkswag is only one of several Afrikaner groups – there is little unity amongst us all yet, though there will be, of necessity. Volkswag is basically pacifist. Other Afrikaner organizations are not – like the AWB. Obviously, as a Volkswag committee member, I know in broad terms what their overall strategies will probably be, their strengths, et cetera. We're in touch with these organizations and our analysis is updated as often as we get information. But I am not a military strategist – I'm a political scientist.' She ended firmly.

Jesus. 'Will you tell me what you know?'

She sighed. 'No, darling. That's confidential. But any qualified military man could make an intelligent guess for you. Ask the Department of Strategic Studies at the university.'

Oh Jesus, Jesus.

She turned on her side. 'And now shall we stop talking about how incompatible we are? And do what we *are* compatible at? Remember soon you become celibate, except for quickies behind the barn.' Then she giggled. 'Oh, you're going to love my family. If you survive it's going to be a case of true love . . . '

75

From Hopetown you turn south-west into the hard-arsed heart of the Karoo. Vast desert vistas of stunted mauve bush, the flinty earth flashing by, distant koppies mauve against the mercilessly blue sky. Then up over the horizon comes Prieska, a town as joyless as it sounds, and if you've got any sense you bypass it. You carry on, and on, in the blistering sun, and then on the horizon comes Marydale, and then Putsonderwater, which means 'well without water', dusty dry hamlets. Mahoney looked at the desert flashing by and it depressed the hell out of him; but Katrina was aglow with enthusiasm for it. At Kenhardt the road crossed the railway line that runs from Sishen in the north to the Atlantic port of Saldanha Bay.

'Sishen is our iron-mining town – the whole mountain is made of iron, we just bulldoze it out in layers, it's very rich. We'll have one of the biggest steel industries in Africa in our volkstaat. Israel never had advantages like that! Nor did Israel have a railway line through the heart of the state, nor this excellent network of roads. Hell – this is ideal.'

Ideal? Okay, but he didn't want to live in Israel either. And then in the far distance he saw a stripe of green and a church steeple rising up

'And now, ladies and gentlemen, our *piéce de resistance* – the wine route commences . . . !'

Mahoney was astonished. Suddenly the desert bloomed, thousands of acres of green vineyards spread out before him, criss-crossed with cement canals, big waterwheels slowly turning. The town of Kakamas nestled among the vineyards, neat and green. To the north was a long range of cliffs.

Katrina said proudly: 'There's a twenty-mile tunnel through those hills, carrying water from the Orange to here. It was dug in 1904, just after the Boer War, by Cornish tin miners. And we'll do the same again.' She placed the map over the steering wheel. 'Here's the Orange. She traced her finger. 'Now, if we dig a canal across this land – ' she traced her finger south – 'and dig another tunnel through these hills, we'll irrigate this whole vast desert area we've been driving through today.' She looked at him brightly. 'Good stuff, huh?'

Mahoney nodded. Yes, it was impressive, what could be done. Even exciting. But where was the money coming from to dig that tunnel?

She said: 'That's part of my job too, sir. The money's in the banks, where it always is. And in bonds the volkstaat will float. And remember that that money will circulate in the form of wages – the project will create a lot of work. Okay?'

'Okay.' He wished she wouldn't demand his agreement after every bit of wishful thinking.

'Liar!' She flicked his knee. Then she held up a finger. 'But now I'm going to show you something that is definitely Okay!'

They drove out of Kakamas, heading west. Vineyards rolling all the way. Towering koppies and cliffs took over, then great, round rocks began to poke up all around, gleaming in the sun; the land was becoming a moonscape. Finally they came to a gate. A uniformed Bushman asked them to sign a roster, and they entered a shaded area of government rest huts. Suddenly he could hear the thundering of the Augrabies Falls.

Clutching a bottle of wine, she led him enthusiastically through towering rocks until they came to a yawning chasm. Cliffs rose up the other side, worn smooth by the waters of countless time. And down into the canyon roared the Orange River, thundering, cascading down into a great boiling, galloping cauldron of water below.

Mahoney was enthralled. It was an extraordinary, dramatic adjunct to the dramatic desert. Katrina shouted to him: 'Great stuff, huh?' Then she grabbed his hand and led him down a rocky trail along the canyon top, as happy as a kid. After a quarter of a mile they came to a steep path that led down into the roaring canyon. They clambered downwards, the Orange roaring and leaping and frothing. She reached a ledge and led him along it to a cave. She sat down and held out her hand like a showman.

'Well?'

Thirty feet below them the Orange roared. A rainbowed mist rose up and filtered down on their sweat like a balm. She extended her arms wide: 'Oh, I love this country! And tomorrow I'll show you our sea . . . '

They drove west across four hundred kilometres of desert, through places called Nabies and Bladgrond and Pofadder and Okiep and Springbok; and then you are in even harsher country, the hard earth windswept from the Atlantic. That hot afternoon they drove into Port Nolloth, the fishing harbour that would one day become one of the volkstaat's ports. They bought fresh fish and drove down a beach track to a cove, where huge smooth boulders protruded into the seething sea. 'Last one in has to be Attorney General of Orania!' Katrina cried. She flung off her blouse, her skirt fell to her feet, she wriggled out of her panties, unhitched her bra, ran down the beach and launched herself into the waves. Mahoney was struggling out of his trousers. He plunged in and struck out after and his hand clawed down on her thigh. She shrieked and he clutched her against him and, oh, the wonderful feel of her cold womanflesh against him.

'So I've got to be Attorney General, have I?'

'Yep.'

'God help Orania.'

'He will, we're His chosen people!'

They built a fire and grilled the fish while they drank crisp wine in the sunset. Afterwards she lay on the blanket and sighed up at the moon: 'And tomorrow we've got to go back to bloody South Africa.'

Mahoney smiled. To her this was already another country. She reached out and fondled his head.

'Do you still think you love me, Luke?'

'Yes.'

'Yes, unfortunately?'

'Yes, *fortunately*.' And he meant it.

She sighed. 'You still don't believe anything will come of my volkstaat.' It wasn't a question. 'And I think I love you. *Un*fortunately – because you're going to break my heart.'

He looked up at the stars. It was the second time she had said that she loved him. He got up onto his elbow. 'How exactly?'

She was looking at the moon. She forced a bright smile, sat up and swept her hand through her hair. Then she plunged her lips onto his and growled into his mouth: 'By being such a goddamn *Englishman*!'

They filled up the cold-box with booze and drove back the way they'd come, and the Karoo was just as bare-arsed, dusty, nitty-gritty dry as yesterday, but today it didn't look so bad because she had told him she loved him. They drank their way across the Karoo and they did not pass a single vehicle until they got back to the wine route again. They stopped at the first winery and had a conducted tour through the towering vats, sampling the firm's fine product. In the late afternoon they came to the town of Upington. Suddenly you leave the green wine route behind, and over on the desert horizon come chimney stacks, and then you are driving along the edge of a sophisticated, industrial outskirt, the factories and warehouses neatly laid out in wide roads lined with trees. Katrina stopped the car.

'That, Mahoney, is one of the most promising industrial areas in the whole of South Africa. Every form of light industry there. Unlimited space for expansion. And it's all done on Afrikaner know-how.'

Yes, Upington was a good little city, the streets wide, big modern shops and office blocks, good hotels, good sports facilities, cafés and restaurants, a good-looking courthouse, a big public library, two schools, a technical college, two good hospitals, a museum to bygone days when this was on the Missionary Road into the heart of darkest Africa, monuments to the long-suffering donkey and the camel who built the area.

'There is everything here a capital city needs: water, industry, commerce, a railhead, a big airport.'

Running through the town was the wide Orange River, with islands and rapids and parklands and pretty houses on its green banks. She drove slowly through the shady suburbs, their lush gardens running down to the water, lawns and frangipani and bougainvillaea growing in profusion. And, oh dear, he knew what she was thinking – 'There's a pretty house' and 'Look at that lovely garden'. When Upington was the capital of the volkstaat, this was where she wanted to live. But no way did he want to live here. What the *fuck* would he do all day? And in bloody Afrikaans?

They spent that night in the municipal rest camp on the bank of the Orange, in a pretty rondavel. They sat drinking wine on the water's edge, watching the sun go down over the vast desert.

She took his hand and said sadly: 'So, unfortunately, I think I have at least convinced you that the volkstaat of Orania is a proposition to be taken seriously, haven't I?'

Mahoney took a cautious breath. Yes, that was true. 'But why is that unfortunate?'

'Because I've also convinced you that I'm to be taken seriously about devoting myself to it, haven't I?'

Mahoney sighed. 'Yes.'

'And that depresses the hell out of you, doesn't it?' she said gently. 'Because you don't want to live in Upington. I saw your expression today.' Before he could answer she continued: 'And I don't blame you. You want to live amongst your own people. Your own culture and language and roots. And, to tell the truth, I don't want to live in Upington for the rest of my life either – yes, I want to live amongst my own people, but I'd much rather do it in a sophisticated, cosmopolitan city. But I have to sacrifice one for the other.' She smiled at him kindly. 'And you don't want to live here while I do that. So, the exercise is a success, because it's proved that. And *that*, darling Luke, is why it's unfortunate. Because no matter how much I love you, there's really no hope for us.'

Mahoney looked at the muddy river. No hope? He had every hope because he did not believe this volkstaat would come to pass. But he had just admitted he took it seriously – and that was true too. He started to speak but she continued relentlessly.

'I know what you're going to say, darling. Namely that it'll never come to pass. There's no point saying it again. Except this much.' She looked at him soberly. 'If it doesn't come to pass, there is even less hope for you and me. Because – although I will do all in my power to prevent it – there will most surely be an Afrikaner rebellion. And in that unhappy event there is definitely no hope for us, is there? Because nobody could expect you to fight for a volkstaat.'

Mahoney snorted softly.

Katrina went on: 'Okay, you think I'm being melodramatic. Well, tomorrow we're leaving this nice, gentle neck of the woods and we're entering the real Afrikaner land – the Western Transvaal, where I come from. And you're going to meet a lot of real, hard-nosed Afrikaners, and if I haven't convinced you there'll be a Third Boer War, those guys will. And I'm not just referring to the AWB – I'm talking about ordinary, God-fearing, salt-of-the-earth farmers, solid Christian citizens who believe President de Klerk is a traitor, who believe they have a moral duty to take up arms to defend their Christian hearth and homes against the godlessness of black Africa – which they believe is going to strip them of their land anyway. And believe me these guys are *prepared*.' She looked at him soberly. 'Now I must make one thing very clear, Luke. Many of those Afrikaners are prepared to fight for the *whole* of South Africa. I am not; I don't approve of them. I believe they're only entitled to a reasonable chunk of it. *But*, when the battle lines are drawn, I'll be stuck with these guys.'

Mahoney looked at her. And, Jesus, he'd had enough of this – here he was, head over heels in love, and being in love was supposed to be *fun*. 'What are you trying to do to me, Kat?'

'I'm trying to be realistic about me and thee. Being in love is a mild though delightful form of temporary insanity.'

'Can we please for Christ's sake cross the bridges as we come to them?'

Her solemn face broke into a grin. 'Right! *Fun!*' She got up from her camp chair. 'I'll fetch another bottle of wine . . . '

76

No hope huh? Well, fuck that.

You drive north-east out of Upington on the old Missionary Road, and you come to Kuruman, the historic oasis where the Reverend John Moffat had his mission, whence Dr David Livingstone set out to bring God to darkest central Africa. Then comes Vryburg, which means Freetown, the one-time capital of the short-lived Republic of Goshen before the British put an end to such impertinence. Then the country suddenly changes. The Karoo gives way to green fields, and there are vehicles again. You are entering the Western Transvaal, the real Afrikanerland. Finally they came to Delareyville, where Katrina's family originally hailed from.

'The gateway to the Western Transvaal,' Katrina said apologetically. 'Don't imagine I can't see how grim this little town is. But these are my people. I don't *agree* with them, but when the chips are down they will be on my side.'

She drove slowly through it. 'By the time the Afrikaner got this far north he'd lost his notions of Dutch graciousness . . . ' They came to the pride of the town, the monument to General Koos de la Rey.

Koos de la Rey. Boer War hero, acknowledged as one of the best military strategists. The man who, having captured Lord Methuen, sent the wounded aristocrat back to England with condolences to his lady. One of the leaders of the 1914 Rebellion. Katrina's great-uncle. Mahoney looked at the big bronze bust of the old man. It was surrounded by tall marble tombstones on which were recorded hundreds of names of men from the area who died during the Boer War at the hands of the British. And, yes, he could see something of Katrina in that countenance. And how did he feel? About Katrina and this man, and what it all meant for the future? He was surprised that he felt a kind of pride. Affection. He glanced at Katrina. She was looking at him with a small smile. 'What?' he said.

'What what?' She took his hand, and led him back to the car. Then she waved her finger at the monument.

'That,' she said, 'is what you're dealing with.'

Mzilikazi's old country: the Western Transvaal stretched on, fields of maize, huge silos rearing up, distant homesteads. In the late afternoon they came to the town of Ventersdorp. As they entered the drab main street, Katrina stopped. She indicated a small white building. It had a large wrought-iron eagle fixed on the wall.

'Headquarters of the AWB. Eugene Terreblanche's office.'

So this was where the plans for the Boer Republic were made?

'Take them seriously,' Katrina said. 'You're stuck with them if you get yourself stuck with me.'

Oh, bullshit. 'You're not stuck with them, Kate. Any more than a German woman in 1938 was stuck with the Nazi Party. You can turn your back on them and stick by your principles.'

'But then Germany went to war, and that German woman was stuck with *that* fact. So she had no option but to toe the line – unless she ran away. And I have no intention of running away.'

Oh fuck her volkstaat. He turned to face her squarely. 'Tell me, if I can take you warts and all – ' he nodded at the AWB offices – 'do you want to get stuck with *me* warts and all? Yesterday you told me you loved me. Is that true, or did you speak a trifle hastily?'

She looked at him. And sighed. 'Truth, right? And the truth is I could be so head over heels in love with you that I'd chuck up everything and follow you to the ends of the earth. But I don't intend doing that. So, I guess I'm guarding my heart.'

Mahoney sat back. 'Okay. That's good enough for me. For the time being.' He waved a finger ahead. 'Advance.'

'But, to answer your question: no, I don't want to be stuck with you warts and all.'

'What the hell warts have I got, a perfect specimen like me?'

She said solemnly: 'Your unhappiness here. You would leave me – and that would break my heart.'

He cried: 'Can we please please please cross the bridges as we come to them? Being in love is supposed to be fun!'

'Right,' she grinned. 'And you're about to cross your next bridge and meet my fun family.'

In the late afternoon they were driving between the dramatic hills. On one side of the road were the Pilansberg mountains, part of the Republic of Bophuthatswana, on the other side was part of the Waterberg range. 'Full of iron,' Katrina said, 'if it hadn't been for the Witwatersrand's gold, Johannesburg would be here.' Shortly before the town of Thabazimbi they came to an ornate farm gate, a thatched archway. A vista of mauve plain opened before them, studded with kopjes. They crossed a cattle grid and wound through more hills. A small plateau reared up in the distance. 'Home.' They wound up it. Tall trees appeared, then orchards, barns and outhouses. They came to a large level area outside a high white garden wall.

'Feeling brave? Just be your charming self and speak Afrikaans.'

She led the way. A garden door opened onto a big lawn. A long single-storey house stood beyond it, with pillars supporting grenadilla vines. To the left was another building. 'Guest wing, where you'll be sleeping.' To the right, the lawn ended at a low wall and a magnificent view of part of the plain. A pine sapling, festooned in Christmas decorations, stood in a pot at the wall. A fountain spouted water from a lion's mouth. Tame guinea fowl and a pair of peacocks roamed the lawn. There was a riot of flowers. The large front door stood open. Suddenly a kitchen door at the end of the house burst open and an old black woman in blue maid's uniform came bustling out, clapping her hands and ululating.

'*Melia!*' Katrina cried.

The old woman came dancing across the lawn to Katrina, ululating, clapping, wreathed in smiles. They flung their arms around each other midst loud laughter and exclamations in Tswana.

'Melia,' Katrina said in Afrikaans, 'this is my big friend, Meneer Mahoney.'

'*Ah! Ah!*' Melia pranced, clapping her hands. '*Too handsome! You love my baby Nkosikazi, hah?*' She burst into peals of laughter.

'That's right.' Mahoney shook hands. 'How do you do?'

'Melia was my mother's nursemaid as well as mine – she's seventy years old, huh, Melia?'

'I change this Nkosikazi's nappy,' Melia howled in glee.

'*Katrina!*' a voice boomed. A large man in a white shirt and tie was emerging through the front door, his arms extended.

'Papa!' Katrina cried. She grabbed Mahoney's hand and whispered: *'He's put on a tie for you. This is serious stuff.'*

The view from the living-room was the panorama of the plain. Steps descended to lawn and gardens extending for two hundred yards before ending in a steep drop. An artificial lake was at the end, surrounded by towering trees and flower beds. The living-room was dominated by a large fireplace, a grand piano and another Christmas tree surrounded by parcels. Mounted heads of lion, buffalo and zebra lined the walls, hides covered the floor.

'Is he English?' the old lady demanded in Afrikaans from the armchair.

'Yes, mother,' General de la Rey said, 'but he was born in South Africa.'

'Is he sleeping with Katrina?' the old lady demanded.

Mrs de la Rey smothered a smile; her husband said sternly: 'Mother, he is Katrina's *friend,* from Hong Kong.'

'Is he after her money?'

'*What* money?' Katrina guffawed.

'No, mother,' Mrs de la Rey giggled. 'And he understands Afrikaans.'

'Let me have a look at him.'

Mahoney walked across the room. '*Aangename kennismaking, Ouma de la Rey,*' he smiled. How do you do, Grandmother de la Rey.

The old lady peered through strong spectacles. Her face was weathered, her hair white. Then she raised a finger. 'Just remember what you did to us in the Boer War, when you're eating our food. You starved us!'

The family burst into laughter. 'I will, Ouma,' Mahoney grinned.

'And put ground glass in our porridge! Come here.' She heaved herself up creakily from the armchair, grabbed his hand and stomped him across the room to a row of big framed photographs on the wall. ('Ouma . . . ' Katrina giggled.) The old lady banged the first photograph with her walking stick and cried: 'That's what you did to us!'

The faded old photograph was two feet long by one and a half deep. It showed a burned-out farm homestead of the Boer War period, the charred rafters, the blackened walls. In the foreground lay rotting horses and cattle, shot by the British troops. In the background were blackened cornfields. 'I'm sorry, Ouma de la Rey,' Mahoney murmured.

'And this!' The old lady tugged his hand and banged the next framed photograph.

'Ou*ma!*' Katrina grinned helplessly.

It showed a score of skinny little Afrikaner children lining a barbed-wire fence, little pinched faces trying to grimace a smile, tattered clothes over spindly frames. Behind them were acres of British-issue tents leading off into a bleak highveld landscape.

'I'm sorry, Ouma,' Mahoney said, and he meant it.

'And this,' she tugged him again. It was a photograph of a tent. A haggard Boer woman held a dying babe in her arms while her other little children clustered pathetically about her.

'And this!' It showed a big cemetery, sad little wooden crosses over fresh mounds of earth, against a background of those vast rows of bleak tents. A Boer woman and her children were weeping around a newly dug grave as another little coffin was lowered. Approaching the cemetery was a group of weeping women and children carrying another little coffin, a British trooper escorting them. Ouma de la Rey cried: 'Twenty-seven thousand women and children you British killed in your concentration camps!'

'Ou*ma* . . . !' Katrina appealed.

'I'm terribly sorry, Ouma de la Rey,' Mahoney murmured.

Katrina's mother led him down the garden towards the lake, sipping from a tall glass of champagne. She said: 'Please excuse my English – I'm rusty and my children got all my brains. Anyway, you are very welcome in our house, Luke, whatever Ouma made you feel.'

'Thank you, Mevrou de la Rey.' He added: 'And your English is perfect too.'

'Rusty.' She stopped to admire her agapanthus. 'And personally I don't care whether you and Katrina are sleeping together or not – I just hope three things: one: that you're discreet. My husband feels very strongly about fornication and I don't want to spoil the Christmas spirit – God knows we may not have many Christmases left the way things are going. Here – ' she plucked a bloom – 'put it in your button hole.' She resumed walking, inspecting her flowers. 'And two: that you don't make her pregnant. That would be the end, in a small community like ours. She's very much regarded as the local girl who made good. And her father would blow your head off.'

Jesus. Mahoney had to work at it to keep a straight face. He took an elaborate sip of his champagne and murmured: 'I understand.' Mevrou de la Rey plucked another bloom, then wandered on. 'It's a magnificent garden. How many gardeners do you have?'

'Me and two others. But we've got eight. They're all old-age pensioners who've been with us for half a century, how can we fire them now that they're good for nothing except being dragged along by a petrol lawn mower?' She stooped, and pulled out a weed. 'And three: that you're not serious about each other.'

Mahoney looked at her back. Then grinned. Mevrou de la Rey wandered on, plucking blooms. Mahoney searched for the right thing to say. 'Well, I'm afraid I'm serious.'

Mevrou de la Rey stopped at a flower in mid-pluck. She contemplated it, then slowly turned to him. 'And Katrina?'

He wanted to laugh and say: I know she's crazy about me too. 'I'm not sure.'

Mevrou de la Rey walked back to him. She said earnestly: 'Katrina has had many suitors. They fall at her feet. Afrikaners, French, German – she's brought them home to meet us. But she eventually turned them all down. None was strong enough for her. She is a very serious, strong woman, Katrina. But she has a weakness for lame ducks – she takes people under her wing.' (Mahoney blinked: was she saying he was weak?) 'Then she has to get rid of them. They all wanted to take her away to live in France, in America, in the Cape.' She looked into his eyes earnestly. 'But Katrina's place is *here*. She must carry on her forefathers' work. And she will. Not only is it her duty, it is her love.' She frowned at him in appeal. 'The Afrikaner has been in this country for three hundred and fifty years – as long as the Americans have been in America. We have suffered but we have survived. It is Katrina's *duty* to ensure we continue to survive.' She let that hang. 'Come, I want to show you something.'

She took a path off to the left. They descended between flower beds, walked a hundred yards through orchard, then came to a clearing. In the middle stood a ruin of a stone house. It had been destroyed by fire many years ago: the roof was gone, the windows and doors burned out. Behind it a barn and outbuildings were in the same condition.

Mevrou de la Rey said: 'My husband's mother – Ouma, up there – she was born in this house ninety-four years ago. This farm has been in the De la Rey family ever since Potgieter sent Mzilikazi packing after the battle of Marico. The British burnt it down during the Boer War. Dragged the women and children out, burnt the house, the crops, the furniture, the books, the bedding, drove off the cattle, the sheep, the goats, the chickens, the ducks, the geese. And herded the women and children off down the road to the concentration camps. They took Ouma off to a concentration camp for two years. Where her mother died of cholera.'

* * *

When he got back to the main house, Katrina was freshly groomed and beautiful in a swirling blue skirt and frilly blouse. 'So – had the garden tour, have you?'

'Lovely. But don't desert me again like that.'

She grinned. 'Did you get the Don't Get Serious About Katrina routine?'

He said: 'Why didn't you tell me about all these Frogs and Krauts falling at your feet? And lame ducks.'

'I told you it was going to be a barrel of laughs. Well, you ain't seen nothing yet – my father wants you to have a drink in his study before the party.'

'Before what party?'

'All the Boers from miles around descend for a braaivleis on Christmas eve. You're going to love 'em.'

'Do all your suitors have to have a tête-à-tête with the old man?'

'Only if they think I'm serious.' (This was the first good news since he'd arrived.) She burst into giggles.

'I want to make it clear,' the old man said kindly in a cultured Afrikaans accent from behind his big desk, fiddling with his glass of whisky, 'that you are very welcome in our house despite all the politics you'll hear. Politics is in our blood. We pray about it, eat and drink over it. Like Ouma's remarks. We have nothing against the English as individuals. Even as a volk. It's the British governments that we're bitter about. Who've landed us in the mess we're in today.'

Mahoney smiled. 'I've got a lot of Afrikaner friends.'

The general held up a finger. 'There's your first mistake. The mistake the whole world makes.' He tapped his breast. 'I am *not* an Afrikaner. Nor are all these people living round here. We are *Boers*. An entirely different volk from those Cape Afrikaners who've given us Boers a bad name.' He fixed Mahoney with a blue military eye. 'Those fancy Cape Afrikaners have dominated the government since Union in 1910. Smuts was a Cape Afrikaner. Louis Botha. Hertzog. Dr Malan. Verwoerd wasn't even *born* in so-called South Africa – he was born in Holland. PW Botha is a Cape Afrikaner.' He shook his head. 'None of them are descended from Boers, the people who trekked off into the interior and founded their own republics of the Orange Free State and the Transvaal.' He raised his finger again. 'And remember, those Boer republics were officially recognised by Great Britain, in 1852 and 1854. And those Boer republics were founded, perfectly legally by international law, on unoccupied land –

the Mfecane had killed everybody off. The only chappie we had to fight was Mzilikazi over here in the west and he was *part* of the Mfecane.' He looked at Mahoney. 'And we Boers never had slaves once the Great Trek started.' He shook his head again. 'We were *legal* republics.'

All this was true. Mahoney gave a judicious nod. The old man sat back. He took a sip of whisky with absent-minded relish, then continued: 'But then the British decided to conquer us. Why? Because *gold* had been discovered in the Transvaal. And the Anglo-Boer War ensued. The mightiest imperial power in the world hurled against our little *legitimate* republics – for the sake of *gold*.' He wrung every drop of shame out of it. 'Gold . . . and after they had finally defeated us – the tiniest volk in the world fighting the greatest empire in the world and very nearly beating them – when it came to the peace treaty, at Vereeniging, the Boers made their greatest mistake.'

Mahoney waited.

The old man sipped, glared, then jabbed a finger. 'The same mistake you made calling us all Afrikaners. The same mistake we Boers made of aligning ourselves with those fancy Cape Afrikaners who hadn't fought the War. We were bamboozled by Smuts into believing that if we made an alliance with them we would be able to cast off the British yoke again and thereby become an independent *"Afrikaner"* volk.' He looked at Mahoney solemnly: 'We were naive. We hoped that if we linked up with those fancy Cape Afrikaners we would recover our independence which Britain had butchered away. A short cut to freedom. So we were bamboozled into joining with the Cape and Natal in the so-called Union of South Africa, as part of the British Empire again. And why? Gold, again. The Cape and Natal wanted our gold. And so did Great Britain. In fact, Winston Churchill – ' he pointed at the great man's memoirs on the bookshelf – 'admits that South Africa's gold financed Britain in both world wars.'

Mahoney wondered where this conversation was heading.

The general continued: 'And those fancy Cape Afrikaners swamped us. And used our gold to finance their concoction of so-called South Africa. And our proud separate identity as Boers, even our *name* got forgotten. We were so bamboozled we even had to fight Britain's war against Germany – and Germany had been our ally in the Boer War. And when some Boers, like Koos de la Rey, mounted the 1914 Rebellion in protest, General Smuts made war on us – and crushed us. Smuts was a Cape Afrikaner. An Anglophile, he wanted to anglicise South Africa, just like Milner did. He was a turncoat!'

Strong stuff, Mahoney thought. He was beginning to see what Katrina meant.

The old man continued: 'And after the First World War the Boers sent a delegation to Versailles in 1919, where the peace treaty was signed, to ask Britain to grant the old Boer republics their independence back. The president of America, Woodrow Wilson, had issued his famous declaration which guaranteed the freedom of every volk, no matter how small, as an unalienable right. So our Boer delegation went off, in their best bib and tucker, full of optimism. And there were delegations from other little countries, asking for the same freedom – Ireland was one of them. They had been under British rule for a century. What happened? Woodrow Wilson refused to even *meet* our delegation. Why? Because the British prime minister, Lloyd George, told him Britain wanted to cling onto us for our gold.' He crinkled his eyes. 'The Irish vote was important in American politics, but the Boer delegation? Oh no, they didn't even deserve a *hearing*!'

Mahoney nodded. *But what's this got to do with me being in love with his daughter?*

General de la Rey continued: 'And then our Boer leaders made their gravest error – they gave up their ideal, and then those Cape Afrikaner bastards really swamped us. They even led us into World War II – again fighting for our British enemy and again with our gold.' He pointed at the bookshelf: 'Read Winston Churchill. It was *Boer* gold that enabled Britain to win the war!' The old man looked at him narrowly. Then slumped back. 'Anyway, our Boer leaders made a terrible mistake in joining with those Cape Afrikaners, betraying the ideals of the voortrekkers. And thereby we got tarred with their apartheid brush.'

Mahoney looked at his future father-in-law. *The Boers got tarred with the apartheid brush?* He waved a polite finger. 'I'm afraid you've lost me there, General.'

The old man sat forward triumphantly. 'You think the Boers were the initiators of apartheid? Wrong! The original Boer republics had almost no black people within their borders. What brought the blacks in? *Gold*, and the British magnates who needed cheap black labour to dig for it!' He spread his hands. 'We country-bumpkin Boers didn't know anything about mining! We were *farmers*. It was you English who knew how, and imported cheap black labour.' He spread his hands. 'We were astonished at all this interest in our little republic. And we were worried. We had no experience in big business. So when you big noises from England and America with all your millions started demanding the vote and God knows what, of *course* we were frightened because it looked like you were going to take over our republic! And we were *angry*, that here come the British again.'

Mahoney took a long breath. 'True, sir, but – '

'Don't call me sir. Or I'll have to call you "judge".'

Mahoney smiled. 'I'm not a judge. Nor do I want to be.'

'Nor do I want to be a sir. I'm Karel de la Rey.'

Mahoney continued with a smile: 'True that the British were bullying you. But it's also an historical fact that you had it enshrined in your constitution that there would be no black voters – "no equality in church or state".'

The old man threw up his hands. 'But so what? Those were the old days. There was no equality between black and white! in Australia or New Zealand or America in those days either! But,' he shook his head, 'the Boers had had *nothing* to do with the Xhosa since the Great Trek – we had trekked to get *away* from them! And we had *nothing* to do with the Zulus once the British drove us out of Natal. And we had nothing to do with the poor old Cape Coloureds – we left the Cape. But we Boers got blamed for the suffering apartheid caused. Oh – ' he held up his palms – 'I admit the Boers supported apartheid, but we had the colour problem *thrust* upon us, by the mining magnates, and by the British, and Union, and the Cape Afrikaners.'

Mahoney shifted in his chair. The old man's historical distinctions were rather metaphysical, though not exactly wrong. And *very* generous to the Boers.

'And now the time has come when the Boers must admit to the world that we were wrong to support apartheid, and explain how it came about. And – now that President de Klerk is talking about the new South Africa and unscrambling the mess that Britain foisted upon us – *we must again demand our old Boer republics back!*'

Mahoney shifted again. The old boy's sincerity was palpable, and he had some legitimate historical and legal grounds, but it was pie-in-the-sky. And unjust. *But what was the point of this lecture?*

'The point of all this, Luke, is that our demand is going to be refused – that traitor De Klerk will not permit it, let alone the blacks. So? So we're going to have to fight for it. Fight for our rights.' He looked at Mahoney. 'The Third Boer War is coming, Luke. And *my* family,' he tapped his chest, 'and Katrina, are Boers. Not Afrikaners.'

The old blue eyes held his kindly. And Mahoney understood: he was being warned off Katrina. He took a sip of whisky. 'I think Katrina really considers herself an Afrikaner.'

The old man shook his head gently. 'Katrina's got her head in the clouds. It happens to these academics, you know. But she is my flesh and blood. And she is the beneficiary of this estate, of which I am trustee. I assure you that under that academic exterior, she is a Boer. And her Afrikaner Volkswag is wet behind the ears.'

Mahoney sighed. 'But if you don't get granted your old republics back, are you prepared to accept a smaller state, like Katrina and the Volkswag want?'

The general stood up to signal the end of the discussion. 'No. We want what is rightfully ours, stolen by the British and those Cape Afrikaners. And if they refuse, we would use the Volkswag's silly bit of land as a military base – *one* of our bases – but we'll never accept it as a substitute.' He smiled. 'Never.' He paused, then repeated kindly: 'Katrina is a Boer. And now, if you'll excuse me, I must get into my Father Christmas uniform.'

77

His Father Christmas uniform? Mahoney went looking for Katrina. He bumped into her grandmother in the passage. She glowered at him. 'Ground glass in our porridge! Twenty-seven thousand women and children!'

'I'm terribly sorry, Ouma.'

'Don't you Ouma me, I'm not your ouma, thank God!'

'I'm sorry. Do you know where Katrina is?'

'She's inspanning the oxen!' The old lady stomped off with her cane.

The oxen? He found his way to the kitchen. Melia and Mrs de la Rey were shrieking with laughter about something as they worked. Mahoney smiled. 'Do you know where Katrina is?'

'Luke!' Mrs de la Rey dabbed her eye with the back of her wrist. 'Are you looking after yourself with drinks? I think Katrina's inspanning the oxen.' The telephone rang. 'Excuse me.' She disappeared.

Melia was still giggling. 'What's this about oxen, Melia?'

Melia turned to him, convulsed with giggles, then held a finger up to his nose: 'You be good man with my baby girl! Only kissy-kissy, no make piccaninny!' She reeled back to the sink.

'Melia,' Mahoney grinned, 'where are these bloody oxen?'

Melia screamed with laughter into the sink: '*No make piccaninny!*' She turned to him, convulsed, her arms out as if holding a shotgun. 'Or Big Baas go *boom-boom*.' She reeled back against the sink: '*Only kissy-kissy . . . !*'

He followed Melia's directions as best he finally understood them: out the backyard, past the barns, through the vegetable gardens. Then below him was a dusty cattle kraal.

An oxwagon stood in front of it: half a dozen oxen were already yoked. Katrina had her back to him, arms akimbo, surrounded by half a dozen black children. She called: 'Mabula!' and out of the pen came the ox by that name, like a martyr. He surrendered himself to being inspanned by the children. 'Vetman!' And Vetman came shuffling out, looking as if he was going to his funeral. 'Baasman . . . !'

Mahoney sat down on the hillside, watching his woman. As the last pair of oxen were yoked, the children went running off in excitement. Katrina spoke into a mobile telephone. A minute later a Land-Rover came grinding round the hill, driven by General de la Rey, resplendent in a red Father Christmas costume with flowing white beard. Beside him were Ouma and Katrina's mother. In the back were several bulging sacks. The old man got out, holding a portable radio. 'Where is Luke?'

'Here I am.' Mahoney began down the slope.

They loaded the sacks onto the oxwagon. 'For the blacks,' Katrina said. Ouma and Mrs de la Rey climbed up onto the front seat beside the old man. Katrina sat on the back, her legs dangling. Mahoney got up beside her.

'*Weg is ons!*' the old man cried, and the wagon creaked forward. Katrina hit a button on the portable radio and 'Jingle Bells' blared up to the African sky.

Mahoney thought it was enchanting. The ox-wagon creaked up the track to the lawn of the main house. There were gathered all the farm labourers and their children, around the Christmas tree, agog. The wagon came toiling up onto the lawn, the natives clapping, the children wide-eyed.

The old man clambered to his feet and cried in Afrikaans: '*Yo-ho-ho! I am Santa Klaus from the lands of snow. I bring gifts for good people only! Are there any good children in this place?*'

Screams of glee, hands waving, all claiming to be good children.

'*Do their parents confirm that they are good children?*'

Cries of confirmation from the adults, white teeth flashing.

'*Is it true they are obedient?*'

Gleeful chorus: '*It is true!*'

'*Is it true they respect their elders?*'

'*It is true!*'

'*Is it true they do their lessons at school?*'

'*It is true!*'

537

'I don't believe it!'

'It is true, it is true . . . !'

Katrina opened the first sack, and pulled out a parcel.

The blacks had gone back to their compound. Dusk was falling. The big lawn filled with people holding drinks, music came from the living room. Smoke rose up from the barbecue. Melia and Katrina circulated with trays of snacks. The only language was Afrikaans.

'What did Pa talk about?' Katrina asked.

'The message was that you're a Boer, not an Afrikaner. And I'm an eminently unsuitable son-in-law, would you believe?' He took her hand. 'Are you a bloody Boer?'

She grinned. 'I'm a bloody Afrikaner. Darling, I must circulate.'

He gripped her hand. 'Kate, I love you. And you love me.'

She smiled and put a finger on his lips. 'Yes, I think I do. And I'm thinking we've got a problem. I'm thinking we've got a lot of thinking to do.' She blew him a kiss and turned away.

Then the commando arrived. They came clattering into the car park, and hitched their sweating horses. They came through the garden-wall door boisterously, half a dozen men in khaki with the AWB's three-legged swastika on their sleeves, pistols swinging in holsters. General and Mrs de la Rey were walking across the lawn to greet them. Handshakes and slaps on the shoulder. They were tanned, jolly and they had been drinking.

Mahoney watched, sipping his whisky. He felt like a fish out of water. Everybody was being very polite to him, but they felt the same about him: *'Katrina se Rooinek*?' – Katrina's Red-neck? And, sure, he liked them well enough – except the guys with the swastikas – they were honest Afrikaner folk, he spoke their language and he understood their history, but, no, he did not feel comfortable amongst them, they were not his folk. Sure, he could accept them, their politics apart, as Katrina's kith and kin, and chew the fat with them and drink beer and eat boerewors and sing Afrikaner songs with them, but he did not want to live with them in their volkstaat, and he certainly did not want to fight alongside them. And he *certainly* didn't want to have anything to do with the guys with the swastikas. They were fucking *objectionable*.

Mahoney looked across the crowded lawn at Katrina being charming. And, Jesus Christ, he didn't like it. Of course he understood that she was being the hostess, and she was being a diplomat – but, oh God, he wanted her to have nothing to do with them. Just then, through the door, came Eugene Terreblanche himself, a bulky man in khaki with a veld hat and beard, and a cry went up from the young men around Katrina.

'Ah Wei Bay! Ah Wei Bay!'

Katrina's parents were greeting him. Katrina made her way to Mahoney. She took his hand: 'Come and meet the great Eugene Terreblanche who's come all the way from Ventersdorp to grace us . . .'

Terreblanche was thickset, handsome, with piercing blue eyes and the easy charm of a man's man. He spoke good English with a heavy Afrikaans accent.

'I like the British. Real fighters. And I like English literature. Shakespeare is wonderful. *King Lear* is my favourite. And some of my best military instructors are British. Excellent men. It's your past that we're struggling against, not your present.'

'I'm a South African,' Mahoney said.

Terreblanche shook his head. 'There is no such thing as a South African, my friend. There is no South African volk, any more than there is a European volk. A Frenchman is a member of the French volk – he is not a European in *nationality*. He is a member of the French volk because the French have a common language, culture, history, and their own territory. Those are the scientific requirements for a volk. But there are fifteen different volk or tribes in this area called South Africa.

'There is no such thing as a South African language – there are fifteen languages. You do not speak South African – you speak English, and maybe one or two others. There is no such thing as a South African culture – all fifteen peoples practise their own culture. And there isn't really a South African territory – we were artificially lumped together in so-called South Africa by the British after the Boer War in the hopes of creating another British dominion. But it's been a hopeless failure – as it would be if you tried to lump all the Europeans together into one state called Europe. It's been a failure in the USSR – all those different peoples want to break away. The USSR is not a volk because all those different peoples have their own languages, cultures, traditions, history and territories. And South Africa is a failure, for the same reasons. The Boers are not South Africans – they are one of the volks that happen to live in southern Africa.'

'So what am I, by your definition?'

'Well, you're not a Boer – unless you marry Katrina and become one of us. And you're not a Zulu or a Xhosa, by the look of you. So you're part of the English volk, but born in southern Africa. And you cherish your English heritage – as we Boers cherish ours. But the difference is that you still regard England as your ultimate refuge. Or you can go to Australia or New Zealand or Canada and live like an Englishman. But we Boers have nowhere else to go. This is it – ' he pointed to the ground. 'Morally and legally it is ours. The so-called South African government unscrambled some of the mess the British forced upon us and gave the Xhosa volk their land and independence back, and the Tswanas, and the Venda, and the Zulus – so there is nothing unusual in the Boer volk wanting their land and independence back too. And if we don't get it, we're going to fight for it. Take that seriously, Luke.'

Oh, Mahoney took it seriously. And, oh, he wanted Katrina out of this. 'And when does the fighting start?'

Terreblanche took a sip of whisky.

'When the Boers' right to self-determination as a volk is finally taken away from him. When our demand is finally, definitely refused. De Klerk is talking about holding the Great Indaba soon. That's when they'll try to force the Boers into the so-called *new* South Africa, just like the British did. That's the day we acquire the moral and legal right to rebel. That's the day the War of Liberation starts.'

Mahoney took a sip of whisky. He believed the man.

Terreblanche continued: 'But fighting will break out long before that, my friend. Because this government is coming apart at the seams. Already it's unable to maintain law and order. Crime is out of control. People cannot sleep securely. The black townships are out of control. Natal is out of control. It will spread to the rest of the country. Why can't the government stop it? Because they have gone soft, they are afraid to apply the only law the kaffir understands: the big stick. Shaka would have controlled it – and Dingaan and Mzilikazi. By sending their big impis in. There's only one way to rule in Africa. But this government is too weak-kneed to do it.' He snorted. 'So chaos is coming, my friend. And that's when we'll have to go in to restore law and order.'

Mahoney said: 'Do you think you can win the War of Liberation? How many fighting men will you have?'

'If I didn't think so, I'd be a fool to start it. I don't want to see the Boer volk defeated again.' Terreblanche's eyes were unwavering. 'The guerrilla always wins, my friend. Look at Fidel Castro and Mao Tse-tung.'

'But Castro and Mao relied on the oppressed peasants.'

'And we'll be relying on oppressed *Boers*, my friend – the blacks will be only too happy to stay out of a white man's war. Because that's what it will be – Boers against this collapsing Afrikaner government. You ask how many fighting men I can rely on?' He gave a wolfish smile. 'How much is ninety per cent of the farmers in the Transvaal and Orange Free State? How much is fifty per cent of the white police force? Fifty per cent of the army and air force? Fifty per cent of the Citizen Force?'

'But will your men be prepared to fire on the other fifty per cent of Afrikaners who remain loyal to the government?'

'Yes, my friend! Because they'll be our enemy, just as the Cape Afrikaners were in the Boer War when they allowed Britain to use their railways to move the British troops up to the front. While their Afrikaner damsels danced with British officers at balls in Cape Town. And after the first few battles many of the so-called "loyal" fifty per cent will defect to us as well, hey.' He looked at Mahoney. 'And how about all those civil servants? All those housewives? All those kids at school?' He smiled with those calm, piercing blue eyes. 'We've got manpower all right, my friend. And we're organizing it.' He smiled wider. 'We have a saying in Afrikaans: "'n Boer maak 'n plan". A Boer makes a plan. The old joke is about this Boer who's out hunting with his son when suddenly this lion comes charging at them. And the old Boer raises his voorlaaier and pulls the trigger. But the powder is wet. So he snatches his son's gun and pulls the trigger. And again the powder is wet. And the little boy says: "What do we do now?" And the Boer says: "Son, now we must make a plan, hey?"'

Mahoney smiled. Terreblanche continued: 'That's the old joke we make about ourselves because we were always such a disorganised volk. That's how we set off on the Great Trek. That's how we went to see Dingaan. That's how we fought Mzilikazi – we didn't even send our cattle off back to Thaba Nchu! Imagine if Potgieter had done so? He would not have mounted another battle against Mzilikazi. He would have stayed south of the Vaal River. Or joined Retief in Natal and really driven Dingaan out, so we had no Zulus today. If Potgieter had made a proper plan the whole of South African history may have been different. But he didn't, so he went back to recover his cattle and he drove Mzilikazi out of the land.'

'Which you now claim.'

'Which we now claim. Mzilikazi abandoned it. We claim it by Right of Conquest – just like Mzilikazi did, fifteen years before, just like the Americans who conquered the Red Indians. But the point is, my friend, the Boer in 1989 does *not* leave his cattle outside the laager. Yes, my friend, we have made a plan. All kinds of plans.' Then he slapped his hands on his knees and stood up. 'Tell you what, my friend, come to see one of my training camps. We're doing a one-day refresher course on the twenty-sixth. Bring Katrina, she's been trained; intellectuals like her are very important to us.'

He could not get her alone until the last guest had left. They stood at the embers of the fire. 'Intellectuals like me, huh?'

'He said you'd been trained at one of his camps.'

'Sure. It's important to know how to defend yourself. Most people round here have been trained – even children. Even my mother. But that doesn't mean we're all members of the AWB.'

'What do they teach you?'

'Usual stuff. Unarmed combat. How to deal with a knife attack, or an axe, or a spear, et cetera. Firearms. How to use a baton. Hand grenades. Tear-gas. Radios. First aid. Leadership – so you can take charge of untrained civilians. That sort of thing.'

'Explosives?'

'On the advanced course, yes – basic demolition work, destroying bridges, railway track and so on.'

Jesus. First Patti Gandhi, now Katrina de la Rey. 'You're going to blow up bridges and railways?'

'I sincerely hope not. I'm only *trained*. I'm also trained in first aid but I faint at the sight of blood. Particularly my own.'

He frowned, 'But then you must be a member of some AWB cell?'

'Luke, I am only a member of a "Reaction Unit" – all farmers round here are. That means if one farm is attacked, the others know how to help and don't go blundering about.'

'And your parents – are they AWB members?'

'No. My parents are not neo-Nazi, Luke. Get that straight. Though they're old personal friends of Terreblanche's family.' She nodded at his glass. 'Better have some more, you won't get any tomorrow, Christmas is a holy day in this household.'

'Do you want to go to see this training camp?'

'No, but it'll be interesting for you. And Christmas is going to be excruciating, the camp will be fun by comparison.'

'Can't we just have a picnic by ourselves somewhere?'

She kissed him on the cheek. 'The following day. I'll take you to my favourite place – my very own waterfall. But before then I want you to meet everybody.'

Mahoney sighed. 'Katrina? Do you really want to be one of those people?'

'No. But I'm going to have to live with them, warts and all.'

He shook his head. 'We can live anywhere, Katie. In Johannesburg.

I could work for Lawyers for Human Rights. Or I can open my own practice. Or we can live in the Cape. You can still come to visit your . . . volk.' He was going to say 'goddamn volk'.

She smiled. 'Luke, I'm like the Jewess who intends to live in Jerusalem. I'm like Ruth, winnowing in alien corn, who wants to go home.'

78

Katrina was right: Christmas day was excruciating.

It began with prayers on the lawn, attended by the entire labour force. Everybody was in their Sunday best, including Mahoney. Breakfast was eaten in silence, but for Ouma's slurping at her porridge. Then they all drove into Thabazimbi, to church. Mahoney was keen that they go in two cars, to be alone with Katrina, but the old man insisted on one vehicle. The journey was a silent one. It was a relief to get to church.

As they walked in, Mahoney could feel five hundred pairs of Boer eyes on him. It was his first visit to a Dutch Reformed church (which he jokingly used to call the Much Deformed Church), and he followed Katrina's lead, knelt and offered up a rusty prayer of his own. Then came hymns he'd never heard, in Afrikaans, which he stumbled through, which Katrina sang joyfully. Then came the sermon, the black-robed young dominee fulminating so rapidly and eloquently Mahoney could only follow snatches of it, bits about the sins of politicians who defy the word of God laid down in 'black and white' in the Bible. The dominee stopped just short of saying President de Klerk was a heathen. There followed prayers for the saviour of Christian values in darkest Africa in these darkest hours. Followed by an appeal for contributions towards the church fund. The final hymn Mahoney recognized as 'Onward Christian Soldiers'.

He followed Katrina out down the thronging aisle, the eyes of Afrikanerdom on him again. An agonizing hour ensued in the church-yard, sweating in the highveld sun, while the De la Rey family talked to neighbours about politics and water and scandalous agricultural prices. Katrina circulated dutifully, Mahoney in tow, smiling bleak smiles, but nobody chatted to him; they whispered about him after he had passed. '*Katrina se nuwe kêrel*,' Katrina's new fellow. '*'n Engelsman.*'

It was a relief to get out of the churchyard for another silent drive back into the hills. Only Katrina's thigh pressed against his made it bearable. Then followed lunch, another solemn and silent affair, except for the lengthy grace that preceded it and followed it, and Ouma's false teeth clacking. Mahoney was dying for a beer. They adjourned to the living-room, where General de la Rey produced a big leather-bound Bible and read aloud. He read from Exodus, about Moses in the bulrushes, about the Jews trekking from Egypt, Moses' rod parting the sea, for an hour. Then everybody adjourned back to the car, and they drove silently back to the church in Thabazimbi. They sang and prayed again, and the dominee fulminated again, this time about Moses, the Promised Land, the heathen Egyptians in pursuit, the Great Trek, the Battle of Blood River, Majuba, the Boer War. Again, the final hymn was the Afrikaans rendition of 'Onward Christian Soldiers'. More standing around in the churchyard, with bleak half-smiles. Then the oppressive drive back into the hills and the silent evening meal, followed by another reading from the big Bible.

Katrina was right: Mahoney could hardly wait to get away the next day to see the AWB training camp.

But it wasn't a barrel of fun. It depressed the hell out of him: the determination in the air, the fight in people's eyes, in their body-language.

'We don't hate kaffirs,' Terreblanche said. 'We only hate the enemy. The enemy is anybody – white, brown, black or yellow – who tries to take our rights away. Against them we will be ruthless.'

No, most of them didn't hate the kaffir, provided he knew his place. Kaffirs who didn't know their place, they hated. And feared. God, it depressed Mahoney. And impressed him. This was no bunch of fools enjoying themselves playing soldiers: these were grim men, all ages and sizes, all giving their best, all convinced of the rightness of their cause. A parade was being held when Mahoney arrived at the farm outside Rustenburg: two hundred men drawn up in ranks in khaki uniform with maroon berets, armed with pistols, rifles, truncheons, knives, all with the three-legged swastika on their sleeves. There were men so old and boys so young they would not have been in any ordinary army, but they were in this one because they *wanted* to be. All snapped to smartish attention, stood rigidly for Terreblanche's inspection. Then came the refresher course, the baton charges, the lunging, the swiping, the hand-to-hand fighting, the dust and the sweat of mock battles midst the yells of instructors.

'And remember many have done military service,' Terreblanche said to Mahoney; 'many have been in real battles in Angola.'

Mahoney could not imagine them winning against a conventional military force, but it was their passion that was impressive. Later a convoy of cars brought the housewives, girls and grandpas and grandmas. They were all armed, all very serious. They formed into different groups and went off to practise their martial skills.

Mahoney followed a group of housewives to one of the target ranges. They ranged in age from early twenties to late sixties. Most wore khaki blouses with the AWB emblem; they all wore holsters. It was all very business-like. They lined up in ranks and offered their firearms for the instructor's inspection. Then the first row advanced. The targets were life-size sketches of a man. The women stood, legs apart, hands at their sides, then, on a barked command, they dropped into a half crouch and clutched their weapons in both hands, aiming. They held the stance whilst the instructor went down the line, correcting any deficiencies in loud military style. Then a barked command – '*Head!*' – and they fired. Then – '*Heart!*' – and they fired again. Another command and each woman dropped to her belly and fired again.

The results were good: each black body had three holes. Critical discussion ensued with the instructor.

Terreblanche appeared at Mahoney's side. 'Come and see the children.'

And the children were the most depressing part of all. 'Give me the youth . . . ' Hitler had said. And now, in the last days of 1989, was not the same happening in the dusty Western Transvaal? Bands of Afrikaner boys, dressed up in their khaki uniforms, sternly marching under the barked orders of instructors, learning unarmed combat, getting stuck into each other with karate chops and kicks and throws; little boys charging at each other with batons, swiping and blocking, scrambling around assault courses; boys at the target ranges zealously firing at paper black men. And the little Afrikaner girls in their neat khaki uniforms, marching, learning self-defence, learning first aid, all very, very serious.

'I'm impressed,' Mahoney admitted.

'This is just a refresher course,' Terreblanche said, 'because we're all on Christmas holidays – but all over South Africa the same thing is going on today.' He looked at him with those blow-torch blue eyes. 'Please tell your friends about today, Luke.'

Mahoney nodded. 'I intend to.'

'But you don't think we can win?'

Mahoney shook his head. 'No.'

Terreblanche smiled. 'You know the saying: one Zulu is worth ten Xhosa in a fight? And the ANC are Xhosa – '

'Nowadays,' Mahoney said, 'everybody's got the AK–47.'

Terreblanche said quietly: 'The difference lies in *here*.' He tapped his heart. 'And in here.' He tapped his brow. 'The Israelis are vastly outnumbered by the Arabs, but they win. Because of here,' he tapped his heart again. 'And there's another important saying: South Africa's future will be decided by the Boers and the Zulus.' He looked at Luke. 'The two fiercest warrior tribes in Africa, if not in the world. Can you imagine how powerful a pact between the Boers and the Zulus would be?'

Mahoney looked at him. 'Are you telling me – ?'

'I'm telling you nothing that isn't written in books, Luke.' He smiled at him. 'The Zulus hate the Xhosa, Luke, and the ANC is the Xhosa. Do you imagine that in the new South Africa the Zulus are going to accept the Xhosa as boss? *Never*.'

'Are you saying that the AWB will make a pact with the Zulus?'

Terreblanche smiled. 'I'm saying we understand each other. In fact, we respect each other.'

Mahoney drove slowly back to Rustenburg in the afternoon, thinking. He imagined Katrina at the target range, imagined her in unarmed combat. Imagined her wielding a baton, a whip.

And suddenly he remembered the witch doctor's warning the night before he left Umtata in disgrace: '*Beware the land of twenty-one . . .*' The AWB's swastika-like emblem was made up of three sevens joined at their feet: three sevens make twenty-one. And the witch doctor had also said: '*Beware the woman who talks of pigs . . .*' Katrina had burst into his life in the Borneo courtroom protesting about the Pig Case . . .

Oh Jesus. And the witch doctor had been right about Patti Gandhi: '*Beware the woman with the red forehead . . .*' The priest had put a red dot on her forehead the night he had married her by Indian custom in Botswana.

He parked outside the hotel and went into the bar. It was empty. He sat on a high stool and drank a row of cold beers, thinking. Thinking about all this, about what he had seen today. About what the hell he was going to do.

It was dark when he left the hotel and started driving back to Dagbreek, the De la Rey farm. He knew what he had to do. And he was grimly happy about it.

There were no lights burning when he got back, but there was a note on his pillow from Katrina saying that she had prepared a lovely picnic for tomorrow.

He woke up late, still happy about his decision.

It was a glorious African day, the sky cloudless blue, the birds twittering through the silence of the highveld. A lovely day for a picnic with his beautiful woman, for crisp cold wine in the sun beside a tumbling waterfall – and, not to put too fine a point on it, for a fuck. Three days without it was about Mahoney's limit. To further improve his spirits he found he was too late for breakfast. Katrina offered to make some, but he wanted to get going.

'Before anybody shows up,' she grinned, 'to argue the Boer War?'

They drove in her father's Land-Rover down into the plain, bumping over winding tracks. Stretches of bush had been cleared to create fenced pastures. They passed a big herd of cattle.

'How many have you got?'

'Only about a thousand. Our real interest is game farming, so most of the ranch is natural bush.'

They came to a fence and crossed a grid in the track. Beyond was bush again. Then Katrina stopped the vehicle and pointed.

Three giraffe were browsing off the treetops a hundred yards away. They contemplated the Land-Rover thoughtfully, then dismissed it and munched on.

'Oh, great. How many have you got?'

'Only seven. When they breed we sell the offspring to other game ranches.'

She drove slowly on, searching the bush. Half a mile later they came to a muddy waterhole. A rhinoceros was nibbling a bush. It turned its head at the vehicle and peered short-sightedly. It had a long curved horn.

'That's Emily. Now, rhinos are profitable.'

'Is she white or black?'

'White. Mild-tempered. We've also got five black rhinos. If Emily was a black rhino she'd have charged by now. We've got two females and a male, bought them last year from the Natal Parks Board. Both females are pregnant. We'll make money selling the offspring. No hunting of rhinos allowed, of course, they're an endangered species.'

'Bloody marvellous,' Mahoney said, watching the animal. 'Do you have any elephant?'

'No. Sometimes they break in, crossing from Botswana, but we shoo them out chop-chop, an elephant has a hell of an appetite. Same with lions, we get rid of them if they come in because they go for our cattle.'

'How do you shoo an elephant?'

She smiled. 'With strong language. Herd them with vehicles back to where they flattened the fence. Lions we have to shoot, unfortunately. We've tried darting them but what do you do with an unconscious lion? Dump him over the fence? The neighbour doesn't fancy him either.'

'Have you ever shot a lion?'

'Me? I couldn't bear to shoot anything. But I've done darting. When we sell a giraffe or some other animal, we dart it with a drug which knocks it unconscious. Then you put it in a crate, haul the crate onto a lorry and cart it off to whoever's bought it. Big job. But fun. That's the limit of my hunting.' She indicated the waterhole: 'If we come down here this sunset we'll see lots of animals queuing up to drink. There're other waterholes, of course, but this is a popular one. Come.' She engaged gears.

They went grinding through the bush until they came to a rise and the plain opened up below them again, mauve under the cloudless sky. Suddenly the world was alive with tawny yellow, and Katrina braked. A big herd of springbok raced towards their track, leaping and bounding, ears up, tails up, startled, following their leader, and when they encountered the track they flew. They went flying through the air in gracious arcs, forefeet up, hindlegs streamlined, perfect golden wide-eyed creatures with white bellies and fluffy tails and exquisite horns, the earth drumming from their dainty hooves. On and on the pretty spectacle went; then the last doe flew across the road and disappeared.

'Bloody marvellous.' Mahoney grinned.

Katrina let out the clutch. 'Now they *are* profitable. They breed prolifically, and hunters pay well to hunt springbok. Particularly Americans. And we have to cull. It's terribly sad, but this ranch has to be commercial to survive. We sell the meat, hides, etc. It's a heartbreaking business but it's no worse than sending cattle off to the abattoirs. It's *better* – the cattle in the slaughterhouse smell the blood and they're terrified. Here it's clean. The refrigeration trucks come, Dad organises a bunch of marksmen, and in they go. They take out two hundred or so, skin them, stick 'em in trucks, and off they go to the supermarkets as venison. The hides go to the tanning factories, the hooves and horns to the gelatine factories. Nothing's wasted.'

Mahoney said: 'How many springbok and impala have you got here?'

'Ask Dad. Basic herd of about five hundred. They double their numbers quickly. Quite apart from the buffalo and the other antelope.'

To the west was a long hill. Katrina turned towards it. They came up onto the crest, onto a flat top. There were the remains of an old cooking fire. Below them was the plain. A huge swathe of land had been cleared of bush and taken over by grass, and in the middle was a vlei, a long stretch of water. On all sides of it grazed hundreds of head of game.

Katrina passed him binoculars. 'Not all of them are down there, of course. But in total we've got a basic breeding herd of about two hundred buffalo and a hundred wildebeest.'

Mahoney put the binoculars to his eyes. 'Zebras.'

'Yes, we've got about twenty zebra all told.'

Katrina had told him about this in Borneo, but he hadn't imagined it as impressive as this.

'Nothing to beat Africa, is there?' she said. 'There're thousands of beautiful places in this world, but somehow there's nothing like Africa. And this,' she indicated the plain, 'is the sort of thing that's going to disappear in the new South Africa. Wildlife will be poached out of existence. Unless we guard it jealously. And a black government is likely to earmark game ranches for re-distribution as cattle land.'

'Do you have much trouble with poachers now?'

'All the time. They cut through the fence and blast off a few buffalo, cut off the meat and run. And they set snares. That's terrible. A long slow death. Not our own blacks: they have a vested interest. Every time we cull they get a percentage: that makes them protective. That's the only way to save wildlife in Africa – commercialise it.' She pointed. 'See that ridge on the other side? That's where my waterfall is.'

Mahoney slowly swept the distant cliffs with the binoculars, but he couldn't see any waterfall. Then, at the far end, miles away, he saw smoke rising up between hills that stood up like pointed breasts. He handed her the binoculars. 'Bush-fire?'

She peered. 'Oh *shit*.' She lowered the binoculars. 'The squatters have come back onto Goodhope. My uncle's land, next door to ours. Oh dear, now there'll be trouble again.'

'What kind of trouble? Eviction?'

'Eviction,' she agreed. 'It's one of the sad stories of apartheid, I'm afraid. My uncle Dan owns a big ranch further away, called Antelope. The ranch called Goodhope – ' she pointed – 'lay between Antelope and our ranch. It was owned by an eccentric old widower who neglected it terribly and allowed lots of squatters to build their shacks there in exchange for cheap seasonal labour – which was illegal. From time to time the authorities would evict them and dump them back where they came from. When the old widower died, Uncle Dan and Pa bought the place, to ranch in partnership. At the same time the government granted independence to Bophuthatswana, and so the squatters on Goodhope became "foreigners", because they were Tswanas, and the government removed them across the border – which is only about fifteen miles away. But from time to time they come drifting back. Poor devils, there's not enough work in Bophuthatswana, and they feel this land is somehow theirs and some of their ancestors are buried here.'

'How many of them?'

'Oh, a couple of hundred maybe. But that fluctuates, they bring relatives and there're always new children. They scratch a living, do a bit of poaching, some find work on neighbouring farms. I feel sorry for them, but they are a nuisance. So, Dad and Uncle Dan have to evict them all over again. Which is a nuisance in itself – we've got to go to court. And there's always unpleasantness, great weeping and wailing and gnashing of teeth. It's awful.'

'Do they resist?'

'No fighting, just passive resistance.' She started the vehicle.

'Are you going to do anything about it?'

'I'll tell my father, and he'll go and talk to them but they'll just say yes, yes, and ignore him.'

They drove back down the hill towards the plain. They passed a small herd of impala on the way and startled a family of warthogs before emerging onto the grassy expanse below. Katrina followed a dirt track. The animals watched the vehicle warily; those far from the track resumed their grazing; then some began to run. They turned with a toss of their heads and went pounding away, and a moment later they all started. In a mass movement hundreds of buffalo and wildebeest were pounding across the plain, galloping around the lake towards the distant cliffs. Katrina trod on the accelerator and went bouncing after them, and more animals joined in the stampede, galloping away, tossing their heads. For a quarter of a mile Katrina went racing, bouncing, jolting after them, then she slammed to a halt and cut the engine.

'Listen.'

The drumming of their hooves filled the air.

'Isn't that a wonderful sound? Look at them.' Below the cliffs the galloping animals swept across the grassland in a great mass of grey and brown. 'And all this,' Katrina waved her hand, 'will go unless the white man stays. And *now* – ' she restarted the engine – 'we come to the *pièce de resistance*, my very own secret place.'

They left the Land-Rover at the cliffs and climbed a gorge, following a little stream that came tumbling down to feed the vlei below. About a hundred feet above the plain they came to the secret place, where the water fell over a ledge into a basin of smooth rocks. An acacia tree gave shade. There was a magnificent view of the plain extending into hazy hills. By the time they reached the waterfall, the animals had come back to the vlei.

'*Voilà!*' she said proudly.

'It's beautiful.' He took her in his arms.

They made a fire and drank cold beer and wine while they cooked the meat she had brought.

'When I was a little girl,' she said, 'I used to dream that one day when I was big I would come up here with my beautiful husband.'

'Well, you're big now. All you need is the husband. *But,*' he admitted reasonably, 'I'm not beautiful.'

She bent and kissed him. 'Yes, you are. In a beat-up sort of way.'

He toppled her down onto the rug beside him. 'And you're beautiful. In the beautiful sort of way.'

She lay, stroking his eyebrow with her fingertip. 'And what about my people, the ones you saw yesterday?'

He shook his head gently. 'Those aren't your people, Kate.'

'No? And my parents? Blood is thicker than water.'

'Indeed. But not in politics.'

'But in a civil war?'

'In a civil war marriage is thicker than blood.'

She sighed. 'Ah, marriage. That's why it's so important one knows what one's in for.'

He didn't want to get into that discussion again right now. He sat up and said soberly: 'Kate, I'm speaking to you as a lawyer now. Your personal lawyer. So please listen carefully.' He paused. 'Kate, starting a civil war is usually an act of treason. Or sedition. Or at least terrorism. All serious crimes. And all carry the death penalty in this country.'

She smiled at him. 'I'll take your word for it.'

'And what I saw yesterday was an act of preparation for sedition or terrorism, Katie.'

'Nonsense. They're learning self-defence.'

'And aggression. Now, an act of preparation is not a crime for which one can be prosecuted. But what I saw was getting very close to becoming an act of consummation, for which one could be prosecuted. And, if so, those people could be convicted. I'm not going to stand by and let you take that risk, Katie.'

She said incredulously: 'Are you telling me that this Afrikaner government would put five hundred Afrikaner men and women on trial for learning *self-defence*?'

'No. But the government might well try a few ringleaders like Terreblanche, to deter others. And I don't want you to be one of them.' He held up a finger to stop her interruption. 'But assuming this government doesn't do it, because of the uproar it would cause amongst the Afrikaners, the next government, the ANC, may not be so squeamish. They're quite likely to be firebrands who would enjoy teaching the

Afrikaner a lesson. And what better way than putting a few of their leaders on public trial?'

Katrina sighed, and started to speak, but Mahoney went on quietly: 'And I heard something else yesterday, which worried me.' He paused. 'Remember why the British hanged those rebels after the Slagter's Nek Rebellion? What was their greatest sin, which shocked even the Dutch? It was that they had tried to enter an unholy alliance with the Xhosa chief – they tried to make a military pact with Ngqika to drive the British into the sea. Right?'

'So?'

'I've got a feeling that history may repeat itself. That your Boer compatriots may make a military pact with the Zulus in order to get their way.'

She sighed. 'Oh, heard that before.'

'It makes sense. The new black South African government will be the ANC – therefore dominated by the Xhosa. The Zulus hate the Xhosa and will never accept domination by them. Nor will the Boers. Therefore the Zulus and the Boers make natural allies. Neither is a threat to each other because the Zulus want Zululand and the Boers want their old republics. Between the two of them they might be able to divide up the country, just like the Slagters Nek rebels intended to do.'

She sighed wearily. 'Sure. Darling, PW Botha tried that when the bloodshed started in Natal five years ago – 'Divide and Rule'. Let the blacks knock the shit out of each other; let the Zulus fight the government's battle against the UDF and the ANC; let the Zulus sort out the Xhosa for us, and then we'll sort out the Zulus. But it didn't work because the UDF also has Zulus – the UDF-ANC alliance is not only Xhosa, by a long chalk. So if the theory wasn't successful for the government, why should it work for Terreblanche?'

'Because the AWB will go in on the side of the Inkatha Zulus with all guns blazing, whereas PW Botha couldn't do that. And I didn't say it would succeed, I only said that history could repeat itself. Slagters Nek didn't succeed either.' He looked at her. 'And I'm not going to let you get mixed up in that, Kat. What are you going to do if it happens, when the Zulus start butchering the Xhosa with the AWB on their side, and you're indirectly on the AWB side because they're on your volkstaat's side? Do you intend to be the AWB's accomplice to a full-scale black-on-black civil *war*?'

She looked up at the sky, weighing her words. Then she turned her head to him. '"Intend to"? No. And I don't think it will happen. But, to answer your question – and I'm glad you asked it – in the final result, the answer is yes. Because it will be part of the civil war. I will do my best to stop it happening, but if that does, I am prepared to fight and therefore I must accept responsibility for it. That's the name of the game, and I won't shirk it.'

Jesus. Yes, it was the name of the game! *And, oh God, what he had decided last night was right.* But he was not going to argue about it further.

He said: 'Be that as it may, last night I made up my mind what I'm going to do about all this, Katrina. About you, about the politics of this godforsaken country, about me.' He turned her face to him. 'And it is this: I am *not* going back to live in Hong Kong. I have to go there in two weeks to tie up my affairs, give notice, but I'll be back inside a few months. And I'm going to stay here. With you. I'm not going to stand by and watch you take these risks without me being here to influence you. To protect you.' He looked at her. 'I love you, Katrina. And I'm not going to let you go.'

She turned her face up to the sky again. 'So introducing you to my people has definitely been a failure?'

'Yes,' he smiled. 'I love you, Katrina. And we're going to get married one day,'

'Married? And what are you going to do about my people?'

'We're our own people, Katrina.'

Katrina took a deep breath: then she rolled on her side and put her arms around him and held him tight. 'Oh thank God. And, yes, I'll marry you. And, oh, I'm so happy . . .'

So Luke Mahoney and Katrina de la Rey became engaged to be married.

No date was set, and she insisted they not tell her parents yet. Mahoney wanted to marry her the very next day, in the Magistrate's office in Thabazimbi; he wanted her to return to Hong Kong with him while he wound up his affairs there, as a honeymoon. But Katrina insisted they wait. She had several reasons: her university work, her Volkswag work, the serious problem of breaking the bad news to her parents. But the real reason was she wanted Mahoney to be sure. But, oh, they were very happy when they got back to the De la Rey homestead in the dusk with their secret, after a wonderful afternoon of making riotous love.

Then the telephone rang. It was for Mahoney, from Splinter Woodcock.

Mahoney took the call in the living-room, with the whole family present. He listened to Splinter, his heart knocking, but he asked no questions. He thanked Splinter and hung up. He turned to Katrina. He was confused to find himself shaken.

'What's the matter?' Katrina asked.

He took her hand and led her out onto the lawn. He turned to her and said: 'As a gesture of goodwill, De Klerk is releasing some political prisoners.' He took a breath. 'Patti Gandhi is being released the day after tomorrow. Splinter says she wants me to meet her outside the prison.'

79

It was unreal. He had had a day to try to get used to the news, to fumble with it, to try to grasp that it was true, that Patti was actually coming out into the big wide world at last, but it was still unreal, like a dream. And his emotions were confused. Not his feelings for Katrina, but how he felt about *her*.

Katrina had been wonderful about it. She had just agreed to marry him, and now he had to rush off to meet the former love of his life, the beautiful tragic woman he had made famous in *Alms for Oblivion*, made the world weep for. Katrina had appeared unfazed. 'Of *course* I understand. Good God, the poor woman's been in prison for over twenty years, of course you've got to go and meet her after all she's been through, it would be callous in the extreme to refuse – and I would be petty in the extreme if I objected. Just please be back here in time to see the New Year in with my family.'

'I love you,' he had said.

'I love you too.'

As he drove Katrina's car through the dark Transvaal night towards Johannesburg he tried to analyse his feelings, tried to rationalise them, but they were too complicated and too blurred for classification. He was overjoyed that Patti was going to be free at last, his eyes burned with joy for her – and with guilt – and, yes, with love. Yes, he loved her – but as a dear friend now, his beautiful courageous friend who had once been his glorious mate, who had endured so much it made him want to weep.

'She's dreadfully excited about seeing you,' Splinter Woodcock had said. 'Don't let her down.'

What did that mean? *Oh Christ, please don't make me let her down. Please God, she understands that we can't get back together after all these years. Please God, I don't break her heart. Please God, give her laughter and joy. Please God, she understands I love somebody else now . . .*

The sun was up over the golden city of Johannesburg when he found his way down unfamiliar byways to the forbidding complex of Diepkloof Prison. It was going to be a beautiful day. It was five minutes to seven, and dozens of cars were lined up outside the gates, hundreds of people waiting. Could these all be people to welcome Patti Gandhi? Surely not. Plenty of other prisoners must be being released today.

Mahoney parked Katrina's car. His hands were shaky. He looked at his reflection in the rear-view mirror, then ran his fingers through his hair. His face was gaunt. There was a tap on his windscreen, and there was Lisa Rousseau, beaming at him.

'*Lisa!*' He clambered out of the car. He put his hands on her shoulders, then clasped her to him. And with this human contact he almost felt like weeping. He kissed her cheek hard, then grinned at her. 'How *are* you? Thank you for coming today . . . '

Lisa laughed tearfully. 'Thank *you*. I was scared you mightn't be able to come, so as I was up here for Christmas I did – I couldn't bear for her to be released into a vacuum. Oh Luke – ' she stepped back and looked at him joyfully – 'I'm so pleased for her! *And*,' she beamed, 'you look great!'

Great? He felt emotionally and physically beaten up. 'So do you, Lisa.' It was true. She must be in her late forties now, but she had not put on weight – she was still a beautiful woman.

Lisa gushed: 'And *Alms for Oblivion* – I *loved* it. Though I wish you'd called me by my real name – what kind of a history siren is called *Elizabeth*? And poor beautiful Patti called Pamela!'

Mahoney grinned. 'I must thank you for indirectly introducing me to Katrina.'

'Oh Katrina . . . ' Lisa wiped her eye with the back of her hand. 'What a brilliant academic mind. Tell me – I've heard a little whisper – are you two – ' she waggled her hand – 'a definite number?'

'Yes,' Mahoney grinned. He felt his eyes burn.

'Oh, Luke, I'm so happy for you. But – ' she cocked her head – 'aren't you on opposite sides of the fence? Be aware of that, darling.'

Just then there was a murmur from the crowd, and Mahoney turned, heart knocking, and he felt pale. He saw the big prison gates open. A black woman walked out. Lisa Rousseau grabbed his hand and said: 'Goodbye, Luke.'

'Lisa!' He turned to her. 'Where're you going? Let's take Patti to lunch together, give her a big welcome – '

'*No*, darling,' Lisa said, 'this is *her* big day.'

There was another murmur from the crowd, and Mahoney turned, but it was another black person who emerged. He turned back. 'Lisa?'

But Lisa Rousseau was walking away down the road. She twiddled her fingers over her shoulder. '*Remember to write!*' she sang.

Mahoney started after her, to drag her back to help him with Patti, but then there was a shout from the crowd, and through the big prison doors stepped Patti Gandhi.

From fifty yards away Mahoney stared, his heart thumping.

The crowd was surging and waving, and now he noticed how many Indians there were, and pressmen – Mahoney was astonished. There were at least half a dozen cameramen in the crowd, snapping pictures. Then he saw Patti above the hands, heads and cameras. He stared. She was walking down the gravel path from the big forbidding fortress – and she looked marvellous. Patti Gandhi came down the path to the gate, waving and smiling her brilliant smile, her long black hair flowing, her face perfectly made up, dressed in an exotic sari. From where Mahoney stood, she did not look a day older. He stood beside his car, staring, grinning, a smile of tearful joy all over his face.

She strode through the gate, arms wide, and people mobbed her. Mobbed her, Indian people throwing garlands around her neck, pressmen's cameras snapping, journalists jostling. Patti Gandhi stood in the midst of them, laughing and kissing, hugging and grabbing hands.

Mahoney stared, tears running down his face, unable to move, not *wanting* to move, *wanting* her to have her welcome. Then she looked up and saw him standing there. For a long moment the world seemed to stand still. Then she made her way through the crowd surrounding her, then stopped. Mahoney and Patti confronted each other, ten yards apart, staring, and a silence fell.

'Welcome back, Patti.' The tears were running down his face.

Patti Gandhi stared at him, her beautiful face still. For a long moment they looked at each other, while the crowd stared and cameramen snapped and pressmen scribbled. Then her face slowly broke into a tearful laugh, and she flung her arms wide and ran to him. Mahoney strode towards her. They collided in each other's arms, and they clutched each other, crying, laughing, hugging.

The 'Welcome Patti Gandhi Reception' in the Sandton Sun Hotel was over. The speeches had been made, the Indian representatives had gone home, the black representatives of the UDF, the handful of white liberals, the press: everybody gone home to ring the New Year in.

Patti stood at the window of her suite and said: 'A fucking *Boer* woman.'

Mahoney said as gently as he could: 'She's a liberal Afrikaner.'

Patti snorted softly. 'How old is she?'

'Thirty-eight.'

Patti nodded bitterly. 'Younger than me. All her hormones intact.' She turned slowly to him. She fixed him with her big brown almond eyes. She said quietly: 'Okay, darling, I understand. Perfectly. A lot of water has flowed under the bridge and so on. As it has with me. We're two very different people now. But let me tell you this, dearest, darling Luke Mahoney – the very same Luke Mahoney who loved me so madly he wrote *Alms for Oblivion*.' She looked at him and shook her lovely head. 'You didn't write that book for money, Luke. You didn't even think it would be published, let alone make you famous. You wrote it because you loved me.'

Mahoney closed his burning eyes. 'True.'

Patti stood by the window, eyes bright. She said softly: 'You can't write something like that – almost like building the Taj Mahal – and then walk away from it unscathed, Luke.'

'I assure you, I'm not unscathed.'

Patti snorted softly. 'My darling, you've no idea what "scathed" is.' She looked at him with brimming eyes. 'For twenty-four years you have kept me sane.'

Mahoney closed his eyes. Tears rolled down his cheeks. He said: 'You never wrote.'

Patti clutched her hands together, then thrust them at the ceiling and cried: 'How could I bear to fucking write?!'

Mahoney's eyes were brimming. And, oh God, he just wanted her to be happy, to rejoice in her freedom.

Before he could muster a reply she said softly: 'And now, after twenty-four years, it's a fucking Boer woman . . . ?' She looked at him with big brimming eyes, then said softly: 'Well, I tell you what, darling: I think you're absolutely right in what you said in *Big Trouble* – give the bastards their volkstaat, and get rid of the sonsabitches! Including your Katrina de la Rey!'

Mahoney closed his eyes. He didn't know what to say, how not to argue. 'I'm so sorry, darling.'

There was a long silence. Then she shook her head and drew herself up and said softly: 'I'm sorry, darling.' She tossed her hair. 'I'm. overwrought. I've dreamed about this day for so long, and now it's . . . *unreal. I'm* unreal.' She waved a hand. 'This hotel is unreal. That sky out there. *You're* unreal.'

Mahoney wanted to sob. 'I understand.'

She looked at him tearfully. She said softly: 'Okay, too much water has passed under the bridge, darling. Even I can understand that. Forgive me. I've been silly.'

Mahoney wanted to weep. He whispered: 'There's nothing to forgive.'

Patti's tears were glistening. She said softly: 'I want to tear off this sari and show you my body and make you make love to me, Luke.' Her voice shook. 'Can I?'

Mahoney stifled a sob. He begged her: 'No.'

'No?.' She sob-laughed and ripped the sari off.

Her glorious silhouette against the window was as youthful as he remembered it, her legs and breasts and belly as beautiful. She stood there a long moment, waiting for him, then she whispered: 'She need not know. I promise you that I won't tell her. You're my friend. And tomorrow I'm flying to London, to rejoin the ANC, darling. All I want is you, now.'

Mahoney had to tear his eyes off her beauty. He whispered: 'I love you, Patti. And you're as beautiful as I remember you. Be proud of that. *Rejoice* in it! But I am not going to make love to you, no matter how much I want to. Because – ' and he had to be brutal and say it – 'I love somebody else now.'

She whispered: 'You *think* you do. But you don't.'

'I do.'

She shook her long black locks at him. 'You're making a terrible mistake, darling. Not only do you really love me, but she's totally wrong for you.'

Mahoney said thickly: 'Goodbye, darling.' He turned to the door, and opened it. He looked back. Patti was still a naked silhouette against the window, staring at him. He whispered again tearfully: 'Goodbye, darling.'

Patti sobbed: 'See you in the new South Africa . . . '

As he closed the door he heard her soft cry. He leant against the wall, and dropped his head and sobbed.

Then he strode down the corridor. He took the elevator to the basement car park, found Katrina's car and drove hard back to the Western Transvaal, for the New Year's celebrations with the De la Rey family. The tears were gleaming on his face.

80

Erik Badenhorst, the former officer in charge of hit squads at Platplaas, had been a very worried man ever since receiving Daniel Sipholo's very first message before his conviction for murdering Hendrik van Rensburg. Indeed that message had finally decided him to get the hell out of the police.

Badenhorst had been a very good officer but it is in the nature of hard men capable of his specialised work to be very independent, often bloody-minded, with superior officers. Over recent years he had made himself unpopular in certain police circles. This had led to his being passed over for promotion. When the message from Daniel reached him, Badenhorst had gone to General Krombrink and urged them to do something for Daniel. 'Pull a few strings, hey, otherwise he'll spill the beans.' But he had been told to ignore Daniel's pleas, to deny everything. 'Nobody will believe him, man.' Badenhorst was not so sure, and he feared that his former superiors would say that any murders attributed to the Platplaas squad by Daniel must be the work of that madman Erik Badenhorst acting on his own initiative. And so he had resigned. His fears seemed confirmed when, on applying for a job, his erstwhile superiors refused to give him a reference. By the time of Daniel's conviction, Badenhorst was scratching a living as a taxi driver. Daniel's messages kept reaching him from Death Row via contacts in the police. And then, on the eve of his execution, Daniel had made his gallows affidavit naming him as the officer who had ordered the murder of Walter Kosagu, among others. Badenhorst was frantic. He disappeared from his home and went to ground: no press-man could find him.

When the Attorney General's investigation began, one by one his former superiors denied under oath ever giving any orders to murder anyone – and Erik Badenhorst could see himself on Death Row. That he had not yet been called to testify confirmed his fear that he was going to be the scapegoat. Then had come Daniel's plea of guilty at the preparatory examination into Walter Kosagu's murder. On Christmas Eve, the Attorney General's investigation had adjourned until the new year. On 2nd January Badenhorst had telephoned Lawyers for Human Rights, the people who had helped Daniel. He desperately wanted their advice, and he wanted Luke Mahoney, who had published Daniel's story internationally, to tell the world that his superiors were lying.

Mahoney and Katrina had just returned to Johannesburg when Splinter Woodcock telephoned. They were sprawled in deck-chairs on the lawn, revelling in being alone together after the festive season, delighted at the prospect of sleeping together again.

The meeting took place the next day at a hotel in Pretoria.

Erik Badenhorst was very anxious to be believed: his coffee cup trembled.

Mahoney tried to calm him: 'Mr Badenhorst, try to relax and answer a few questions first. Now, I take it you've read Daniel's story in the newspapers? Is that story true?'

'It is absolutely true, sir. And I have a lot more to tell you that Daniel doesn't know about.'

Mahoney said: 'So you are a multi-murderer? Crimes for which you will hang if you are prosecuted.'

Badenhorst said tensely: 'Yes, sir. But every murder was carried out on the orders of my superior officers. But they will deny everything, put the whole blame on me and Daniel.'

'So, why don't you just deny everything, like your superior officers, say that Daniel is lying to save his neck?'

Badenhorst leant forward. His cigarette trembled.

'Sir, yes, I'm taking a hell of a chance, hey. But who will believe me? The whole world knows Daniel's story, and the police will blame me. Erik Badenhorst, the trouble-maker, hey?' He shook his worried head. 'How can one man fight the whole police force? They'll find a way of hanging me to shut me up – like they wanted Daniel to hang to shut him up.' He took a deep worried breath: 'The only guys who can help me are you, Lawyers for Human Rights, and the ANC.'

Mahoney was taken aback. 'The *ANC*?'

Badenhorst said earnestly: 'I've thought a hell of a lot about it, hey. The ANC are the only people with the back-up, with the organization to give me the protection I need.' He looked at Mahoney desperately. 'But how do I get to them, hey? How do I convince them that this is not just another dirty police trick so I can walk into their office and blow their heads off, like I would have done six months ago if I'd had the chance? You're my only chance, sir. If I tell you everything, honest to God, and they read it in the newspapers, they'll believe me, because the police would never go about it like that – publicly confess to terrible crimes just to get their foot in the ANC's door to shoot somebody.'

The man was right. 'If you want to talk to the ANC you'll have to leave South Africa to do it.'

'Exactly, sir. And how do I do that except through you and Lawyers for Human Rights?'

'Lawyers for Human Rights are very respectable lawyers and they will not cover up a crime. And I don't work for them. I happen to be a lawyer, but I'm speaking to you now as a writer.'

Badenhorst pleaded: 'Okay, but can you get to the ANC for me, sir? Have you got any contacts? How can I do it alone? They may kill me, in revenge. How can I trust *them*, without you speaking for me?'

Mahoney said, 'Do you want to be paid for your story?'

Badenhorst looked shocked. '*Got*, no man! All I want is a safe conduct. Protection from the police. And,' he added, 'to tell the bladdy truth at last. Get it off my chest. And help Daniel too. *Got*, man, that guy's done a lot of dirty jobs for the police and now he's standing on the gallows they desert him, hey.'

Okay, Mahoney believed the man was on the level. He sighed: 'Yes, I've got a contact in the ANC.'

Badenhorst closed his eyes in relief. 'Many thanks, hey. But it's bladdy urgent, sir – the cops can come for me any moment. How soon can you get hold of him, sir?'

Mahoney sighed again. 'Her,' he said. 'I've got to get your story first. And we've got to get you out of the country. Now, have you got any money?'

'Sir, I've only got a small police pension. No savings.'

Mahoney didn't want to tell the man that he would surely be able to get the *Globe* to bankroll him for a while – he didn't want to encourage him to exaggerate anything. He picked up his pen. 'Okay, let's get the facts. But first: you've read in the newspapers about Richard Barker's murder? Do you know who killed him?'

'No. But I've got a bladdy good idea.'

'Who?' Mahoney demanded.

Badenhorst said: 'The same people who murdered Anton Lubowski in Namibia. And Matthew Goniwe. The Civil Cooperation Bureau.'

'The Civil *Cooperation* Bureau? Who the hell are they?'

'The army's hit-squad boys. I don't know anything about them, jus' like nobody knew about Platplaas until Daniel talked.'

'So how did *you* hear about them?'

'I haven't heard much, but it doesn't take much imagination – every army has its special forces, even Britain. *Got*, man, this country's been at war for sixteen years in Angola and Mozambique – of course our army has the same thing.'

'But how do you know it's called the Civil Cooperation Bureau?'

'It's something like that. They're not in uniform, but they're ex-army. Tough guys. They have ordinary jobs as well, or businesses, all over Africa, but they take their orders from the Defence Force.'

'All over Africa?'

'All over the world. Other countries have embassies, their intelligence officers work as clerks but really they're spies. Well South Africa cannot have embassies in many countries because of apartheid, so the government sets up their agents as businessmen in Kenya, or Paris – but really they're spies, hey.'

And in Hong Kong? Mahoney thought. 'But who told you it's called the Civil Cooperation Bureau?'

'When I left the police I was desperate for a job, hey. One day I heard there's one going at a private security firm. I rush there, but a guy tells me the job's been taken. But he says as I'm an ex-policeman there may be a job for me in the Defence Force, in the Civil Cooperation Office. Or Bureau, or Department. He said: "Doing anything from breaking a window to rubbing out somebody." He said he'd speak to somebody he knows and told me to come back next week. I did, but he had already left the firm. Nobody knew where he had gone. So I telephoned the Defence Force and asked to speak to the Civil Cooperation Bureau and the guy said there was no such thing. None of my old friends in the police knew anything. Anyway, at that stage I got a job as a taxi driver.'

Mahoney sighed. 'Okay. We'll come back to that later. Let's get to work.' He looked him in the eye. 'Only the truth. If you're not sure of anything, say so.'

It was a hair-raising story. All the details would take a week to get, but after three hours Mahoney had the broad outline noted, enough to present to Patti Gandhi.

He was confident of the *Globe*'s support: it would be a scoop. But the ANC would be wary. At noon he left a very tense Badenhorst and drove into Johannesburg, to Hugo Wessels' office at *Vryburgher*. He wanted a prestigious Afrikaans newspaper to be in on this story too. Hugo was delighted. He gave Mahoney the ANC's telephone number in London. Mahoney drove to a hotel. Ten minutes later he was connected to Patti Gandhi. 'Hullo?' she said.

Mahoney said: 'Two questions: do you know who this is, and is your line safe?'

There was a pause. Then Patti whispered: 'Yes to both questions.' Then: 'I knew you'd call.'

Mahoney took a deep breath. 'Please listen carefully, without asking questions. I need an answer from your head office tomorrow. The next day may be too late, the informant may be arrested. You must send your answer to the fax number I'm about to give you. You must send it from a *public* fax machine, not your office. And it must be coded, to look like a business deal, no names mentioned. Your answer must be a *guaranteed* yes, or no. And if your people let us down the press will tear them apart. Have you got that?'

A pause. 'Got it. But Luke?'

'Yes?'

'I love you,' she whispered. 'I knew you'd call.'

Mahoney's mind fumbled with how to handle this. Then he heard himself say: 'I love you too, Patti. But too much has happened.'

A long pause. Then: 'Okay, shoot.'

81

The next morning her fax arrived: '*We guarantee the goods will be accepted provided we are satisfied as to quality and manufacturer's future reliability. If we are not so satisfied, goods will be rejected but left intact.*'

Erik Badenhorst put his hands to his face in relief.

The next priority was to get him out of the country to a place where he'd be safe from the police while he was fully debriefed and his story written. Mahoney had told Katrina nothing about all this last night, and he couldn't do so until the story was published. But he had to explain that he was going away. He telephoned her at her Volkswag office.

'Yes?'

'Katie, please don't ask any questions, but I've got to go away for a few days. This afternoon. Following up details of Daniel's affidavit. I can't tell you anything for professional reasons, until I come back, then I'll tell you everything.'

She appealed: 'Going *away*? Oh *shit*, Luke, must you? – I've been thinking about you all morning, getting all hot and bothered. Can't it wait?'

Mahoney grinned. 'No, it's very important.'

'Oh, *damn*. Is it really only for three days?'

'Well,' Mahoney said, 'maybe four.'

'Oh, *shit*. Where the hell are you going?'

'To Swaziland.' He added: 'By car.'

There was a pause. Then: 'Swaziland. That's where you used to go with her. Mahoney? You're not meeting *her* there, are you? She hasn't taken it into her pretty head to fly out from London on a sentimental journey, has she?'

'No, darling. This is strictly writing.'

She snorted. 'You wrote a hell of a lot about *her*, remember?' She sighed. 'Okay, darling, but please hurry it up. I'll count the hours, starting now. Who am I going to get romantic with tonight?'

'Nobody, I trust.'

'Your trust, sir, is well founded.'

That afternoon Mahoney drove his rented car out to Jan Smuts Airport. He parked in the basement. He saw Badenhorst waiting, as instructed, near the telephone boxes. Hugo Wessels was sitting ten paces away. They all boarded the flight to the island of Mauritius, in the Indian Ocean.

Erik Badenhorst was a very nervous man. He had half-expected to be arrested at the immigration desk and charged with murder. He went through first. Mahoney's eyes darted around the throng. But Badenhorst got through the barrier without a hitch.

It was no coincidence that their hotel was the very same in which Mahoney had holed up with his British Airways hostess years ago. It was the only hotel he knew, and it was secluded. Palms lined the white crescent of private beach. The hotel was almost full, the garden bar always jolly, there were lots of pretty ladies in bikinis and at night there was dancing to a steel band. It was a very romantic place, and Mahoney wished he could have brought Katrina with him. But it was all work.

Erik Badenhorst was a nervously exhausted man but a euphoric one. They had been unable to talk business on the aircraft, but once they got to the island it came tumbling out. He was desperate to be believed, to offload his conscience.

It took Mahoney and Hugo three days' hard work to get the story into coherent sequence. They sat at the far end of the tropical beach with tape recorders. Two machines recorded everything Badenhorst said, while Mahoney and Hugo made notes and cross-examined him.

It was an awful story. About a police force which had been given so much power by its political masters that it had grown to believe it was above the law it was sworn to uphold. A police force grown so arrogant that it believed any ends justified the means. It was a story of cold-blooded murder, burglary, theft, assault, torture and perjury.

'Those years when I was based on the Swaziland border, those sabotage jobs I did inside Swaziland, blowing up the odd ANC safehouse, the odd ANC vehicle, kidnapping ANC people, all that was just psychological training, hey. So when I was promoted and took over Platplaas I was toughened, ready to take over the sharp end . . .

'Daniel was bladdy good, hey. We were available to any police station to do any special jobs and between jobs the askaris – those are the ANC terrorists we captured and persuaded to work for us – they went into the black townships and mingled, picking up information. The askaris were valuable because they could recognise terrorists they'd seen in training camps, in Cuba and so on . . .'

And it was a story of cold-blooded callousness. 'The first chap I actually had to murder was Sipho Mondile.' Sipho, an ANC suspect, had been arrested in Grahamstown and during the course of robust interrogation he had taken the unusual step of diving through a window with his hands manacled behind his back. Landing on his head. The doctor advised the police that Sipho had suffered brain damage, that they had 'another Steve Biko case here'. When Sipho recovered consciousness he was officially released, immediately unofficially kidnapped, and driven to the Botswana border.

'General Krombrink telephoned me saying I had to dispose of a problem person. So I went to collect some "knock-out drops" from him.'

Badenhorst proceeded to the Botswana border, where he met other local officers. Sipho had already arrived, handcuffed, a very sick man. He was told he was to be deported across the border as soon as it was dark, and given a drink containing the drops. When he fell asleep, he was shot through the head. A funeral pyre of old car tyres was prepared, the body placed on top.

'Who shot him?' Mahoney demanded. 'You?'

'No, it was a sergeant called . . . I'm not sure of the name, hey.'

Jesus, Mahoney thought, you witness a murder by one of your colleagues and you're not sure? 'But you were supposed to be the hitman?'

Badenhorst said: 'Ja, but *Got*, man, I was a bit squeamish and this sergeant was keen to do it, he hated kaffirs, hey.'

'And,' Hugo said, 'how did you feel?'

Badenhorst sighed. 'How do you feel when you go to the movies and see James Bond shoot one of those Russian spies, hey? Or push him into the swimming pool with all those piranha fish? You think James Bond is a good guy, hey . . . ?'

Although Sipho's hands, feet and head were quickly consumed by the flames, it takes about nine hours to reduce a corpse to ashes in a cremation like this one. The policemen settled down to wait, drinking and grilling chops around another fire.

Mahoney interposed: 'D'you know who killed Ruth First? She was the wife of Joe Slovo, leader of the South African Communist Party. She was killed by a letter-bomb in Mozambique.'

'No. The police have got an expert who can make any kind of umbrella-gun, letter-bomb, time-bomb, and so on, but I think Ruth First was killed by the CCB, the Civil Cooperation Bureau.'

'What's this CCB?' Hugo said.

Mahoney said: 'He thinks it's an army hit squad, part of Military Intelligence, that operates worldwide.' He told Hugo what little they knew, then said to Badenhorst: 'And Albie Sachs? He was a senior ANC officer, in Mozambique. He got his arm blown off when he inserted his key in his car door.'

Badenhorst said, 'That must have been a CCB job. Nobody at Platplaas would know how to rig a bomb to a car door.'

'Did the police have other hit squads, apart from Platplaas?'

'Possibly. I once heard of a place called : . . something-plaas, but I knew nothing about it.'

'Do you know who shot Dulcie September? She was the chief ANC official in Paris, gunned down outside her office.'

'That would be CCB. General Krombrink wouldn't send a dumb cop like me to Paris, hey. *Got*, I'd get lost.'

Mahoney smiled. 'And Anton Lubowski? He was a lawyer in Namibia who was a top SWAPO officer. He was gunned down outside his house just before Namibia got its independence from South Africa.'

Badenhorst shook his head. 'That must be a CCB job too.'

'But why? The war against SWAPO was over, South Africa had already announced that Namibia was getting independence.'

Badenhorst shrugged. 'Maybe he was helping the ANC.'

Mahoney said to Hugo: 'This is bloody important. When I'm back in Hong Kong you must follow this story up, Hugo.'

'Damn *right*.'

And it was a tale of astonishing inefficiency.

'An ANC member called Mike was captured. But he was a tough guy and didn't break under interrogation. So General Krombrink decided to get rid of him. The plan was that we'd say Mike had been turned and joined us, but then deserted. Askaris didn't sign any forms when they joined us, so there were no official records. I was called in to bump him off. Now, we also had an askari called Paul, who nobody trusted, hey. He had joined the ANC, deserted, and we had picked him up and tried to turn him into an askari. But he could do nothing right. So General Krombrink called me to his house one night and told me I should get rid of him at the same time as Mike. I had some poison which I had acquired for another case but never used – it's supposed to cause heart attacks. I wanted to try it, because I don't like shooting. I decided to do the job on a farm near the Mozambique border, where the police have a post under Captain Fourie. I told Mike I was deporting him across the border after dark. I stopped in Nelspruit, went to the municipal dump, and filled the vehicle with old car tyres to cremate the bodies. We proceeded on to the farm. I handcuffed Paul to Mike, and told Paul he was guarding him. We then offered them beers. Captain Fourie secretly poured the poison into their drinks. We settled down to our beers, waiting for them to have their heart attacks.

'But nothing happened, hey. No effect at all. We lit a fire for a braaivleis. So the next day I told Mike we hadn't deported him yet because he didn't look well. Paul still thought he was guarding Mike, still handcuffed to him. That afternoon we opened more drinks and put the poison in, lit a fire for a braai and settled down to wait. But again nothing happened! By the time we wanted to go to bed, Paul and Mike were still in perfect health. *Jesus*. So I decided to go back to Krombrink the next day to ask if he had any poison handy. I went to his house. But the maid told me Krombrink and his wife had gone shopping. She asked me to wait in his study, because she was cleaning the living-room. I waited and waited – the maid brought me coffee. Finally I couldn't wait any longer and drove back to the border. We lit a fire for a braai, squirted a triple dosage of poison into the drinks for Paul and Mike. We really expected them to drop this time. *But again nothing happened . . . !*

'So. So I decided we just had to shoot them, hey. But I couldn't do it in cold blood. I still had some old knock-out drops – they just put you into a deep sleep. We doped two drinks, and after a while they fell over asleep – those knock-out drops work fine. Captain Fourie put his foot on Mike's head. I had to look away. He shot him behind the ear. Then Paul. In the morning we shovelled the ashes into the river . . .'

82

Hotel guests swam and played and sunbathed as Mahoney, Badenhorst and Hugo worked under the palms. It was on the third day that a lone figure appeared, a woman in a bikini, a large straw hat and large sunglasses. She was beautiful. She had a voluptuous, sun-tanned body, with full breasts, long shapely legs, her hair pulled up. She walked slowly past them along the water's edge. Her appearance interrupted the work under the palms. '*Wow!*' Hugo said. She walked to the end of the beach, then turned and began to retrace her steps.

There were many people round the garden bar when they returned in the late afternoon. The woman was sitting alone at a table with a tall exotic cocktail, reading a magazine. She was still wearing sunglasses but she was in a colourful dress now.

They went to their respective bungalows to change. As Mahoney stepped out of the shower there was a knock on his door. 'Who is it?' He draped a towel around his waist and opened the door.

The beautiful woman stood there. Smiling. Her long hair was loose now. She took off her sunglasses. 'Hullo, Luke.'

Mahoney stared. And his pulse tripped.

'Patti . . . ' he whispered.

She walked in, smiling. 'What are you doing here?' he said. His heart was knocking.

She walked to the window and looked out at the sea.

'Just a little holiday.' She turned. 'I deserve a holiday after twenty-four years in jail, don't you think?'

Mahoney was shaky. Bemused. And the sexual impact of her was enormous. 'Yes, of course.'

'But why *here*?' Patti smiled. She walked to a chair and sat. 'Not such a coincidence really, Mauritius is a popular holiday resort.'

Mahoney was bemused. Before he could think what to say she continued: 'Well? Are you pleased to see me?'

'Yes, of course I am.' And he was.

Patti smiled. 'But Katrina wouldn't be if she knew? And furthermore you don't believe me. Quite right.' She tossed her head back. 'Okay, I'm here because the ANC sent me, darling. To check this guy Badenhorst out before we let him into our midst. In case it's another police dirty trick to blow all our heads off at once.' She looked at him, amused. 'There, you believe me now, don't you?'

Mahoney was half-grinning. 'Shouldn't I?'

'Sure. Strictly business, that's the purpose of my sleuthing you, not your magnificent body.' She held up a hand. 'Strictly business, Luke – I'm over that romantic nonsense of the last time I saw you. I've adjusted to the real world again. Had a couple of fucks and I feel fine. Okay?'

He was confused to feel a stab of jealousy. Almost shock.

He said: 'But how did you know I was here? Nobody knows, not even Katrina. We didn't tell the ANC.'

'The ANC has its sources, darling.'

He took a deep breath. 'But why did they send *you*?'

'Because,' she smiled, 'they trust my judgement about *you*. And I can get to you, because you'll trust me. Whereas you would refuse to even speak to a stranger. Okay?' Then she blinked her beautiful eyes play-fully. 'Though I must confess I volunteered for the mission.'

She dropped her head and giggled. 'Your *expression*! Now you don't know what to believe? Okay.' She put on a sober face. 'Okay, so put on some clothes and come to my room, I'll send for a bottle of wine. Then we can discuss this case in comfort.' She got up and turned to the door.

Mahoney was still shaky. 'I can't talk to you about it without Badenhorst's permission.'

She had her hand on the doorknob. 'The journalist's code of ethics?'

'And the lawyer's.'

She straightened. 'Do you trust me, Luke?'

He did not know. And he did not trust himself to be alone with her. He said: 'You must trust *me*.'

She leant forward. 'I *do* – but the ANC doesn't! They've learnt to trust nobody.' She shook her head. 'And you haven't exactly got a good track record with the ANC, Luke, after dumping them twenty-odd years ago, and after all the derogatory stuff you've written about Africa.' She shook her head again. 'In fact they're only prepared to listen to this story because it came through *me*.' She paused. 'You are not to ask Badenhorst for his permission, Luke, let me make that clear. That would defeat the purpose of me being here – I am here as a *spy*, to make an assessment of his credibility through my friendship with you *before* the ANC exposes itself to another possible dirty trick. And I must make something else very clear, Luke: if Mr Badenhorst's story *is* another dirty trick, he's going to find himself very much out-gunned. His bits and pieces will be far and wide. And yours are likely to be next, because you'll be seen as an accomplice.'

Mahoney had almost recovered his composure. 'Are you threatening me?'

Patti smiled. 'On the contrary, I'm trying to protect you.' She looked at him. 'And there's another detail I must tell you: I don't know who they are, because the left hand does not know what the right's doing in this business, but I do know that I'm not the only ANC person on this island interested in Mr Badenhorst's story, and you.'

Mahoney frowned. 'Are you telling me – '

'That the ANC has got heavies on the island keeping an eye on you? Of course. We're not fools, to let a possible viper into our midst so trustingly. I am just the frontman, to do the initial brain work and advise whether Mr Badenhorst appears a reasonable investment, or whether he's a time-bomb.' She lifted a finger. 'And if *that* is suspected, his feet won't touch the ground, he'll be spirited away for interrogation in a manner with which I'm sure he's familiar. And your name will not only be mud, it could be blood. And I, darling Luke, care for you far too much to want it to be blood.' She turned the door handle and arched her eyebrows. 'Strictly business. Please come to my room as soon as you're dressed.'

Strictly business? His mind was in turmoil when he made his way to her rondavel. But, yes, it was strictly business. He managed to recover from her impact, got his old feelings for her in perspective, but he had to work at it, to keep his mind off her beauty, off his instinctive reaction to her presence, off memories of long ago.

She sat opposite him at the table on her little verandah, a file open, wine in an ice bucket, a glorious sunset going on behind the palm trees, riotously beautiful in a blue sari that clung about her perfect breasts, her golden midriff bare, her long black hair hanging. She was a very exotic woman whom any man would desire, but she was all business. And Mahoney got himself under control. She listened intently as he summarised the facts, jotting notes on a pad, cross-referring to her file, cross-questioning him.

'You'll be sued by Krombrink,' she said.

'Possibly, yes.'

'There's no corroboration. The bodies have been cremated, and all the other policemen Badenhorst mentions will say he's lying. The ANC will not be able to assist you with legal costs.'

'Okay.'

'So you're satisfied that Badenhorst's telling the truth?'

'Yes.'

'Very well. Good.' She made a note. 'Next case?'

Mahoney looked at his notes. 'Mary Tombi,' he said. 'She was an ANC office bearer in Gaborone, Botswana.'

Patti turned to the index in her file, then turned to the relevant pages. She read the ANC's evidence concerning the attempted assassination, then said: 'Okay, shoot. If you'll pardon the pun . . .'

It was almost midnight when they finished. Dinner had been sent to the bungalow. There were four empty wine bottles. Patti said: 'Okay. So far I think your Mr Badenhorst is on the level. Only a few discrepancies with our information, but they're to be expected. When will you be finished getting the rest of his story?'

'Tomorrow morning. But I'll still have to type it up.'

'So, we meet again here tomorrow afternoon?' It wasn't a question.

Mahoney nodded. 'And will you be able to give your judgement then?'

She smiled. 'You mean my *recommendation*? I'm just the Girl Friday around there. But I think I can advise them now that Mr Badenhorst is probably not another dirty trick. I intend phoning them in the morning.'

'And what happens then?'

'Then, assuming we get the green light, we proceed to London tomorrow night. And Mr Badenhorst is interrogated by the big boys.'

He noted the 'we'. 'And if the big boys believe him?'

'Then he's got nothing to worry about. He gets ANC protection and they'll help him find a job in England until he can return to South Africa when the ANC takes over the country.'

'Can I have that in writing, please.'

She frowned. 'You already have it in writing in my fax to you.'

'That was in code. I need it in clear language now. I'm in a peculiar dual position, Patti – both the journalist and a lawyer. Badenhorst is both my informant *and* my sort of client.'

Patti smiled. 'Okay, I'll give you that in writing. Because, darling Luke, the ANC is a *trust*worthy organization – '

'And if your big boys don't believe him? What happens then? At that stage my "client" is sitting in your head office, defenceless.'

'Then he's very much on his own, I guess.'

'You *guess*?' He shook his head. 'Lawyers don't deal in guesses, Patti, when their client's life is at stake. I insist – *we* insist – on a commitment in black and white, a "safe conduct". And what do you mean "*very much* on his own"?'

She said quietly: 'It depends on why they don't believe him. If they think he's just trying to save his neck – like the police say Daniel is doing – they'll just kick him out into the street. But if they think he's a spy, or another dirty trick to get into their midst to blow them to smithereens, he can't expect to be treated as anything other than the enemy.'

'Meaning?'

'I don't know, Luke. Not my department.'

'That's not good enough, Patti. Your coded fax said that if he was disbelieved he'd be released unharmed. I insist on knowing what's the bottom line when he walks into the lion's den.'

She looked at him. 'Luke, neither you nor Mr Badenhorst are in a position to insist on anything. He's a self-confessed murderer. He can be extradited from almost any country to face trial and hanged. And the South African government is likely to do just that, as part of their claim of innocence. Or one of their hit squads could be sent after him. So your Mr Badenhorst wants protection from the ANC and forgiveness for murdering ANC personnel? Okay, if he's on the level, he'll get both – which is bloody big of the ANC. Of course, we're doing it for the propaganda value, but we'll *have* that anyway when you publish the story. So Mr Badenhorst should be bloody grateful to us.' She raised her eyebrows. 'But if he's *not* on the level . . . ?' She shrugged.

Mahoney shook his head. 'As a lawyer I cannot advise him to accept that. The man's life is at stake.'

'So were the lives he murdered in cold blood.'

Mahoney jabbed a finger. 'And so were lives when you imported explosives into South Africa twenty-odd years ago.'

There was a shocked pause. She stared at him.

'Those explosives were intended for the sabotage of military installations only – '

'But they weren't used for that! They blew up innocent commuters on Jo'burg's railway station!'

'I promise you I did not know that was going to happen. And I don't believe that was an ANC job!'

'But you took the risk, knowing – you must have known – that there was a possibility of it being used against innocent civilians.'

Patti said slowly: 'I swear to you by all that's holy, Luke Mahoney, that I did not believe there was that risk. Military installations *only* was the ANC policy in those days. *And* I was fighting a just war against the fascist barbarism of apartheid.'

'And Erik Badenhorst believed he was fighting a just war against the communist barbarism of the ANC.' He added: 'Against the barbarism of Africa.'

She glared at him. 'Of Africa, huh?'

Mahoney sighed. 'Patti, as a highly intelligent woman you know that Africa is a great big corrupt Marxist dictatorial fuck-up.'

She enquired softly: 'And that's what you think the ANC will be?'

Mahoney sighed again. 'Let's talk about Badenhorst. And I swear to you that he's on the level.'

Patti said quietly: 'Then you'd better come to London and plead his case to the *"barbaric"* ANC, hadn't you, instead of throwing him to the wolves?'

Mahoney was taken aback by this. Then he saw the veiled pleading in her eyes. And, oh God, he wanted her.

'I'm not going to London, Patti. It's not necessary – '

'You're his lawyer!'

'No, I'm not in private practice, I can't represent him – '

'His *de facto* lawyer; you've been giving him legal advice and laying down the law to me about his safe conduct!'

'As any journalist would in my position.' He stood up.

'Then stand by your man by deed as well as word as any journalist would!' She glared at him impotently, and her eyes filled with tears. Then she blurted: 'Once a hack, always a hack, huh? You fucked up one career in journalism by being in the wrong bed at the wrong time, and now you're about to do it again!' Her lip trembled, and she waved a hand. 'This is a big story, Luke, and what the ANC do about it, what happens to Badenhorst, is a *scoop*, it can go for weeks, months, *years*! This is only the tip of the iceberg of assassinations the South African government's been carrying out – and will continue to carry out – the ANC has a mine of information which you can get your hands on if they trust you! We *need* publicity and I promise you we'll easily get another journalist to carry on the story if you don't. It's a *golden* opportunity, Luke, but what do you do? You scoop the first part, let it sink or swim and rush back to the arms of your new-found Boer lover!' Her bright eyes brimmed with tears, then she blurted: 'Well I tell you, Luke Mahoney, you'd better stick with being a beat-up lawyer in Hong Kong and forget about South Africa because you're too much of a *hack* at everything now. You're too out of touch with the real world to *care*, you're too softened by the fleshpots like all those other Somerset Maugham characters! So take my advice, Luke.' She held up a finger, eyes brimming. 'Take my advice and go back to your soft Hong Kong job where you belong, because the drama of Africa is wasted on you!'

Mahoney was staring at her. She stared back at him, aghast at what she had said. Then she dropped her tearful face into her hands and cried: '*Oh, forgive me, Luke* . . .'

Mahoney swallowed, and stood still. 'That's all right, Patti.'

She sobbed into her hands. 'No, it's not all right – I've hurt you! And it's not true. You're *not* a hack-anything, I only said it to hurt you and I'm ashamed of myself . . .'

Mahoney said softly: 'Maybe it is true.'

'No!' She stared up at him tearfully; then she blundered towards him and flung her arms around him. '*No it's not, Luke! I was just trying to hurt you because I'm jealous, I'm screwed up.*'

Mahoney closed his eyes and he felt his arms slide around her. And, oh, the feel of her against him, her perfect heavy breasts, the wonderful satiny feel of her bare back, the contour of her hips, and his knocking heart turned over in compassion for her, for the awfulness of twenty-four terrible years in prison, and with all his heart he admired her, and he desired her, and, oh God, he had to get out of here if he wasn't going to get into all kinds of trouble . . .

'Let's get some fresh air, walk along the beach.'

She held him, her body suddenly rigid; then she stepped back and swept her fingers through her hair. She forced a smile. 'No . . . Thanks, but I'm okay again now. And it's late and you've got a lot of work to do tomorrow.' She flashed him another smile. 'Okay, please go now. I'm fine. Thanks. Good night . . .'

Mahoney walked through the moonlit gardens. There were still people around the thatched bar, some couples dancing, the tinkle of laughter. No lights showed in Badenhorst's or Hugo's windows. He came to his bungalow. Beyond, the palm-fringed moonlit beach curved away to the far promontory, the sea silver-black. He stripped off and threw himself down on the bed.

He lay in the balmy dark, eyes closed, trying not to think about Patti Gandhi. Trying not to think about why she had tried to hurt him, sting him into going to London, trying not to think about her hurt, trying not to think about twenty-four awful years in prison, of her courage, his admiration for her; trying not to think of his guilt. *There was no reason for guilt, nobody can be expected to wait twenty-four years.* And trying, *trying* not to think about her body, about the feel of her in his arms.

Think about Katrina!

Oh yes, Katrina. He knew he loved Katrina. But Katrina had not suffered, he felt no *guilt* about Katrina. She nursed no dreadful *hurt* that demanded his compassion.

Try to stop thinking about Patti and go to sleep!

But he could not make it. He swung off the bed, went to his refrigerator and got out a beer. He slung a towel around his waist and stepped out into the palm-shadowed moonlight.

He set off along the beach, swigging beer without tasting it, trying to think only about his scoop, how to maximise its impact, its headline, its phrases, its punch-lines, trying to think of the book he would write about it, the title, the jacket. He tried to think about anything except Patti Gandhi, the sheen of the lamplight on her loins, the shadowed swell of her breasts, the fragrant smell of her. But he could not make it, and he came to the end of the beach and he wanted to bellow to the starry sky: '*Not guilty, Patti Gandhi!*'

He ripped off his towel and ran at the silvery sea, and he hurled himself into it. The warm water crashed over him and he swam underneath, his eyes open, the silvery ribbed sand swirling past below him. He swam and he swam, until his lungs were bursting, trying to blast out his guilt about Patti Gandhi, then he broke surface and swam hard, arms thrashing. He thrashed and he thrashed, and he passed the end of the promontory, then he rolled onto his back and turned towards the beach. He swam towards the shore, trying to exhaust himself, trying to thrash out his guilt and his lust. When he was twenty yards from the beach something grabbed his wrist tight. He gasped, and twisted, and there was Patti Gandhi, grinning at him.

'Hullo, Luke.'

He stared at her, treading water, his heart knocking. She was naked, her long black hair floating in clouds. He could glimpse her breasts under the silvery surface, and he could feel his loins hardening.

'*What are you doing here?*'

'Same as you. Trying to forget.'

His mind was fumbling, his erection hard, his heart knocking. 'This isn't the best way of going about it.'

'No . . . I was sitting on the rocks, I saw the way you swam. You were desperate.'

'Yes.'

'And so was I . . . ' And she thrust her satiny nakedness against him, her breasts against his chest, her belly against his erection, her thighs writhing against his, and, oh God, the bliss of the fleeting feel of her. With all his heart and loins he wanted to possess her and ravish her, and he clutched her and they sank underwater. For a desperate bubbling moment there was nothing in the world but her glorious nakedness and her wide laughing mouth plunged against his, then they had to let go and break surface, gushing, gasping. They trod water for a moment, panting into each other's faces, eyes desperately locked; then she turned and started swimming towards the beach, her long legs and buttocks silvery in the moonlight.

Mahoney kicked and thrashed after her, his heart knocking, and his hand came down on her ankle and he wrenched her towards him. She twisted back into his arms in a flash of silvery womanflesh, and now his feet were on the sand and he clutched her against him, his mouth plunged onto hers, his hands sliding desperately all over her, her back, her hips, her buttocks, her loins, her breasts writhing desperately against him, joyously gasping. Then she broke the kiss, panting, gasping, and turned out of his arms and seized his hand. They went lunging through the water to the beach, urgently wading, and she threw herself down on the hard wet sand. Mahoney collapsed down beside her and desperately took her in his arms, and he rolled on top of her and she clutched him tight, opened her long golden legs to him and wrapped them fiercely around his.

* * *

Afterwards, lying spent on their backs in the sand, the warm sea lapping at their feet, she whispered: 'Do you love Katrina?'

And, oh God, he knew what he should say, he knew what he wanted to say, but he had to be honest, with himself and with her. And with Katrina. He said: 'I don't know.'

She whispered: 'Do you love me?'

And he knew he should say no, if only to give himself time to clear his mind, to unconfuse himself; he *knew* he should tell her that too much had happened for him to be able to think about that question yet; he knew he should only tell her that he admired her more than any other person, that he desperately desired her, but she deserved his honesty at least.

'I don't know.'

She closed her eyes and gave a soft sigh, and her hand squeezed his. She was silent a moment; then she said to the moonlight: 'What are we going to do?'

He stared up at the starry sky.

'I don't know.'

83

He woke up before first light, exhausted, sprawled on top of the crumpled sheets, and for a moment he did not know where he was; then he felt her warm nakedness beside him. And the night was like a feverish, beautiful dream. He lay still, his nerves crying out for more sleep, desperately trying to go back to sleep so as not to face the day, not to face last night, not to face what it meant for tomorrow. Finally he swung off the bed and looked down at her.

And, oh yes, she was beautiful.

She lay on her side, one long leg bent, the other stretched out as if she were posing, one arm outflung, her black hair splayed out across the pillow, her lovely face in soft repose – and, oh God, he did not know how he felt. He tore his eyes off her, picked up his towel, slung it around his waist and turned towards the door.

'I love you, Luke,' she whispered.

He slowly turned. He did not know what to say. He did not know anything, except that his heart was breaking.

She was still sprawled on her side, eyes closed. 'Please come to England tonight.'

He took a deep, tense breath.

She lay motionless, as if holding her breath, the silence hanging. Then: 'Okay, go and finish your story. Then please come back.'

He spent the morning with Badenhorst and Hugo getting the last of the facts, sitting under the palms ten paces from where he had made wild love to Patti last night. He had great difficulty concentrating. It was mid-afternoon when he finished typing up his story, with the assistance of a row of cold beers. He ripped the last page out of his typewriter and slumped back, trying not to think. Then he flung open his door, and listened. Hugo's typewriter was still clattering in the next bungalow. He pulled on his swimming trunks, then ran down onto the beach, and hurled himself into the sea. He emerged ten minutes later and threw himself down under the palms and stared up at the big blue sky.

And, oh God, with all his loins he knew what he wanted to do – and maybe his heart also: he wanted to go to England. And with all his heart and loins he knew what was wise and what he *really* wanted to do, and that was go home to Katrina . . .

He heaved himself up and stomped back into his room. He snatched up his story and walked to Hugo's bungalow. Hugo and Erik were slumped around a mess of beer cans, looking whacked. Mahoney thrust a copy of his latest writing to each of them. 'I'll be at the bar when you've checked the facts.'

Twenty minutes later Badenhorst came to fetch him. Mahoney returned to Hugo's bungalow. 'Okay?'

'Okay,' Hugo said. 'But mine's better written, of course.'

'Of course.' Mahoney turned to Badenhorst: 'Erik?'

'Ja,' Badenhorst said. 'Fine.' His face was strained.

'Anything to add? Or change?'

'No.' He sighed tensely.

'Stop worrying,' Mahoney said. He shoved the story into a big envelope, and sealed it. He held it out to Hugo. 'To be hand-delivered to the editor of the *Globe* in London personally, tomorrow. For publication the same day as your newspaper publishes.'

Badenhorst said: 'And if the ANC doesn't believe me?'

'Then it's up to our editors to decide. But I think they'll say publish and be damned. And I think the ANC will believe you, Erik.'

'Christ, man, I wish you were coming with me, hey.'

Mahoney sighed. He held out his hand. 'Hugo will be with you. Goodbye, Erik, and good luck. And call me collect in Johannesburg if you're in trouble.'

'And you'll phone my wife? And tell her what's happening.'

'The moment the story is published.' He turned to Hugo. 'See you in Jo'burg when you get back from London.'

He went back to the bar and had a stiff whisky. Then he walked to Patti's bungalow and knocked. 'It's me.'

'Come in.'

Her bag stood by the door. She had just showered and she lay on the bed in a sarong, her long tresses wet, splayed out on the pillow to dry, water still glistening on her. She did not move. She said gently: 'Come here.'

He closed the door, and walked to her bedside. He stood looking down at her smouldering eyes.

She said softly: 'Are you coming to England?'

He shook his head slightly. 'No, darling.'

She looked up at him steadily. 'You're making a mistake, Luke.'

'I'd be making a mistake if I came.'

'You can't have another chance at such happiness, after so long, and not go for it, Luke.'

He closed his eyes. *The words he had used to her twenty-five years ago. The words he had urged on Katrina.*

She whispered: 'You really love me, Luke.'

He took a deep, tense breath. 'But too much has happened, Patti.'

She had not moved. Her beautiful smouldering eyes were steady. She whispered: 'Please make love to me one more time.' She looked at him, then she swept her sarong off and rolled onto her back. She parted her knees wide and held out her arms to him. Her eyes were full of pleading. And she was the most gloriously naked woman in the world – and, oh God, he could be madly in love with her all over again. He whispered: 'I'm not going to England, Patti.'

Her hand reached up to his loins. She whispered: 'You're rock-hard for me.' And she swept up onto her knees and she ripped the towel from his waist and pulled down his swimming trunks, and she grabbed his penis and plunged her hot wet mouth down onto it.

And she sucked and she sucked, her head going up and down, up and down, her teeth vibrating and her tongue frantically working and her wide lips grasping, her shoulders writhing, and she pulled his thighs against her breasts and her hands reached up to his nipples and kneaded them. And Mahoney groaned, eyes closed in anguished bliss, and his hands went to her face to try to lift her off him, and she shook her head fiercely and her fingernails gripped so fiercely into his thighs he gasped. She sucked and sucked savagely, and then there was nothing in the world but the searing, desperately mounting bliss; then he crescendoed into her hot mouth, and the sky began to tumble. He slumped down onto the bed, panting, his hands clasping her head against his belly.

She looked up at him, her eyes big and moist. She whispered: 'No?'

He squeezed her gently. 'No . . . '

She lay still a long moment, then got slowly to her knees. She wiped her wrist across her sensuous mouth. She smiled faintly.

'Okay, darling. See you soon in the new South Africa. But you ain't seen nothin' yet . . . I didn't dream about you, and jerk off about you, for twenty-four years to be foiled by a Boer woman.' She smiled brightly and put her fingertip on his lips. 'So long.' Then she turned and threw herself down onto her stomach.

He stared at her. And she was so beautiful, lying there, her long golden legs, the luscious mound of her buttocks, her golden back. 'Patti?'

She said against the pillow: 'I've said it all, Luke. For the time being. I love you. Don't answer that, just remember it. Please go now. Go home to your Afrikaner lady. See you soon. In the new South Africa.'

With all his heart he wanted to comfort her, to tell her how much he admired her, how much she meant to him, but, oh God, she was making this easy for him, and he only whispered: 'I love you too, Patti. But too much has happened.'

'You've said that. I just don't believe it, that's all. Please go now.'

He got up off the bed and pulled on his swimming trunks. He turned to the door and opened it. He stepped out into the afternoon. As he walked away he heard her sob once.

84

That night was bad. The hotel was full of holiday-makers, but to Mahoney it was empty, ghost-ridden. And guilt-ridden. He wanted to be alone but he could not bear his empty bungalow: he walked along the beach in the moonlight, trying to rationalise his feelings, for Patti, for Katrina, trying to rationalise away his guilt towards both. But the beautiful beach cried 'Patti' at him, the very sand was party to her body. She had lain *here*, and the lapping sea and the moonlight and the palms were accomplices to his confusion and passion and guilt. He walked back to the jollity at the hotel. A light was burning in her bungalow. He felt a stab that was almost grief, almost anger that strangers should lie in the bed where she had lain last night with him.

He wanted a crowd of pretty people around him, and he sat alone at the garden bar and drank a row of cold beers, watching the pretty people dancing, trying not to think about Patti Gandhi, trying to think only of Katrina. Katrina was beautiful, Katrina was just as admirable in her way, and as courageous in her way, and, yes, he loved Katrina. And he had been drinking since before noon, he had been drinking for five days . . . And, oh God, he didn't know what to think . . . He went to bed late, and drunk, and exhausted.

But in the morning he got it straightened out. When he woke up at noon the last five exhausting days seemed like a dream, and beautiful Patti Gandhi was a dream too. And today he was going back to Katrina. He lay there trying to evade his guilty conscience, trying to go back to sleep, his nerves stretched tight; but he could not, and there was only one way to treat a hangover like this. He went to the garden bar and began another row of cold beers, staring out at the sea. And he began to get it straight in his mind.

Surely the bizarre dream was a good one. It had been lovely, and exciting, and surprising, and wildly erotic, and sad, and *good* because he had confronted that emotional confusion of her again and he had dealt with it. It was good because now he knew that, lovely though it had been, wildly erotic though it was, he could not go back to her. *You cannot go backwards in this life.* And that it was sad was good too: it would be bad to have an experience like that, meeting the woman you had loved so madly long ago, and find it meant nothing anymore. And that was good for Katrina too, because he knew now how he felt about Patti, and about her. So there was no reason to feel guilt, what had happened was *good* . . .

And it felt good that the crisis was over, and that the work was over, and that today he was going home to Katrina. *Home.* Yes, he loved her. This afternoon he was going *home*.

It was eight o'clock when his flight landed in Johannesburg. He recovered his car and roared onto the road into the city, smiling. He was excited about getting back to Katrina. It was nine o'clock when he pulled into her yard.

The house was in darkness. Her car was not there. He tried the garage door, but it was locked. He mounted the steps and inserted his key. He groped for the kitchen light switch. He walked into the dining room: there was no note on the table.

She said from the darkened living-room beyond: 'I'm here.'

'Kat . . . !'

She was sitting in the gloom, a silhouette against the window. She was holding a glass of wine. She said: 'And how was sunny Mauritius?'

He stared at her silhouette.

'How do you know I was in Mauritius?'

She said quietly: 'There's a fax for you. It arrived an hour ago.' She indicated the coffee table.

Mahoney picked it up. He took it to the light of the kitchen, his mind fumbling.

'*Your merchandise is totally acceptable this end. Advertise with confidence. Mauritius was wonderful. Love, Patti.*'

The paper trembled in his hand. Then he mouthed, *Bitch*. How the hell did she know Katrina's fax number? Then he realised: she'd got it from Hugo or Badenhorst. He turned back to the dark living-room. He said: 'Kate, I promise you I didn't know she was going to be there.'

She had not moved. 'You told me you were going to Swaziland, Luke. And I even asked you if you were meeting her. I meant it as a joke. But it seems my female intuition has a nose like a pointer.'

Mahoney closed his eyes. 'I told you I was going to Swaziland because it may be that your telephone is tapped. I was going on a very big story of national importance.' He looked across the gloom. 'Erik Badenhorst's story, the guy whom Daniel names as his officer in charge at Platplaas? Every journalist in town was looking for him, remember, including me. Well, he showed up at Lawyers for Human Rights. He wanted to spill the beans. We decided the only safe course for him was to get out of the country immediately.'

'I see. But why was Patti Gandhi there, pray?'

He took a deep breath. 'Because,' he said, 'Badenhorst had decided the only people who could protect him were the ANC. I contacted Patti on his behalf. But I swear I did not know the ANC was going to send her out to Mauritius to check on his story.'

Silence. Then: 'I see. But I wonder why they sent *her*. The beautiful Miss Gandhi of Miss South Africa fame?'

'Because she's a senior member of the ANC now.'

'Or,' she said, 'because she has a big pull with you?'

Mahoney sighed. 'Yes, that's another reason, I think.'

Katrina smiled thinly in the dark. 'And, I think she volunteered for the job.' Mahoney took a deep tense breath. Before he could respond, she said: 'And?'

'We compared Badenhorst's evidence with the ANC's own information.' He held up the fax. 'And it was evidently a successful meeting, Kat.'

Katrina looked at him across the dark.

'Did you make love to her?' The question hung; then she said: 'No, I don't want you to answer that. I won't believe you if you deny it, and I don't want you to lie.'

Mahoney was grateful for the darkness. And, oh God, what was the merit in being truthful? It would only hurt, and he knew exactly how he felt now. But he was to live to regret his decision. He said quietly: 'No I didn't, Kate.'

There was a short silence. Then: 'She's still very beautiful. Why not? The love of your life? All that passion you poured into *Alms*.'

'But that was over twenty years ago.' He looked at her. 'It was nice seeing her again, Katrina. And, yes, there were a lot of memories. But only *memories*. Because now I'm in love with you.'

Katrina sat there, an immobile silhouette against the distant street lamplight. The cricking of night insects. Then she said: 'I don't care whether you made love to her or not. All I care about is how you feel now.'

'I love you, that's how I feel. I've loved you ever since I asked you to marry me in Borneo.'

She was silent. Then she got to her feet. She walked towards him, and her arms were outstretched. She slid them around his neck and held him tight. She whispered: 'Welcome back, darling. And congratulations on your scoop. And . . . ' She plunged her mouth onto his and kissed him hard. 'And I'm *mad* with jealousy.'

Mahoney clutched her tight, and his heart seemed to turn over. *'There's nothing to be jealous about.'*

She squeezed him, then leant back in his arms: 'And I'm grateful to her.'

'Grateful?'

She smiled tearfully. 'I've been black with jealousy. And that's good. Because it made me realise how much I love you.' She plunged her mouth onto his again, her sensuous lips crushed against his, her tongue writhing into his mouth, her loins pressed tight against his, and he clutched her and clutched her and kissed her and, oh God, he was happy.

He pulled her head back and said: 'Let's get married tomorrow. Without telling a soul. Chuck in your job at the university and fly back to Hong Kong with me and we'll work off my resignation period together. We'll have three glorious months as a honeymoon . . . '

She leant back in his arms, her lovely eyes smouldering: then she grinned at him. 'My answer to your marriage proposal is still yes. Yes, yes, yes!'

She flung her arms around him, and kissed him again, hard and writhing, then leant back in his arms again and said tearfully: 'I'll marry you when you come back. If you come back from Hong Kong and still want to marry me, volkstaat, civil war and all, I'll be the happiest voortrekker lady in the whole wide world . . . '

PART XII

PRESIDENT DE KLERK ANNOUNCES
NEW SOUTH AFRICA

NELSON MANDELA RELEASED

CIVIL COOPERATION BUREAU UNCOVERED

JUDICIAL INQUIRY INTO
HIT SQUADS APPOINTED

NATAL VIOLENCE SPREADS TO
JOHANNESBURG

85

Erik Badenhorst's revelations were published the day Mahoney got back to Hong Kong, bringing further uproar and fresh demands for a judicial inquiry. Just two days later the Attorney General delivered his report, declaring that on the evidence presented to him no hit squads had ever existed, that Daniel Sipholo and Erik Badenhorst were telling a pack of lies. There was rejoicing in the police but the public uproar redoubled.

Two days later Hugo telephoned Mahoney. 'Thought you'd like to know that the police have arrested a man for the murder of your friend Richard Barker. And another man for the murder of Anton Lubowski. Old Floris Klaasens – the man who interviewed you about Barker's murder? – he arrested them. Not much detail yet, except that both arrested men claim to work for the army. For Military Intelligence.'

Mahoney stared out of the window down at the magnificent harbour. 'Jesus Christ, that must be the Civil Cooperation Bureau that Badenhorst told us about. I passed on the information to Klaasens when I got back . . . Pick up the ball and *run* with this story, Hugo – there's nothing I can do out here.'

'Of course I'm going to run with it. I'm going to be famous, like you.'

'What else do you know about this CCB?'

'Not much, but it was part of the Total Strategy syndrome. The buzz is that it operated world-wide, dealing with enemies of the state. Its chain of command leads all the way up to the State Security Council and the president himself. Now we know who killed Dulcie September in Paris, et al.'

'Jesus. So President de Klerk knew.'

'Maybe not, he's only just taken over. But old PW Botha knew. De Klerk has given orders that it be disbanded.'

'Oh sure – they'll just go underground. *Run* with this story, Hugo. Do you know anybody in the army?'

'Sure, but nobody's talking.'

God, it made him want to get back to South Africa.

That same night Katrina sent him a fax of the newspaper report. Across the top she had written: *I wonder whose side these guys will be on when the civil war starts?* Oh, it worried him that she took this civil war for granted. The next night she telephoned him.

'Hullo, darling!' he cried.

'I love you,' she said.

He laughed. 'I love you too!'

'Well, you're going to have to love me an awful lot. If you're having any second thoughts about coming back to this witches' brew, now's the time to think.' She sighed. 'It's serious, Luke. All these police hit squads, and now the CCB, it's just the tip of the iceberg. Darling, this country is run by securocrats. Those guys are not going to disappear. Anybody who imagines that there's not going to be a civil war is kidding themselves. So the question for you is: do you want to give up everything for that?'

'Do *you* want me to come back?'

'Of course! But you're giving up a career to be with me. I love you and I don't want that to be spoilt because you regret the decision when South Africa becomes a bloodbath. I want you to know what you're in for.'

Mahoney felt his eyes burn. 'I,' he said, 'am in for *you*.'

Pause. 'Warts and all?'

'You haven't got *warts*, have you? Where?'

'Oh, darling, be serious! I know what you're grinning about – you don't think there'll be a volkstaat! Well, I'm trying to tell you that you're so *wrong*! And the price we pay for it is going to be in *blood*!'

Mahoney's eyes were moist. He said: 'Kat, I'm coming.'

Silence. Then: 'Okay, I've done my duty, tried to warn you. But, darling . . . ? Has *she* been in contact?'

'No, darling.' Thank God it was true.

'She hasn't popped over from London for a spot of sweet and sour pork?'

Mahoney laughed. 'Darling, England *is* twelve thousand miles away.'

Silence. Then she sighed. 'But seriously, how do you feel about leaving Hong Kong? Is it sad?'

'It's beautiful. And boring. It always was boring.'

'Ever since AIDS?' She laughed. 'Darling, I'll do my best to make you happy. As a founding father I'll have all kinds of pull. Attorney General at least, for you!'

'Heaven forbid! I'm coming back to have fun.'

*　*　*

Beautiful and boring? Absolutely true. And the bullshit colonial social life gave him the screaming jim-jams. When you're lying in the arms of the woman you love beside a tumbling waterfall, with the mauveness of the African plain stretching out around you, full of game, and you feel this country is in your bones, it's easy to say to hell with fucking Hong Kong, I'm an African really. To hell with all that colonial bullshit, those black-tie dinner parties, the one-upmanship, the money-talk and the extravagances. But when you're back in old bullshit Hong Kong and you're packing up a whole life, selling your car, your yacht, packing up your books, and you look out the window and there's that magnificent harbour and there's all that money to be made and there're all those friends you really love – then it's not so easy. And when you read about the bloodshed, the Inkatha impis knocking the living shit out of the UDF impis, the crack of police guns and the clattering of AK–47s – you think, Am I crazy? And then there're all the cocktail parties where your friends say: 'But why *South Africa*? Is there a woman involved?'

He did not tell them about the woman involved, for that would have made it sound crazier. *A Boer woman?* No, she's an Afrikaner – but nobody would have understood the difference.

And then came 2nd February, 1990, when the South African parliament resumed, and the difference between an Afrikaner and a Boer became apparent.

It was about midnight in Hong Kong when parliament reopened in South Africa with the usual pomp and ceremony: it was two o'clock in the morning when Mahoney's telephone rang. 'Darling!' she shouted. 'President de Klerk has just announced that he is *unbanning* the ANC, the PAC, the Communist Party, the works! And he's committed the government to negotiating a new constitution with all parties! And Nelson Mandela is to be released . . . !'

Mahoney stared across the dark room. Down there the lights of Hong Kong were twinkling on the harbour. 'Good God.'

'Do you *realise* what this means? The Great Indaba at last. This is the new South Africa!'

The ANC unbanned? It was hard to believe it had happened at last. 'Good God . . .'

She said more soberly: 'And do you realise what else? Now the trouble really starts. Did you hear that?'

Yes, now the shit was going to hit the fan, Africa-style. 'But anything is better than fucking apartheid.'

'Oh yes! Luke? I've got tears in my eyes. There's dancing in the streets here! Singing. Jubilation. It's on television right now, there's a special morning programme. Even Archbishop Tutu is toyi-toying!'

Mahoney's eyes were burning too. 'And the right wing?'

'Oh, the Conservative Party stormed out of parliament in protest, saying they're going to devise a strategy against this "capitulation". The AWB has called it "Collapse without honour".' She sighed. 'There's going to be trouble, but I'm so relieved. I didn't believe it was going to happen so completely as today. Now we've *got* to talk to them, to the ANC and the others, and get this show on the road. That's the way the Afrikaner will get his volkstaat. So the sooner we start negotiations the better. Yes, I'm relieved. But there's going to be a hell of a lot of trouble.'

Oh, if only he could talk her out of this volkstaat. He said: 'And not only from the right wing. Now the Zulus and the Xhosa are *really* going to get stuck into each other.'

'Yes, we're in for a bloody time. But, God, I'm still happy it's happened. That something is happening at last. Luke?'

'Yes?'

'Are you sure you want to come back?'

'There's only one thing I'm sure about: you.'

He could hear her smile.

'I love you too,' she said.

The next morning it was across the front page of the *South China Morning Post*: 'THE NEW SOUTH AFRICA IS ANNOUNCED. *In a speech that has taken the world by storm, astonished left-wing political parties, the President of South Africa yesterday unbanned . . .'*

It was across the front pages of the world, the editorial pages, the television screens: FW de Klerk making his dramatic speech in parliament, the Conservative Party storming out in protest, the dancing in the streets, the furious faces of Dr Treurnicht and Eugene Terreblanche, the excited commentaries. Mahoney stared at the screen in a confusion of joy and wonder: wonder that this was actually happening at last after forty awful years! And for the moment he did not care about what was to come, the bloodshed, all that mattered was that the awful hand of apartheid had been lifted. And, yes, he was glad he was going back. That night he wrote in his journal:

History was made yesterday, and history repeated itself yet again. Yesterday the final miles of the Great Trek were begun. 150 years ago the Afrikaner defied the known world and trekked away into the unknown to find his freedom. He finally found it, at tremendous cost in blood, misery

and hatred, and for the last forty years he defended it fiercely in his laager.
But yesterday he disassembled his laager to trek again. Again it is into the
unknown.

The next week Nelson Mandela was released.

It was a glorious summer day. Newsmen from around the world were outside the Victor Verster Prison, the road lined with thousands of people, black and white.

The television reporter said: 'The atmosphere is charged with excitement and emotion, as we wait for the dramatic moment when the world's most famous political prisoner is released. Through these forbidding gates Nelson Mandela will shortly walk, after twenty-seven years. The eyes of the world will be upon him, and stay upon him as he leads his people into the new South Africa. He is likely to be the most important force in that massively important process: indeed the hopes of all Africa sit upon his shoulders, for the new South Africa will be vital for the regeneration of this desperate continent. It is the man's importance that accounts for the delay in releasing him: it is now a week since President de Klerk's dramatic announcement. He could have been released the very same day, but it was important that he not be released into a vacuum, important that his reception be prepared, his trumpets blown so that his stature is recognised by all South Africans, black and white.'

And then, down towards the gates, the great man came.

His hair was white. He was wearing a dark suit and by his side, holding his hand, was his wife, Winnie Mandela. And the roar went up from the crowd. Amid the cheering and the waving and the shouting and the clapping, Nelson Mandela smiled and waved as he stepped through the big gate and began his walk to freedom. He walked down the long avenue of excited people, waving and reaching out to shake eager hands, calling out thanks and greetings, smiles all over his handsome old face, and beside him Winnie walked proudly, waving and laughing also.

Twelve thousand miles away, in Hong Kong, it was after midnight. Mahoney sat in front of his television watching the historic scene, and his eyes were moist. He could feel the emotion in those crowds, he could almost feel what was going on in that man's breast: the triumph, the joy of being free at last. He watched them walk that mile of happiness through the cheering crowds, and for the moment all he felt was the joyous relief that apartheid was over, and he felt no fear for what was going to happen now, what was going to happen to the boiling pot now the lid was off.

At the end of the tumultuous avenue of people a limousine was waiting. Nelson and Winnie Mandela climbed into it, waving, smiling: then off they slowly drove, to roars of applause, towards Cape Town to make the speech the world was waiting for.

It was to be made in the Grand Parade, against the background of the City Hall and dramatic Table Mountain. It was to be high drama, an historic speech by a brave man whose voice had been strangled for twenty-seven years; and the world rejoiced that at last he could make it. But its profound importance was that it was also to be a policy speech of the ANC, spelling out their grand plan for the new South Africa. A massive crowd waited for Mandela in the Grand Parade, and a mighty roar went up as his motorcade arrived. He appeared on the City Hall balcony to mighty applause as the crowd beheld their hero. Finally silence fell, and the world waited for Nelson Mandela to begin his historic speech.

And that speech made Mahoney close his eyes and groan. And curse. Curse the whole of incorrigible Africa!

'Incorrigible!'

It did not really matter that Nelson Mandela announced that despite the president's peace initiative the Armed Struggle would continue. That you could swallow: every army keeps its powder dry. What infuriated Mahoney was that there stood the grand man of African politics, the Hope of Africa, black and white, announcing to the world – the world that had seen the Berlin Wall come tumbling down, the world that had irrefutable proof that communism was a monstrous failure, a bankrupt economic policy that flew in the face of human nature, that denied fundamental human freedoms and human initiatives, that guaranteed the aggravation of impoverishment of his black people – the great Nelson Mandela declared to this world that the new South Africa would be a socialist state where the whole 'commanding heights' of commerce would be nationalized, that the land would be redistributed amongst the proletariat, and that until a democratic government was installed economic sanctions against the racist government of South Africa should continue.

'Shit!' Mahoney cried.

He stared at the grand old man of Africa and he could not believe – did not *want* to believe – that he meant what he said. That the man could be so naive, so unwise as to proclaim – internationally – that he was going to commit the country to economic suicide! *Good God, surely the man knew about the economic chaos of Russia, of Eastern Europe, of Cuba, surely he knew about the economic ruin of the whole of Africa, the backwardness of China!*

He *must* know, he's not stupid. So surely he's just posturing, this is just a tactic to keep the government guessing, just a stick to intimidate them at the Great Indaba. *Please God, this is just a tactic!* But if it *is* a tactic the man is being terribly irresponsible to utter the threat at a time when South Africa needs to encourage international investment to alleviate the very poverty he complains his people are suffering.

'*Shit!*' He grabbed the telephone and dialled.

'Hullo darling!' Katrina cried. 'Have you seen the news . . . ?'

'He can't mean it. But he's playing with dynamite!' he said. 'He's raising the expectation of the masses that they're all going to be rich when he's nationalized everything and there's going to be hell to pay when they find out it's not true.'

She said soberly: 'I think they *do* intend to nationalize. That's always been their policy.'

'But that was before the Berlin Wall came down!'

'Luke,' she said, 'the guys running the ANC have been in the bush for forty years, feeding their souls on the slogans of the Cold War. And over half their national executive are Communist Party, for God's sake. And the African is an absolutely natural candidate for communism – it's a myth that Africans aren't natural communists. Sure, they're possessive about their cattle and goats, but the *land* on which they graze is owned by the *tribe*, like the water and sunshine. The *land* is the basis of their economy and it's perfectly natural to them to own it communally. So the same applies to the factories upon the land and the mines beneath it.'

'But Mandela isn't a peasant who can't think further than cattle – he's had twenty-seven years to think!'

'And twenty-seven years without any practical experience. And the ANC's only experience is in running a liberation movement in the bush. The ANC has no experience of running an economy, they've only run a welfare organization, all their money has come from aid – they don't even have the experience of earning a *living*. Yes, I think they're naive enough to imagine they can succeed in nationalization where the rest of the world has failed.' She added: 'Don't get me wrong, I'm glad they're unbanned, that we're going to talk to them at last and hammer out a new, *just* South Africa, and I'm glad Mandela is out and I wish the man happiness. I'm just telling you that I believe he means to nationalize.'

'Well, then there's no hope.'

'The hope, Luke, is that we negotiate them out of it. Bully them out of it – the government will never agree to a socialist constitution. And they'll have the Western world behind them – the West will read Mandela the Riot Act about nationalization when he comes with his begging bowl. *That's* the hope.'

'But constitutions get torn up in Africa.'

'Yes. And that's another reason why it's so important that the Afrikaner gets his own volkstaat.'

'They can tear up any agreement about that as well.'

There was a moment's pause. Then: 'From now on begins the most important period of South Africa's history, Luke. The culmination of what South Africa's three hundred and fifty years of bloodstained history has been all about. And I intend to be in on it. And it is going to vitally affect the rest of Africa, and I intend to be in on that too. I'm an African, Luke, not a colonial – I'm fifteenth-generation African. I'm staying, come hell or high water. Darling, if you're having doubts – and I wouldn't blame you if you were – please tell me now. It will break my heart, but I would rather know now than later.'

Mahoney felt his eyes moisten. 'I have plenty of doubts about South Africa, Kat – there's plenty to be doubtful about. But that I love you I have no doubt. Got that?'

'Got it.' She smiled across twelve thousand miles.

'And I also know I am an African, and I also intend to be part of this historic time. And Africa needs all the people of goodwill it can get, and I'm one of them. Got that?'

Katrina sighed happily. 'Got it,' she said.

But, alas, Africa is a cruel place and it will not hesitate to be cruellest of all to people of goodwill, and it will not care afterwards that it was not necessary.

86

A lot of things happened in those three months.

While the world applauded, while the media reported on Nelson Mandela's every move, through the triumphant motorcades and the massive crowds, the toyi-toying and the ululating, while churchmen and politicians around the world preached peace and rapprochement, and offered the lifting of sanctions to revive the economy for the benefit of the blacks, midst all this goodwill the words of Nelson Mandela rang out telling his people that the Armed Struggle would continue, that the commanding heights of the economy must be nationalised, telling the world that sanctions must continue – and the nihilism broke out.

The mindless violence. Violence for the sake of it. Mahoney saw it on television: the swarming in the Ciskei and in Bophuthatswana, the running battles, mobs attacking the factories where they worked, the shops where they bought their food, burning the schools where they got their education, attacking the farms, attacking police stations, petrol-bombing post offices and houses, burning and looting in an orgy of violence, the smoke barrelling up, the flames leaping. For five days the anarchy reigned in an orgy of celebration at the release of Nelson Mandela, an orgy of rebellion. Then the smoke cleared, and South Africa stared, appalled. Mahoney wrote:

> *Maybe it wasn't much of a job they had at those factories, but at least they got paid at the end of every week. But now they have nothing.* Why did they do it? *Was it an outburst of democratic joy at Mandela's release, a rebellion against their own black authorities who are the product of apartheid? Yes, it was partly both, but I fear it is more: it was a glimpse of the Mfecane all over again:* destroy the enemy. *But it is even more ominous: there was no thought that tomorrow there would be no factories to earn their wages in, there was only the lust to annihilate, to hack, to burn, because they believe that in the metaphoric tomorrow the skies will start raining bicycles and transistor radios and bank notes because Mandela is released and everything will be nationalised.*
>
> *This is the prelude to the new South Africa?*
>
> *This is what the voortrekker trekked away from, this is why – or one of the reasons why – he built the laager of apartheid. And now, as soon as he opens his laager, his worst fears are confirmed . . .*

AND MEANWHILE, IN NATAL, VIOLENCE REDOUBLES

> *Chief Buthelezi has applauded the unbanning of the ANC, applauded the release of Nelson Mandela, called for the lifting of sanctions, called for the cessation of violence. But he has warned that it is likely to increase now as the ANC exiles start coming back into the country 'with their AK–47s'. And he's damn right.*
>
> *The power struggle has taken on a new fury as each side furiously seeks to bludgeon the other into submission. The hills of Natal are resounding with the clatter of gunfire and the slash and crash of axes and sticks and assegais, the impis swarming over the hills, Inkatha impis attacking the ANC, ANC impis attacking Inkatha, buses being machine-gunned, kraals and houses burned, petrol-bombs flying, thousands fleeing. Sixty* thousand *people are homeless, the hills alive with people running away from the dreadful violence, penniless, hungry, frightened, thousands streaming*

into the white towns seeking sanctuary, refugee centres being set up in
schools and church halls. It is the worst violence Natal has seen since the
Mfecane.

'It *is* the Mfecane all over again,' Katrina said. 'And neither Buthelezi
nor Mandela *wants* to stop it! Both piously call for peace, but Mandela
has refused to appear on a political platform with Buthelezi in a joint
appeal despite outcries from the press – '

Mahoney snorted. 'Politics, Africa-style. The ANC doesn't *want* to give
Buthelezi stature by appearing on the same platform as him – and they
want to show their muscle now they're unbanned.' He sighed grimly.
'But where's the massive police presence to stamp out this veld fire?'

'While they're stamping out the fire over here another one breaks
out over there.'

'Sure,' Mahoney said, 'and I'm sure there are roadblocks and sirens
and baton charges and tear-gas, but where's the *massive* police presence,
to knock the living shit out of the impis, where's the iron fist? Or does
government also want to let the ANC feel the muscle of Inkatha? Let
the two biggest black parties knock hell out of each other. Divide and
rule has always been the government's strategy. Do you think De Klerk
intends the Afrikaner to be marginalised in the new South Africa?
Bullshit!'

That night he wrote in his journal:

I have no doubt that such is the case: De Klerk has no intention of
committing political suicide through his reforms. He has no intention of
letting the white man, let alone the Afrikaner, be trampled underfoot.

Then at last it burst across the headlines: MANDELA AGREES TO PEACE
RALLY WITH BUTHELEZI. And there were pictures of the massive crowds in
the Durban stadium, the ANC flags and Inkatha flags, the chanting and
the ululating, spears and shields and pangas and axes and knobkerries
bristling, and there on the platform were Nelson Mandela and Chief
Buthelezi shaking hands before the roaring mobs, Mandela publicly
thanking Buthelezi for demanding his release, for refusing to negotiate
until he was free, Mandela calling on the people to stop fighting, telling
them to throw their pangas into the sea. But on the way home from the
stadium the violence erupted across the land even more bloodily.

The world is bewildered, but South Africans are not – we knew it was
going to happen: there is no political tolerance in Africa. The only question
is, can this change? I am staking my personal future on the hope that it

can – but I am not optimistic. The only hope of achieving such change is if the black leaders, particularly Mandela and Buthelezi, enforce it. But have they got sufficient control of their followers? At the moment the answer is clearly no. And do the black leaders really want *their followers to change? And, if they* personally *want it, do their lieutenants? I bet the answer to that is also no.*

And then another Peace Rally was announced, again to be addressed by both Mandela and Buthelezi – but it has been cancelled at the last minute by the ANC 'because the situation is too tense'. Buthelezi declares himself 'absolutely astonished', claiming the ANC are trying to manipulate the international media into believing that Inkatha is responsible.

Is there any good news at all about the new South Africa?

POLICE OPEN FIRE ON HOSTILE ANTI-RENT DEMONSTRATORS

Twelve people were killed and many wounded in Sebokeng when the police opened fire on an armed mob of 50,000 blacks demonstrating against rent increases by their local black authority.

ANC STILL REFUSES TO SUSPEND THE ARMED STRUGGLE

Despite the violence, despite a call from Archbishop Tutu, Mandela has again publicly declared that the Armed Struggle will continue 'until a democratically elected government is in power'. Even President Kaunda of Zambia has called on the ANC to disband their army to help President de Klerk defuse the belligerence of the Afrikaner right wing, to no avail. Meanwhile both the PAC, with their motto 'One Settler One Bullet', and AZAPO say that their own armed struggles will continue until they have seized the entire land and given it back to the blacks . . .

The telephone rang. 'Hullo, darling!' he cried.

'Have you heard the bad news?'

'I've heard nothing but bad news. What now?'

She said: 'Mandela has broken off talks with the government in protest at the police shooting those blacks who were demonstrating in Sebokeng against the rent. And unfortunately he's right. The police didn't use tear-gas first, some trigger-happy cop panicked, then others followed suit. Most of the dead and wounded were shot in the back!'

'Oh *Jesus!*'

'Right. *This* could be another Sharpeville . . .'

In numerous statements the ANC has repeated that it will 'stimulate economic growth through the re-distribution of wealth', ensure the state 'assumes a leading role in the economy', that 'conglomerates will be dismembered', industry and agriculture 'restructured', while 'organised workers' will play a 'key role in a mixed economy'. The ANC's political partner, the Communist Party, has published a document entitled 'Has Socialism Failed?' It argues that the collapse of communism does not prove that Marxism is flawed, that socialism could undoubtedly be made to work in South Africa without the 'negative practices' which led to its downfall in eastern Europe. Meanwhile the Communist Party has announced that the party will maintain its underground structures as it expects to become a prime target of a right-wing backlash.

The fax machine rang, and then over twelve thousand miles came Katrina's hand-written scrawl: *Thought you'd get a laugh out of this. I love you, please call me tomorrow, XXX.*

The cutting was an article from the *Spectator* written by a prestigious London journalist, reporting on an interview with Joe Slovo, the leader of the South African Communist Party:

I asked him what faith could be put in his political judgment. He had, after all, mistaken (Russian) tyranny for freedom, and scarcity for plenty, during nearly half a century: he had systematically denied evidence of famine, mass murder, forced labour, repression, terror and brutality.

'We all make mistakes,' Joe Slovo said. 'Haven't you?'

When Mahoney telephoned her the following night he said: 'Yes, but the comedy is tragic – the guy really means it! And these guys have been hand in glove with the ANC for forty years.' He shook his head. 'These guys are unrepentant, unabashed, unembarrassed communists – they shrug off fifty years of failure and intend to ride to power on the ANC's back. And that's why Mandela is repeating time and again that they're going to nationalise the economy.'

'They'll change their tune – the world isn't going to put any more aid and investment into a black communist country now that the Cold War is over – '

'That,' Mahoney said, 'is the only hope.'

'*That*,' Katrina said, 'and an Afrikaner volkstaat.'

* * *

Under a huge banner proclaiming 'The Third War of Freedom', a massive national summit of the Conservative Party held at the Voortrekker Monument denounced the reform process, saying that if 'constitutional ways to fight the political changes are closed to us, we will regard ourselves as an oppressed volk, and we will have no choice but to fight. . . ' They warned the government: 'Don't force us on a road we refuse to travel. We will not allow you to force integration down our throats.' It would be 'easier to stop the ocean with a broom than to halt our move towards freedom.'

The telephone rang. 'Hullo, lover!'

'Well,' she said, 'at last here's some good news: the ANC is talking to the government again.'

'Thank God.'

'De Klerk has promised a judicial inquiry into the police shooting of those twelve blacks in Sebokeng last month, and so the ANC has agreed to resume talks. They're all flying down to De Klerk's official residence tomorrow. And,' she said, 'get *this*: De Klerk has bowed to public pressure and is appointing a judicial commission of inquiry into police hit squads and the Civil Cooperation Bureau. So you've been instrumental in making history, darling.'

Mahoney felt his excitement mounting. 'So maybe we'll get the truth at last!' And, *God*, it made him want to hurry back to South Africa.

'But don't get too excited. Because listen to this: the judge can only inquire into hit-squad activities *inside* South Africa. Not into anything that happened beyond the borders.'

'Oh *shit*!' Mahoney cried. 'So we'll only get a fraction of the story. It's a cover-up! And the rest of the CCB structure outside the country will remain intact.'

'But the ANC's army remains intact outside South Africa too. I think,' Katrina said, 'both sides are keeping their powder dry.'

The next day the report was hanging out of the fax machine:

THE GROOT SCHUUR MINUTE IS SIGNED!

At an historic meeting between the ANC and the government, designed to clear away obstacles to the Great Indaba, agreement has been reached which commits the government and the ANC to resolving the existing climate of violence and intimidation, to working for 'stability

*and a peaceful process of negotiations'. Leading political exiles will be
allowed to return to take part in these negotiations . . .*

Mahoney put down the fax and stared out of the window.

Well, thank God the Great Indaba was getting on the road at last. But
now what?

Down there, where the fairyland lights of Hong Kong sparkled, he
made a lot of money as a senior government lawyer – until the end of
next month. And then what?

Then it was the FW & Nelson Show, that's what. The Only Game in
Town. You pays your money, but you has no choice, that's what. And
all the exiles are coming home, including MK, with their AK–47s, that's
what. And that's going to make Chief Buthelezi and his Zulus *very*
uptight, that's what. If you think you've seen bloodshed up till now,
you ain't seen nothin' yet.

That night he saw the television footage of the historic Groot Schuur
meeting, and his heart missed a beat. For there, in the line-up of cabinet ministers and the ANC hierarchy, was Patti Gandhi. She was beautiful, in a sober suit, her long black hair pulled back. For a moment the
camera held on her as the commentator murmured: ' . . . a former
political prisoner for twenty-four years, great-niece of the famous
Mahatma Gandhi . . . ' Then the camera moved on.

Mahoney stared, not hearing the words of De Klerk and Mandela,
just wanting the camera to move back to Patti. And what did he feel? A
mixture of astonishment and pride. Pride and astonishment that she
was there, with President de Klerk and Nelson Mandela. And astonishment at his reaction to seeing her again – the confusion of emotion.

Mahoney felt the blood throb in his face. He got up abruptly, and
poured himself a whisky. He took a big swallow.

'*I'll get you back,*' she had said. '*See you in the new South Africa.*'

Then the telephone rang. 'Hullo, lover,' Katrina said. 'Did you get
my fax? About the Groot Schuur Minute?'

'Yes, thank you.'

She said: 'Well, thank God we're getting somewhere at last. For a
while after the Sebokeng shooting I thought the ANC was going back to
the bush and the whole stand-off was going to happen again – sanctions redoubled, bombs exploding, the right wing up in arms.' She
paused. Then: 'Patti Gandhi was on television. At Groot Schuur. As part
of the ANC team, did you know that?'

Mahoney took a breath. 'Yes, I've just seen it on satellite.'

'Oh. So you saw her? And? Did you know she was so high up the
ANC totem pole that she's at such an historic meeting?'

'No.'

'She didn't tell you in Mauritius?'

Mahoney closed his eyes. 'As I remember she described herself as the Girl Friday.'

'She was being modest. Evidently she's going to be a big wheel in the new South Africa. Minister of something.'

'Probably.'

Katrina sighed. Then: 'She looked ravishing.'

'And so are you.'

She snorted softly. 'And what did you feel when you saw her?'

Mahoney said grimly: 'Compassion.'

'And that's all?'

'Yes, Kat. That's all.'

Silence again. Then: 'I wish I believed that, darling. There must be more, after all that famous passion in your book. And she has an enormous sexual presence.'

'Compassion. And benevolence. I only want her to be happy.'

Silence again. Then: 'But I wonder what *she's* thinking?'

'I'm thinking about you, Kat.'

'And about my volkstaat?' She gave another sigh. 'Luke, please don't break my little Afrikaner heart.'

He smiled. 'It's a deal.'

There was a pause. Then: 'Well, I have a suggestion to make. Shouldn't you . . . wouldn't it be . . . fairer to all of us, if you went to see her again before committing yourself to me?'

Mahoney was taken aback. And no way did he intend putting himself through that ordeal again. 'No, Kat.' He added: 'And I *am* committed to you.'

Pause. Then: 'Okay, I don't want you to see her either, but I'm glad I said it.' Then: 'Oh, darling, I'm counting the days. Only forty-six to go.'

Bill Summers, his publisher, called from New York.

'Good news, Luke! There's a humdinger offer for the film rights of *Alms for Oblivion*! Two hundred thousand US dollars, plus three per cent of producer's profits. Plus fifty thousand if you act as technical advisor on the set, plus a separate fee, yet to be negotiated, if you write the film script. What do you say?'

What did he say?! He was overjoyed. 'Grab it! Who are these guys?'

'It's a purpose-formed American company called Galloway Productions – that's normal these days: a producer forms a special company for tax purposes. The producer is called Mike Galloway, and he wants to use a well-known British director, Peter Lennox, who made that excellent movie *Justification*. They want to use that famous Indian actress Mila Singh for Patti – I mean Pamela – and she's a knockout, and big box-office. And they want to stick to your story almost as is – that's unusual. They're wild about it. But get this – they don't just want to make a two-hour movie, they want to make it into a mini-series for television *as well*, at least eight hour-long episodes, maybe ten, bringing the story up to date to include the modern South Africa. The publicity you're going to get is fantastic. It's all this new South Africa that's brought attention back to *Alms*. And another unusual aspect of the deal is they aren't just buying a twelve-month *option*, they're buying the *rights*, *outright*. That means they're serious. Two hundred and fifty thousand as soon as you sign the contract, Luke!'

'Sign it for me!' Mahoney exulted. 'You've got my power of attorney.'

'So when can you start work on the film-script?'

'As soon as I get back to South Africa at the end of next month!'

'Okay,' Bill Summers said. 'Meanwhile please keep the copy coming for the journals – sounds like all hell's breaking loose down there in South Africa. But, Luke, you realise you what this movie's going to do for the sales of *Alms*? They'll go through the roof again. So Luke? Listen, Pamela is likely to be released from prison soon – I mean Patti – '

'She's out,' Mahoney said.

Moment's pause. Then: 'My *God* – she was the gorgeous Indian gal we saw on television. Of *course*! Oh *wow* . . . !' Then he snorted happily. 'Look, Luke – my boy, now's the time for the sequel to *Alms*. The movie is going to bring South Africa up to date, so you might as well write the book too. So you must make contact with Patti – '

'I've seen her,' Mahoney said.

Astonishment. 'You've *seen* her! And . . . ?'

'And,' Mahoney said, 'it's over, Bill. No, I couldn't write that book.'

'But,' Bill said, 'if you're writing the film script it's the same thing!'

'It's not. With a film the actors do all the hard work, portray the emotions, et cetera. With a book *I've* got to do it. And I'm not up to it. *Alms* is already written. The sequel ain't. No can do.'

'Couldn't,' Bill Summers appealed, 'you *try*?'

'No,' Mahoney said firmly. He added: 'I'm going to marry Katrina, the woman I've mentioned. And I don't want to complicate that by having an imaginary love affair with Patti.'

Bill Summers sighed. 'Sure, the Wild Lady from Borneo. And congratulations and best wishes. But that doesn't stop you *inventing*.'

'It does . . . ' Mahoney smiled.

'But you will write the film script?'

'Yes. If they pay a fair fee.'

Immediately afterwards he telephoned Katrina.

'*A movie deal . . . !*' she shrieked joyfully.

87

Every second day they spoke on the telephone: every day she faxed him the leading newspaper stories for inclusion in his journal:

INQUIRY INTO HIT SQUADS IS A DEBACLE

The judicial commission of inquiry into hit squads is so restricted in its terms of reference – confined to actions taken within South Africa's borders – that it is a farce, say Lawyers for Human Rights and others. Evidence of hit-squad activities comes to a dead stop at South Africa's borders because the judge cannot legally listen to what happened after that . . .

Mahoney telephoned Splinter Woodcock.

'Luke, these guys from Military Intelligence sit in the witness box with false beards and dark glasses, refusing to answer awkward questions on the grounds it may incriminate them – and Judge le Roux has no power to force them to answer, not even to fine them for contempt! And when he demands to see their Military Intelligence files, they say they're missing, don't know where they are! The judge is virtually powerless to do the job De Klerk gave him.'

'Of course they've gone missing – they're not likely to leave incriminating files around, are they? They'd have a standard procedure for getting rid of evidence like that.' It made Mahoney seethe: *he had broken this story.* And he was angry with President de Klerk who had said: 'We will cut it to the bone' – but he had so restricted the judge's investigative powers that he was toothless! 'And what are we finding out about the CCB?'

'We're only glimpsing the tip of the iceberg but the evidence so far reveals that the CCB operates worldwide. Every spy or hitman is technically a civilian, operating "legitimate" money-making businesses which are funded by the taxpayers' money. The CCB has its men in ten regions: western Europe is Region Five, for example, South Africa itself is Region Six. In total they have sixty-four "offices" worldwide, employing hundreds of agents, and they have links with outfits like

601

Israel's Mossad *and* the numerous neo-Nazi organizations all over the world. The chain of command starts with our illustrious Minister of Defence – though he stoutly denies everything – and descends through the Chief of the Defence Force down to another General who is called "the CCB Chairman". Below him comes the commanding officer who is called the "Managing Director", a colonel. Below him we have a "Regional Director", who presides over *sixteen* South African "cells". The colonel who is Regional Director for Region Six is masquerading as the manager of a Johannesburg hotel. His minions – the hitmen – are not known to each other: only two men in each cell know each other and they work as partners in crime. *Crime* being the operative word, Luke. And each of these agents hired *"unconscious"* agents, petty criminals to do their dirty work without knowing why.'

'Go on,' Mahoney said.

'Well, these guys in false beards and sunglasses are only admitting to kids' stuff under our cross-examination – like hanging a monkey's foetus on Archbishop Tutu's door, putting an unsuccessful bomb in the Early Learning Centre in Cape Town – apparently it was an ANC front. Another agent admitted that he'd hired a Coloured criminal code-named "Peaches" to put poison in the drink of Nelson Mandela's lawyer – but good old Peaches stoutly denied it. But he *did* admit to cheating the CCB by taking two thousand rand to burn an "ANC" minibus – and it's proved that the minibus never even *existed*. Luke, it's a circus – the CCB are just feeding the judge little titbits while the *important* stuff is denied.'

Mahoney seethed. And *God*, he would love to be back there, getting his teeth into this alongside Splinter. 'And no evidence as to who killed Richard Barker?'

'No, nor who shot Anton Lubowski, because the judge is not allowed to hear evidence of what happened outside South Africa's borders. Jesus – what a cover-up! The ANC's lawyers are up in arms, as am I. However the police lawyers have been allowed to introduce evidence about sixty murders committed by *ANC* hit squads, and Buthelezi's lawyers have announced they intend to lead evidence that ANC hit squads have murdered over a hundred senior Inkatha leaders.'

'Oh, *really*?' Mahoney was pleased to hear that. 'The ANC loves to claim they're lily-white. If you'll pardon the pun.'

'Yes, this inquiry is turning into a two-edged sword for the ANC, they've got egg on their face too. A police expert has testified that they can attribute over five thousand political murders to the ANC. And, by the way, on the very day the ANC was unbanned they started a massive operation, called Operation Vula, which means "Open Up" – smuggling arms into South Africa from Mozambique.'

Mahoney grinned. 'Oh, *yeah*. The ANC is lily-white. It's going to be a lovely Great Indaba.'

'*Mean*while,' Splinter said, 'the AWB are staging marches protesting that the nation's heroes in the CCB are being persecuted, and *mean*while some bright pressman says he's uncovered an AWB plot to murder Nelson Mandela at the airport when he returns from America. And De Klerk has got ants in his pants – '

'Jesus,' Mahoney said. 'Somebody bumps off Mandela and the prairie fire *really* starts.' He sighed. 'But the real question is: what happens to the CCB and the police hit squads after this sham? Do they vaporise in embarrassment or do they continue to knock off their enemies before the Great Indaba?'

Splinter snorted. 'That's exactly the question. De Klerk has piously announced that the CCB is being disbanded – '

'Oh *sure*. Closed down, missing hitmen, files, missing corpses and all, plus all the securocrats of the Total Strategy, all the generals who've spent a lifetime fighting the ANC, all gone happily into retirement to play with their grandchildren – '

'Exactly, it's bullshit,' Splinter said, 'and even as we speak there've been over ten political murders of potential witnesses since the inquiry *began*. The government's underground network is in panic, confusion reigns. And we've now got evidence that even the *Johannesburg City Council* had its own spy network! – spying on left-wing rate-payers, even City Hall had a fully fledged spy department involved in skulduggery – that's how paranoid South Africa has become! Jesus, Luke, we're only scratching the surface but South Africa is *rotten* with apartheid's paranoia. We've developed a whole covert culture under apartheid's Total Onslaught mentality.'

'And it's not going to go away when we start the Great Indaba.'

'Christ, no. It's *entrenched*. The CCB may be technically disbanded, but the whole organization is untamed, worldwide. All those thousands of agents, all those bank accounts holding millions? And the chain of command is intact. We've created a Frankenstein that could be worse than Renamo. A terrible right-wing threat, with tons of money at its disposal. This puts a different complexion on the ANC's theory of a Third Force.' He sighed. 'I wish you were helping me with this, mate, not sitting on your arse in Hong Kong, I've got so much work.'

Oh, Mahoney wished so too. 'And when is Daniel testifying?'

'Some time yet. He's still on Death Row. He's become a born-again Christian, written letters to Jimmy Swaggert in America, the guy who said he saw Jesus striding across the highway nine hundred feet tall? Badenhorst of course refuses to return to South Africa to testify, so we'll all have to go to England to continue the inquiry there.'

God, it made Mahoney want to hurry back. He would *love* to be involved in this.

MANDELA ON DIPLOMATIC OFFENSIVE

Nelson Mandela is the world's favourite martyr. He is on the diplomatic warpath, talking to heads of state in Germany, Holland, France, Britain, receiving the honours of martyrdom. He beats the drum, urging them all to maintain sanctions against South Africa, claiming that the reform process is not irreversible, that the 'pillars of apartheid' are still standing. 'I still do not have the vote!' he proclaims. Now he has been accorded a ticker-tape welcome in New York. Not even visiting heads of state get such treatment. And Mandela is a statesman who has yet to prove himself. So why? The answer is not that Mandela is such a wonderful statesman – we haven't seen him for twenty-seven years, so how would we know? – but that apartheid was such a beastly system.

Apartheid made Mandela; Mandela did not unmake apartheid. Had he been sentenced to death twenty-seven years ago it is doubtful whether we would even remember his name. And the ticker-tape parade was the decision of David Dinkins, New York's first black mayor, who rode beside Mandela in the limousine. A bonanza of publicity for Hizzonner.

Katrina shouted gleefully down the telephone: 'Have you heard what Winnie Mandela did in New York?'

That night Mahoney watched the parade on television. There was Winnie Mandela sitting in the open limousine between her famous husband and a beaming David Dinkins, the streamers streaming and the confetti falling like snow, the crowds waving, cheering, adoring. Mahoney too was caught up in the emotion of the scene. He felt for Mandela and he wished him well. But then there was Winnie Mandela standing on a platform, dressed in a Gucci camouflage suit with soldier's cap on her head, her fist upraised, shouting into the microphone: 'And if we do not get what we rightfully demand, I will lead my people back into the bush to continue the Armed Struggle!' The television camera followed her down Fifth Avenue on a shopping spree, accompanied by her retinue of bodyguards and admirers. She entered one of the most prestigious stores in New York. And then there was Winnie Mandela plucking dresses off racks to oohs and ahs from her retinue, swirling and twirling, Winnie Mandela emerging from changing room and jumping up and down in delight, her entourage clapping.

Winnie Mandela swept out of the shop, all smiles, and the television reporter was standing in front of his cameras and saying in wonder: 'Mrs Winnie Mandela bought clothes to the value of several thousand dollars. But when it came to paying, one of her entourage suggested to the owner that they be given to Mrs Mandela as a gift. The owner agreed.'

Mahoney gaped. 'Good God,' he whispered. *'Already?'*

AND NOW FW DE KLERK IS ON DIPLOMATIC OFFENSIVE

FW and Mandela have a gentlemen's agreement not to steal each other's thunder. While one is touring the world collecting accolades the other stays at home collecting his wits. With Mandela back from ticker-tape parades, FW is now off to press the flesh and tell the world that Mandela's talking crap . . .

Katrina said: 'Daniel started his evidence to the commission of inquiry yesterday. I'll fax you the newspaper reports tomorrow. But the police lawyers gave him a tough time under cross-examination, and Splinter Woodcock says he wasn't a very impressive witness, the judge doesn't seem to believe him.'

'Oh Christ,' Mahoney said.

'The police lawyers are saying that he committed the murders on his own initiative, in collaboration with Erik Badenhorst, without orders from higher up. And they're hammering the fact that he only made his confession the night before he was due to hang. And, of course, he *is* a self-confessed murderer – he's admitted now that he did murder Van Rensburg.'

'But that's to his credit! If he admits now that he was correctly sentenced to death he must surely be believed!'

'Okay, but he gave evidence on oath at his trial that he *didn't* murder Van Rensburg. So the argument is, why should we believe a self-confessed perjurer? And he can only be hanged once, but he may not be hanged at all if he blames his superior officers.'

Mahoney seethed. *Bloody lawyers* – they made him sick. God, he was glad he was getting out of the game. 'Well, he'll be corroborated by Badenhorst when he gives evidence.'

'Two murderers corroborating each other? Both with a strong motive to blame their superior officers?' She sighed. 'I'm worried, darling. I'm worried about you being sued for libel by the police if Badenhorst and Daniel aren't believed.'

Mahoney snorted. It worried the hell out of him too. 'Anyway, apart from that jolly news, what else is happening in sunny South Africa?'

She sighed. 'Oh, shit, Mahoney, the violence is terrible. Now that the ANC's unbanned they're really getting stuck into Inkatha. And vice versa. Outside Pietermaritzburg there're open gun battles in full view of the city, tens of thousands of refugees living in churches and community halls. ANC and Inkatha gangs fighting it out in the townships, no-go areas everywhere. And if you give the wrong password you're dead.'

'But where's the fucking *army*? Why hasn't De Klerk sent his big battalions in to put a stop to this bullshit – his army's got nothing to do since we've pulled out of the Angolan war!' He took an angry breath. 'Because he doesn't *want* to stop the ANC and Inkatha killing each other! Let them *exsanguinate* each other so that they're less of a threat to the Afrikaner. It's history repeating itself!'

There was a short silence. Then: 'Please don't imagine that nobody's thought of that before, Luke. Even as we speak, Nelson Mandela is busy proclaiming it to the world – claiming the government is *encouraging* this violence for purposes of Divide and Rule, *sponsoring* a so-called "Third Force" of right-wing elements to attack the ANC and support the Inkatha warlords.'

'And Mandela could be right.'

Katrina said quietly: 'It's bullshit, Luke. The violence is typical African politics at work, and the ANC is embarrassed because it looks as if blacks are incapable of democracy, so they claim they're innocent victims of evil government forces. But remember it was the *ANC* who publicly – on Freedom Radio – declared war on Inkatha, saying the head had to be chopped off the "Buthelezi-snake". And it was the ANC who called for "the country to be ungovernable". And it was Mandela who refused to meet Buthelezi to stop the violence – Buthelezi was willing! And what I resent, Luke, is you – a writer and therefore an opinion-maker – lumping all Afrikaners together as one big bad scheming tribe, sponsoring a Third Force of butcher-boys to shoot up innocent women and children – '

'Kate, I didn't intend that – '

'Well it certainly sounded like that. Look, I have no doubt that there are rogue elements in the police and army who're turning a blind eye to the violence. Maybe even giving it a helping hand. And I have no doubt right-wingers like the AWB are delighted that the blacks are fighting each other. But I sincerely hope that you make it clear to your readers that there are many decent, moderate Afrikaners – and I am one of them – who would never *dream* of supporting a Third Force, and I'm sure De Klerk is one of them. And for you to imply, as Mandela is doing, that De Klerk's responsible for a Third Force of butchers is doing the man a *gross* injustice, and doing *immense* harm to the prospects of peace . . .'

The faxed newspaper report read:

HIT SQUADS INQUIRY MOVES TO LONDON

The commission of inquiry has flown to London to hear the evidence of Erik Badenhorst.

The evidence was heard in the South African Embassy in Trafalgar Square, before a gallery full of pressmen. Badenhorst testified to masterminding the murders carried out by Daniel Sipholo and others. Under heavy cross-examination by police lawyers, Badenhorst denied he bore a grudge against the police, denied that he entertained 'delusions of grandeur', denied he was imagining himself as 'some reformed hero in a James Bond-type international drama'. He denied that he had carried out the murders on his 'own wicked initiative' and that, now Daniel Sipholo had spilt the beans, he was trying to save his own neck by conducting a smear campaign against the police, trying to pull down the whole edifice with him. On the contrary, Badenhorst said, he was willing to return to South Africa to face trial provided his erstwhile superiors stood in the dock beside him. At one point the judge interjected that one of his answers was 'crap'.

'"*Crap*"?' Mahoney echoed on the telephone to Splinter Woodcock.

'Well, it slipped out. To everybody's amusement.'

'But is the judge impartial, for Christ's sake?'

'Oh, he's a good judge. But he clearly doesn't believe Badenhorst, any more than he believed Daniel. And I must say neither made very impressive witnesses under cross-examination. Badenhorst was very nervous, inclined to gabble, as if he'd rehearsed his story.'

'Of course he'd rehearsed his story. He'd already told me.'

'Sure. But instead of admitting when he's confused, or saying he's forgotten, he tries to bluster his way out of it. And then he gets angry when he's not allowed to complete his story because the rest takes place outside South Africa's borders.'

'Oh Jesus.' And Mahoney could feel the cold hand of bankruptcy on his gut. This was his story – and his solvency depended on it. 'So, what's going to happen? A white-washing of the police?'

'I very much fear so.'

Mahoney closed his eyes. Seething, sick in his guts. 'And so the fucking police are going to sue me for libel.'

'Well,' Splinter said, 'keep your fingers crossed. I'll always give you a job at Lawyers for Human Rights.'

But maybe Splinter's offer of a job wouldn't be a joke: the next week came Black Tuesday, when the stockmarkets of the world crashed, and Luke Mahoney lost a whole bundle of money.

Mahoney did not belong to the government's pension scheme – 'Who would trust a Hong Kong government pension after Red China takes over in 1997?' And Mahoney was not a saver: all his life he had spent his money like a sailor. 'Easy come, easy go.' Nonetheless he had, over the years, entirely by good luck and not at all by good management, accumulated a stock-market portfolio of something like a million dollars. 'On a good day,' his stockbroker said. Black Tuesday was a terrible day. In one morning Mahoney's speculative shares were almost wiped out.

'*Shit!*'

'Luke, we'll climb back up,' his broker said.

'*Sell!*' Mahoney barked. 'I need the cash. I'm starting a whole new life at my age, for Christ's sake!'

'Luke?' said Max, the Director of Public Prosecutions. 'Shouldn't you reconsider, old buddy? Hang on to your well-paid job for a few more years? Persuade this Katrina woman to come out here and be a rich Hong Kong wife.'

'*No*, Max. The die is cast. You don't go back on decisions like this. And you only live once.'

'I just hope you live at all. All that violence? And if the South African police sue you?'

'*Fuck 'em*,' Mahoney said. 'Cross the bridges as we come to them.'

'Does Katrina know you lost your dough?'

'No.'

'Maybe if you told her she'd come to Hong Kong?'

'Max,' Mahoney sighed, 'she's a *Boer*.'

'I thought you said she was an Afrikaner! Same thing now?'

'*No* . . . Max, you won't understand, you're a dick-head Australian, you guys shot all your Aborigines. In South Africa we've still got ours, we only shot a mere *handful* . . . ' He added: '*Shaka* helped, of course, so did Mzilikazi. So did the British. So did the Xhosa national suicide. But, Max, in South Africa we're *Christians*. Katrina won't come to godforsaken Hong Kong. She's got a mission in life.'

Max sighed. 'And,' he said, 'you've got your film. Thank God for those movie-rights being sold. I guess that keeps the wolf a long way from the door.'

It was all a bad start to his return to South Africa, the threat of being sued by the police, plus Black Tuesday. And then, the next week the news got worse: the violence that had been racking Natal broke out around Johannesburg.

88

It happened overnight.

Suddenly the war erupted around Johannesburg as the black townships became raging battlefields between Xhosa and Zulu, ANC and Inkatha, ANC and AZAPO. Overnight there were the mobs confronting each other with sticks and spears and pangas and AK-47s, the impis boiling out of the hostels, the smashing down of doors, the crash and whoosh of petrol bombs, the swipe of clubs and pangas midst the screams of women and children and the leaping flames, the wailing of police sirens and the rumble of the Caspirs, the stink of tear-gas and the thud of riot guns and the clatter of gunfire.

For a whole weekend the carnage raged, over five hundred people were killed, over four hundred unidentified bodies lay rotting in the mortuaries. The ANC blamed Inkatha and the police, Inkatha blamed the ANC, the police blamed both of them, Mandela personally blamed Buthelezi, Buthelezi personally blamed Mandela. There was a mass funeral organised jointly by the ANC and AZAPO, but when the AZAPO representative got up to speak he was howled down by the ANC, and AZAPO mourners were attacked with deadly weapons. The next day AZAPO officials demanded: 'Is this a glimpse of the new non-racist South Africa the ANC is planning?' And a horrified press demanded that Mandela and Buthelezi meet on a public platform again, but Mandela refused, declaring Buthelezi 'wants a sea of blood to promote his political ambitions', and he blamed the police for 'fanning the flames', declaring to the world that 'the government's hands are dripping in blood'. The international media proclaimed their disgust with Mandela for refusing to meet Buthelezi, the *Daily Mail* in London calling him 'a prideful old man, a worn-out old Marxist who has brought his country to the brink of civil war'.

Then a new tactic of terror appeared – black gunmen opening indiscriminate fire during the rush hour in downtown Johannesburg, mowing down blacks at bus stations and train stations, blasting at them from speeding vehicles.

Mahoney saw the ghastly pictures on television: the bodies, the blood, black women and children and old men, the flashing lights of police cars, the ambulances, the weeping, the shock. Oh Jesus, he had not expected it to be as bad as this, and the more he thought about it the more he was sure that this latest savagery was *not* simply African democracy at work – there must be a Third Force operating.

The war in Natal, mind-boggling though it was, made some kind of sense: there, the ANC were fighting Inkatha for political turf, so that when the first elections came the electorate would be firmly intimidated. That was African-style democracy: the black victim knew very clearly who was intimidating him, he got the message who he had to vote for. But what was the message when faceless black gunmen open fire from unmarked vehicles during the rush hour? The black people in those bus queues were Xhosa, Zulu, Sothu, Tswana, Swazi, Venda, Shangaan – so *who* were the gunmen intimidating? If the gunmen were ANC they risked shooting ANC supporters. If the gunmen were Inkatha, they risked shooting their own supporters. It didn't make sense. Therefore the only reasonable deduction was that these faceless gunmen were trying to intimidate *everybody*. Their only purpose could be the creation of chaos and fear.

Fear of the future. And fear of the future makes anybody want to cling to the past. However bad the past was, it was nothing like as bad as this mayhem. Mayhem by *black* gunmen. Therefore Black is Bad: Black is Chaos. That was the message the gunmen wanted to send.

Was he being too subtle? Would the black populace think like that? But for sure the *white* populace would think like that. And be so afraid of black chaos that they would insist on clinging to the past? Insist on martial law? So that the Great Indaba would be cancelled? Were whites who wanted the Great Indaba cancelled employing these black gunmen? If so, who were these whites? Right wing, obviously. But did they have a *structure*, a chain of command? An organization? Or were they just a handful of thugs, sowing mayhem on their own dreadful initiative? Or both?

Well, Mahoney thought, we know from Badenhorst and Daniel that there were police hit squads. And we know that the Civil Cooperation Bureau was a bunch of international hit squads run by generals. So what about a similar organization run by elements within the security services? A cabal of right-wing officers bent on creating chaos so there would be a military coup? If so, who could their black hitmen be? Well, how about their Angolan mercenaries in 32 Battalion who were bivouacked in a tent city in the Western Transvaal, with nothing to do now the Border War was over?

It was five p.m. in Johannesburg. The streets were thronging, clogged with cars and minibuses, whites hurrying home to their suburbs, blacks streaming to the trains and bus stations. One thousand four hundred trains run every day from Johannesburg, carrying black workers to and from the teeming townships of the Witwatersrand. In the rush hour the huge railway station is packed, people surging to board the spartan carriages, cramming in; as soon as one train departs another pulls in. And, usually, as each train pulls out, the singing starts: tribal songs and hymns.

Sam Mbene – the nephew of Aunt Matilda who had been burned alive in Natal, the club-foot boy whom Jill Dawson had picked up on the road 'looking for a better land' – Sam Mbene had made his way to Johannesburg and had found a job as a gardener in the white suburbs. This afternoon, after work, he squeezed himself into one of the railway carriages, making his way back to his shanty in Soweto. There was a church group in the carriage, and before the train departed the bibles had appeared and the singing started. Mamas in woollen caps, young women in modern clothes, old men and young with deep voices, clapping as they sang their praises to the Lord. It was beautiful singing, and Sam clapped too, although he did not know the words. When the train was hurtling through the industrial area towards Benrose station all hell broke loose.

Suddenly the doors at each end of the carriage crashed open, and in burst black men yelling in Zulu *Kill all the dogs*. There was a shocking blast of gunfire, then the men slashed their way into the mass of screaming people, hacking with their pangas, stabbing, swiping, roaring *Kill all the dogs*, smashing open heads, guns fired point-blank into faces. A wave of terrified people blundered down the carriage, trampling each other underfoot, blood gushing, people scrambling under seats and flinging open windows and leaping out of the hurtling train.

Sam scrambled desperately down the carriage, clawing over bloody, screaming people, but an impenetrable mass was trying to claw towards him. He screamed and tried to scramble under a seat, then saw a panga on high coming down at his head and he threw his arm up and felt the blow jar through his body. He scrambled up wildly and lunged for the door. He flung it open and screamed as he launched himself out into the hurtling dusk.

On the train the attackers continued to hack and swipe their way down the carriage until the train slowed as it came into Benrose station. People wildly leapt out, but on the platform another gang was waiting and the carnage resumed, screaming people chopped down as they fled. Then suddenly the attackers turned and ran, leaping off the platform onto the tracks. They ran away into the dusk towards Johannesburg.

Benrose station was a battlefield, bodies sprawled, blood everywhere, people reeling. Twenty-six people lay dead, more than a hundred people were mutilated, sixty more lay along the railway track.

It was the first of many train massacres in the new South Africa. It brought the political death toll for the month up to seven hundred and thirty.

The massacre happened during Mahoney's last week in Hong Kong. When he came home, late, he found Katrina's fax. And he wanted to shout with rage: *Jesus, this is the new South Africa I'm going back to . . . ?*

He tried to call Katrina but got her answering-machine. He poured himself a big whisky and snapped on the television. And there, relayed by satellite, was the horrific scene.

The television journalist said: 'But who are these savage people – and what is their purpose? Everybody says the attackers spoke in Zulu – but their only words were *"Kill the dogs"*. Maybe the attackers were non-Zulus who used those few words to create the impression they were Inkatha supporters. If they were Zulus how did they know they were not killing fellow Inkatha supporters? Conversely, if they were from another tribe, they may have been killing fellow tribesmen, fellow party-members. Neither scenario makes sense. So, who are they? Hired guns? Hired by whom? It seems their only purpose can be terror, the creation of chaos which will stop the promised Great Indaba in its tracks – '

'*Right!*' Mahoney cried at the television.

' – even make the country ripe for a military takeover as has happened in so many countries in Africa. Perhaps the answer to these shocking events lies in the question: who would *want* all that to happen? This is Lynda Grace, CNN, Johannesburg.'

'The right wing, Lynda!' Mahoney cried 'The Third Force!'

God, this was what he was going back to? This was the new democratic South Africa he had chucked up everything for?

The telephone rang.

'Hullo, Luke,' Patti Gandhi said, 'I'll only disturb you a moment. But first – I've heard on the grapevine that *Alms for Oblivion* is being made into a movie! Congratulations, I'm so pleased for you. I'm thrilled.'

'Thank you, Patti.' His heart was knocking.

'*And,*' she said, 'I'm thrilled for me – I'm *dying* to see my story on film. Do you know which actress is going to play me?'

'They're hoping to get Mila Singh. She's box-office.'

'Oh, wow. And which actor is playing you?'

'I don't know yet.'

'Well, they'll have a job finding anybody good-looking enough, won't they, darling? Robert Redford is too old. Anyway, that isn't what I called about. Have you heard about the train massacre?'

'Yes.'

'I just want to make sure you know what you're doing. About whose side you're joining. Luke, that train massacre – which I'm sure is only the first of many – is directly or indirectly attributable to the South African government – '

'Bullshit, it's attributable to the right wing, Patti.'

'Luke, I'm just telling you the facts. We have evidence that recently *many* truckloads of Zulus have been transported up to the Johannesburg area from Natal, armed to the teeth, and deposited in Zulu hostels. The police did nothing to stop it, because the government *wants* the power struggle against the ANC that's raging in Natal to spread to the Transvaal. Mandela is furious. He's demanded the government use their powerful security forces to end it.'

'So the government's turning a blind eye?'

'Or worse. What other explanation is there for a huge convoy of Zulu warriors arriving without the police stopping them? And we *know* that the government has been training hit-squads of Zulus at two secret camps, in the Caprivi Strip and northern Natal – that's why your friend Richard Barker got shot down.'

'But we can't prove it.'

'We will. It all proves that the government is waging war on the ANC. It proves they're using their old policy of Divide and Rule.'

Mahoney said: 'It doesn't prove that De Klerk knew about it. It only proves that *somebody* unlawfully used taxpayers' money to train Inkatha warriors.'

'I'm not going to argue with you. President de Klerk *must* know – if not, he's out of control of his own forces. But at the very least it proves the Third Force exists, and it is helping Inkatha, *with government resources.*' She paused. Then: 'I want to make sure you know what you're getting mixed up in.'

Mahoney sighed. 'How am I getting myself mixed up in this, Patti?'

'Luke, however conservative you sometimes appear, you are a moderate, who supports the reform process. That means, at the end of the day, that you deep down support the ANC – '

'I don't, because they're dominated by communists.'

'Be that as it may, you certainly don't support the right wing. And the Third Force is part of the right wing. And the Third Force is making allies out of the Zulus in what is a civil war against the ANC. And the Afrikaner Volkswag is part of the right wing, Luke. And Katrina de la Rey is a leading light in Volkswag. So, whether you admit it or not, Katrina is indirectly on the side of the Third Force and the Zulus. Indirectly, she is party to this violence. And to the civil war that is quite possibly coming.' She paused. 'That is what you're getting yourself mixed up in, Luke. And you don't belong there.'

Mahoney sighed again. 'Katrina intends to do everything in her power to avoid a civil war.'

'Yes, I know, I've had her checked out, and she's regarded as a pacifist and a moderate – '

'You had her checked *out*?'

'Certainly. I want to know what I'm up against, not only for personal reasons but for when the Great Indaba starts, Luke. But the point is, if the right wing don't get their volkstaat there is going to be a war. And your Katrina is going to be mixed up in it. And what are *you* going to do, Luke?'

Mahoney took another deep breath. He said, without conviction: 'I think there may be a rebellion, a bit of IRA-type activity, but people of the calibre of Katrina will talk them out of it.'

Patti snorted. 'Who're you kidding, Luke? You're trying to persuade yourself that you haven't fallen in love with the totally wrong woman. I'm convinced that you have. And I have your interests at heart. Because – not to put too fine a point on it – I love you. However, I accept what's happened. But stop deluding yourself about the difficulty you're in, Luke. Oh, don't get me wrong, I believe she's a very nice person. Very sincere, et cetera. And very beautiful – I've seen photographs of her. She's quite stunning. And, as it happens, I personally consider that some kind of Afrikaner homeland mightn't be such a dumb idea, to keep them quiet. But that's my personal view and I don't see the ANC agreeing to it. And so I see civil war – not just the minor rebellion you so optimistically envisage. And you, my darling, are going to be in big difficulties.' She paused. Then: 'Okay, I've said enough. Oh, except this . . . do you know that she's bi-sexual?'

Mahoney said grimly: 'I know she's had a few liaisons with women, yes. As – I seem to remember – *you* have. I believe it's not that unusual. Or sinister. Nor, I happen to know, is it a problem with her. Okay, Patti?'

Patti grinned. 'Okay, *touché*. So it doesn't bother you. But just tell me this: does it turn you on?'

Mahoney smiled, despite himself. 'Go to hell, Patti.'

She laughed. 'Oh no I won't! I'll see you in the new South Africa. Till then, bye now. And Luke?'

'Yes?'

'I don't love you *that* much!'

'What do you mean by that?'

She laughed. 'Not enough to seduce your Afrikaner lover in order to get back into your bed. *But* – I *do* love you . . . ' The telephone clicked.

Mahoney hung up. And slumped back in his chair. And tried to get the throbbing out of his breast.

By God he wanted to talk to Katrina. To tell her he loved her. And, by God, he wanted this week over, to get on his way.

89

And then, at last, the last day came.

He had been up till late, drinking for the last time with the boys at the Foreign Correspondents Club, and he was up early doing his last-minute packing. At nine o'clock the shippers arrived to take his last packing cases, and the apartment was bare but for the Hong Kong government's soulless furniture. At nine thirty the taxi-driver rang the bell, and took his two suitcases. He looked around the apartment for the last time, and he looked down at that magnificent harbour, and he felt no twinge of sadness. He had had enough. It was beautiful but it was impermanent. Borrowed Place, Borrowed Time. In six years the communists were coming to take it back. And a government apartment is never a home. He hadn't had a home in fifteen years, and he was glad he was going to make one now. And in twenty-four hours he would be in the arms of his home-maker. And, oh God yes, he was glad to be getting his show on the road at last, for better or worse.

He walked out of the apartment, walked out on a life, towards the new South Africa.

He had to change aircraft in Harare, Zimbabwe, which in his day had been Salisbury, Rhodesia, as Qantas was not yet allowed to fly to the new South Africa because Nelson Mandela wanted sanctions to continue. Mahoney had several hours to kill. He changed some money at the airport, getting over eleven Zimbabwe dollars to the pound – it had been two dollars to the pound in his day – and took a taxi into town.

He was surprised how good the city still looked – because the country as a whole had gone downhill since independence. Harare looked okay, but the fact remained that Zimbabwe was virtually a one-party state, all the newspapers owned by the State, corruption abounding, the economy tottering, basic foods in short supply, unemployment rife, the bloated bureaucracy inefficient. The fact remained that the white farmers were under loud constant threat of having their land seized for distribution to peasants as window-dressing for a collapsing economy. The fact remained that President Robert Mugabe was still an unabashed Marxist, and anybody who drove past his official residence in the suburbs between dusk and dawn was machine-gunned by his palace guards. The fact remained that he was driven at breakneck speed wherever he went with sirens blazing and all traffic had to pull over, or else. The fact remained that he had reduced his once-strong currency to Mickey Mouse money – and the value of a country's currency, like the acceptability of a businessman's cheques, is a sure-fire indicator of success or failure.

Mahoney went to the Impala for a beer, one of his old watering holes, where the foreign correspondents used to solve the problems of the world. His was the only white face. His bar stool had a big rip in the vinyl cushion. The blacks were noisy but friendly. There was a big portrait of Comrade President Mugabe on the wall. Mahoney ordered a whisky, but there wasn't any. He sat drinking a beer out of a chipped mug.

Is South Africa going to be like this? he wondered. Eleven rands to the pound, presidential sirens wailing, land confiscated . . . ? No, it won't be, for several reasons. Firstly, there are over five million whites in South Africa, not the couple of hundred thousand there were in Rhodesia. And South Africa has a vast economic infrastructure, which Rhodesia didn't. South Africa has vast tourism potential, five big ports and thousands of miles of good highways and railways and umpteen airports, which Rhodesia had not. And the Berlin Wall has come tumbling down, communism is dead, which wasn't the case in Rhodesia's day. And the South Africans are not a militarily defeated people, which the Rhodesians were. And the South Africans are going to *negotiate* their future, not have it thrust upon them by Britain. The world now acknowledges that Africa is a fuck-up, which it dared not do in Rhodesia's day. The new ANC government will be bound to good behaviour – it won't have money thrown at it, as in Rhodesia's day.

And, above all, South Africa has the Afrikaners – *three million of the fuckers* . . .

Mahoney sat there in the noisy black bar under the photograph of Comrade President Mugabe, drinking a row of beers out of his chipped beer mug, about to take another wired-up taxi on bald tyres to catch his plane to his very own, very beautiful Afrikaner, and he thought: *Thank God for the Afrikaners* . . .

It was sunset when he looked down on the mine dumps surrounding the golden city, on the sprawling townships of Soweto and Alexandria where the blood ran in the rutted streets, and he saw the fires, the smoke, and he could almost hear the screams and the clatter of gunfire. Welcome to South Africa. Just miles away, in the pretty suburbs of Sandton and Houghton, cars streamed along the roads, uninvolved.

He emerged from the Customs hall, pushing his laden trolley, a grin of anticipation, his eyes darting. He could not see her. He passed the barricade, and stopped. Then: '*Mahoney!*' she cried, and there she was, hurrying down the long marble hall, dressed to kill, a smile all over her lovely face. Mahoney abandoned his trolley and ran towards her, and they clutched each other, laughing.

Seated on a bench twenty paces away, another beautiful woman watched them over the top of her newspaper.

Patti Gandhi's heart was breaking.

PART XIII

90

It was highveld winter, the sky cloudless, the air crisp, there was snow on the Drakensberg and at night the fire crackled in the grate. Katrina had been burning the midnight oil for weeks to get her work out of the way; Mahoney had been doing the same. Both were in a holiday mood.

It was a honeymoon. The first two days they spent entirely at home, and almost entirely in bed. 'There's food and booze for a week in the fridge, and it's cold outside.' Outside, in the sprawling black townships, in the vast highveld and the rolling downs of Natal, in the mauve hills of the eastern Cape, the violence continued; but here in Johannesburg's pretty avenues it was cosy, drinking good wine, just talking about each other. In the morning the newspaper was pushed under the door, the news was on radio and television, but it was mostly about the violence and they did not want to think about it now.

'We've become inured to it,' she said. 'We lose track of where it was going on yesterday, where today's outbreak was, tomorrow's is anybody's guess. And we shake our heads in our nice white suburbs and say I told you so. Everything we feared would happen is happening and this is only the beginning, and we'll be powerless to stop it unless we declare martial law. So don't let's talk about it.'

'But why doesn't De Klerk send the army in?'

'He daren't do it yet. Because the ANC would be up in arms about soldiers shooting "innocent civilians". The ANC *wants* the violence, to show their strength – they've been underground for a long time and they want to show their colours. And Inkatha wants it because they're scared of the ANC. And I think the government wants it because it can say to the world, "See – this is why we want protection of our minority rights, so how about more sympathy?" Anyway, let's talk about the lovely things we're going to do next week.'

And then, the next day, Operation Iron Fist was announced.

Operation Iron Fist: a massive deployment of soldiers and police throughout the sprawling townships, curfews, armed roadblocks, house-to-house searches for dangerous weapons, helicopters clattering, radios rasping and sirens wailing, the hostels sealed off with hedges of razor wire. The piles of confiscated weapons at the roadsides, spears, axes, pangas, knives, sticks, pistols, home-made guns, AK–47s, hand grenades. Additional courts were set up in the townships and a Joint Unrest Monitoring Programme was launched with representatives of the security forces and all political parties to monitor the violence, advise the government, arbitrate disputes, mediate. It was an impressive display of the government's will to crush the violence; but Nelson Mandela was the first to cry foul, only days after demanding that the government use 'its powerful, well-equipped forces'. Mahoney angrily sat down at his new desk and typed.

He insists that the police and soldiers don't carry arms at all, but use only water-jets and tear-gas. The use of razor wire to seal off the hostels, which are a major source of the violence, he condemns as a 'reckless measure, hazardous in the event of fire.' He condemns the curfew 'because it restricts civil liberties', calling it 'the reintroduction of the State of Emergency by political sleight of hand'. In the same breath he damns Iron Fist as 'totally ineffective' and as 'a licence to kill us indiscriminately' and 'shoot us like game'. He immediately departs overseas where he tells the world that 'the South African government is waging war on the ANC'. The confiscation of weapons he damns as the government's efforts to disarm the ANC; he darkly warns that his 'patience is not unlimited' and that he will 'undo all that has been achieved if government does not display the will to control the violence'.

Jesus Christ. What's wrong with this guy Mandela? And where's his own will? He refuses to meet Buthelezi to make peace. We know he's intelligent, so we can only conclude that either he's as time-warped with prejudice as the right wing, or he is cynically causing confusion and animosity because he wants the violence to continue to show ANC's muscle before the Great Indaba.

The government has declared itself 'speechless' at this double-speak. The Star described Mandela's self-contradictions as 'mock-worthy'. Even British Labour MPs have damned Mandela's refusal to meet Buthelezi as political chauvinism, adding that he's frightened to call for peace lest it show that his writ does not run to the black townships. The Daily Mail in London has described him as a 'worn-out old Marxist'. Meanwhile, the violence rages on.

More wild shootings from vehicles in downtown Johannesburg, more train massacres, faceless blacks bursting in, hacking, blasting, killing; now

*it only takes somebody to shout 'The Zulus are coming' and people leap
from the hurtling trains.*

Out there in the black townships there were the Iron Fist roadblocks
and foot patrols; but the townships are vast and in the rutted byways
were the Comrades, the ANC youths, their heads full of the new South
Africa, their blood hot with the pronouncements of their leaders, and
gangs of young Inkatha warriors, their blood hot with the insults their
leaders had suffered from the ANC. Both lay in wait and challenged the
people hurrying home and pointed at their noses and said in English:
'What is this?' And the people had to make a desperate decision
whether to answer with the Zulu word '*Ikhalo*' or the Xhosa word
'*Impumelo*': and the wrong word meant death.

Sam Mbene got off the crowded train in Soweto and hobbled after
the throng on his club foot. At the exit were armed policemen, black
and white, body-searching for weapons. He hurried down the road,
heading for his hostel. He came to a police roadblock and he was
searched again. He hurried on, going with the throng, through the
rows of little houses, then he turned off towards K section. He passed a
foot-patrol of soldiers. He turned to take a short cut when the gang of
youths ran out of the lane. Sam turned to run, wild-eyed, a stick
swiped his head, and he crashed into a wall. The leader pointed at his
nose and said in English: 'What is this?'

Sam's heart was pounding; it was impossible to tell whether they
were Xhosa or Zulu. They surrounded him, weapons raised, one holding a car tyre, malicious grins on their faces, shaking their boxes of
matches: and Sam was faint with terror, not knowing which word to
say. He opened his mouth but nothing came; and the leader whipped
back his stick and swiped him on the head again. Sam crashed back
against the wall, his head reeling. The leader pointed at his nose again:
'*What is this?*'

Sam clutched his bloody head, faint, vomit of terror rising, and he
opened his mouth, and the youthful black faces lit up: and he croaked
the Xhosa word: '*Impumelo.*'

There was a moment's disappointed silence, then the gang turned.
They ran down the lane, brandishing their sticks, carrying their tyre.
They clustered at the end, peering out for their next victim; and Sam
started to run in the opposite direction, his stomach heaving, joy and
terror all over his face.

* * *

Texas Khumalo, who had been Sally Freeman's landlord, was neither Xhosa nor Zulu: he was a Shangaan, his homeland up in the north-eastern Transvaal. Texas wanted nothing to do with politics: he was an entrepreneur. He had saved hard all his life and bought his first mini-bus. He had tried to avoid the taxi war that raged in Soweto in the 1980s, failed, got his head chopped open and his taxi burned. Now he paid protection money , which gave him guaranteed routes without daily threats from the Black Cats and the Tip Tops and Three Million Dollar gangs: Texas only wanted to get on with earning a living. He was even prepared to pay taxes.

Texas started work at the Soweto taxi-rank at four a.m. Mini-bus by mini-bus ground forward as the long crocodiles of people clambered in: he took their fares, then off he drove towards the skyscrapers of Johannesburg and the East Rand, hurtling between the mine dumps. When he got to his destination, he took on passengers for the journey back to the West Rand. From long before dawn to well after dark Texas Khumalo drove his mini-bus around eGoli. It was on his seventh routine trip into Phola Park one Thursday afternoon that Texas came to grief.

There was a crowd around the taxi rank: a man was addressing people in Xhosa, there was shouting. Texas hardly spoke any Xhosa. He climbed out of his mini-bus and stretched, then called in Fanagalo, the pidgin language all black people learn to speak: *I am going to Soweto.*

A man in the crowd turned, and pointed, and shouted: *There's one!*

All heads turned to Texas; then a group of men broke away and came towards him, shouting in Xhosa. Texas retreated towards his vehicle; he held up his hands in peace and shouted: *I am a taxi-driver, men, I am a Shangaan . . . * Now the whole crowd was coming at him, men, women and children, and now some were toyi-toying in excitement, women ululating, youths were shaking match boxes, one carried a motor-car tyre. Texas retreated, repeating that he was a Shangaan – then the first stick swiped him.

It was a blinding blow across the ear, and Texas reeled, and another stick smote the other side, and he sprawled. He collapsed midst the shouting and toyi-toying and he tried to clamber up, arm curled over his head, as sticks gleefully swiped at him, then a hand grabbed his collar and they dragged him into the rough ground beyond the taxi rank, the crowd following. They threw him down and kicked him and swiped him, sticks and boots flying; they beat him and kicked him until his head was covered in blood, then the ringleader bellowed at him to stand up. Texas clambered to his feet, gasping in terror, reeling, crying: *I am a Shangaan – I am not a Zulu – * And the trial of Texas Khumalo before a Peoples' Court began.

Texas staggered in the middle of his mob of accusers, bloody, terrified, trying to deny the charges that he was a Zulu, denying that Shangaans were sell-outs, that the Shangaans supported Chief Buthelezi, denying that he was a member of Inkatha, and with each demand somebody pranced forward and swiped him. Then the ringleader pranced forward, his stick on high, shouting for silence, asking the people if this man was guilty. There was a roar of affirmation. The man pranced around the circle demanding confirmation, then he turned on Texas and swiped him again, and he sentenced him to death. And the youths gleefully pranced around him, holding the car-tyre aloft like a noose; then they rammed it over his bloody head. Texas screamed in terror and tried to wrench it off, and they grabbed his wrist and got the tyre under one armpit. Then they bound his wrists with barbed wire, wrenching the spikes into his flesh; and all the time the toyi-toying and the ululating, the youths shaking boxes of matches. Then a can of petrol was fetched, and the execution began.

Texas was shoved down onto his buttocks. His wrists had been bound in front of him so he still had some use of his hands, for one of the most enjoyable things about a necklacing is watching the condemned trying to pull the molten tyre off himself. The petrol was poured inside the tyre. Texas wept and cried out for mercy. Then the executioner opened his box of matches and selected one. He held it up to the crowd, they burst into new ululating. Then he held it up for Texas to examine. *'Is this a good one, Zulu? Or you like another one?'*

Texas's bloody face was contorted in terror. *'I am not a Zulu, Nkosi, I am not a Zulu . . . !'*

'Is this a good match, Zulu?'

'I am not a Zulu, sir . . .'

The executioner began to toyi-toyi, shaking the box, flourishing the match; he danced towards Texas, making mock strikes with the match, then danced away again; he pranced round the side of him, and Texas frantically tried to turn to face his tormentor. The executioner danced up behind him and rattled the matches in one ear, then pranced away and rattled them in his other ear. Now the crowd was very excited. The executioner danced up to Texas one last time, rattling the box and feinting; then he held up the match, for all to see again, then he struck it. The match flared, and he waved it back and forth: then with a shout of triumph he dropped it on Texas.

The tyre burst into yellow flames, black smoke barrelling, and Texas screamed. He screamed from the bottom of his lungs, the flames scorching his head, and he sucked in the searing fumes, and he screamed again in the terror of suffocation, his bound hands grabbing at the flaming tyre, he screamed again as his fingers buried into flaming rubber, and he collapsed onto his side. He heaved himself up again, frantically shaking his burning head, and he tried to use his hands again but now they were on fire with melting rubber, and he collapsed onto his other side. And he tried to scramble up to run, and he collapsed onto his stomach and his scream was cut off in agonised choking. He writhed over onto his back and sat up again, frantically trying to pull the blazing tyre off with his bound blazing hands.

The black smoke had reached 300 degrees C now, destroying the tissue of his lungs as it suffocated him, and now molten rubber was running down his back and chest, burning into his flesh. But still Texas tried to pull it off, his burning hands wrenching at the molten blazing mass, his flesh ripping from his fingers, his bare bones clawing, the flesh tearing off his chest and shoulders and face, his skull exposed, his lips and nose and chin burning off. And all the time the toyi-toying and the ululating, the children skipping and clapping their hands.

It took Texas Khumalo twenty minutes to die. He was unidentifiable when the police found his charred body, his head and torso destroyed, his fingers burned off. Nobody they questioned knew anything about it. There had been over three hundred necklacings that year, apart from all the other violence: it did not even get a mention in the newspapers.

91

The following day the university Easter vacation began, and Katrina and Mahoney left for the Wild Coast.

It was fun all the way. She had wanted to drive down via Orania to see how her trees and volk were getting on, but that sounded too serious and they went via Natal. Mahoney had bought a second-hand Land-Rover. They left mid-morning with a cold-box of booze and as soon as they left the mine dumps behind they cracked the first bottle of champagne. They sped through the Orange Free State with its vast wheat fields and its tall silos and its dramatic kopjes: then they descended into the rolling green hills of Natal, following the path of the voortrekkers a hundred and fifty years ago. It was beautiful, rolling country. It was hard to grasp that beyond this swathe of highway war was raging, Inkatha impis waging battle with ANC impis, that out there in those hills thousands of desperate homeless people were fleeing the violence of the new South Africa.

'Why aren't we seeing any of that violence?'

'Because it's a black man's war now. The white man's no threat anymore. So it's the Mfecane all over again.'

The sun was setting when they left Natal, the land of the Zulus, and crossed the river into the Republic of Transkei, where Mahoney was born, the land of the Xhosa. Just beyond the river is the splendid Wild Coast Sun Casino, and they checked in for the night. It was jolly with holiday-makers. Mahoney and Katrina showered, then went into the dining room to settle down to a long dinner to celebrate the start of their holiday.

It was not a coincidence that Patti Gandhi was also in the hotel: she had employed a firm of private detectives to report on their movements. She sat four tables away; Mahoney had his back to her, which is how she wanted it: it was Katrina she wanted to see. Patti was wearing tinted spectacles, a scarf over her head. It was when they started their Irish coffees that Patti got up and languidly walked to them.

'Hullo, Luke. What a surprise to see you here.'

Mahoney was astonished. And again, as in Mauritius, the world seemed to stand still for a moment. Then he stood up, his heart knocking. 'Patti,' he said hastily, 'this is Katrina de la Rey . . .'

Patti smiled down at Katrina. 'I know. How do you do? Forgive me for intruding, I'm just passing.' She turned back to Mahoney. 'You're looking *great*. You haven't aged much in twenty-five years, have you?' She turned to Katrina. 'I was in prison for the last twenty-four years, you see.'

Katrina's face was a mask of bemused politeness. 'Yes, I know. Won't you sit down?'

'No, I must away.' She gave a brilliant smile. 'Just wanted to say hi, and meet you. I've heard so much about you. And to tell you how glad I am that Luke has somebody as lovely as you to look after him in the new South Africa.' She looked down at Katrina with a liquid smile. 'You're very, *very* beautiful.'

Katrina was blushing. 'Thank you. So are you.'

'If somewhat faded. But not yet jaded. But, alas, some years older than you. However, isn't it great that in the new South Africa we can all be friends – *legally* at last?'

'It is,' Katrina said.

Mahoney was still standing. He could still feel the flush in his face. He was astonished all over again that she could still affect him like this.

Patti continued: 'And you've no idea what an absolute joy it is for me to be able to meet you in a place like this – to be allowed in here is a tremendous novelty. And I have a Pavlovian reaction every time – I still expect a policeman to appear.'

627

Katrina was smiling at her with bright sympathy: 'I can imagine.'

'*Can* you? *Anyway*,' Patti went on brightly, 'I look forward to seeing you both again. Do give me a call when you're back in Johannesburg.' She snapped open her handbag and produced a few visiting cards. They read, '*Patricia Gandhi, African National Congress National Executive, Shell House, Johannesburg*'. She said, as an afterthought: 'I believe you're going to be on the Volkswag's negotiating team at the Great Indaba, when it starts.'

Katrina was surprised. 'How do you know? It hasn't been announced.'

Patti smiled. 'Ah, the ANC has its sources, we know everything about everybody we're interested in. *Any*way, I'll be seeing a lot of you, because I'm on the ANC delegation.'

'*Are* you?' Katrina was very interested.

'And I think it's all to the good if everybody at that negotiating table knows each other as well as possible, so we get to trust each other, don't you agree?'

'Absolutely,' Katrina said earnestly.

Patti said brightly: 'So let's meet for dinner, or lunch, and compare ideas for the new South Africa. You never know, out of understanding each other's point of view agreement may emerge.'

'Quite,' Katrina said earnestly. She opened her bag and pulled out a visiting card. 'Both my office and my home numbers.'

'Excellent.' Patti smiled. 'And,' she added, ' – but this is off the record – I'm beginning to think that maybe an Afrikaner homeland within a federal-type structure mightn't be such a bad idea.'

Katrina looked taken aback. Then delighted. 'Really?'

'That's my personal view, not the ANC's, and I'm not to be quoted please. I'm still thinking about it. But I've read all your Volkswag literature, and I know my South African history – and politics – and I've *studied* Luke's excellent book *Big Trouble*, and it seems to me that a homeland of sorts for the Afrikaner might be the simplest solution. To defuse the crisis and allay fears. We've got too much fear in this country.' She added: 'Provided there's no apartheid in your volkstaat, of course.'

'There won't be,' Katrina promised. '*Won't* you sit down?'

'No, thank you, I must get some sleep, we'll talk about it over lunch one day. Where're you off to, or are you going to squander your money here in the casino?'

'To the Wild Coast,' Mahoney said. 'To Qora. My father's camp.'

Patti sighed. 'Oh, how lovely.' To Katrina: 'My parents and I used to sneak off to the coast there a few times in the bad old days. God, how often I used to think about it in prison – running along those beaches, free as the air, diving into that surf! I'll think of you enviously.' She turned to Mahoney. 'And how's our movie coming along? Have you started writing the script yet?'

'Our' movie, Mahoney noted. And he was surprised she knew he was commissioned to write the film script. 'No, I'm starting now, at the Wild Coast.'

'Make it a good one, Luke. Just follow *Alms*, don't change it a scrap. Do you know where they're shooting it?'

'I'm told in Umtata, Jo'burg and Swaziland. And what are you doing in this part of the world?'

'On my way to Umtata – a bit of family business, Gandhi Garments still has a factory there.' Then she held out both hands, one for each of them, and squeezed each. 'Well, work hard. And – ' to Katrina – '*au revoir*.' She turned away with a dazzling smile.

Mahoney watched her go. He sat down slowly. He was shaking.

Katrina was looking at him, with a small smile. 'Well?'

Mahoney was aware that he was blushing. 'Well what?'

'Well, *wow*. What was that all about? And have I really got a potential ally on the ANC executive? And what a stunning-looking woman.' She smiled. 'Oh, I know very well what it was about – that was *loaded*. The lady was making her dramatic presence felt. And sizing up the Other Woman. Because, she's still in love with you, Luke.'

Mahoney's face still felt flushed.

'I assure you it's over. Twenty-five years is a long time.'

Katrina nodded sagely. 'Indeed, it's been a very long time for *her* – for twenty-five years she's had nobody but you to think about. To dream about. You've been enormously important to her. Now she's out and you've been cruelly snatched from her arms by another woman. And an *Afrikaner* woman – one of the tribe who put her inside. Who robbed her of her youth. Of her freedom. And now robbed her of her man. Her sense of injustice must be enormous.'

Mahoney sighed. 'Okay. She's had an awful time. And I admire her enormously. But it would be extraordinary for a relationship to survive twenty-odd years, and surely she accepts that.'

'I'm not worried, darling – I feel secure. But I'm not sure she's accepted it. However . . . yes, I admire her, too, anybody who's endured all that time in prison for her cause warrants admiration. And I even agree with her cause. Apartheid was wrong, and she fought it. And paid dearly for her courage.' She sighed. 'Yes, I feel very sorry for her. And guilty. For what my people did to her, and now for what *I've* done to her.'

Mahoney took her hand. 'You've done nothing to her, Katrina.'

She picked up Patti's card. She said pensively: 'A member of the ANC executive thinks an Afrikaner volkstaat mightn't be such a bad idea, huh? God, this could be important. Do you think she meant that? Or was she just being diplomatic?'

Mahoney sighed. 'She's a very independent, forthright person. I can't imagine her saying something like that to be polite. However, it's only her personal view.'

Katrina nodded pensively. Then: 'From little acorns great oaks grow. Yes, I'll certainly take her to lunch. Start nourishing that little acorn. And, I feel sorry for her – she's a lonely person.' She added: 'Even though I think she wants to make her presence felt by you through me. Don't you?'

Yes, Mahoney thought so too. 'I don't know,' he said.

'Do you mind? If I take her to lunch, and water that acorn?'

Mahoney gave an inward sigh. Yes he did mind, because he was guilty and worried that Patti may tell Katrina about Mauritius. And, God, he regretted that lie. And, God, he didn't know whether it was wise for him to see Patti if she had this impact on him every time.

'Of course I don't mind. You're your own person and know womankind better than I do. And, yes, she's lonely. I want her to adjust, and anything you can do to help her will be good. But I wouldn't expect too much out of it.' He rubbed his chin. Then smiled at her: 'I love *you*.'

'I love you too.'

He nodded soberly. 'Yes, do it. Be kind to her.'

Katrina said: 'And show her that not all Afrikaners are awful people.' She added brightly: 'And, who knows, I might persuade her that a volkstaat would be an absolute *bargain* for the ANC.'

92

The Transkei was not the land of green rolling downs that he remembered. Because of the shortage of thatch-grass most huts were roofed with corrugated iron now, and everywhere was the degeneration caused by apartheid: the land over-populated, over-grazed, the cattle and goats thin, jagged scars of soil erosion in every fold. And the people did not wear red blankets or brass bangles anymore, the women did not smoke pipes. They all wore white man's tatters now. And the villages which, when he was a boy, were small nuclei of white civilization were now run down, with rusted shells of cars, plastic bags fluttering, goats and pigs scavenging, the street thronging with unemployed, their only economy the worn-out hills.

'Lord,' Mahoney said, 'it used to be beautiful country.'

It was midday when they pulled into Umtata, his old home town. It was further evidence of the mistake of apartheid. The pretty Umtata he knew was just another black man's town now: black people thronging everywhere; traffic hooting and jamming; the Victorian shops of Main Street now grubby; the good old Grosvenor Hotel closed down, the windows broken, squatters on the verandah; the lovely old town hall's gardens now a market; the grand old Imperial Hotel a flophouse. And everywhere blacks, blacks, blacks, not a white face to be seen. But, ah yes, in the town centre was the black man's notion of grandeur: the old Magistrate's Courthouse had been bulldozed down and replaced with towering steel-and-glass offices to house the thousands of black bureaucrats.

'Jesus, why do they do it? Can't they *see* it's ugly? Why do they have to make a sow's ear out of a silk purse?'

Katrina said: 'But all Third World people are the same – in Europe the *nouveaux riches* are the same. And the Afrikaner too – look at our awful modern Dutch Reformed churches, built like triangles, look at our ugly little Afrikaans towns – the Afrikaner has been in Africa so long he's forgotten about gracious old architecture. So don't be too hard on these Xhosa.'

He drove past his old school. The grounds were thronging with black children. Mahoney sighed. This was where he had been head prefect once upon a time; this was where he had eyed the girls' legs; this was where Lisa Rousseau had everybody drooling over her while his heart burst with possessive pride. All gone. A whole way of life, a whole history, all gone.

Katrina smiled. 'Don't show yourself to be a prejudiced, racist South African.'

'But this is my old school. Wouldn't anybody feel the same?'

'Sure, we're all racists up to a point.'

He drove past the girls' hostel. It was still there. 'That's where it all began.'

'You randy bitch, Lisa! Screwing a *schoolboy*, forsooth.'

'See that window? That's where she hung a towel out as the all-clear sign. And that drainpipe – that's the bastard that let me down. If it hadn't been for that drainpipe, my whole life would have been different. I'd have won a Rhodes scholarship, probably be a respectable history professor now. I would never have met Patti again. I'd never have met you in Borneo. And I wouldn't be trying to write up the same journals I seduced Lisa with.'

'Thank God for that drainpipe!'

He couldn't bear to go and look at his old house.

It was late afternoon when they got near the sea. The hills began to turn greener, the cattle and goats a little fatter, the huts had thatch again, and women were wearing red blankets again. Then they saw the sea in the distance. They came over the last hill, and the Qora river burst into view.

'Oh wow!' Katrina said.

The sea opened through the river mouth into a blue lagoon that meandered around sandbanks and little islands, through steep forested gorges up into the hills. On top of a grassy ridge overlooking this lagoon was the Mahoney camp, a cluster of thatched huts.

'It's *beauti*ful!' Katrina cried. 'Oh, we're going to have a *lovely* time.'

They did have a lovely time. Five miles to the south was the small Haven Hotel, but a wide river, with no bridge, separated them and no tourists came their way. Every day black children brought fresh oysters for sale. In the mornings they lay late in the deep feather bed. 'It's a holiday,' she said, 'we don't have to get up at all if we don't want to. We can drink champagne and make love all day, those oysters really *work*.' The first two days they did stay mostly in bed, getting up only to get more oysters, fetch another bottle of wine, make a sandwich; maybe oysters really do work – it seemed to Mahoney he just couldn't get enough of her.

'Better open more oysters, Luke, if you're serious about this.'

Finally they began to get organised. One day, about mid-morning, they made it out of bed and he went to catch a fish while she tidied up the camp. He cast into the gully that had never failed him as a boy and within half an hour he had two good fish. He would have loved to continue, but he felt guilty taking more from the sea than he needed. He cleaned the fish, then walked back up the grassy hill.

'Don't tell me I'm not a helluva provider, woman. Don't tell me I'm not a helluva big wheel.'

'*My hero!*'

After breakfast they tried to do a few hours' work. He started on the film script with a new ream of paper, a copy of *Alms for Oblivion* and a book called *Profitable Screenplay Writing*. He found it easy. In addition, he devoted about an hour each day to his journals. With their papers spread out at each end of the dining table, Katrina prepared Volkswag's arguments for the Great Indaba while Mahoney sorted out recent events, marshalling his facts, trying to weave them into the big picture of South Africa.

MORE TRAIN MASSACRES

There have now been five massacres by unknown assassins since the violence spread to the Reef – despite police on the trains.

AT LAST MANDELA AGREES TO MEET BUTHELEZI

Nelson Mandela has finally agreed to meet Chief Buthelezi to seek a peace accord. The government has applauded, adding that 'it has taken him a long time to reach it, at a high cost in human life'. Meanwhile, in three speeches, the ANC again accuses the government of 'using every vile tactic', claiming that 'the vicious violence is aimed at making us bow down to their bayonets and jackboots. Operation Iron Fist is aimed only at stripping us of our civil liberties.'

VIOLENCE, VIOLENCE, DESPITE IRON FIST

WIT WOLWE HOWL DOWN TELEPHONES AT GOVERNMENT MPS

NOW MANDELA SNUBS BUTHELEZI

Christ. For months Mandela has refused to meet Buthelezi to promote peace because that would give the Zulu leader stature. Berated by the international press, Mandela eventually announced that he would. Now the ANC has announced that Mandela will only meet him 'as part of a delegation of other homeland leaders'. This is amazing arrogance, implying that all other leaders, including Buthelezi, are merely old tribal chiefs – and it's calculated to fan the flames.

Predictably, Buthelezi has rejected the ANC's invitation.

ANC CONTINUES TO RECRUIT SOLDIERS DESPITE IRON FIST

Meanwhile . . .

ALL BLACK ORGANIZATIONS ACCUSE POLICE OF SIDING WITH ANC

Every hour they listened to the news on his portable radio. The news was bad, and Mahoney seethed, but the truth is he was very happy. He was a *writer* again, and big bad news is the stuff writers feed on. He was a fulfilled man for the first time in many years, being back in Africa, devoting himself to it again. It was great to be sitting here worrying, and it was *wonderful* to have the woman he was mad about sitting at the other end of the table, also worrying about her African thing, her goddamn volkstaat. It was exciting to be in on this dramatic stage of African history, working on it together. He had never been happier in his life. And, oh yes, he loved her. And, thank God, he'd got all that emotional, *sexual* impact of seeing Patti Gandhi again into perspective.

When the sun was lower they went down to the blue lagoon. They swam naked, and if any children were peeping from the forest they did not care. It was lovely wallowing in shallow clear water, drinking good wine, the satiny feel of her drifting against him, her lovely long legs, her breasts, her blonde hair floating about her shoulders – and talking, *talking* about anything and everything.

'You know why I love you, Mahoney, apart from those beat-up good-looks? It's that handsome brain of yours.'

'And you have the prettiest ears attached to each side of your handsome brain; I am very proud of your ears.'

'And I'm very proud of your silver tongue.'

'When it comes to tongue, Professor, I'm your only man.'

'Yes please!'

Sometimes they drifted across the lagoon to the long white beach, and went surfing. High curling breakers half a mile long came rolling in from the Indian Ocean, crashing up onto the pristine sand. They ran into the sea and dived, hearing the waves crash over them, striking out, side by side, diving under the next wave, swimming on until they were beyond the breakers, where the big swells were still rearing up. And they trod water, waiting for the really good one, every seventh one, riding up the other swells, waiting. And there is nothing like it as the wave comes towards you, growing higher and higher, and then you are rising up the slope, up, up, up, and there is the precise moment when you must kick and strike out with her – and you go roaring with her, on your belly, head up, skidding for hundreds of yards, and it is one of the most exhilarating sports in the world.

But that was kid's stuff compared to her windsurfing. On the fifth day she lugged her new windsurfer down to the beach. The sea was flat but there was a good breeze. She rigged it and first tried it in the lagoon. She went flying up towards the gorges. Then she floated it down to the river mouth, and put out to sea. Mahoney was half a mile away fishing. Katrina flew past him, half a mile out, with a cheery wave, her lovely body taut. She executed a smart about-turn and headed straight out to sea.

'*Hey*,' Mahoney yelled, '*don't go too far!*'

She could not hear him. She kept going, as Mahoney watched with mounting alarm. '*Hey, there're sharks out there!*'

She kept going, getting smaller and smaller. Mahoney watched in consternation. '*Come back!*' When she was a mile out she turned and headed south. She went creaming along his horizon, a tiny triangular shape. Mahoney stared, horrified. She disappeared beyond the southern headland.

'*Jesus!*' Mahoney leapt down onto the sand and began running along the beach.

It took him an hour to reach the headland, the sand pulling at his feet, running until he just had to walk to get the hammering out of his chest, then running some more. Katrina had not reappeared. He was very worried now. He toiled up the steep headland, rasping. Then he crested it, and below was the river mouth, beyond were the rondavels of the Haven Hotel. Half a dozen people were clustered around Katrina on the beach, chatting.

Mahoney slumped down in a heap, and thanked God. Getting the knocking out of his heart. Then he heaved himself up, waved his arms and bellowed: '*Kat!*'

The wind was against him. He hollered and hollered. Then he cursed and began to clamber down the headland. He was going to swim across that fucking river mouth and tell her that no way was she going to fucking windsurf back – he was going to get the Land-Rover to *drive* her infernal machine back to camp. When he was halfway down Katrina got up and carried her board back into the water.

'*Hey!*' Mahoney roared. But nobody heard him. She pulled up the sail and headed out to sea again.

'*Jesus*!' He went scrambling frantically back up the headland.

By the time he reached the top again, gasping, she was halfway home on a windward tack. Then she turned and went skidding across the sea towards their river mouth.

An hour later Mahoney toiled up to the camp. Katrina's passion-pink wetsuit lay on the grass alongside the windsurfer. She was at the dining table, surrounded by her books and notes.

'Hullo,' she said, 'where've you *been*?'

* * * *

635

She waited until the boozy lunch was going strong before telling him. 'You'll never guess who was on the beach over at the Haven Hotel this morning: Patti Gandhi.'

Mahoney was astonished. 'Good God.'

Katrina smiled. 'Arrived yesterday. Just decided on a whim to have a holiday at the hotel. But don't imagine that it's a coincidence, darling – the lady intends to make her presence felt. So, I invited her over for lunch.'

'You invited her *here*?'

'Of course. I'd do it in Jo'burg, why not here? The sooner we get over the confrontation – if that's the word – the better. I'm quite sure she intended driving over here anyway.' She raised her eyebrows at him. 'Will it upset you to see her again?'

Mahoney sighed. 'No, Kat. I don't want *you* to get upset.'

'Well, I'm confident I can handle it, if you can. Can you?'

'*Yes*.'

'And,' Katrina said, 'I'm confident of you.' She grinned. 'If she wants to come on with her big battalions – I refer to her sexual charm rather than MK – I'm ready for her.' She reached for the wine bottle. 'Actually, I think she's very nice. And she's certainly a very valuable contact in the ANC. But if she tries to shake that gorgeous arse of hers at you – she'll get as good as she gives!'

Oh Jesus. Mahoney smiled wanly: 'When is she coming?'

Katrina giggled. 'I'd say any time. Maybe tomorrow. I just hope I have a couple more days to work on my tan!'

93

But Patti Gandhi did not come the following day. Nor the next.

'She's doing her number,' Katrina said. 'She knows we're waiting for her dramatic entrance, she knows I'm trying to look my most ravishing best, and she's letting the tension mount.'

'Bullshit.'

'You don't know *women*. Excuse me, I'm going back to the sun to get this tan up.' She giggled. 'You better work on yours too.'

But he did not go down to the lagoon to join her. Because that day the radio announced the results of the commission of inquiry into hit squads in South Africa. He listened to the radio with consternation, his pen flying across his notebook. Then he strode onto the ridge, cupped his hands and bellowed: '*Katrina! Come up. I'm in big trouble.*'

She came toiling up into the main hut. Mahoney was sitting at the table with a large glass of whisky. 'What trouble?' she demanded anxiously.

Mahoney said grimly: 'The commission of inquiry has finally delivered its report. And it declares that Erik Badenhorst is a liar. With delusions of grandeur, and a hatred of his former police superiors. And that Daniel was lying on the eve of his execution. Platplaas, the judge finds, was a legitimate police base only used for gathering information.' He looked at her. 'Realise what this means? Now the police will sue me and Hugo for libel. Individuals like General Krombrink, who I said gave Badenhorst his orders.'

Katrina sat down slowly. Aghast. She took his hand. 'Oh God.'

Mahoney turned to his notebook. 'However, the judge does say that the CCB *may* have been responsible for certain political assassinations – like Richard Barker – "although no firm evidence had been laid before him". But that doesn't help me because I didn't write anything about the CCB. He exonerates the Minister of Defence. However, he did complain that he had been unable to arrive at the "full truth" because "willing, trustworthy witnesses did not come to the fore".' Mahoney put his hands to his face. '*Of course no fucking witnesses came forward! The police and the CCB made sure of that!*'

Katrina squeezed his hand. Mahoney took a deep, angry breath. 'The police are cock-a-hoop. But nobody is fooled!' He banged his notes. 'Prestigious academics, opposition politicians, the press are all up in arms. The National Association of Democratic Lawyers has denounced the commission as a huge cover-up. The whole thing reeks! The Centre for Human Rights at the University of Pretoria said that the report is an "opportunity lost" to restore the status of judges – the populace will believe Judge le Roux was participating in the cover-up!' Mahoney groaned. 'And he had to make his decisions on only a fraction of the evidence. As soon as Badenhorst testified to crimes committed *outside* South Africa the judge was not allowed to listen to it. So he only got a fraction of the picture. It made the inquiry a *farce*.' He slapped the table. 'And the blame for that lies squarely on President de Klerk for refusing to extend the enquiry. He *deliberately* handicapped Badenhorst – *and* the judge. And witnesses had the right to refuse to answer questions. *Jesus!* The whole process reeks.' He put his hands to his face. 'De Klerk has only himself to blame now if nobody believes him when he denies that the government is promoting the violence through a Third Force.'

Katrina said anxiously: 'But surely the police won't sue you – they'll sue *Vryburgher*, *they* published the story in South Africa. They won't proceed against the *Globe* and you, surely?'

Mahoney snorted. 'Why not? Make an international case out of it?' He glared out the window at the sea.

Jesus, he had to get his act together and find out about this Third Force. When he was sued he didn't want to have to rely solely on the evidence of Badenhorst and Daniel.

Several other things happened that afternoon. There was another train massacre, Mandela declared it the work of a hit squad, and even President de Klerk admitted: 'There are forces which do not want peaceful negotiations.' The press announced that the gunmen firing from vehicles were both black and white men, and that amongst the Zulu impis that attacked Phola Park was a white man who was killed, whose body mysteriously disappeared. The United Nations Secretary General announced that right-wing elements in the police were assisting the Zulu impis, providing transport and logistical support.

And that afternoon Patti Gandhi arrived.

They heard a car pull up on the grass slope outside the kitchen.

'Oh, God.' He was in no mood for subtle confrontations. For loaded conversations about 'our movie'. For discussions of the disastrous hit-squad report. He wanted to be *alone*, to think as a lawyer.

'Shall I tell her this is not a good time?' Katrina said.

'No.' Mahoney sighed. 'Let's get it over with.'

He poured a big dash of whisky, while Katrina went out to greet her. He heard polite laughter. Then Patti entered.

She wore a bikini under a bright beach robe, and she was ravishing. And, despite himself, Mahoney felt the sexual impact of her all over again. 'Hullo, Patti,' he glared, 'welcome.'

She said soberly: 'Luke, I won't stay – but I heard the bad news on the radio about this hit-squad report and decided to come because I knew you and Katrina would be worried. Luke? I'm quite sure the ANC will stand by you if you're sued. We know Badenhorst and Daniel are telling the truth, we've got independent corroboration of their stories. We stuck our necks out in accepting Badenhorst and it's our credibility that's on the line too.'

Mahoney suppressed a sigh. Sure, the ANC would be behind him, but he was damn sure they wouldn't pay the legal costs.

'Thank you, Patti. I'm sure you've got corroboration of aspects of Badenhorst's story, but that won't help me, or Hugo. Because we'll be sued by *individual* police officers – though the police will gladly pay *their* legal costs. And those individuals are people like General Krombrink – who put you in jail – and who Badenhorst says gave him his orders.

The ANC has got no corroboration to prove *those* facts. Only Badenhorst was present when orders were given.' He took a tense breath. 'So, my defence will rest entirely upon the evidence of Erik Badenhorst. And he's been found to be a liar.'

Patti said earnestly: 'Okay, but I want you to know that you're not alone, Luke, and though I can't speak officially for the ANC yet, I think they'll help you with legal costs.'

Mahoney was absolutely taken aback. With the *legal* costs? This was too good to be credible. *Communist money?* He did not know if he wanted to believe it. Before he could fumble a reply, Patti continued resolutely: 'And if the ANC won't, I personally will.'

Mahoney was taken aback again. So was Katrina. Before he could muster a protest, Patti held up her hands and said: 'We're not going to talk about it anymore, it may never happen. I just want you two lovely people to know you've got friends. I assure you I can afford it – I haven't spent a cent in twenty-five years, my shares have increased a thousand-fold, I'm a very rich lady. *So* – ' she grabbed both their hands tight – 'no more morbid discussions about libel actions, please. We can talk about anything you like, about what a shit life is, about Buthelezi and Mandela, but no more worry about Badenhorst and his silly hit squads.' She reached for Katrina's glass of wine, sipped and added: 'Anyway I must go, I know you want to be alone.'

'*Nonsense*,' Katrina said. 'You're staying for lupper.'

'Lupper?'

'A boozy juxtaposition of lunch and supper!'

And it was boozy. Katrina was in a mood to drown her worries. So was Mahoney. He had just had his story thrown out of one court and he was very likely to be thrown into another one. He didn't know what to believe about the ANC being supportive, and he certainly wasn't sure whether Patti's help was a good idea. But it was a hell of a comfort at this stage.

And he was keen to get some information on the ANC's views, and so was Katrina. And Patti was very interested in their views. 'But who are these people in this so-called Third Force, how're they organised?' Mahoney demanded. 'Are they simply rogue elements in the security forces – handfuls of individuals, or are they an underground structure with a formal chain of command? Or both?'

'Both,' Patti said. 'Formal and informal.'

'But what *evidence* has the ANC got?' Katrina demanded. 'Apart from Badenhorst's story?'

'God, how much more evidence do you want? We would certainly be naive to assume the CCB doesn't exist anymore just because President de Klerk ordered it to be disbanded!'

'But how far up do you think the chain of command extends? Right up to De Klerk himself?'

'No – ' Mahoney began.

'*Yes*,' Patti said. 'Or certainly as far as the Minister of Defence. Perhaps, psychologically, the president doesn't *want* to know, so his conscience is clear, but he *really* knows.'

'And approves?' Mahoney demanded.

'Of course. Because it's to the government's advantage that the blacks appear to butcher each other in the name of democracy. So the government can claim to the world that whites must be protected with "minority group rights", separate residential areas, veto rights over uncongenial legislation, et cetera.' Patti snorted.

Katrina said: 'I'm sorry, I simply don't believe President de Klerk is sanctioning mass murder.'

'Nor do I,' Mahoney said.

'*Lord* – I wish I had your faith in my fellow man. De Klerk's an Afrikaner *politician*, for God's sake, and now he's fighting the Third Boer War. Only this time he's trying to appear respectable. But he's fighting the old battles nonetheless, for the white man's survival, and I don't believe for a moment the guy would be squeamish about shedding a bit more black blood.' She snorted. 'And do you know where the chain of command ends in the *informal* Third Force?'

'Where?'

Patti held up a finger. 'The top of Afrikaner society, Luke. Top members of industry, the legal profession, doctors, accountants, teachers, civil servants.' She put her hand on Katrina's. 'I trust this doesn't annoy you?'

Katrina smiled. 'I'm a political scientist. Nothing shocks me.'

'Good.' Patti continued earnestly: 'The ANC knows that a cabal of high-powered civilian Afrikaners exists dedicated to the preservation of white supremacy at any cost. And they're associated with the "*formal*" Third Force – the guys in the security forces – and they discuss strategies, and provide funds.'

'But what *evidence* has the ANC got? Can you find out? Because I need this information.'

'I doubt the ANC will open its files to you, Luke. But I can try.'

'That would be wonderful.'

Patti continued: 'And then there's the AWB. Of course Eugene Terreblanche is in contact with both the "formal" bunch – the elements in the security forces – and the "informal" bunch – captains of Afrikaner commerce. And then there are the *really* informal Third Force: the right-wing splinter groups. There are at least forty-eight groups, like the Order of Death, the Wit Wolwe, hate-filled fanatics, who could turn the country into an inferno with just one act of terror, like assassinating Mandela. So?' She raised her eyebrows. 'All these chains of command thread back to the "formal" Third Force, the rogue officers in the security forces. And *they* take their orders – indirectly – from the Minister of Defence.'

Mahoney shook his head.

'Bullshit, Patti,' Katrina said, 'the chain of command stops at those rogue officers.'

Patti sighed. 'Look, the civil war in Natal has been raging for years. It was the government's duty to stop it. But they didn't. Because PW Botha and his securocrats, time-warped by decades of apartheid, saw a convergence of interests in this conflict – let *Inkatha* crush the ANC and its allies! So they just sent in token amounts of troops – and wrung their hands. But now we know about Inkathagate – that the government trained an elite corps of Zulus as urban guerrillas in the Caprivi Strip. And then the ANC is unbanned – and what happens? The violence immediately spreads from Natal up to the Johannesburg area. As if by spontaneous combustion. Bullshit! We *know* that truckloads of Zulus suddenly arrived – and the police did nothing about them. And suddenly Zulu hostel-dwellers are attacking the ANC. And we hear all kinds of stories that the police are helping the Zulus in this violence – '

'But no hard evidence,' Katrina said, 'only hearsay.'

'But look at the rest of the evidence: we *know* there were police hit squads; we *know* there are CCB hit squads; we *know* that South Africa was and is *still* run by securocrats. De Klerk hasn't fired them. All the way down the line those securocrats are still in position, with all their dirty-tricks mentality. Have those leopards changed their spots? And we *know* that '*they*' trained those Zulu warriors in Caprivi. We *know* that suddenly truckloads of Zulus come up from Natal and the violence breaks out on the Reef. White men are seen amongst the Zulu marauders. Then gunmen start shooting at blacks in bus queues. And then these dreadful train massacres start.' Patti frowned. 'You stack all that evidence up and what do you conclude? *That the government is sponsoring this Third Force, assisting Inkatha.* So that when the Great Indaba starts the ANC is in disarray. *That's* the irresistible conclusion!'

Katrina sloshed more wine into their glasses. She said: 'Patti, the ANC is as guilty as Inkatha and this Third Force. Because this violence is about who will wield power in the new South Africa. When Mandela was released he snubbed Buthelezi – because acknowledging him would make Buthelezi appear an important political player. Even *now*. Why doesn't Mandela meet Buthelezi at a public peace rally – shake hands with him, sign a peace treaty? Why does he run around the world piously blaming everybody else instead of using his prestige to put a stop to the violence? Why? Because the ANC wants to get as much political advantage out of the violence as possible, to *show* its strength.'

Patti's beautiful eyes widened: 'Bull*shit! Inkatha* started it – '

'Non-*sense*!' Mahoney said. 'The ANC publicly declared Inkatha and KwaZulu legitimate targets, remember, Patti? And remember that the ANC also has its private army – the MK. *They* haven't been disbanded, have they? So of *course* Inkatha will muster its own army. And MK was trained and armed by Russia. Compared to the vast sums Russia gave the ANC, what South Africa did for Inkatha is a drop in the fucking ocean!' He held up a finger. 'And remember that when the government launched Operation Iron Fist the ANC was the first to cry foul. Because the ANC *wants* the violence to continue!'

'No! It's because Iron Fist was excessive!'

'The only way to stop these blacks fighting each other is to be tough! The way Shaka would have done it. Declare martial law, send the army to shoot it out, street by street, block by block. And what a world outcry there would be if we did that! The ANC would have screamed blue murder.' He shook his head at her. 'This is an *African* war, Patti, and the only people who can stop it are Mandela and Buthelezi. *Sign* a fucking peace treaty midst international fanfare. *But*, Mandela won't do it – until he's got all the political advantage he can out of it.' He snorted. 'It's called the African Way, Patti.'

She said archly, 'Like the government is doing with their Third Force?.'

'I think,' Katrina grinned, 'we've arrived back at Square One.'

But it was a good-natured argument, well oiled with wine. It was after midnight when Patti said: 'Guess I'd better hit the road back to the hotel.'

'You are *not*,' Katrina said, 'going to drive, alone, thirty miles through the Transkei, in the middle of the night, after all you've drunk. There're plenty of beds here.'

'Absolutely right,' Mahoney said.

'You're both absolutely right,' Patti said.

'Which makes us,' Katrina said, 'in agreement on at least something. So how about an Irish coffee?'

'That sounds absolutely right.'

'You're both absolutely right,' Mahoney said.

'So where, I ask myself, will this meeting of great minds end?'

'Under the table?' Patti enquired.

'You're absolutely right.'

It all seemed terribly funny. It was three Irish coffees later when Mahoney made his way to bed leaving the two women in profound contentious discourse about Adam Smith and Karl Marx, with a lot of other eggheads thrown in. 'You're *absolutely wrong*!' were the last words he heard from Katrina as he tried to blow out his bedside candle, followed by Patti's 'You're absolutely wrong that I'm *absolutely* wrong!' Followed by shrieks of laughter. '*Eggheads,*' were Mahoney's last words to himself.

Dawn was breaking when Katrina inefficiently clambered into bed beside him. She lay on her back, staring up into the dark rafters, then said: 'I love you.' She added, by way of clarification: '*You.*'

Mahoney didn't hear a thing. She elbowed his back. 'Did you follow all that?'

'*Mmm,*' Mahoney mumbled. Katrina stared up into the darkness.

'She's great. I really like her. In fact I even lent her my toothbrush! *Howzat?*'

No response from Mahoney. She dug her elbow again. 'I lent her my *toothbrush. Howzat* for an Afrikaner? I don't lend *anybody* my toothbrush, except you, *once,* in an emergency. *Howzat?*'

'Mmm,' Mahoney groaned. Katrina continued: 'That *proves* I'm not a racist. We brushed our teeth together, at the water tank. *First* me,' she admitted reasonably, '*then* her, but I still lent her my effing toothbrush. Doesn't that prove that not only do I have a heart of gold, I'm not a racist? *Doesn't* it?'

'Mmmm.'

'*Doesn't it?*' She was silent a long moment. Then: 'And you know something else, Mahoney? She kissed me goodnight.' She paused dramatically. 'That mightn't sound a big deal for a non-racist after lending her my effing toothbrush, but it was on the *lips.*'

Mahoney did not respond. She waited, then gave him another nudge. 'Did you follow all that? I don't want to have to repeat this.'

'*Mmm,*' Mahoney agreed.

'I said she kissed me on the mouth. At her hut. It was only a brief kiss, but it was definitely a *passionate* one.'

No response from Mahoney. Katrina nudged him.

'Did you get that? And as I lie here in my inebriated state I can think of at least four important things about that. Are you listening?'

'*Mmmm.*'

'The first is, I know she really likes me. She's *not* insincere. She's not a bullshitter.' She paused. 'The second is: she really *fancies* me. Sexually.' She paused again. 'Me, as *well* as you.' She paused. 'Are you reading me, Mahoney?'

'Mmmm,' Mahoney murmured.

'And the third important detail, my Lord, is she ain't gonna get you. You're *my* man now.'

There was a long drunken pause, then she ended: 'And the fourth significant detail is that I *let* her kiss me. I didn't kiss her back, but I *let* her kiss me. Okay? Does that mean I liked it?'

There was a long silence. Then, in an instant, she was in a drunken sleep.

Mahoney mumbled: 'And when the government does try to clamp down, mark my words that Nelson Mandela will be the first to cry foul.'

94

Mahoney remembered none of that in the morning.

The sun was high when he woke up. Katrina was not beside him. He tried to remember how the night had ended; then he swung out of bed and held his head. He wished he hadn't done that so suddenly. He got up more slowly, and draped a towel around his waist.

On the dining table was a note: '*Down at the lagoon. Love you, K.*'

He was in no shape to trudge down to the lagoon without a beer to kick-start his heart. It went down into his ravaged system like a balm. He had a cold bucket-shower, and decided to have another beer while he sat in a heap at the table, staring into the middle distance, trying not to think about being sued by General Krombrink. *Fuck 'em.* Cross the bridges as you come to them. He got a third beer, and set out into the glaring sun for the lagoon.

He was halfway down the steep path when he heard Katrina's laugh. And he glimpsed them through the trees. Katrina and Patti lying on their stomachs in the shallow clear water, beer cans in hand. Both were topless, their bikini tops flung up onto the sand.

Mahoney stopped. He had presumed that Patti had gone back to her hotel. And he sighed. He was in no shape for jolly talk yet. Certainly in no shape for politics. Even if it was as stimulating as last night. *Particularly* if it was as stimulating as last night. He turned, and climbed back up the path, to the camp.

He got another beer, then sat down at his typewriter.

An hour later he heard Patti's car start, then drive away. He had just finished listening to the news on the radio. Katrina entered in her bikini, her long blonde hair matted with salt water. 'Hi! Didn't you see my note? She's just left – we thought you were still dead to the world. How're you feeling?'

'The doctor says I'm now allowed visitors provided I don't get excited.'

'Poor *baby*.' She held his head to her breasts. They were warm and smelt erotically salty. He fondled her sun-warmed thighs, then slipped his hand inside the back of her bikini. 'You're making me excited,' he warned.

She kissed him and her mouth tasted of wine. 'Can I have a drink first?' She sprawled on the chair beside him, her long legs apart. 'Wow, what a night. Who's your doctor? What did we eat?'

'You fried up a whole pile of fish and chips.'

'Ah. Remember now. I'm a hell of a cook. Mahoney?' she grinned at him. 'I'm getting drunk again, where's your doctor?'

'How long have you been up?'

'Hours. Heard Patti washing the dishes, decided we'd better tackle the job with a hair of the dog. Then decided to have a swim with the entire dog – we killed a six-pack and two bottles of wine, your doctor was very wise to keep you in bed.' She slapped her hands on her knees. 'Enough of this decadence – what do you want for brunch?'

'Why didn't Patti stay for brunch?'

'Uh-*uh*. Enough of a good thing. It was a great evening, we're all very relieved we got on like a house on fire – but last night was enough for starters. She's smart enough to know that too. Smart lady. Like yours truly. Cool lady. Nice lady. Nice, cool lady.' She added: 'She's off to America next week.'

'America? What for?'

'Heavy-duty ANC business. She's a big wheel. Very modest about it. And *therefore* –' she pointed a jolly finger – 'potentially valuable to me!'

'So, what did you talk about?'

She grinned. 'You mostly. Our hangovers? Everything under the sun. Politics mostly. She's one hell of a political scientist. She's read everything in prison, from Aristotle to Kingdom Come. Impressed the hell out of me. And I'm not easily impressed. But you know what her problem is?'

'What?'

'When it comes to the nitty-gritty, to *applying* her vast knowledge, she's just a theorist. Without any *hands-on* experience, as the Americans say. And why should the poor girl have? She's spent the last twenty-odd years in prison. *But* – ' Katrina shook her head sagely – 'admirable though her academic knowledge is, she's a greenhorn. *Like,* unfortunately, Nelson Mandela is – after twenty-seven years in prison he's got no experience either! Like the rest of his cohorts. They've all been living in *exile,* living in an artificial world of *theory,* in London and Stockholm and Lusaka, running a *welfare* organization, training some kind of army which never fought a battle. And living on *handouts* for forty years, from Russia and Sweden . . . ' She shook her head. 'People like your Patti have no *idea* of the real world, Luke.'

My Patti? But Mahoney distinctly let it go. Katrina sloshed more wine. 'They're all still talking the dead Latin of forty years ago, Luke, still talking about nationalizing anything that makes money. Everything except private swimming pools!' She threw her arms wide: 'It's *bullshit,* Mahoney! Even Mr Gorbachev knows that now. But the ANC? For*get* it.'

'Patti's still talking like that?'

'Exactly like that!' Katrina leant forward and held a finger at his nose cheerfully: 'Know what I want to do with that smart lady? – *drag* her by the scruff of her neck out of the dark ages and teach her a few facts of *life.*' She snorted. 'She still believes that the Communist Party – riding to ultimate power on the back of their ANC partners – can turn South Africa into a socialist paradise! Nationalize everything and *pow* – South Africa will bloom!' She held her finger out again. 'Know what I want to do with that lady? *Shake* her! Shake some 1991 realism into her! This is *my* country she's talking about, not just *hers.*' She snorted aggressively. 'And I'm going to do it!'

'How?' Mahoney grinned.

'Christ, my job is educating people. And I'm going to educate her if it kills me. Not just because I like her, but because she represents the thinking of the ANC. And the goddamn Communist Party. And maybe if I get through to her it'll get through to the rest.' She snorted. 'Jesus – what a hard-headed brainstorm she is. Trouble is she thinks the world's flat.'

'You told her that?'

'Certainly I told her that. All night I told her that.'

Mahoney grinned. 'But it was good natured?'

'Good *natured*?' She sloshed more wine into their glasses. 'We have a hundred things in common. Not least of which is you!'

'What about me?' Then he wished he hadn't said that.

She grinned. 'What a stud you are. How you were wasted in Hong Kong – how responsible she feels for you having to stay out of South

Africa all these years, what a contribution you might have made, how glad she is you've come back, writing again . . . ' She looked at him cheerfully. 'And, how did *you* feel? Still lust after her?'

The image of Patti's nakedness in Mauritius flashed across his mind. 'No,' he smiled.

'Bullshit, all men lust after beautiful women, and she's got one of the best bodies I've seen.'

'If I had any lust left after yours, I'd be a sexual maniac.'

'*Aren't* you?' she grinned. Then she tipped more wine into her glass. 'Oh, I'm having a lovely day. It's a very good thing I didn't invite her to brunch, or we'd have got very drunk. And we'd have probably all ended up in bed together!'

Mahoney snorted into his beer mug. He wondered if he'd heard that right. Katrina burst into giggles. 'Your *face!* Don't tell me you've never thought about it. Patti tells me she suggested it to you once. Remember Gloria Naidoo?'

Mahoney grinned. 'You two got pretty pally down there today.' And he knew what Patti was up to. And it was wildly erotic. And highly dangerous.

'Oh, I know all your murky past.' Katrina dabbed her eye. 'Cool down, lover, no way am I giving you the chance to get enthusiastic about that gorgeous body of hers again.' She kissed him on the nose. 'So don't get your hopes up.' She took a noisy sip of wine. 'And I can't believe she's that much of an optimist either – she knows I'm not a dumb blonde. In fact I think she's over you. She talked about you in a such a matter-of-fact way.' She grinned. 'In fact I think it's *me* she fancies.'

Mahoney was astonished. 'You?'

She jerked her breasts indignantly. 'And what's so unattractive about me, buster?'

'Nothing at all.' Mahoney grinned. 'But why do you say that?'

She burst into giggles. '*Because it takes one to spot one?!*'

'Seriously.' Mahoney grinned.

Katrina dabbed her eyes. 'Oh, I'm having a lovely day. Shall we say fuck work, get drunk over a long lunch, make wild passionate love and sleep it off?'

'Absolutely.'

She looked at him, her eyes wet with mirth, trying to be serious. 'Don't you remember what I told you when I came to bed last night?'

'No?'

'So you really were asleep? Despite that erection I tried to make you do something sensible with. Mahoney – I told you she kissed me. Goodnight.'

'Kissed you?'

'Yep. Only briefly. But long enough for there to be no mistake about the invitation inherent therein. *But,* instead I came to bed, told you like the honest Injun I am and tried to interest you in a bit of carnal knowledge.' She added: 'Of me.' She added further: 'Unsuccessfully.'

Mahoney smiled. 'But how did you feel?'

She giggled again. 'It's turning you on, isn't it? The thought of our two female bodies interlocked in sexual passion, with you rumbling all over us?' She got up and kissed him again, hard, on the mouth. 'Well forget it, honey-child, Ah ain't such a bimbo! But to answer your question – no, that kiss did nothing for me. It neither offended me nor pleased me, like somebody nudging your foot under the dinner-party table. "Uh-oh," you say, and you move your foot away, right?'

'Right. I always say "Uh-oh," and move my foot away.'

'Right. You think, "Here comes another one of those tiresome randy ladies", right?'

'Right. Every time.'

'Right. Anyway all I wanted was to crawl into bed with you. And have carnal knowledge of you. Which I attempted. Unsuccessfully. So what you gonna do about it, big boy? And don't move your foot!' She put her fingertip on his lips. 'Anyway, the danger is passed – she's being sent to America on ANC business, tub-thumping around raising money by telling the gullible Yanks how beastly De Klerk is and how sanctions must continue. So – ' she kissed him hard on the mouth – 'forget any erotic fantasies over her, lover. If it's *fantasies* you want – ' she tapped her breasts – 'talk to me. Starting whenever you like, I'm in the mood.' She looked at her watch. 'And forget the news, it will only be bad.'

That was the first year of the new South Africa.

PART XIV

NATIONAL PEACE ACCORD SIGNED

PILLARS OF APARTHEID
COME TUMBLING DOWN

ECONOMIC CRISIS LOOMS

BLACK LAND-HUNGER TO BE REDRESSED

WINNIE MANDELA TRIED FOR MURDER

GORBACHEV DISBANDS COMMUNIST PARTY

GREAT INDABA TO BEGIN AT LAST

95

The months that followed were a big bad time for the new South Africa, but for Luke Mahoney they were good times. Despite the violence raging out there, despite the daily despair, the desperate plight of the economy, despite all that shit, he was very glad he had come back. He had thrown in his lot with this dark continent he loved and despaired over, and every day was a treasure trove of stimulus, to worry about, argue about, make judgments about, *write* about. And, oh yes, he was in love.

He had thought he was in love in Borneo, he had suspected he was still in love when he had come here 'to investigate her', he had thought he was in love when he had finally resigned from the Hong Kong Government; now he *knew*, with all his heart. Patti Gandhi had come and gone, he had withstood her impact because he had known that he really loved Katrina. And, it was *great* to love Katrina. It was great to be in love with somebody who loved Africa as he did.

And it was wonderful to make love every day to that lovely body, lovely to lie on the bed watching her get undressed, watching as she sat before the mirror in her underwear and took her make-up off as she told him more about the things that had happened that day. She always wore stockings, never pantyhose which she considered unfeminine and sexless. Her panties were brief and her brassieres were frilly. She took her time as she talked, she enjoyed flaunting her body for him; and when she finally came to bed, a smile all over her face, the sheer beauty of her nakedness was a fresh marvel each time. And it was lovely waking up together in the mornings, the ritual of getting ready, sharing the shower, seeing her get dressed again, putting on her make-up again, brushing her hair, getting into her high heels, dashing off to work looking like a million bucks, knowing that in ten hours she would be coming home and the whole lovely ritual would start over again.

And it was great to know that he had ten solid hours to work on the film script and on his book without having to go into court, without a queue of policemen to consult him, without lawyers to give him a hard time, without law to look up and judges to argue with and juries to worry about. Once a week he went to Lawyers for Human Rights to give a day's voluntary work; sometimes he had to go to the university library to look up a point of history, or to the *Star*'s newspaper library, about once a week he met Hugo and Shortarse Longbottom for a pub lunch to sort out the problems of the world; but for the rest he sat in his study and worked on his book, doing again what he had always wanted to do, be a writer, an historian, a chronicler, an opinion-maker. It was great to hear the busy buzz of the printer, it was great to achieve in one day what had taken him a week in Hong Kong. And it was great to get the day's news as it happened, not the next day in truncated form. The news was bad, but that was good too because bad news is what good writers like to worry about.

A National Peace Accord was signed midst great fanfare, between the government, the ANC and Inkatha, wherein good conduct was promised and committees were created to resolve political disputes: and in addition a commission of inquiry into violence was set up under the Honourable Mr Justice Richard Goldstone, supported by a big staff of lawyers and senior police officers, to get to the bottom of the political mayhem – but none of this seemed to be worth the paper it was written on. The violence raged on, the insults and allegations flying, the ANC blaming Inkatha, Inkatha blaming the ANC, the government blaming both of them. The president told parliament that sixty thousand troops were deployed to stop this black-on-black violence, that the ANC had launched over six thousand attacks on the security forces and had killed 130 policemen.

But midst the clamour the pillars of apartheid came down: the government repealed the Group Areas Act, the Black Lands Acts, the Internal Security Act. Habeas corpus was restored, and now black people could buy land and live anywhere they liked. And then desegregation of education began. And the right wing was in an uproar, bombs exploded at several schools, the Conservative Party announced that blacks who bought in white areas would be dispossessed when their party came to power. The government upgraded existing black leaseholds in the townships to freehold, 500,000 hectares of state land was given to black farmers, plus a further 100,000 hectares repossessed from white farmers who had not repaid their loans. It was a massive act of magnanimity, but the ANC demanded that all farmers who could not repay their loans immediately should be bankrupted and their farms distributed. The Farmers Agricultural Union vowed to take up arms.

Jesus, why does the ANC make such an inflammatory demand at a time like this? The ANC knows a valid loan cannot be called in on a whim – so it's an inflammatory scare tactic and thoroughly irresponsible.

'*Outrageously* irresponsible,' Katrina said angrily when she came home. 'They'll bring a hornets' nest about their ears. I think they *want* trouble. And *that's* why we need a volkstaat – because when the ANC takes over they'll fly in the face of the law and call in all land loans whether it's legal or not.'

That night she telephoned her parents. She emerged from her study half an hour later, grim-faced: 'Everybody's up in arms. Pa's gone into Brits to a farmers' meeting. They're talking war, all right.' She gave a tense sigh. 'So, I'm going up tomorrow for a family discussion. They think De Klerk is a traitor, and the only way to deal with a traitor is to rebel – *that's* what they're talking about tonight in Brits, you can bet.'

'But is your family in debt to the Land Bank?'

'All farmers are in debt to the Land Bank, Luke. And there's been no rain this year.'

'But deeply in debt?'

She said apologetically: 'Family business.'

The next evening she telephoned to say she would not be home until the day after next. 'Big indaba, the brothers are here, so are half the farmers in the area. Congratulate yourself you're not – the Boer War is being refought, no Englishman would be safe. How're you, darling?' She sounded tense and tired.

'How're you, is the point.'

'Very busy trying to pour oil on troubled waters. These guys are girding their loins for war, and I'm scared.' She took a tense breath. 'Okay, I must go now, back into the fray, more oil to be poured.'

'Katrina – are the De la Reys going to be okay over this Land Bank business?'

'The De la Reys,' Katrina said, 'are in deep shit. Unless we're very lucky we're *all* going to end up in my cottage in Orania! Okay, got to go now. Bye, I love you.'

She arrived back looking tired and worried. She kissed him then leant back in his arms.

'Congratulate your heroine. My oil worked – for the moment. The rebellion is postponed. Ask me no more, all confidential. *But* – ' she turned and walked towards the house – 'I'm going to have to sell this

653

place. Fast. To save the ranch. My brothers are selling their houses too. I've already been to the estate agents and put it on the market.'

Mahoney was astonished. 'How much have you put it on for?'

'It's worth every bit of three hundred thousand, but I'll take two hundred for a quick sale.'

'*That* urgent?'

'That urgent. Now, have we got anything to drink in this house?'

He followed her inside. 'Kate, I'm going to buy this house.'

She slumped her forehead against his shoulder and giggled. 'Oh no you're not! This is a De la Rey problem and we'll solve it. Oh no – how are we going to bargain, you and me?'

'I'll give you three hundred thousand for it.'

'Oh no! I'd never get that much in this chaos and I'm not taking your money.' She kissed him hard. 'And can we please stop talking about it? I've been thinking about it for months. The ranch has been in debt for years.' She slumped into an armchair.

The next day Mahoney walked to the nearest estate agent's office. In the window was a photograph of Katrina's house: the asking price was R275,000, 'for quick sale'. He went inside.

'I want to buy that place. Through a nominee. Subject to the condition that the present occupants rent it back off me.'

An hour later he returned soberly to the house. Well, he was committed now. As he walked in Katrina called out. He found her sitting tearfully at her desk.

'Well,' she blurted, 'I think I've sold it!' And she burst into tears.

Mahoney feigned astonishment. 'So fast! God, you're *lucky*. What did you get?'

'Two hundred and seventy thousand,' she sobbed.

'That's wonderful!'

'I *know*,' she wailed.

'Have you accepted it?'

'I said I wanted to talk to you about it . . . '

'Well, you get your sweet ass round there right now and sign!'

She sobbed: 'But there is a bright side. He wants us to rent it back from him for a year – for only a thousand rands a month.'

'That's a *bargain*. Grab it, woman.'

'*But what about my beautiful house?*' she wailed.

'Cry all the way to the bank.'

She cried all the way to the estate agency. Over a long boozy lunch at the Steak House to celebrate she said: 'Oh darling, such a weight has fallen off my shoulders. This deal will keep the wolf from Dagbreek's door. And that's very important – and not only to me. Because, believe me, Dagbreek is a very emotional focal point out there in the Western Transvaal because Pa's such a big wheel. If Dagbreek were forced into bankruptcy and dished out to the blacks the fat would be in the fire.' She shook her head. 'If the government doesn't roll over these loans and give those guys another year of grace, oh boy.' She took his hand across the table. 'So today is very good news . . .'

But there was plenty more bad news. That week half a million civil servants announced that the government could not rely on their loyalty unless their jobs in the new South Africa were guaranteed.

Katrina said: 'And they can paralyse the country. Paralyse the airports, the railways, harbours, hospitals, schools, police, courts – and the security forces. One man can paralyse a whole ministry by putting a glitch into the computer system. Imagine what they could do to the Income Tax Department.'

And the economy was in dire straits, the Reserve Bank warned that unemployment would make South Africa ungovernable in five years because the black population was growing at 2.5 per cent per annum: 16.3 million blacks were living below the 'minimum living levels', 45 per cent of blacks were unemployed, Operation Hunger was feeding 1.6 million people daily, including 20,000 whites.

The cause of it all was sanctions and the economic boundaries created by 'Separate Development': the chickens of apartheid had come home to roost. South Africa needed massive foreign investment; the chairman of the mighty Anglo-American Corporation said South Africa could be an economic miracle like the Pacific Rim, absorbing all its unemployed, if sanctions were lifted and the violence ended – but still the ANC cried out that sanctions must remain 'until the reform process is irreversible'.

'But it *is* irreversible,' Mahoney groaned. 'How can the government go backwards now? All the pillars of apartheid legislation have been repealed!'

'Mandela himself,' Splinter said, 'still does not have the vote.'

'But before that there's got to be a new constitution – that's what the negotiations are going to be about. If De Klerk went back on the reform process now the world would come down on him like a ton of bricks!'

'You think that would worry the right wing? The AWB? The Conservative Party? The Boerestaat Party and the Wit Wolwe and the other forty-odd splinter groups? There could be a military coup tomorrow. Of course sanctions must continue, we need them as a stick to wave at government.'

'What about the youth whose heads are full of expectations – another two million are entering the job market next year, but they'll find nothing because of sanctions. What's Mr Mandela going to do about that little problem? Does he want to inherit the ruins?'

Trade delegations from fifty countries visited South Africa, but none invested because of the violence. But a number of sanctions were lifted that year: the ANC was outraged and announced that when they ruled the country they would be 'reluctant to repay international loans made to the present government'. Then they announced that they would make all whites pay one-third of all their assets as a tax to redress the imbalances created by apartheid. And the Congress of South African Trade Unions, the ANC ally, announced they would strive for a socialist South Africa despite the collapse of communism. They mounted 885 strikes that year. There was an international outcry denouncing all this 'archaic thinking', and President de Klerk grimly assured the world that he would never agree to a new constitution which permitted such 'provenly failed practices'. And then the government introduced VAT and the ANC went into spasm and mounted a two-day general strike. There was massive intimidation which left eighty-four blacks dead at one mine alone, and the country lost two billion rand in production. And all the time the violence, and Mandela cried out that elements in the police were a 'killing machine acting in terms of Mr de Klerk's wishes.'

Then the trial of Winnie Mandela began, on charges of the kidnapping and murder of Stompie Seipei, the fourteen-year-old activist who'd died at the hands of her Mandela United Football Club.

'Now *there*,' Mahoney said, 'is a piece of good news.'

There on the television screens were the chanting mobs of ANC supporters outside the Supreme Court, the limousine arriving to roars of applause, Winnie Mandela stepping out, beaming, clenched fist aloft, dressed to kill, Nelson Mandela beside her looking sombre. Mahoney felt sorry for the man. He was conducting himself with the dignity befitting his office as president of the ANC, but Winnie was making a spectacle of the event, she looked like a woman who did not believe any judge would dare convict her now.

The case against Winnie Mandela was strong, and it got stronger every day, but each day Winnie emerged from the Supreme Court to the roars of her supporters, beaming, her clenched fist aloft. And then the State closed its case and Winnie Mandela got into the witness box. She denied everything, denied her Mandela United Football Club was her own hit squad, denied she had ordered Stompie Seipei's kidnapping and beating, denied she was even in Johannesburg that day. Under cross-examination she was shown to be a 'composed and unblushing liar', as the judge put it in his judgement. She was convicted of kidnapping and being an accessory after the fact to assault and sentenced to six years' imprisonment. But when she emerged from the court, on bail pending appeal, she was beaming and giving her clenched fist salute to her roaring supporters. But Nelson Mandela looked very sombre indeed.

'Lord. She's just been convicted of an awful crime and she laughs about it, for the whole world to see. She's worth a million dollars to the government in adverse publicity for the ANC.'

Katrina watched the woman on the screen. 'The Afrikaner just won't accept a woman like that as First Lady.'

'I think,' Mahoney said, 'that Mandela will have to dump her.'

'But he's devoted to her. For twenty-seven years she's been the only woman he had to think about.'

'The ANC will make him dump her – this is bad news for them.'

And there was more bad news.

That night Hugo telephoned. He said grimly: 'Well, my friend, the police are suing us over our hit squad story. The documents have just been served on us. General Krombrink is suing me and *Vryburgher* for saying Badenhorst got his murder orders from him. You'll be sued next. Three million rands he wants, plus costs.'

Mahoney stared across the room, aghast. And he felt the cold hand of bankruptcy on his gut. Then he felt his lawyer's blood rise. He slapped the desk and said: 'This isn't bad news – this is good! *Good*. This gives us a second chance to prove our story. The commission of inquiry whitewashed the police – now we've got another chance!'

Hugo said: 'And if we fail we're fucked.'

'But we *won't* fail. Our story is *true*. Badenhorst is telling the *truth*. Think *positively*.'

That night he explained it to a very worried Katrina. 'Look, Krombrink's suing *us*, so *he's* got to prove that our story – Badenhorst's story – is *untrue*. The burden of proof is on him – *the police* – to prove to the court that he did *not* give Badenhorst his orders.' He spread his hands. 'How does Krombrink prove that? The best he can do is to take the oath and say it's a pack of lies. And maybe produce something like a diary to show he was out of town that day – an alibi. Big deal. But all *we've* got to prove is that on a balance of probabilities Badenhorst is telling the *truth*. *Why* would Badenhorst admit to committing murder if it wasn't *true*?'

Katrina massaged her brow. 'As *long*,' she said, 'as he doesn't make an asshole of himself in the witness box again. Otherwise we're ruined.'

The telephone rang, and Mahoney's pulse tripped when he heard the voice. Patti said, from England: 'I've just heard about Krombrink suing *Vryburgher*. And I want you to know that I'm on your side. Like with money, for legal fees?' She added, before he could protest: 'It doesn't matter whose money. Who do you think is paying Krombrink's legal fees? The police. And where do the police get their money from? The taxpayer. So there'd be nothing wrong with you accepting help from the ANC, Luke, as we were involved in this case from the beginning. But call it my money, if you like – it's *my* money.'

Mahoney's eyes moistened. 'I really appreciate that, Patti. But Krombrink will only go after me if he wins against *Vryburgher*. Let's wait and see. The important thing now is that *Vryburgher* win.'

'But for that we need Badenhorst to be a much better witness than he was before. Will you be coming to London for that part of the trial? The guy sure needs coaching – and he's *your* witness, you got the story from him. He respects your opinion.'

'It's not for me to coach a witness, Patti. Just tell him to be calm. Not to get flustered. No exaggerations. And if he doesn't know the answer, say so. Just be entirely truthful.'

She cried: 'Luke, the guy needs *you* to tell him. A lot hangs on this case – for him, for you, for the newspaper, for the ANC. For South Africa – we must have the *truth*. Look, your airfare and expenses will be arranged – '

'Patti,' Mahoney said, '*Vryburgher*'s lawyer will give him the advice he needs. Tell him to remember we *know* the police are lying. It's *Krombrink* who needs to be nervous, not Badenhorst. The truth will out.'

She cried: 'And if it doesn't you're going to be very poor indeed! *Think* about it.'

It did not bear thinking about.

But there was some good news. The wind of change that was blowing in the south was being felt in other parts of Africa and democracy was breaking out all over. In Zambia, Kenneth Kaunda, president since 1964, was swept from power in a general election, leaving a ruined

Marxist economy behind him. In Kenya President Daniel-arap-Moi was forced to permit multi-party politics. In Zimbabwe, President Mugabe was facing increasing resistance to his rule, and the same was happening to President-for-life of Malawi, Dr Hastings Banda. In Russia, President Gorbachev formally disbanded the Communist Party, causing the South African Communist Party, the ANC's ally, to go into a spasm of embarrassment, prompting Joe Slovo, the Secretary General, to accuse Gorbachev of 'colluding in the chorus of vilification of Lenin, the greatest world revolutionary', attacking him for the 'indecent haste with which he is rushing to make friends with racist Pretoria'. And he rushed into print with an essay titled 'Has Socialism Failed?', writing: 'We firmly believe in the future of socialism. Marxism remains valid . . . an indispensable guide. The weaknesses which have emerged are the results of distortion. They do not naturally flow from Marxism, whose core is essentially humane and democratic.'

Humane? Democratic?

The Western world guffawed – and that was bad news for the ANC.

And then the trial of General Krombrink versus *Vryburgher* began in the Supreme Court in Johannesburg.

And that, too, was good news. At the end of the first day of Krombrink's evidence Mahoney was jubilant.

'He's a very bad witness under cross-examination!' he exulted when he got home to Katrina. 'He's blustering and stammering and shifting! He denies that Badenhorst's ever been to his house – and claims Badenhorst knows what the inside looks like because you can see into it from the street – but today it was proved that you can't! And he can't explain how Badenhorst knows what his study looks like – the photographs on the wall, et cetera.'

The second day Mahoney came home even more jubilant. '*Vryburgher*'s lawyer made mincemeat of Krombrink!' He punched his palm. 'All it needs now is for Badenhorst to make a good impression.'

Two days later the court flew to London to hear Erik Badenhorst's evidence. The next night the telephone rang.

'He was excellent!' Patti cried. 'He's calm and convincing – I'm sure he's making a good impression on the judge, he's standing up to cross-examination very well. *Vryburgher*'s lawyers are very pleased!'

Mahoney closed his eyes. '*Oh thank God.*'

'They expect to fly back to South Africa tomorrow night. Judgment will be next week, after the court's heard argument.'

Mahoney took a deep, happy breath.

'Patti? I'm very grateful for all your moral support.'

'Think nothing of it – I just wish you and Katrina had come over for the excitement, I'd have loved to see you. How is she?'

'She's well. Working hard at Volkswag.'

'And as beautiful as ever? Well, give her my love.'

He was touched by her concern. And overwhelmed with relief. So was Katrina. That night they drank a very good bottle of champagne.

'She's a *very* nice person, Luke. A loyal friend to you. And when she comes back we're going to be very nice to her.'

But despite the good news, it was a very worrying week waiting.

There was grim-faced tension in the Supreme Court on judgment day, as the plaintiff, General Krombrink, and his cohorts, the South African police, gathered in the courtroom alongside the defendant, the editor of *Vryburgher*. On today's judgment hung the credibility of the South African police: and the credibility of the South African government. Did the South African police commit murder, or did they not? Did, therefore, the South African government sanction murder, or not? Was Daniel going to hang or not? Had *Vryburgher* and Luke Mahoney made assholes of themselves, or not? And were they going to be bankrupted?

Mahoney was sick with tension as he filed into the Supreme Court that morning. Pressmen from around the world were there for this cause célèbre. Then there was the rap on the door, the registrar called 'Silence in Court', and the judge walked in.

Mahoney sat beside Katrina and Hugo, his elbows on his knees, his brow in his hands, listening to the judge's summary of the evidence with dread in his heart. Then a smile began to creep across his face.

It was clear the way the judgement was going: Krombrink's evidence was being torn apart, his demeanour unfavourably commented on, his evasiveness described. And then: 'By contrast, I find the evidence of Erik Badenhorst to be demonstrably true for the reasons that follow . . .'

Mahoney could not bear to sit still anymore. He got up impulsively and hurried out of the courtroom. He reached the corridor and slumped against the wall, a tearful smile all over his face. Katrina emerged, and clutched him joyfully.

'*We're not going to be bankrupt!*' she sobbed.

Inside the courtroom the judge was concluding his reasons for believing Badenhorst. He ended: 'Accordingly, this action is dismissed, with costs.'

And the noise broke out. The pressmen scrambling to file their stories, the editor of *Vryburgher* congratulating his lawyers, General Krombrink berating his. Mahoney slumped against the wall and held a tearful Katrina tight.

'We're not going to be bankrupt!'

That night the mother of all parties was held at *Vryburgher's* offices. In the midst of the noisy festivities the telephone rang for Mahoney. It was a tearful Patti Gandhi, calling to congratulate him: 'I thought I'd find you there!'

'Don't congratulate me, I didn't do anything.'

'Except rush in where angels fear to tread! Is Katrina there?'

'Of course she's here.'

'Let me speak to her . . .'

Ten minutes later the telephone rang again. Again it was for Mahoney. 'Hullo?' he shouted happily above the noise.

There was a moment's pause; then came the sound of a wolf howling.

'*Fuck off!*' Mahoney roared, and slammed down the receiver.

And then, at last, towards the end of that good big bad year, despite all the violence, despite all the furore about hit squads, despite the accusations of double agendas and Third Forces, it was announced that the Great Indaba would start its first session the week before Christmas. And it was to be called CODESA, the Convention for a Democratic South Africa.

And the world heaved a sigh of relief.

It was the month before CODESA started that Patti Gandhi came back.

97

Her faxed letter was addressed to Katrina.

> *Darling*
> *I am bursting with excitement at coming home next week –*
> *forever! No more assignments abroad. Please don't meet me at the*
> *airport – I know how busy you are – but I insist you both come to*
> *my house-warming party the following night. There will be all*
> *kinds of interesting people, some top ANC brass, SACP, DP – and a*
> *lot of odds and sods of all hues and political persuasions. I believe*
> *those of us who're going to face each other across the table at*
> *CODESA can only benefit from knowing each other beforehand.*
> *And, I'm dying to see you guys. So don't let me down!*
> *Love*
> *P*

'I think we should meet her at the airport,' Katrina said. 'We owe her that, after her offers to help us. And after all she's been through.'

Mahoney sighed. 'Kate, you've got to stop feeling guilty for what the government did to her all those years ago. And remember she *was* guilty of smuggling explosives, even if she didn't think it was going to be used to blow up innocent people.'

'Okay, but today she's a heroine, and she protected you.'

'Indeed, but if you want to meet her at the airport, do so because you like her, not out of guilt.'

'I do like her. Okay, I feel guilt too, not least because I've deprived her of you, but she's a gutsy lady who's been through hell and I want to help her. And she finds it very difficult to make friends – she's a loner, and twenty-four years in jail has made her more so. She told me at the Wild Coast. She's desperate for friends.'

'Yes, she was a loner at school. The only Indian girl in town. That's what started her off as a rebel.'

'Well, she's not a rebel now, she's on the side of the new big battalions, the boot's on the other foot. And that's another good reason for befriending her: it's good diplomacy, Volkswag needs all the friends in high places it can get at CODESA.'

Mahoney thought she'd need a hell of a lot more than Patti Gandhi on her side for that one. 'I wonder where she's bought a house? Somewhere very nice, I imagine.'

'I wonder if Mandela himself will be at her party?'

'That would be a coup.'

Katrina smiled. 'Like your presence will be, darling. The famous author who wrote the famous book that made her famous.'

'Ex-author. People have forgotten my name.'

'Who's going to make a hell of a come-back with his new book.' She smiled. 'Patti's dying to show you off at her party.' She kissed his ear and growled: 'I don't mind it going to your head, but not to your loins.'

Mahoney was surprised to see a number of pressmen at the airport. But Katrina was not. 'After all she did make a hell of a name with that Miss South Africa hoohah. And her dramatic trial. And all her other trials. And that name does happen to be Gandhi. And she *is* very beautiful.'

She was very beautiful indeed as she came sweeping through the glass doors, a porter pushing her laden trolley. And, again she made Mahoney's heart miss a beat. Her sexual impact was astonishing.

She was wearing a lime silk trouser-suit that clung at her waist to accentuate her bust and her perfect hips and her long legs, sexy high-heeled sandals, her black hair cascading. She was clutching a large straw sun-hat to her head, wearing large sunglasses and her wide, dazzling smile. The cameras flashed, and she rushed to greet the black men going forward to her. She flung her arms around the first one, laughing, and Mahoney was surprised to recognise him as Chris Hani, the vaunted commander-in-chief of MK. Then a stocky white man was embracing her with big smiles, and it was Ronnie Kasrils, the head of MK's Military Intelligence. Then a pretty black girl was embracing her, and Katrina said: 'Recognise her? That's Zindzi, Mandela's daughter – '

'Patti's bigger-time than I realised,' Mahoney muttered.

Then she turned and her face lit up afresh as she spotted Mahoney and Katrina. '*Luke! Kate!*'

She rushed to them, her arms wide, laughing. '*Oh, thank you for coming.*' She flung her arms around Katrina and gave her a big kiss, sparkling, laughing hullos and how-wonderfuls, then she turned into Mahoney's arms. '*Oh thank you for coming to meet me – you shouldn't have bothered . . .*'

The cameras flashed as she planted a big kiss on his cheek and she flung her other arm around Katrina and laughed at the cameras: '*This* is the man who wrote that wonderful book *Alms for Oblivion* – and *this* is the lucky lady – ' she squeezed – 'who looks after him now as he writes the screenplay for the movie. Watch out for it!'

A pressman shouted: 'How about a photograph of you all together, with Mr Hani and Mr Kasrils.'

'Yes!' Patti grabbed Hani's hand, and Kasrils', tugged them to a grinning Mahoney and Katrina. She flung one arm around Katrina and the other around Hani, and the photographer asked Mahoney and Kasrils to crowd in, fling their arms around everybody's and say *cheese*.

A portrait of the new South Africa? Mahoney thought to himself.

The ANC officials drove Patti to her new home. Mahoney and Katrina parted in the car park: they had come in separate vehicles because Katrina had to go on to her office.

Mahoney said: 'It was a great home-coming for her.'

'Yes. And I'm glad I was there to put in a good word for Afrikanerdom.'

'When those pictures appear in the press, will it upset the Afrikaner Volkswag? You arm in arm with Hani and Kasrils?'

She smiled. 'Darling, it may upset some Afrikaners, but not the Volkswag. We've decided to rejoin the human race.'

98

Patti's house was in the prestigious suburb of Illovo. The sweeping drive was lined with cars. The garden was lit up by flickering candles. There was a hubbub from a multitude of faces, white, brown, black and yellow. Waiters circulated with trays. A maid admitted Mahoney and Katrina, and led them through the throng to Patti on the terrace. '*Darlings*!' Patti cried.

She was radiant in a turquoise sari, her hair piled up on top of her head, gold earrings dangling, her smile brilliant. She took their hands and threaded them through the guests, heading them down onto the lawn. And Mahoney was astonished to find himself being introduced to Nelson Mandela. 'How do you do, Mr Mandela. A belated welcome back to the world.'

Mandela astonished him further by saying: 'Ah, Mr Mahoney, the man who wrote that book. And Miss Gandhi, I believe, is the heroine?'

'If in fictionally glamorised form, Nelson,' Patti laughed.

'On the contrary,' Mandela said, 'I don't think the book did you justice, good though it is!'

'I bet you say that to all the girls, Nelson!'

'Never fails!' He turned to Katrina. 'And you're one of the famous De la Reys, I believe?'

Katrina grinned. 'Without the voorlaaier and the laager, Mr Mandela.'

'*I'm mighty relieved to hear it.*' Everybody laughed. Then Mandela solemnly took her hand in both of his: 'I'm so glad we're talking to each other at last, Miss de la Rey. I look forward to seeing you at CODESA. If the rest of the delegates are half as charming as you, it's going to be a delightful new South Africa.'

Mahoney had been taken around, introduced, had shaken many hands, even autographed a few old copies of his book. He said to Ronnie Kasrils: 'Tell me, are you guys serious about nationalization?'

Ronnie said: 'Deadly serious.'

'But,' Mahoney said, 'what about the failure of communism world-wide? Doesn't that put you off?'

Kasrils said: 'Communism has not failed. It is mankind that has failed communism. Marxist-Leninism remains an invincible, logical economic and political theory. And communism has not failed in China, my friend. Nor in North Korea, nor Vietnam. Nor Cuba.'

Not failed? Jesus. 'Communism's successful there, is it?'

'Though they've made mistakes, like we all have.'

'So, South Africa is going to be a communist country?'

Kasrils put his hand on Mahoney's shoulder. 'Don't worry, we're not going to take away your swimming pool. Or your cook-boy. That's kid's stuff, Luke – it's the mines we're after, the banks, the insurance companies, Anglo-American.'

'And the press?'

'There will be freedom of the press.'

'Even if they criticise you?'

'Provided the criticism is fair.'

'Like in Russia? And China?'

'We will have an open society, an open government. Democracy.'

'Lenin's idea of democracy is a dictatorship by the proletariat, the worker. Is that what you'll have?'

'We will permit opposition parties to function.'

'For how long, Ronnie?'

'Forever, Luke.'

'Or until such time as the proletariat want to change the constitution? And make it a one-party state.'

'Well, the people are sovereign, they can change anything, Luke.'

'The constitution should be sovereign. As in America.'

'Even in America the people can change their constitution.'

'Not fundamental democratic rights. Such a change would itself be unconstitutional and therefore illegal.'

Mandela had left. Mahoney saw Katrina in conversation with somebody he didn't know. He wandered over the lawn to Chris Hani, commander-in-chief of MK. 'So, what's new, Mr Hani?'

'Call me Chris. Hey, you're the guy who wrote *Alms for Oblivion* – tell me, are you still on our side?'

Mahoney wondered if he'd heard that right. 'On the Communist Party's side?'

'The ANC alliance. The Struggle.'

Mahoney said: 'I'm on the side of justice and fair play. That was clear in *Alms*.'

'But you joined the ANC once, in Botswana.'

Mahoney was surprised such a senior official knew that detail. 'Yes, twenty-odd years ago. But your guys gave me such a tough time screening me, I thought better of it. And they intended sending us straight back to South Africa, into the lion's den, even though we were on the run from the police. And Patti, to her credit, did not try to dissuade me when I refused. In fact she tricked me into leaving the country. She obeyed orders, went back and immediately paid dearly for it.'

Chris grinned. 'Didn't have the guts, huh? But you had the guts to fight for Moise Tshombe in the Congo.'

So the guy probably had read the book. 'I fought for Tshombe for three reasons, Chris. One, I was penniless. Two, I was joining my equivalent of the Foreign Legion, to get over Patti. Three, Tshombe was the legal prime minister of the entire Congo, lawfully elected, not a rebel anymore, and he was fighting against the communists and their Simbas.'

Chris Hani smiled. 'You'd fight for Tshombe, but not for us?'

Mahoney frowned. 'The two situations were somewhat different.'

Chris Hani smiled: 'The moral difference escapes me. Tell me – your lady-friend is demanding an Afrikaner volkstaat. Do you consider that Zululand, for example, would have a right to secede from the new South Africa if they don't get what they want at the Great Indaba? And the Boers?'

Mahoney saw the connection with Tshombe. 'It would depend entirely on the circumstances. If the constitution were unfair, or if the rest of South Africa became ungovernable, they may *acquire* a legal and moral right to secede. That's International Law.'

'And do you think that may happen?'

'I sincerely hope not. But anybody who doesn't consider it's a possibility is deluding himself, given the political climate and the history of the Zulus and the Boers.'

'Hmmm,' Hani said. 'Your lady-friend, Katrina – charming woman. But she seems to think it will happen if the Boers and the Zulus are not granted an independent state. I hope you're doing your best to dissuade her.'

Mahoney smiled. 'Katrina hasn't got to be dissuaded. She's simply reporting what she believes the Boer nation will do. I *hope* she's wrong, but Katrina is a hell of a smart lady. She knows her people much better than you and I do. I trust her judgement. And I think the Afrikaner will only be pushed so far.'

'And what,' Hani asked, 'is that point?'

Mahoney said: 'The Afrikaner is a legalistic soul. He believes in his dominee and political leaders, and expects them to be upright men. And he believes in his God-given right to be an Afrikaner. At the point where that right is taken away, he will rebel. And that point is reached when, *one*, CODESA refuses to give him his volkstaat, and *two*, *this* government, his own Afrikaner government, hands over power to a black government.'

Hani nodded. 'So you think the Afrikaner should be granted his volkstaat at CODESA?'

Mahoney said: 'Not what the Conservative Party is demanding, the old Boer republics. But the volkstaat that the Volkswag wants, the northern Cape, is a reasonable demand.'

'*Reasonable*?' Hani echoed. 'A perpetuation of apartheid?'

'Not at all. Speak to Katrina. There'll be no apartheid, no forced removals, no discrimination. The Coloureds and blacks already there are Afrikaners by culture.'

This was evidently news to Hani. 'Then why the hell don't they just muck in with the rest of us in the new South Africa?'

'Because they want to govern themselves. Like the Jews want Israel.' He added: 'And it would be a bargain for the ANC.'

'*Bargain*? You think the Afrikaner can be trusted to keep any bargain about no apartheid? Why would it be a bargain?'

'Because, by giving away a piece of semi-desert you would take all the wind out of the Afrikaner's sails. He can't complain anymore. He's got his political address if he wants it. If he elects to stay in the new South Africa, he'll just have to muck in.'

'And you think the Conservative Party and the rest of the right wing will be content with that? They want their old Boer republics.'

'Tough. Can't have them. Take the northern Cape, or leave it, sir. That's what you say, Chris.'

Hani snorted. 'And then they fight. So why give them anything in the first place?'

'Because it's the smart, diplomatic thing to do.'

'And give them a military base to fight us from?'

Mahoney said: 'Chris, if they rebel they'll have *plenty* of bases. The Mozambique border? The Botswana border? Zululand border?' He shook his head. 'But most of the Afrikaners would not fight, Chris, if they feel they've been given a chance of self-determination. Only the hard core, the bitter-enders.'

Chris Hani took a sip of his drink. 'And on whose side will your Katrina stand when the rebellion starts?'

Mahoney smiled. 'Ask her. But I assure you she's not a warmonger, she's a peacemaker.'

'And on whose side will *you* be?'

'That's the big drama of South Africa, isn't it? The *tragedy* of Africa. On whose side are you when the bloodshed starts? On the side of law and order, or on the side of justice?'

'There's a difference?'

'Of course there is. For decades *you* have been on the side of justice, but not on the side of law and order.'

'But in the new South Africa they will be the same thing.'

Mahoney raised his finger. 'That's the other half of the god-awful African tragedy, Chris. Nobody's sure they can believe you on that one. Just like you guys feel you can't trust the Afrikaner. We only have to look at the rest of Africa to be very worried indeed. One-party states.'

Hani said: 'South Africa was also virtually a one-party state. The white party. And Mandela has said that he's spent his life fighting white discrimination and he'll spend the rest fighting black discrimination. But you haven't answered my question: if the Afrikaners start a civil war, on whose side will you be?'

Mahoney looked him in the eye, with a smile. 'On the side of justice,' he answered. 'And I'm not sure which side will have that.'

Hani smiled. 'That means you'll be on our side. We could use a popular novelist. Let's have lunch some time. Bring Katrina.'

Mahoney detected the hand of Patti in this. *'Sure.'*

Katrina was talking to Ronnie Kasrils. Mahoney saw Hugo talking to Richard Barker's girlfriend, Janet. Hugo beckoned.

He said: 'If the army has been training Inkatha warriors on the Caprivi Strip, there's no reason why they shouldn't also be supplying arms to Renamo. But I think I'm altering Richard Barker's theory on that. I think those arms Richard saw were destined for the right wing.'

Mahoney frowned. 'But Richard saw Renamo soldiers pick them up.'

Hugo held up a finger: 'Renamo were picking up those arms on behalf of the right wing. Renamo are hand-in-glove with the militarised right wing! Renamo are bandits and hire-guns who'll happily fight for the Afrikaner rebels. Look: Richard's Land-Rover was stolen in Swaziland after he escaped, remember. Well, it's been found. The police picked it up at a roadblock during Operation Iron Fist in Soweto. Being driven by a known car-thief. A false floor had been welded onto the back part, obviously for smuggling purposes. The cops traced the vehicle back to Janet through the engine serial number. The thief said he'd stolen it from a farm in the Western Transvaal. The police checked out the farmer, called Van Niekerk, but he denied all knowledge. But Richard's insurance company suspected Van Niekerk was involved in a cross-border car-theft ring, so they sent a private investigator to check him out, a guy called Wainwright. He found the Land-Rover's tracks all over the farm, so Van Niekerk is lying. And Van Niekerk is a commando leader in the AWB. The tracks led to a dry stream where there was freshly dug earth. The insurance company is sending Wainwright back tomorrow night to see what's buried there. They don't trust the police to investigate this. And I'm going with Wainwright. Because what I think we'll *find* – ' he tapped Mahoney happily – 'is *arms*.'

Mahoney frowned. 'But, the plane was coming from the direction of South Africa. If people in the army were delivering arms to the AWB, why would they deliver to Mozambique?'

'Because,' Hugo said, 'a parachute drop direct into the Transvaal would be detected by Civil Aviation radar. And the arms came all the way from Angola. Mozambique is wild and it's largely under Renamo control, so it's safe to drop the arms there. The security forces and Renamo were hand-in-glove. So if my theory is correct, Renamo picked up the arms on the instructions of right-wingers and delivered them somewhere along the Mozambique border. From there they got distributed inside South Africa. And Richard's vehicle was used to transport some of them. And they're buried on Van Niekerk's farm. Waiting for the revolution. And *I*,' he tapped his breast, 'intend to nail him.' He smiled: 'Are you in?'

Mahoney grinned, 'Of course I'm in!'

The party had thinned down to a dozen guests. But the buffet table was still laden with food. Mahoney said to Katrina: 'Did you have much of a talk with Joe Slovo?'

'A few minutes. Quite a nice old guy, pity he's a communist.'

'Did you ask him how he felt about the good old Berlin Wall coming down? And dear Mr Gorbachev?'

'I'm too polite, I'm trying to make *friends*. But I asked him about his economic policy, and he turned the question around, asking me Volkswag's policies.'

'Well, I don't think you missed much. Manage to talk the dear man into giving you a volkstaat?'

'Not yet, but I got an A-plus for Charm and Effort, which was the purpose of the exercise tonight. No, he's dead against the idea – he's even hotly against any form of federalism.' She tucked in her chin and made her voice deep: 'He wants a *unified* South Africa. Tribalism must *end*. Zulus and Xhosa and Tswana and Venda and Shangaan and Afrikaner and English must all forget what they are and become *Azanians*! And winner takes *all* – none of this power-sharing crap that De Klerk is talking about.'

Mahoney smiled. 'Winner-takes-all, with the communists dominating the ANC from within. Great. A silent coup. Did he ask you what would happen if you don't get your volkstaat?'

'No, but they're expecting all kinds of trouble from the Zulus.'

'How very perspicacious, so he's right about something.' Mahoney emptied his glass. 'Do you think it's too early to leave?'

Katrina said, 'I think Patti's rather upset about so many people leaving early, half the food's untouched. It's only nine thirty, I feel sorry for her, but I'm whacked.'

She went through the house looking for Patti. She went to the main bedroom where all the ladies' coats were. Then the kitchen. She spied her in the darkened pantry. 'Patti?'

Patti turned with a bright smile. 'Hullo!'

Katrina peered at her through the gloom. 'What's wrong, lady?'

Patti tossed back her hair, and dabbed her eye. 'Nothing! Thank you for coming, everybody was delighted to meet you, even Nelson told me, and Chris Hani. So!' She forced her bright smile: 'Have you also come to say goodnight?'

Katrina's heart went out to her. '*No*, I was just wondering if I could help you with something?'

Patti leant back against the refrigerator. She sniffed. 'Fetch yet more food? Seen it all out there?' She grinned tearfully. 'You've come to say goodnight, haven't you?'

'*No.*'

'Yes, you have.' Then she put her hands to her face. 'Oh, I'm sorry, I'm being a fool. I was so excited about coming home I made the mistake of imagining everybody was equally excited.'

Katrina put her arms around her. 'It's a lovely party, Patti!' She held her tight. 'Don't cry.'

Patti slid her arms around her. Then she tossed back her hair and smiled tearfully. 'I'm being an awful *girl* about this. Guess I'm tired too. Jet-lag, this whole thing was a mistake. But it seemed such a good idea and I wanted to come home with a *bang*.'

Katrina said: 'How about meeting me for lunch tomorrow? Or dinner's better, Luke's got to go away.'

Patti snorted wanly. 'When we've got all this food going begging? Come here for dinner, we'll go out another time.' She opened a drawer and pulled out a plastic bag. 'Here – ' she picked up a cold chicken and shoved it in – 'take this for lunch.'

'*No –*'

'*Please.*' She kissed her finger and put it on Katrina's lips. 'Please. And now,' she smiled brightly, 'I'd better get back to my humdinger of a party!'

99

Steve Wainwright was a tough, clean-cut man, about forty years old. He had been in the famous Selous Scouts during the Rhodesian War. He had told them to wear tennis shoes and bring a flashlight each. And to be prepared for a five mile hike.

They went in two vehicles, Mahoney following alone in his Land-Rover. He had a map, and as the journey ground on, his concern mounted: they were getting closer and closer to the De la Rey ranch, Dagbreek. When Wainwright finally halted, on a deserted track, Mahoney estimated they were only ten miles from Dagbreek, as the crow flies. As instructed, Mahoney parked deep in the bush, and they proceeded on to Van Niekerk's farm in Wainwright's vehicle.

It was after ten o'clock when they stopped, on the banks of the dry Limpopo River. Wainwright pulled off into the bush. He produced three shovels, a pick-axe and a crowbar. 'Hope you guys know how to use them. Are you armed?'

'No,' Mahoney said.

'Mind if I verify? If there's going to be any shooting I'd rather I did it.' He quickly frisked him, then continued: 'Single file. No talking. No flashlights. If I crouch, you crouch. If I run, you run like hell after me, unless I shout "scatter".'

It was a moonless, cloudy night. They climbed through the farm fence and set off through the dark bush. There were no distant dogs to be heard. Now and again a cow loomed ahead. It was midnight when Wainwright halted. He pointed at a silhouetted kopje.

'About a mile the other side is the homestead. The streambed is just this side of the kopje. Wait here, I'm going to recce – it's just possible that the site is guarded. No talking.'

They sat down on the sand. Mahoney wondered how Katrina and Patti were getting on.

They were getting on just fine. Katrina was very relieved that Patti had cheered up; she had slept off her jet-lag and had a 'good' first day in her new ANC office. She seemed to have put her disappointing party behind her. She was getting along with the champagne.

'It wasn't *such* a bad show, was it?' Patti said.

'People only left early because it was a weekday. And I met some very important people.'

'And you made a *very* good impression, Katrina. Nelson – he phoned me today to thank me – Nelson mentioned how impressed he was with you.'

Katrina laughed. 'I don't believe he even remembers me!'

'My darling, you're very hard to forget. You're very beautiful. And Joe Slovo phoned, said how charming you were. And so did Chris.'

'Bullshit,' Katrina grinned.

'Darling, I swear by all that's holy. They knew you were coming, unofficially representing Volkswag, they're briefed on guest-lists as a matter of routine. And they were very interested to meet you. I think they thought you'd have two horns and a tail.'

'Well, you're very kind introducing me to these heavyweights.'

'It's part of my job to get to know as many people as possible in the opposite political camps. Sort of PR and intelligence-gathering combined, so that at CODESA we've got an idea who we're dealing with. Just like you want to meet our side. It's all sound diplomatic practice.' She smiled tipsily. 'But more important, you're about the only friends I've got, you and Luke, I want you guys to be part of my life and I want my people to like you.' She looked at her solemnly. 'You've no idea what a hell of a time I'm having adjusting.'

'I can imagine.'

'No, you can't, darling. But – no more talking about it. I'm free and I'm lucky to be alive. Instead of an unmarked grave I've got – ' she waved a hand – 'this lovely house, a good job, lots of money, so what the hell am I complaining about?' Her eyes moistened, then she took Katrina's hand across the table impulsively. 'Kate, promise me one thing?'

'What?' Katrina smiled.

Patti said: 'That we'll never let our political differences come between us. It's quite possible for people of opposite political persuasions to remain the best of friends, isn't it?'

'Of *course*.'

'It's even *healthy*, even if you have hell-fire rows, it's not only intellectually stimulating it's actually bonding – you end up agreeing to disagree if the friendship is important, loving each other despite the differences.' She looked at her earnestly. 'Right?'

'Right,' Katrina smiled.

Patti squeezed her hands, then sighed. 'You guys seem the only family I've got.'

Katrina's eyes moistened also. She said: 'And, you know, I don't think we're really in such opposite camps, you and I? I don't think there's anything irreconcilable between the Volkwag's demand for a reasonable volkstaat and the ANC's position. We expect to be part of the new South Africa too, in some kind of federal structure – like the United States. Economically and legally.'

Patti sighed. 'I know, darling, I know. And truth to tell I can't find much fault with it because I suspect a federation is how we'll end up after CODESA – not a unitary state. And as you pointed out at the Wild Coast it would probably be a bargain, to defuse the Afrikaner crisis. I've told Nelson so. And Joe. And Chris.'

'You have? And?'

'Oh, they won't hear a bar of it. This is off the record, but I don't want to bullshit you. Actually Nelson – who does not treat me as his closest confidante by the way – but Nelson nodded and said something to the effect that everybody was entitled to their say at CODESA, though he was against the volkstaat idea because it smacks of apartheid. And because South Africa needs the Afrikaner.' She held up a finger. '*There.* I've just given you my first piece of inside information about the ANC's thinking. Though it's doubtless nothing you didn't know already. You can tell Volkswag, but it's not for publication. Is that a deal?'

Katrina smiled. 'Deal. Though, as you say, it's nothing we don't know already.'

'Right, but it's from the horse's mouth. But – ' she grinned – 'they really like you, Kate. They're bowled over.'

Katrina threw back her head and laughed.

Wainwright came creeping back. Mahoney and Hugo followed him through the dark bush. Ten minutes later they arrived at the dry streambed. Wainwright pointed: even in the dark, Mahoney could see that the soil had recently been turned over, then covered in brush. Wainwright prodded the ground with his crowbar, demarcating the perimeter.

'Start there. I'll start here.'

They began to dig. Within minutes Mahoney was panting. But it was his shovel which struck wood first, eighteen inches below the surface. He cleared the sand with his hands. Wainwright shone his flashlight: it was plank, painted grey. '*Yes!*' They resumed digging.

A few minutes later they had uncovered the first crate. It was four feet long by two wide. On either side of it were others. Wainwright wedged the crowbar under a plank. It lifted with a loud creaking. Mahoney winced. Wainwright pulled the plank back.

They were looking at gleaming AK–47 rifles, packed tight against each other. 'Jesus.'

'Dig!'

They dug feverishly, the sandy earth flying. Fifteen minutes later they had uncovered the whole site; eight crates lay in the big shallow hole.

'There may be more underneath,' Mahoney whispered.

'This is plenty of evidence. Open a plank on each crate.'

Mahoney prised up a plank on the next crate. More AK–47 machine guns. Five minutes later he had each crate partially open. Each contained the same. 'Get out of the hole!' Wainwright pulled a small camera out of his pouch. He raised it and there was a flash. He snatched up one of the AK–47s.

'Put all the planks back and start filling in the hole.'

It was almost midnight.

It had been a good evening, but Katrina was tired now. She had tried to leave an hour ago but Patti had pressed her to stay for yet another bottle of wine, and she was anxious not to hurt her feelings. Patti was wide awake, sparkling, wanting to talk, talk, talk. 'You can't *imagine* what it was like having almost no intellectual conversation for all those years – when I came out I was positively garrulous, button-holing all and sundry and I was terribly frustrated when they couldn't talk about Gross National Product and the economic laws of Adam Smith. I was an absolute *bore*. In London I'd go to pubs alone and drink all kinds of booze in the hopes of finding somebody intelligent to talk to, then be terribly hurt when they only wanted to talk about *sex*.'

Katrina smiled. 'After twenty-four years in prison I'd have thought that sex was pretty high on your intellectual agenda.'

'Oh it was, but we can get sex whenever we want, simply by crooking our finger! And I did. And what an anti-climax it was. I'd been without a man for so long I'd forgotten how.'

'Yes. Sex must be one of the worst aspects of prison.'

Patti snorted. 'Yes, it was grim. And masturbation gets so *boring*. The only alternative was turning to other women.'

Katrina waited. Then: 'And? Did you?'

Patti twirled her wine glass, a small smile on her lovely mouth. 'I'm not a lesbian.' She grinned. 'I think Luke will confirm that. But, yes, in twenty-four years I did have two relationships. One was with a wardress. She was very nice – an Afrikaner, called Anna. She was very serious about rehabilitation of prisoners, she was studying criminology. Not like the usual dykes you find in the prison service. Anyway, when I became a "tame prisoner" I worked with her in the administration offices. She was kind. She smuggled in goodies for me, newspapers, books on different subjects I was studying. When she was transferred I really missed her. She used to come back occasionally to visit me, to cheer me up.'

'Have you seen her since you got out?'

'Not yet.' She sighed cheerfully. 'And the other one was an Indian girl who was my cellmate for a few years. She was in for manslaughter – shot her husband. Nice girl. When she was paroled I really missed her. Because we were actually living together it wasn't like the furtive affair I had with Anna.'

Katrina took a sip of wine. 'But did you . . . *love* them?'

Patti gave a smile. 'No, darling. Only lesbians fall in love. We were just good friends who needed each other physically, to make life bearable. Most women are potentially bi-sexual. That's why we're so aware of our own femininity, and other women's, why we study fashions and borrow each other's clothes – we're naturally more physically intimate with each other than men are. After all, our first imprinting is to our mother's breast.'

Katrina took a sip of wine. 'Yes, we had a long boozy discussion about this at the Wild Coast, as I recall.'

'Did we? My recollection is hazed by all the alcohol.' She smiled. 'I remember dawn breaking. And, I do remember kissing you goodnight outside my hut.'

Katrina wanted a cigarette. 'Yes. You did.'

Patti said: 'I hope I didn't offend you.'

Katrina was aware she was blushing. 'No.'

Patti was silent a moment, staring at her wine glass. Then: 'Did you like it?'

Katrina's mouth twitched as she suppressed a smile. 'I don't remember. My recollection is hazed too.'

Patti smiled widely. 'Maybe I could refresh your memory?'

She leant forward and her hand cupped Katrina's breast.

Katrina closed her eyes. She said: 'It's really time I went. Luke may be home already. And this feels somewhat incestuous.' Then she felt Patti's lips gently close on hers. Her mouth widened into a grin and she kissed Patti fleetingly hard, then stood up. She grinned. 'Not only is this incestuous it's very undiplomatic – we're facing each other at CODESA soon!'

Patti sat back and giggled. 'True!' She slapped her own wrist. 'Did you hear that, Hand? *No cheap thrills at CODESA!*'

Katrina laughed, then put her hand on Patti's shoulder. 'And now, before this conversation gets too frivolous – '

'And incestuous?' Patti grinned.

'Incestuous and serious – '

'And erotic!'

'Incestuously seriously erotic – '

'With the usual attendant solemnity!' Patti giggled.

'Before all that happens – '

'*Before we carry diplomacy too far?!*' Patti banged the table.

'*Before,*' Katrina laughed, wagging her finger, 'we fuck up CODESA and the whole of the new South Africa with extravagant diplomacy – '

'Before I talk Nelson into giving you the whole fucking Transvaal!' Patti laughed. She dropped her hands on her knees. '*Before all that comes to pass –* '

'*I must go home!*' they chorused. They threw back their heads and laughed.

'Oh.' Katrina dabbed her eyes. 'It's been a lovely evening.'

Patti dabbed her eyes too. '*Must* you go?'

'Yes, yes, *yes*.' Just then the telephone rang. 'That's probably Luke, wondering where I am.'

Patti walked into the living-room, still giggly. She picked up the portable telephone and said: 'Is this Big Bad Luke?'

There was a moment's silence. Then a bloodcurdling howl of a wolf ululated over the receiver. '*Woh-woh-woh-woh-wo-oh.*'

Patti stared, her heart knocking. Feeling the blood drain from her face. Then she turned, the receiver still to her ear, and walked back to the terrace. She looked wide-eyed at Katrina, then passed her the receiver.

Katrina put it to her ear. Then her face filled with fury. '*Fuck off!*' she yelled. She clicked off the telephone. She looked at Patti furiously. '*Bastards.*'

Patti slumped down in her chair and held her face. 'Oh God.'

Katrina grabbed her hand.

'*Bastards!*' she cried. '*Racist pig bastards!* Ignore them.'

Patti held her face. Taking deep breaths. She whispered: 'Oh God, this sort of thing terrifies me.'

'Bull*shit!* Luke and I have had two calls like that and nothing's happened. It's just psychological warfare because you're who you are. To *hell* with them! They're just the last kick of a dying mule!'

Patti whispered: 'God, why did I buy a big house all to myself?'

Katrina sat down beside her. '*Patti*, we'll call the police right now.'

Patti snorted tearfully. 'The police, don't make me laugh. Anyway, I've got a private security service, they send a squad car if I press the panic button.'

'Then *call* them. Wouldn't the ANC provide security?'

Patti dropped her hands and dabbed her eyes.

'I suppose so. I'll arrange it tomorrow.' She sniffed. 'You go home, I'm over the shock now, I'll be okay.'

Katrina squeezed both her hands. 'Look, come and sleep at our house tonight. Luke's probably home by now. There's a spare bed.'

Patti took a deep breath that quivered.

'No, I'm over it now, and I've got to get used to living on my own.' She waved a tearful hand at her house. 'I can't let myself be driven out by stupid phone calls on my third night, can I?'

'That's *right*!' Katrina said.

Patti smiled at her tearfully. Then put her hands around her neck and sobbed: 'Oh *shit*, what a homecoming!'

'Patti . . .' Katrina began.

Patti looked at her, her eyes full of tears, then blurted: 'Instead of me coming to your place, won't you stay here for tonight? To . . . give me courage? I'm not going to let these *bastards* frighten me away!' She added tearfully: 'In the spare bedroom, I mean, please don't worry about *that*.'

100

The shovels flew, filling in the big shallow hole. Then they trampled all over it, compacting the sand down again. 'Now the brush!' They started hauling the big branches of brushwood back. They were almost finished when the voice rasped in Afrikaans:

'*Stand still! Hands up!*'

Mahoney whirled, heart pounding – then crouched. He could see nobody in the darkness. He groped for his shovel, as a weapon. He looked desperately for Wainwright: he was four paces away, a gun in his hand, Hugo beside him. Then Wainwright shouted in Afrikaans: '*Put down your guns and come out. We are the police. You are surrounded!*'

'*Jy praat kak, man!*' And there was the crack of a gun and a bullet smashed through the brush beside Mahoney. Wainwright shouted: '*Scatter!*' And they scrambled up and ran.

Mahoney ran flat out, trying to keep low, clutching his shovel. Gunfire crackled behind him. He ran and he ran, swerving around trees, leaping over logs, rasping, gasping; somewhere over there were Hugo and Wainwright. He looked wildly over his shoulder and saw flashlights jerking. He ran and ran, rasping, gasping, desperately dodging trees, and now exhaustion was wrenching at his guts and legs. He looked back and saw the dog. It was a white blur racing towards him, and Mahoney reeled around, shovel raised. As the dog hurled itself at him in a terrible flash of snarling jaws, Mahoney swiped, and felt the

677

blade thud. The animal yelped and sprawled. Mahoney turned to run again, but the dog scrambled up and came at him again. Mahoney gasped in terror and swung the spade again wildly, and the edge connected with the animal's head and it crashed, writhing.

Mahoney turned to stagger on again, chest heaving, rasping. The flashlights were only fifty yards away now. He ran, his lungs wrenching, then ahead he saw the fence. He looked wildly for Hugo and Wainwright but all he saw was dark bush. He stumbled up to the barbed wire, swung his leg over, and collapsed onto the other side. He scrambled up and lurched onto the dirt road and started to run, and he tripped. He lay a moment, gasping, trying to get the thudding out of his heart, then scrambled up again. The flashlights were scattered. All he saw was the track disappearing into darkness; all he knew was the thudding of his heart. Wainwright's vehicle was at least a mile away and no way could he run it. To the left was the riverine foliage of the Limpopo. He went crashing through bushes down the dark bank, then he sprawled, and rolled. He came to a stop just above the riverbed. He lay, eyes closed, sucking in air, legs trembling.

Above the hammering of his heart he heard voices. Then footfalls as they ran down the track. He closed his eyes in heart-thudding relief. Then, in the distance, he heard Wainwright's vehicle starting up. Then shouts. The vehicle roaring away. The distant sound of gunfire. Then, silence.

Oh shit – now what?

He lay there, trying to let the exhaustion soak away into the earth before the bastards came back and he had to run for his fucking life again.

Please God, they thought he'd escaped with Wainwright. Please God, they didn't come looking for him.

Katrina had left a message for Mahoney on the answering machine explaining she was spending the night at Patti's house, and why.

She stayed up for one more drink, to steady Patti's nerves, then they said goodnight and she went to the spare room. She got undressed and climbed into bed. She lay in the dark, trying not to think about that bloodcurdling wolf howl. Trying not to listen for strange sounds. Trying to convince herself that there was nothing to be afraid of from these Wit Wolwe bastards.

She must have fallen asleep because she did not hear her door open. The first she knew was the figure silhouetted against the window, and she gasped. Then she saw the female curves through the night-gown, silhouetted against the window.

'I'm sorry, I did scratch on the door,' Patti whispered.

Katrina untensed. 'Are you all right?'

'I can't sleep.'

Katrina got up onto her elbow and whispered: '*Forget* about them.'

'I keep hearing things.'

'But it's only imagination.'

Patti whispered: 'Will you come and sleep in my room? In the big bed?'

Katrina closed her eyes. No, she did not dare do that.

'Come sit here for a minute and calm down.'

Patti moved to her side. She sat down. Katrina could not see her expression in the half-darkness. She began to speak but Patti put her finger on her lips. Then she picked up Katrina's hand, and gently placed it on her breast, and held it there.

Patti whispered: 'Please.'

Katrina closed her eyes, and took a deep sighing breath. For a long moment they were quite still; then Patti stood up. She wordlessly pulled her night-gown up over her head, and dropped it on the floor. Then she pulled back the blankets. She looked down at Katrina's nakedness, and silently got into bed beside her.

Mahoney lay in the undergrowth, listening to the sounds of his pursuers returning down the track. They were talking, but he could not make out what was said. He heard them clamber over the fence. Their footfalls disappeared. He slowly untensed.

Well, they thought he'd got away. Thank God.

And it was a dead certainty what they were going to do now: they were going to dig up that cache of arms before the police arrived.

So, the cache was going to disappear. No seizure. Maybe a prosecution of the farm-owner, on the evidence of Wainwright's photograph – but could that prove beyond reasonable doubt that the farmer *knew* it was buried on his land? It was a long way from his homestead.

Mahoney took a deep, tense breath. Trying to avoid the decision. Oh God, no way did he want to go creeping back, trying to get close enough to see the bastards' faces so he could say in a court: 'That is the man I saw digging up those crates.' And, anyway, how reliable could his identification be, in the dark? Even if they used lanterns?

True. But, oh God, what might he see if he went back . . . ?

With monumental misgiving he heaved himself up.

He found the place where the dry stream crossed the track. He crept under the fence, back onto the farm. He crept up the streambed. Thank God it was a cloudy night. God, was he crazy? He crept and crept, trying to listen above the knocking of his heart. He crept for twenty minutes, stopping, listening, peering, then he heard the crunch of a shovel, and froze. Then a flashlight lit up a patch of bush for a moment, and he realised he was only about forty paces from the bastards.

He crouched in the half-cover of a bush, heart knocking.

He could just make out four dark forms. The flashlight came on again. Three men crouched in the hole, a fourth holding the torch. But he could not make out faces. Half a dozen of the crates were standing beside the hole. Then another crate appeared as the men hefted it out. Muffled speech. Then the men began to lift again. Mahoney glimpsed something that looked like a cutlass. White. Then he recognised it as an elephant's tusk.

Ivory?

He stared. More tusks were being hefted out. And he understood. *Ivory for guns.* And who had arms to sell for ivory? The fucking army! They had all the captured AK–47s from the Angolan war.

Then he heard the sound of a distant engine. For a wild moment he thought it was Wainwright returning with the police. Then he identified the sound as an aircraft's. He searched the sky. The sound got louder. Then he identified the sound as that of a helicopter. Then he saw it.

It was coming from the north, flying low, with no lights. Then suddenly a vehicle's headlights lit up the scene. He had not seen the vehicle in the dark. The men were spreading a large rope-net on the ground. Now the helicopter was lining itself up above them, hovering, its downblast blowing sand everywhere. Mahoney crouched under his bush, desperately trying to see. The men were loading the crates into the net. A cargo hook was descending from the helicopter. Mahoney desperately shielded his eyes, trying to read a marking on the fuselage, but he could not because of the angle. Now the men were throwing the ivory into the net. Desperately Mahoney tried to keep his eyes on the fuselage through the swirling grit. Now the hook was going upwards. Now the net was lifting off, the downblast harder, grit fiercer. The net was level with the treetops, and the fuselage turned sideways, showing its number – and the vehicle's headlights were switched off.

The headlights went off at the crucial moment, but not before Mahoney thought he got the number. He wanted to bellow a curse because he was not sure. The helicopter turned its nose and began to clatter away.

Mahoney slumped, desperately trying to wipe the grit out of his eyes, desperately repeating the number he thought he'd seen, desperately scratching it in the sand. The figures were filling in the hole.

Mahoney got up and began to retrace his steps. As he reached the fence there was a flash of lightning, then a crack of thunder right above his head.

Two hours later he reached his Land-Rover. He was soaked and cold and exhausted. Wainwright and Hugo were waiting in their vehicle. Wainwright was furious because he'd lost his camera. 'What the fuck happened to you? We were about to call the cops.'

Mahoney slumped into the backseat. 'I think the cops arrived.'

'Jesus!'

He told them what had happened. Wainwright said: 'We've got the helicopter's number. So we can probably nail down which police are hand in glove with these guys.'

Hugo said: 'So what do we do now?'

Mahoney said wearily: 'In a sane world we would report the whole thing to the cops.'

'The cops?!' Wainwright was incredulous. 'You've just seen the cops! Putting them in charge of this is like putting a rabbit in charge of a lettuce patch.'

Mahoney said: 'Not the entire police force is right wing, there are many honest ones – '

'Yeah, and how do you pick the honest one? If I go to the Commissioner himself – who does he appoint to investigate? How does *he* know who's honest when it comes to right-wing sympathies?' He shook his head emphatically. 'No way.'

'Then report it to the Goldstone Commission of Inquiry into Violence,' Mahoney said, 'you can trust Judge Goldstone.'

'Yeah and how do we know the cops can't pull the wool over *his* eyes? He's a judge, for Christ's sake, not Sherlock Holmes. *Already* the evidence is gone – all we've got is an empty hole. And now the rain's even washed out all footprints, and I've lost my camera.' He shook his head emphatically again. 'No, this is my case. And you, Luke – ' he held a finger out – 'you've given me your word not to publish any story until I say so. Right? Not a word to anybody, not even Katrina.'

'Right,' Mahoney sighed.

The rain teemed down all the way back to Johannesburg.

Mahoney was surprised that Katrina's car was not there when he got back at dawn. He walked to their bedroom. He stopped in the doorway: the bed was made. He walked back to the living-room, looking for a note. Then he saw the red light flashing on the answering machine. He was very relieved to hear Katrina's voice:

'Darling, I'm spending the night at Patti's because she's nervous about being alone. Explain later. I love you.'

Patti nervous? He looked at his watch: only six o'clock. On a Sunday morning – too early to telephone. He turned towards the bedroom, then the answering machine clicked again. There was a moment's heavy breathing, then a male voice said: '*You fucking whore, sleeping with the fucking enemy.*' Then came the bloodcurdling wolf howl. Mahoney froze, listening to the terrible sound. Then the message continued: '*And shacked up with that writer bastard who's a traitor to South Africa. Traitors must die.*' And the howl came again.

The machine clicked off. Mahoney stood, eyes closed, his anger rising through the knocking of his heart. And he suddenly understood what Patti had been nervous about – she had received a call from the Wit Wolwe too. So the bastards had seen Katrina's car there. He snatched up the telephone and stabbed out Patti's number. He waited tensely. It rang five times, then Patti's voice came over her answering machine inviting the caller to leave a message. He slammed the receiver down and headed for the back door.

He drove through the teeming rain to Illovo. He swung into Patti's gate. There was Katrina's car. He parked, then ran through the rain. He rang the bell.

He waited a minute, then rang again. Then he turned and hurried through the rain down the side of the house. He knew which was the spare bedroom. The windows were open. He stepped across the flower bed, reached through the burglar bars, and pulled back the curtain. 'Kate?'

Through the gloom he saw a figure suddenly sit up with a gasp. He sighed with relief. 'It's okay, darling, it's me, Luke.'

But it was Patti who came to the window. 'Luke?' She clasped the curtain across her bosom. 'Oh, you gave me a fright.'

Relief. 'Are you guys all right? I got Kate's message.'

'We received a scary phone call, that's all.' She put her finger to her lips. 'Katrina's still asleep in the other room. Or do you want me to wake her? Come in out of that rain.'

'No, let her sleep, I'll go home to bed. You go back to sleep.'

He turned and ran back through the rain to his Land-Rover, thanking God.

He opened the door, then stopped. God, he was cold and wet and tired and did not want to drive home to an empty bed. Patti was still standing at the window, the curtain to her bosom, smiling. He walked back through the rain.

'Yes, I think I will come in, please.'

A minute later the front door opened. Patti was wearing her night-dress. She had run a brush through her hair. 'Come in.'

He took his muddy shoes off. 'Sssh!' Patti said. She led the way through the living-room to her bedroom door.

Mahoney whispered: 'Why's she sleeping in your room?'

Patti put her mouth to his ear. 'Because I'm a scaredy-cat. I couldn't sleep so I got into bed with her in the spare room. But evidently she found it too small.' She quietly turned the handle.

Mahoney tiptoed in. Katrina was sprawled diagonally across the double bed, her blonde hair awry, fast asleep. Patti blew him a kiss and silently withdrew.

Mahoney took a happy breath and undressed. He peeled back the covers and slid noiselessly into bed beside her. He wanted to take her warm body in his arms but he did not want to wake her.

In an instant he was asleep. Katrina stirred. She felt the body beside her, and looked up. Then she smiled and collapsed back onto her pillow. She snuggled up to him.

'I love you,' she whispered. 'I love you and I love you.'

It was early afternoon when he began to wake up. The rain was still drumming down – but it was not that which woke him, it was a deli-cious erotic dream about plumbing the warm sweet depths of a woman. And then he became aware it wasn't a dream – he *was* plumb-ing the depths of his beautiful woman, her soft loins astride him, smil-ing down at him, her blonde hair hanging down to his chest, her lovely breasts brushing his face, her hips slowly going up and down and round and round. And he smiled up at her and pulled her down tight against him as she writhed.

They were not aware of Patti entering the room. When Katrina felt the hand trailing slowly down her back she thought it was Mahoney's. When Mahoney felt the hand trailing up his leg he thought it was Katrina's. It was not until Katrina felt the hand gently tilting up her head that she realised Patti was there.

Patti was naked. She tilted Katrina's head back slowly, then she slowly kissed her. Then, confidently, she knelt one knee on the bed beside Mahoney's shoulder, then lifted her other leg slowly across him. Then she cupped Katrina's breasts. She lowered her loins onto Mahoney's face, and her hands slipped down to Katrina's hips and began to move them.

'Trust me,' she murmured into Katrina's mouth. 'Trust me . . .'

And the rain beat down.

PART XV

PART XV

101

A lot of things happened in the year that followed. Down in the Transkei, in his old home town of Umtata where the filming of *Alms for Oblivion* began, Mahoney sat in his hotel and piled up the headlines: CODESA STARTS. VIOLENCE ESCALATES. CLASHES AT CODESA . . .

Codesa. It was an unprecedented gathering of all shades of political opinion, to discuss, to bargain, to make deals, to arrive at 'sufficient consensus'. Every day it was on television, the huge hall at the World Trade Centre, the pomp, the two Supreme Court judges presiding to see fair play, the party representatives gathered round the massive circle of tables, the Afrikaners, the Zulus, the ANC, the Democratic Party, the Labour Party, the Indian Congress, COSATU. And all their advisers banked up behind them, and all the observers. On the first grand opening day there was the new Minister of Constitutional Development, Roelf Meyer, at the podium, for the first time in South Africa's bloodied history formally apologising for apartheid.

'It was not the intention of the South African government that the political science of apartheid would result in indignity and economic and personal suffering. Indeed the opposite was intended. However, that was the unhappy result. And we, the government of South Africa, wish to place on record that we regret this.'

Jesus. *Wonderful*. There, against a huge mural of a dawn breaking over a multi-racial land, were the hundreds of party delegates, the gallery jam-packed with press and television men. There at the ANC part of the table, sitting five seats away from the great Nelson Mandela, was Patti Gandhi, looking absolutely beautiful.

The television camera held on her for a moment, the commentator intoning softly: 'Miss Patricia Gandhi, well known as an anti-apartheid activist during her colourful youth, recently released from a life-sentence in prison, great-niece of Mahatma Gandhi . . .'

The camera panned the observers' tables and for a moment Mahoney glimpsed Katrina, making notes furiously:

' . . . representatives of the Afrikaner Volkswag, who are only present as observers at this stage. Notably absent today, even as observers, is the Conservative Party, which has announced that under no circumstances will they "negotiate with communist terrorists" . . . '

A lot of other things happened during this big bad time of the burgeoning new South Africa. Steve Wainwright telephoned to report that he had been unable to trace the helicopter which had been seen airlifting the cache of arms – Mahoney had noted the number wrongly, no such registration number existed. And there was no record by the Civil Aviation Authority of a flight in that area that night. 'But, of course, they would have flown low, under the scan of radar,' Wainwright said.

Mahoney cursed. 'But the farmer – Van Niekerk – he must still be prosecuted for illegal possession of weapons. Our evidence will be enough to convict him even though you lost your camera.'

'Mr van Niekerk,' Wainwright said, 'is dead. We can't prosecute a dead man. The very next day burglars broke into his farmhouse. Shot him in the ensuing struggle. Between the eyes.' He added: 'No witnesses, just the body. Found by his housemaid.'

Mahoney stared across his hotel room. Images of hit squads flashed across his mind. '*Burglars,* huh?! You believe that crap?'

'Police enquiries,' Wainwright said dryly, 'are continuing. I've told them all I know.'

And there was more infuriating news: President de Klerk announced in parliament that he was introducing an Indemnity Act, granting immunity from prosecution to all government servants who had committed crimes of violence in the course of their duties provided they made a clean breast to an indemnity board, the hearings of which would be held in camera, in secret. The time had come for reconciliation, he said, for forgive and forget – the new South Africa could not afford the bitter recriminations of Nuremberg-type trials.

Mahoney was furious. '*Christ, guys like General Krombrink getting off the hook?*' he fumed on the telephone to Katrina. There was an outcry in the press. If this was to happen, several editorials said, the confessions must at least be made in public, for all the world to hear – there must be a Truth Commission if there was to be reconciliation: 'If there is to be forgiveness we must know what it is we are forgiving – and particularly the families of the victims must know what happened to their loved ones.' '*Hear, hear!*' Mahoney said. The ANC was outraged and they vowed to repeal the legislation when they came to power, vowed to prosecute everybody who had been granted indemnity.

Mahoney said maliciously: 'Oh boy. Imagine what the likes of General Krombrink are thinking about this. Should they, shouldn't they?'

'I don't believe the ANC meant it,' Katrina said on the telephone, 'it wouldn't be legal to revoke amnesties.'

'No, but I doubt that would stop them. The Nuremberg Trials weren't strictly speaking legal either – there was no precedent in international law for those trials, but the world was so outraged by the Nazis that they brushed the point aside. And imagine if Hitler had issued a decree in his last days in his bunker granting immunity to his war criminals? The world would have thrown the decree out the window. Well, I think the same will happen with this Indemnity Act.' He smiled maliciously. 'And what I *love* is the thought of the likes of General Krombrink worrying their black hearts out, trying to decide whether to apply for amnesty or not. The temptation. If they go for it and the ANC revokes, their confession will be there in black and white. Their agony, deciding whether to go for the bird in the hand and risk the vulture in the bush.'

And then the result of Winnie Mandela's appeal was announced, and that was infuriating news too: the Appellate Division of the Supreme Court reduced her sentence from six years' imprisonment to a fine of twenty-five thousand rands. The right wing was outraged, the newspapers astonished.

'*Jesus*!' Mahoney fumed. 'What's happening in this country? First De Klerk tarnishes its image with his Indemnity Act, letting murderers off the hook, now the Appellate Division tarnishes its image. How can a fine of twenty-five thousand be an adequate punishment for kidnapping?'

'It's a political judgement,' Katrina said. 'Imagine the riots we would have from her supporters if Winnie was actually sent to jail.'

'The courts are supposed to be above politics.'

'It was a judgement of Solomon,' Katrina said. 'South Africa can't stand more blood. And it doesn't need any more martyrs. Let's be grateful that the ANC will have to dump her now, they can't afford to have a convicted kidnapper in their hierarchy.'

Twice a week they telephoned each other, almost every day they faxed each other, if only to say 'I love you'. Every night Katrina typed up her notes of the day's proceedings and faxed a copy to Mahoney. He wrote in his journals:

> I was astonished when Volkswag announced that they were not going to participate in CODESA at this stage, but I now see they were wise to let the government take the brunt of the winds of change – because the honeymoon period is definitely over and angry clashes and recriminations have begun.
>
> The government is demanding a federal constitution based roughly on

tribal lines, each with its own legislature (which is almost what Volkswag wants) with an overall federal government confined to foreign affairs, defence, roads, railways, harbours, communication, etc. In addition they want 'protection of minority rights,' and veto powers over uncongenial federal legislation. But the ANC is demanding a unitary state, *one central government which rules the whole of South Africa – the Westminster model which Britain thrust upon all her African colonies, and which in every case immediately resulted in a one-party dictatorship. This winner-takes-all-forever formula is what the government and the Zulus and the right wing are determined will not happen here.*

And all the time, while the leaders are negotiating, the violence rages on, the ANC and Inkatha butchering each other. And white South Africa watches in horror and asks, Is this the new South Africa? Is this what De Klerk has let us in for? *And the Conservative Party rants up and down the land at packed meetings, denouncing the government as traitors, denouncing CODESA as* CONDEMNSA, *declaring that the government has no mandate for these dastardly reforms, pointing to the violence as the result of this perfidy, trumpeting the whites back into the laager, demanding a general election.*

Katrina said on the telephone: 'And there's little doubt that the Conservative Party would win. The violence up here is appalling. God, how's it going to end up? Like the Congo? The Afrikaner is running back into the laager in droves, and a hell of a lot of English-speakers too. Ma and Pa came down to Jo'burg yesterday – Pa's got a face like thunder and tells me the war-talk in the Transvaal is very serious stuff indeed.'

'And Volkswag, what are they thinking?'

'Paradoxically, all this mayhem is to our advantage – it's getting us international sympathy for our modest demand, as compared to the extravagant demands of the Conservative Party who want to turn back the clock. And De Klerk has his back to the wall, making him fight harder for his federal constitution, which is also to our advantage. And he can wag a finger at the ANC and say "See, this violence is what your black democracy is like, that's why we need a federation and protection of minority rights!" The ANC is highly embarrassed by the violence, because it looks as if blacks are incapable of behaving democratically even whilst their leaders are negotiating about it, so that puts them under pressure to be more reasonable – '

'But are they scared of the Afrikaner?'

She snorted. 'The ANC knows that if the Afrikaner rebels the fat will be in the fire. They know that if the situation deteriorates to the point where De Klerk is forced to call a general election he'll *lose*, the new South Africa goes out the window and the ANC goes back to the bush – and they *know* they've never beaten our army in a battle yet, nor could they ever. And this time the ANC won't have Russia supplying them. And they know the world is losing patience with Africa now that the Cold War is over – '

'And the ANC is still claiming they're quite innocent of all this violence, of course?'

'Oh, they're as pure as the driven snow, it's all the horrid Zulus' doing – and the government's, who's sending in its Third Force to create the impression that blacks are incapable of democracy.'

Mahoney sighed. Okay. Except she didn't know as much as he did.

'And Patti – what does she think?'

'Well, I don't see much of her. I do at CODESA, of course, and occasionally we have a coffee, but usually she's closeted with her ANC delegation – but my guess is she doesn't believe all this Third Force crap either. She knows this is typical African politics, but she's got to put a brave face on it.'

'And? Is she still of the opinion that a volkstaat might not be a dumb idea?'

Katrina sighed. 'In private, yes. But at CODESA she toes the official ANC line – a unitary state, no federalism, winner-takes-all. We're leaving it to the big guns to argue about it for the moment.'

Mahoney hesitated, then said: 'So, what else do you talk about in private?'

There was a pause, then she grinned. 'In private? That really turned you on last time, huh?' Before he could reply she said: 'Darling, forget it. File it away as a pleasant incident, but don't expect it to happen again. It's just too complicated. And she's a complicated lady.' She changed the subject: 'So, how's the movie going? How does it feel?'

There are certain subjects you don't pursue. 'Eerie.'

Yes, it felt eerie, watching the story of his life being enacted. Eerie watching an actor portraying him as a schoolboy, young Luke trying to tear his eyes off the girls' legs, young Luke unable to tear his eyes off the beautiful Miss Rousseau, young Luke galloping past the girls' hostel to impress Miss Rousseau, young Luke dredging up historical facts with which to waylay Miss Rousseau, young Luke having his first sexual experience with Miss Rousseau, writhing on top of her jodhpured loins, young Luke shinning up her drainpipe every night, young Luke being beaten up with hockey sticks. And interwoven was the young

Patti Gandhi helping out in her father's store, lonely young Patti without any friends, young Patti illegally attending the convent, young Patti not allowed to play sport, not allowed to the dances and the cinema, young Patti defiantly diving into the municipal swimming pool, the brutal South African police reduced to stripping to their underpants to effect an arrest.

Yes, it was eerie, looking back on his youth. He saw more knickers on the actresses than he'd ever been lucky enough to see as a schoolboy, and Miss Rousseau's sex-talk on celluloid was so forthright that the real young Luke Mahoney would have been terrified. And her celluloid history lessons were downright bullshit: where was the teacher who held her class spellbound?

'*No*,' Mahoney said to the director, 'you're missing the point and not doing either Miss Rousseau or the Battle of Blood River justice. Miss Rousseau is very representative of the new South Africa that is still thirty years ahead, but you're portraying her as an Afrikaner *tart*. What I wrote in the script – '

'Luke, the audience doesn't give a shit about the Battle of Blood River, what they want to see is *action* – and Miss Rousseau's pussy. Sexy school teachers are highly erotic – '

'You are paying me,' Mahoney said, 'as a consultant – '

'Is it a nice day for filming?' the director demanded.

Mahoney frowned. He even looked up at the sky. 'Sure.'

'Okay, so now I've consulted you!'

It was frustrating. And at times it tugged at his heart. The young Indian actress playing Patti did her job very well, and wrung every tear out with her loneliness, and she was very sexy. And when she was put on the bus and waved goodbye to the little white town that had treated her so badly, real tears were burning in Mahoney's eyes. And, *God*, he felt sorry for the real Patti.

And, yes, it was boring.

Boring. Up at sunrise, on the set all day, only three minutes of film in the can at the end of it – five if you're lucky. The fucking about. The cameraman trying this angle and that. The re-writing of the fucking script. The fucking debates. The arguments. Mahoney bellowed: '*Why don't you do it as I wrote it?!*'

'Luke,' the director said, 'why don't you go back to the fucking hotel and have a nice rest until I send for you.'

He did end up spending most of the time in his fucking hotel. He was not allowed, in terms of his contract, to go anywhere else without the director's permission, and most weekends were spent re-writing the script. In between times he wrote up his journal for his American publisher, keeping abreast of the news by radio. When he'd finished that chore he tried to write the sequel to *Alms for Oblivion*, as he'd finally undertaken to do. And that was eerie too, and complicated by the eerie business being re-enacted just up the road at the film-site. *Sexually* complicated.

Yes, sexually. Mahoney was a highly sexed man, and all the beef and knickers he was seeing up at the film-set didn't make his celibate life very comfortable, though he could resist temptation – he wasn't going to complicate his life by a fling with a starlet. (The actress playing Miss Rousseau was being knocked off by the producer, and Mila Singh, playing Patti, was having it off with the director.) But – all that sex-bother aside – Katrina was quite right in saying that their unexpected sexual encounter with Patti Gandhi had preyed on his mind. Vividly. Had turned him on. *Of course it had* – what man wouldn't have been sexually enthralled by the spectacle of two beautiful women wrapped around each other, while he had his rampant way with both of them, until they all sprawled in a tangled mass, panting, sated.

Then had come the remorse: Katrina's. 'Your Calvinist Dutch Reformed Church remorse?' Patti had cajoled.

But, yes, Mahoney had had remorse too, though not because of his Calvinist conscience: his had been identified with Patti. It did not worry him that Katrina had been sexually impassioned, he was confident of her, he understood her bi-sexuality and he understood entirely her physical attraction to a woman as beautiful as Patti Gandhi. It was about Patti that he felt remorse. For he knew Patti was still in love with him, and he wanted to do nothing, *nothing*, to inflame, to encourage that. Because he knew with all his heart that he loved Katrina now. Oh, he loved Patti too, for her suffering and for all the many lovely and terrible things of long ago, and with all his heart he wanted her to be happy (and, thus, assuage his guilt) – but he was in love with Katrina now, and no way could he go back on that commitment, nor did he want to. Nor was he tempted to. But, oh God yes, he was tempted by Patti's body. Her sexual hold on him was enormous. And, yes, Katrina was right: he had thought a lot about that extraordinary episode. And, oh yes, he wanted it to happen again. He tried to file it away in his mind as just a delightful memory, as Katrina had warned – it was a complicated and dangerous game to play. But, trying to write the sequel to *Alms* in his lonely hotel room, with the story of Patti Gandhi being re-enacted just up the road, trying to write the new story of what happened to her when she came out of prison into the new South Africa and met the love of her life again, it was very hard not to think a great deal about that extraordinary afternoon. And, oh yes, he wanted it to happen again. *But*, no way did he want it to complicate, let alone endanger, his relationship with Katrina. No *way*.

And then, one afternoon, there was a knock on his door. And there stood the lovely Patti Gandhi.

'Hullo, Luke.' She smiled her brilliant smile. 'Just popped down to check out Gandhi Garments. And the movie.'

They had dinner together in the hotel restaurant.

'How is my new book going?' she smiled.

Her new book? 'How did you know I was writing it? Even Katrina doesn't know.'

'Bill Summers told me.'

He was amazed. 'You've spoken to Bill Summers?'

'I went to see him in New York. Just out of curiosity. After all, he is the man who published our story. And, he was very charming. Took me to lunch.'

'He didn't tell me.'

'I asked him not to. In case you thought I was being pushy.'

Pushy? 'I see. And?'

'And, we talked about you mostly. What a great book *Alms* was. And he told me you'd finally agreed to write the sequel, because the movie was being made. I was thrilled. Why doesn't Katrina know?'

Mahoney sighed.

'Because,' he said, 'writing a book is a very emotional business. For me, anyway. I've got to put myself into the skin of the characters, to bring them alive. I've got to do a lot of brooding. And I don't want Katrina to feel that I'm brooding about you.' He added: 'I'll have to tell her sometime. But not yet. And I don't want you to tell her, please.'

Patti said solemnly: 'Of course. I understand.'

'And,' Mahoney said, 'I may never finish it.'

'Oh!' Patti said. 'You *must*, Luke. It'll be a wonderful story.'

He snorted. 'What *is* the story?'

Patti twirled her wine glass.

'It's a sad story,' she said.

Oh God. 'Yes. Sad.'

She said: 'When Pamela comes out of prison, Jack is in love with somebody else.'

Oh God. 'Yes. But is that a story?'

'Of course. A heartbreaking story.'

'But what happens then?'

Patti twirled her glass. 'Well, what?'

'Exactly.'

'Just tell it as it is, Luke.'

He took a deep breath. 'Mauritius too?'

She snorted softly. 'No. That will hurt Katrina.'

Oh, he liked her for saying that. He gave her a bleak smile: 'Exactly. So you see my difficulties.'

Patti said to her wine glass: 'But the rest, Luke. Just write it as it's happened. It's a poignant story so far. Our conspiracy.'

Mahoney looked at her.

'Our conspiracy?'

Patti glanced up at him. She said hastily: 'I don't mean anything underhand – any secret between you and me. I just mean the secret the three of us shared that afternoon.' She looked at him, moist-eyed. 'It was lovely, wasn't it?'

Mahoney closed his eyes. Yes, it was lovely. He desired Patti. But no way was he going to be underhand to Katrina again. Tonight or ever again. He smiled tensely: 'Yes, of course it was.'

Patti looked at him earnestly, and smiled. 'Oh, darling, there's nothing to be uptight about. Oh, I know you, Luke. I've had twenty-four years in prison to analyse you. And your books helped. And I know that for all you're a helluva wild guy – or used to be – deep down you're an honest-to-God faithful sort. Faithful to your friends. And faithful to your lover – once you've settled down to her. As you now have, at last. And I want you to know, Luke, that I'm also a faithful friend. I accept what's happened between you and me as inevitable, and I would do nothing to undermine you and Katrina. All I want – and expect – is to be your friend.' She looked at him with big beautiful moist almond eyes: 'Your friend.'

'Of course you're my friend, Patti.'

'Yes, you're a loyal soul, Luke. And, God, you don't know how much that means to me. You're the only sort of family I've got.'

It tugged at his heart, her saying that. And the way she said it: her eyes. Although her voice was composed and she smiled, it was a cry from the heart. He wanted to give her that, but he did not know whether he could withstand her sexuality. He said: 'Of course you're my family, darling.'

Patti smiled. 'And I think Katrina understands that. And that I'm not a threat.'

Not a threat? No, she wasn't. Except sexually. He said: 'Have you discussed it with her?'

'Yes. We've seen quite a bit of each other. And I made my position clear.' She smiled. 'And I'm sure she believes me.'

Katrina hadn't reported this to him, she'd only said Patti was a complicated lady. 'What did she say, exactly?'

'Whole conversation? Too long.' She sighed, then smiled sadly. 'But I said that even though we were married by Indian custom, I had no claim on you. It had no legal effect. Only an emotional tie.' (Oh God.) She went on: 'And I'm sure she believes me.' She looked at him. 'Of course, that little detail was on her mind. Did she ever discuss it with you?'

He wished this hadn't come up. 'Yes, once. It was all in *Alms*.'

Patti said: 'And I assured her that the child was not yours.'

Oh, why was she bringing all this up? 'But it was?'

'Of course it was. But I lied to her, to put her mind at rest.' She added: 'The same way I lied to you all those years.' Her eyes were moist. 'And I still want your mind to be at rest. What's happened can't be undone, and I don't want to use any emotional blackmail. In fact I'm sorry I tried the day I came out of prison, but I was distraught, I was trying to hurt you. It was silly and unfair of me and I'm sorry.'

Mahoney took her hand. 'You've got nothing to apologise for, Patti.'

She dabbed her eye with her napkin. 'Okay. But anyway, I told her all that to reassure her. So that your lives are not complicated by any of that old shit.' She looked at him, moist-eyed. 'All I want is to be your friend, Luke. I accept my position.'

Knew her position. Oh, that was self-effacing. It tugged at his heart. And, oh, the guilt. He squeezed her hand.

'Our house is your house. But, Patti, you must think positively. You're a ravishingly beautiful woman. And so intelligent. And courageous. Patti, you're going to meet somebody soon and fall in love.'

She extricated her hand and sat back. She folded her arms. She said quietly: 'Think positively? I'm an expert on that – how do you think I got through those years in prison? Knowing you were out there sowing your wild oats. How do you think I managed to stop myself writing to you?' She snorted. 'You don't understand, Luke. I don't *want* to fall in love, I don't want to go through that trauma all over again. I've been in love, I've had the best, I don't want second-best. I'm like – ' she waved a hand – 'like a widow, who finds remarriage unthinkable.' She frowned at him. 'I'm calm about it now. Yes, I was screwed up for a while. Like when I saw you in Mauritius. But I'm back under control now.' She said wanly: 'Oh, for my first month in London I screwed myself black and blue. How *pathetic* can a girl *get*? But I'm over all that nonsense now. All I want is to do my duty to the new South Africa. And friendship.' She added: 'And do you know that in all my frantic fucking after I came out of prison I didn't have one orgasm?'

Oh, Mahoney didn't want to hear all this. His stab of possessiveness, of sadness, was intense.

'Not even with you in Mauritius. I faked it. I was too uptight – in love – or thought I was. Now I know it's a different sort of love – the love of friends. And *then* I had my first orgasm: with you and Katrina.'

And, oh, this was heart-wrenching.

Patti smiled wanly: 'And, you've no idea how wonderful it was, Luke. How . . . *explosive*. With not only relief but . . . *warmth*. A wonderful feeling of warmth, and affection and *safety*.' She smiled at him, moist-eyed. 'I knew I was with *friends*. *Doing* it with dear friends.' She grinned at him, half blushing, half tearful. 'You've no idea how wonderful that was, after all those years in prison.'

Mahoney had tears in his eyes. He said: 'I'm glad.'

'I walked on air for weeks. Had a hard time looking serious. And Katrina had a wonderful experience too. Even if she did burst into tears afterwards.'

'She didn't burst into tears. She was only . . . remorseful.'

'Yes. Which is nonsense, Luke. What's to be remorseful about making a gift of such happiness? To your friends?'

'Yes. But she's a Calvinist.'

'Yes, we had a long talk about it. She's a complicated lady, Luke. But a very sincere one, darling. And I like her enormously. You be good to her.'

Katrina complicated? 'Of course I'm good to her.'

'Yes, you are. She thinks the world of you. And she's a very smart lady. Boy, is she intelligent. But uptight, about her Calvinism. Luke?' She looked at him earnestly. 'I don't want anything like that to spoil our friendship. It's all I've got. And all I want.'

Oh, it tugged at his heart. 'It won't,' he said.

She said earnestly: 'It needn't. Not at all. It's just a gift. Do you want it to happen again?'

He snorted softly. How could he deny it? 'As long as there's no tension.'

'Exactly. And there's nothing to be tense about.' She looked at him moist-eyed. 'I don't want to meet somebody else and fall in love, Luke. But like everybody else I do need sex from time to time. And if I can have that with you guys, that's wonderful. But if it's a problem, forget it. I promise you I don't want anything silly to spoil our relationship.'

Yes, he believed that. And he didn't know what to believe. And when, late that night, he escorted her upstairs to her room, and kissed her goodnight on her cheek, and hugged her and fleetingly felt her lovely body against him, he was under control. And so was she. And

Patti did nothing to destabilise it. Perhaps it only needed her to do one little thing to make it all different, and very complicated, and fraught with guilt, but she did not. For an instant they were pressed close together, and he felt her gorgeous breasts and thighs against him, then she stepped out of his arms and blew him a kiss with a ravishing smile. 'Good night, darling.'

'Good night, Patti.'

It was almost two o'clock in the morning when he got back to his room, but he picked up the telephone and called Katrina.

'Sorry to wake you, but I just had to call to tell you that I love you.'

'Oh, I love you too!' Katrina cried. 'And I wasn't asleep, I'm up working on CODESA.'

'I love you.'

'I love you too!'

His eyes were burning. 'And,' he grinned, 'how's fucking CODESA?'

102

And CODESA was fast turning into a fuck-up.

Chief Buthelezi had stormed out because the Zulu king was not allowed a separate vote, the ANC accused the Zulus of being responsible for all the violence, the Zulus accused the ANC of being responsible, the ANC accused the government of supporting the Zulus, the government accused the ANC of continuing the Armed Struggle, the Zulus accused the government and the ANC of making secret deals, the ANC accused the government and the Zulus of making secret deals, the government accused both of them of fucking up the peace process, the ANC accused the government of trying to perpetuate white minority rule with federalism, the government accused the ANC of wanting a winner-takes-all constitution, the ANC accused the government of wanting a loser-takes-all constitution. The PAC raved that CODESA was a sell-out, the only solution was one-settler-one-bullet, the Conservative Party raved that CODESA was a sell-out and the only solution was apartheid, and the AWB raved that the only solution was war. Meanwhile, out there in the black townships the violence raged on.

Katrina said: 'Volkswag was right to keep out of CODESA at this stage – the ANC are seeing how dangerous the Conservatives are, and we appear positively moderate – we don't want to get caught up in a slanging match at this stage. After the government and the right wing have taken the heat it will be the right time for us to walk in with our sweet reasonableness.'

And then two government members of parliament died, the Conservative Party won the resulting by-elections easily, loudly proclaiming that De Klerk had no mandate for his reforms, that the white electorate was deserting him in droves, loudly demanding a general election, loudly declaring that De Klerk was a lame duck. And then, to everybody's consternation, midst all this clamour, the headline burst across the press: REFERENDUM! And an astonished world was told that President de Klerk had thrown down the gauntlet to the right wing and was calling a national referendum amongst the white electorate to determine his support.

'*Good God – is he mad*?' Mahoney cried. 'He could easily lose this referendum! Then he'll have to call a general election and he'll lose that too! Then the Conservative Party will be in power and there'll be chaos. The blacks will rise up. The world will come down on us like a ton of bricks, more sanctions . . .'

'Darling, he has no choice,' Katrina said soberly. 'He's lost two by-elections, he has to prove that he speaks for the majority of whites.'

'Nonsense! He holds the majority in parliament, he has the legal power to *ram* through these reforms.'

'But not the *mandate*. The Conservative Party is quite correct when it says he didn't get a mandate at the last election for all these reforms, he's stolen a march – '

'But he's got the *legal* power! Parliament is the supreme law-maker – he should not risk losing that power.'

'But if he wins he'll have so much more power to negotiate – '

'*If* he wins! If he doesn't we're ruined!'

Mahoney wrote:

> This is the most desperate decision in South Africa's bloodstained history. On this referendum hangs South Africa's future – a hope of living or definitely drowning in blood. And De Klerk is terribly wrong forcing this decision on the land. And – mark my words – as the referendum builds up, so will the violence as the Third Force creates more havoc to drive the electorate back into the laager . . .

The campaigning was fast and furious. Across the land the banners and posters spread in a rash, *Vote Yes*, and *Vote No*, and *Vote Yes For a Better Future*, and *Vote No Against Chaos*. The political rallies everywhere, the rhetoric, the ranting, the stink bombs, the fisticuffs, the booing and the cheering. And, as Mahoney predicted, across the land the black-on-black violence redoubled, the train massacres, the pitched battles, the necklacings, the gunfire.

'Patti is convinced that this increase in violence is being provoked by the Third Force to drive the whites back into the laager – '

'*And she's right.*'

On voting day Mahoney watched the continuous news coverage on television. With dread. If the vote today was No, all hell would break loose. The new South Africa in flames.

And if the vote today was Yes? The new South Africa in flames also?

There, on the screen, were the crowds queuing at the polling booths. The *Yes* and *No* banners everywhere. The loud last-minute haranguing as the voters arrived. Policemen everywhere, the AWB in their uniforms.

At nine o'clock that night the last polling booths closed and exhausted anxiety descended on the land. Mahoney telephoned Katrina.

'What do you think?'

Katrina sighed. 'Oh darling, there're a lot of frightened voters in this country. God, I'm frightened of a No vote.'

'And Patti? What does she think?'

Katrina snorted. 'The ANC are keeping a low profile. Letting De Klerk do his thing. In fact she appreciates his courage. But it's back to the bush if the vote is No.'

At ten o'clock the next morning the first result was announced in Cape Town. Newsmen from around the world were gathered in the City Hall auditorium. Across the land people were at their television sets.

Into the auditorium came the Commissioner of Census. He sat down and read the first result: 'To the question "Do you want the government of South Africa to continue on its present course of negotiation for a new non-racist constitution?" the result from the electoral district of Port Elizabeth is: Yes, 27,862: No, 8281.'

There were cheers. But nobody was cockahoop, because Port Elizabeth was a safe district.

All day the results came in, and one after another they were majority Yes-votes. The excitement began to mount. As the overall percentage crept upwards the euphoria began. And as it crossed the fifty per cent mark the beautiful voice and joyous face of Marike Keuzencamp, one of South Africa's top vocalists, burst across the screen singing '*Dit is 'n Land.*' It is a Land, called South Africa.

Mahoney was weeping as he telephoned Katrina: 'Well, it looks like we've made it, baby!'

Katrina sobbed: 'I'm in floods of tears. It is *the* land, darling.'

At four o'clock the last result came in. It was from the Pietersburg electoral district, where Katrina's parents lived. And it was the only area which returned a No vote.

'Darling, I'm sorry,' Katrina sob-laughed, 'but I told you so.'

But the overall result across the land was known: 68.89 per cent of South African whites had voted Yes, 31.11 per cent had voted No.

And then there on the television screen was President De Klerk, on the front steps of the Houses of Parliament for his victory speech, his cabinet clustered behind him, and as he went to the microphone the crowd burst into 'Happy Birthday'. By coincidence it was indeed the president's birthday.

He listened, beaming, and as the song ended he said: 'And Happy Birthday to the new South Africa! The day the Book of Apartheid was closed forever.'

In a bar in Pietersburg a big Afrikaner picked up his beer bottle and hurled it. It smashed the television screen and President de Klerk disappeared in a shattering gurgle. The man bellowed in Afrikaans: *'And that's how he will disappear from South Africa!'*

103

And so CODESA resumed. And the film unit of *Alms for Oblivion* finished its work in the Transkei and relocated to Johannesburg to make the rest of the movie. And, *God*, Mahoney was glad.

Glad to leave the haunted Transkei with its black decrepitude, the spoilt memories, the loneliness of his hotel room. It was wonderful to cross the river back into South Africa where everything still worked. And when at last he began to mount the escarpments of the Drakensberg and the rolling Natal countryside began to give way to the flat Orange Free State, and then at last to the distant lights of the mining cities of the gold reef, and the flyovers across the highway began to proliferate, he was grinning with excitement at being with Katrina again and he was overjoyed that he was coming back to this throbbing cosmopolitan heart of darkest fucking Africa. When Katrina came running out of the back door, her blonde hair flying and joy all over her beautiful face, he did not care about anything but her.

It was a Friday night. They had two whole days before she had to return to CODESA. It was lovely lying in the big bed together, the highveld winter outside; lovely lying in the whirlpool bath together, drinking wine; lovely sitting round the kitchen table talking, talking.

'Don't talk about bloody CODESA,' Katrina said. 'I'm up to here with it. The Zulus have stormed out, the PAC are still ranting about one-settler-one-bullet, the Conservatives won't negotiate at all, so CODESA is reduced to the government and ANC, and they're at loggerheads. The ANC wants an election immediately to elect a "constituent assembly" to draw up the new constitution. The government wants the constitution to be drawn up by CODESA. And so on.'

'And the government's right,' Mahoney said. 'CODESA must decide on the constitution, like the founding fathers in America did. The ANC would win any election and then write any constitution they liked. Then we'll have a one-party state.'

'Well, the ANC is threatening to walk out now.'

'The right wing will love that. But do you think they're serious?'

'Patti says they're serious.'

Patti. Just her name made that afternoon come back to life. 'And how is she?'

'She's much better. She's got her teeth into her job. But she's still *very* lonely. She hasn't any real friends.' She paused. 'How did it feel, filming her early life? Did it make you . . . nostalgic?'

'No. I wasn't in love with her when I was a schoolboy.'

'Just in lust?'

'I was in lust with anything in a skirt.'

She smiled though the billowing steam of the whirlpool bath. 'Are you still in lust with her?'

Uh-oh. Mahoney grinned. 'I'm in lust with you. And in love.'

She smiled. 'A man can be in love and still lust after another woman.' She looked at him with a twinkle in her eyes. 'You must have thought about that afternoon the three of us ended up in bed together, surprise-surprise?'

No point in denying it. 'Yes.'

'It turns you on.' Not a question.

'It would turn any man on. Unless he felt insecure.'

'And, do you feel insecure in my affections?'

No doubt where this conversation was heading. 'No. Should I?' He added: 'Does it turn you on?'

She raised her eyes and held his.

'You know my past.' She added: 'But I feel secure in your affections, too. You didn't look like a worried man.'

'No. Were you a worried woman?'

She looked at her wine. 'No. Or I wouldn't have permitted it.' She shook her head. 'But I guess no woman feels comfortable seeing her man enjoy another woman.'

He was silent a moment. Then: 'Has it happened again?'

She raised her eyes to his. She said: 'I swear it has *not* happened again. But only because I have not permitted it. Patti has certainly wanted it to happen again.' She paused. '*She* is in lust with me, darling.'

Oh, dear. He didn't want Patti to get hurt. The words hung. But, oh yes, they were erotic. And dangerous. 'Why, what's she done?'

Katrina grinned. 'There're no sexy details.' She took a sip of wine. 'But, we've seen quite a lot of each other. At CODESA, of course, but she drops around here quite often. She's lonely, and so was I with you away.' She looked at him. 'Yes, she did make one pass at me, soon after you left. But I rejected it. And we discussed it, frankly, as mature people. And I said, in short, that I would not be . . . unfaithful to you.' She looked at him with a wisp of a smile. 'That may not sound very mature, but that's how it would seem to me. Since then, no further passes. She's a very controlled person. But I can feel her tension. But, she's got a big thing about me, darling.' She paused. 'In fact she's almost besotted with me.'

'Be*sott*ed?' Oh Christ.

Katrina smiled, and waved a hand. 'Infatuated. In lust. The dividing line is blurred at initial stages, people invest the subject of their desires with all kinds of romantic qualities. But Patti's case is complicated by the fact that she hasn't led a normal life – her psyche, her emotions, have been distorted by years in prison. During which time she had nothing but female companionship. Plus the notion of you, which she clung to. Now she's free, but she's lost you. So that leaves only female companionship. And that, at the moment, is me. I have assumed a disproportionate importance in her life. And *that* is doubtless because I am part of you.'

Mahoney sat back. He felt guilt.

'And when you rejected the pass, what did she say?'

Katrina twirled her wine-glass. 'She asked if you would think me unfaithful if you were *involved*.' She waved a hand. 'As a fun thing, now and again.' She smiled. 'I lied. I know damn well you wouldn't mind having two women in bed occasionally. But I said I didn't know. So, she suggested I try the idea on you.'

Mahoney smiled. Guilt, yes. But it was also very erotic. He said: 'Which you are now doing?'

Katrina shook her head. 'No, I'm just giving you an honest report. To make of what you will.' She looked at him soberly. Then said: 'Patti wants a ménage-à-trois, Luke. And that's dangerous.' She added: 'It's common enough, particularly amongst artistic people, but it's a dangerous game.'

A ménage-à-trois. And this was the threshold of potential trouble Mahoney knew he was crossing. Had he pulled back at this threshold this story may have been entirely different.

'"To make of what I will" . . . ? What do *you* want to make of it?'

She smiled wanly. 'What do you want, Luke?' She waved a hand. 'Oh, I know what you'd like, don't bullshit me, Mahoney.' She looked at him half-smiling. 'I notice you don't deny it.'

'Oh, I do deny it.'

'Oh sure. Absolutely. Cross your heart, and all that.'

He grinned. 'My heart, I assure you, has nothing to do with it.'

She smirked. 'No, it's your loins. Your heart, I think, I am confident of. Though no woman should be over-confident of her man, I suppose.' She looked at him. 'And? Are you confident of my heart? And my loins?'

'I am very confident of your beautiful heart and loins; I would proudly take them anywhere.'

'Even unto Orania?'

'Even,' he said, 'unto Orania.' There was a silence. Then: 'Well? How do your loins feel about this?'

She smiled. 'My loins are in excellent shape. And so is my heart. So it's my *head* that matters, pal.'

'And what does your beautiful head say?'

'You're awfully interested in how this discussion is going to turn out, aren't you, darling?'

Warning bells rang. Mahoney spread his hands innocently. 'You raised it.'

Katrina laughed. 'And you, my darling, walked straight into my trap!'

Mahoney frowned. 'Your trap?'

She slid across the bath and crushed her mouth onto his, then laughed at him. 'Just testing! Testing how you felt about having the gorgeous Patti Gandhi romping in bed with you again. Oh, I don't blame you. But – in answer to your question, my head says No!' She grinned down at him. 'Sorry to disappoint you, my darling.'

Mahoney was taken off guard by all this. But he kept a straight face. Bravely concealing his disappointment. '*Me* disappointed? Not so. Just an intellectual exercise, Professor.'

'Nothing to do with your loins, huh? *Good.*' She kissed him again. '*Liar*,' she growled into his mouth, 'sex-mad liar, I know you'd love it!'

'And you wouldn't?' he grinned into her mouth.

'It's *you* we're discussing, buster!' She kissed him hard, then straightened, and tapped her lovely breasts. 'Fantasies you talk to *me* about, got that? Is it leather? Plastic raincoats? See-through silk underwear? Name it, you've got it. But beautiful Asian sex-sirens – for*get* it. It won't happen again, darling . . . '

104

But it did happen.

That week CODESA broke down, Nelson Mandela angrily declaring the talks 'a waste of time'. Patti Gandhi broke the news the night before, on the telephone.

'Well, prepare for fireworks tomorrow, darling. And you can blame the bloody-minded government with their demands of a senate-of-losers to have veto powers over legislation they don't like. And now their insistence that the new constitution receive the approval of seventy-five per cent of the constituent assembly instead of the seventy per cent we suggest. De Klerk is just too cock-sure of himself since his referendum victory, he thinks he can bully us – blame *him*, darling.'

Katrina groaned. 'So what happens now?'

Patti said grimly: 'Mass Action, that's what. You'll hear all about it tomorrow. Mass Action for three months – strikes, marches, boycotts, to bring the government to its senses.'

Katrina was aghast. She cried: 'For God's sake – that'll ruin the country! Three *months*! Your VAT strike lasted two days and it cost two billion rand in lost production – and God knows how many lives!'

'That's what the bosses have decided, honey-child.'

'For God's sake, do they *want* to inherit the ruins? And have a flood of new blood? There'll be massive intimidation – '

'There won't be any intimidation by the ANC – '

'*Oh come off it, Patti!*'

'Well, if FW would be reasonable he could avoid all this – '

'Is the ANC being reasonable?! To walk out and declare economic war – and more bloodshed – just because they're not getting their way at CODESA? Is that what negotiating is about?! No, negotiating a country's future requires statesmanship and bargaining and patience – '

'But what do you do when you reach the end of the road, wise gal?'

'You haven't reached the end of the road – you've reached a deadlock, that's all! Christ – okay, I agree the government's been difficult, so walk out in a huff, sure, leave FW looking silly with nobody to negotiate with, but for Christ's sake don't break a deadlock by creating mass *havoc!* It's *utterly* irresponsible!'

There was a moment's silence. 'Irresponsible?'

'And immature! God, I thought Mandela was a man of stature. It's worse than irresponsible, it's despicable.'

'Despicable, huh?'

'*Yes, goddamnit!*'

Patti said coldly: 'I have a difference of opinion with Mandela on this one, but despicable he is not. We have no vote yet, no parliament in which we can make our voices heard – '

'CODESA is better than parliament because the eyes of the world are on it and *anybody* can make his voice heard! Christ, is this the way Mandela's going to run parliament when he's in power – call down the wrath of God every time he doesn't get his way!?'

Patti said icily: 'Is that what you think of us?'

Katrina fumed: 'That's how you're making yourselves look! Mandela will lose a lot of international sympathy over this Mass Action! The world will think South Africa's going to be another typical African disaster!'

'So Mandela's just another typical kaffir politician, is he?'

Katrina closed her eyes in exasperation.

'For God's sake, I didn't say that.'

'It sounded very like it to me. Once a South African, always a South African, huh? A leopard doesn't change its spots?'

Katrina took a furious breath. 'I never had any apartheid spots, Patti! Get that straight. And I think we'd better change the subject, before we start getting unkind!'

'"Unkind"? Well I think we'd better terminate this entire conversation. Sorry I troubled you with some inside information.'

'Patti . . .' Katrina sighed.

'Good *night*.' The telephone clicked.

Katrina slammed down the receiver. '*God spare us!*'

Mahoney was equally angry when she told him the news.

'Has Mandela no conscience?! In this climate of violence to announce Mass Action! The *bloodshed* it will cause! It's not only despicable, it's *insane*!' He jabbed a finger. 'Patti was right – Mandela *is* just another African politician if he goes ahead with this!'

'She said "kaffir".'

Mahoney snorted. 'Oh Jesus. Maybe that's how she sees it in her secret racist heart – Indians are more scared of the blacks than we are! Look what happened to them throughout east Africa!'

The next day Nelson Mandela dramatically announced that the ANC was walking out of CODESA, angrily accusing the government of trying to cling to power indefinitely. It was headline news all over the world. But there was no announcement of Mass Action.

'Maybe they've thought better of it,' Katrina said.

'No way,' Mahoney said grimly. 'They'll wait for a day or two to get international sympathy from their dramatic walk-out, which makes De Klerk look like a shit, then they'll piously announce that as he hasn't backed down they're "*forced*" to resort to this "*peaceful*" Mass Action.'

And then Boipatong happened.

Boipatong. It is just another black township most whites had never heard of, somewhere out there on the gold reef around Johannesburg, another teeming area of little concrete houses beside shanties and joyless hostels. But that week Boipatong became an international name. That week some Zulus were involved in a dispute with some Xhosa in Boipatong. The following day a rumour spread that the Zulus from KwaMadala Hostel were about to take revenge. People locked themselves in their shacks and houses. But the police did not go to the hostel to investigate, they did not send out extra patrols. That night the Zulu impi erupted, hundreds of warriors went rampaging through the township, smashing down doors, dragging out people, hacking and swiping and clubbing. Forty-five people were massacred, dozens wounded, eighty-five houses burned, before the Zulus ran away into the night.

That night it was on television: there in the glaring arc lights were the pools of blood, the police, the hacked bodies being loaded into ambulances, the horrifically wounded, the journalists' dramatic reports.

'Oh *shit*,' Mahoney groaned.

That night Nelson Mandela called a press conference at his mansion in Houghton.

In measured, angry tones he announced to the world that the ANC was not only walking out of CODESA, it was breaking off negotiations entirely because of the massacre in Boipatong. The government, he said, was responsible for the hideous butchery, like it was for all the violence ravaging the land, because it failed to take adequate security measures to stamp it out despite repeated demands. He said a Third Force was promoting the violence and the government was tolerating it because it served the nefarious purpose of divide-and-rule whilst also promoting the international impression that black people were incapable of behaving democratically. Add to this, he said, government's intransigence at CODESA, its attempts to emasculate any future black government with 'power-sharing' and a senate-of-losers with permanent veto rights, and it became obvious 'even to a blind man' that the government had a hidden agenda to thwart the democratic process.

Accordingly, the ANC had no alternative but to embark on a programme of peaceful Mass Action for three months, consisting of strikes, marches, boycotts.

'Oh *God*,' Mahoney groaned.

The next day it was front-page news and without exception the editorials denounced Mass Action as highly irresponsible, dangerous to life, destructive of the economy and the welfare of the people the ANC claimed to champion. The government angrily denounced it as 'in conflict with the spirit of honest negotiation and the National Peace Accord', calculated to lead to 'mindless violence, destruction of lives and property, and large-scale economic destruction'.

'*And the fucking rest!*' Mahoney cried. '*How about civil war?*'

The next day the government announced new security measures to protect the state from the havoc: protection of all national key points would be increased, troops would maintain essential services, the Citizen Force and Commando Units would be on stand-by to back up the thousands of soldiers already deployed across the land. And the ANC alliance denounced the call-up as 'evil and hypocritical', demanding the order be withdrawn, saying it 'rejects with contempt' the government's 'war talk' which is 'extremely sinister and suggests they are trying to create a war psychosis to enable them to crack down on peaceful mass action,' accusing the government, big business and the media of 'whipping up a storm of protest against the attempts of our people to challenge an intransigent, corrupt and ruthless clique who are refusing to surrender power. Democrats have no option but to devise methods to challenge this bully-boy attitude and pressure it towards bona fide negotiations.'

'Jesus Christ,' Mahoney said. 'This could be the end. This could result in such chaos that martial law is imposed, and that will be the end of CODESA. This is exactly the opportunity the right wing is waiting for – such chaos that there's a military coup.'

As South Africa braced itself a new bill was rushed through parliament to strengthen the police, empowering them to tap telephones and intercept mail.

'*Jesus*,' Mahoney said, 'now we're going back to the bad old days of the Total Strategy.'

The legislation was denounced by the media and lawyers as a negation of the spirit of CODESA ('*What* fucking CODESA?!' Mahoney cried) and the new South Africa ('*What* new South Africa?' Mahoney cried. 'This is typical African politics all over again, the big impis, the big laager!') But the most dangerous provision was the section that banned private armies.

'Good *God*.' Mahoney groaned. They were in the whirlpool bath, listening to the evening news on the radio. '*Disarm private armies?* The government is going to send its army in to disarm the AWB? And simultaneously disarm the ANC? And the Zulus?.' He shook his head in wonder. '*That'll* be when the civil war really starts. Separating the Boer from his gun?'

Katrina massaged her brow. 'De Klerk daren't do it. He simply daren't *infuriate* the right wing further. And disarming them would even infuriate the moderate Afrikaners, they would rush back into the laager – that would cost him half his support – '

'And disarming the Zulus is going to cost him *all* their support – and they're his natural allies against the ANC.'

Just then there was a knock on the back door.

'Ignore it,' Mahoney said. But Katrina got up, and draped a towel around herself. She walked to the kitchen, dripping.

'Who is it?'

'It's me,' Patti said.

Katrina sighed, and turned the latch.

Patti stood on the verandah, smiling uncertainly, a bottle of champagne in her hand.

'I'm sorry,' she said.

Katrina closed her eyes. 'Me, too,' she smiled.

They embraced each other.

Of course a lot of other things happened in South Africa that Saturday night. Forty-eight people were murdered, slightly lower than normal. There were 87 political arsons, 403 house-breaking, in Johannesburg there were 97 car-thefts, mostly at traffic-lights; Evi was raped and so were 107 other women nation-wide; a total of 87 witch doctors illegally cast spells using human parts to bring victory in battle, and 17 people were killed in car smashes. Frikkie van der Merwe found a scorpion in his shoe. Willy Madlala ate his grandmother's liver to make him lucky at gambling. Regina Mpofu was stabbed in a shebeen because she wore an ANC tee-shirt; Alice Ndhlovu was stabbed in a shebeen because she wore an Inkatha tee-shirt. There was another train massacre but only three people were killed this time, leading the analysts to a spasm of optimism that train massacres were on the decrease. Patti Gandhi and Katrina de la Rey and Luke Mahoney got drunk together in the whirlpool bath. Mrs Jefferson-Smythe had a row with her maid Lilian over missing sugar. A gardener called Matthew Zabada caught his toe in his master's mowing machine. Lilian stabbed Mrs

Jefferson-Smythe with a breadknife but only hit her shoulder-holster. Patti Gandhi went to bed with Katrina de la Rey and Luke Mahoney.

Afterwards, when he tried to remember how it started, the details were blurred. He remembered Katrina's foot sliding up his leg; he remembered his own foot feeling its way up between Katrina's thighs and finding Patti's hand there; he remembered Patti's hand holding his rampant penis, he remembered Patti fondling Katrina's breasts, he remembered fondling both their breasts; but the sequence was lost in the drunken eroticism of it all. He remembered the two women silently getting up out of the bubbling bath, bodies sheening, steam rising off them; Katrina holding her hand out to him. He remembered walking silently together into the bedroom; falling wordlessly onto the big double bed together. He remembered the magnificent spectacle of two beautiful female bodies entangled, arms and legs sliding and writhing, long blonde hair and long black hair; the wild eroticism of possessing both of them.

Afterwards, as they lay in an exhausted, satiated, drunken tangle, Mahoney said:

'If this is called Mass Action, I'm all for it. I never knew you could have so much fun without laughing.' It seemed terribly funny and they all laughed uproariously. Katrina said, 'I'll fetch more champagne,' and Patti said, 'I'll have to sleep here tonight, I'm too drunk to drive,' and Mahoney said, 'Absolutely, but you won't get much sleep,' and that was uproariously funny too.

105

A ménage-à-trois can be tricky. Not so difficult to initiate, because many mature adults, aware of their limited youthfulness, begin to regard their bodies less as temples and more as workaday corporeal assets with a questionable spiritual future. As Patti Gandhi said, such a person is capable of making a brief gift of their body as a kindness to a friend. If that act of giving is also enjoyable, so much the better. If that act of kindness is also the fulfilment of a fantasy, then great. If fulfilment of that fantasy is uncomplicated by feelings of insecurity, then absolutely great. If that uncomplicated enjoyable act of kindness comes accompanied by a sense of loyalty and trust, then perfect.

'The best of both worlds,' Patti said.

'That's the up-side,' Katrina said soberly. 'The down-side is the complication.'

'I promise *you*,' Patti said earnestly, 'there will be no complication from *me*. I had twenty-four years to rationalise Luke, and I expected nothing from him if I ever got out. All I want is to be his friend. If I can also be his sexual partner from time to time, along with you in a ménage-à-trois, then great. He's a great fuck, and *you're* a great fuck. And I know *I'm* a great fuck – and I've got a lot of fucking to catch up on. And I don't want to do it around town and get AIDS. So to me it's just a fantasy come true. Okay? Uncomplicated.' She smiled at Katrina. 'I like you far too much – and you two are the only friends I've got that I care about. If I'm a complication,' she waved her hand, 'I'll never darken your doors again. And I'll put it all down to life's bitter-sweet tapestry. I don't want to ruin Luke's life all over again. *Or* yours. Okay?'

Katrina held her eye. She said: 'I believe you, Patti. And we're also fond of you. But I don't want it to happen again.'

'But you enjoyed it?'

'Yes.'

'And Luke enjoyed it.'

'Luke? Of course.'

'So what's the problem, if you believe me?'

Katrina said: 'The problem, my darling, is that it's immoral.'

'*Immoral?*' The beautiful eyebrows went up.

Katrina said quietly: 'Patti, I'm a Calvinist girl. I love Luke and have a great relationship with him. It's morally wrong to do anything to jeopardise that. QED.'

'*Jeopardise* it? So you don't believe me? Or you don't trust Luke? I'm a threat to you?'

'I don't think you're a threat, Patti. Or am I too trusting a soul? But, it's immoral.'

Patti frowned. 'But how can nature be immoral?' She waved a hand. 'All human beings are bi-sexual – you told me that yourself at the Wild Coast. Most people are unaware of their bi-sexuality because the opposite gender is available. But if no opposite gender were *ever* available, almost every woman on this earth would become a lesbian. Because we all need orgasms, darling. Like we need food, and sleep. It's very simple. It only becomes complicated when love enters the picture. Love is a device dreamed up by Mother Nature to keep man and woman together for the purpose of rearing children. The human child takes a minimum of ten years to rear before it can fend for itself, so Man ordained marriage and dressed it up in Love. And Love is fine – I'm not knocking it. But no procreation – and therefore no "marriage" – applies to our ménage-à-trois. To the simple fact that I'm sexually attracted to you, and you to me. And both of us to Luke.' She smiled. 'And Luke, not to put too fine a point on it, is happy as a pig in shit. In short, darling, we all are sexually constituted in such a way that we want to have a romp in bed together now and again.' She spread her hands. 'No big deal. Right?'

'Your logic is correct. But I'm not going to do it.'

Patti looked at her, appealing. Then she whispered: 'Look.' She slid forward on the sofa and pulled her dress up over her thighs. Then she raised her lovely legs and parted them. Her panties were white lace.

She said softly: 'You like that, don't you? Well, so do I. Nothing to be ashamed about. Just fun.' She held Katrina's eye. 'What you see has held kings and tsars and prime ministers and peasants spellbound since time began. It's the great common denominator.'

Katrina said: 'Sigmund Freud is part of my stock-in-trade.'

'So enjoy. It's a gift.'

Katrina held Patti's smouldering eyes and grinned. 'Go to hell, Gandhi. Put your beautiful loins away and have a drink. Luke's not here. That was the deal.'

Patti slumped her legs together and laughed.

'Quite right – that's the deal.' She got up, crossed the room and gave Katrina a big kiss on the cheek. 'I love you guys. Now, what've you got to drink in this crummy house?'

And Mass Action rolled.

Out there in the townships the war for political turf went on, ANC versus Inkatha, Zulu against Xhosa, the running battles, the gunfire and the pangas and axes and clubs, the train massacres, the bus-queue massacres, the necklacings, the blood, the screaming, the fleeing, the sirens of ambulances, the rumble of military vehicles. And then, midst all this mayhem, the ANC announced the centrepiece of their Mass Action Programme.

They would mount a massive rally in King William's Town which would march across the border into the independent Republic of Ciskei, occupy the capital of Bisho until the dictator Brigadier Gqozo surrendered power and permitted free political activity. Thereafter there would be a massive march on the KwaZulu capital of Ulundi to force Chief Buthelezi's government to do the same. Thereafter they would march on the Republic of Bophuthatswana.

'*Good God – is Mandela mad?*' Mahoney cried.

There was an outcry in the media condemning the marches as madness, *guaranteed* to provoke massive bloodshed, guaranteed to fail to achieve their objectives, guaranteed to destroy the National Peace

Accord, guaranteed to destroy CODESA, guaranteed to destroy investor confidence and wreak enormous damage on the economy, guaranteed to drive the white man back into the laager, guaranteed to lose the ANC international support. 'Worse political folly, worse lack of statesmanship, guaranteed to bring the ANC into contempt, is hard to imagine.'

'*Despicable!*' Mahoney seethed. '*Typical African politics.*'

There on television was the venerable Nelson Mandela reading his announcement, and there was the beautiful Patti Gandhi defending it at a press conference.

'The ANC's patience is not unlimited. We can no longer tolerate the situation where in large parts of our country petty despots, like Brigadier Gqozo, who came to power in a military coup in the so-called Republic of Ciskei, refuse to permit the ANC to operate – '

'But the Republic of Ciskei is not part of South Africa anymore,' a newsman interjected, 'it's independent – '

'That's fictitious nonsense, sir. The rest of the world does not recognise Ciskei as independent and nor does the ANC!'

'But the South African government does – the people of Ciskei were asked in a referendum whether they wanted independence, and they were officially granted it. So it *is* legally independent, whether the ANC likes it or not. So surely the ANC has no legal right to overthrow the government – '

Patti jabbed a finger. 'We have every *moral* right – to assert our *democratic* right of free political expression, which is what the new South Africa is supposed to be about. We all know that Ciskei only survives through the billions of taxpayers' dollars that are poured into their corrupt, white-elephant administration by the South African government – '

'But the ANC only survived through billions of dollars donated by the Soviet Union and other socialist countries – '

Patti retorted: '*Socialism*, sir, has a highly *moral*, *Christian* base! There have been certain failures, but the moral high ground remains intact. Apartheid on the other hand has a thoroughly *immoral* base. The so-called Republic of Ciskei has survived only on the blood-money of apartheid, of millions of black South Africans who have been brutally oppressed and denied the opportunity to self-betterment. The ANC, sir, has not the slightest compunction in damning such a government and saying "*We will march on you, Beelzebub!*"'

Another reporter demanded: 'And are you also going to march on the Republic of the Transkei which is also a military dictatorship under General Holomisa – but who happens to be pro-ANC? Or does the ANC *approve* of that dictator?'

Patti ignored the question and pointed to another reporter. 'Yes, sir?'

'*Jesus Christ . . .*' Mahoney groaned.

The reporter demanded: 'But how do you justify marching on KwaZulu and Bophuthatswana – both those states have *elected* governments?'

'But no *democracy*, sir! The ANC is unable to campaign in Bophuthatswana because of harassment. And KwaZulu is notorious – it's a well-known fact that Buthelezi and his Inkatha party are trying to crush the ANC – '

'But the ANC started it! The ANC and Inkatha were allies against apartheid, but then the ANC openly declared war on Inkatha. Is that because Buthelezi had the audacity to disagree with the ANC about communism? It's a well-known fact that the ANC declared war on him to *prevent* him getting his political stronghold there – Radio Freedom said: "Chop the head off the Buthelezi snake"!'

Patti jabbed her finger. 'Inkatha started it! Anyway, the fact remains that, right now, free political expression is not possible in Natal because of Inkatha, and now Inkatha has exported its impis from the killing fields of Natal up here to Johannesburg to wreak the same havoc – they arrived here by the lorry-load! And what the ANC is saying, sir, is that all this political oppression has got to stop! And as the black people have no voice, and as CODESA has broken down through the intransigence of the government with their preposterous demands of a senate-of-losers, and as there is no freedom of political expression in places like the Ciskei and KwaZulu, the ANC is forced to march peaceably on them – '

'"*Peaceably*"? How can you expect that to be *peaceable*?'

'The ANC will be unarmed. If there is any blood it will be on *their* hands, sir, not ours. The ANC marches in *peace. For* peace. Now if you'll excuse me . . . ' She marched off the stage, looking like a million bucks.

'*Stupid bitch!*' Mahoney shouted at the television. He turned to Katrina. 'What are we *doing*,' he demanded, 'romping in bed with a bitch like that?'

But he knew why: she was irresistible.

106

In the bad old days of the Kaffir Wars, King William's Town was a military post, part of a cordon sanitaire between the white frontiersmen and the Xhosa. Today King William's Town lies on the border of Ciskei, which is separated only by a corridor of rolling bushland from Transkei, both independent of South Africa, both Xhosa countries, both military dictatorships. The only difference between them was that the Transkei dictator, General Holomisa, perceiving on which side his bread would be buttered in the new South Africa, supported the ANC, while the Ciskei military dictator, Brigadier Oupa Gqozo, was anti-ANC because he knew they would take his domain away from him. Brigadier Gqozo, therefore, aligned himself with Chief Buthelezi, who insisted that KwaZulu remain autonomous in the new South Africa, and with President Mangope, who insisted that Bophuthatswana remain independent and, ironically, with the Afrikaner right wing, who insisted that they be given their old Boer republics back.

The Ciskei's purpose-built capital of Bisho is a grandiose conglomeration of parliamentary buildings, supreme court, civil service blocks, a sports stadium, the presidential palace, military barracks, all surrounded by the houses, huts and shacks of the ordinary Ciskeian. Bisho is only a few miles from King William's Town. King William's Town is normally a sleepy little place. But this Monday morning it was swarming.

At sunrise the convoys of buses started to arrive, bringing ANC people from far and wide. The ANC had rented King William's Town's sports stadium as a gathering point; by noon it was packed with eighty thousand excited supporters. Up onto the platform came the leaders, Chris Hani, commander-in-chief of MK, Ronnie Kasrils, Joe Slovo, Patti Gandhi, and a roar went up. The speeches began, railing against 'the De Klerk regime', against 'these Boers', against apartheid and all its works, against the so-called Republic of Ciskei and its tyrant Brigadier Gqozo – all evils that must be torn out by the roots. For two hours the speeches railed on to roars of applause, the excitement mounting. Then the people came pouring out of the stadium with their banners. They formed up into a massive phalanx half a mile long, and the march on Bisho began.

A few kilometres away the Ciskei Defence Force waited, where the tarred highway swept along the border. The South African army and police also waited, just outside Ciskei territory, to contain the violence that would surely spill over. Along the side of the highway was a high hedge of razor wire, blocking all access into Bisho, except a short road that led directly into the sports stadium. This was where Brigadier Gqozo intended to contain the marchers.

There were many pressmen and television crews waiting to record the bloodshed. The atmosphere was tense. Radios crackled with reports from King William's Town. They had been waiting for hours, hearing the roars rising up from the stadium.

Mahoney and Katrina had driven down from Johannesburg overnight to witness it. Mahoney said to Hugo Wessels: 'Why is Gqozo going to let them into his stadium, I wonder?'

'To contain them? They've got to go somewhere, and he can hardly put razor wire around the whole of Bisho, or he'll be effectively under siege. But if he bottles them up in the stadium they'll eventually get bored and piss off home? That'll make the ANC look pretty silly. Their march will be a very damp squib.'

Mahoney shook his head. 'It's a death-trap.'

'I think so too,' Katrina said worriedly.

Mahoney pointed. 'Once they're inside the stadium, Gqozo surrounds the place with his army, and he's got them at his mercy.'

'Machine-gun eighty thousand people?' Hugo said. 'No way.'

'No,' Katrina said, 'but once he's got them trapped, anything can happen – they may riot, start smashing the place up in frustration, he tear-gases them, pandemonium ensues, people get trampled to death, they try to break out, and that gives Gqozo an excuse to shoot.'

Mahoney studied the Ciskeian forces beyond the razor wire. Most were concealed in the long yellow grass, or behind buildings, or in dugouts. A few white officers were walking around. He walked a hundred yards up the road to speak to an officer of the South African forces.

'Excuse me, captain, can you tell me what the Ciskei's strategy is?'

'No, sir,' the officer replied in a heavy Afrikaans accent, 'but it doesn't take much imagination.'

'So what's going to happen when the ANC marches into that stadium?'

'I don't know, sir. You'd better ask the officer commanding the Ciskei forces.'

'Do you know him? Can I speak to him on your radio?'

'I don't know him personally, sir, except he's Colonel Harry Stegmann.'

Mahoney frowned. 'Harry Stegmann? Was he in the Congo army?'

'He's been in everybody's army, sir.'

Mahoney grinned. 'Please let me speak to him on your radio.'

Half a minute later he was saying: 'Harry Stegmann, this is Luke Mahoney. Did we fight together in Tshombe's army? Over.'

There was a moment's silence. Then: 'Well Jesus Christ!' Harry said. 'You old reprobate! Over.'

Mahoney laughed. '*Me* reprobate? Still a soldier of fortune, huh? Do you ever come up to Johannesburg? I've always got a bed for you. Over.'

'Who needs Jo'burg when all the fun's down here? Over.'

'Harry, can you tell me your plan?'

'You know I can't, Sergeant. Over.'

Mahoney said: 'Harry? Please don't open fire. Over.'

'*Me* open fire? Colonels don't open fire. Colonels sit in front of computers these days.'

'Today could start a big fire, Harry.'

Harry said: 'Who's starting it? Not us. We're the independent Republic of Ciskei, Luke, legitimately defending our territory against an illegal ANC invasion. If they want to defy the Law of Nations, it's their problem. How about a drink in the Officers' Mess here tonight? Over.'

'You're on,' Mahoney grinned. 'If we're all still alive.'

'Just keep your head down, Luke.'

Mahoney walked on up the road. He came to the short avenue of razor wire that led into the stadium. Nobody challenged him. He walked up the dirt track to the big main entrance.

The tiers of seats rose up on all sides, the big football field in the centre. Silent and waiting.

'*Lord*!' Katrina said. She had followed him. 'It's a perfect killing field.'

At the far end of the silent stadium was an exit. It led into Bisho. The big barred gate was open.

'*Open?*' Mahoney frowned. 'Why is it open if Gqozo intends to bottle them up in here?'

Katrina said worriedly: 'They march into the stadium from this end, see the exit, run out into Bisho in a stream. And the Ciskei soldiers shoot 'em.'

'Oh, *God*.'

Just then they heard the roar rising up from King William's Town as the mighty march began.

The marchers appeared at the bottom of the long hill in a mighty phalanx the width of the highway, stretching out of sight down into the city. Up the long hill towards Bisho they came, marching, chanting, television crews filming them. On and on up the hill they came, their noise getting louder and louder. And then Mahoney could identify Patti. She was on the edge of the front row, wearing jeans and a denim shirt, her long hair flowing.

Katrina went striding down the hill towards them. Patti gave a wide surprised smile. 'What are you doing here, darling – come to join us at last?'

Katrina fell into step beside her. '*Listen, tell your people not to go into the stadium – stay on the highway.*'

'Of course we're going into the stadium, the highway is in South Africa. It's no good demonstrating against Gqozo in South Africa, darling – '

'*Listen, there're Ciskeian soldiers lying in wait everywhere!*'

'We know, darling, we know – we've done a recce.'

'*Well for Christ's sake don't go out the other end of the stadium because you'll be mown down – it's a trap!*'

'You mean,' Patti smiled, 'Mr Gqozo *thinks* he's set a trap. Thanks for your concern, darling, but we know what we're doing – '

Katrina cried: '*Promise me you won't try to march out the other end of the stadium or you're in very big trouble!*'

'Darling, trouble is my business – always has been.'

Katrina stood on the verge as the noisy mass marched and toyi-toyed. Then she jogged to rejoin Mahoney.

'Did you convince her?'

'*Stupid bitch!*'

They stood, impotently watching the massive column dancing past them. Then, up at the front, the leaders turned off the highway and led the way down the avenue of razor wire into the big gateway of the stadium.

The rest was shocking.

The massive column followed their leaders through the bottleneck, into the huge stadium. Then they barrelled out, scrambling up onto the tiers of seats. Suddenly, there was Ronnie Kasrils running towards the open gate at the other end, shouting, waving his arms. Then the mob was scrambling down off the benches to follow him. They ran in a great mass across the football pitch towards the bottleneck of the exit. Ronnie Kasrils ran through it. He burst out into the open ground beyond, into Bisho, to lead his people into the heart of the dictator's capital to lay siege to it. And the gunfire broke out.

Suddenly the day was filled with the shocking clatter of rifles as the Ciskeian Defence Force leapt up from hiding and opened fire; the day was filled with the screaming and the collapsing, people throwing themselves flat, people fleeing back towards the stadium, crashing into each other, trampling each other underfoot. For an eternity of three minutes the gunfire clattered, screaming people collapsing all around; then there was a shocked pause; and the screaming and wailing rose up to the sky. Then there was another burst of gunfire. For another three minutes the killer cacophony raged as the wounded writhed and belly-crawled to cover and the rest of the mob frantically scrambled and fled.

Then the gunfire ceased, and there was only the screaming, the uproar, the wailing, the blood, the bullhorns bellowing, the mob surging leaderless back onto the highway. Outside the stadium, in Ciskei territory, lay twenty-nine dead, over two hundred wounded.

'*Patti*!' Mahoney roared. '*Patti!*'

Patti Gandhi had been running after Ronnie Kasrils when a bullet smashed her off her feet. Her head hit the ground, and all she knew was the shock, the gasping, the blood on her chest, the bodies crashing all around her midst the clatter of the gunfire. She raised her head and bellowed: '*Stop shooting, you bastards!*' Then her head reeled and she clutched her bloody breast, and she fainted.

The rest was very confused. The orders bellowing over the bullhorns, the South African ambulance crews running through the stadium, the television crews everywhere. Mahoney burst out of the stadium into the battlefield of Bisho, looking wildly for Patti. There was blood and bodies everywhere.

Patti!' he roared.

He saw her body beside a dead youth, her long black hair splayed, her blood pumping out of her chest. He ran to her frantically. '*Oh Christ, Christ, Christ!*' His fingers found the wound and he thrust the fabric of her shirt into it to staunch the blood. He heaved her up. Clutching her in his arms, he started to run. He went staggering towards the stadium. He lurched through the archway onto the sports field, gasping, rasping, sobbing: '*Oh you stupid bitch . . .*'

Those shocking six minutes were seen across the world. The bodies sprawling, crawling, the blood, the screams, the outrage. Across the newspapers of the world were the headlines, the condemnations, the angry editorials. On the television screen was Nelson Mandela furiously blaming President de Klerk for the massacre because the tyrant Gqozo was his puppet, denouncing De Klerk for all the violence racking the land. On television President de Klerk was angrily denouncing Gqozo and angrily denouncing the ANC for provoking bloodshed, for cynically sacrificing lives for propaganda, angrily reiterating that Ciskei was legally an independent republic, that South Africa had no power to depose the tyrant. And across the world there were angry editorials denouncing all three of them – '*A plague on all your houses!*'; denouncing Gqozo as a butcher; denouncing the ANC – '*The ANC has signed the National Peace Accord committing itself to peaceful negotiation: how can marching on an enemy's stronghold with the avowed intention of overthrowing him be considered peaceful?*'; denouncing the government for creating the independent state in the first place – '*The chickens of apartheid are coming home to roost.*' And there was the tyrant, Brigadier Gqozo, announcing that if the ANC marched on his country again they would get more of the same. And there was Eugene Terreblanche of the AWB loudly offering the services of his army to Gqozo to defend Ciskei. And then the ANC were loudly announcing that they would now march on the KwaZulu and Bophuthatswana capitals also, and occupy them, until Buthelezi and Mangope surrendered power, and there were Buthelezi and Mangope both warning the ANC that Bisho would look like a Sunday-school picnic if they tried.

And the ANC, 'bloodied but unbowed', had egg all over its face.

PART XVI

107

The good news was that the bullet that felled Patti Gandhi missed her lung; it made a bit of a mess of some ribs, but left only small wounds.

'Hairline scars!' the surgeon said proudly, 'and underneath that lovely complexion you've got the cutest ribs I've ever seen. You can come back anytime!'

'I bet you say that to all the ANC warriors, doc.'

'If the warriors look like you,' the doctor said, 'I'm going MK!'

Patti was confined to hospital for only two weeks. 'Heaven,' she declared to Katrina, 'I haven't slept like this for years. When's the party? I'm full of get-up and at-'em.'

But she had to convalesce for a month. Mahoney felt they should offer to let her stay with them, but Patti declined. 'No, I want to remain your friend. I got myself shot, I get myself unshot. I'll visit you when I need solace, don't doubt it. But please come and minister unto me frequently.'

Twice a week Katrina dropped in on Patti's house, on her way back from work. Patti was taking it easy but working on piles of ANC material. ANC bodyguards protected her premises now. 'How's the madam, today, Amos?' Katrina smiled as she got out of her car.

'Madam fine, madam,' Amos beamed.

'Not marching to KwaZulu today?'

'No, madam,' Amos giggled.

'Why not, Amos – is she chicken?'

Amos thought that was hilarious. 'Ah! Chief Buthelezi too much-i skellum, madam.'

'Darling,' Patti cried, as Katrina walked into her study. 'Look at my sexy scars now.' She dropped the back of her sari and presented her golden shoulders for admiration.

'Wonderful.' The wound was now just a pencil line. 'That surgeon was bloody clever.'

'And this.' Patti turned and exhibited her breasts. The scar was almost invisible.

'Wonderful.'

'Feel it.'

Katrina stroked her finger across it. '*Ex*cellent.'

Patti grinned. 'I think all that's necessary for it to disappear completely is for you to kiss it better!'

Katrina laughed. 'Go to hell, Gandhi. You know the deal.'

'Just one little teeny kiss?' Patti put her hand behind Katrina's head tenderly.

Katrina yielded, and kissed the little scar. 'There.'

She straightened and Patti whispered brightly: 'It would be awful nice if you bent a little lower and kissed my rampant nipple.'

'No way, kid, I know what'll happen.'

'But you'd *like* to?' Patti grinned.

'Where's my drink, I've been slaving over a hot desk all day.'

'If it's Luke you feel guilty about we can phone him right now and I'm sure he'll be here in a flash!'

'I'm sure he would.' She turned towards the kitchen, smiling. 'Where's my drink?'

Patti grabbed her elbow and pulled her around. Katrina slumped against the wall, taken aback. Patti looked at her, smouldering: 'I don't want Luke around either.' Then her hands ripped Katrina's blouse out of her skirt. She ripped the blouse up to her neck, then plunged her hands onto both her breasts.

Katrina stared at her, chest heaving. Patti kissed her fiercely and she thrust her breasts against hers. Katrina stood there, rigid; then Patti's hands reached down and pulled her skirt up to her hips. She thrust her hand between Katrina's thighs. She panted into her mouth: 'Oh, *yes*, you're wet for me.'

'No . . .' Katrina whispered into her mouth.

'*Yes!*' Patti unclipped Katrina's skirt at her waist. It fell to her feet. She stood there in her stockings and suspenders, her breasts heaving. Patti's sari was hanging off her hips. She whispered: 'Rip this garment off me.'

'No . . .' Katrina closed her eyes. Then smiled. 'No.' She stooped to recover her skirt.

'*Yes!*' Patti wrenched her sari off and flung it across the room. And there she stood, gloriously naked, her eyes afire. For a moment they stared at each other, smouldering: then Patti plunged her mouth on Katrina's again and collapsed her backwards onto the sofa. She sprawled on top of her, her pelvis thrust down against Katrina's, their breasts hard against each other's. Then she writhed down Katrina's body, kissing it.

Afterwards, they lay on the floor, hair awry. Patti whispered: 'I'm sorry. But cheer up, darling. Nothing terrible has happened. There's nothing wrong in making a little love in this sad world of ours.'

Katrina sat up. She hugged her knees. 'You weren't making love,' she said.

'I *was*. I love you and Luke!'

Katrina snorted softly. 'You love Luke.' She began to get up but Patti's hand gripped her knee.

'*Yes. And you.*'

Katrina snorted again. 'What have I done to deserve your love?' She turned to her. 'You weren't making love, you were *lashing* out at the world for the shitty hand it's dealt you – you were expressing your anger sexually – getting your own back. Taking some revenge – *sexually*. And particularly your anger at the Afrikaner for what we did to you.' She got to her feet and stooped for her panties. She stepped into them and wriggled them up her hips.

Patti said, from the floor: 'Oh, you're so beautiful. But you're wrong, Dr Freud. But even if you're right, so *what*? Almost everything in this sad life has its roots in animal sexuality. But believe me, beautiful Afrikaner lady, when you've been sitting in loveless prison for twenty-four years you don't give a shit about the *roots* – what you want when you come out is *love*, wherever you can get it. And you're immensely grateful for any crumb of it you get! And I'm immensely grateful to *you*.'

'To *me*?' Katrina picked up a stocking. 'Don't stretch credulity. I took your man away from you.'

Patti sat up. She appealed: 'But I understand that. God – I may be a soppy dumb-dumb but I'm not a fool! Of course I dreamed about Luke for twenty-four years – but I'm also pretty smart and didn't really expect him to be waiting with a bunch of red roses when I got out. Lisa Rousseau had warned me – about *you*, amongst other things. Of *course* I'm grateful to you – you could have been a bitch and cut me off dead and stopped Luke having anything to do with me. But you didn't. You were *kind* to me. You treated me as . . . ' She waved a hand. 'Like an important person who deserved *respect*, because I was kind of part of Luke's . . . *family*, almost. And I *loved* you for it. And I still do.'

Katrina was pulling on her second stocking. 'Yeah?'

'*Yeah*. Jesus, what other family have I got? What other friends like you, who I can talk to?' Then she stifled a sob. 'Acquaintances by the hundred, sure, people I work with – but friends? Look – please have a drink and let's talk about this.'

'Another time. I want to go home.'

'And do what?'

Katrina knew exactly what she wanted to do. Confess what had happened to Luke and beg his forgiveness.

Patti said softly: 'And tell Luke, huh?'

'Yes.' Katrina pulled on her blouse.

Patti looked at her. She said: 'But you wanted to do it too. You enjoyed it.'

Katrina tossed her hair off her face. She buttoned her blouse and didn't answer. Patti whispered urgently: 'And that was a *sin*? To . . . give a fellow human being, who loves you – and who you love too, in your tense Calvinist way – to give her a little physical love?'

'It wasn't *love*. It was anger. Expressed in . . . ravishment.'

Patti said: 'You could have hit me.'

'I've never hit anybody in my life.' She looked down at her angrily. 'I feel terrible! Guilty as *hell*. But, yes, I enjoyed it. Satisfied? But I've betrayed Luke!'

'So you're going to confess it?'

Katrina put her hands to her face.

Patti looked at her. Then she got up and slid her arms around her. She whispered: 'Oh please don't be a fool. Please don't create a crisis when there needn't be any. A sin? Darling, your exquisite Dutch Reformed Church conscience has no *idea* of sin in this awful world.' She held her tight. 'Do you imagine that on this tiny speck in the infinite universe we call Earth the act of . . . *kindness* you permitted matters the tiniest jot?'

The good news was that the ANC did not dare march on Bisho again, nor KwaZulu, nor Bophuthatswana. But their Mass Action still rolled, in fits and starts and with a lot of bloody noise, clanking down the stony slope towards the ruin of South Africa. The strikes, the boycotts, the students' marches, the sit-ins, the intimidation; and all the time the rattle of gunfire, the arson, the violence, the fighting for political strongholds. The killing fields of Natal ever bloodier, massacre matched by massacre, screaming women and children and infants gunned down first by one side, then the other; and up there on the Reef the ANC Comrades, armed to the teeth, terrorising, the impis of Inkatha, armed to the teeth, retaliating. It was a hell of a time that year, after CODESA broke down and the ANC and Inkatha fought it out for political territory in the African Way. And the international investors watched in horror, and white South Africans packed their bags in droves.

'The Congo all over again,' Mahoney said.

And there was more bad news. That year, as the ANC's Mass Action bloodily clunked, corruption scandals rocked the government as the Auditor General unleashed new accounts to parliament with overwhelming evidence that forty years of undisputed rule had resulted in Afrikaners treating South Africa as a pork barrel, a fountain of jobs for the boys, taxpayers' money siphoned off in scams and fictitious purchases, kick-backs for civil servants, bribes, government tenders awarded to pals, rake-offs, the Transport Department taking bribes from airlines to avoid landing fees, civil servants in cahoots with lawyers to plunder the Third-Party Vehicle Insurance Fund, palatial new government buildings standing half-used, billions poured into corrupt homeland administrations, inferior textbooks prescribed because they were written by pals, colossal overruns on state projects, thefts, overtime abuse, billions spent on secret Defence budgets for the likes of the Civil Cooperation Bureau. It was a shocking year of skeletons tumbling out of government cupboards, and the ANC rubbed its hands in glee.

'*God*,' Mahoney said. 'We're just as bad as the rest of Africa.'

'*Except*,' Katrina said, 'these abuses stem from the bad old days of apartheid. You can't blame the *present* government for them.'

'Bullshit!' Patti cried. 'The leopard might have changed its spots, but it's the same *leopard*.'

And then it was the ANC's turn to squirm. Nelson Mandela announced his legal separation from his wife, Winnie, after a series of embarrassments dating back to her 'necklace' speech, her Mandela United Football Club, her conviction for kidnapping Stompie Seipei, culminating in exposure of letters written to a young man alleged to be her lover. She had to resign all her powerful official positions, as head of the ANC's Woman's League, head of their Welfare Department. And Winnie Mandela looked as politically dead as a dodo.

'Thank *God*,' Mahoney said. 'But I feel bloody sorry for Nelson. He spends twenty-seven years in prison and finds this awaiting him.'

'*Nobody*,' Patti said, 'can reasonably expect anybody to remain faithful for twenty-seven years whilst their spouse is in prison.'

Mahoney said: 'But we can expect her to be discreet. Caesar's wife must be above reproach. And how can South Africa have a First Lady who is a convicted kidnapper? Who publicly approves of necklacing?'

'She's had a hell of a life,' Patti said. 'Is it any wonder she's a bit unstable?'

And then the scandal broke of ANC prison camps, and it was the government's turn to rub their hands. Back from exile came angry MK soldiers who went to the press and told horrific tales of the ANC's

727

military camps in Angola and elsewhere, tales of torture by Mbokodo, the security men of the ANC, torture of anybody suspected as a spy, who complained about the food, about boredom, about inaction, about not being sent back to South Africa to fight the Boers; stories of floggings, overcrowded prison cells with overflowing toilet buckets, solitary confinement, denial of food and water, incarceration in metal tanks in the blazing heat, suffocation, shattered eardrums, electric shocks, men tied upright to trees for weeks, backbreaking forced labour, summary executions. And what made it more scandalous was that the exiles said the topmost ANC leadership had known about these abuses – Chris Hani, the commander-in-chief, Joe Slovo, head of the Communist Party, even Oliver Tambo, acting-president of the ANC, all visited the camps but did nothing to curb Mbokodo's abuse of power.

There was a rash of denunciatory editorials, even in the liberal overseas press, and the government rubbed its hands in glee, and the right wing belly-laughed and the Conservative Party trumpeted that to negotiate with the ANC was suicide, that Mbokodo, the 'Boulder that Crushes', would crush all opposition in the new South Africa.

Mahoney said: 'If this is what the ANC did to their own soldiers, imagine what they'll do to their critics once they're in power.'

Patti said sullenly: 'What about the government's bullying for forty years?'

'I agree – both the government and the ANC are typical African political bullies. A plague on both their houses. The sooner we all emigrate to Australia the better.'

'There will be,' Patti said, 'no Mbokodo in the new South Africa. We will not repeat the injustices of the present government – '

'No Mbokodo in the new South Africa?' Katrina cried. 'No security police? Oh, wonderful! So we can all relax. And all because there'll be no more trouble in the new South Africa. The Zulus, the AWB, Buthelezi, they'll all beat their swords into panty-hose? Treurnicht will return to the pulpit and preach Love Thy Black Neighbour?'

'The ANC,' Patti said, 'is appointing a commission of inquiry into these torture camp allegations. Fully fledged lawyers.'

The next day, Nelson Mandela was on television solemnly announcing his commission of inquiry, and the world applauded; and then he announced the composition of the commission and the world groaned. Two of the lawyers were ANC stalwarts, and the hearings would not be public. And, as De Klerk had done, he had made the terms of reference so restricted that the commission could only hear evidence surrounding one camp.

'An inquiry by ANC lawyers? In private? About only one camp?'

But the ANC's commission reported that the witnesses were telling the truth; and then Amnesty International instituted its own inquiry and it delivered a report condemning the ANC for its human rights abuses. So the ANC had egg all over its face again. But, as Patti pointed out, at least it had the moral high ground of accepting blame. 'Unlike De Klerk, who for a long time *refused* to appoint a commission of inquiry into police hit squads, and then so restricted it that the truth could not be uncovered! And all those bastards who masterminded those police hit squads – and the CCB thugs – they're still in their jobs. Whereas all those Mbokodo people will be fired by the ANC.'

'Yeah? Joe Slovo too? Chris Hani?'

'*They* had nothing to do with torture!'

Mahoney sighed. 'Look, Patti, the ANC's army is totally under the control of the communists. The recruits were indoctrinated, had political commissars over them, communist officers, the Revolutionary Council was staffed entirely by communists. And Mbokodo men were all communists. And who controlled the Communist Party? Joe Slovo and Chris Hani. Both of them visited the camps. Hani was involved in crushing the mutiny. And Oliver Tambo. Of course they knew. *And they not only still hold their jobs, the Communist Party continues to dominate the ANC!*'

Katrina held up her hands. 'Can we please stop shouting?'

And then, whilst the government was rubbing its hands at the ANC's discomfort, the scandal broke that the Civil Cooperation Bureau had not been disbanded. The CCB was alive and well, now called the Department of Covert Collection, staffed by senior officers of Military Intelligence, until the Goldstone Commission got wind of them, raided their offices in Pretoria, seized files which proved that they were plotting to discredit the ANC by involving them in prostitution and drugs. And so the government had egg all over its face again – and the ANC rubbed its hands in glee.

'*Nobody* can now dispute that a Third Force is causing the violence,' Patti said.

'"*Exploiting*" the violence,' Mahoney said, 'not *causing* it. What's *causing* the violence is the age-old African way of power politics.'

'Bullshit – ' Patti cried.

'*Bullshit?* And all the violence that's racked Africa since time began – since the Mfecane, the violence in Kenya, Uganda, Nigeria, the Congo, all that was caused by a nasty Third Force too?'

'These declarations of bullshits,' Katrina groaned, 'are becoming a frequent occurrence.'

Mahoney said: 'Patti, what *isn't* nonsense is what this Third Force *intends* doing – namely, mounting a rebellion when the time is right!

What we've uncovered so far – police hit squads, the CCB, now the Department of Covert Collection – it's just the tip of the iceberg. The rest of it stretches across South Africa, in right-wing cells and whole regiments of the Citizen Force, half the police, half the army, plus massive arsenals. Plus all the military blueprints prepared by the experts of the Total Onslaught era. Plus all their sympathisers in the civil service who can bring the country to a standstill.' He shook his head. 'Have we put an end to the Department of Covert Collection because the Goldstone Commission raided them? Have we hell. All we've done is verified their *existence*. Have we put an end to police hit squads? Have we hell. They're all still available, waiting for the go-ahead. *That's* what I'm worried about. And that's what you guys in the ANC should be worrying about, instead of gloating about De Klerk's latest embarrassment.'

'Go,' Patti said, 'and teach your grandmother to suck eggs.'

'And *you*,' Mahoney said, 'advise *your* grandmother that if she wants to avoid this civil war she'd better agree to giving the Afrikaner his precious volkstaat *when* CODESA resumes. *If* CODESA resumes. If the ANC's Mass Action hasn't driven us *all* back into the laager. Or else the Afrikaner will wipe the floor with your grandmother.'

'I'm hot for you.' Patti smiled across her wineglass.

'Luke,' Katrina smiled sweetly, 'is not with us.'

'Go'n wake him up.'

'No. He was up all last night on the film-set, he needs his sleep.'

'Did you tell him about last time?'

'No. I didn't want to complicate matters.'

'Complicate what matters?' Patti frowned. 'I don't want to *live* with either of you. Just a romp now and again. You're the only sexual part-ners I've got. And all I want, thanks very much.'

Katrina smiled. 'You're too kind, darling.'

Patti grinned. 'It's true. Why would I want to go out there and scrounge for fifty-year-old married men who might give me AIDS? And I'm not interested in anybody *younger* – what the hell would we talk about? Do they know a fraction of what I know? Have they suffered? No, they've been living on the fat of apartheid all these years with their eyes closed. What have I got in common with them? And as for young studs – forget 'em. Had half a dozen in London and not only were they brainless they suffered from premature ejaculation.' She added: 'But don't worry, I had myself tested for AIDS and I'm okay.'

Katrina smiled. 'That's good.'

'And I haven't had anybody but you since I came back to South Africa.'

'Good.'

'Nor do I intend to.'

Katrina sloshed more wine into her glass. She didn't respond.

Patti said: 'I'm quite happy the way we are.'

Katrina sighed. Patti continued: 'I get my jollies, and I've got my dear friends. And my job. And I'm well off. And I'm *free*.'

Katrina felt guilt burn. 'Patti,' she said, 'Luke and I are really very fond of you.'

'"Fond"?' Patti grinned from across the room. 'What a milk-and-water word for good old *lust*. For *laughter*. For *fun*. For . . . ' Her eyes moistened. 'For *loyalty*.'

Katrina smiled. 'Okay, you out-word me. But we are.'

Patti grinned. 'For *orgasms*?' She shook her head at her. 'Almost nothing is more fundamental in this animal life we lead than happy *orgasms*, is it?'

'True.'

'Patti got to her feet. She pulled up her dress to reveal her lovely legs. 'So, how about a bit of fundamental friendship, madam?'

Katrina threw back her head and laughed. 'Luke's asleep!'

'Then I'll go'n wake him, shall I! The sonofabitch must be a friend of mine after all he owes me.'

She swept through to the bedroom. Mahoney was out to the wide world. Patti swept back the blankets.

'Luke!' she cried cheerfully. 'Some *good* news at last.'

The good news was the spin-off of all these scandals. The ANC realised its image was tarnished and the goodwill of the world was not inexhaustible, that their righteous Mass Action rang terribly. And the government realised that its image was tarnished and that the world's goodwill for them was not inexhaustible either. And so it came to pass that the two of them, their tails somewhat between their legs, managed to get together at a *bosberaad*.

A *bosberaad* means a Bush Consultation, the sort of gathering the voortrekkers summoned when deciding how to knock the living shit out of the kaffirs and the British, an event characterised by much strong drink, roasted meat, and pejorative language. In this *bosberaad*, however, it was all smiles. Government limousines fetched the ANC negotiating team and whisked them off to luxurious accommodation on some rich Afrikaner's farm with all mod cons.

The result was published, all smiles, as a 'Record of Understanding'. The government dropped its demand for a senate-of-losers. And it agreed that the new constitution would be drawn up by an elected Constituent Assembly. (*'Shit,'* Mahoney cried.) The ANC agreed in principle to 'regionalism' instead of a winner-takes-all unitary state. Both sides re-committed themselves to reconvening CODESA. The ANC agreed to abandon their Mass Action Campaign. ('Thank *Christ.'*) And the government agreed to prohibit the carrying of dangerous weapons, which meant disarming the Zulus.

'*Disarming the Zulus!*' Mahoney cried in wonder. 'What's Buthelezi going to say about *this?*'

And Chief Buthelezi had a lot to say. He announced that the mighty Zulu nation would never return to CODESA because the government and the ANC were striking private deals. He threatened that KwaZulu would unilaterally declare its independence of South Africa and defend it to the last man. He defied the government to try to disarm the Zulus. ('*Yeah . . .* ' Mahoney agreed.) And fifty thousand Zulus in battle dress marched through Johannesburg, armed to the teeth, chanting blood-curdling war cries, and descended on the principal police station, inviting the authorities to disarm them. There was not one arrest.

And then Winnie Mandela denounced the ANC 'leadership clique' for striking private deals with the government, for 'climbing into bed' with the government to enjoy the 'silken sheets', saying she pitied her estranged husband for being 'so naive'.

And then the formation of a new political axis called COSAG was announced – the Concerned South Africans Group.

It consisted of the white Conservative Party and its numerous Afrikaner allies, including Katrina's Volkswag, plus the black parties of Inkatha, Bophuthatswana and Ciskei. Its purpose was to present a united military front at CODESA against the government-ANC 'clique'. To fight for the territorial rights of the Afrikaner, the Zulu, Tswanas, and the Ciskeian Xhosa.

It was an impressive line-up of conservative resistance to the new South Africa that was going to be hatched when CODESA resumed. It represented almost half of the population of the old South Africa.

'And now,' Mahoney said, 'the battle lines are truly drawn . . . '

108

It was Justin Nkomo who had broken the scandal of the ANC's detention camps to the press.

It had taken Justin five years to make it from Luanda across the vast war-torn Angolan bush, then across the Congo, then across into Kenya, to Nairobi. To cover that distance he had begged, borrowed, stolen, walked, hitch-hiked, stowed away on barges, buses, trains. In every place his fear had been the ANC – being recognised by somebody who had known him in Zambia, in Cuba, in Angola, in MK. He had no travel documents and, usually, no money. It was not until he reached Nairobi that he got any reliable information on what was happening in South Africa, from newspapers: this new man called De Klerk was turning South Africa on its head by talking about a Great Indaba. Justin had scraped up a few shillings and written two air letters. One to his bank in Miami, instructing them to telex all his money, which he estimated at about two thousand dollars, to Barclays Bank in Nairobi; the other was a back-up, written to his wife, Sally, care of her parents in Atlanta, Georgia, begging her to lend him a thousand dollars and telex it to Barclays Bank, Durban, Natal, South Africa.

Justin Nkomo had done a lot of thinking in the four years since he had escaped from the ANC prison in Nova Instalacao, and it boiled down to this: no *way* did he want to see the ANC as the new government of South Africa, no *way* did he trust them, and no *way* was he a communist. Justin Nkomo was going to take his services to Chief Buthelezi of Inkatha.

It had taken Justin another seven months, after his money had finally arrived in Nairobi, to make his way, still without travel documents, down across Kenya, then across the border into Tanzania, then across into Mozambique. The extent of the collapse of Tanzania's economy under Marxism had shocked him, but the devastation of Mozambique under the combined impact of Marxism and Renamo appalled him. When he crept across the border of northern Natal, into South Africa, at dead of night, he had absolutely no doubt about which side he should offer his services.

But it was his experiences in the ANC military camps that Justin wanted the world to know about and which he offered Inkatha in exchange for a respectable place in their organization. And Inkatha snapped him up: Justin went to Johannesburg under an assumed name, and set to organising the Returned Exiles Committee, collecting affidavits from other disaffected MK soldiers. He did so with relish.

One of the angry people who came forward to his committee was

Albert Mpofu, who had been one of the leaders of the Soweto Riots of 1976. Albert had also had a gutful of the ANC: he had deserted after two years in one of their detention camps. He had made his way to Dar es Salaam in Tanzania and joined the rival PAC.

Justin and Albert had not known each other during their unhappy service in MK but they had a lot in common because of it. In the six weeks they worked together collecting evidence before breaking the scandal, they became friends. Both had the common purpose of discrediting the ANC, but for different reasons. Justin wanted the truth to be known so that the ANC's abuse of power did not re-occur in the new South Africa, and he wanted their domination by the communists made known. Justin wanted the ANC to fail because he believed that the only way that the new South Africa would survive and escape the oppressions of the rest of Africa was as a federation of largely autonomous states, like America. That was what Inkatha wanted, whereas the ANC wanted a unified state where they held all the power. Justin Nkomo had no wish to derail negotiations at CODESA: he just didn't want the ANC to come out on top – he wanted co-existence of ethnic states to win the day.

But Albert Mpofu wanted to discredit the ANC for a different reason: the ANC was a multi-racial organization and that was anathema to Albert. He had joined the PAC because he was a black racist who wanted Africa for the Africans: that, more or less, was what Steve Biko and his Black Consciousness movement had striven for. Albert did not object to the communist influence in the ANC because the PAC was also a socialist organization which demanded that all the land be returned to the Africans: he wanted the ANC destroyed because it was making a deal with the white man at CODESA, and he wanted the white man driven into the sea. Albert wanted CODESA derailed and destroyed in a bloodbath.

He helped Justin collect affidavits from angry MK soldiers; then, once the story was broken and the ANC had egg on its face, he disappeared. His destination was his cell in King William's Town where his mentor, Steve Biko, had started Black Consciousness twenty years ago. Justin had known nothing about this: he was mystified by Albert's disappearance. And he would have been horrified had he known what he was about to do.

And there was another surprise for Justin when he completed his assignment and returned to Ulundi. There, awaiting him, arms akimbo, was his long-lost American wife, Sally Freeman Nkomo, breathing fire.

'*You sumbitch!*' she hollered, before collapsing in tears into his astonished arms.

*   *   *

Albert's first bomb exploded in the Queen's Arms, a blue-collar pub in East London. The death toll was only six, but twenty-four others were badly wounded by flying shrapnel, and the bar was a ruin. For his next trick Albert went upmarket: he hit the Selkirk Country Club.

The Selkirk Country Club is a very pleasant, genteel place: a spacious clubhouse, a large bar, a tasteful lounge, a reading room, an excellent restaurant, all surrounded by gardens, squash courts, tennis courts, a golf-course. For generations the club had been for whites only, but since De Klerk's historic speech two years ago the members had voted to make it multi-racial, though no non-white person had yet applied for membership. The club was a popular place; on weekends it was crowded, the parking area full. It was on a quiet Wednesday night, however, when there was little chance of being pursued, that Albert struck.

There were golfers at the bar but there was only one private dinner party going on in the dining-room, a dozen people, the guests of a local lawyer. They were on the main course when Albert and three men, wearing balaclavas, burst in the side door with AK–47 rifles, and opened fire. In a prolonged blast they gunned down the dinner guests, sending them sprawling in splats of blood, blasting them off their chairs and across the table. Then, for good measure, Albert lobbed a hand grenade into their bloody midst, and the gang turned and ran.

They ran across the golf course to a dirt road beyond, jumped into a waiting stolen vehicle, and sped away into the night, making for the Republic of Ciskei a few miles away. By the time the police arrived at the country club, they were safely over the border.

Albert's purpose was to make the PAC a force to be reckoned with when CODESA resumed. His plan relied on the creation of such terror as to make the white man panic, flee back into the laager, and thereby destroy CODESA, to make the white man so furious that he rebelled against his government's reforms so that martial law had to be declared, so that the ANC would rise up, so that chaos would ensue, in which the white man and the ANC would destroy each other. When that process was completed, the PAC could begin rebuilding the new socialist South Africa, for the Africans. So Albert and his APLA cells began attacking remote Afrikaner farms.

In the ensuing months Albert's hit-and-run teams attacked a score of farms, killing dozens of whites, and their cry *'Kill the Boer! Kill the farmer!'* reverberated across South Africa. And his strategy looked like working: the farmers were up in arms, the AWB got many new recruits and announced that the borders of the new South Africa would be drawn in blood.

109

The saying is: 'The future of South Africa will be resolved by the Boers and the Zulus.' And when CODESA resumed it looked as if the saying was coming true: here were the Zulus and the Afrikaner right wing, as members of COSAG, the Concerned South Africans Group, lined up as allies against a new common enemy, the South African government and the ANC. What COSAG demanded was autonomous states for each ethnic member of their group: and if they didn't get their way there was going to be big trouble. And, as Professor Katrina de la Rey said in one of her many addresses to CODESA, 'a single spark can start a prairie fire.'

'Is the delegate for COSAG threatening us?' Patti Gandhi enquired sweetly from across the hall.

'On the contrary, madam,' Katrina retorted, 'the Afrikaner volk wish to *avoid* a prairie fire! We wish to *avoid* the clash of ethnicity which has characterised Africa to date, we wish to respect other nations' differences, live in harmony with them, as equals, as good neighbours! We want to avoid the horrific civil war that is happening as we speak in Yugoslavia where Serb, Croat and Muslim fight each other to the death, we want to *avoid* the violence and hatred and misery of Ireland, we want to *avoid* the animosities of the rest of Africa where different tribes were lumped together by colonial powers drawing nice straight lines on the map of Africa – with the result that post-colonial Africa has been at war with itself ever since! We wish to *avoid* repeating all those old mistakes by being realistic, recognising the healthy cultural forces of ethnicity and allowing different ethnic groups to govern themselves as much as possible – '

'Sounds like the perpetuation of apartheid to me,' another ANC delegate said.

'I can assure the honourable delegates that it is *not* the intention of the Afrikaner Volkswag to repeat the disasters of apartheid. There will be no discrimination of any sort in *our* volkstaat. All people will have equal rights, be they white, black, brown, yellow, ANC, CP, communist, or whatever – '

'And is that what the Conservative Party wants too?' a black delegate enquired.

Katrina retorted: 'I cannot speak for the Conservative Party, you must ask that of Dr Treurnicht – '

'But you're all allies now in COSAG, you're all in bed together.'

Katrina's eyes flashed. 'The honourable delegate knows perfectly well that the different members of COSAG have somewhat different agendas, though they do have the common denominator of wanting autonomy for their respective groups. But to imply, because we are presenting a unified front against the ANC-Government juggernaut, that we all therefore wish to perpetuate apartheid is not only downright untrue, it's also downright trouble-making!'

'What would be downright trouble-making is giving the Afrikaner an independent volkstaat – because he's not to be trusted! He'll start his apartheid all over again!'

'Order!' the chairman said wearily. 'Professor de la Rey has the floor.'

The COSAG members indeed had different agendas. The Afrikaner Volksunie, which included Katrina's Volkswag, only wanted a semi-autonomous volkstaat in a federation with the new South Africa; the Conservative Party wanted a completely independent state, where only whites would be citizens, in a loose confederal association with the new South Africa; the Zulus and the Ciskei wanted to be almost independent in a federation with South Africa, and Bophuthatswana insisted on remaining completely independent. The government wanted 'regionalism', where provincial-style governments had extensive powers over their areas; the PAC demanded that the whole of South Africa be returned immediately to the blacks under a Marxist government. COSAG and the government and the ANC demanded that the PAC disband their army if they wished to participate in CODESA, and the PAC demanded why the hell should they while COSAG had its AWB army, Inkatha its impis, the government had its security forces, and the ANC had its MK. The ANC demanded that elections be held immediately for a constituent assembly which would draw up the final constitution for the new South Africa. The COSAG members insisted that the new constitution be finalised before the first election.

And all the time, during the noisy slug-fest of the conference, the violence raged on out there in the black townships and in the killing fields of Natal and the Orange Free State, Inkatha fighting the ANC, the ANC fighting Inkatha and the PAC, the PAC massacring white farmers, the AWB bellowing that it would declare war if one more white was killed.

And then Chris Hani, the Secretary General of the Communist Party, and a putative heir-apparent to Nelson Mandela, was gunned down.

It was a beautiful South African day. In the town of Boksburg, where Chris Hani had bought his modest suburban home, it was Saturday-morning-as-usual: children riding their bicycles, blue-collar whites fixing their hire-purchase cars, housewives going off to the supermarkets. That's what Chris Hani did this Saturday: he went shopping for his wife. He took his teenage daughter with him.

Chris Hani had given his bodyguards the weekend off because he intended staying at home. Returning from the supermarket, he turned into his short drive, and parked. His daughter went inside with some groceries. Neither noticed that a car had stopped just beyond the gate. Chris Hani hefted his groceries out as a white man stepped into his gateway.

'Mr Hani?'

Chris Hani turned. The man pulled his hand from his pocket, levelled a pistol and fired.

Chris Hani was blown off his feet. He sprawled and the gunman strode up to him and fired three more shots into him. Then he ran back down the drive, got into the waiting car and drove away.

An Afrikaner housewife who lived opposite the Hani family heard the shots. She ran outside. She saw Chris Hani lying in his drive, saw the car pull away. She frantically memorised the number. She ran inside and telephoned the police.

Ten minutes later the police stopped a car in Boksburg answering the description given by the Afrikaner lady. It was driven by a white man called Janusz Waluz. He was known to be a member of the AWB. He refused to answer any questions. He was still carrying the pistol, which ballistic evidence subsequently proved was the weapon that killed Chris Hani. When his apartment was searched a typed hitlist was found containing, *inter alios*, the names and addresses of Chris Hani, Nelson Mandela, Joe Slovo and President de Klerk.

While the police were searching the apartment the telephone rang. The caller was a man named Clive Derby-Lewis. He was a former member of parliament for the Conservative Party, and a member of World Apartheid movement, a neo-Nazi organization. When his house was searched a copy of the same hitlist was found. The pistol that killed Hani had been adapted to have a silencer fitted, and the gunsmith who did the job was traced to Cape Town. He told the police that the person who had brought it to him for adaptation was Clive Derby-Lewis.

The outrage that followed the assassination of Chris Hani should have been the spark that started the prairie fire of South Africa – and Mahoney thought it was going to be. That night the security forces were everywhere, white people stayed at home with their guns to hand; but within hours Nelson Mandela and President de Klerk were on television, side by side, appealing to the people to resist giving vent to their rage, to realize this atrocity was intended to create chaos, to derail the negotiations for the new South Africa in an explosion of blood. Mahoney wrote in his journal:

> . . . it is to the credit of Mandela that he did not exploit the situation, refrained from rhetoric, and exhorted his bloody-minded constituency to follow suit. Of course the ANC has every reason to wish to avoid the chaos, for they are, by and large, dominating the negotiation process, and will no doubt win the first elections that will follow it soon. Martial law would have brought that process to a juddering halt, probably for years as the Generals ruled, as in South America. Nevertheless, he genuinely did not want more blood spilt. Mandela went up in my estimation tonight. And so, also, did De Klerk. If ever he had second thoughts (as he must have done, in view of the violence) about sharing democracy with blacks, if ever he had the opportunity to correct mistakes and let the African Way separate the men from the boys, to apply the ultimate law that might is right, to impose his political will, to enforce by martial law his notions of how the new South Africa should be (as every other African president would have done), today was his chance. But he proved himself genuinely dedicated to the process of negotiation.

The murder of Chris Hani could have sent things out of control in South Africa; and, oh yes, there were the rabble-rousing speeches at his funeral, the ANC out in force, the Inkatha impis waiting, the security forces waiting, and the world held its breath again as the television cameras recorded the great funeral cortège, the lying-in-state at the massive football stadium, the outraged speeches, the roars for blood, the spears and axes and AK–47s and the war dances; and as the massive procession set out from the stadium to lay Chris Hani to rest there was the pillage, the mobs of mourners breaking into shops and looting, the arson, the gunfire from the Inkatha hostel en route mowing down a couple of dozen, and there were the crack of police tear-gas guns, the wail of ambulances, the running battles: but, for all that, the crisis passed off without major alarm, and to the world's relief CODESA resumed.

It was a screamingly tense time, but one of the spin-offs was that a new sense of urgency entered the labyrinthine deliberations of CODESA. And then the dramatic announcement came: the government and the ANC had agreed that the first one-man-one-vote general election would be held on 27th April, of the following year; that the constitution for the new South Africa would be drawn up by the elected representatives; that a Transitional Executive Council consisting mainly of ANC and National Party appointees would effectively rule the country pending those elections.

Mahoney was aghast when he heard the news. His publisher demanded on the telephone: 'What the hell does this dramatic announcement mean, Luke?'

'It means,' Mahoney said, 'that the government and the ANC have ridden rough-shod over the demands of COSAG, over the Afrikaner right wing, over the Zulus, over Bophuthatswana, over the Ciskei – the ANC/Government juggernaut, has decided to bulldoze ahead with their own deal and fuck everybody else. It means that De Klerk has told half his Afrikaner volk to like it or lump it – plus the Zulus, the Tswanas, and the Ciskeians, who altogether represent almost half the entire population. It means, in short, that De Klerk has dropped them in the shit. And it means, in short, that the shit is going to hit the fan.'

110

Katrina was outraged. 'The *bastards*! They just got together behind our backs and made a deal without our consent, *without* finalising the new constitution first. It's a complete breach of trust. But the two big guns have decided they've had enough of listening and just steam-rollered over us! Do you realise what this means?'

Mahoney realised very well. 'No volkstaat, for a start.'

'And it means that when the ANC wins the election – as it doubtless will – they'll probably have a sufficient majority to write any goddamn constitution they like – '

'Not quite,' Mahoney tried to soothe her, 'CODESA is still going to prepare a list of constitutional principles which the ANC must adhere to – and there'll be a Constitutional Court to decide whether it conforms or not – '

'But where is this list of constitutional principles? Yet to be drawn up! Who by? The same two bastards who rode rough-shod over us today! What about the constitution the Zulus want? The Afrikaners? For Christ's sake, a constitution should be written in *stone* before an election – De Klerk has completely abandoned his responsibilities to give the nation an iron-clad constitution *before* handing over power!' She paced furiously across the living-room. 'The only thing we can be certain about is that there'll be no volkstaat – not even a *"region"* in which Afrikaners predominate! And you realise what *that* means?'

Mahoney had written the book on it. 'Big trouble.'

Katrina seethed: 'The Afrikaner will feel betrayed – and not just the right wing, I mean ordinary moderate Afrikaners who wanted to abandon apartheid but who also wanted their own identity. Jesus, can you imagine the trouble if you created a United States of Europe and didn't give the French local self-government?' She snorted. 'Many, *many* moderate Afrikaners are going to desert De Klerk and flock to the right-wing laager now.' She looked at him grimly. 'And do you know who's going to unite them? The Generals.'

'What Generals?' Mahoney said.

Katrina said grimly: 'Who do the Afrikaners traditionally turn to in times of crisis? During the Great Trek? During the Boer War? During the 1914 Rebellion? During the Total Onslaught era? Their *military* men. Their generals. And this country has a good few generals to take up the traditional mantle. And they have many, many friends in the security forces.'

Mahoney frowned. 'But is this a fact – that the Generals are going to take over the right wing now?'

'It will happen, I assure you. And *then* the potential for civil war is greatly increased.'

'And your father? Is he one of these generals?'

She snorted. 'With a name like De la Rey?'

'But have you spoken to him about it?'

'My father,' Katrina said, 'has spoken about little else for years.'

'But have you spoken to him about today's developments?'

Katrina sighed. 'Darling, I can't tell you any more until it's formally announced. Suffice it to say that I'm worried sick.' She clenched her fist. 'And *furious*.'

And so was Mahoney worried. God, he wanted her out of this. 'But what happens next? CODESA isn't over yet, even though COSAG stormed out in protest today.'

'Oh, we'll storm back to CODESA. And make a loud last-ditch stand against the folly of this conspiracy. And we will doubtless fail, as you've always said we would. And then,' she sighed grimly, 'anything could happen.'

The next day the surprise agreement was front-page news. Most of the English-language press applauded that finality was in sight at last, but some warned of the dire consequences of riding rough-shod over COSAG. 'May we remind Mr de Klerk and Mr Mandela,' one editorial said, 'of the saying that the history of South Africa will be determined by the Boers and the Zulus?' 'It is folly,' editorialised another, 'to imagine that the Zulus and the Boers (not to mention the other stalwarts of

COSAG), are going to take this out-of-hand rejection of their political aspirations lying down.' 'To many,' opined another, 'it will appear that Mr de Klerk has thrown in his hand to Mr Mandela's trump card that international sanctions must continue until an election date is set. To them it will appear that President de Klerk has sold his guns – and his gunners – for rancid butter.'

And the next day the formation of the Afrikaner Volksfront, and its Committee of Generals, was announced.

It was a committee of five retired generals, from the army, the air force and the police, to draw together the different factions of Afrikanerdom, weld them into a united front, to make a last-ditch stand at CODESA for Afrikaner self-determination.

'It is our sincere hope,' General Karel de la Rey said at a televised press conference, 'that the Afrikaner does not have to resort to arms to secure what is rightfully his.'

The next week the AWB took CODESA by storm.

They came from far and wide, three thousand armed and uniformed men converging on Johannesburg. They assembled half a mile away and fell into columns with their banners and drummers. Eugene Terreblanche took up his position at the head in his Landcruiser, and the march began.

They came tramping down the tarred road in the crisp winter morning, and the beat of their drums rose up. A hundred yards from the high fence surrounding the World Trade Centre stood the first line of armed policemen, white and black, stretched across the road: but the AWB column did not falter, the police officer did not order his men to resist, and the first line of defence crumbled. Fifty yards from the gate was the second line, and the AWB marched triumphantly on to it, and the second line of defence crumbled. And the AWB marched on to the gates. There was the third line of defence: policemen across the opening, armoured vehicles on either side. But still no command came, the AWB men shoved their way past and went streaming into the big compound, and the assault on CODESA began.

Mahoney was in the public gallery, listening to the acrimonious debate, when he heard the commotion outside. All the delegates looked up. Mahoney hurried out of the hall into the big atrium.

Through the long glass walls of the atrium he saw the mob flooding into the compound, the policemen scattered amongst them in disarray; he saw Katrina's father in the midst of the mob, waving his arms and shouting, trying to restrain them; then he saw the Landcruiser belonging to Eugene Terreblanche mount the pavement and charge the glass doors.

The Landcruiser jolted up onto the pavement outside CODESA, the AWB mob surging behind it; then the driver trod on the accelerator, and the vehicle crashed into the big glass doors. And the glass shattered in great cracks and shards, and the driver roared the vehicle forward again. In a mass of flying glass, the Landcruiser burst into the atrium.

Mahoney turned and ran back to the conference hall, to protect Katrina. AWB men were running to take up strategic positions on the stairs and balcony and in the upper corridors, guns ready. And Eugene Terreblanche strode for the hall.

The hall was in uproar. Delegates were snatching up their papers, hurrying for the exits. The leading Government and ANC delegates had run into the same office, one frantically telephoning President de Klerk, the other Mandela. Mahoney saw Patti hurrying out. He looked for Katrina: he could not see her in the mêlée, he thought she had already run for it. Then he saw her: she was still sitting at her place, eyes grimly closed, her brow propped in both hands. Mahoney ran across the hall to her.

'*Come on, get the hell out of here!*' He started snatching up her papers.

Katrina looked up at him angrily. 'Like hell I will! I'm going to tell *them* to get the hell out of here!' She scrambled to her feet furiously.

'*Kat!*' Mahoney grabbed her arm across the table but she wrenched free and started striding towards the entrance as the last of the delegates scrambled out the exits. At the same moment Eugene Terreblanche and his men burst into the hall.

'Get out of here!' Katrina screamed in Afrikaans. '*Don't you realise the damage you're doing to the Afrikaner cause?!*' The AWB men ignored her, charging into the hall, kicking over chairs, overturning tables. '*Get out! We're trying to negotiate a volkstaat and you make us look like barbarians!*'

Mahoney vaulted the tables, onto Katrina's side. There were AWB men everywhere now. He strode after her as she advanced furiously on them. '*Barbarians!*' Mahoney grabbed her arm. She wrenched free and leapt up onto a table. '*Barbarians! Is this the image the Afrikaner wants to show the world?!*' Mahoney threw both arms around her from behind, and slung her over his shoulder midst loud AWB laughter. '*Let me go!*' Katrina shrieked, and she beat her fists on his back. '*Let me down!*' Mahoney strode grimly down the row of tables for the exit, clutching her kicking legs. '*Get out of here, you stupid barbarians!*' Katrina yelled at her countrymen as Mahoney carried her through the door.

Katrina's office was down a corridor. Mahoney shoved it open, dumped her on the desktop, turned and locked the door. Katrina clutched her head.

'*Oh God, God, God.*'

In the conference hall the wrecking went on, tables being over-turned, papers scattered, water glasses smashed, slogans spray-painted on the walls: '*Eie volk, eie land*' – 'Own people, own country.' Down the corridors AWB men were beating on doors, menacing delegates. Outside in the compound the rest of the mob chanted their slogans and brandished their weapons and waved their banners. The police stood tensely by. Some were mingling with the crowd, talking and joking. Some AWB men started a noisy braaivleis in the grounds, and some policemen were joining in.

For two hours the AWB mob occupied CODESA whilst their leaders harangued delegates, handed over written demands for an Afrikaner volkstaat. The telephone lines were hot. Then Eugene Terreblanche re-entered and announced that he had negotiated a safe conduct for them, and he called them to prayer. And the mob of uniformed, armed men with the swastika emblem stood with heads bowed. In ringing tones Terreblanche called upon Almighty God to hear them, to grant them their just prayer for a land of their own in this continent of chaos and corruption, as He had given unto the Jews their own promised land in the midst of the heathen. The heartfelt prayer rang out in the echoing hall; then it ended, and the national anthem, '*Die Stem van Suid Afrika*', was sung. The AWB men snapped to attention, and so did the white policemen present, and the stirring anthem swelled through the build-ing. It swelled out of the shattered atrium, out into the noisy compound, and three thousand people came to attention and sang.

Mahoney had left Katrina in her office with Patti; he was in the shat-tered atrium again. He saw the mob standing righteously to attention as they sang. There were hundreds of white policemen standing to atten-tion also; but no black policemen. They stood at sullen ease. Then tramping from the convention hall came Eugene Terreblanche, leading his stormtroopers. They tramped over the glass shards, out onto the terrace, and the roar went up again from the mob, the salutes, the weapons on high, the banners aloft. Then the national anthem was sung again. It rose up to the clear highveld sky.

Mahoney watched the spectacle through the shattered glass wall, and he thought: *Oh God, God.* The anthem came to an end, then orders were barked, the mob fell into ranks.

The AWB marched out of the compound triumphant, to the beat of drums. Behind them lay the ruins of CODESA. And the police watched them go.

111

For days the spectacle of CODESA being smashed down was on the television screens of the world. It was, as Katrina fumed, worth a billion dollars of free publicity to the ANC, showing the world in glorious Technicolor why the Afrikaner should not be trusted with a volkstaat. It gave the ANC more reason to deride the Afrikaner Volksfront at CODESA, it gave President de Klerk justification for abandoning that part of Afrikanerdom. For days the furore raged in the press about how disgraceful it was that the police had not raised a finger because they were afraid of antagonising their right-wing brethren. For days there were calls for the Minister of Law and Order to be fired. For days there were learned arguments from journalists how the disgraceful behaviour was to be dismissed as unimportant desperate voices in the wilderness. But Mahoney saw it differently. He faxed Bill Summers in New York:

> What many dismiss as an unimportant voice in the wilderness is in fact a very important battle cry and warning of what is to come. What we saw yesterday was but the tip of an iceberg which will wreck the ship of State if it is not given passage. It was a dramatic display of Angry People Power and it will not go away by belittling it, any more than the IRA or the Basques will go away by piously pronouncing what shits they are. The press is howling for the blood of the Commissioner of Police for not suppressing the outrage, but the press are howling up the wrong tree: President de Klerk knows that to resist would not only have resulted in a dreadful gun battle, it would have been the spark to ignite the prairie fire. De Klerk knows his (ex?) people and judged it best to let them do their thing. I sincerely hope that Mandela was only posturing when he threatened to call out MK to arrest the malfeasants, for nothing would please the AWB more. I hope both Mandela and De Klerk don't make the mistake the media is making in dismissing the incident as something to be ignored in the headlong rush to hold an election and get sanctions off South Africa's back.
>
> The AWB assault on CODESA is proclaimed a failure because, 'bloodied but unbowed', CODESA has tidied up the mess, reconvened and confirmed that the elections will be held on schedule, no matter what the Afrikaner right wing, their Committee of Generals, COSAG, the Inkatha Freedom Party, Bophuthatswana, Ciskei and the rest of them want. Well, the AWB assault was not a failure, folks: as a demonstration of their destructive potential it was a success. That we will see more of it is certain.

And then, midst all the violence racking the land, the Cape Town church massacre occurred.

Kenilworth is a pretty, upper-class suburb of Cape Town. The St James Anglican Church stands in an avenue of oaks. It is a modern building, with a large amphitheatre of varnished pews, blue carpet and tapestries. There were 1,400 worshippers attending the evening service on Sunday, 5th July, 1993, a cold Cape winter night. 150 of them were Russian seamen off a visiting trawler fleet. A duet from the choir was singing 'More Than Wonderful' when the massacre started.

Suddenly the door beside the altar burst open. There stood a black man wearing blue overalls; behind him were four others. The man threw a hand grenade into the midst of the astonished worshippers, and then all five started firing. There was the shocking explosion of the grenade midst the clattering gunfire, then another shattering explosion from another hand grenade, and the pandemonium broke out.

The bloody chaos, screams midst the horrific clattering, the scrambling, men, women, children throwing themselves down behind the pews midst the splattering blood and flying flesh, bibles flying, bodies blown apart, screaming, fleeing people mown down in the aisles. For an eternity of thirty seconds the carnage raged, fire spurting from the muzzles of five automatic weapons; then suddenly it ceased, and the gunmen ran.

Twelve people were killed in the massacre, three of them Russian seamen, a hundred and forty-seven were badly wounded. There was blood everywhere.

The St James Church massacre was, to date, the lowest point of South Africa's transition to democracy, rendered more horrific by having happened in a place of worship. 'If we cannot go to pray in safety,' the Democratic Party said, 'how can we go to the polls in safety?' 'Thoroughly evil', 'Unimaginably callous', 'Mind-bogglingly brutal', 'The most despicable act imaginable', 'A new horrifying nadir'. were some of the fulminations from the press, politicians, the government, the ANC, the international media. President Clinton laid the blame 'on those seeking to thwart negotiations,' and called for 'aggressive' police investigation. President de Klerk challenged 'all political leaders to join hands in combating violence'. General Constand Viljoen, head of the Committee of Generals which led the Afrikaner Volksfront, deplored the brutal massacre but warned that such incidents would continue until a political settlement was reached which catered for all political parties.

'Which,' Patti said, 'is exactly what the massacre was intended to achieve. To plunge the country into a bloodbath of reprisals which would derail CODESA. And who would want to do that?'

'If you're implying,' Katrina said dangerously, 'that the Afrikaner Volksfront did it, I'll get mad. Nor do I believe the AWB did it. Whatever you think of Eugene Terreblanche, the man's a Christian.'

'Kate,' Mahoney said, 'we're not implying that the Afrikaner Volksfront or even the AWB *officially* did it. But one of their members may have done it of their own initiative. Because the question is: *who* would benefit from a bloodbath of reprisals which plunges the country into such chaos that the military take over, thus putting a stop to CODESA?' He spread his hands. 'The ANC? No – they're winning over-all. The government? No – they're forging ahead with CODESA. Who does that leave? Inkatha? It's possible. But the most likely candidate is the extreme right wing of Afrikanerdom. And their Third Force.'

'Exactly,' Patti murmured.

Katrina glared at them. '*Or*,' she said, 'it could be the PAC. The bastards who shoot up innocents in the Selkirk Country Club and the Queen's Arms in East London, and schoolgirls and farmers in the Orange Free State. To create a reign of terror. To terrorize the white man into capitulating.'

'It's a possibility,' Patti conceded, 'but it begs the question: how would the PAC benefit if there was a military coup d'état and CODESA was thrown out the window? There's no way the PAC could take on the Defence Force.'

Katrina said dangerously: 'If you imagine that, as a political scientist, I haven't thought all this through by my little fat self, you are doing my intellect a grave insult.'

'Darling,' Patti said, 'we have the highest regard for your intellect! *But – who* did it?'

112

Sally Freeman Nkomo had no doubt who did it. It was Inkatha, that no-good outfit her no-good sumbitch of a husband had joined! *Abso-fucking-lutely definitely*. The ANC wouldn't have done it, she explained loudly to her fellow Coloured students at the University of the Western Cape where she had enrolled after that sumbitch of a husband had made it clear that too much water had passed under the bridge for them to get it back together – the ANC wouldn't have done it because the fuckin' ANC was winning at CODESA. The fuckin' right-wing Afrikaners wouldn't have done it, because the fuckin' Afrikaner wouldn't have shot down honkies.

'What about the PAC?' Priscilla asked.

'No *ways*,' Sally said. 'The PAC don't mean that jazz, that's just fightin' talk to scare the shit out of the honkies. It was Inkatha, I lived with those Zulu warriors for four weeks and I married one of the sumbitches, I should know!'

'I thought you married a Xhosa prince, Princess Sally?' Priscilla teased.

'Yeah, but I'm divorcin' the sumbitch and gettin' rid of my title, whereas you'll have to undergo major cosmetic surgery to get rid of yours, JAP.'

The University of the Western Cape, near Cape Town, had been set up for Coloured, half-caste, people in the bad old days of apartheid under the Extension of University Education Act. Sally Freeman Nkomo had enrolled there because – having one Irish grandparent – she had decided that it was amongst the Coloureds of Africa that her roots truly lay, the Xhosa and Zulu having treated her so fuckin' *shittily*. The university now admitted white students too, though precious few had applied. Priscilla Cohen was one of the few.

Priscilla was a Jewish lass from New York, a sociology graduate who had come to South Africa to do a year's post-graduate research for her Master's degree: 'The Potential of the Coloured People in the New South Africa' was her subject. JAP, in Americanese, is a slightly derogatory expression meaning Jewish American Princess, but Priscilla wasn't like that at all: she was an earnest, energetic, shy girl who did not flaunt her money, who wanted to live amongst the Cape Coloureds, understand them and their problems. She was liked well enough on campus and she earnestly participated in student activities, but her social life was disappointing. Much though she liked the Coloureds, she found she had little in common with them off-campus. Priscilla came from a prosperous American background where middle-class sophistication, manners and conversation was taken for granted; the Cape Coloureds, by contrast, were what she reluctantly described as lower class. Their homes were clean but usually smaller and poorer than those of poor blacks in America, and the formality with which she was treated was the behaviour of people who felt ill-at-ease entertaining somebody from a higher social stratum. She didn't get to *know* them. Though some Coloured boys made bold and flirted with her on campus, none asked her for a date. The Coloured girls were friendly, but tended to hang on her words. They were inhibited by class. So when bouncy Sally Nkomo showed up on campus and hailed her as a fellow American, the two fast became firm friends: they had the whole American experience in common. 'Princess Sally' and 'Princess Prissy' they called each other.

Sally moved in to Priscilla's apartment and soon had the joint appropriately decked out. She hung no more colourful blankets on the wall, no more African handicrafts, but photographs of Coloured personalities were plastered everywhere, politicians and musicians from around the Cape and around the world. Typical Cape Coloured cuisine emerged from the odiferous kitchen, Cape Coloured music resounded, she learned all the Afrikaner songs, she began to study the Afrikaans language and she studiously cultivated the Cape Coloured accent. Princess Sally was a godsend to Priscilla: she soon had a flow of Coloured students passing through the apartment, the pair of them were soon invited to student dances and barbecues and picnics, and Priscilla began to make real friends, really get to know the Coloureds, and have fun. She wrote happily to her parents:

> I love it here. The Cape is so beautiful, mellow, with its oaks and its vineyards and its old Dutch architecture, and the people seem much more gentle than in places like Johannesburg. It is in the Cape, of course, that the saga of South Africa all started 340 years ago, and the hedge of bitter almonds planted by Jan van Riebeck to keep the whites and natives apart is still to be seen. This is where the Cape Coloured race began through miscegenation between Dutch settlers and Hottentot women and slaves. They are an attractive 'race', most of them looking like brown white men, but they seem to have the colourfulness of the blacks – though most of them want to forget their black ancestry. They aspire to a white man's way of life and indeed live like white men in every way, financial considerations aside.
>
> What surprises me is their politics: before apartheid collapsed the Coloureds were pro-ANC, but now most of them seem to support President de Klerk and his National Party – their former oppressors! This is doubtless because, being brown white men, at heart and by culture, they are as afraid of the blacks as the whites are, and as anxious to maintain white standards. Of course, this is largely because of the worrisome track record of the rest of Africa, and the violence here is horrific. It is less in Cape Town than elsewhere, but nonetheless there is constant upheaval in the black squatter townships of Kayelitsha and Crossroads, near here. This shift to the National Party amongst the Coloureds has also happened amongst many liberal whites, who were formerly fiercely anti-government. Last week Sally and I drove to Stellenbosch University to visit her friend, a Professor Lisa Rousseau, and she too, now that the oppression of apartheid is over, ardently supports

De Klerk's National Party whereas formerly she supported the
ANC. Of course, this is partly because the National Party leopard
has changed its spots and hijacked the liberal Democratic Party's
platform, but I'm sure the greater reason is a fear of the black man
now that ANC rule is nigh. Even dear Princess Sally, who has done
her utmost to find her African roots, has changed her tune and now
not only loudly supports the National Party but speaks Afrikaans
whenever she can! (She really is remarkable: she speaks Xhosa
quite well too, and a smattering of Zulu.) Myself, I remain
staunchly pro-ANC: only a strong unified government can end these
tribal divisions and only a new-broom ANC government will be
able to sweep away the economic injustices of the past.

That is what Priscilla Cohen wrote to her parents the day before she
was murdered.

That day Priscilla and Sally drove to the university as usual. After
lectures they attended a political meeting convened by ANC students
on the campus. It was well attended and there was the usual heckling
and argument but it was mostly good natured.

'What you *ous* gonna do about the violence, hey?' somebody
shouted at question time.

'The violence,' the ANC student replied, 'is not the ANC's doing, man,
it is largely caused by the Third Force, by the PAC and by Inkatha – '

'Bullshit, man, there're hardly any Zulus in the Cape – it's caused by
the bleddy Comrades, the ANC youth with their heads stuffed full of
bleddy nonsense because the ANC says it will nationalise the economy –'

'I can assure the questioner that the ANC will not nationalise – '

'How can we believe you when the ANC is dominated by the
Communist Party, hey?'

Priscilla found the courage to stand up. 'Mr Chairman, may I make a
point as a sociologist, albeit a foreigner? It seems to me that the
excesses of the youthful Comrades are not to be blamed upon the ANC
but upon the apartheid government which brought about a whole
generation of under-educated youth who became rebellious because
there was no hope for them. And it is only a populist ANC government
who can offer them that hope by affirmative action and thereby bring
them back under control – any other government, particularly one
dominated by the National Party, would not be trusted by them – '

Sally jumped up. 'So what my Yankee friend is saying is if you can't
lick 'em join 'em?! What an ass-about-face argument *that* is – '

It was just after dark when Sally and Priscilla left the campus in
Priscilla's car, heading back to their apartment. They were approaching

the highway, when they came round a bend and saw the roadblock in their headlights. Suddenly the road was full of black youths armed with sticks and axes, prancing and posturing and shouting. Priscilla slammed on the brakes. *'Oh Christ,'* Sally cried, *'here're your Comrades!'* The car came to a sharp halt. Priscilla frantically rammed the car into reverse gear, the vehicle leapt backwards, and it stalled. And the mob ran at them. *'Locks!'* Priscilla shouted. *'Explain to them in Xhosa!'*

The car was surrounded by a mob of angry black youths swiping the car with sticks, shouting: *'Kill the farmers! Kill the Boers!'*

Sally desperately shouted in Xhosa: *'Greetings, brothers, we are one of you! We are students at the university!'*

'Kill the farmers! Kill the Boers!'

'We are Americans!' Priscilla shouted. *'We are ANC. Viva Mandela!'*

'Kill the Boers!' the leader shouted and his axe smashed the window. In a crash of splinters the glass shattered, Priscilla shrieked and twisted the ignition, the axe swiped again, the window burst apart and the leader reached in and wrenched open the door. He seized Priscilla and dragged her out. *'I'm an American – I'm not a Boer. I'm an American –'*

She scrambled up off the road, and then everybody was swiping her. Sally shrieked: *'She's Americano – leave her alone!'* Priscilla Cohen reeled across the road under the rain of blows, crouched, her arms curled over her head, gasping, crying *'I'm not a Boer!'* The mob pranced after her as she staggered and reeled and sobbed, having their sport, letting her stagger away a little, then giving her a swipe that sent her reeling again. They swiped her across her shoulders and back and chest and buttocks and legs, shouting *'Kill the Boers!'*

Sally screamed *'Leave her alone!'* and she ran at the mob, fists flying, and a blinding swipe across the head felled her, and she sprawled unconscious. And the mob proceeded to murder Priscilla Cohen.

They beat her to the ground, and Priscilla screamed and tried to curl herself up into a ball under the rain of blows, and then the kicking started. Joyful kicks in her back and guts and chest. Then the leader shouted: *'Bulala!'* – Kill – and he wielded his axe behind his head and swiped it down on Priscilla's back. Priscilla's spine smashed in a gaping spout of blood, and she screamed again; then half a dozen axes and pangas proceeded to swipe down on her.

They chopped Priscilla Cohen's head right open, then they ran away into the night, shouting: *'Kill the Boers!'*

PART XVII

FREEDOM ALLIANCE FORMED

AWB BOMBS STAGGER SOUTH AFRICA

ZULUS REJECT ELECTIONS

RIGHT-WING AFRIKANERS
DECLARE OWN PARLIAMENT

BOPHUTHATSWANA AND
CISKEI REJECT ELECTIONS

AFRIKANERS SPLIT OVER ELECTIONS

113

In the big bloodstained tapestry of South Africa the details of what happened at the resumption of CODESA do not matter now – the last-ditch stands, the slug-fest, the angry rhetoric, the newspaper headlines that raised hopes one day and dashed them the next – what matters is that a new organization was formed to challenge the government-ANC juggernaut, and it was called the Freedom Alliance.

It was what Mahoney had feared: the alliance of the Boers and the Zulus, the two fiercest warrior tribes in Africa, joined by Bophuthatswana and Ciskei. What all four demanded was their own independent states and they vowed they would fight together to ensure each member got it. What matters is that the potential for rebellion, for treason, was now multiplied, and what worried the shit out of Mahoney was that Katrina was in the thick of it. What matters is that the mounting violence, the St James Church massacre, and the brutal murder of Priscilla Cohen gave the two big guns at CODESA, the government and the ANC, a new urgency to wrap up their deal and foist it upon the furious Freedom Alliance. What matters is that the Afrikaners' demand for a volkstaat, the Zulus' demand for an independent KwaZulu, was finally bulldozed down again. What matters is that CODESA ended in anger, while De Klerk and Nelson Mandela shook hands before the television cameras and announced to the world that the new South Africa was truly at hand, confirming that elections would be held on 27th April, 1994, that the South African government would hand over power to a Transitional Executive Council, a body which would effectively rule the country until the elections. What matters is that the constitution of the new South Africa was not finalised but was left to the coming elected parliament to decide, on thirty-three principles laid down by CODESA. What matters is that the ANC came close to getting its way. What matters is that the Freedom Alliance was up in arms.

And so the electioneering for the new, non-racist, one-man-one-vote South Africa began. Mahoney wrote:

Will we never learn? Must the history of this blood-stained land, this blood-soaked continent, repeat itself yet again?

It is madness to hold elections in this climate of rampant violence. There is no way they can be 'free and fair'. Intimidation, the big stick, the big impis, and bloodshed will be rife, as it has always been in this unholy land since the days of the Trekboer, Slagter's Nek, the Kaffir Wars, Shaka, the Mfecane, Vegkop, Blood River, the Great Cattle Killing, Majuba, the Boer War, the 1914 Rebellion, the Defiance Campaign, Sharpeville, the Soweto Riots, the Vaal Uprising, the Armed Struggle, the Natal Killing Fields, the Reef Violence, the whole nine yards. And now, on top of all this, we're going to have additional violence from the Freedom Alliance. So what the hell are we doing, trying to hold 'free and fair' elections now, folks? It's a betrayal of the principles of democracy. A betrayal of CODESA. A cruel betrayal of the People, black and white, who have struggled and suffered so long for democracy.

So surely to God the elections should be postponed until the violence is stamped out, until they can be free and fair? Surely to God this crisis with the Freedom Alliance should be defused first?

Yes. But no. They cannot be postponed, because the expectations of the masses have been raised: on 27th April their new South Africa will dawn, they will be masters of their destiny. And many expect the skies to start raining milk and honey, bank-notes, bicycles and transistor radios. There would be riots across the land if the elections were postponed. The only way to postpone them would be to declare martial law, send the army in to stamp out the violence, disarm the populace, shoot it out street by street with the warlords: and what a mess that would be. And, apart from all that shit, the ANC would scream blue murder. And 'go back to the bush'. And renewed sanctions would hammer down on our heads. Because the ANC wants these elections to go ahead on schedule, because they know they're going to win.

So these elections are going to go ahead on schedule. So we're going to have an unfree and unfair result. And if by some miracle the security forces manage to keep the peace and stop intimidation on voting day, so what? The blacks are already intimidated. The only question for the Independent Electoral Commission to decide is how unfree and unfair is good enough for unfree and unfair Africa. What is an acceptable level of political death? And fuck the consequences. And the consequences are going to be fucking dire. Because the Afrikaner has not got his volkstaat and the Zulu hasn't got his Zululand. Even if, by some miracle, the elections go off without major trouble – as appeared to happen in Zimbabwe after their war – the new South Africa has bargained a whole new history of big trouble for itself with the same reckless, indecent haste as the British decolonised the rest of Africa.

And so the die is cast. And now the Afrikaner Volksfront has defiantly held their own election for their own independent volksraad which will fight to the death for their independent volkstaat.

'Luke?' Bill Summers shouted excitedly on the telephone from New York. 'what's the significance of this volksraad the right wing has elected?'

It was midnight in Johannesburg, six p.m. in New York. Mahoney had just returned from the film set, pissed off. Katrina was still at work. He was frying some eggs while he drank a stiff whisky. 'Bill,' he said, 'why don't you use the telephone?'

'Telephone?' Bill shouted, mystified. 'I *am* telephoning you.'

'Oh, I thought I was hearing it straight.'

'Very funny. So what's all this mean? And why haven't you sent us an update?'

'It means,' Mahoney sighed, 'that to many Afrikaners De Klerk has let them down – he has not nailed down a new constitution giving each people its autonomy within a federation, he's capitulated to the pressures of the violence, and international pressure. In other words it looks like the ANC are going to get their way and have a strong central government at the expense of the powers of the "regional" governments. And this is bad news for South Africa – just like it would be in Yugoslavia. Imagine if you tried to make all those Muslims and Serbs and Croats re-unify again? Folly. And it's folly in South Africa which has a *dozen* different nationalities who have *never* got along together. That's what the problems of South Africa have always been about.' He added: 'And it's quite illegal to force reunification, by the way – Bophuthatswana and Ciskei are independent republics, so it's absolutely illegal to force them to rejoin South Africa. So they have every right to resist by force. You can't say the same for the Zulus and Boers, because they never had independence, but now they've got the excuse that their allies are being treated illegally.'

'But what's the significance of the Afrikaners electing their own parliament – does that mean they're declaring themselves independent, like America did two hundred years ago?'

'Not yet,' Mahoney said, 'but it's the first step. And it's history repeating itself – it's the same thing the voortrekkers did a hundred and fifty years ago when they gathered at Thaba Nchu and elected their governor, before going on to do battle with Mzilikazi and Dingaan. This new volksraad is deciding where their volkstaat is going to be, drawing the boundaries, et cetera, organising their army, then trying to bully the government into recognising their independence. If they fail at that, they'll probably declare themselves independent.'

'And then the shit will hit the fan?' Bill Summers said hopefully.

'Yes. But the shit's going to hit the fan anyway because the Zulus, Bophuthatswana and Ciskei are refusing to let the elections be held in their territories.'

'So what's the government and ANC going to do about that little problem?'

'Big problem. First they'll try to starve them into submission – cut off their financial support. That'll create chaos. If that fails, send the South African army in to conquer them. That's when all the Freedom Alliance members will rush to each other's military aid.'

'But they can't win, you say.'

'No. But they could make such a hell of a mess that they force the government and the ANC back to the negotiating table, with guerrilla tactics. Already the AWB has set off a lot of bombs, blowing up electrical pylons and so on. And the combined military strength of the Freedom Alliance is not inconsiderable. The Generals' Club knows its job. And they've got a lot of friends in the Defence Force and police. Then there are the AWB – they're loose cannons who're probably an embarrassment to the Generals' Club but they could inflict a helluva lot of damage. Then Bophuthatswana and Ciskei both have standing armies mostly under white officers – though we don't know how loyal they'll be if their salaries aren't paid. And then there are the Zulus. Most of them will respond to their king's call that Zululand must be a sovereign kingdom – they'll fight. They haven't got an official army because they're not legally independent, but they've got thousands of men who've been trained unofficially. And they've got KwaZulu police. And then there're all those Zulu warriors.'

'Jesus,' Bill Summers said happily. 'Fax us all this stuff, Luke, we must be ready to hit the streets. And Katrina? Where does she stand in all these new developments?'

Mahoney sighed. 'In the thick of it.'

'Is she a member of this new parliament – this volksraad?'

'No,' Mahoney said. 'She refused because she believes the Afrikaners should participate in the forthcoming elections to prove their strength and so they've got a voice in the new South African parliament, to continue to press for a volkstaat. So she's frantically working behind the scenes with like-minded people, trying to persuade volksraad members to form a separate party which will contest the elections. It's going to be called the Freedom Front.'

'Jesus – *another* political party, these Afrikaners are always splitting up, huh? And, how do you rate her chances?'

Mahoney was tired. His fried eggs were now cremated. He said testily: 'She thinks they're getting some important people on their side. She's working with a few Conservative Party MPs and two of the generals. They're working day and night trying to cobble together a whole new political party, prepare party principles, a list of candidates, et cetera. It's a hell of a big job. And the party's got to register within the next two weeks – the elections are less than two months away. I hardly see her.'

Bill Summers did not catch Mahoney's testiness over six thousand miles. He said brightly: 'And how's the beautiful Patti Gandhi?'

Mahoney sighed. 'Also working hard. Haven't seen her for weeks.' He added: 'She's a candidate on the ANC list for the forthcoming elections.'

'Hardly see her?' Bill sounded disappointed, as if hoping to hear of romance. 'And, how's my new book coming on – *Return to Alms*?'

Mahoney didn't want to talk about it. 'So far I'm just adapting the episodes of the screenplay into prose.'

'Can I see some chapters?'

'No, Bill.'

'Why not? Too personal? Good. That's what made *Alms* so distinctive – you put your heart into it. But just tell me . . . ' He hesitated, then: 'Is Patti – the . . . *drama* of Patti – is it coming to life? In *Return*, I mean.'

Mahoney sighed. 'Yes, Bill.' He added wryly: 'Don't worry.'

'Of course I worry. If she doesn't come to life – her drama, I mean – if *you* as the writer don't feel that drama – '

'Relax, Bill. If you don't want to publish it, that's okay by me.'

'Oh, I want to publish it! I can't wait.' Then: 'And . . . ?'

'And what?'

Bill sounded embarrassed: 'I mean, how do you feel about her?'

'Which "her"?'

'*Well*,' Bill said reasonably, 'I suppose I mean Patti. She's the book.'

'Katrina's also the bloody book, Bill.'

'Of *course*,' Bill said earnestly. 'I meant: I hope all this isn't complicating your life with Katrina?' He decided to change the subject. 'And, how's the movie going?'

Mahoney sighed. 'Oh, they're fucking up my story.'

Yes, the director was fucking up the story. Almost every day Mahoney was instructed to re-write passages of his script to meet the requirements of 'political correctness': almost any scene or piece of dialogue that showed blacks as anything other than earnest, democratic souls had to be rewritten at the last moment. Everything the black actors said now had to be courageous rectitude, because that's what the folks wanted to see in America.

'You're asking me to write nonsense,' Mahoney protested to the director: 'Africa is a fuck-up, not a success story. Africa is largely populated by uneducated peasants, nice people, but peasants nonetheless, who don't understand democracy yet. You've seen the violence here.'

'*Yeah*, but we can't *show* it. That's not box-office.'

'Fuck box-office, I refuse to write crap.'

'You want us to get another writer, sacrifice your script fee? You want your three per cent of profits don't you?'

'There'll be no profit if you screen bullshit!'

'Oh yes there will be,' the director crooned. 'Political correctness, that's what the great unwashed public wants to see.'

And, yes, Mahoney wanted his script fee. So, yes, out of the script came the big bad Africa, out came the Congo, out came Idi Amin in Uganda – the Mau Mau of Kenya weren't even mentioned but the white Rhodesians got a roasting – out came the bloodshed, oppression, corruption of African politics and in its place came sweet reasonable politicians who righteously blamed all the troubles of Africa on colonialism and the apartheid regime.

'I refuse!' Mahoney stormed. 'Go'n get yourself another writer!' He stomped off the set. He stomped to the nearest bar. An hour later he stomped back. 'Okay,' he shouted, 'what crap do you want me to write now?!'

The failure of communism, the collapse of the Berlin Wall 'and all that jazz' were 'politically correct', so his scenes about that were allowed to stand, but his dialogue about the communist influence in the ANC was a no-no. 'Nelson Mandela,' the director said, 'and the ANC are box-office. They're sacred cows.'

'*I refuse!*' Mahoney stomped off the set. The next day he stomped back. '*Okay, the ANC is a sacred cow . . .* '

And the Afrikaners and the Zulus were the bad guys. (Bophuthatswana and Ciskei didn't even rate a mention – 'Too complicated for the audience to understand,' said the director, who didn't understand either.) All Afrikaners were khaki-clad beer-swigging louts who kicked the 'kaffirs' all over the barnyard, while the Zulus were noble savages gone wrong, suborned by the wicked white man's trinkets into supporting apartheid.

'*Bullshit!*' Mahoney cried when he read the edited script. 'Buthelezi has *never* supported the government! And the Zulus are a proud people. And most Afrikaners are decent God-fearing folk!'

Mahoney won his battle on that one, after telling them to stick their soap opera up their collective ass. He was much mollified when he was persuaded to come back: he could do it his way. Maybe it wasn't turning into such a bad soap after all. Maybe the director wasn't such an asshole. For almost a week he got along with him. But then came the final scenes where Pamela was released from twenty-four years in prison; where Jack tells her he is in love with somebody else now, with the beautiful Afrikaner called Elsa van Niekerk.

It was a painful scene for Mahoney to write. All the guilt he had felt came flooding back, his pity, his admiration for this courageous woman, the pathos in her plea, her heartbreak. And, oh, her beauty as she stood in naked silhouette against the window: he wept as he wrote it. And, oh, he wanted Patti to be happy now. And he felt guilt on top of guilt because he was still in her life, that she was denying herself the chance of proper happiness by still clinging to him: guilt that he permitted it. All her life she had been on the outside looking in, lonely, struggling for her rights, and she had paid with the best part of her life. And now she was still paying the price of compromise, still knocking on the door, clinging to what she could. It was terribly, terribly sad, and he was permitting it. He *would* put an end to it, for her sake. Patti Gandhi had to be made to go out and seek her proper, rightful happiness.

It was a heart-rending scene, a fitting ending of the series of *Alms for Oblivion*. He had it delivered to the director, and proceeded to get amongst a bottle of whisky. He was desperate to get this movie finished, so he stopped living in the past.

For the rest of that day he was under the influence of those scenes; it was a good thing that Katrina was out of town so he did not have to explain his mood. And he did not want Katrina to read the scenes; he did not want her to know how he had really felt that awful day. And then the telephone rang, and it was the dreaded director.

'Luke, it's a great scene, but I want you to change the ending. It's simply not right for Jack to drive off *tearfully* back to Elsa – he must have more *doubt*. He's throwing over the *heroine*, for Christ's sake. We've decided he's gonna see the light and go back to Pamela in the final episode. You make Elsa too much of a goodie-goodie – she's a *Boer*, for Christ's sake, she hasn't got the heart of gold you give her, she's got a swastika engraved on it. A leopard doesn't change its spots – *that* must be the message in the final episode. And that's what makes Jack return to his senses and go back to Pamela. As the new South Africa dawns. They rush into each other's arms.'

Mahoney closed his angry eyes. 'Leaving Elsa to do what?'

'Leaving Elsa in her laager with her Boers. Facing the inevitable. Except she doesn't know it – she still thinks the Boer can win. Fade. Sunset. Theme tune. Credits.'

Mahoney said: 'And Jack and Pamela rush into each other's arms? On a hilltop. Silhouetted against a blazing sunset?'

'Or better still a sun*rise*,' the director enthused. 'How about that? The sun of the new South Africa coming up. Now that's *box*-office, Luke.'

'Leaving misguided Katrina in her laager, facing her just deserts?'

'Who's Katrina?' the director demanded.

'I mean Elsa.'

'*Yeah*. Elsa facing her just deserts, you got it, Luke! Jack sees the light and joins Pamela in the ANC.'

'And that's box-office?'

'*Right*. We'll make a bundle!'

'And everybody lives happily ever after in the new South Africa? Except Elsa, who dies a Quixotic but well-deserved death?'

'*Well*,' Al said, 'don't be too hard on her as an *individual*. After all, she is a *femme fatale* herself. But you got the picture, Luke! Now, how long will it take to write this last episode?'

'Oh, not long at *all*,' Mahoney said reasonably. 'Because I won't be writing such crap, Al. What I've written is the natural end of the movie, and it's good.'

'The contract,' Al said, 'calls for you to write twelve episodes. You've only written eleven.'

'I've written more than *twenty* episodes but you chucked out the ones on the Congo and Uganda! And the contract calls for *about* twelve episodes, the final number to be decided by agreement between me and you. And I'm not agreeing to any more. Goodbye, Al.'

He banged down the telephone. It rang again immediately but he refused to answer it. And proceeded to get drunk. At eight o'clock there was a knock on the back door. And there stood Patti Gandhi.

'It's a beautiful scene,' she said. 'We're not going to change a word.'

Mahoney was astonished. Her sexual impact was confused by her statement. He said: 'What have you got to do with this series?'

Patti walked in. She shut the door behind her and leant back against it. 'Darling, it's my story. I own it. I'm the one and only shareholder in Galloway Productions.'

Mahoney stared. At a loss for words. Patti continued solemnly: 'And I've told the director to cool it. We're going to do the scene your way. The *right* way. And we're going to do the final episode our way.'

Our way? Mahoney was bemused. '*You* bought the film rights?'

'Yes, darling. I always wanted *Alms* to be made into a movie. I thought about it for years in prison.' She grinned, and dabbed the corner of her eye. 'I even wanted to play Pamela.'

'Jesus. You paid me all that money?'

'Have you got an open bottle of wine?'

'Jesus.' He turned to the refrigerator. 'All that money.' He extracted a bottle.

'It's worth every penny. It's going to make a lot of money.'

He turned back to her in wonder. 'But why didn't you tell me?'

She took the glass of wine, and leant against the wall.

'Because, I didn't want you to feel beholden to me. I didn't want you to feel that I was . . . clinging to you.'

Oh Jesus, Jesus. That's exactly why she bought the rights. And, oh God yes, it made him feel beholden to her. Worse than that – it made him feel a fraud. Jesus, he'd lost most of his money on the stock exchange, so he had been able to afford this house, this lifestyle, only because Patti had bought the film rights to *Alms*.

'And you probably wouldn't have sold the rights to me had you known. Because you'd have felt compromised. That I was . . . clinging.' She looked at him. 'Which I was not. Did I give one hint that I was the owner? Have I used that as a lever?'

He shook his head. 'Does Katrina know?' Did that explain anything?

'No. And I don't want you to tell her. I don't want her to feel beholden to me either.'

'So why're you telling me now?'

'Because you've walked off the job again. And you were right. You haven't always been – you've sometimes been too tough on the blacks and the ANC, but you've moderated that. This time you were entirely right. I don't want you to change the story.'

He was still bemused. He sighed. Oh, what story? What happens from here? What happens in the final hour, the final episode?

'You don't need another episode, Patti. The ending I've written is perfect the way it is.'

She said: 'It's perfect, but not the perfect ending, Luke.' She added: 'You can't let me down now.'

Oh God – let her down . . . ? 'You said we'll do the final episode "our" way. What's that mean?'

'The way it's happened, between the three of us.'

Mahoney closed his eyes. Oh no. He didn't want to write that story. Not for Bill Summers, not for Patti. He said: 'And how does it end?'

Patti looked at him. 'Yes, how? That's the question, isn't it? That's for you to decide.'

Oh no. He tried to sound impersonal: 'And you. You own the rights, you insist on another episode.'

She said softly: 'Or maybe it doesn't end. Maybe that's the real story.'

He snorted. 'So in the final scene they all walk away into the sunset together, into the new South Africa. Nothing resolved. Fade. Theme music. Credits. Not a dry eye in the house.'

Patti closed her moist eyes. 'If that's the way you want it.'

If that's the way he wanted it? No it wasn't. And he was going to resolve this right now. *End* this heartache. End her pain. *And* his. He searched for the right words, but she interrupted: 'Or maybe that's not box-office. Maybe there must be resolution.'

'Oh fuck box-office!'

She waved a hand earnestly, her eyes bright. 'Yes, resolution! And it must be poor Pamela who loses out. It's *her* story, her *tragedy*, after all. She must be the one to suffer. That's the pathos. After all those years in prison she still had hope. And so does the audience – the audience *wants* her to live happily ever after at last with her true love. But Jack finally chooses Elsa.'

Mahoney's heart was breaking. 'Patti, your true love is somewhere out there waiting – '

'And why does Jack choose Elsa?' Patti whispered. 'Not just because she's beautiful.' She shook her head. 'Not just because she's a nicer person – which she probably is – you don't spend half a lifetime in prison and come out entirely unembittered. No, Jack chooses Elsa because of *politics* . . . Because of his secret *racist* heart. Because despite his protestations about wanting the end of apartheid, he's still a South African. *Afraid* of the new South Africa. So when the chips are down he chooses his own kind. And the audience knows he's making a tragic mistake. *That's* the pathos.'

Oh Jesus. 'Patti, please listen to me – '

'No – *you* listen to me, Luke.' Her eyes were full of angry tears now. 'And why is Jack making a tragic mistake? Not just because he really, deep down loves Pamela. Not *just* because they were always really meant for each other but tragically torn apart.' She looked at him tremulously: 'Jack is making a tragic mistake because Elsa is going to *fail*, Luke. Elsa, for all her beauty and her brains, is a quixotic character. She is an *anachronism*, who's trying to hold back the march of history with her make-believe volkstaat! In fact she's a *tragic* figure, because her so-called Freedom Alliance is going to fall apart at the seams. The Freedom Alliance is a house of cards, and Elsa is going to fall apart with it! The Freedom Alliance is a *liability* to her, because they're going to collapse after the first bloody battle and precious Elsa is going to get trampled underfoot! And what makes her doubly tragic is the nefarious partners this tragic heroine of yours aligns herself with – worthless people like the AWB and the tyrants of Bophuthatswana and Ciskei!' She frowned, her eyes full of tears: 'How *unworthy* Elsa makes herself, Luke. What a *waste.*' She looked at him tremulously: 'And so Jack wastes himself too. That's the pathos.' She glared, eyes brimming. 'Maybe that's how you should write the final episode, Luke.'

Mahoney took a deep breath. And, oh God, his heart was aching. He said softly: 'We can't go on like this, Patti.'

Patti stared at him; then she put her hands to her ears. 'I've said enough. So I'll go now. Goodnight.' She dropped her hands and turned to the kitchen door.

'Patti, we can't run away from this any longer. *This* is a waste. Of *your* life. It's *you* who's got to make your own life. You must stop compromising.'

Patti had her back to him, her hand on the door-latch. She turned slowly to him. The tears were running down her beautiful face. 'Do you want that?'

Oh God, no he didn't. 'Yes, I want that.'

'You don't.'

'I do. For your sake.'

The tears glistened. She said softly: 'You don't understand, darling. I accept compromise. Like many a woman before me. Like many a mistress. My whole life has been a compromise. Ever since I was a girl in Umtata without a single friend. The whole compromise of our affair when we were young. The *dreadful* compromise of prison.' She shook her head at him. 'I'm an old hand at compromise, Luke. And I'd rather have that than nothing. That's what every mistress in the world ends up accepting.'

Mahoney said thickly: 'But you're not my mistress.'

Patti looked at him tearfully. 'No, I'm better than that. I'm your *fantasy.* And you're mine. All those years I fantasised about you. For twenty-four years I dreamt about you. Had long conversations in my head with you. Kept myself beautiful for you.' She shook her tearful head at him. 'I can wait a few more.'

Oh God, darling. 'For what, Patti?'

She looked at him steadily. 'You'll leave Katrina one day. Not because she isn't a lovely person – she is. A crazy Afrikaner, but a lovely person. And she's my only friend. But friendships get trampled under-foot in affairs of the heart, Luke – plenty of people fall in love with their best friend's husband or wife. And I was your friend long, *long* before Katrina ever was. And you'll leave her because she's the wrong woman for you.' She looked at him. 'I can wait. You'll come back to me. Not like in our movie.'

Mahoney's heart was breaking. He steeled himself and said: 'It's over, darling. I'm not coming back to you. Please understand that.'

Patti flinched. But then her moist eyes were steady again. She whispered: 'You love me, Luke. Nobody could write that love scene, where Pamela comes out of prison, and not love. You love *me*, not the lovely Katrina – you only think you do. I'm good for you and for *us*, and for the new South Africa. Katrina isn't. She's simply not. No matter which way you decide to write the final episode.'

It broke his heart to say it, but he had to: 'I don't love you, Patti.'

She clapped her hands to her ears again. 'I don't hear you, Luke Mahoney. And it's bullshit.'

Mahoney wanted to weep. 'We're not going to see each other again, Patti. And you're going out into the big wide world to find your own true love.'

Patti clamped her hands to her ears harder and cried: 'I don't hear you! I'm going now. Goodnight, darling.' She turned for the door.

Mahoney rasped tearfully: 'I'm not going to write the final episode.'

She froze, then she turned to him slowly. 'You deny me even this?' She stared at him, her eyes bright with pain. 'First you deny me your love. Then you deny me even your friendship and tell me to go out into the world. Now you even deny me my story.' New tears welled. '*My* story, which I paid for in blood, by twenty-four years in prison. Which I paid for with the love of my life. And which I then paid a lot of money for. And now, in the final hour, you desert me . . . ?' She looked at him incredulously, then she dropped her face in her hands and sobbed.

Oh God. 'Patti – '

Patti threw her hands wide and cried: 'I need you, Luke! If I can't have you as my lover I still need you as my friend! And I need you to finish my story. My movie. *Our* movie – the story of our life. What have I got to do to earn your loyalty – go down on my knees and beg? Be your slave? Tell me what I've got to do to earn your loyalty and I'll do it! Because I *need* you, Luke. *Please* don't turn your back on me. *Please* don't throw me out of your life.'

Oh, her self-effacement broke his heart. He had a sob in his throat. 'Of course I'm your friend, Patti. I'm not turning my back on you.'

She looked at him, then she blundered across the kitchen. She flung her arms around him and clutched him tight, and burst into racking sobs. Mahoney held her tight, his heart breaking for her, his guilt swamping him. 'I'll never turn my back on you, Patti . . .'

She sobbed: 'Then don't ever say that again.'

He held her tight, his heart aching. 'I won't.'

She nodded tearfully against his shoulder. 'And you can write the final episode any way you like.' She sniffed. 'And I'm sorry I said those things about Katrina. She's a lovely person. I was speaking in hot blood. I was trying to diminish her.' She took a quivering, resolute breath. 'I said it nastily, and I'm sorry. But what I said is true: Katrina's going to fail. It's all going to blow up in her beautiful face.' She held him tight. 'You're worth so much more than that, Luke.'

Mahoney closed his eyes. *But you still want to marry her*? The question was unspoken, but he could feel it in her tense body. For a long moment she was rigid: then she whispered: 'You want to make love to me.'

Mahoney felt his heart turn over. He whispered: 'No, darling.'

She whispered ardently: 'Yes, you do. I can feel you against me.'

'But no, darling.'

She held him. 'I want to feel you inside me.'

He held her tight. And with all his breaking heart he just wanted to possess her, to mount her, to feel her envelope him, demanding him, consuming him, her whole glorious body wrapped around him – oh yes, he wanted to make love to her, but he whispered: 'No, Patti.'

'Yes!' She thrust her pelvis against him, then she seized his hand and pulled it down to her loins. '*Feel* me. Feel how hot I am for you.' And, oh, the soft, hot, blissful feel of her through her dress. 'And *this* – ' She thrust his hand against her breast, and, oh, the fullness of it. She seized her dress and pulled it off her shoulder, and her beautiful breast was bare, and she thrust his hand against it and plunged her mouth back onto his and thrust her loins against him. '*Yes* – ' And she slithered down him, to her knees, then she toppled over onto her back, her long black hair splayed out on the kitchen floor. She pulled her dress up to her hips, and bent her knees and parted her lovely legs, and she held out her arms to him. And Mahoney sank to his knees beside her, his hands wrenching at his belt, and she tore her panties off ; and they came together in a lunging, gasping, mass on the kitchen floor, and she cried out in joy – and, oh, the bliss of each other.

Afterwards, sitting at the kitchen table, in the emptiness of after-love, she said: 'Please don't feel guilt.'

Oh, of course he felt guilt. About Katrina, for betraying her, about Patti, for breaking her heart. And he was angry for confusing himself all over again.

She said softly: 'Don't feel guilt about me. I love you. With all my heart. And what we did gave me great happiness. There is no reason to feel guilt for giving happiness in this brutal world.' Mahoney took a breath, to speak, but she went on: 'And I'm not going to ask you what's going to happen. I'm not going to put any pressure on you. But don't tell me I've got to go out into the big wide world.' She frowned at him. 'I don't *want* to love anybody else, Luke. Please grasp that simple fact. The idea is totally repugnant to me.'

Oh God. 'And what about Katrina?'

Patti clasped her hands on the table. 'I really, *really* like Katrina. She's a wonderful bonus.'

Mahoney frowned at her. 'A *bonus*?'

'Shh, darling . . . And *listen* to what I'm telling you. And I'm not telling you anything you don't know very well already.' She looked at him, her eyes moistening. 'I love you, Luke – fact number one. Fact number two: I must accept what's happened. That you think you love Katrina now. Fact number three: I must accept the compromise you want me so courageously to eschew. Fact number four: I would rather compromise than wither on the vine. This may sound pathetic, but it's so fucking *true*. But it's my life, what's left of it, and I'll live it as I wish. And *that* – ' she smiled tearfully – 'is how I hope you write the final episode of my movie.'

Mahoney's heart was breaking. Patti continued: 'Fact number five: the beautiful Katrina has stolen your heart.' She looked at him mistily. 'Whether I like it or not, she's a *fact*, Luke, part of you, and I've got to live with that. And therefore she's very important to me. And, believe me, I'd rather have to live with a nice person than a nasty one, somebody who refuses to let me be part of your life.'

Mahoney said: 'And part of our sex life.'

Patti looked at him steadily. 'Yes, that's part of the bonus. I need sex, like everybody else. I need you, and that Katrina is like me is an added bonus. So? The best of both worlds. What I share with you two is wonderful. And I'm grateful.'

Grateful? Oh, that word tore at him. The self-effacement. 'You're a beautiful woman who should have her own beautiful life.'

'The only life I want is you. As I can't have you, I want this one. Why shouldn't it last forever? We wouldn't be the first ménage-à-trois in history to last a lifetime.' She paused. Then: 'However, I know how it's going to end.'

He looked at her. 'How?'

Patti said quietly: 'There's going to be war, Luke, and you and Katrina are going to be on opposite sides. Because Katrina is not going to be able to shed her baggage of the AWB, so her political party will not be respectable. And you will not be on her side, because you'll be unable to bring yourself to stand by her people. You're not a Boer.' She ended: 'I don't believe you're going to marry Katrina, Luke.'

Mahoney looked at her grimly. 'I'm marrying her, Patti.'

Patti smiled gently. 'When? After the war? Or before?' She stood up. 'All right, I'd better go now, I've said too much, as usual.' She walked around the table, stooped and kissed him lingeringly on the cheek. 'Goodnight, darling. Write a wonderful script. Any way you like.'

Mahoney did not move. 'Goodnight.' He heard the back door click behind her, her high-heels click across the stoep, her car start.

He hung his head. He could still smell her perfume, on his hands, on his shirt. Smell her body. Feel her underneath him. Still feel the sweet hot depths of her . . .

He got up abruptly and walked through to the bedroom into the bathroom and turned on the shower. He stood under the jets, scrubbing the smell and feel of her off him. And, oh God, he wanted Katrina to come hurrying home. He wanted her out of this volkstaat business. Out of the war zone. He just wanted her to get her precious Freedom Front Party off the ground, fight the election, lose, come home with her tail between her legs and live happily ever after with him.

He stepped out of the steaming shower and reached for a towel. 'Hullo,' Katrina said.

She was sitting in the wicker chair beside the whirlpool bath, long legs crossed, a tall drink in her hand. She looked exhausted. 'Darling, you're back!' Mahoney went to her, stooped and kissed her.

'Was Patti Gandhi here?' she said.

Mahoney blinked. It was on the tip of his guilty tongue to lie. 'Yes. Why?'

Katrina smiled thinly. 'And what did she want? Apart from your body?'

Mahoney flinched inwardly. He had promised Patti not to tell Katrina that she owned the film rights to *Alms*. Nor did he want to discuss that ending with Katrina. 'Just to see us.'

Katrina asked quietly: 'Did you make love to her?'

Mahoney flinched again. 'No. Of course not.'

'Why "of course"? She's a very desirable woman. And she'd screw you at any opportunity.'

'Because I'm with you. I don't want to open a Pandora's Box.'

Katrina smirked sadly. 'We've already opened it. Did you kiss her?'

Mahoney put on a frown. 'Yes. On the cheek, like I always do.'

Katrina put her hand in her pocket and pulled out a gold earring. 'I found this on the kitchen floor.' She opened the clip and snapped it on her own ear. She tugged it. 'Strong clip. Take more than a kiss on the cheek to get it off.'

Mahoney's grim sigh belied his sinking heart. Did his shirt, lying on the floor, have lipstick on it? 'I don't know how the hell her earring fell off, Kate.'

Katrina looked at him. Then sighed.

'Okay. Life isn't worth living if you can't believe your lover.' She put the earring on the shelf, got up wearily and began to get undressed. She slung her skirt into the bedroom, got out of her underwear and dropped them on the floor. She stepped into the whirlpool bath. She lay back, eyes closed. 'Are you coming in?'

'Sure.' He dropped the towel and got in. He lay down next to her.

She reached for her drink, took a sip and said: 'Did she tell you what she's up to in Bophuthatswana? Fomenting riots by telling the civil service they won't get their salaries and pensions.'

'The ANC's doing that, hardly Patti.'

'Patti's one of the organizers. Like she was at Bisho. And d'you know what their purpose is?'

'To topple Mangope, force Bophuthatswana into rejoining South Africa.'

Katrina snorted softly. 'More than that. They're trying to provoke a bloody confrontation with the Freedom Alliance – because we'll have to go to Mangope's aid if he can't cope. So? So the Freedom Alliance will have to rush in, guns blazing. There'll be bloody battles. International outcry. Blood on Afrikaner hands. Freedom Alliance portrayed as Nazis. South African army has to go in. Further battles. Freedom Alliance defeated, in disgrace. End of Freedom Alliance. End of Afrikaner Volksfront, Inkatha, Bophuthatswana, Ciskei – all defeated, all in disgrace. End of self-determination, end of volkstaat, end of KwaZulu. End of story.' She looked at him. 'That's the ANC's little scenario.' She paused, then added with a wry smile: 'And Patti's got an additional little scenario of her own: *I* will be disgraced, in your eyes. And you'll leave me.'

Oh Jesus. Almost exactly what Patti said.

'You disgraced? You don't want the Freedom Alliance to go in to Bophuthatswana?'

'God, no. Mangope's a despot. He's an embarrassment, like the AWB and Ciskei. But we'll have to go in. That's the deal.'

'And you'll support them?'

'Of course. You have to take the rough with the smooth in love and war.'

Mahoney sighed. Oh *Jesus*. He said earnestly: 'Kat, you don't. For God's *sake*, give up this Freedom Alliance connection now. For God's sake, register your new party *now*, and contest the election as best you can and keep your hands clean.'

'That's exactly what General Viljoen and a few others like me are trying to do.'

'Then *do* it – *now*. And cut your connections with the Freedom Alliance before Bophuthatswana blows up in your face and you've got blood all over your hands. Because after that there'll be a similar blood-bath in Ciskei. Then in *KwaZulu*.'

'You don't understand the work involved in organising a credible political party, darling – and it's hopeless if it's not credible, particularly to the Afrikaner. And you don't desert your allies until you've done your utmost to persuade them to follow you.'

'Kat,' Mahoney sighed, 'you've done your utmost. If they won't follow you into legitimacy, for Christ's sake leave them now. Bophuthatswana could blow up tomorrow. And if you can't register tomorrow, for Christ's sake give it *all* up now. Give up this volkstaat. There *is* a middle-ground to occupy.'

Katrina smiled sadly. 'Which you want to occupy?' It wasn't a question.

Mahoney closed his eyes. '*Yes*. There *can* be inter-tribal harmony. The Afrikaner has *not* got to be the exception to be happy. We *can* all live together harmoniously if we work at it!'

'Can we? Sure, *I* can. But can the Zulus? Will the Afrikaner? *Should* they, morally, be forced to do so, when you look at all the strife of Yugoslavia. The Irish. The Kurds. Pakistan and India. The Basques. Russia. The tribal chaos of the rest of Africa.' She shook her head. 'I don't believe so, darling. Look at the violence right here, right now. Can there be a free and fair election? If not, is that *just*? If it's not just, why should we accept an *un*just way of life?'

'It's better than civil war.'

'Sure – temporarily. "If rape is inevitable, relax and enjoy it." But *permanent* rape? Permanent civil war, like Ireland? Do you really believe there will ever be inter-tribal harmony and middle-ground in South Africa, just because we hold a violent, unfree and unfair election?'

Mahoney looked at her. '*Yes*. Eventually. Because of *Ubuntu*, and the African tradition of human kindness, and forgiveness.'

Katrina smiled: 'I know all about *Ubuntu*, darling. But *Ubuntu* hasn't served the rest of Africa very well over the last forty years, has it? *Millions* of people slaughtered.' She looked at him. 'Isn't it better to stick to your guns – to your *principles* – from the beginning, and try to *avoid* the mistakes of the past – avoid all that bloodshed?'

Oh, *God*. Mahoney said urgently: 'For God's *sake*, to avoid being *responsible* for bloodshed, cut loose from the Freedom Alliance now.'

Katrina stretched out and pressed the jet-button. The steaming bath suddenly erupted in bubbles. She slid down and sank beneath the frothing hot water. She lay there submerged in the turbulence, her long blonde hair swirling in tempestuous clouds on the surface, her lovely breasts and thighs awash. Then she sat upright. She stood up with a gush, hot water and steam rising off her lovely body, her long hair plastered sodden to her golden shoulders. She was beautiful.

'I love you,' he said.

She smiled down at him sadly, then bent and kissed him hard. She said into his mouth: 'You stick to your writing, darling, and leave me to my political troubles. And now let's go to bed and sleep, sleep, sleep.'

Mahoney cupped her hot breasts, then slid his hands down her gleaming thighs. 'I want to make love.'

She kissed him again. 'Only if you don't talk about the crisis anymore.'

She stepped out of the bath, glistening.

114

Bophuthatswana. The patchwork of little regions dotted down the western half of South Africa, notionally welded together as a republic legally independent of South Africa since 1978. Bophuthatswana was normally a quiet little higgledy-piggledy country except for the grandiose new capital of Mmabatho and the magnificent casinos, its people docile under the iron hand of President Mangope, its little army and civil service subservient under his patronage. There was no democratic nonsense in Bophuthatswana: it was ruled the African Way. But this week Bophuthatswana was not docile: the ANC was determined to dismember the Freedom Alliance, piece by piece. And the easiest way was to tell the civil service that their salaries and pensions would not be paid unless Bophuthatswana was reincorporated into the new South Africa.

It worked fine. Much better than Bisho. Immediately, the strikes began, the hospitals closed down, the postal services, the broadcasting corporation blacked out, barricades thrown up, the police firing tear-gas, and live ammunition. For two weeks it went on, but President

Mangope refused to give up power. And the unrest redoubled. That third week ten thousand Bophuthatswana civil servants bussed into Pretoria and marched on the Union Buildings demanding their reincorporation into South Africa. That same day the Bophuthatswana police went on strike, refusing 'to kill their brothers', and the looting began. The smashing and grabbing, shop windows shattering, excited people streaming down the streets carrying their swag, smoke barrelling skywards midst the stink of tear-gas as the Bophuthatswana Defence Force tried to do the job of the police. That evening President Mangope telephoned his Freedom Alliance partner in Pretoria, the Afrikaner Volksfront, to ask for military help to restore law and order.

The Afrikaner Volksfront's private army, under the command of General Viljoen, was a very different kettle of fish to the maverick AWB. The AWB refused to submit to General Viljoen's command, and he was trying to distance himself from their loutish image. President Mangope, when he called for help, specifically asked that the AWB not be included. But that did not deter Eugene Terreblanche: this was what *his* army had been waiting fifteen years for. His orders went rasping out on telephone and Radio Pretoria, and from all over the environs the AWB scrambled into their uniforms, snatched up their weapons, jumped into their vehicles and headed off into the night for Bophuthatswana to restore law and order.

Katrina de la Rey was an admirer of General Viljoen – and so, reluctantly, was Mahoney, who had met him twice through Katrina. The man was a gentleman, highly intelligent, very experienced in his science, personable, sincere and made of political steel. Katrina and the general agreed that the Afrikaner had to participate in the forthcoming elections in order to have a voice in the new South Africa's parliament, to enable them to fight legitimately for a volkstaat. In this they were in a small minority within the Afrikaner Volksfront, most of whom were bent on forcing the new South Africa, at the barrel of a gun, to grant their demand. The general regarded the gun as their last resort.

Katrina was speeding down the motorway at 7 a.m., on her way to her office, when she heard the news on her car radio that the Afrikaner Volksfront had responded to President Mangope's plea for military help. She was horrified. This was a confrontation she had dreaded. And for what? To prop up an embarrassing ally like the dictatorial Mangope! It was madness – there would be a bloodbath which would bring the Afrikaner into further disrepute, further imperil their chance of a volkstaat. She frantically called General

Viljoen's home on her carphone but got no reply. She telephoned his office and got no reply. She tried the Afrikaner Volksfront office, but it was too early to get a response.

It was then that she got the hourly news on Radio 702: *'In the small hours of this morning, commandos of the AWB and the Afrikaner Volksfront crossed into the nominally independent republic of Bophuthatswana to restore law and order.'*

'Jesus Christ!' Katrina cried 'The AWB too?!'

'Having mustered overnight on the Bophuthatswana border in response to President Mangope's plea for help, Freedom Alliance commandos seized control of the airport, strategic buildings and installations, and the Megacity shopping complex, where widespread looting and destruction has been going on.

'The occupation of the airport was achieved without resistance from the Bophuthatswana Defence Force because of President Mangope's request. However, when it was discovered that AWB commandos were amongst the right-wing forces and that they had occupied the capital, the Bophuthatswana commander ordered them to withdraw forthwith, explaining that although the AVF forces were welcome the AWB's racist presence would not be tolerated by the Tswana populace. The AWB leader, Eugene Terreblanche, was visibly angered by this, claiming to be here at the request of President Mangope, and refused to obey.'

'Jesus!' Katrina cried.

'As a result, the AVF forces seem to have remained at the airport, whilst in Mmabatho mayhem has begun. AWB members are driving around there and adjoining Mafikeng in scores of vehicles bristling with gunmen, shouting obscenities, breaking up mobs of demonstrators, chasing people off the streets, shooting at looters and stone-throwers. Many people have been wounded, an unknown number killed. Gangs of resisters are throwing stones and throwing up barricades but at the moment the AWB gunmen seem to be in control of the town, as the police stay out of sight and there is confusion amongst the Bophuthatswana Defence Force as to their orders. Meanwhile, the South African army has occupied the South African Embassy and more troops are said to be on their way . . .'

Katrina trod on the accelerator and swung off the motorway, onto the road for Bophuthatswana.

Got, man, this was exactly what Frikkie van Aswegen had been waiting for all his life, hey – a chance to shoot kaffirs *legally*, guest of President Mangope, restoring law and order in a kaffir country, showing the ANC who's fokkin' boss, hey, showing the fokkin' *world* they can't fok around with the Afrikaner, hey . . .

Spirits were high in Frikkie van Aswegen's carload of stormtroopers as they roared out of Ventersdorp that Thursday evening in a noisy convoy of vehicles. Morale was good as they rocked up at the hotel near the border to muster with stormtroopers from other areas and to have a few more drinks before taking on the kaffirs. Morale was at fever-pitch when they got their marching orders, debouched from the boozer and scrambled into their vehicles and went roaring across the border, into Mmabatho.

Frikkie van Aswegen had joined three friends in an old blue Toyota so he could have both hands free to shoot. And Frikkie had never had so much fun in his life! Before dawn they had secured all the strategic installations, and then the real *skop, skiet en donner* started, hey, when the kaffirs started showing up at sunrise. Kaffirs everywhere, shouting and throwing stones and trying to make roadblocks, kaffirs running and regrouping. *Got*, man, it was *lekker* roaring around the town with all the other AWB vehicles, hooting, shouting, shooting, chasing kaffirs off the streets, hey, seeing them run terrified. But the best part was when they threw stones and you had the excuse to shoot to kill – that was *lekker*, seeing them hit the dust!

Frikkie crouched in the backseat of the Toyota, blasting out of the window at any kaffir who showed himself, and when there were no kaffirs, just blasting at buildings to show the bastards who was boss. All morning the fun went on as the AWB vehicles roared through the streets and by-roads of Mmabatho and Mafikeng, sending kaffirs running for their lives, their dust and gunfire rising up midst the pall of smoke of looted shops. Then, at noon, the Bophuthatswana Defence Force rallied from their confusion to recapture their city.

And, *Got*, Frikkie had never been so astonished in his life. *Got*, one moment they were roaring around town doing their job for the Freedom Alliance and Mangope – an' doin' it bladdy well, hey – the next moment there's all these armoured vehicles full of kaffir soldiers threatening to shoot, shouting '*AWB out!*', pointing rifles, then suddenly there's kaffirs everywhere shouting and throwing stones and jeering.

As a major in the AWB, Frikkie scrambled out of the backseat and strode towards the armoured vehicle indignantly, waving his gun and shouting: '*What's going on, hey?*' His response was a rattle of gunfire, dust spurted up around his feet, and Frikkie got the message. He went running flat out back to the Toyota, and Gerrit swung around and went roaring off down the road to roars of jeering and ululating. Frikkie and the boys drove away angrily, bewildered, and then, *Got*, suddenly there were armoured vehicles everywhere, blocking side roads, AWB vehicles milling: and the rout of the AWB began.

It was a confusing, humiliating retreat. Frikkie was furious. Here they were restoring law and order for Mangope and now his fokkin' army is chasing them out? All over Mmabatho and Mafikeng AWB commandos found their paths blocked by outraged soldiers and mobs shouting '*AWB out!*', and experienced the ignominy of finding themselves suddenly outgunned and herded down the roads by menacing armoured vehicles bristling with angry soldiery. All over town AWB vehicles were roaring down roads in confusion, being herded out of town. *Got*, it was *outrageous*!

Frikkie's vehicle was the second-last in the angry convoy that found themselves being driven out of town in clouds of angry dust, shouting defiance and obscenities at the jeering mobs, loosing off the odd last defiant shot. Frikkie's mind was reeling with the injustice of it all when they came around a corner and saw the bunch of international journalists busy filming their ignominious retreat. And Frikkie saw red. Here were these bastards of the foreign press giving the Afrikaner a bad name – and Frikkie barked an order and Gerrit slammed on the brakes. He rammed the vehicle into reverse, went roaring backwards up the road to sort out the fokkin' journalists.

The vehicle slammed to a halt and Frikkie and Klaas and Dries leapt out, brandishing their pistols. The journalists scattered, the AWB chased them, and the punch-up began. Angry journalists and outraged AWB men trading punches and kicks, and Frikkie and Dries and Klaas grabbed their cameras and threw the film on the ground, *donnering* the foreign press, hey. Then suddenly there was a burst of gunfire from across the street, bullets flying, angry journalists scattering, and Frikkie threw himself flat on the concrete. Dries and Klaas raced back to the car and threw themselves in, horrified, and Gerrit slammed his foot on the accelerator, and roared away down the road, following the end of the routed convoy. Leaving Frikkie lying there on the ground. Frikkie had never felt so alone in his life, hey, surrounded by all these hostile foreign press and kaffirs, hey. And he stopped playing dead and leapt to his feet, and he *ran*.

He ran flat out for the nearest side-road, then threw himself behind a dustbin, rasping, gasping, terrified, all alone. Frikkie did not know it then, but his life had just been saved.

Gerrit and Klaas and Dries sped up the dusty road after the rest of the fleeing convoy, guns ready. Ahead was an intersection manned by an armoured vehicle, the streets thick with yelling Tswanas, a bunch of journalists clustered on one corner. The convoy roared through them under scattered fire, yelling, scattering people, firing back. Gerrit's heart missed a beat as he saw the mob ahead, but he trod on the accelerator to catch up with his kinsmen, waving his pistol out the window, Klaas and Dries at the ready. To the right was a police station and they blasted off at it defiantly – and there was an answering fusillade from all sides, and the Toyota jolted and Gerrit's windscreen disappeared in a mass of flying glass. There was a gasp from Klaas as a bullet hit his neck. Gerrit came to a juddering stop on the corner of the intersection, astonished, terrified. And at this same moment Katrina roared up.

The rest was very shocking. Afterwards, when Katrina tried to reconstruct the scene, it seemed to have happened in terrible slow motion. There was Gerrit's shattered Toyota juddering to a halt midst gunfire, the journalists snapping photographs. There were the Bophuthatswana police coming running, the mob shouting and ululating. Then the front passenger door opened and out toppled Klaas, blood pumping from his neck, slumping to the dust unconscious. Then more gunfire, and the back door opened and out clambered Dries, also wounded, and he slumped down onto the dirt, his head propped against a wheel. Then the driver's door opened and out fell Gerrit, wild-eyed, astonished at the blood, and he lurched around the car to his wounded companions as the pressmen's cameras clicked and the policemen came running. There was Gerrit, crouching beside Klaas, his hands up in surrender, his mouth working, pleading for an ambulance. Then there was a policeman raging at him: '*You killed two people! Who do you think you are?! What are you doing in my country?! I can take your life in one second!*' Then a second policeman was sweeping his gun in an arc, screaming he wanted to shoot '*these fucking dogs who killed women.*' There was Gerrit, shaking with fear, turning away and lying face down on the ground in surrender.

From where she sat behind her steering wheel ten paces away, it looked to Katrina as if the tableau had stabilised, that nobody else was going to be shot. The journalists were urging the police to call an ambulance, asking the AWB men their names. Then Dries muttered 'Black bastards!' and a policeman went berserk. With a shriek he fired a shot into the back of Klaas's head as he lay unconscious; Gerrit looked up, horrified, then slumped his face onto his hands in terror, and the policeman shot him dead through the head. Then a second policeman was screaming at Dries, firing from the hip, and Dries's body bucked as half a dozen bullets killed him.

The rest was very confused. The shock, the blood, the shouting, the journalists diving for cover; Katrina scrambling out of her car, aghast, shouting '*Stop! Stop!*', running at the gunmen, hands up. Then two arms were thrown around her waist and she was wrenched off balance in the midst of the converging mob, and there was Patti Gandhi pulling her back towards her car shouting: *'Get the hell out of here before they shoot you too – '* She flung open the passenger door, shoved Katrina in, then ran to the driver's side, scrambled in and went roaring backwards up the road. Patti reversed two hundred yards, then swung the car around and went roaring up the road, out of harm's way.

'So – Bisho again?' Katrina demanded furiously. She was shaking.

'Just doing my job.' Patti slammed on the brakes. 'Now get the hell out of here, sweetheart, or you're gonna get your sweet self shot – '

'Doing your job?! Fomenting violence!'

'Darling, your Nazi boys started it.'

'They are not my boys and you fucking know it!'

'But those blacks back there don't, you're tarred with the same brush so get your sweet ass out of here. I better get back.' She began to get out of the driver's seat.

'You bastards started this! Stirring up the Bophuthatswana civil service about their pensions!'

'But, of course, darling. With, I might add, the connivance of the South African government. Mangope has to be got rid of somehow, and toppling him with his own people is surely better than having a blood-bath like Bisho.'

'So you foment a revolution! It's fucking illegal! The ANC is utterly despicable. It just breaks the law when it feels like it. By law Bophuthatswana is an independent state, a foreign country, but you don't like it so you just go in there and overthrow it. Is this how the ANC's going to rule the new South Africa? The *African* Way. If there's a regional government you don't like you're going to overthrow it illegally?!'

Patti said quietly: 'Mangope is a tyrant who refuses to let his people take part in the elections – '

'Oh *Christ*, I know *that*, woman, I shed no tears for Mangope. It's the *principle* I'm talking about – the ANC's lawless conduct. You're a bunch of political bandits who trample the law underfoot whenever it suits you!' She pointed out the back window furiously. 'Look what you've done! Look at that smoke. Now they're not protesting about pensions, they're ransacking. Millions of rands of damage you've caused!'

'Small price to pay for democracy, darling.'

'Oh *shit*!' Katrina shouted. '*Shit, shit, shit!* There's no talking to you ANC. *You* aren't paying! Small price to pay? Like Bisho? Like all the thousands of schools the ANC's destroyed over the years? All the houses you've burnt? All the blood you've shed? All the people you've roasted alive? All a small price to pay so that the ANC can steamroller over all of us in the African Way?' She stopped, and took a deep angry breath. 'Jesus – do you want to inherit the ruins? Yes I think you do – you don't care as long as you win! Jesus, you make me *sick*. And frightened.' She jerked her head. 'Go on, get back to your fire – I've got work to do, trying to put it out!'

Patti smiled sadly. 'Have you finished?'

Katrina's eyes flashed. 'Not quite!' She thrust her hand into her pocket and pulled out Patti's earring. 'Yours, I believe?'

Patti blinked. Then: 'Oh – there it is! Where did you find it?'

Katrina said softly: 'When did you notice you'd lost it?'

Patti was taken off guard. 'Oh, I can't remember, two weeks ago maybe.'

'So that would be the last time you were at my house?'

'I suppose so?'

Katrina said softly: 'You're lying, Patti. I found this large and valuable gold earring in the middle of my kitchen floor five nights ago when I returned unexpectedly. Why're you lying?' She looked at her grimly. 'Because you fucked him, didn't you?'

Patti's beautiful eyes gave nothing away. She said softly: 'Yes, I lied, darling. Because I didn't want to hurt you – I didn't want you to think that I'd visited Luke whilst your back was turned. But I did – just for a chat.' She looked at her. 'I lied to protect you and Luke. Because I love you.' She shook her head earnestly. 'You say I want Luke. Yes, but not that way, darling. As I sit here now, I have your happiness in my hands. All I have to say is, yes I fucked Luke, and you will storm away, vowing never to see him again, and then I'd have him.' Her eyes moistened. 'Not so?'

'Damn right!'

'So I could lie, darling, and say yes, and then I could have him, right? As simple as that.' Patti smiled sadly, then shook her head. 'But I don't want Luke that way. I don't want to be second-best, darling. Second-best I've already got. If Luke ever comes back to me, I want it to be because he *chooses* me, not because I tricked him. So it's with an absolutely clear conscience that I look you in the eye and say, No, darling, not only did I not fuck him, but I wouldn't play such a dirty trick on you. And you – ' she raised a finger – 'better believe that. And *now*, if you'll excuse me, after rescuing you from big shit, I'd better get back.'

She flung open the door and swung out. She bent and said through the window: 'And you go home, darling. This is no place for a white Afrikaner.' She blew her a kiss. 'And remember I love you guys.'

She turned and went striding off down the road.

Closeted all day in his study, writing, Mahoney knew nothing of all this until he switched on the television at eight o'clock for the evening news:

'*South African Defence Force have now occupied Mmabatho and Mafikeng, mopping up bands of right-wing commandos and escorting them out of the territory, and delegates of the Transitional Executive Council have flown in to put into place a temporary administration. Hereupon it was learnt that embattled President Mangope had agreed to the reincorporation of Bophuthatswana into South Africa and to allow elections –*'

'Thank God!' Mahoney cried.

'*– only to withdraw his promise half an hour later after receiving a telephone call from the president of the Afrikaner Volksfront, Dr Ferdi Hartzenberg, telling him he was selling his birthright –* '

'Oh Christ!'

'*– but within hours President Mangope had again changed his mind, under the pressures of reality, promising yet again to allow elections.*'

'Thank God.' Mahoney sighed. Thank God? Thank God that a lawfully independent republic has been unlawfully overthrown by Machiavellian strategies with the connivance of the South African government? Jesus Christ, this was gutter politics. But wasn't he also thankful? Thankful that a cornerstone had been unlawfully kicked out of the Freedom Alliance wall, thankful that therefore his woman was going to have to give up her Freedom bloody Alliance. *Thank Christ for the African Way.*

And then the images of the battle for Mmabatho and Mafikeng came on the screen, the AWB vehicles careering through the dusty streets bristling with yahooing gunmen, the crackle of gunfire, the pall of smoke rising up from the looted shops, the bodies, the stone-throwing mobs, the rout of the invaders – and then the shocking images of Gerrit and Dries and Klaas roaring up to the intersection, guns blazing, the fusillade of answering gunfire, the juddering halt, the blood, the shouting, the arguing, the blood-crazed policemen, the shocking execution, one, two, three.

'*Jesus!*'

And suddenly Mahoney knew where Katrina was – in fucking Bophuthatswana! He hurried for the telephone and frantically dialled her office – he got the answering machine. He dialled General Viljoen's home, and got the answering machine. He dialled Radio 702 – and to his immense relief he was told that there were no reports of a white woman being killed.

Mahoney banged down the telephone, went through to the kitchen, poured a large whisky and took a big gulp.

Then he heard Katrina swing into the backyard. He flung open the kitchen door.

Katrina was walking wearily across the lawn. Mahoney ran down the steps and flung his arms around her. 'Where've you *been?*'

She slumped against him. She said flatly: 'You know about Bophuthatswana?'

'Is *that* where you've been?'

She sighed wearily. 'I have been,' she said, 'with General Viljoen, registering the Freedom Front as a political party for the elections, before the midnight deadline.' She leant back in his arms and smiled wanly. 'Congratulate your heroine. And General Viljoen. We've broken with the Afrikaner Volksfront and the bloody AWB. Their behaviour today was the last bloody straw. We're now respectable. We're contesting the elections instead of going to war.'

Mahoney stared at her. Then closed his eyes.

'Oh, thank *God.'*

'Are you sure you mean that – "Thank God"?'

She sat opposite him at the kitchen table, with a large gin and tonic. She had shadows under her beautiful blue eyes. She had told him the whole awful story.

Mahoney sighed inwardly. Yes and no. No, because he had hoped this bloodbath today would make her quit.

He said: 'Christ yes. You're now a legitimate political party and you've shucked off your disastrous AWB baggage.'

She said soberly: 'But do you realise what this means to us? It means I'm probably going to be an MP for the northern Cape region, darling – arguing full-time for a volkstaat under a new Thirty-fourth Principle. Not just a university professor with a theory anymore, but a full-time legislator who has to put her body and soul where her mouth is. And I'll have to live amongst my people.' She waved a weary hand. 'I'll have to give up this place – no more cosmopolitan Johannesburg, it'll be somewhere like Kimberley where I'll have to live, darling. *And* you, if you still want to live with me.' She folded her hands on the table and looked at him soberly. 'Starting in about two months. Straight after the elections. How does that appeal to you?'

How did that appeal to him? Oh Gawd. As long as she was out of the war it didn't matter? Living amongst all those Hairies?

Before he could muster how he felt Katrina continued: 'And think well before you answer, darling. You've got about two months to decide. But then it's crunch-time. This isn't theory anymore, me driving you around my volkstaat showing you its pitiful wonders while you sit there smiling benevolently, humouring me because you don't believe it will ever happen. This is for real, now, my darling. Under the proportional representation system the Freedom Front is going to win a number of seats in the regional parliaments – and in the national parliament – and yours truly is going to be elected to one of the seats in the northern Cape parliament, because sure as hell the Afrikaners there are going to vote for my Freedom Front Party. And so that's where I've got to live.' She looked at him. 'It's almost crunch-time, darling. Do you want to live like that, with my people?'

No, Mahoney did not. But he still couldn't believe it had to be like that. She raised a hand to interrupt him and continued: 'And don't say we can live here and commute to Kimberley once a month – we can't. And another thing.' She took a deep weary breath. 'The threat of war isn't over, darling. It's only been averted for the time being, for as long as it takes to argue our case in the new parliaments. Our purpose in entering this election at this eleventh hour is to prove our strength, to prove to the world that there're a million South Africans out there who want self-determination, who demand their own piece of this earth. Armed with that mandate we're going to argue like hell for our rights. But we're keeping our powder dry, Luke – the general is a gentleman who intends using all the legitimate channels to get his volkstaat, and then go the extra mile, and then another mile. But when we reach the end of that road, if we don't get them to agree to our volkstaat, there'll almost definitely be war, Luke. And when it comes to war, the general knows what he's talking about.' She looked at him: 'So don't be too euphoric that we've dumped the AWB, darling, because we certainly have not dumped the military option as a last resort. That is a most important detail for you to put into your calculations when you utter "Thank God". Because although we've gone respectable the battles are only beginning.' She looked at him soberly. 'Think about that, please. Is that a fight you want to be involved in, Luke? I don't think so. You don't belong there.'

Almost exactly what Patti had said. He frowned. 'What are you saying to me, Katrina?'

'Up to now you've been saying we'll cross the bridges as we come to them. On the assumption that it was safe to be in love with me because my volkstaat would never happen. Well, you're at the bridge now, darling, and my volkstaat is on the other side of it. I'm saying that the time has come for you to decide whether you really want to cross that bridge.'

Mahoney took her hands across the table. He said: 'I love you.'

She smiled sadly. 'Me too. But love isn't enough. You've got to cross the bridge as well. That's our little tragedy. It's the tragedy of Africa, in microcosm – Africa is a continent of extremes, it forces you to choose sides, you have to be on one side or the other.'

He said ardently: 'There's *middle* ground you can be on.'

She shook her head. 'No, darling. What is about to happen is the culmination of three hundred years of South African history – the culmination of the Great Trek. People in the middle get nowhere politically in Africa. You see – you're still thinking, *hoping* that I won't have to cross the bridge, that therefore you won't have to face the problems that I tried to show you when you first came out from Hong Kong. You said being in love is supposed to be fun. So I let myself fall in love, I let my heart rule my head. And yes, it's been fun, lovely fun – but we're *there* now, and you've got to be on one side of the bridge or the other.' She looked at him. 'And I don't believe you belong on my side, darling.'

He frowned. 'You're telling me you want us to break up now?'

She said quietly: 'I'm telling you you can't avoid it any longer. And I'm asking you to think hard about it now.'

He squeezed her hands. '*Marry* me, Katrina. Tomorrow. And we'll live happily ever after as best we can on whatever side of the bridge we have to, live with the imperfect future that's been thrust upon us. And we'll live well, Kat – this soap opera of *Alms* is going to make a lot of money!'

Her eyes were moist. 'Oh, darling, you're not listening – '

'Oh *fuck* the bridges – '

'And fuck the volkstaat too – because it'll never happen?' She shook her head wearily. 'But I haven't finished telling you about the bridge, darling.' She looked at him. 'What about Patti?'

Mahoney closed his eyes. With foreboding. 'What about her?'

Katrina said quietly: 'I'm not going to ask what she means to you, because I don't want to hear the truth and I don't want to hear a lie. I couldn't bear either.' She looked at him. 'But I know that she has a great hold over you. And I want you to be clear that she is part of the bridge, Luke. When you cross the bridge – if you cross it – you leave her behind. It's over. In fact it's over right now as far as I'm concerned.' She held up a palm to stop him interrupting. 'But that's not why I mention her. I want to make a clean breast at the threshold of this bridge.' She paused, then: 'I want you to understand that I've been a whore, Luke. And why.'

Mahoney was taken aback by this. 'A *whore*?'

Katrina took a breath.

'Please don't interrupt, let me tell it straight.' She paused questioningly. Mahoney nodded. She continued resolutely: 'I've had to live with the legendary Patti Gandhi ever since I fell into bed with you in Borneo. With the knowledge of her as the great love of your life in *Alms*. And live with you writing that movie about her. And I've had to live with the knowledge that you fucked her in Mauritius.' She held up a palm. 'Please don't deny it. I knew you had to go through something like that when she came out of prison. And it hurt me like hell, but it's one of those things in this imperfect life you can't do anything about.' She paused. 'And I've had to live with her sexually since you've come back to South Africa. And that's what I want to make a clean breast about.'

Mahoney was staring at her. Katrina continued: 'My problem was threefold. One, I'm sexually attracted to her because that's the way I am, and I can't help that. Two: I *used* her, Luke. I *used* her sexuality, not only for my own gratification, but like a doctor uses a virus when he inoculates you – to make you immune. I reckoned that after all that passion in *Alms*, and after all that sexuality confronting me – threatening *us* – the best defence was inoculation. Don't fight it, *deal* with it. And maybe that would inoculate you against her as well. And three. I fucked her for politics, Luke.'

Mahoney stared at her. Katrina continued, moist-eyed: 'Yes, for politics, darling. Don't look so surprised. Sex has motivated all aspects of life, including politics, since time began. Read Sigmund Freud. Sex made the caveman go out, hit his mate on the head and claim his bit of territory. Sex made him build his family clan. Sex made the clan become a tribe. Tribal sex made the tribe become a nation. Sex has made princes marry princesses for political expediency, made kings marry their queens to weld nations together. Sex made the Afrikaner people what it is, an African tribe which imagines itself to be white but which is half mongrel-brown. The whole of humankind is no different – or better – than the rest of the animal kingdom rutting in the springtime, except we've got more intelligence. And so I used Patti's sexuality – *and* mine – *and* yours – for tribal purposes. Like many a politician before me I saw an opportunity to get behind the rival tribe's battlements through Patti Gandhi and try to honey-talk them into a treaty.' She smiled at him wanly. 'And I've failed. All my blandishments, all the tricks of the courtesan, have failed. So that only leaves tribal conflict. Not because I want it, but because it's beyond my control. Now.' She looked at him: 'Do you still want to marry me? Knowing I've been a political whore.'

Mahoney was staring at her. He said: 'But you liked her as well?'

'Oh yes. And I admired her courage. And I felt very sorry for her. And I felt very guilty. All that. But from the day I first saw her, at the hotel when we were on our way to the Wild Coast, I saw my opportunity to use her. But I was also scared of her – scared of the threat she posed to my happiness. So it took me some time to put my wicked plan into action. I had many misgivings along the way.'

Mahoney said: 'And Patti? Was she a whore too?'

'Oh yes. She used my weakness – my sexuality and my political aspirations – she used me to get at you.'

'But she genuinely likes you.'

'Oh yes. She's genuine when she says we're the only real family she's got. And she's turned on by me. But she really means *you* are the only family she's got – I come as part of that. And she's obsessed by you. And she's tough, darling. All is fair in love and war, for her. She'll sacrifice her feelings for me the moment she's got you back.' Katrina smiled sadly. 'She's a patient hunter. She's played a clever waiting game, Luke. She's convinced that sooner or later you'll realise that you can't cross the bridge with me, and then she'll be waiting for you, when you step back from the brink. That's why she was so supportive when we argued for the Thirty-fourth Principle, to allow for the possibility of a volkstaat. She wants me to have to cross the bridge, leaving you behind.' She looked at him solemnly. 'And maybe isn't that where you really belong, Luke?'

Mahoney was astonished. 'With the *ANC*?'

'*No*, with Patti. You could lead a normal life, in your own culture. With me, across the bridge, you couldn't. That's what you've got to consider urgently now, darling.'

'Jesus.' Mahoney's eyes were burning. He'd had enough of this drama. He frowned: 'Do you love me?'

'With all my little volkstaat heart.'

And suddenly Mahoney wanted to laugh.

'Then that's good enough for this imperfect world! Love will find a way.' He got up and pulled her to her feet and held her tight. 'We're getting married in the morning, woman.'

She grinned at him, her eyes full of tears. 'No, I ain't, lover, not yet.'

'Yes you are!'

She leant back in his arms. 'Are you prepared to be a volkstaater, Luke?'

'I'm a South African. And so are you.'

She smiled tearfully. 'Oh darling, there ain't any such animal as a South African. So. Answer my question, please.'

He sighed, then said: 'Oh, I hate to say this, and I feel so sorry for you after all your hard work. But, darling – there isn't going to be a volkstaat.'

She looked at him tearfully. Then she turned out of his arms. She said: 'You're wrong. And if you're right, there will be no peace.' She turned and smiled at him sadly. 'But you've answered my question. And your answer is no.'

Oh Christ. Mahoney closed his eyes.

'Wrong. My answer is yes. Yes, I'm prepared to live in your volkstaat if that's what it takes to live with you.'

Her eyes were moist. 'But you don't believe that's going to be necessary?'

'Correct.'

Katrina smiled. Then walked to him and put her arms around him. She said: 'I love you. And I'll marry you the day you cross the bridge. But if you wanted to do that today, I wouldn't let you, because I wouldn't want you to make a mistake.' She smiled at him. 'But you aren't at the threshold of the bridge today. The elections are still six weeks away. A lot of water can flow in six weeks.' She squeezed him wearily. 'And now, take me to bed. I've got a lot of work to do when I wake up.'

PART XVIII

ELECTIONEERING IN TOP GEAR

VIOLENCE, VIOLENCE, VIOLENCE

AFTER BOPHUTHATSWANA,
CISKEI COLLAPSES

ZULUS MARCH ON
JOHANNESBURG – MASSACRE

STATE OF EMERGENCY DECLARED

INTERNATIONAL MEDIATION
BY KISSINGER FAILS

VIOLENCE, VIOLENCE, VIOLENCE –
DEATH TOLL SOARS

BLOODBATH IN RWANDA

SA WHITES STOCKPILE FOOD – MANY FLEE

115

Those six weeks were bad, though there was some good news.

The good news was that, after the Bophuthatswana bloodbath, the Republic of Ciskei surrendered without a fight, and that meant the Freedom Alliance had lost yet another ally. The bad news was that now KwaZulu would be the ANC's next target. Mahoney had rented a cellular-pager which vibrated on his desk and reported the latest news in a little window as it happened: and the news was bad. The blood flowing in KwaZulu as the ANC and Inkatha butchered it out, as Chief Buthelezi demanded a cast-iron federal constitution before he entered the elections, as the ANC tried to destroy him; as the Afrikaner Volksfront vowed to support him to the death. The bad news was the president of the Afrikaner Volksraad fulminating to his volk that there must be no compromise, that they must boycott the elections, that they must gird themselves for war; the bad news was bombs, as the Afrikaner right wing blew up electricity pylons, post offices, government buildings. The good news, as far as Mahoney was concerned, was that his woman was out of it. The bad news was the bloodshed around Johannesburg as Zulu hostel-dwellers and ANC comrades gun-battled for political turf; 137 policemen were killed that month, 342 other people. The bad news was Buthelezi demanding that the elections be postponed. The bad news was the Goldstone Commission of Inquiry into Violence pronouncing that three top generals in the police were implicated in the Third Force, in running guns into KwaZulu. The bad news was that KwaZulu was training thousands of warriors in the forests. The bad news was the bloodshed and the bombs, the gunfire, the necklacings, the stink of tear-gas, the screams. The bad news was the violence at electioneering meetings, ANC and PAC youths breaking up Democratic Party meetings, hounding the candidates off their turf. The bad news was Chief Buthelezi announcing that unless a federal constitution were laid down, there would be the 'final fight to the finish with the ANC'. The bad news was King Goodwill of the Zulus entering the political area and demanding the whole of his old kingdom. The very bad news was Nelson Mandela vowing that under no circumstances would the election date of 27th April, 1994 be postponed; 'That day is sacrosanct,' he declared.

And the bad news was the mayhem in Rwanda, the massacres, the genocide as the Hutu tribe slaughtered half a million of the Tutsi tribe, the bloody chaos as hundreds of thousands fled across the borders. The bad news was the thousands of whites leaving South Africa for fear the same was to happen here. The bad news was the Great Zimbabwe Land Grab, the lands of white farmers being seized in the name of the peasants but dished out to cabinet ministers and civil servants. The bad news was Winnie Mandela's rabble-rousing, telling the people that Eugene Terreblanche's farm would be the first to be seized and distributed to the people in the new South Africa.

But, for all that shit, there was some good news.

For the very first time in South Africa, democracy was really trying to go to work, trying its bloody best to get out there and inform the people: Voter Education programmes on the radio and television and newspapers, the officials and volunteers going out there into the faraway hills and valleys trying to educate the people about democracy, telling them their rights, explaining about the secret ballot, promising them on the souls of their ancestors that nobody would know how they voted, that no party thugs would be able to find out and beat them, kill them, burn their houses, maim their cattle if they did not vote for their party. The good news was twenty-six registered parties campaigning across the vast country, from the big battalions of the ANC and the Nationalist Party down to KISS, the Keep it Straight and Simple Party, people of all political persuasions going out there amongst the simple folk who had never voted before, telling them their policies, trying to woo them with promises of a better life, more housing, schools, hospitals, dams, roads, electricity, land, jobs, money.

'Which is good,' Mahoney said on the telephone to his publisher, 'it's democracy at work, but it's also dangerous because it's only possible with massive increase in taxes and massive aid, and even then it's going to take a long time and most of those simple people expect it to happen immediately. Expectations of the masses are being raised and there's going to be trouble when they realise that it's not forthcoming for years.'

'Will it ever be forthcoming?'

'Depends on how much the ANC interferes with the economy. The Afrikaner fucked it up for forty years with the profligate waste of apartheid, but South Africa is a rich country and can rebound provided the ANC practices a market economy and no communist bullshit, no nationalization, doesn't appoint unqualified blacks to powerful positions in the name of "affirmative action". And provided they don't frighten away investors with high taxes and all the usual African insanity which bankrupted the rest of the continent. The ANC claims they've abandoned all communist notions now, but the trouble is their executive is riddled with unrepentant, unabashed communists. And the ANC's Reconstruction and Development Programme – to solve the massive problems of housing and jobs and social upliftment left behind by apartheid – *will* require government interference in the economy, and massive taxes. The ANC says their programme will only cost thirty-nine billion rand, but economists are saying it'll cost double or more. And the ANC has announced that they're going to appoint a hard-nosed lefty to implement their programme in the Johannesburg region, and he says he doesn't intend to let the International Monetary Fund or the World Bank bully him into a "bourgeois democracy" and a "so-called free market" system.'

'*Charming*. And what's going to happen to the Zulus now that Bophuthatswana and Ciskei have collapsed?'

'The bad news is that the ANC is now trying the same trick on KwaZulu, Bill, fomenting strikes over pensions, et cetera. That's *very* bad news, because if the Transitional Government sends the army in to restore law and order and topple Buthelezi there'll be hell to pay. KwaZulu has a helluva lot of warriors who're loyal to their king, and they've got a big loyal paramilitary police force with all kinds of guns who all hate the ANC, and they've got those tough-guys trained during the Inkathagate scandal, and now they've got a guerrilla army of five thousand who're being trained in the forests by mercenaries. If Buthelezi sounds the clarion and sends his impis into war it'll make the bloodbath of Bophuthatswana look like a Sunday stroll. And the Afrikaner Volksfront will go in to support them with all guns blazing.'

'And when's this likely to happen?' Bill Summers said hopefully.

'In the next few weeks leading up to the election. If Inkatha don't get their demands.'

'And what exactly are their demands?' Bill demanded.

'Inkatha demands a federal constitution which guarantees the autonomy of KwaZulu-Natal and the position of the Zulu king, and they demand that that constitution be finalised *before* any election is held – not left to the new parliament to decide because that will be dominated by the ANC. And now King Goodwill is demanding that his whole kingdom be returned to him, dating back to the boundaries Dingaan established in 1834. So they're demanding that the elections be postponed until all this is finalised. And there'll be war if the elections go ahead without them, Bill. But the ANC accuse Buthelezi of brinkmanship, saying he's scared to face an election because he knows Inkatha will do badly.'

'So the shit's going to hit the fan?' Bill Summers said happily.

'My educated guess is that after the ANC's won the election they're going to send the army in to crush the Zulus once and for all. Finish off the job the Boers started a hundred and fifty years ago.'

Bill snorted. 'The ironies of history. Fax us all this urgently, Luke. Meanwhile what are the Boers doing?'

'Well, the Afrikaners are split now that the Freedom Front Party has entered the elections. The Conservative Party is boycotting the elections, while the AWB and the other extreme right-wing groups are noisily preparing for war.'

'And you still take them seriously?'

'Hell, yes. Only a blind optimist wouldn't. And there's not much to be optimistic about in all this violence.'

'And Katrina?'

And Mahoney hardly saw Katrina these days. Most days she was on the road, organizing party offices in Afrikaner strongholds in the Transvaal, Orange Free State and the northern Cape, organizing committees, holding meetings, distributing party literature, campaigning, fund-raising, explaining. Her principal area was the northern Cape, persuading the scattered farmers and townsfolk that a volkstaat could prosper, but her principal target was the Coloured community, trying to convince them they had nothing to fear from a volkstaat, that they were Afrikaners too. She was keeping a punishing schedule, and when she was back in Johannesburg she came home late, too tired to talk, all she wanted to do was collapse into the whirlpool bath then fall into bed beside him and sleep.

'But she's happy. She's doing what she truly believes in and doing it the correct way, through the elections, to prove the Freedom Front's strength so they can argue their case. And they've already wrung a significant concession out of CODESA at the last moment – the new constitutional rules, which used to have thirty-three principles which the constitution-makers must follow, now includes a thirty-*fourth* principle: namely that a parliamentary "committee", called the Volkstaat Council, will be set up to examine the possibilities of creating an Afrikaaner region – where, how, et cetera. It doesn't mean they'll get it, but it opens the door to discussion. But Katrina is bullish when she's got the strength to talk about it. She's convinced they'll get sufficient number of seats in the new parliament to enable them to put up a good fight for the volkstaat. And unfortunately I think she's right.'

'Why unfortunately? I thought you favoured giving the Afrikaner his volkstaat.'

'I do, I just don't want my woman dedicated to it – I don't want to live in a volkstaat, amongst a bunch of hairybacks, Bill. And if they don't get their precious volkstaat they'll probably resort to the military option – and I certainly don't want Katrina mixed up in that.'

Bill Summers sighed happily. 'Luke, all this personal dilemma of yours is great stuff for your sequel to *Alms*. Please get your ass to an anchor with that book. Meanwhile keep faxing us an update every day for those journals. Especially describing the terrible violence.'

And then the terrible violence got worse. The next week the Zulus marched on central Johannesburg.

They came from far and wide, on foot and by train and bus and mini-cab, fifty thousand angry, sweating, chanting Zulus from the hostels and goldfields and factories and townships, armed to the teeth with their spears and axes and knobkerries and shields, swarming through downtown Johannesburg, a great mass of seething Zulu humanity with its fighting blood up, advancing from all directions in massive phalanxes into the heart of the city, to the Library Square Gardens, to demonstrate their solidarity with their king and Chief Buthelezi, to hear a rabble-rousing speech from their local leaders. Fifty thousand Zulus overflowing the Library gardens, flooding jubilantly down the main streets and side-streets, the roar of their deep voices rising up to the skies. For an hour they waited for their leaders to speak, then suddenly the bloodbath began.

Suddenly there was the *crack crack crack* of gunfire coming from the rooftops of the skyscrapers, indiscriminate gunfire blasting down into the seething mass of humanity below. Suddenly there were the shocking splats of blood, the shouts, the bodies collapsing, the massive surging of people trying to find cover, shoving, trampling; then came the frenzied answering gunfire of the Zulu warriors shooting furiously up at the buildings, plaster flying and windows shattering midst the pandemonium, people throwing themselves behind benches and parapets and cars and trees. And the sniper gunfire crackled on murderously, the answering gunfire crackled back.

For the next two hours the central district of Johannesburg was a war zone as furious Zulus raged through the streets, looting, drinking, smashing midst random sniper fire from the rooftops. First they swarmed on the ANC regional offices and had three shoot-outs with security guards, then they swarmed on the ANC national headquarters two blocks away. They came from three directions, brandishing their weapons, a great mass of Zulu warriors descending on the towering ANC office block; the ANC guards fired warning shots in the air, then gunfire raked the building. The Zulus stormed the headquarters and the ANC opened fire to kill, and the carnage continued. And the streets of central Johannesburg were a battlefield, bodies, blood, shattered glass everywhere. Fifty-one people were killed that morning and many more were wounded.

'For Christ's sake, Luke, what's happening?' Bill Summers shouted. 'Who were those snipers on the rooftops?'

'Inkatha says it's the ANC. The ANC denies it – but Mandela refused to let the police enter the ANC headquarters to search for weapons and gunmen! And the tragi-comedy is the police and De Klerk accepted his refusal. Jesus, this is the new South Africa? Anyway, the police have no evidence yet. But my guess is the Third Force did it, the same guys who organized the train massacres, right-wing hoodlums trying to create chaos to derail the elections. They wanted to infuriate the Zulus into attacking the ANC.'

'The AWB?'

'Could be, but there're dozens of right-wing organizations, each as bad as the next, the AWB just happens to be the biggest. Or it could be rogue elements of the police and army. The Goldstone Commission has just fingered three police generals as being involved in the Third Force, gun-running to the Zulus to prepare them for civil war.'

'And what are the Zulus doing after this massacre?'

'The violence has increased, of course. A State of Emergency has been declared in KwaZulu-Natal. On the East Rand it's a war zone as Inkatha and the ANC comrades shoot it out, and in Natal the bloodshed's worse now that King Goodwill has virtually called the Zulus to arms. A summit meeting's been called between De Klerk, Mandela, Buthelezi and King Goodwill to persuade Buthelezi to take part in the elections, and they offered to entrench King Goodwill's powers as constitutional monarch of the Zulus, but Buthelezi insists that the election be postponed and a federal constitution written in stone first. And now he demands international mediation. Mandela and De Klerk refused. So the deadlock remains and the blood continues to flow.'

'So what's going to happen?'

'The bloodshed's going to get worse, that's what. It's Buthelezi's only chance of getting his way. Now the Inkatha Youth League have announced they're going to stage a massive protest march on Johannesburg on Friday – "Rolling Mass Action" they call it. They're going to march on the ANC's headquarters again and lay wreaths for their slain warriors. Can you imagine what's going to happen?'

'Jesus. You stay away from downtown Johannesburg on Friday, Luke, we need you alive. So what exactly does a State of Emergency mean?'

'It means the army is sent in.'

The armoured vehicles rolling into the green hills of Zulu country, the military roadblocks, the patrols of soldiers, the helicopters clattering, the radios crackling: but the violence continued even worse; the guerrilla wars in townships and forests and hills and vales resumed after the patrols had passed, and the death toll soared. And in Johannesburg the police and army rigged high razor-wire barricades in dreaded anticipation of the Inkatha Youth League's march, turning the city centre and the ANC headquarters into a fortress. Political leaders around the world called on Buthelezi to call off his youthful warriors, to avert a bloodbath and civil war, but Buthelezi refused – the ANC had used plenty of Rolling Mass Action in the recent past, he pointed out reasonably, particularly in Bisho and Bophuthatswana. Then the ANC and the government gave in: they agreed to international mediation, though still refusing to postpone the election. And Buthelezi called off the march. And the world heaved a sigh of relief. A high-powered delegation, which included Henry Kissinger and Lord Carrington, immediately flew out to South Africa midst fanfare to mediate. But on arrival they found that Buthelezi still insisted that the election be postponed: the ANC and the government wouldn't hear of it, Buthelezi walked out, the high-powered mediators flew home.

'Oh Jesus,' Mahoney said. 'It means, Bill, that Buthelezi has overplayed his hand. He expected to get the elections postponed by the international mediation. He's failed and now he's completely finished – he's out of the race and he's handed KwaZulu-Natal to the ANC on a plate. And that is a disaster.'

'Does this mean war?' Bill Summers said excitedly.

'Unless a miracle happens.'

And then, the next day, one week before the elections, the miracle happened.

As South Africa braced itself for the bloodbath, the news broke that Buthelezi had agreed to enter the elections. There on the television screens was a wearily smiling trio of Buthelezi, De Klerk and Mandela on the steps of the Union Buildings of Pretoria, announcing to the world that disaster had been averted.

'I am doing this for the sake of South Africa,' Chief Buthelezi said. 'Of course, as we are agreeing to participate only one week before the elections, whereas all the other parties have been campaigning for months, it will be a miracle if my Inkatha Freedom Party does well . . . '

And then, immediately, another miracle occurred: the violence stopped. Overnight the gun battles between Inkatha and the ANC comrades spluttered out. Overnight the gangs and impis disappeared. Overnight the no-go zones became open zones, the blood-letting ceased, and a brittle peace descended on the land.

'*This is wonderful news,*' Mahoney faxed to Bill Summers. '*Though a cynic may say it only means that General Mandela and General Buthelezi have agreed to suspend politicking the African Way. For the time being?*

'*But this means the Afrikaner right wing, the so-called Freedom Alliance, have lost their last and most potent ally, the Zulus. For the time being? I think we can now expect some violent reaction from them to show their muscle.*'

And then came Black Sunday.

116

The bomb contained ninety kilograms of mining explosives, the weight of a big man. It was packed in a stolen car that was driven through the Sunday morning streets of central Johannesburg by a tall skinny white man with long blond hair. He parked near an intersection, one block away from the ANC national headquarters, the same distance from their regional office, in an area of old Johannesburg that is a mixture of apartment buildings, shops and office blocks. There were a few people on the quiet Sunday street as the man lit the fuse, then hurried away into the morning.

Thirty seconds later the bomb exploded. The percussion was felt right across the golden city. It blew a hole two metres deep in the street, shattered buildings all around, smashed windows for three hundred metres in all directions. Nine people were killed instantly in a mass of flying flesh and blood; ninety-two were wounded.

Mahoney was alone in his house when he heard the distant explosion. He was about to leave for the film set. Katrina was in the northern Cape, winding up the Freedom Front's electoral campaign. Mahoney snapped on the radio and television. But there was no information yet. Then, within minutes, his cellular pager vibrated, and the detail appeared on its little screen:

'*Oh Jesus, Jesus.*' He ran outside to his vehicle and drove into the city to see for himself.

It was noon when he returned from the shocking scene, sick in his guts. From the rubble and twisted steel and shattered glass, the blood, the bodies, the cries, the grief, the ambulances, the cops, the crowds, the journalists from around the world who outnumbered the cops. Three of the dead were little black children. Their mother hysterical with grief. '*Oh Jesus, Jesus, please spare this land from more of this.*' As he walked into the house, to write up his journal whilst his blood was still hot, he saw the light flashing on his answering machine.

Patti's voice came on, thick with emotion: '*Luke, I know you're alone but this call requires no response – I just beg you to think about it. You and I know who did that terrible bomb blast – the right wing. We also both know that Katrina and her Freedom Front had nothing to do with it. But the fact remains that when all the chips are down those murderous right-wing bastards are going to be on Katrina's side. Those are the people you're going to be associating with, Luke. And you don't belong there. Just like you could not associate yourself with the ANC all those years ago. Luke, you're blind if you can't see the impossible situation you're placing yourself in. And if you can't see the moral danger today, you certainly will tomorrow. All right, goodbye.*'

Mahoney closed his eyes. And snapped the button to wipe the message off. Sick in his guts.

Oh Jesus, Patti.

But no, she wasn't being a bitch – that emotion in her voice was genuine. *And, oh God, the sickening fact was that she was right.* He could not bear Katrina to be associated with those murderous swine, just like he'd been unable to be associated with Patti's bombers all those years ago. *He wanted Katrina out of this volkstaat business. And what did Patti mean about tomorrow?*

Mahoney knew what was going to happen tomorrow, Monday, the day before the elections started: Katrina had told him about the petition her father was rushing through the Supreme Court for the eviction, once again, of the squatters on Dagbreek ranch before the forthcoming ANC government turned the rights of property-owners upside down. The eviction notice ordered the squatters to vacate the land by ten o'clock on Monday, 25th April, failing which to submit, in a peaceful manner, to the arrangements made by the sheriff for their removal.

Those removal arrangements were made at the expense of General Karel de la Rey, which he could ill-afford. He hired a fleet of lorries to take them back to their former homes in what used to be, until last month, the Republic of Bophuthatswana. He also provided a lorry of maize to feed them when they got there.

It was no secret in Katrina's neck of the woods that the AWB was going to march along with the sheriff to ensure the eviction was successful; but the first Mahoney knew about that detail was when he came home from the film set and found Katrina's weary, tense message on his answering machine:

'Darling, I won't be home tonight after all, I'm going to Dagbreek to try to do something about the bloody AWB interfering in the squatters' eviction. And now I hear the ANC are going to be there as well.'

'Oh, Jesus.'

The ANC were there unofficially, several lorry-loads of men. And Patti Gandhi was there: she had organised the resistance on her own initiative. That Sunday afternoon, the day before the eviction notice expired, her contingent arrived and started organizing one thousand squatters, the women and children into front-line passive-resistance units.

It is uncertain how much Patti Gandhi's motivation was genuine and how much was a desire to embarrass Katrina de la Rey and thus demonstrate vividly to Luke Mahoney that he did not belong with her. Dramatic trouble-making had always been her hallmark – though certainly she did not intend the tragic consequences. She intended the battle of Dagbreek to be a passive-resistance exercise, as the great Mahatma Gandhi had practised in South Africa before overthrowing the British Raj, thus laying the stepping stones for the destruction of the British Empire, the end of the Colonial Era, thus laying the stepping stones for the Cold War in Africa, the intrigues and rebellions and wars from the Red Sea right down to the Limpopo, from the Indian Ocean to the Atlantic, thus laying the stepping stones for the collapse of Africa to communism, the destruction of the African economies, the reduction of the people to poverty. But it matters little that Patti Gandhi's dramatic intentions were passive. What matters is that the Zulus had decided at the last moment to enter the election and had thus deprived the right wing of their most potent ally in their demand for self-determination. What matters is that a killer bomb had exploded in Johannesburg and the people were angry, the new South Africa was at hand and they were full of expectations of land. What matters is that CODESA had ended with a denial of an Afrikaner volkstaat. What matters is that Winnie Mandela had pronounced in a rabble-rousing speech that farms of the likes of Eugene Terreblanche would be the first to be seized by the new government and given to the people. What matters is that nobody from Katrina's neck of the woods was going to take any more shit.

Katrina had driven to Dagbreek to plead with her father to postpone the eviction. To no avail. 'Pa, the mood of the blacks is explosive – this could turn into a bloodbath and from there anything could happen.'

'I don't want blood,' the old man said, 'I only want my land. Free of thieves stealing my cattle and poaching my game and chopping down my trees and polluting my waterholes. They have had plenty of warning, I have done everything legally, and I am even providing a removal contractor.'

'*But there will be blood, Pa!*'

'Then they will be the first to spill it, girl, my friends are under strict orders. But if it's blood the ANC want it will be mostly theirs I'm afraid.'

'Your friends in the AWB have strict orders to be *gentle?!*'

'Almost everybody around here is AWB at heart, girlie, it's hard to find a friend who isn't. But they won't be marching in uniform, they're only there to back up the sheriff. And the police will be there in case there's a breach of the peace.'

'*A breach of the peace?! Christ, a bomb has just exploded in Johannesburg –* '

'No blasphemy, please – you've been listening too much to that Englishman you live with in sin – '

'*Jesus!*' Katrina thumped her breast. '*I*, your daughter, *personally* beg of you in the name of common sense to postpone this eviction until the country quietens down! *Any* incident now could be catastrophic. Mandela and De Klerk both appealed for calm – '

'*Nelson Mandela?!* My goodness! The Great Man *himself*? The man who planted all those bombs years ago? That terrorist whose so-called army had been planting bombs all these years and blowing up farmers and innocent women and children – he's suddenly a nice reformed character and complaining about people who follow his example? My goodness, how strange the world is. And his little friend President de Klerk went along to the television station also, to tell the Afrikaner people that they must be nice quiet people while their country is given to that reformed character Mr Mandela and his godless communists?' He fixed his daughter with grim blue eyes and shook his head. 'What has this country come to, what a *terrible* state of affairs where the president of the Afrikaner volk has got to trot along to the South African Broadcasting Corporation to beg the black people not to get nasty with the white people who brought civilization to this country, just because some angry Afrikaners give Mr Mandela and his henchmen some of the same medicine they've been dishing out to the white people for years.'

'Oh Christ!' Katrina sat down and clutched her head.

The general said grimly. 'Don't misunderstand me – I deplore innocent people being the victims of bombs. What I am telling you is that such things are *inevitable* when you try to suppress a volk – it's absolutely *predictable*. And there'll be plenty more until the Boer gets his justice, and I just hope that Mr Mandela remembers the lesson of all his own bombs when he tries to suppress us.' He shook his head at her. 'I don't approve of bombs, but I am a realist whose business is war and peace. Don't ask me if I shed any tears over the inevitable.'

'I'm not asking for tears! I'm asking you to wait until the country's quietened down.'

The old man shook his head. 'This country is never going to quieten down, girl. Your friend President de Klerk has opened a Pandora's Box and the lid will never close again – the blacks will never stop fighting each other, and the communists will never rest until they rule the country. There will be no democracy, girlie. There will be no more freedom for black or white, thanks to your Mr de Klerk. *Now* is the time to get those squatters off my land – while the white man is still in control. When the ANC is boss, it'll be too late.'

Then Katrina drove to the squatter camp. It was a hive of activity. To her astonishment she saw Patti in discussion with a group of ANC stalwarts. Patti was equally surprised when Katrina strode up to her.

'What are you doing here? Don't tell me you've driven all the way from Jo'burg to offer your condolences to the homeless?' She glanced around. 'Is Luke here?'

'Sorry to disappoint you. This is my neck of the woods and I'm here alone to try to prevent mayhem. Can I speak to you alone, please?' Katrina turned and strode back to her car.

Patti walked after her grimly, her arms folded. 'What's your brilliant strategy, darling? Call down the angels? If you want to get this called off you'd better speak to your pals in the AWB, not me.'

Katrina controlled her anger. 'This is my family's land, and my family are not AWB. However, I've tried to persuade my father and failed.'

Patti made big beautiful eyes. 'Oh! So you want us to surrender?' She waved her hand. 'These poor people who have nothing in the world but the tatters they stand in, you want them to submit meekly to being thrown into trucks like cattle and dumped back across the so-called border into Bophuthatswana?'

Katrina took an angry breath. 'I'm asking you to avoid bloodshed. I'm *begging* you to persuade them to start packing so that when the lorries arrive in the morning the AWB won't have any excuse to throw their weight around. And I will personally accompany them into Bophuthatswana to help resettle them.'

'You *seriously* expect us to start packing, to give in to *Boers*.'

'I'm deadly serious. The alternative is a potentially disastrous confrontation.'

Patti's eyes flashed. 'My answer is *no* to such blackmail. And *their* answer – ' she pointed behind her – 'would be *no* even if I agreed! They intend to stand up for themselves for the first time in their miserable, impoverished lives. But it'll be passive resistance. The women and children will be lying down. They will not raise a finger – it'll be your Boers who start any fight!'

Katrina kept her temper. 'And *your* MK warriors? And the squatter men? Armed, ready to leap up to protect their women and children?'

'What do you expect men to do when their women and children are manhandled? You can't expect to separate a black man from his traditional weapons, darling. Even the mighty South African police didn't dare try to disarm the Zulus when they marched on Johannesburg two weeks ago.'

'Exactly! So your resistance is *not* going to be passive! And what about your ANC men – how are they armed?'

Patti closed her beautiful eyes. 'We are here in an advisory capacity only. If we are armed it is for self-defence only – '

'*Bullshit!* You wanted blood! Just like you wanted blood at Bisho, so you could be martyrs – '

Patti flashed: 'We don't *want* to be martyrs – we *are* martyrs. We *want* to be normal human beings like you with a place in the sun. Not a hundred thousand acres, like you, just these few pitiful acres – '

'Oh *Jesus!*' Katrina slumped back against her car and pressed her fingertips to her eyes . 'Oh Jesus, Jesus. Well, I'm going to talk to these people myself!'

Patti waved a hand. 'Go ahead, it's your land. Just don't expect a very friendly audience – the name De la Rey isn't very popular around here.' She walked away, hips swinging, arms folded.

Katrina strode into the squatter camp. She raised her hands above her head and hollered in Tswana: '*Everybody, listen to me! Everybody, please gather around! I want to tell you what's going to happen tomorrow! I want to tell you what to do so there is no bloodshed tomorrow –* '

A stone came flying. It was thrown by a ten-year-old boy. It caught Katrina on the temple and she lurched, clutching her face. A gasp went up from the people; then Patti was running. She flung her arm about Katrina and yelled: '*Who did this? Bring him to me. This woman is my friend. She came here in peace!*'

An ANC man grabbed Katrina's arm and pulled her towards a lorry. The boy had been grabbed by another ANC man. Katrina slumped against the vehicle. 'I'm okay.'

Patti prised Katrina's fingers from her brow and looked at the wound. It was only a shallow gash but bruising had appeared already. 'Get the first-aid box! We'd better get you to a doctor.'

'I'm okay. Give me a mirror. Just give it a dab of disinfectant.'

'One of my men will take you home – '

Katrina turned on her. 'I am *not*,' she said angrily, 'going home with an injury, or you'll have my father down here like a crack of thunder – they think I've driven back to Jo'burg. I'm staying right here until this business is over! And right now I'm going to talk to these people!' She shoved herself away from the lorry and held up her hands again. She shouted in Tswana: *'Now listen to me!'*

117

It was ten o'clock that Sunday night when Mahoney got back from the film set and heard Katrina's message. Before dawn on Monday morning he was on the road for the Western Transvaal.

The squatter camp at Dagbreek was already alive with people tensely preparing. With the first sunlight Katrina awoke in the back seat of her car, stiff and cold. The swelling had gone from her forehead but the bruise was livid. The ANC man who had been detailed to guard her gave an unsmiling 'Good morning'.

'Good morning. Thank you, you can go off now.'

She climbed into the front seat, adjusted the rear-view mirror and began to brush her hair. She was almost finished when Patti tapped on the window. 'How are you?'

Katrina rolled down the window. 'I appeal to you one last time – '

'Darling, we discussed it last night into the wee hours. Do you want some breakfast?'

Katrina looked at her angrily. 'You're really looking forward to blood, aren't you?'

'No, darling. We're looking forward to justice.'

'For Christ's sake, the court's issued an eviction order!'

'The South African courts are just?' Patti smiled. 'Breakfast?'

Katrina looked at her venomously. 'I despise you for what you are about to do. Because today *you*, Patti Gandhi, descendant of the great pacifist Gandhi, are going to cause *blood* to make political capital. And

I,' she glared, 'am now driving off to try to prevent it. No breakfast thank you!' She twisted the ignition key.

Patti pulled open the door and dropped to her haunches. She seized Katrina's hands. 'Please believe me when I say I *honestly* disagree with you. I respect what you say, but this stand must be taken today for these poor people – '

'*Lies!* You're taking it for the big bold image of the ANC. Like you did at Bisho!' She pulled the door closed.

Patti leant in the window and put her hand on her thigh. She pleaded: 'I love you!'

Katrina looked up at her. Her face bruised. 'You love yourself. And *Luke*.'

'No! I really love *both* of you – I want to be your friends *forever*! In the new South Africa.'

'Sure.' Katrina let out the clutch. She roared backwards, swung the car around and went roaring up the track.

She drove into the glorious sunrise towards two hills called Sheba's Breasts. She stopped between them, swung her car across the track, blocking it. It was then she glimpsed the sun flash on the binoculars on the top of one of them. She reached into the glove compartment and pulled out her own binoculars. She scanned the two hills.

She could make out nobody up there. She lowered the binoculars. Then she put her hands to her face and tried to pray.

They had started out from Dagbreek early, thirty lorries and a score of vehicles carrying AWB men. In front drove a Land-Rover carrying four white policemen and a deputy-sheriff of the Supreme Court. They encountered Katrina's car, and pulled up.

The policemen and deputy-sheriff got out. Katrina was standing, feet apart, hands on hips. She demanded in Afrikaans: 'Who's in charge here?'

A police officer touched his cap. 'I'm in charge of keeping the peace here, madam. This gentleman – ' he indicated the sheriff – 'is in charge of the civil procedure of evicting these squatters.'

'And you're in charge of those AWB men behind you!'

'No, madam,' the policeman said, 'and I don't know whether they're AWB men or NP or DP or ANC. I have no power to stop them being here.'

'*Bullshit!* You can order them to disperse under the Riot Act. And you can fire tear-gas at them if they refuse!'

'Madam, there is no riot. And this is a free country, and this is private land – '

'A free country!? *Hah!* Officer, I beg you, in the name of God to order these people to go home or there *will* be a riot!'

The sheriff walked forward. 'Professor de la Rey, I hereby request you to move your car – '

'And I hereby request you to get rid of this AWB mob before you not only kill people but fuck up the whole of South Africa!'

The sheriff walked to her car and grabbed the door handle. It was locked and Katrina had the keys: the car was in reverse gear and the handbrake was on.

She leapt up onto the bonnet, threw up her arms and shouted: *'In the name of God, I beg you to stop!'* Then she leapt down and began to run back to the squatter camp.

She ran and she ran. She looked back and saw twenty men bunched around her car, manhandling it out of the way. She ran into the squatter encampment, panting.

A thousand pairs of eyes looked at her. In front of her, spread over an area the size of a football pitch, lay the prostrate bodies of six or seven hundred women and children, all heads raised at her. Beyond them, where the shacks began, lay the men, several hundred of them. Silence. Katrina stopped at the front line, panting. She could not see the ANC men and their vehicles.

She shouted in Tswana: 'They're coming! Now I beg you in the name of your ancestors not to resist them! I beg you to let them pick you up and place your belongings in their vehicles! I beg this of you in the name of peace. In the name of the new South Africa that is coming. I beg this of you in the name of Chris Hani who died for you. And I promise you I will accompany you to your old land and help you with money!'

A figure rose up from the ranks. It was Patti Gandhi. She swept her hand through her long black hair and walked towards her.

'Well said, Kate. I admire you, and so do these people behind me. Now get the hell out of harm's way, darling.'

'Like hell I will!' Katrina stepped around her and marched into the midst of the prostrate women and children. *'In the name of your children, I beg you to surrender!'*

Patti grabbed her elbow. 'Get the hell out of here, darling. Get right back there – ' she pointed into the trees – 'and keep your pretty head down.'

Katrina wrenched her arm free. 'Where are your ANC men?'

'Never mind.'

Katrina pointed back furiously at the hills. 'They're up there, aren't they?! Laying ambush!' She turned and yelled at the prostrate bodies:

'You're planning a battle you cannot win! You are throwing yourselves in front of death – '

She looked back and saw the convoy begin to move, her car on the edge of the bush now. She turned and she ran, leaping over prostrate bodies. She ran towards the advancing vehicles, waving her arms. She came to a panting halt outside the encampment.

The Land-Rover stopped and the sheriff climbed out. He had a document in his hand. He began: 'By order of the Supreme Court of South Africa. It is hereby ordered – '

'To hell with your orders!'

Katrina turned and ran back into the squatter camp. She stopped at the first line of prostrate bodies. She thrust her hands on her hips. The sheriff climbed back into his vehicle. The convoy started again. Katrina planted her feet apart defiantly, her bosom heaving.

Patti shouted from behind her: 'Get out of there!'

'Like hell!'

The convoy had almost reached the camp when Mahoney caught up with the rear of it. He had just heard on his radio that another bomb had exploded at a black taxi-rank in Germiston, flesh and blood flying, buildings shattered. He slammed to a stop and scrambled out. He started running.

The convoy came to a halt fifty yards from Katrina. Men began jumping off lorries. The deputy-sheriff and the policemen walked towards the encampment. The other men followed in a solid phalanx. They were carrying batons and sjamboks. The sheriff carried a loud-speaker.

He halted ten paces from Katrina, held aloft his documents. 'This is an eviction order! We have come to remove you from this land and to take you back to where you came from.'

Katrina shouted: 'They surrender! They'll come peacefully!'

'No!' a male voice shouted, and a ragged cry of No went up all around.

'Yes, they will!' Katrina turned on the mass of prostrate bodies and shouted: 'Get up! Up! Go fetch your belongings!'

'No!'

'Yes!' Katrina turned frantically back to the sheriff. 'Yes, they will! Just give them time – '

'Like hell we will!' Patti shouted. She climbed to her feet midst the mass of bodies.

'They surrender!' Katrina shouted. She ripped open her white shirt.

'*Surrender!*' She ripped it off her shoulders. She waved it above her head: '*See this? It's the white flag of surrender – just give them time to collect their things –*'

Mahoney shoved his way through the mass of men. He took the sheriff's arm. '*Wait – let me speak to her!*' He strode towards Katrina. '*Kate –*'

'*You keep out of this!*'

Mahoney stopped in front of her, panting. 'Now look. These guys,' he jerked his thumb over his shoulder, 'mean business, and want you out of the line of fire –'

'*You tell her, Luke!*' Patti shouted.

'And so do these people mean business!' Katrina jerked her head behind her. 'And I'm trying to stop it, in the name of God!'

'Kate, there's going to be a fight and these squatters will see you as the enemy, the landlord's daughter. Now you've done your duty –'

'*If you do your duty you'll stand beside me!*'

'For Christ's sake!' He turned and faced the sheriff, both hands raised. 'Give us a few minutes, please! I'm a lawyer and I'm trying to negotiate a peaceful settlement!' He turned to the mass of prostrate blacks. '*Please listen to me! I'm a lawyer, trying to help you . . . !*'

Katrina hissed: '*Tell them to surrender, for Christ's sake!*'

Mahoney shouted: '*The Supreme Court has ordered your eviction. If you wish to appeal against it I will help you, free of charge, but to resist now is unlawful. I will lodge your appeal after the election, which starts tomorrow. Right now, for the sake of your women and children I advise you to cooperate with the authorities to avoid trouble –*'

'*No!*' Patti shouted. She stood up dramatically.

The stick that struck Katrina was wielded by a twelve-year-old youth. It was Patti's shout that triggered him. In a flash he scrambled to his feet, his stick on high, furiously yelling, '*No!*', and he bounded and swiped. The stick struck Katrina a blinding blow across her head; she reeled, gasping, and Mahoney spun on the youth, shocked, furious, and he swung his fist wildly. He hit the youth on the chest, but the stick swiped again and caught him on the head, and a roar went up. Blacks were leaping up everywhere, and Mahoney turned back to Katrina, desperate to protect her, and he saw her on her knees. She was trying to get up, a wild bunch of blacks around her, sticks flashing on high and swiping, and somewhere in the midst of this was Patti Gandhi screaming '*Stop! Stop!*' And Mahoney bellowed. It was a bellow of fierce outrage and hate – '*You black bastards!*' – and he charged.

Mahoney charged into the midst of them, his fists swinging wildly, murder in his heart. He seized the nearest black man and slung him aside and his fist crashed down on the head of the next man like a club.

He slugged his way through the mass of black bodies towards Katrina. She had collapsed onto her side, blood flooding out of her mass of blonde hair, sticks flashing down at her, Patti Gandhi clawing and kicking and screaming. Mahoney bellowed, the primitive roar of a man fighting his way to the defence of his woman, and he slugged his way into the mass of flailing sticks, and all hell broke loose.

The rest was very confused. All he knew was the mass of sticks raining down on him as he crashed to one knee beside Katrina to lift her up, to get her out of here, the screams of Patti somewhere in there, the roar of the AWB men coming, bodies thrashing and fighting everywhere. Then the *crack crack crack* of gunfire midst the pandemonium. Then suddenly there were no more blows, suddenly blacks were fleeing everywhere, AWB men pounding after them, sjamboks flashing. Mahoney wrenched Katrina over onto her back, gasping. Her head was covered with blood. '*God God God* – ' All around were screaming people, white men fighting black people, policemen shouting and grabbing. In the midst of it was Patti Gandhi, flailing about with a stick. 'STOP!' Mahoney roared. 'FOR CHRIST's SAKE STOP!' He wrestled his arms under Katrina, and heaved her up. He staggered to his feet. He started carrying her out of this madness, tears brimming in his desperate eyes. The fighting seemed to have nothing to do with him anymore. He lurched between the bodies, all he knew was he had to get her out of this, get to his vehicle and rush her to a hospital.

He staggered with her towards the convoy, trying to run. And suddenly he realised he was running towards gunfire, the earth spouting up about him. '*Stop* – ' he tried to shout but it came out as a rasp. It was coming from Sheba's Breasts. He ran, staggering, lurching, for the police vehicle, to get her out of the gunfire, rasping: 'Please God! Please God!', and he sprawled. He crashed on top of Katrina, scrambled back up, heaved her up again and lurched to the vehicle, his heart pounding. He lowered Katrina to the ground, flung open the back door, heaved her up again, whimpering: '*Please God.*' He shoved her inert body into the back seat, then he plunged his ear to her breast and tried to listen. He could just hear a heartbeat above the clamour of the camp. '*Oh, thank God . . .*' He could not bear to examine her bloodied face. He scrambled out and slammed the door. The ignition keys were in position. He snatched them out and locked the vehicle. Then he turned and started running up the track to fetch his Land-Rover, to bash it through the bush and bundle his woman into it and rush her to the nearest hospital.

Mahoney's vehicle was two hundred yards up the track, at the rear of the convoy. He was halfway there when the police vehicle burst into flames. Then the lorry behind it exploded also.

They burst into flames in mighty whooshes, flames barrelling upwards as their fuel tanks were ignited. Mahoney stumbled to a stop, staring, aghast; he glimpsed men running away through the trees. And he bellowed in horror and started to run back to the police vehicle.

He ran wildly, bellowing '*Katrina* – ' Great yellow-black flames were belching up. He ran wildly up to it, and the heat hit him like a blow, a searing wall that made him throw up his hands across his face. And he flung himself at the back door. For an awful instant he saw Katrina's bloodied face on the back seat, her clothing on fire, and he bellowed in outrage and wrenched the handle, and it was locked. And he roared in fury and wrenched the key from his pocket, rammed it into the door, wrenched it open. He grabbed her by the armpits and heaved.

Katrina's inert body hit the road in a thump, and Mahoney dragged her. He dragged her frantically through the beating heat off the track, rasping, gasping. He dragged her twenty yards into the trees, lurching, then he crashed to his knees beside her and began to beat at the flames on her. He beat and beat, slapping frantically with his palms, until the flames were all out and his hands were blistered. Then he ripped open her skirt and heaved, pulling the smouldering fabric off her.

Katrina de la Rey lay there, her face a mass of blood, her body a mass of wicked bruises; down her shoulder and arm and thigh the angry welts of blisters were rising. Mahoney stared, tears of shock and horror running down his face. Then he wrestled his arms underneath her, heaved her up and staggered to his feet, and began to lurch through the bush towards his vehicle.

Then he heard the noise. But it was not the sound of the battle; it was the roar of fire. The crackling roar of flames leaping with the wind from the burning vehicles, leaping off into the bush, the roar of grass and trees catching fire in a massive wave. Mahoney stopped.

A great wall of fire was running through the bush on the other side of the track, great belches of flame and smoke leaping up towards the African sky, towards the squatter camp. Mahoney stared, aghast: then his mind reeled red-black in fury, fury at the wounds on the body of his woman, fury for those brutalised squatters down there fleeing in all directions, fury at the raging fire that was going to sweep across this country; and he threw back his head and bellowed: '*God spare this land . . . !*'

118

That night yet another bomb exploded in a middle-class black bar in Pretoria. The first day of voting for the new South Africa was just dawning when the matron gently insisted he leave the hospital. *'Please, Mr Mahoney.'*

Mahoney said: 'I'm paying for this private room, and I'm staying.'

'Agh asseblief, Meneer Mahoney. Laat haar rus.' Let her rest. The matron put her hand under his elbow.

Mahoney let himself be persuaded to his feet. He had two days' growth of beard, his eyes were gaunt. He said thickly, in English: 'Will you look after her?'

'Of course, Mr Mahoney.'

Mahoney sat down on the chair again. He said: 'I want to be here. When you wash her – ' he closed his eyes – 'I want to see that you comb her hair properly. And put some lipstick on.' He pointed. 'She's got no lipstick. And you must cover those hideous stitches with her hair. Like this.' He fluffed Katrina's golden locks across her forehead. 'Like this – see? Only better! Ladies know how to do this sort of thing – '

'Please, Mr Mahoney.' The other nurse took his wrist and gently pulled it away. 'Please, go home now, leave her to us.'

'Home?' Mahoney's voice caught. He could not bear to think of home.

'General de la Rey has his car waiting for you, with a driver.'

He wanted to say: *Fuck General de la Rey. Fuck all you Afrikaners. And fuck Africa.* He said: 'Please thank the general.' He got to his feet. He pointed at Katrina. 'When I come back I want her to look beautiful.'

He walked out into the neon-lit corridor. Nurses were hurrying in both directions, efficient, crisp in their white uniforms. Mahoney walked down the antiseptic corridor, numb, exhausted, his heart breaking. He came to the big foyer. Out there, through the big glass doors, the sun was rising. He walked out, into the new South Africa.

He saw General de la Rey's car in the parking area, but turned away and started walking down the steep tree-lined street. He did not notice the car of Patti Gandhi. The first he knew was the clip of high-heels behind him, then the tug on his arm.

'Luke . . . ?'

He stopped.

'Oh God I'm sorry, Luke,' Patti said. The tears were streaming down her face.

Mahoney looked at her, exhausted. Patti was exhausted too. Her tear-filled eyes were gaunt. He did not know what he wanted to say.

There were so many things to say. He wanted to say, It's all your fault, and he wanted to say, Thank you, and he wanted to say, Get out of my sight. He said: 'Yes.' He turned and walked on.

Patti hurried after him. She grabbed his arm. 'I loved her too, Luke.'

Mahoney stopped. Yes, he half-believed that. 'Sure.' He turned and started walking again.

Patti grabbed his arm again. 'I did, Luke! I *do*. She was one of the most real, *worthwhile* people I've met. She also wanted the new South Africa. We could have all lived together in harmony.'

Mahoney looked at her. 'Yes. And you bastards killed her.'

Patti flinched. She said tearfully: 'You know that's untrue!'

Tears were suddenly running down his face. And, oh God, he didn't know what the truth was anymore. He heard himself say: 'In Africa nothing is true or untrue, since recorded time began. It's all the African Way.' And he wanted to shout at her, to bellow at the sunrise about the Big Impis, about the African Way that had killed her. But he turned and walked on down the sunlit street.

Patti hurried beside him. '*Please*, Luke. Let me drive you home.' She added tearfully: '*Your* home, not mine. I'm asking nothing of you. Just let me take you home.'

Home? Oh Christ, he couldn't go home, he never wanted to go home. All he wanted to do was turn around and walk back to that hospital, where they were looking after her, washing her, putting lipstick on her, covering her stitches with her flaxen hair. Home was right here in the street outside Thabazimbi Hospital in the sunrise. Home was where the undertaker took her. Oh Christ no, the only place he wanted to be was right here, the last place he had seen his woman. 'No thank you, Patti.'

She whispered: 'I'm there whenever you need me.'

He turned and walked away. The pretty streets were empty. The sun was rising on the new South Africa. The tears were running down his face.

No, he could not bear to go home. He could not bear to walk into that silent, pretty, empty house and see all her pretty things, her dresses hanging in the wardrobe, her jumble of pretty underwear, the shoes and boots, her jars of creams and lotions on the dressing-table, the frilly stool where she sat, the mirror she peered into when she put on her make-up. He could not bear to see the bed she had lain in, where she had given him such bliss, he could not bear to see her feminine bathroom, the brass taps, the big whirlpool bath steaming, the pretty hanging plants. He could not bear to walk down the empty passage and see the telephone answering machine with her voice on it, her last message telling him she was rushing up to Dagbreek to do something about the AWB and the squatters. He could not bear to hear her voice, but, oh God no, he could not bear to wipe it off the tape – he would keep it for the rest of his life. He could not bear to walk into her silent study and see her desk exactly as she had left it, her scrawled notes, her papers, her books. He could not bear to see that life-size photograph of her on the wall, her perfectly sculpted golden body tensed, her back, her shoulders, her buttocks, her lovely long legs, her golden hair shiny. Oh God no, he could not bear to go home.

He walked down the quiet early-morning streets, the sun glinting on the treetops, the eastern horizon aglow. He walked and walked, taking any turn that came his way, and all he wanted to do was turn around and walk back to that hospital, the last place he had seen her, and sit with her again, but they would not allow him to be with her anymore and soon the undertaker would take her away. He walked and walked, and now white people were emerging from their early-morning houses, and now many blacks were coming out onto the streets, and they were all walking quietly in the same direction as he was. He walked alongside them, alone amongst the people. '*Goeie môre, meneer*,' some of them said, but he was hardly aware of them. Then ahead were the grounds of the school, and all the people were streaming through the gate, and joining a long queue; and he realised that they were lining up to vote in the first elections of the new South Africa.

Mahoney stopped at the school fence and looked at the long line of people queuing. And then he noticed that most of them were old people, and the infirm, black and white and brown, many on crutches and in wheelchairs, supported by younger people. And then he remembered that this first day of voting was reserved for the enfeebled, and the sight of all those weathered faces queuing up to vote brought new tears burning up to his eyes. And what was so noticeable was that they all looked so good natured. Happy. There were smiles and greetings, everybody was so placid, so patient. Mahoney looked at them, new tears welling, tears of wonder. And he just wanted to walk into the school grounds and join those people, embrace them, stand in line with them to vote for the new South Africa. And, oh God, he wanted Katrina to see this! He wanted to hurry back to her and tell her the wonderful thing that was happening. And he felt the grief well up, and his chin begin to tremble, and he turned away.

He walked away, past the gate, through the people streaming from all directions towards it. He walked and walked, fast, and his heart was breaking. He came to the edge of the pretty early-morning town, where the road led south towards Johannesburg or north to Zimbabwe. Black people were streaming down the road from both directions, the old and infirm, little old black ladies hobbling, white-haired old men with their sticks, old people who had walked from far and wide to vote for the very first time in their lives, all heading for the school.

It was nine o'clock when he found the Last Chance Café & Bottle Store at the roadside with its big red Coca-Cola sign. He had been walking for three hours. He went inside, into the jumbled hodgepodge of canned foods and wilting vegetables and yesterday's bread and newspapers and sweets, and its odiferous counter of stews and sadza and fried fish. There was one formica table, a television set on the wall. Behind the counter was a small array of booze bottles.

'A half-jack of whisky please,' he said.

'Not till opening hours at ten o'clock,' the Portuguese said. 'Liquor Act. What kind of whisky?'

'Any kind of whisky is all right.'

The Portuguese put a half-jack of Johnny Walker on the counter.

Mahoney sat at the formica table and drank cheap coffee laced with Johnny Walker, and watched the television, the tears glistening on his cheeks and his heart breaking. For there on the screen was the bright morning, the sky blue, the sun shining bright on the same highveld that had greeted the voortrekkers a hundred and fifty years ago, the highveld of Piet Retief and Hendrik Potgieter with their wagons and volk. Then there was the sun glinting on the treetops of the suburbs and the skyscrapers of eGoli, Johannesburg, the place that had caused all the trouble, and then there was the theme music and the whirling logo of *Elections '94*, and he listened to the elated SABC anchorman:

'It's a glorious day for the birth of the new South Africa, as millions of elderly people of all colours and political persuasion queue side by side across our land to vote. The wonderful feature of this glorious day is the spirit of democracy that pervades our land. South Africans, black and white, brown and yellow, are coming together busting out all over with goodwill as they line up and wait for their first-ever chance to vote. It is a wonderful atmosphere that pervades our beautiful land as, contrary to all expectations, contrary to the doomsayers that there would be bloodshed and mayhem, South Africans of all hues are coming out of their huts and shacks and cottages and apartments and suburbs and mansions, lining up together to await their turn to cast their vote. It is an extraordinary exhibition of multi-ethnic togetherness as South Africans, so long riven by racial and tribal divisions, seem to have thrown all that aside to participate in the new South Africa . . . '

And then the massive car-bomb exploded at Jan Smuts Airport. Exploded in a shocking blast that was felt thirty miles away, blasting the

South African morning wide open, blasting bricks and marble and glass in all directions. Mahoney stared at the television, at the devastation, the ruin, the blood, the dust, the weeping and wailing; and he wanted to leap to his feet and bellow his towering outrage that such a terrible thing could be done on such a day. He stared at the horrific scene, aghast: then he dropped his head on the table, and up it erupted, his grief. His grief for his woman, his grief for this bloodied country.

But then, as he wept, something absolutely extraordinary happened: the miracle of this day refused to be shattered by that outrage, the feeling of *Ubuntu* refused to go away. Between updates on the dreadful bombing – 'police believe they are very close to making a number of arrests' – the television cameras flashed around the vast, beloved country, from Johannesburg in the heartland to the slopes of Table Mountain in the very south, from the arid north-western Cape to the lush rolling hillsides of Natal, from Umtata and the Wild Coast to the far north hard by the Limpopo: the long lines of people queuing in snaking columns miles long, lining up to cast their vote. And in all these queues, these comings-together of the people, there were the smiles, the patience, the goodwill: the *Ubuntu*.

It was like a dream. Mahoney sat at the formica table on the outskirts of Thabazimbi in the heartland of Katrina de la Rey's Afrikanerdom, watching the long lines of people, and the tears were running down his face, and his heart was breaking. And, oh God, he wanted Katrina to see this, he wanted to hurry back to Katrina and tell her what was happening, burst into the hospital and tell her how wonderful it all was, hold her tight and hug her, point at the television screen and laugh with her that this was how it was going to be, *beg* her to give up her volkstaat, cry: *'Darling, look – maybe everything is going to be all right after all . . . '*

Inca Gold

Clive Cussler

THE INTERNATIONAL
NO. 1 BESTSELLER

A desperate call for help from a stricken archaeological expedition brings Dirk Pitt to a sacred well high in the Andes. What he discovers as he attempts to rescue two divers lost in its perilous depths leads him into deadly confrontation with a ruthless band of international art-thieves, who plunder ancient sites for their precious arte-facts.

Dirk Pitt's extraordinary adventures take him to the fabled Lost City of the Dead, lead him in search of a Spanish galleon washed miles inland by a giant tidal wave centuries before, and eventually set him on the trail of a fabulous hoard of Inca Gold. But Pitt will need all his skills and tenacity simply to survive as he races to track down the sacred site – before the richest prize known to man is lost to the world for ever. . .

'Clive Cussler's hero Dirk Pitt is made of strong stuff, handling the improbable with nerves of steel . . . he is one of the best adventure heroes around.'   *Today*

'Clive Cussler is the guy *I* read.'   TOM CLANCY

ISBN 0 00 647909 X

Without Remorse
Tom Clancy

THE *SUNDAY TIMES* NO. 1 BESTSELLER

It is 1970. Back in the US after serving as a Navy SEAL in Vietnam, John Kelly meets a woman who will change his life forever. She has recently escaped from a nightmare world of unimaginable suffering, yet before they can plan a future together, the horrors of her past reach out to snatch her from him. Kelly vows to gain revenge – but finds there are others who have need of his deadly skills.

In Washington a high-risk operation is being planned to rescue a key group of prisoners from a POW camp deep within North Vietnam. Kelly has his own mission; the Pentagon want him for theirs. As he attempts to juggle the two, he must step into a netherworld as perilous as any he has ever known – from which he may never return. . .

'Clancy's latest action thriller is certain to join his unbroken string of bestsellers . . . a master storyteller.'

New York Times

'Sure to thrill . . . outstanding suspense. Satisfying, engrossing, chock-full of meticulous knowledge of the military, war heroics and nail-biting action.'

Boston Herald

'The reader becomes enthralled . . . politically fascinating. Great fun.'
Observer

'Heart-stopping . . . the product of a master.'

Washington Post

ISBN 0 00 647641 4

Other paperback titles by HarperCollins include: